About the author

James Warden was a teacher for forty years, and retired in 2006. He now enjoys his retirement as much as he enjoyed his time in the education service, and is catching up on those things which he left undone and ought to have done – in particular, his writing. He writes every morning between nine o'clock and noon, for thirty-six weeks of the year.

He is fortunate enough to be able to act in several Norwich theatres – the Maddermarket, the Sewell Barn and, with the Great Hall Players, at the Assembly House – and this experience informs his writing. His stage adaptation of Laurie Lee's *As I Walked Out One Midsummer Morning* was performed at the Sewell Barn Theatre in November 2009. His original play, *Letters from a Boy in the Trenches*, which was based on the letters of a WW1 soldier, was performed in Marchington, Staffordshire in 2015.

James is married – for the second time – and lives in Norfolk. He and his wife travel as much as possible. They have visited Italy (where they were married in 2002) several times, Canada, Bermuda, Egypt, India, the Czech Republic, New England, Poland, Slovenia, Antarctica, Alaska, the Galapagos Islands and the Falkland Islands. They have also taken several holidays in various Mediterranean resorts – the basis for his first novel, *Three Women of a Certain Age*, which was published in July 2010.

During his years in education, he wrote about twenty play scripts for children. These included the one that formed the basis for his children's story, *The Great Gobbler and his Home Baking Factory at the North Pole*, which he wrote in 1982 and published in December 2010.

He has three sons by his first marriage and they inspired two of his novels – *The Vampire's Homecoming*, which was published in 2011, and *The One-eyed Dwarf*, published in 2012. With them and his first wife, he also travelled to the southern states of North America, France, Germany (West and East), Estonia and what was Czechoslovakia.

His other writings include a novel, *The Age of Wisdom*, and the autobiography of Bill Pieri, *The Boy in the Photograph*.

Swinging

IN THE

SIXTIES

by

JAMES WARDEN

Grosvenor House
Publishing Limited

This book is published by
Grosvenor House Publishing Ltd
28-30 High Street, Guildford, Surrey, GU1 3EL.
www.grosvenorhousepublishing.co.uk

A CIP record for this book
is available from the British Library

ISBN 978-1-78623-917-4

To
my friends and fellow students
63–67
in memory of our dreams and aspirations

Acknowledgements

In referring to incidents in the lives of public figures I have used their autobiographies, authorised biographies or, in one case, a book written about them. These books are:

Cliff by Patrick Doncaster and Toby Jasper; Sidgwick and Jackson 1981

The Way the Wind Blows by Lord Home; Collins/ Fontana 1976

Malcolm X: By Any Means Necessary by Walter Dean Myers; Scholastic 1993

Mandy by Mandy Rice-Davies with Shirley Flack; Michael Joseph/ Sphere 1980

Just As I Am by Billy Graham; Harper Collins 1997

Grand Inquisitor by Sir Robin Day; Weidenfeld and Nicholson/ Pan Books 1990

The Making of a Prime Minister by Lord Wilson; Weidenfeld/ Joseph 1986

The Crossman Diaries by Richard Crossman; Hamilton & Cape/ Magnum 1979

The Rise of Enoch Powell by Paul Foot; Cornmarket Press 1969

John by Cynthia Lennon; Crown Publishers 2005

Lennon: The Definitive Biography by Ray Coleman; Pan Books 2000

Keith Richards: Before They Make Me Run by Kris Needs; Plexus 2004

David Frost: An Autobiography by David Frost; Harper Collins 1994

I Have a Dream: Story of Martin Luther King by Margaret Davidson; Scholastic 1986

Michael Ramsey: A Life by Owen Chadwick; Oxford University Press 1990

Long Walk to Freedom by Nelson Mandela; Abacus 1995

Fighting All the Way by Barbara Castle; Macmillan/ Pan Books 1994

I should like to thank family and friends, past and present, for giving me an insight into the training of nurses in the 1960s; oversights and misunderstandings are mine, not yours. I am also indebted to Joan Woodcock's excellent first-hand account, *Matron Knows Best*, which put me right on procedures and practices. Her book is published by Headline Review, 33 Euston Road, LONDON, NW1 3BH.

I should, also, like to thank Jim Roberts for his painting, which I have used for the cover of this book and also on my website (www.jameswarden.co.uk).

Chapters

Principal Characters

**Students at County of Staffham Teacher Training College
(Coseley College of Education from September 1965)**
<u>Final Year Students (1962 Year Group)</u>
Pete Campbell
Barry Glover

<u>1st Year Students (1963 Year Group)</u>
Stephen Last
Desmond Smith
Simon Wiseman
Paul Crisp
Michael Harrison
Susan Paget
Jenny Pryce
Marguerite Bannister
Stella Aldridge

<u>1st Year Students (1964 Year Group)</u>
Amanda Harrelson

Elizabeth Sturlson, Des's girlfriend

Hughie Spragg, a member of the Appalachian Four

Student Nurses at Staffham General Hospital:
Kate Walsh
Miriam Davison
Joan Whiting
Heather Burton
Sheila Pratt
Christine Dixon

1963

CHAPTER ONE

First steps on a long walk

Stephen Last stepped down from the bus into the swirl of autumn leaves that greeted him at Cotes Warren Church. As the bus pulled away he looked up, smiling to himself, and saw the white-walled blocks of the County of Staffham Training College. He was here at last, suitcase in hand, and taking the first steps on what he supposed would be a long walk. The desire to teach had sprung suddenly, but apparently fully-formed, into his head as had stood by his locker at Ipswich Civic College. He had just come from one of Martin Lewis's frenetic geography lessons; as he talked, the lecturer's eyes had flashed with enthusiasm, his joy had filled the classroom and his hands had carved glaciated valleys in the air. He was an inspiration to Stephen, who was seventeen and wondering what to do with his life. If he could make his subject, English, as fascinating as Martin made his, Stephen felt that he, too, could inspire generations of children. He was the first one in his family to have the chance of an education beyond secondary school, and had turned down a university place because he felt a teaching diploma would prove more useful.

He was aware that he was also beginning his personal road to freedom – education being the only road he knew – as he walked towards the college gates. Collingwood

Hall was a dilapidated sprawl of H-shaped blocks; the students' bedrooms and washrooms were situated down the long strokes of the letter and a kitchen and common room filled the centre stroke. He had been allocated to A House, which was one of the three blocks for men; the other blocks – and he remembered being told, by a second year student, at his interview that there were thirteen in all – were allocated to the women. He'd never had a girlfriend – not in any real sense, not someone who had been special beyond all others in the groups with which he spent his time – and he thought that it might be much the same here: mixed groups rather than particular friendships.

In the common room he found Simon Wiseman, who Stephen had met at interview. They'd travelled up on the train together, sharing a fascination with the James Bond novels and talked about *Dr No*, which had just 'burst onto the screen', as the papers liked to express it. Stephen had liked Simon, who now uncurled himself from what appeared to be a lotus position, came over and shook Stephen by the hand.

"Good to see you. Have you signed in? No? We have to – across in the main block. I'll walk over with you. You took your college father's advice did you, and didn't buy half the crap they told you to on the college lists? The Bible! What for, I'm doing English. Even then you're not going to read the Complete Works of Shakespeare, are you?"

"By the time I got his letter, I'd spent nine shillings on the very rough Spring Books version," replied Stephen, with a laugh.

"So had I. Still, it'll be a useful door stop. Did you buy your rugby, football and cricket kits?"

"I take it you didn't?"

"I've avoided sport since I left primary school at the age of eleven. No-one's going to get me on the field ever again. Anyway, if you need one, the second years are flogging theirs off cheap in the main block."

The main block was buzzing with new student life. Among those seeking his attention, Stephen came across the National Association of Schoolmasters rep: a tall youth with a permanent grin and rubbery lips.

"Are you in a union?" he asked.

"No," replied Stephen.

"You'll need to be – and one that represents your interests as a man teacher. You're looking puzzled? There are far more women than men in teaching as I expect you've already realised looking round. Well, the NUT, with so many women involved, can't represent men properly, can it? We're the main bread winners, and we need our own union if we're to get a fair deal. They'll be after equal pay soon, if we don't watch out ..."

It had never occurred to Stephen that men and women teachers were paid differently, and he said so.

"Well, they're not as good as us, are they?" replied the rep," They can't be, can they?" he laughed, "They have a period every month, don't they? And that means that for at least three or four days of the month they're under the weather and performing under par."

Stephen had no idea what a period was let alone that it resulted in a woman "performing under par" – another phrase that might, he thought, open new worlds.

"I'll think about it," he riposted and passed on.

On Jermyn Street, near Piccadilly Circus, a taxi pulled up alongside Andrew Oldham, the manager of the Rolling Stones. The window was wound down, quickly, and John Lennon called out:

"We've got some numbers that might be right for the Stones."

"What's it called," replied Andrew, getting into the taxi.

"*I Wanna Be Your Man.*"

At Ken Collyer's club the two groups – presented by the press as being in opposition to each other – ran through the new song. The recording session progressed with the Stones doing a Beatles number written just for them.

When they'd finished registering, Simon suggested that they went to the Red Room – a communal room shared by all the students – and they settled down to a cigarette. It was the beginning of term, they were flush with their LEA grants and it was a Peter Stuyvesant they passed around. Stephen had only smoked for a year – the second one of his A level course – and he enjoyed doing so. 'How good to be sitting here,' he thought, 'free in this unknown place – suddenly the stretched elastic is eased and the tension is reduced.' He didn't quite know what the thought meant, but it was good to be away from home.

"Did you go on the march this year?" asked Simon, leaning back in his chair.

"No," replied Stephen, quietly, catching a glimpse of Simon's CND badge as the other spoke. He'd never liked marches: to him, those on them were just an organised mob, and he loathed mobs. He was also sceptical of the motives of those who marched. All right, among them were sincere people led by their principles but many went for the laugh and only because their mates were going; it was just another way of being part of the gang.

"You missed a good one. Spies for Peace distributed their leaflets and we all stormed the RSG at Warren Row."

The network of underground bunkers, called Regional Seats of Government, had outraged the country because they smacked of the ruling classes – those who would have brought a nuclear war about in the first place – looking after themselves in case it happened. Thanks very much!

"I suppose I should have marched after the Cuban Missile Crisis last autumn and with the Yanks sailing into Holy Loch … but no, I didn't. To be honest, I'm not convinced it does much good."

"It does a bit more good than sitting around just talking about it," cut in a rather tall, lean youth with baby-faced cheeks, "Hello. I'm Des – Des Smith, pleased to meet you." His remark, which could have been taken as offensive, was relieved by a warm, broad grin. Both Stephen and Simon reached over, without standing, and shook his hand. "I'm from Middlesbrough," he continued, as though this established his place in the world.

"What you mean the Norf," chuckled Simon, deliberately emphasising the 'f', "where they hew wood and draw water? Simon Wiseman. Om from Borehamwood: the cradle of culture. Pleased to meet yer. And this is Stephen Last."

Stephen could only admire the way in which his new-found friend had cottoned on to the situation and thrown out the national stereotypes to oil the conversation.

'Simon's a fashionable dance,' he thought, 'and changes his costume when the lights go down.'

Des pulled over a chair and introduced the youth who was with him.

"This is Mike Harrison. He's from Liverpool. Where're you from, Stephen?"

"Suffolk. Hello. We're pretty evenly matched then? Two from the south and two from the north."

"Have you seen the talent round here?" said Mike, running his tongue over a pair of full, red lips from which protruded the longest canine teeth Stephen had ever seen outside a horror film. "I don't think we can fail to score, lads."

"They'd hop into bed thinking you were tired," laughed Des, "It's their first time away from home and it's one reason a lot of them come to training college." He looked at Stephen as he spoke, aware that here was someone who needed educating in the social arts. "To find a husband," he continued by way of explanation.

Stephen had never thought about the matter. It seemed to him that you came to college to train as a teacher, and he realised just how naïve he appeared. It worried him but only slightly, and he grinned at Des and Mike. The smile lit up what was, otherwise, a somewhat serious face. As they sat chatting, and with so much ease between them, Stephen realised that the next three years (they were the first group of students to be offered the three-year training course) were going to be the best of his life.

"What a gas!" chortled Simon.

Michael Ramsey, Archbishop of Canterbury, walked the streets of his city in a battered overcoat and with his old clerical hat shoved onto his head. He liked to wander in this way – greeting those in his care and visiting the SPCK bookshop, where the manager, on seeing him coming, would remove some of Ramsey's own books in order to encourage the belief that they were selling. He carried a stick, which he did not use, and chatted with the visitors to the cathedral. He made his way to the public library where he sat down to read the local paper.

Back in A House, everyone was settling in. Their trunks had arrived – brought over by the porters – and the goodies packed by their parents were being passed around. One youth called Bob (intensely serious but with a friendly manner), who appeared to be in some way responsible for the running of the house, which accommodated thirty students, was trying, above the chatter, to make the regulations clear.

"Don't forget, if you go out in the evening you must sign out and then sign in again *when you get back. Do not* sign out and in before you go out because some fireman might perish in the flames looking for you ... and make sure you're in by eleven o'clock. Everyone must be back in house by then."

"It's no joke," cut in another second year, speaking as though he'd seen someone smiling, "a woman student was knifed and thrown in a ditch last term. If we hadn't known she was still out after hours, no one would have gone looking for her."

As Bob enumerated the dos and don'ts, Stephen wondered whether the knifing story was true; where he came from such things just did not happen. He looked at the speaker who was a tall youth with an unusually large

head. The hair was cut close to the skull, and this emphasised the forceful boniness of his appearance. He walked
with a stoop, appearing to lean forward from his shoulders, and was so delicately balanced that Stephen thought
the extra weight of a cigarette in his mouth might cause
him to topple forward. The youth's eyes were large and
brooding.

"Here," he said, catching Stephen's eye, "come and
meet John. I'm Pete, by the way, Pete Campbell."

He led Stephen from the common room, passing by
the small kitchen and communal washrooms and so to
John's room. Stephen noticed that Simon had followed
them. Pete knocked and entered without waiting to be
asked, and it occurred to Stephen how absent was
any 'ceremony'; at home, none of his family had been
allowed to start eating until his father joined them at the
table.

The room was an organised clutter of artwork. From
the ceiling hung a crushed and rusted milk-crate – one of
the old, metal ones. Rust dripped from the crate onto a
piece of canvas on the floor.

"John's into conceptual art," chuckled Pete.

"Hello," said John, nodding towards Stephen and
Simon, "that's ready for my special study. I think it sums
up the pathos of the mother-child relationship beautifully."

"Cool," responded Simon.

"Sit down ... you're first years, are you?"

There was only the one chair by the table, which stood
in for a desk, and the bed. Pete sprawled across the bed,
and Simon slouched against the wall, his back supported
by a large cushion. Stephen perched on the table.

The room, small and cramped though it was, had been

made extraordinarily comfortable by the use of cushions, fabrics and table lamps, which cast their light downwards, leaving the ceiling and upper part of the room in a complexity of shadows.

As they talked – or, rather, as John and Pete talked – Stephen thought back to his bedroom at home. His father – on learning that Stephen had persuaded his mother that it was worthwhile to continue his studies instead of going to work immediately to bring home his first wage packet – had begun to make him a desk. It was beautifully made – the work of a master cabinet-maker – but had never been finished: nothing short of perfection was good enough for Stephen's father, and that always seemed to be just out of reach.

When Pete left "to get ready", Stephen wandered to his own room and unpacked. Someone had said that the walls were held together only by the tape that kept the wallpaper in place, and that may have been true, but Stephen soon had his room cosy. He, too, had brought a lamp and placed it on the dressing table into which he carefully put his clothes, and onto which he placed his clothes brush, alarm clock, electric shaver and other toiletries. A small wardrobe behind the door took his trousers, shirts and coats. He arranged his books along the window sill and on the shelves of the too-small bookcase. He hung his dressing gown over the foot of the bed to soften the appearance, and his pseudo-sheepskin coat on the door hook. He arranged his pens and pencils in place on the table with his notebooks and the novel he was reading currently – Muriel Spark's *The Ballad of Peckham Rye*. Looking round, he decided to replace the lamp onto the table where it would cast light on his work. In the circle of light, he arranged his proudest possession – the portable typewriter that had cost him £17 and for which he'd worked at potato picking all summer. He'd been the only one at college with a typewriter, and his speed was remarkably fast for someone untrained. Stephen unzipped the case with its pattern of brown and white squares and removed the neat, trim, grey-green machine. After locating the case next to the leg of the table, propped against the side wall, he slid a sheet of white paper under the roller, turned the furled knob to wind it in, flipped up the lever and slid the carriage to his right.

He was still typing, when Simon knocked at the door. It was early evening.

"Are you coming down the Red Lion? Everyone is. Evidently, Pete plays down there. He's got a folk group."

The local pub was reached by a narrow road that crossed the back of the college grounds. Stephen and Simon soon joined hordes of students, laughing and chatting as they wound their way drink-wards. Few of them had cars – a mere handful made up of the sons of businessmen – but a car would never have made it through the crowd, anyway.

Pete Campbell rocked on a stage at one end of the long room; he was amplified and the sound was shattering. He sang and played guitar, while another student kept the rhythm on bass; at least, that was what Stephen, who knew nothing about music, thought was happening. Pete was playing a mixed bag of popular tunes from the folk tradition – Dylan's *Blowin' in the wind* and Seeger's *If I had a hammer* – tossed together with the skiffle numbers of Lonnie Donegan and the popular ballads of Buddy

Holly. He was obviously a regular and the entertainment was going down well.

There was barely space to move in the long room. Stephen glanced around and saw Mike Harrison sitting with a group at the far end; they were settled nicely into one corner. Stephen nodded that Simon should join them, and then went to the bar for a couple of pints. He paid his three shillings and, pints in hand, squeezed his way through the crowd. Several of the girls made oohing sounds as he eased by them, their faces aglow with expectation and alcohol.

"Are you Stevie?"

The girl who spoke had a tumble of mouse-blonde hair framing a pale, snub-nosed face and a pair of light, blue eyes. At that moment, Stephen thought she was the most beautiful thing he had ever seen, especially when her face lit up with a dainty smile. No one had ever called him "Stevie" before.

"This is Jenny, Steve," cut in Mike Harrison, "we were just telling her about you."

"There can't have been too much to tell, can there?" Stephen responded.

"Ooh, we learn quickly," replied Jenny, delivering her smile again, "Squeeze in here. We can make room for you."

Stephen eased himself in against her thigh, and a shudder of desire passed through him. 'Don't read too much into it. You've been caught before.' The thought flashed aside and he smiled.

"This is my friend, Marguerite," said Jenny, indicating a slender girl who sat, elegantly poised, beside her, a bemused smile on her face, "We're Home Economics students. Have you got a light, Stevie?" Jenny held his hand around the match as he lit her cigarette, and she smiled into his eyes. "Marguerite's from Newcastle," she continued, exhaling the first puff of smoke.

"Missing home, are you? You'll soon get used to it. We'll have to plan something for the weekend." Mike spoke with his toothy grin. "I've got a car."

"Sarfend 'ere we come," offered Simon to no one in particular.

Marguerite and Jenny exchanged glances and smiled.

Pete Campbell began singing *Where have all the flowers gone?* They all joined in, and Stephen downed his pint in one as the song finished.

"You drink like the lads at home," jibed Marguerite, her smile a tease, "I didn't think you southerners could down a pint in one."

"I'm from the east coast – a mongrel mix of Saxon and Angle …,"

"Oh, I thought Mike said …,"

"No, that's me," chortled Simon, "I'm yer Londoner – darn from the old Bull and Bush and bottle-fed on yer Watney's Red Barrel."

They all laughed and chorused the television jingle "Watney's Red Barrel", as Des crossed the room from a small hatch that served the end nearest the bar. "Room for one more?" he asked.

"You can sit next to me, Des," suggested Jenny, "but stay away from Marguerite because she's engaged to a lad back home."

"That right, pet?"

"Aye – I've known my Bobby since we were at school together."

Stephen took an instant liking to Marguerite, and he could see that Des felt the same. There was something imperturbable about her that was immediately attractive. Besides, from Des's point of view she was one more student from the north.

"You have a lovely name," said Stephen, suddenly, "The marguerite with its long white rays of petals."

"Ooh, Stevie, you are romantic," interjected Jenny.

"It's a beautiful flower."

"The ox-eye daisy?" laughed Marguerite, "My mum named me after the wartime cook."

"Ever been put down, Last?" said Des, "You can't flirt with these northern lasses."

"Anyway, after Bobby her heart goes to Cliff."

"Cliff Richard?"

"He's gorgeous, but not ready to marry he says."

"How do you know that?" asked Stephen.

"Cliff wouldn't do anything without consulting his fans," Jenny offered as an explanation, "When he came to Wolverhampton, we stood in Queen's Square and screamed and screamed. When my dad saw it on the telly, he said he'd never seen the likes of it. Little did he know I was one of those doing the screaming."

The evening tumbled along, and they all settled comfortably with each other into the padded seats and the beer. Moving across the long room to the bar always involved an intimacy that was a delight and a challenge. Des and the other northern lads he attracted criticised the beer, comparing it unfavourably to northern beers and claiming they "wouldn't use it to water daisies". Joules – a distinguished Staffordshire brewery based in Stone was dubbed "Foul Joules" for no other reason than it was a midlands brew and the northern lads felt obliged to demean it in favour of their own beers. Stephen knew it was going to be like this for the next three years and, for the second time that evening, he was glad. As closing time approached, Pete and his friend moved the singing towards numbers like *Goodnight, Irene* and the sentiment of strangers enveloped the night.

They romped home together, arms linked, singing their way through the hamlet of Cotes Warren without a thought for the locals who might be asleep, blissfully unaware of the world around them, rocking their souls "in the bosom of Abraham".

When Stephen and Simon stumbled back into the common room, some of the second year students were already settled to a game of cards; others sat, reading or chatting, while a few watched television. The newscaster was presenting an account of a bomb blast in an Alabama church:

"... four young black girls died and more than twenty others were injured when a bomb exploded in the 17th Street Baptist church in Birmingham, Alabama ... Civil rights leader, Dr Martin Luther King, said he would go to Birmingham to preach his philosophy of non-violence. Dr King also said he has sent a telegram to Governor Wallace blaming him for the continued loss of life ... Dr King's cable said: 'The blood of four little children and 13 others critically injured is on your hands'."

A quiet bustle of activity followed this announcement; apart from expressions of condemnation, there seemed little else that anyone could usefully contribute. Meeting Bob's approval, they signed in. Simon flopped into a chair, and offered a cigarette to those nearby. Without thinking, by force of habit, Stephen went to his room, and pulled off his coat. He slipped into his long, tartan dressing gown, made a pot of tea in the small kitchen, and poured himself a cup. He placed the cup on its saucer – part of the set of crockery his mother had bought him for college – and walked into the common room.

"There's a pot of char in the kitchen, if anyone fancies a cup," he proffered, as a friendly gesture, and the other lads looked up.

There was a silence he didn't understand, and then a big youth called Brad called out "It's Lord Astor!" Simon looked up and grinned, and Stephen realised the other lads were all holding mugs. In his dressing gown, cup and saucer in hand, he must have struck what appeared to be an aristocratic note. He smiled back, grateful there was no malice in any of the faces. It was a name by which the older students were to know him until they left to begin teaching.

Stephen sat down next to Simon and the conversation drifted onto the Christine Keeler affair. She and a friend, Mandy Rice-Davies – immediately dubbed by the gutter press 'Randy Mandy', and by television programmes as 'Randy Mice-Davies' – had, it was claimed, gone down to Lord Astor's place where they'd been paid for sex. One paper alleged that the women had pocketed £200 a time.

"How on earth can anyone afford to pay £200 a shag?" thundered Brad.

"And the rest," chimed-in Bob.

"It'd take a teacher about five months to earn that. Christ, things need sorting out in this country. The toffs have had it their way for too long."

"It wasn't just Profumo who was caught with his pants down; the whole bunch closed around to protect him and they've lied their way out of government."

"The Establishment is on the way out. Our days of being led by 'those who know best', by 'the natural party of government,' are over. Make way for the New Order."

Suddenly, the whole common room burst into song; it was a number sung by Millicent Martin in *That Was The Week That Was* earlier in the year. They'd watched it apart, but now shared it together:

"See him in the House of Commons
Making laws to put the blame
While the object of his passion
Walks the streets to hide her shame."

It was sung to the tune of the music hall song *She was poor, but she was honest*, and laughter rocked the room as it had once rocked theatres.

Chapter Two

Caring for my patients

Kate Walsh, flattening the front of her new uniform for the umpteenth time, was breathless with trepidation. She glanced furtively around her at some of the other eager faces, and recognised a few from her days as a cadet nurse. In one way or another they were all fidgeting. Only one figure seemed completely calm. She was older than the others and wore a frilly cap. She stood, hands relaxed on her long-sleeved blue dress, gazing towards a door at the far end of the room. Kate looked down at her own uniform; this was her student nurse's uniform – her first ever! The starched, white apron, the blue dress and the white, starched cap fitted perfectly. Kate was pleased. Her cadet uniform had been awful, but they'd been measured for the new ones. She fiddled with the chain that fastened her pocket watch into one of the breast pockets, and then checked that her scissors and pen were still in the other. The nurse in the frilly cap caught her eye and she stopped; it was only a sign of nerves, of course, and a nurse ought not to be nervous.

As though at a given signal – and, later, Kate realised that it was the clock, not the door, at which the frilly-capped nurse had been gazing – the older woman turned and looked at each of the students in turn.

"I'm your Home Sister," she said, "Sister Maitland, and I will be responsible for supervising your preliminary training. You will walk each morning from here to the training school where you will complete your twelve weeks PTS before being allowed to continue your training on the wards of Staffham General. You will, of course, be in uniform as you walk through the town, and that means that you will process with decorum at all times. You will walk in pairs, following closely behind the ones in front of you. Should you need to speak, you will do so in well-modulated tones. Remember you are nurses and that your behaviour – at all times – reflects upon the good name of Staffham General."

Sister Maitland paused, as though expecting someone to contradict her – indeed, almost hoping that someone might summon up the temerity to do so – and then continued:

"You may have been attracted to nursing by such programmes as *Emergency Ward 10*, but you will find that the real thing bears little resemblance to what you might have seen on television. Few of the doctors will prove to be heart-throbs, and even if they do you will find little time to swoon over them. Real nursing requires strength of character, dedication and a selfless and abiding care for your patients. Nursing is not a part-time job. It is a vocation ..."

Sister Maitland paused as she said the word and looked around at the young women before her, as though letting them know she could spot a charlatan a mile off and before breakfast.

"At least half of you will fail to complete the twelve weeks preliminary training. When you arrive back here at the nurses' home at night you will wonder how you are ever going to stand on your two feet again. The external door will be locked by one of the Home Sisters at ten o'clock and lights-out will be ten-thirty ... There will be no late passes while you are in PTS. Anyone found out of bounds after ten-thirty will face instant dismissal. Is this understood?"

"Yes," mumbled a dozen somewhat awestruck voices, unaware that they had joined the army or that there was a war being waged.

"Yes, Sister!"

"Yes, Sister."

The heavily-fortified police van – a steel divider separating the white from the black prisoners – took Nelson Mandela to the Palace of Justice in Pretoria. To avoid the enormous crowd of supporters at the front of the building, the prisoners were driven to the rear and taken in through great iron gates. As he descended from the van, Nelson could hear the crowd singing and chanting.

The courtroom was jam-packed with journalists both local and international. Nelson looked down at his prison clothes – the khaki shorts and the flimsy sandals – and felt disgusted. Moreover, he had been in solitary confinement for months, and had lost almost two stone. He looked up and smiled at the gallery.

The charges were read out by the deputy attorney general of the Transvaal – a small, dapper man whose voiced squeaked when he became emotional – and Nelson listened as he and his fellow prisoners were accused of "complicity in over two hundred acts of sabotage aimed at facilitating violent revolution and an armed invasion of the country". If convicted, the penalty was death by hanging.

Nelson's defence lawyer stood up and asked for a remand "on the grounds that the defence has not had time to prepare its case. A number of the accused have been held in solitary confinement for unconscionable lengths of time, the state has had three months to prepare its case, while we have only received the indictment today".

The judge, sitting in his flowing red robes beneath the wooden canopy, gave a three-week adjournment – that is, until October 29.

A fine drizzle paved the way to the training school, and Kate and her fellow students were glad of the long, navy woollen cloaks with the purple lining. The training school was a pleasant enough building that might, at one time, have been the town house of someone well-to-do. Rambling and sandy, it formed part of a crescent of houses in what had once been a select part of the town and, even now, bore a distinguished appearance.

They were met by two Sister Tutors – Sister Moore and Sister Codsley – and the look in both their eyes removed any idea that anyone was in for anything but a hard time. Sister Codsley was small, shrew-like woman and she scuttled along hallways and corridors as soundlessly as a mouse; she might have been any age from thirty to fifty. Sister Moore, an attractive woman who was, apparently, much younger, and who was immaculately groomed, had the look of someone who had "come up the hard way", bloodied but unbowed. She wasted no time in getting down to business:

"You arrived late this morning. Don't let it happen

again. Your day will start at 8.30 sharp and you will have lectures or tutorials until one o'clock when you will break for lunch. After lunch you will resume your studies until six o'clock when you will return to the nurses' home. Some days you will be on the wards or on what we call 'field trips' ..."

Sister Moore paused on the word as though such an experience might have held an unspecified threat.

"Now, I will hand you your timetables. Generally, you will be together for lectures on anatomy, physiology and nutrition, knowledge of diseases, hygiene and care of your patients ..."

She paused again, so that the final phrase could sink in, and then handed out the individual timetables.

"For practical sessions, you will work in smaller groups. These will cover such things as how and where to give injections, correct lifting techniques, how to set up trolleys for drips, catheters and nasal gastric tubes and the application of dressings ... to name but a few of the skills you will acquire to become a competent nurse."

Kate was pleased to hear the word 'acquire'. Despite her tone, Sister Moore seemed to have no doubt that these skills would be 'acquired'. Once the timetables had been given out, Sister Codsley stepped forward quietly and asked the students to follow her into one of the practical rooms. This had been set up as a small ward. There were six beds, a sterilising room, a sluice room that housed urinals, bedpans and a bedpan hopper. At one end of this room was a cupboard, neatly packed with enamel bowls, instruments and linen. Two of the beds were occupied by dummies; the titter this caused in several of the girls was quelled immediately by one look from Sister Moore, a look that paralysed two of the students on the spot. No one found the skeleton funny! There were metal poles on wheels in one corner; in another, two-tier trolleys of stainless steel.

"Now, nurses," said Sister Codsley, crisply, "Sister Moore and I are going to show you how to make a bed. Nurse Walsh, you will time us, please."

How she was known by name Kate was unaware, but she reached for her breast-pocket watch and smiled. In less than three minutes, working together, the sisters had stripped the bed and re-made it. There wasn't one student who wasn't impressed.

"What did you notice, nurses?"

For a moment no one spoke – some out of modesty, some out of ignorance, others because they did not want to appear too knowledgeable in front of their friends. As the eyes of the two Sister Tutors bore into them, Kate – who had been a cadet nurse for two years – spoke up:

"You worked as a team, kept the bottom sheet as taut as a drum-skin, shook the blankets as little as possible, started at the top of the bed, had the counterpane hanging equally on both sides and made sure that the folded corners were exact triangles."

Sister Moore's left eyebrow rose half-way up her forehead and her lips pursed. She wasn't sure whether this one was taking the mickey or not. Kate wasn't sure, either, why she'd rattled off her experience in such a fashion; what she did know was that her action had been inspired, in some way, by a desire not to be put down.

"Well spoken, Nurse Walsh," said Sister Codsley.

"Perhaps you would care to demonstrate your expertise with the help of a friend," pursued Sister Moore,

"... and explain what you're doing, and why, as you proceed."

"I'll help you," said a student who had been watching Kate closely. She was a tall girl with a soft, pretty face that had a bird-like quality about it. Kate nodded to the other girl, indicating that she was to copy her every move, and then went to the bed. They stripped it, laying the sheets and blanket – all folded into three – on two chairs the Sister Tutors had previously placed at the foot of the bed.

"We ensure that the bottom sheet is taut because wrinkled sheets are the main cause of bed sores. We shake the sheets and the blanket as little as possible to avoid creating dust and spreading infection. We ensure that the corners are neat and that the counterpane hangs correctly because the ward looks tidier."

Kate glanced over the bed and smiled at the student who had offered to help her; at that moment an intimacy was born between them. Sister Codsley stepped over and examined the bed.

"It always pays to start at the top," she said, running her hand along the counterpane, "In that way, you're sure of leaving enough of the top sheet to make good corners. Have you anything to add, Sister Moore?"

"As Nurse Walsh has said, wrinkled sheets are the main cause of bed sores – despite what you might have heard to the contrary – and bed sores are a result of poor nursing care ... and no one wants or deserves such care." She paused and looked at Kate, who thought a faint smile might be hovering about the Sister Tutor's lips. "Well done," she continued, "and in under three minutes, thirty seconds. We shall expect much of you, Nurse Walsh."

Cynthia Lennon had suffered enough at the voice of John's Aunt Mimi, and move out to a bed-sit in Hoylake. It was a grim, little, five-pounds-a-week bed-sit and Cynthia smiled to herself, ironically, thinking that John was touring the country living in luxury hotels while she remained in virtual hiding with his son, Julian. John was expected to be 'available' to his girl fans; a Beatle with a wife and (heaven forbid!) a child might have turned off the teenagers.

'Why do you put up with it? Are you afraid of John?' Someone had asked her that once, but it wasn't true. The Beatles manager, Brian Epstein, had insisted that she remain out of the picture. It was true that John had struck her – years before, when he'd caught her dancing with his friend. He'd punched her in the face, knocking Cynthia's head back against pipes that ran along the wall behind her, and then walked away. Three months later he telephoned, asking her to go back to him and apologising for what he'd done.

Now, she and her mum pushed Julian round and round in his pram, desperate almost to the point of hysteria to keep him quiet so as not to disturb the other tenants who were old and rather cranky. Cynthia was pleased not to be doing anything that might harm John's career.

"Thank you," said Kate to her new-found friend as soon as the group was released for lunch, "I'm Kate Walsh."

"Joan Whiting – pleased to meet you. I just felt that she was hoping you'd fall flat on your face, and I didn't want that to happen."

"I think Sister Moore cares passionately about her

26

work and her profession. She'd rather sort us out now than have us harm a patient later. I like her."

Joan Whiting looked shrewdly at Kate and thought that it wasn't usual to cement a friendship with a disagreement.

"I came across her sort at boarding school. There was always an element of the bully about some of the staff. I don't mean they'd actually hurt you, but more that they always had to be in charge and everyone had to know it. Only in that way, they felt, could any kind of order be kept."

"You went to boarding school?"

"Yes, daddy and mummy were away a lot. He worked in the diplomatic service, and they thought that boarding school would give us a settled 'home life'."

"Us?"

"My sister, Rosemary, and I."

"How exciting. I always wanted to go to boarding school."

"It wasn't, and you wouldn't have – not after you'd been there for a term. It was mind-bendingly boring. The one thing I did get out of it, however, was the time to read."

"I enjoy reading. My favourite writer is Georgette Heyer. I'm reading *The Toll-gate* at the moment, but my favourite is *Bath Tangle*."

Joan looked at Kate and smiled. Suddenly, without any hint of her intentions, she reached over and hugged Kate round the shoulders. Kate blushed, but did not like to pull away. She was sure there was nothing wrong with the affection Joan was showing.

"Try reading Jane Austen," said Joan, "and see if you like her. I've got all six of her books. I'll lend you one."

The lunch – a new word for the midday meal that Kate's family had always called 'dinner' – was ample beyond anything she could have imagined. Potato and leek soup was followed by sausage and mash with peas, and this was rounded off by spotted dick and custard. The students barely had time to eat it before they were herded off for the afternoon session – a lecture by Sister Codsley on the control of diseases. "Cleanliness, nurses," she concluded, "is, indeed, next to godliness – and it starts with yours. Bath daily – if a bath is available, and if it isn't strip wash at the sink. There will be enough foul smells on the wards without you adding to them."

Lord Home had a problem. When he visited Harold Macmillan in the nursing home, the Prime Minister had asked him if he would consider taking on the leadership of the party and, therefore, the job of Prime Minister. Alec was quite happy in the House of Lords and with his work in the Foreign Office. Besides, it involved renouncing a peerage that had been held for hundreds of years; it meant finding a new constituency and fighting a by-election in order to be able to sit in the House of Commons. Alec was not sure, also, about the state of his health; he'd suffered from tuberculosis and was having trouble with his eyes. He had no training in economic matters, and these were likely to figure significantly in the next General Election, which could not be put off forever. He had once, jokingly, told a journalist that he did his sums with matchsticks. Harold Wilson, an ex-grammar schoolboy and leader of the Labour Party, "was not likely to miss a trick like that".

Kate found herself sharing a room with a quiet girl called Sheila Pratt. Sheila had said little during their first day at the training school but her concentration had been intense. She was pale and underweight, and looked almost sickly – one of those people who were always suffering from 'the sniffles' (as Kate's mother put it) or tonsillitis. As they settled in that first evening, it was Kate who did most of the talking and she soon discovered that Sheila came from Leeds.

"Isn't there an infirmary there?"

"Yes – a good one."

"But you didn't want to train there?"

"No."

"Glad to get away from home?"

The pause was enough to tell Kate that she'd hit some nail or other on the head, but she got no further with Sheila and decided to seek out Joan, who had a room of her own – small enough to qualify as a broom cupboard – at the top of the house where the servants would have slept.

"It's going to be bloody cold when the weather turns," said Joan, her voice a blend of exasperation and resignation, "Who are you in with?"

"Sheila Pratt."

"Oh, Miss Intensely Working-Class."

"You're quick to judge people."

"I've met her sort before. There were one or two at boarding school, sent there because their parents – who would have scrimped and saved, no doubt, to do so – thought that a bit of culture might rub off. We soon knocked that out of them. At boarding school there are the rich and the poor, but you're all one class."

Kate had never met anyone quite like Joan before; to her all those who went to boarding school had rich parents. Her own mother had had a hankering to send her to a "posh" school but "the money wasn't there", as she explained.

"I'm not sure you're right about Sheila," she whispered, "I think she's just withdrawn. She'll come out in time."

"You're a nice person, Kate Walsh, and you'll make the best nurse among the lot of us ... Do you know what made me go into nursing?"

Kate waited, quietly.

"Stubbornness! My parents wanted me to go to a finishing school. Can you imagine! Anyway, I finished my A levels – English, Law, French and European History ..."

"You read Law?"

"Daddy insisted. In fact, he chose three of my A Level subjects. I insisted on English, and I had to take that as a fourth ... You looked puzzled, Kate ... Dad's a conservative with both a big and a small 'c'. Lord Home – pronounced 'Hume', for some reason best known to the family – has been saying for some years that we need to join the European Community. You remember de Gaulle snubbed us when we were set to sign the Treaty of Rome? Well, daddy is convinced that we will join, and what better qualifications could I have when the time comes than the three A Levels he chose for me? All the family are lawyers, in one way or the other ... and so I decided to become a nurse!"

She laughed, and Kate thought she had never heard more abandoned and joyous mirth in her life.

In the common room at A House, Stephen Last and Simon Wiseman, sitting with the whole house around their small television set, roared with laughter as *TW3* came to its end that evening. David Frost, using that punishing, gimlet-like voice of his was pillorying Sir Alec Douglas-Home, who had accepted the premiership:

"... you are the dupe and unwitting tool of a conspiracy: the conspiracy of a tiny band of desperate men who have seen in you their last slippery chance of keeping the ladders of power and influence within their privileged circle ... you have always drifted with the tide ... and that tide has eventually left you naked and exposed on the shore ... you, in your sixty years, have foreseen nothing ..."

The laughter almost choked them as David Frost summed up with a quick ad-lib "So that's the choice before the electorate. On the one side, Lord Home; on the other, Harold Wilson. Dull Alec versus Smart Alec. Good night."

Robin Day, sitting in the TV lounge of the Royal Hotel, Scarborough, watching the programme late on Saturday night during the Labour Party Conference, observed a clutch of Labour Party notables – among them Barbara Castle and Dick Crossman – also roaring with laughter at *TW3* as it abused the Tory government.

"Marvellous stuff! Marvellous!" said Dick Crossman, afterwards, "But of course the BBC won't be allowed to get away with it when Labour is in power."

CHAPTER THREE

Friday, November 22

Stephen Last was just entering the washroom – a large space with a double row of sinks along the centre, each served with its own tap from a common pipe, and toilet cubicles against the walls – when Simon Wiseman, rushing from his own room with a peculiarly distressed smile on his face, accosted him.

"Have you heard the news? President Kennedy has been shot."

"He can't have been," replied Stephen, only realising much later how inane the response must have sounded.

"It's just been on the radio."

They both walked slowly to the common room where other students were watching the news on the BBC. "Dallas, Texas – the whole world in shock – shot in the head – sitting next to his wife, Jenny – several shots rang out – the presidential motorcade ..." It was more than anyone could take in. It wasn't just the death of one man; it was the death of a dream.

Martin Luther King was in his upstairs bedroom, packing for a trip. The television was on in the background, but he was only listening in part until an emergency news bulletin interrupted the programme. For seconds only, Martin stared at the screen, and then called out to his wife.

"Corrie," he yelled, "Corrie, President Kennedy has been shot – maybe killed."

Coretta King rushed up the stairs and into the bedroom. They sat side by side on the bed, listening to the news, taking in its awful import. 'The President is dead.' Martin turned to his wife.

"This is going to happen to me, too," he said, quietly.

Kate Walsh had been off duty for almost a couple of hours and was absolutely shattered. She rested on her bed, waiting for the various aches to pass from her feet and arms and legs and back.

It had been a long, hard day, beginning in the Sister's office with the ward report. The nurses going off duty had given the usual report on every patient. The night staff had already placed the 'nil by mouth' signs on those patients due for surgery. Kate, working with a third year nurse, had the job of bathing the patients ready for surgery, changing them into their theatre gowns, pulling on the white socks and covering their hair with a paper hat. She helped to strip the beds and remake them with freshly-laundered sheets. She'd placed on the bed the special canvas sheet with the slots down each side into which the porters could insert the wooden poles to lift the patients onto the theatre trolley. Making the patients comfortable and speaking a few words of reassurance was what Kate enjoyed; it was why she had become a nurse.

It was always a traumatic time for the patient as they waited to be taken to the theatre. The uncertainty, combined with the unfamiliar procedures, was unsettling.

Patients had to be checked to see that false teeth were removed, as were jewellery and make-up. Only wedding rings were allowed and these had to be taped carefully.

"You'll need to keep calm, Nurse," the third year nurse reminded her, reassuringly, "Sometimes we get behind with the pre-meds and the anaesthetists can get stroppy. It's best to ignore them and let them rave. The patient comes first and some of these old dears can't do much for themselves. We'll have to collect each one from the ward, as well, and make sure their airways are clear. They're vulnerable with that down their throats and they could choke. So we stay with each patient until they come round …"

Kate listened as the more experienced nurse talked and demonstrated. She couldn't but admire the other young woman's confidence and poise. One day, she thought, I might – just might – reach that level of competence myself.

Harold Wilson, on a speaking tour in North Wales, was hurrying to the nearest BBC station, having been asked to record his reaction to the news of President Kennedy's assassination, when he stopped off at a fish and chip shop to get a bite to eat.

"Good Evening, Mr Wilson. You seem in a hurry, sir. You've heard the news, I take it?"

"I'm on my way to the BBC now."

"It's a bad business."

Harold reached into his pocket for change, but the owner put out a restraining hand.

"Have that one on the house, Mr Wilson. Put it down as my contribution to the memory of Jack Kennedy."

Lord Home, now Alec Douglas-Home and Prime Minister of the United Kingdom, arrived at Broadcasting House with only three minutes to spare before he was to pay his tribute to President Kennedy after the nine o'clock news. He was still in a state of shock and the sense of loss pervaded him. He and Kennedy had been in tune about world affairs ever since he'd been received at the White House.

Alec got into the lift, which moved upwards slightly, juddered to a halt and stuck. The lift attendant tried various buttons, and it moved not upwards but downwards. Thinking himself lucky, the Prime Minister raced up three flights of stairs, his lungs bursting, his heart beating overtime, and made it to the studio just in time.

At the Globe Cinema, Stockton, the Beatles were playing to an audience who could hear nothing but their own screaming. *With the Beatles* had just been released and the Fab Four were reprising their days in Hamburg with Chuck Berry's *Roll Over Beethoven*. The squealing irritated John Lennon. He felt they might as well not have been singing; four waxworks dummies, shaking their Beatle hairstyles, would produce the same effect. The concerts were nothing to do with music, he thought, as the teddy bears, dolls and jelly babies came hurtling onto the stage. A tribal chorus of screaming resounded around the hall as they reached the end of the song, and John let out an obscenity.

Kate Walsh, cocooned from the world in her room, sat on the edge of her bed swapping stories with Heather Burton about their first day on the wards. Kate had learned earlier that Heather had stayed on at grammar school and attained sufficiently high grades for a university place without having any intention of going to one. "I thought I deserved a decent education," she laughed, "whether I was going to be a nurse or not. Why should teachers get all the best grades!" It wasn't a question.

"I started off doing the TPRs," she was saying, "God – I couldn't even find the pulse of the first old man. His wrist was so bony, I felt sorry for him. He was a nice old boy, though. He kept smiling to reassure me that he had one! There were about thirty patients on the ward. It took me over an hour and a half to get their temperatures, pulses and respirations."

Kate smiled to herself; during her cadet days she had learned that it could, and should, be done in a third of that time.

"I enjoyed feeding the patients, I must say," Heather continued, "I was told off for standing up, but I just didn't like to sit down until the ward sister told me it was best."

"Otherwise the patients felt you were hurrying them?"

"Yes. I really felt I got to know my patients during mealtimes. The wards are so big and everyone has their private space, and so you could talk, and let them talk, without anyone over-hearing."

"You've Florence Nightingale to thank for that," Kate cut in, "She was responsible for the design of these words. Plenty of fresh air – give the patients space! And the curtains help, of course."

"The ward sister told me that it's important to keep an eye on the patients, whatever else you may be doing, and she insisted that there was a nurse on the ward at all times. If anyone had to go out to the sluice room, for example, she said they were not to leave the ward before ensuring that there was another nurse on there."

Kate remembered her own impression of the wards, as she listened to Heather talking. She had been surprised at how quiet they were especially in the afternoons when the physicians had finished their visits. She'd appreciated her cotton dress at such times because the wards tended to be warm. She'd liked the busy orderliness of the ward: the Ward Sister doing her rounds, clearing the flowers from the centre table at mealtimes so that those patients who wanted to do so could eat together, even the urinal round when you wore pink gowns over your uniform and completed the I and O charts recording intake and output!

"You enjoy nursing, don't you," said Heather, smiling at Kate.

"Yes," she said without any reservation, "I do. We can make the world a better place by providing good patient care. That's what I'm here for. There was a time when working class people couldn't afford treatment. We've moved on now, thank the Lord, and let's keep moving."

Heather seemed about to say something when there was a knock on the door and Miriam Davison burst into the room, transistor radio in her hand.

"Have you heard?" she enquired.

"Heard what?" queried Kate.

"President Kennedy has been shot."

"What? We've been on the wards all day. I never knew."

"It's on everywhere. It's on the radio now," Miriam hollered, adjusting the tuning knob and placing her transistor on Kate's bedside table. "... the crowd's cheers turned to screams – the President's wife crawled over the back of the limousine – Mrs Kennedy cradled her husband in her arms – sirens screaming …"

Kate looked around her small room – her bed squashed against one wall, Sheila Pratt's against the one radiator, and with barely space to swing a cat between them, the wardrobe shoved behind the door, the little side table with her travelling alarm clock, the rickety chest of drawers that served as a desk and on which they were supposed to keep their books and to study, the family photographs pinned to the walls of fading yellow – and realised that this would remain her image of the President's death.

"It's terrible," screeched Miriam, "to think that anybody could actually kill the President of the United States … Do you remember what he said in his inaugural speech?"

Kate and Heather looked at her, struck dumb by her passion, waiting to hear. As Miriam spoke, Joan appeared at the door and rested against the jamb.

"He said – and I'm paraphrasing, you understand – he said something like we were a new generation and that the torch of freedom had passed to us, that we were disciplined and purposeful and committed to change the world for the better, that we'd meet any hardship and bear any burden and support any friend to achieve that end …"

"He also brought us to the brink of nuclear war," interrupted Joan, in her implacable voice, "Had Khrushchev not had the sense to back down, we could all be dead by now. Kennedy's Americanised manhood got in the way of common sense."

Miriam looked at Joan: puzzled, bewildered, not believing anyone could speak like that of a dead man who had been a hero. She said "He said 'ask not what your country can do for you, but what you can do for your country'."

"He pushed us to the edge of nuclear war," repeated Joan.

"He brought us to the edge, or he saved us," said Heather, quietly, "We can debate it endlessly, but what is certain about Jack Kennedy is that he knew we all inhabit a very small planet, we all breathe the same air and we all cherish our children's futures ... he was a beacon of hope, a way forward ... and now he's dead."

She looked up at Joan, daring her to contradict. Joan said nothing.

Mandy Rice-Davies, who was living at her parents' home, heard the knocking and the scuffles on their doorstep. The press had sought her opinions on almost everything since the Profumo affair exploded in the papers and on the television screens, but she wasn't expecting a visit that evening. When she opened the door and saw a dozen reporters standing in the driveway, she could scarcely believe her eyes or ears.

"Mandy," they chorused, "What do you think of the assassination of President Kennedy?"

Billy Graham had just teed off for the fifth hole at the Black Mountain course in North Carolina, when the manager of the Christian radio station he owned there drove up and shouted out "The President has been shot!"

Billy had liked Kennedy; the President had endeared himself to him by smoothing the way for his crusade in Colombia. The attendance at their meetings had been as high as twenty thousand. He'd last seen the President at the 1963 National Prayer Breakfast where, realising Billy was suffering from flu and shivering in the cold without his overcoat, Kennedy had excused him a meeting with great graciousness.

Billy had been troubled about the President's proposed visit to Texas. It wasn't a state that was friendly towards Kennedy. The Republican candidate, Barry Goldwater, had created quite a groundswell of support in the state. 'Don't go to Texas!' Billy's foreboding had borne no fruit; it was a foreboding, nothing he could put his finger on, and he'd been unable to contact Jack Kennedy.

Hearing the dreadful news, Billy rushed to the station's studio where he was handed the latest teletype; the news was inconclusive. Billy decided to go on air and pray for the President and his family, and read scripture. As he did so, a scrap of paper was held up against the glass. 'He's dead,' it said. Minutes later, Walter Cronkite broke the news to a traumatised nation. Billy Graham turned to the friend with him, and they spoke of the President and prayed for his family and for the new President, Lyndon Baines Johnson.

Lyndon B Johnson – the fifty-five year old Texan and, until that moment, Vice-President of the United States of America – was aboard the presidential jet with Jenny Kennedy, her clothes still stained with her husband's blood, and with Jack Kennedy's body. Before it had taken off, he took the oath of office.

When the jet touched down in Washington, he told reporters "I will do my best; that is all I can do. I ask for your help, and God's."

Stephen laughed and passed Simon a cigarette. 'The guitar, the magic guitar that eases all pressures ... Pete is the pivot of the evening – strumming, singing, talking, drinking ... an evening like any other. The air gently warmed by beer and companionship. The pleasure of leaning against a girl's thigh as she sits on the mantelpiece ... the pleasure of being crushed as the pub fills, and the heat building patches of moisture against the girls' blouses with their dark bra straps ... the students gathering ... the night closing in on us, the music becoming louder, the singing lustier and split with throaty, beery sounds'.

Trays of beer swayed from the bar, held aloft over talking, singing, snogging heads. Someone stands suddenly, and two pints of special bitter shower down covering Des's trousers. He grins that boyish grin of his and squeezes his groin past girls' backs. Jenny laughed up at him over her gin and lime; her eyes were wide, expressive and free. Knots of girls stood about the room, giggling, their eyes seeking a walk back to college, their mouths chattering.

"I saw Crisp snogging tonight," spluttered Simon.

"When?" asked Stephen, without too much interest.

"When those lads opened the window behind us to get out to the bog. Crisp's had a few birds since he's been here, hasn't he?"

"Yeah," was all Stephen replied, but it said everything.

Simon handed his cigarettes round. The term was pressing on, and they were now smoking Silk Cut; Peter Stuyvesant would have to wait until for the new term; only the children of grocers and publicans could afford them now. The smoke hung from the ceiling to just above head level. A great shout went up.

"Go on, Josie!"

The girl – very pale and dressed completely in tight, black clothes – sat on the piano, dangling her legs, enjoying her moment. Someone passed her a pint and she swung her legs.

"Fifteen seconds!"

She raised the glass and pushed out her breasts. Even the guitar playing had stopped. She placed the rim on her lips and tilted the glass until it was empty.

"Twenty seconds," everyone roared.

She stood and stretched out her arms. A gang pushed their way towards the piano. The girl's eyes flickered and she fell from the piano into their waiting arms – out cold. They carried her to the car. All was still until someone pushed forward for more beer and the guitars were strummed and they all started to sing.

A final year student, Barry Glover, sitting next to Stephen, leaned over and whispered in his ear.

"She's a diabetic."

He shook his shoulders and gave Stephen a grin, as if to say 'you make your own choices in life'. Barry Glover was what Simon termed a 'professional northerner'. His region circumscribed his identity. He was the kind of person who supported Newcastle United through thick and thin, bad or good and to the end of the world. Nothing north of Northallerton Gate could have anything bad said against it, or anything south anything good said about it.

The twisting network of talk and laughter and song now focussed on Pete and his girl and their crowd. 'Scores of minds reduced to one consciousness,' thought Stephen.

"If I had a hammer,

I'd hammer in the morning
I'd hammer in the evening
All over this land,
I'd hammer out danger,
I hammer out a warning
I'd hammer out the love between my brothers and my
sisters
All over this land."
Somehow, he felt that it should go on forever.

It was bitterly cold in New York, when the news came that the President had been murdered. The first thing the blacks wanted to know was whether a black man had been responsible. John F Kennedy had been the most popular president among blacks ever since Franklin Roosevelt.

Malcolm X had given his views – the President had recognised the successors of South Vietnam's President, Ngo Dinh Diem, and his brother, Ngo Dinh Nhu when the president had been killed in a military coup, and thought that Kennedy "never foresaw that the chickens would come home to roost so soon." He felt the atmosphere of violence in the United States had been tolerated by the Kennedy administration, and that it was this atmosphere that had claimed the life of the President.

❋

Twenty four hours had passed when Stephen eased himself against the wall, coffee mug in hand, and settled into the hushed atmosphere. *That Was the Week That Was* had started, and in the common room hands of cards were un-played on the tables, darts hung from the board, newspapers were folded or dropped casually to the floor and books hung on the arms of chairs. No one was expecting jokes that night, and no one was disappointed.

They'd been talking all day, and now they wanted someone outside themselves to bring it all together. Just as Dylan's words caught the thought or feeling you couldn't express yourself, so it was hoped that David Frost's team might catch the spirit of broken hope and despair that Kennedy's assassination had created.

When they'd arrived back from The Red Lion, Simon had talked all night.

"It's the shock. No one could have foreseen this. The man was a beacon of light – he showed the road forward, the road to a new kind of freedom. Whether he understood that fact or not, he engendered it in all of us – it wasn't just the Americans. It wasn't what he had done, but what his presidency made possible for the future ... I feel empty, Stephen ... I feel as though part of me has simply stopped functioning ... It shouldn't have happened ... In some ways, I can't actually believe it has happened ... Anyone else, but not Kennedy ... He gave us the chance to dream ..."

He'd spoken like this all night, over and over, as though grieving the loss of a personal friend or a close member of his own family.

Watching now, the thirty students in the common room heard David Frost open the programme, and then tributes came from Roy Kinnear, David Kernan, Kenneth Cope, Willie Rushton, Lance Percival – names familiar to all of them. David Frost, himself, offered a summary that captured the mood exactly.

"...with the murder of John Kennedy, death has become immediate to people all over the world. For the first time, because of the nature of the man and the nature of a shrinking world, people everywhere feel they've lost someone they'll miss ..."

When Millicent Martin began to sing Herbert Kretzmer's song *The Summer of His Years*, Stephen got up, quietly, and left. He found the lane that ran down behind the college and made his way to the little bridge that crossed the stream from the field. Sitting under the bridge, his eyes hot, watching the sluggish stream lose itself in the mud, he searched his pockets, slowly. 'Cigarettes and matches.' The cigarette drooped between his lips. He lit it and drew the smoke deep into his lungs. 'Stale and dry as sun-bleached hay.' He tossed the match into the stream and watched it become the colour of mud. He removed the cigarette from his mouth, stubbed it out, replaced it in the packet and then crushed the packet, forever. 'I want to cry, and then pass on.'

Chapter 4

Everything that is nice
and decent

The serving hatch clattered upwards, the queue leaned forward and the bored old lady raised her arm and dropped cabbage onto the first plate. Stephen waited, his eyes scanning the dining hall. Jenny Pryce was sitting with friends – other girls who were part of the large Home Economics Department. They always looked so clean and cool and efficient – yes, and attractive in their pink overalls. They didn't seem to have a hair out of place – ever. He'd arrived late for one of the Education lectures and quickly shaved with his electric razor at the side of the room. One of them had actually complained to Des about "Stephen performing his toilet" in the lecture room, as though he'd urinated on the floor. At the time, it had made him feel dirty, and he didn't need that; as it was, he felt awkward enough with women.

His long conversations with Des had also unsettled him. They'd got to know each other quite well since the beginning of term – both being in the same English and Education groups brought them together a great deal, and Stephen envied Des his ease with women. They'd talked a lot about more or less everything, including their relationships with women.

"I like them young, myself," Des had said, "You can mould them to your ways. If they've had experience, they can be a bit awkward. Takes them longer to get to know what you like. Christ! When Elizabeth and I first got together she was bloody useless – in a snog, you know …"

Stephen didn't; he'd never had a snog – a kiss, yes, but never a snog.

"… stiff as hell she was. She'd sit on my knees stiff as a board … You can loosen them up working from scratch."

Everything in Des's room was neat and tidy rather as one imagined an old maid's room to be: clothes were neatly folded, books stood in piles and even the record player was parallel with the edge of the table on which it stood. 'Sitting in a garden shed, warm on a winter's day,' thought Stephen, not knowing from where, or why, the thought came.

"Being free, Last, you're a lucky bugger. They're some well-stacked birds here."

"I can't say I'm too keen to get involved," Stephen had replied. It wasn't true, of course, but he'd meant it in a certain way, without fully understanding what he meant. He added "I suppose having a steady bird has its advantages."

"One thing Elizabeth has given me has been a sense of purpose. That's one thing a woman does for you – gives you something to aim for."

"It sounds a bit narrowing, put like that."

"You have to have had a woman to know what I mean. It's fantastic how much you learn about women from just knowing one well … in fact, it's difficult to know much about women at all until you've known one of them really well ... Look at Crisp. Look at the number of birds he's had since he's been here – and what does he know about women?"

Without knowing why, Stephen had said – on that evening or another (he could never remember) "I suppose I learned ... a bit ... from Una."

Stephen took his loaded plate, ignoring anyone he might know and sat alone in the corner of the dining hall. He wanted to be alone to enable him to absorb the embarrassment of that moment. He knew why he'd said it, of course. Thinking about it later, Stephen realised that he'd wanted to impress Des with the knowledge that he, too, had known one woman well; but he hadn't – not in any real sense of the word.

Una had been a foster child, and Stephen had met her in his early teens. She had been his first love, his first stolen kiss. They'd hung around together, as part of a group but special to each other. She'd been pale and blonde with grey-blue, dreamy eyes and their feelings for each other had been what adults term – somewhat, and unnecessarily, contemptuously – "puppy love". They'd spent hours outside the corner shop, under the lamplight, talking. Una had been unhappy with her foster parents and wanted to get away. Stephen had written the letter to the Child Welfare people for her, and Una had been moved to a large, happy family home.

"You wrote the letter," Des had queried.

"Yes. Una was frightened to ..."

"And you persuaded her? ... You sound like a bloody martyr, Stephen. I wouldn't have done that ... the girl

wanted someone to talk to – nothing more. But you …
No, it wouldn't be fair."

"Come on."

"No, no, I could be wrong."

But he hadn't been. Des had somehow guessed that Stephen's motives in writing the letter for Una had been because he didn't want to get further involved. Problem sorted – cut and dried, done and dusted. Looking back, Stephen realised that, in Des's perception, there was some truth.

"Pleading guilty to charges of conspiring to pervert the cause of justice, and also of perjury, Christine Keeler was sentenced to nine months in prison at the Old Bailey today."

Listening to the news item, Des had been amazed at the severity of the sentence. Christine Keeler, a prostitute, had been found sleeping with John Profumo, the War Minister, and Eugene Ivanov, a naval attaché at the Russian Embassy, at more or less the same time. The aristocracy had got involved and embarrassed themselves, Profumo had lied to Parliament, and everyone in the press and on television had had a field day. It had been "a gas" – as Simon Wiseman liked to express it. Profumo had been forced to resign, Macmillan's government was on the verge of toppling, the old order was standing around with shit on its face and it looked as though a young woman – whose favours they'd all been gagging for – was paying the price..

"The twenty-one year old broke down in tears as the judge pronounced sentence."

Des turned off the radio and reached for his guitar. He begun to strum and then to sing the Hank William's song:
"Hear that lonesome whippoorwill
He sounds too blue to cry
The midnight train is whinin' low
I'm so lonesome I could cry"

Kate Walsh had got to know Sheila Pratt, her room-mate at the nurses' home, quite well, despite the girl's reticence. 'She's downtrodden,' thought Kate, 'unsure of herself.'

"I'm very ordinary," she'd said one evening when they were both tucked up in bed reading through their lecture notes on the digestive system, "my parents never really expected much of me."

"They must be pleased that you're training as a nurse," replied Kate, looking up with some interest because this was the first time Sheila had shown any willingness to talk.

"Not really. Mum thinks I'd be happier working in a shop and dad says it would bring in more money ... Everyone else always seems more intelligent than me. I can't always join in their conversations because I don't know what they're talking about ... you're not laughing at me, are you?"

"No," said Kate, rapidly, because, in a way, that was exactly what she was doing. She felt sorry for Sheila, but the other girl sounded like some doe-eyed dog that'd been told off. "You mustn't think so little of yourself, Sheila. Confidence is half the battle."

"I don't see what my life would hold if I did what mum and dad wanted," continued Sheila, "I would end up being just a wife and mother – like mum. There's nothing wrong with that, but it … it doesn't lead anywhere, does it?"

"I've not thought about it in that way," murmured Kate, "I suppose I'll get married one day but I want to be a nurse."

"There you are, you see – you're sure you'll get married one day. I've never been sure of anything. I've always felt that if I opened my mouth I'd say the wrong thing."

"Everyone feels like that at some time or other."

"I always feel like that – all the time."

"You mean with people like Joan around?"

"Yes – she scares the life out of me."

"She doesn't mean to – it's just her way. She's been educated at a private school, and so she sounds sure of herself but it doesn't make her any better than you."

"I don't want to be anything special," offered Sheila, after a longish silence as they thought about Joan, "I failed the 11+ and went to an ordinary secondary modern and so I know I'm not in the top drawer where brains are concerned, but I do want to be a good nurse … But what I don't want to do is to … is to turn my back on my roots. It's there that I belong."

Kate did laugh then and Sheila looked over, her eyes almost brimming with tears.

"What's so funny? I thought I could speak to you."

"Sheila," replied Kate, going over to the other girl and putting her arms round her shoulders, "I'm laughing at your foolishness in thinking you've got nothing to say to anyone. What you've just said is quite breath-taking. It would knock the guts out of any company. You want to 'be a good nurse but not turn your back on your roots'.

That's quite breath-taking, Sheila – it contains a whole vision of what we are about. We're the first generation of our families to be able to do this."

Sheila looked puzzled, but knew she'd found an ally.

Nelson Mandela, back in court charged with treason, sensed that Justice de Wet had grown more hostile to him and the other leading members of the African National Congress. He suspected that the judge's previous stance had brought down the wrath of the apartheid government.

Nelson felt more comfortable than previously. His attorney had objected to the arrested men having to wear prison garb, and they'd won the right to appear in court in their own clothes.

They were charged with "recruiting persons for sabotage and guerrilla warfare for the purpose of starting a violent revolution". It was alleged that they had "conspired to aid foreign military units to invade the republic in order to support a communist revolution. "The orders for munitions on the part of the accused were enough to blow-up Johannesburg."

When asked how he pleaded, Nelson stood and said "My Lord, it is not I, but the government that should be in the dock. I plead not guilty."

Desmond Smith wondered about Stephen Last and about his own relationship with Elizabeth Sturlson. Last had a way of putting things that was unsettling – ignorant because he had little experience of women, but still unsettling. "It's one helluver responsibility going to bed with a bird," he'd said, "Once the sexual element becomes involved, the relationship moves to another level." He spoke like that – almost in abstractions; in an older man it would have sounded pompous, but he did say what no one else would dare to utter.

Des didn't go along with the spiritual side of things. Last – Stephen (why the hell do we call each other by our surnames?) – had said that the sexual side of a relationship lifted it to a spiritual level. He clearly felt that the degree of intimacy between a man and a woman involved in physical lovemaking was an experience almost akin to the religious. Des didn't believe that: he thought things would be far healthier if people just treated sex as part of a relationship instead of wrapping it up in coloured paper and keeping it in their bottom drawer.

Des had told Stephen that he read too much D H Lawrence, and he'd laughed. However, he was one of the few people around with whom Des felt he could have a meaningful conversation; Stephen Last did make you think.

It did make you feel more responsible towards the woman, didn't it? He and Elizabeth had first had sex that summer before he'd left for training college, and she clearly expected a certain commitment from him because of the turn in their relationship. It was no longer simply a boy-girl friendship. Had it moved to (stuff Last!) another level? In all honestly, Des felt it must have done, and that was what unsettled him.

Since arriving at Collingwood Hall he'd become aware of Susan Paget. He'd noticed her first when a group of them went swimming one Saturday at the public pool in Newcastle-under-Lyme. She was a PE student. She'd walked past in a tight, black costume, a brightly-coloured towel dangling from her left shoulder, unaware, he was sure, of the effect she was having on him or anyone else.

They'd passed looks in the Red Room, she'd laughed at his jokes and joined in the folk songs he accompanied on his guitar; they'd found themselves together in groups that went to the Red Lion, sitting together and drinking. They'd laughed together and there'd been a warmth between them.

And then there'd been that night. A group of them had been staggering back to college. Simon had done a cartwheel and he'd followed on along the road with a forward roll. They'd all been singing, their voices clanging against the cold air, rattling the brittle trees. "Home, home on the range." The refrain swelled and he and Simon had led a soft-shoe shuffle. Susan had just been part of the group, until Stephen disappeared and left him in a right mess. Later, he discovered his friend had forgotten his coat and gone back for it, but that didn't help at the time.

He'd found himself walking with Susan to her residential block – H House where many of the PE students were housed – and standing in the porch with her. Des had glanced across at the other porch and saw another couple saying goodnight. His eyes swung to Susan and she was watching him. Her mouth was gaping, soft and wet. He was sure she'd slid her arms round his neck, and then he'd dropped one arm to rub her back. What a back! He'd never felt such a warm, firm glide of muscle in his life. She'd gasped and moved her hips forward, and he'd kissed those lips and felt those thirty seven inch breasts against his chest. He'd gripped her waist and held her close. How long they'd kissed he couldn't remember but it had seemed an age. After that moment came the calm. Susan had smiled and touched his cheek, and turned away and closed the door as though something had been agreed between them.

Now the term was coming to an end, and Elizabeth was waiting for him in Middlesbrough.

Susan Paget glanced at the letter, askew by its envelope, for a second time, screwed it up and threw it in the waste bin. 'I cannot wait to see you again, darling,' it had said, 'Make sure you get the train as early as possible. I'll meet you on the platform. If only you knew the agony I've been through since you've been away. On Saturday, we'll make up for all that.'

Susan wondered what her new friends – the crowd – would make of Rodney, especially with that silly beard he was growing when she left in September. Her father didn't like him: he thought he was 'affected'. He was always trying to make an impression, particularly at parties, organising more rounds – but he was fun, he was nice. His letter had finished 'Look after yourself, Dido.' Why did he always call her 'Dido'?

Des slid down the window of the train and looked out along the platform. Through the hissing of steam, the shower of smuts and the rushing and shouting of the porters, he saw Elizabeth, waiting and quiet. The girl was enveloped with a calm contentment. He picked up his battered suitcase, reached out to move down the handle of the carriage door and stepped onto the platform. She ran towards him and clung to his arm so that he could reach his ticket only with difficulty.

The sun burned red behind the gas tanks as they walked to his home from the station. Smoke hung in the air and would do so until rain brought it down, streaking the pavements in black. Men in dirty overalls, their faces grimed, clumped from work. They were miners and heavy-metal workers, and Des felt proud

"There goes our inheritance," he said, "Whatever you might say about my father, he bloody well fought. I couldn't be anything but a socialist."

They crossed the bridge to the town centre, caught up in the flow of men from the factories.

"Our dad's off work again," said Elizabeth, "He caught his hand on a machine. It had no guard. The union's suing for negligence. You ought to see him sitting about."

"Moping, is he? He doesn't like being away from work, does he – your dad? That's more than you can say for my bugger. If he can stir it up he will – but they've got his number now. He was in the Party, once, you see ... what my mother's had to put up with."

"They're not in at the moment," said Elizabeth, "We can stop off at my house. It's been lonely up here without you, Des."

Des caught her eye and smiled.

"Aye, lass," he replied, "I've missed you, too."

Elizabeth lay back on the settee and Des thought how lucky it was that her mother was out for the night. Elizabeth's dress was on the floor and her bra strap down around her waist. 'A belly-full of syrup – that's how it feels. They can flower it up all they like. This is what it's about – a girl and a settee. I've been away from this for a whole term. It'll be four years before we can get married. Why is it the man who has to put on the brakes? She was frightened in case her parents returned suddenly. What's the argument against sex before marriage, anyway – that it leads to promiscuity? Outdated moral standards foisted on us by the ruling class through religion.'

"I'll go," he said, kissing her gently on the forehead, "I don't want to be here when your mum gets back."

"No. I'm going straight to bed now," replied Elizabeth.

The ceiling of the folk club cellar hung low with synthetic dust covering the hay baskets. 'Bank clerks and teachers – hobos for the night,' thought Des. Elizabeth was snuggled into his arm and they were waiting for the group to finish tuning up, when Mark and David, two friends of Des's from his schooldays, walked in.

"Hey man – good to see you," they said, quietly and almost off-the-cuff. They was some quiet chest thumping and arm punching, the beers were replenished and they sat down.

"How's teacher training college, then?" asked Mark.

"Nowhere matches it for apathy and off-the-peg ideas," replied Des.

"Come on, man, it can't be that bad – not with you there."

"It's OK."

"You mean you no longer see Britain as being 'the most class-ridden society under the sun', and education the only remedy?"

"You haven't met the types I've met at training college."

"Like?"

"Like bevies of girls who haven't a thought in their heads except to get a husband, and pseudo-intellectuals who haven't got a basic grasp of politics."

"And that 'basic grasp' is?"

"That the country has to change – that there is no longer a 'natural party of government', that the boys from the grouse moors need to be replaced by people who know what they're doing."

"Harold Wilson and the Labour Party?"

"It's a start, but what we really need is a population that is no longer content to sit back and let themselves be governed by just anyone. Only education can achieve that end."

"Des is right," said Elizabeth, "people are happy to deceive themselves into thinking that everything will be all right because it's obvious that those who rule us are not out-and-out villains. Corruption in this country is not blatant and, therefore, people are happy to believe that it does not exist. Just because we don't put our protestors into mental asylums or concentration camps doesn't mean that everything is OK. Unless education turns the tide, all that will happen is that the ruling classes will find other ways to rule. What we need to do is to change the way people think about being ruled."

"Bloody hell, pet, that was a mouthful," said Des.

"I may have stopped trudging pavements while you've been away, Des, but I haven't stopped reading."

"George Orwell," remarked David, with a laugh.

"Among others," replied Elizabeth, and she grinned.

Mark looked at his friend and envied him Elizabeth. 'She's such a ... permanence – that's the word. He must be enjoying himself more than we are – having to actually work for a living. We've all had to grow up a lot lately what with leaving the sixth form and all."

"You've got Dylan's latest – *Freewheelin'* – I take it. What do you think?"

"I like *Girl from the North Country*," Des replied, "You feel it's based on something personal. It sounds as though he's carried it around with him for a long time."

"His *A Hard Rain's A-Gonna Fall* is the one the gets to me," cut in David, "It's only just over a year since the Cuban Missile Crisis and I still wake up sweating about what might have happened with those two bastards facing each other off."

"Kennedy couldn't let the Russians get away with planting missiles on Cuba, Dave."

"No, but peace gained through a balance of terror is no way forward. You've only got to have someone who's unbalanced with his finger on the nuclear button, and we're all done for."

Elizabeth said nothing as she sat soaking up the conversation of these men who had only recently been boys and who she had known more or less all their lives. It was because of them that she'd joined the Young Socialists and trudged endlessly round streets knocking on doors. Suddenly she laughed, and the men stopped talking and looked at her.

"What's up, pet?" asked Mark

"Do you remember when we printed off all those leaflets," laughed Elizabeth, "and found we'd written 'socalism' instead of 'socialism'?"

"It wasn't so bloody funny at the time," said Des with a broad grin.

"Oh it was," chuckled Elizabeth.

"Yes – it was," said Mark, and they all joined in her laughing.

Stephen Last knew that he should not have watched what was reported as being the last *That Was The Week That Was* with his father, but he'd been determined to see the final shafts of abuse pouring from the screen. The BBC had decided to axe the programme because 1964 would be an election year and 'the political content of the programme ... will clearly be more difficult to maintain'. Nobody actually believed this; almost everybody was aware that politicians did not like being laughed at, and that pressure had been applied somewhere from someone. Even the *Daily Mail* – his father's 'office' paper – through one of its leading journalists, Peter Black, had called it 'a win ... for the crypto-fascists who cannot bear to see authority mocked'.

The final programme had been well up to its usual mark and even Stephen's father had laughed when he recalled David Frost and his team announcing, some weeks previously, that *Andy Pandy* would also end because 'it is felt that in an election year the political content of this programme, which is one of its most successful ingredients, will be more and more difficult to maintain'.

After the team had disappeared from view in their sports car, however, Stephen's father had felt obliged to denigrate the programme and those things for which it stood.

"It was rubbish," he said, folding his copy of the day's *Daily Mail* neatly on the side table, "Those idiots were sneering at everything that is nice and decent. Some of us have fought a war to keep this country a fit place to bring up our families, and then you get a load of clever dicks peddling their filth on your television set. If that's all they learn at university – I expect most of them went to Oxford or Cambridge – then it's a sad state of affairs. It was full of blasphemy, the kind of jokes schoolboys tell behind the cycle sheds, lavatorial humour and undergraduate smut. We can do without that, thanks very much."

Stephen knew he wasn't expected to respond; had he done so, his father would have put him down on the basis that he had lacked experience and wasn't in a position, not having fought a world war, to express an opinion. With everything put to rights, Stephen's father said goodnight and went to bed.

Stephen sat thinking for a long time. He was ignorant – he knew that – but not in the way his father supposed: his ignorance was more in his lack of knowledge about the way society works. His abiding interest had always been literature, and he'd absorbed many of his views from books and plays. Whenever he'd felt uneasy, it was because what the writer was supposed to stand for was belied by his words. Osborne and Amis were the 'angry young men' of their generation, but neither seemed to have an understanding of any class other than the one from which they came. Osborne's much-lauded hero was a weakling who cuddled his teddy bear and abused his wife; his anger led nowhere and changed nothing. Lucky Jim, Amis's hero, who'd had Stephen in stitches and bursts of admiration for his tilts at academics still living in the past, was fair enough; but Amis himself clearly abhorred the idea that university education should be expanded to include more students – 'That's the trouble with having so many people here on Education Authority grants'. In Amis's view 'more' would inevitably mean 'worse'; the idea that these very students may have been denied a decent education by the existing system wasn't something he wanted to contemplate: they were merely 'too stupid to pass their exams'.

Elsewhere, Robin Day took a more measured view of the BBC's decision to axe *TW3*. He thought that the programme had been unjustly licensed to lampoon politicians and mock religion, and that the 'BBC standards of fairness and accuracy went out of the window'. While other programmes were obliged to respect those very standards upon which the BBC had gained its charter, 'Frost and company were privileged to indulge their snide and mocking pleasure.' He recalled, in particular, the programme in January 1963 when David Frost had introduced an item called 'The Consumer's Guide to Religion' – an item he felt then, and now, that was calculated to offend everybody.

Miriam Davison had volunteered to work over the Christmas break, and she had enjoyed her experience thoroughly. She was a devout Christian and her special moment had been on Christmas Eve when the hospital staff, carrying lanterns, had toured the wards singing carols. The wards were, more or less, in darkness and the light of the lanterns produced an effect that verged on the mystical. Miriam sat by the bed of an elderly patient and held the lady's hand as the choir sang *Silent Night*. Miriam felt the hand she held tighten with pleasure.

When the carol came to an end, the patient whispered in Miriam's ear:

"They wouldn't sing *Away in a Manger* would they? I used to love that song at school, and my grandchildren sing it and I shan't be with them this year."

Miriam approached the Ward Sister, passing on the request, and there was a bustle of appreciation among the doctors and nurses. The song carried its own magic for Miriam as she thought of home and her family all off to the Crib Service. The old lady's voice, tremulous with excitement and husky with age, joined in the singing. When she reached the last line, "*and fit us for heaven to live with thee there*", tears ran down her cheeks and she smiled at Miriam. 'This is it,' thought Miriam, 'this is why I have come into nursing.'

1964

CHAPTER 5

The times they are a-changin'

The holidays had not gone well for Susan. They'd started badly at Euston Station and careered downhill from the moment she and Stephen Last had stepped onto the platform. Rodney had been waiting for her, waving a copy of *Popular Mechanics* to attract her attention, more or less ignored Stephen, whom she'd grown to like during their first term, and then proceeded to denigrate him.

"Who the hell was that? Did you see his tie – and that tweed jacket? Obviously a teacher in the making: probably a born teacher. I could scarcely believe he was with you, Dido. Part of the provincial crowd, is he?"

She'd been laughing with Stephen all the way back. He might be a bit intense, but he'd at least credited her with some intelligence. She'd never spent a whole train journey before discussing books, films and the theatre. Most of the lads at college seemed to think that any girl in the PE department must be fit and healthy and gagging for a shag, but not Stephen. Moreover, he obviously liked Des as much as she did, he was a great source of information about both Des and someone called Bob Dylan and he listened when you spoke.

Rodney had steered her to the parking space at the rear of the station, and opened the door of what was obviously his car. He did have good manners.

"New car," she'd asked.

"Yes, the old man was rather generous. Little beauty isn't she? I've arranged for us to go to Alistair's party tonight, darling. Hope you feel up to it. Actually, it's mainly in your honour. I think Ally rather fancies you himself. Good to be back?"

"Yes ... I suppose the old crowd will be there?"

"Lord, yes."

"Your beard's growing nicely."

"Not bad is it? I expect they'll reach the provinces in a year or two. What's it like up there among the miners?"

"I haven't seen a mine ... They tell me they're further north."

"I still don't see why you didn't apply to a training college nearer home – or, better still, a university. You're not really going to teach, are you?"

"Yes, I am – and you have to go where you can get a place."

"Oh really, Dido! People do get into London colleges you know. It's not simply a matter of A Levels."

Everything he said and everything he stood for cut right across the grain – and the worth, and the aspirations – of people like Stephen and Des. Who was this man to whom she had once thought she might get engaged?

The party had spiralled with jazz and clothes: groups posed in the large lounge of Alistair's flat, record sleeves hung limply from fingers, a group of men (or were they boys?) stood by the record player discussing cars (nobody discussed cars at college – few had a car). Rodney left her and joined them, chortling and rubbing his beard. She had giggled as Alistair greeted her.

"Gin and tonic with a twist of orange, isn't it? How are you, Sue? It's good to see you again. Oh, we're not all here yet; bags of folks to come. Wait until you meet Marcus and his wife. Wow. You haven't met anyone until you've met Marcus. Like the flat? Nice, isn't it?"

"Yours?" she'd asked, sliding a word in quickly, edgeways.

"Actually, dear old dad gave me the first years rent as a twenty-first. He said I'd have to fend for myself after that."

The evening had dissolved into dancing and chit-chat. Rodney had claimed her and they'd been the first couple on the dance floor. He'd moved from toe to toe, keeping his heels exactly two inches apart and his feet at right angles to each other. 'Someone has taught him to dance or he's read about it in a magazine, but he doesn't feel it,' she'd thought, as she leaned slightly forward and swayed her hips, raised her arms, bent her elbows and twitched them. Other pairs joined in until only one couple was left on the sheepskin rug, mouthing each other. The dancers writhed in a jangle of colour – eyes glazed, faces stretched. During the smooches, Rodney kissed her on the mouth. Experience had taught her to keep her teeth quite close together, unless she wanted a wet tongue thrust into her mouth – and she didn't. 'The world watched through a camera lens,' she thought, without quite knowing from where the thought had come.

Sometime late into the night there had been a tap on the door, and Alistair had leapt to his feet crying "It must be him!" as though some messiah had come knocking. "Marcus," Rodney had whispered in her ear, licking crumbs off his beard, "He's been imported especially to impress you."

Marcus wore a long, buckskin coat, tasselled and transferred. The girl by his side, who Susan discovered was his wife, was dressed identically. They both grabbed at the food on the coffee table and thrust fistfuls into their mouths before sitting cross-legged on the sheepskin rug. Alistair introduced Susan, while Marcus and his wife washed down the food with great gulps of beer. When they'd finished, Marcus reached for his wife's hand and held it gently. "He sees things in it," whispered Rodney, with a snort, "you'll hear some beauties in a minute."

"Marcus and his wife believe in free love," explained Alistair.

"But you are married?" asked the girl who'd been snogging on the rug during the dancing and whose name was Anna, a school friend of Susan's.

"We believe in the fidelity of the relationship," said Marcus, "It was right for us to marry, and so we married. If we had not, the fidelity of our love would not have been impaired. We believe in the sacredness of love between all people. This is a feeling of the spirit – you cannot explain it in intellectual terms. Love for us is soul, not mind."

"It's so much a matter of sensitivity," continued Marcus's wife, who had not been introduced and whose name Susan did not know, "Harsh words are anathema to Marcus. I have seen him wince at unkindness. Love is a force. When Marcus is low, my breasts are the batteries of his soul."

"It flows between us ... Anna, take our hands and you, too, will feel it pulsing along your arm."

Susan had laughed, quite raucously, and embarrassed herself and Alistair. She apologised profusely, as her breeding had taught her to do, but Marcus and his wife remained unperturbed.

"Please don't let strife cut us off from each other and the eternal truths," pleaded Marcus, "Susan, take Anne's hand. Connect with Rodney. Love is a current, and we generate so much energy. It recharges the dead batteries until they can generate for themselves. Join the circle. Let your selves flow into each other."

"Let the people sing," chanted Marcus's wife, and they all repeated her words, "Let the people dance, Let the people feel, Let the people love."

At the end of a long evening, Susan had found herself with Rodney, parked on the heath near her home. Before she realised, he'd been kissing her and unbuttoning her dress. He kissed her mouth, her neck and then her breasts as her dress opened. "Rodney, please," she'd heard herself say, and then his hand had slid up and along her thigh and attempted to pull her tights down. "I've a rug in the back," he'd said, unbuttoning his trousers in a rush and loosening his underpants until his 'thing' had leapt out.

"Rodney, I can't."

"What? What's wrong? I thought you loved me. You said you loved me. What are you frightened of? Let's prove our love."

"Prove?"

She'd pushed open the car door and fallen out onto the heath, as he stood, open-mouthed and open-trousered. Susan buttoned her coat, gasping for breath, not wanting to scream, not wanting this boy to stick his 'thing' into her: just wanting to get home, say good night to her parents and go to bed.

They hadn't seen each other again over the whole of Christmas, and now she was back at Collingwood Hall wrapped in her duffle coat and long, striped college scarf. Here, there was some purpose to life and she'd found it.

Holdalls and suitcases muddled the floor and chairs as usual: some placed precisely, others strewn. The students in A House sat between and on them, talking over mugs of tea. Split packets of biscuits, provided by their mothers, lolled on the tables. Years of scudding chairs had threadbared the carpet and cigarette smoke mingled with the fresh smell of lavender polish. Darts thudded into the board. Stephen Last breathed in with a huge sigh of relief. 'Home,' he thought, 'I'm home.' He got up, more contented than he had imagined possible since he'd left childhood, and wandered to his room.

He'd barely stretched out on the bed with his copy of Alan Sillitoe's *Saturday Night and Sunday Morning* when he heard a hurried tap at his door. Simon Wiseman entered almost before Stephen had answered; excitement was in every line of his body and every resonance of his voice. Stephen laid aside the book, smiled and looked up.

"What's up, youth?" he asked.

"Well," he gasped, "I did it."

"Did what?"

"Had sex."

Stephen stared, speechless, at his friend. 'You don't have to say that, you don't have to pretend, you've nothing to prove.' He knew it was a lie, and a lie that demeaned them both. Every anxiety Simon must have felt stared out from his eyes.

"It was great – bloody marvellous."

'Show surprise. Go on, show it. Express admiration and ... humour.' Stephen found he couldn't.

"Where did it happen," he asked.

"Well ... I was at this party, see ... uuuuur, uuuuur ..."

The laughter, intended, Stephen supposed, to sound both grateful and lascivious ground out from Simon's mouth.

"... and when the others had gone, you know, I hung around and she said "Would you like to stay, Simon? ... uuuur ... She'd even drawn the bed down, and we went in and had it."

At that moment, Pete Campbell knocked and poked his head round Stephen's door.

"You lads coming down the Red Lion tonight?"

"Yeah, we'll be there," said Simon, "I was just telling Steve ..."

"What was that, youth?"

"... I had sex over the Christmas break."

"Good for you, youth," replied Pete, glancing at Stephen with a puzzled look in his eyes, and then leaving.

"You fancy a cup of tea, Si?" asked Stephen, "I'll go and make one. I won't be a minute."

Des was strumming his guitar, aimlessly, 'She almost worships me. I'm not a god, I'm a person.' He sang:

"I wander the highway, with you by my side.

We're crossing the river; we glance at the tide.

The seaway is pulling, the water sinks fast ... "

'But I'm lonely for Elizabeth.' He watched his fingers, thin and knotted, on the neck of the instrument.

Susan turned as the door clicked. Marguerite paused, her hand on the latch.

"Rodney and I are finished," said Susan, "Yes, we finished over the holiday." She moved from foot to foot as she spoke, twiddling her fingers, her back stretched high, giggling.

"Another girl?"

"No, nothing like that – nothing so decent – just a man being a man. You know ..."

"Are you all right, pet?"

"Oh yes."

"Don't let it get you down."

"Oh, I won't. Some of us really go in for broken hearts ... Aren't men pigs, Mags? Do you know, all the time he was tugging at my zip, he was justifying himself – talking about proving our love. I begin to wonder what love is. We haven't met yet."

Marguerite watched her friend. Her Bobby had never tried anything like that on; he respected her, and she was glad.

In the Red Room after dinner Des said to Stephen:

"What do you make of Eliot's *Waste Land*?"

"It's a depressing piece of writing, to say the least."

"Do you agree with his comparison of our society to Cleopatra's? He doesn't get round to mentioning the fact that hers was built on slavery and ravished by disease."

"No," said Stephen, not wishing to be drawn.

"It is his central theme in the poem, isn't it – the disintegration of our society? Personally, I think our society has more potential now than ever before."

"Go on," prompted Stephen.

"A rotten society decays, and another takes its place," continued Des, Eventually …"

"A perfect society will evolve," Marguerite suggested.

"That's right, pet – yours and mine."

"I don't think Eliot was contrasting now and then in quite the way you suggest," proposed Stephen, "You're crediting him with what he didn't say, and then criticising your own suggestions rather than what he actually said …"

"Ooh, are you reading for a distinction, Stevie," said Jenny Pryce with a laugh.

Des glared at Stephen and then grinned. He'd have a chat with him afterwards; it might improve his grades.

In his room, pulling on his thick coat and gloves, Stephen listened to the radio. The announcer was talking about the visit of Pope Paul V1 to the Holy Land:

"… his historic three-day pilgrimage reinforced his message of unity and reconciliation … he met with the head of the Eastern Orthodox Church … Pope Paul and Patriarch Athenagoras … were the first leaders of their respective churches to meet since the fifteenth century …"

Stephen smiled to himself and turned off the radio.

Having completed her twelve week PTS course, Kate Walsh found herself back on the surgical ward and was pleased to find that Joan, who had helped her that first day with making the bed for Sister Moore, had been placed with her. They passed a grin but no more, as Sister Trevelyan welcomed them before beginning her morning report, detailing which patients were going home and which were to be prepared for surgery.

One young man, who had been there since the previous summer following a motorcycle accident, was still showing no signs of recovery. His parents would come each day, hoping to stimulate some response, but he remained unable to speak or walk. Kate smiled at him each time she passed, but he only frowned. When she tried to feed him, he would push the plate away and attempt to punch her in the face. It was awful to see someone so young so dependent upon others to sustain him. As she watched the food dribbling down his chin, Kate was reminded of an old film starring Fredric March playing both Jekyll and Hyde. She felt that this young man had both within him, and that his accident had released the demon side. His parent apologised and Kate reassured them. She was a nurse – at least a student nurse – and this was her vocation.

She and Joan found themselves working together taking blood pressures, temperatures and pulses – the routine stuff that was the backbone of their work. Sister Trevelyan pointed out that what they must note were the variations.

"Any fool can take readings," she explained, "but it takes a nurse to note the significances. A high pulse rate and a drop in blood pressure following an operation could indicate ...Well?"

"Internal bleeding," offered Kate.

"Internal bleeding, Sister."

"Internal bleeding, Sister," said Kate, correcting herself.

"Well done, Nurse Walsh. Your time at the Preliminary Training School has obviously not been wasted ... Nurse Whiting, what would a high temperature following an operation possibly indicate?"

"Post-operative infection ... Sister?"

"Good. I've obviously been blessed with student nurses who have listened to their tutors ... Oh, and Nurse Whiting ..."

"Yes ... Sister?"

"There's no need to pause before the word 'Sister'. It's been earned the hard way, as you will come to know."

As their first day on surgical progressed, the truth of these words were borne out many times. The manic pace, always conducted in a leisurely manner so that calmness prevailed for the patients, drove both Kate and Joan to exhaustion. Thirty beds were made and remade as necessary, medicines were dispensed, drips and catheters were checked and re-checked, observations were made and bedpans were handed round and emptied. At one point, half-way through their shift, Kate found Joan in the sluice room leaning against one of the sinks and gripping it tightly with her eyes closed.

"Are you all right, Joan?"

"Yes – don't fuss, Kate. I'm tired, that's all"

"OK – no need to bite my head off."

"Sorry – I've always been a bit snappy. It's my time of the month, that's all, and the pressure, today, is not helping."

At his weekly audience with the Queen, Sir Alec Douglas-Home continued to be impressed by Her Majesty's extensive knowledge on every national and international problem. Doubtless her Private Secretaries were skilled in the selection and presentation of whatever she needed to be apprised, but nevertheless there remained a mass of fact and information that needed to be absorbed by her Majesty. Alec found her experience, which was placed so readily at his disposal, to be encouraging and invaluable. He looked forward to these regular meetings with pleasure.

Before making his way to the Red Lion, Paul Crisp admired himself in the long mirror on the common room wall of C House. It had been a good Christmas holiday. He'd gone up to Liverpool for a few days, and he and Mike Harrison had picked up a couple of birds from the convent. They'd been panting for it! He recalled Mike's laughter. "She handed them to me on a plate! They were a couple of right ..."

He'd left the sentence unfinished.

"Admiring yourself, Crispy," laughed Des, coming into the room and ruffling Paul's hair.

"Shove off, Smith."

"I was looking for Mike."

"He'll be here in a minute," replied Paul, re-combing his hair.

Des watched as Paul Crisp adjusted his pullover, straightening out the wrinkles in the sleeves and levelling the bottom. 'He's a tailor's dummy,' thought Des. "The girls cannot but admire him.'

"How do I look, Des?"

"Bloody marvellous."

"Pullover all right?"

"Immaculate."

Paul slipped into his top coat and flicked some possible dust from the shoulders.

"Shoulders OK?"

"You look great, Crispy," said Mike Harrison, as he entered the common room.

"Do you remember those convent birds at Christmas, Mike?"

"Bragging again, are we, Paul bach?" yelled a Welsh youth who had sat watching the performance from in front of the television set. Bryn Edwards was a rugby player and a singer of rugby songs. If anyone epitomised Welshness – and there were many Welsh students at the college – it was Bryn, who lived life to the full. "You'll have your tongue on the floor, in a moment, man."

"It takes me a long time to pluck up courage to talk to a girl," said Cliff Richard, "If a girl makes the first move – I'm off!"

He'd enjoyed a long-term boy-girl friendship with Jenny Irving, a dancer he'd met while he was doing his show at the London Palladium, and had considered marriage, but both he and she knew that it was out of the question. "It will annoy your fans," she'd said. He didn't know many girls and had liked her company, but that was all. He didn't want to hang around with the other fellows all the time, and he and Jenny had gone out together.

Now he was in the Canary Islands filming *Wonderful Life* and his co-star, Susan Hampshire, was the centre of press attention. Susan had spoken her mind to the reporters and photographers, saying that movie life was not a bowl of cherries.

"It's sheer hard work from dawn to dusk," she exclaimed, "Most nights I'm in bed and asleep by nine o'clock."

He hadn't written to Jenny – not even a postcard – since he'd been away filming. He thought to himself that his wife – should he ever marry – would have to put her foot down with him. He'd need someone who would speak her mind and not be afraid to say what she thought. Somehow, he couldn't see himself marrying for a long time. What he was doing now was so valuable for him as a man and so valuable for the things he believed in; they had to come first.

Standing in the toilet cubicle, Stephen Last breathed softly. He could hear the noises of the residential block, as students returned from the pub. He heard the toilet seat in the cubicle to his right lowered.

"Cor, hurry up babe. I can't wait for it," gasped the voice of Pete Campbell, "I want it really bad tonight."

Stephen waited until he heard the two doors open, and supposed that Pete and his girl, Glenda, had passed through to Pete's room. Women were not allowed in the men's houses after a certain time at night, but Stephen didn't suppose that would trouble Pete too much. Pete had been around before he decided to take up teaching as a career, playing folk clubs in the north.

Stephen walked to his room, passing Bryn Edwards on the way. Bryn was hurrying a girl along the corridor, and she looked down as Stephen passed them. Every inch of Bryn's muscular frame was tense with expectation.

He and Bryn, both first years, had little to do with each other during college time – Bryn being in the PE department and Stephen in the English – but they'd struck up a casual friendship in the common room; for no reason at all, a natural trust seemed to exist between them. Bryn, his face full of brotherly concern, had once said to him:

"You want to get busy, man. Dip your wick a bit. Before you're married, see. You won't have a chance, then. Wouldn't be fair on your wife, would it?"

"You're a rum bugger, you are," Stephen had replied, not knowing what else to say, and Bryn had laughed.

"Why? It's all right until you're married, man. They enjoy it! But it wouldn't be fair on your wife, now would it?"

Stephen walked along the corridor, wishing a girl was waiting in his room. He closed his door with quiet precision and picked up Bob Dylan's latest album, *The times they are a-changin'*. He placed it carefully on the turntable of his record player, and moved the needle arm across. The grating voice sang out thoughts he'd had but could not articulate – at least not with Dylan's lyrical clarity. Stephen wasn't concerned with the politicians – Dylan's senators and congressmen – although there was a battle outside and it was raging; he felt that time would settle those issues. It was Dylan's plea to mothers and fathers that attracted Stephen's attention most – "... and don't criticize what you can't understand." They couldn't, but that didn't place Stephen, or many of his generation, "beyond their command". They had, after all, fought a war for the freedoms Stephen's generation now enjoyed. Shouldn't their voices be heeded? Shouldn't their standards be respected? Their old road was rapidly aging, and a new one (or new ones) was opening up. It was just a question of whether the shackles could be shed, and the new one walked.

CHAPTER 6
Vestments

Michael Ramsey, Archbishop of Canterbury, faced a serious problem. The Church Assembly had passed the measure by large majorities, and it was going forward to Parliament. He knew what would happen. His experience of the political situation told him that the measure would be opposed; a campaign was certain to be mounted to throw out the measure, and the matter would be raised to the level of a national disaster. He could see the headlines now – 'MPs fear a drift to Rome'.

The purpose of the measure was straightforward: it was to legalize the wearing of certain vestments – the chasuble and the alb – in parishes where the priest and laity wished it. Michael well knew that the matter, though straightforward, was not simple.

The Prayer Book of Elizabeth 1 ordered that all priests should wear these vestments when taking mass and the Prayer Book of 1662 had reiterated that order; but no one obeyed it. When, during Victorian times, some priests had reverted to doing so, there had been an outcry against it in many parishes, since it was considered not to be in keeping with a Protestant church. In 1877, the Judicial Committee of the Privy Council – which was at that time the supreme court of appeal for the Church of England – tried to settle the disputes by ruling that the vestments in question were illegal. The clergy, however, ignored the ruling and carried on in accordance with their individual consciences.

When Michael became Archbishop of Canterbury in 1961, he was of the opinion that about twenty-five percent of the clergy wore the vestments and were, in effect, in breach of the ruling. The proposed measure would ease the minds of those clergy and parishioners who felt that their way of worship was in breach of the law of the land. He was, therefore, going to have to ask Parliament for permission for his clergy to wear vestments that a quarter of them already wore.

It wasn't simply the ridiculousness of this which kept him awake at night; it was also his awareness of the heated debates that would ensue over what would appear to the public at large to be a trivial matter. Had the Church of England nothing better with which to occupy its time? He could hear many voices raised in anguish: many would see it as a move towards Rome, some would simply find it shocking that such garments were to be legalized and others would wonder why the clergy needed to dress up at all. It would be raised to the level of a national disaster.

Everyone was aware that a general election was due, and opinion polls showed that Alec Douglas-Home's government was on the point of collapse. MPs, fearful of losing their seats, would not vote for a measure that might antagonise their constituents – particularly for a measure that would be deemed unnecessary since it would change nothing. Michael could hear his friends in Parliament begging him to postpone bringing the measure before Parliament or, at least, leaving it until the next session. Michael, however, felt that he could not be seen making a decision for what amounted to political reasons. He had no wish to make himself appear an ass before the Church Assembly.

Stephen Last fidgeted in his new suit, rubbing his back against the artificial well in the grounds of Knutton Gardens Ballroom. The well was in the centre of a cobbled courtyard that shone with recent rain. He looked around him at the old, yellow, white-washed walls, the round arches, the wrought iron gate and the red roof. In the distance, he could hear the sound of the band. Couples burst in and out of the ballroom to snog in the cloisters that surrounded it. Stephen pushed open one of the gates and walked through the archway until he reached the lily pond. 'I can't dance, and there's no point in my being here,' he thought. He'd been desperate to get out of the ballroom but, since giving up smoking, had no reason at all to leave. He felt awkward as he interrupted another couple who were talking, intimately, by the side of the pond. The bloke nodded to him. He didn't recognise the girl, but thought she was one of the nurses who usually came to these dos from the hospital in Staffham. The bloke was Barry Glover, a final year student. He was the kind of man who would be described, with a laugh, as a 'professional northerner' by Simon Wiseman, who, Stephen thought, could equally well be described as a 'professional southerner'.

"Hot in there, Steve?" enquired Barry.

"So-so. It's the noise of the band that drove me outside, though."

"Yeah, right. Excuse us."

With that remark, Barry took the girl's arm and led her back onto the dance floor. Stephen watched them go – not without some envy in his glance. As the door opened, the sound of the lead singer's voice, yelled out across the courtyard:

> "*Now let me tell you just one more ti- ime,*
> *You little baby you're gonna be mi-ine,*
> *I wan' you to twist and sha-ake*
> *I wanna you to be my da-ate,*
> *Mm – oh yeah, mm-oh yeah, mm-oh yeah*
> *Yeah, yeah. Yeah, yeah. Oh yeah.*"

Somehow, he thought, it didn't turn out to be as easy as the singer imagined. 'You're never sure if the girl will say yes, and if she said no how would you feel?'

In America, the Beatles were having no such problem. When Pan Am's flight 101 from London touched down and the door of their plane swung open the adulation of the fans swept over them; Brian Epstein had done his work well, pursuing the record companies and television stations. The screaming at New York's Kennedy Airport was intoxicating. Cynthia Lennon, who was with her husband on this trip, wondered how so many young people could be caught up in such a 'wave of emotion' over what to her were four 'boys'.

At the press conference – the largest they'd ever attended – the questions were fired in rapid succession, and were parried, easily, by the wit of the group. The streets leading to their hotel were crammed with teenage fans – mainly girls – who screamed themselves hoarse and waved whatever came to hand – T-shirts, Beatle wigs, banners and photos.

Security was tight and invasive; within their hotel, the

Beatles and their entourage were more or less imprisoned. Telegrams, letters and cards from well-wishers piled up at the door; limousines carved their passage through the streets. There wasn't a young girl in America, it seemed, who didn't wanna hold their hands or whatever else they could grab.

Heather Burton had liked Barry Glover when she and the others had first come to Knutton Gardens in the autumn, and they'd seen each other on several occasions in Staffham when he'd come into town on a Saturday. She hadn't said much to the other girls because they were still somewhat immature in the way they thought about men – something with which she'd never had a problem. She recalled one cringe-making night when they'd all gathered in Kate's and Sheila's room and giggled over a medical book that showed an erect penis. There had been lots of talk about 'It' and 'hard-ons', and Kate had said that her mother had told her "never to lift her dress to a man" after she started her periods. Sheila Pratt had actually asked if anyone had "gone all the way". Her question, so inept it was embarrassing, had been followed by a long silence. Heather hadn't, but didn't feel it held the horrors expected by Sheila and one or two others. Certainly, she felt that if came to the point with Barry she might well enjoy the experience; but she wasn't ready for that – not yet.

Barry was a blast of fresh air to Heather. Brought up almost exclusively in the leafy suburb of Barnet, Heather had led a charmed existence but a narrow one. She'd been clever at school and done well in her A levels; the teachers had liked her; her parents had been kind and supportive (seeing that, if she wanted to dance, she went to dancing lessons or, if she wanted to be musical, she took up an instrument); the boys she'd known had all been decent middle-class lads from decent middle-class homes.

In Barry, she'd found a world that had, before, only existed in books and the writings of people like George Orwell. Barry had talked about his childhood with love – a love filled with both admiration and anger. He'd talked of going to the corner shop to buy his weekly comic (something called the *Hotspur*) or a pennyworth of sweets; he'd talked of his dad sitting on the doorstep of their terraced house smoking Woodbines; he'd talked of walking to school on fog-filled mornings when smoke from the factories choked the air and hung from slate roofs; he'd talked of standing for hours on the street corner under a winter lamp with his mates; he'd talked of his mum keeping a family of five fed on very little (fresh, seasonal vegetables from his dad's allotment, always potatoes and, hidden in the potatoes, some meat); he'd talked of rag-and-bone men with a horse and cart; he'd talked of going to the fish and chip shop for some chips and a pennyworth of scraps; he'd talked not about himself so much as the world from which he'd come – the world from which he wanted to give children the chance to escape.

"Education's the way forward, Heather," he'd said, in that quiet way she found so attractive, "if our children are to escape the grinding poverty of that world, they must have the chance of a decent education – learning isn't just for the rich."

"But you sound as though you love that world," she'd answered, "You sound as though you want to return to it."

"I do. I admire it – it's a way of life – but it wouldn't hurt to take a bit more money into it, and the only way the kids of the future are going to do that is by getting an education that will get them the best jobs – the jobs of the future."

He'd held her hand across the table of the coffee house as he spoke and, afterwards, he'd drawn her into a side alley and kissed her; it had been a gentle kiss, as though he saw it as a privilege. Somehow, it was at that moment Heather realised she loved him.

Back on the dance floor, she saw Kate and Joan and Sheila all dancing with lads from the training college. Hips jerked and thighs twitched in sudden movements. There was much grinning and much thudding of heels on the floor. Waves of hair shook in the spinning lights, heads rolled and arms stretched and clasped the necks of partners.

Stephen Last, crossing from the bar with a pint of beer was grabbed by Jenny Pryce, who stood his beer on a nearby windowsill and drew him onto the dance floor. Simon was prancing around like a gigolo, doing his Mick Jagger impression – genitals thrust suddenly forward, a leer from ear to ear, lips pouted. Des's fingers entwined themselves in Susan's hair. She made a soft, whimpering sound and smiled.

"I haven't seen many of those since Christmas, pet," he said.

"Seen what?" she replied, unnecessarily.

"Smiles," he replied, with just a hint of wanting to know in his voice.

There were some final, shattering thuds of music from the band and the dance collided to a halt. The group – 'The Pus' – grinned from the stage.

"There you are, you see," Des continued as they stood

facing each other on the silent floor, "You've stopped the band."

Susan grinned, and made no attempt to sit down with the others who had collapsed around their collective table, Jenny eyeing Stephen, Marguerite smiling at everyone, Simon lolling against the radiator and handing Stephen his beer, Mike looking across the dance floor for Paul Crisp who was coming towards them with a nurse on each arm – who he introduced as Kate Walsh and Sheila Pratt.

The women eyed each other, rather caustically Stephen thought, but the conversation was friendly enough. The nurses, it appeared, were all in their first year as students and were training at the Staffham General. As they talked, another of them came over to the table with a final year student, Barry Glover, and introduced herself as Heather Burton. Stephen looked across to the dance floor and caught Des's eye as the newcomers joined in the talk around the table. 'Here's the future,' he thought, 'dancing together.' It was something he and Des had talked about – often.

The band struck up after a while and they drifted onto the floor as a group. Stephen hesitated but only for a moment. Simon's shout "Come on, Last, you miserable bugger – even you can Conga" and the tugging of Jenny on one arm and Marguerite on the other propelled him to the floor. Lost in the melee, he found he was enjoying himself.

Billy Graham picked up the phone; a member of the Republican Party was on the other end of the line. He'd just read a newspaper article to the effect that Billy was "considering running for President."

"... we have enough support to nominate you," he said.

Billy paused before answering. He'd been urged by a few friends to consider making such a move, but had no idea how it how been leaked to the press. He knew what his father would say:

"You've got to call a press conference and stop it."

He knew his wife, Ruth, would agree with her father-in-law. After all, he and Lyndon Johnson were friends; he and Ruth had spent evenings at the White House with Lyndon and his wife, Lady Bird. His father was right; he had to call a press conference and stop the speculation. Billy knew what he would say:

"... if nominated I will not run; if elected I will not serve. God has called me to preach."

The morning air was besotted with drizzle which dripped from the branches of trees and from the rusted, twisting wire of the tennis courts. Des ducked under the fence and made for the dining hall.

"Ooh, I am honoured," said Susan, as he sat beside her and asked for the salt.

"I couldn't find anywhere else to sit, pet," he replied, smiling, "What's up?"

"Nothing," she began, and then continued, "I finished with Rodney over Christmas ... When do boys become men, Des?"

"When they begin to understand women, I suppose. What happened?"

"He tried it on, and I didn't like it ...Does that make me ... unnatural, Des?"

"It's up to you – there's no obligation."

"But men do expect it, don't they?"

Des couldn't say 'no' to her question – or could he?

"No," he said, "it's the wrong word to use – 'expect'. It's up to the couple concerned. Some do, some don't."

"But the woman has more to lose, hasn't she? It's her who carries the can if anything goes wrong."

Anything going wrong had always been at the back of his mind whenever he and Elizabeth were together in that way; anything going wrong wasn't to be considered.

"Yes," he agreed, reluctantly, "I suppose she does ..."

The conversation seemed to stagger to a halt. Susan watched Des pick at the corner of his boiled egg and cut a small piece from it. She smiled to herself at the fastidious way he was eating – almost like an old aunt of hers.

"Had you known him long?"

"We were at school together ... we could have just slipped into marriage without realising it," laughed Susan.

"People do break up," urged Des, hoping to raise a smile, "How many girls arrived here wearing engagement rings last September, only to meet someone else – someone different – when they arrived? How many broke off their engagements over Christmas?"

"Have you got someone at home, Des?"

"Yes," he replied, almost hoping the answer would go unnoticed.

"Are you engaged?"

"No."

"Do I sound prudish?" asked Susan, wondering what Des and his girl had been doing over Christmas.

"No ... you mustn't think of it like that ..."

"There're a lot of girls here who do ..."

"Do they?" he interrupted, "I shouldn't believe all you hear around college ... You took a positive decision, Sue. It's your life, and you made a choice for yourself ..." Not sure how to continue, he grabbed a phrase of Stephen Last's "It's your road you're seeking."

"I feel better, now," she laughed, her snub nose twitching, "I'm just going down to the village. Would you come with me?"

Des was delighted – pleased that he'd restored Susan's confidence, even more pleased to be walking with her to the village shop.

Not Fade Away was climbing the charts rapidly. The Rolling Stones were still singing covers, but Keith's song-writing partnership with Mick was progressing. He was glad his manager, Andrew Oldham, had made him sit down and write what Keith thought of as horrendous songs.

"We'd farm them off to somebody else," he told Kris Needs, "'cos we didn't wanna know ... You've gotta get all that shit outta your system before you can really start writing."

Marianne Faithfull had been pleased to be given *As Tears Go By* (it had been a big hit for her) and Gene Pitney ("a big mate of ours") had also had a big hit with *That Girl Belongs to Yesterday*.

"*Tell Me* was gonna be flogged off – it was cut as a demo – but we bunged it on the album. It's doing well as a single in the States," explained Keith, "Mick and I have been writing songs together for about a year now. We didn't make a lot of fuss about when we started – we just began working at it because it was something we liked doing. At the moment, we've got about a dozen songs sort of half-finished. Most of them are intended for our next LP, but we've got a lot of work to do on them yet and it gets more and more difficult to find time every week."

Pete Campbell was desperate to make it as a singer/songwriter. If only he could just get the break he needed. Playing down at the Red Lion for students was one thing, but it wasn't going to buy any bread – let alone butter it. He was coming to the end of his time at college. Soon he'd be qualified as a teacher, but that was a fall-back position; what he really wanted to do was make it on the music scene.

As he walked into the King's Head in Staffham, he saw Stephen Last and Simon Wiseman, glasses nearly empty, huddled over the beer puddles on their table – well, Stephen was huddled and Simon lolled back in his chair. Simon caught his eye as Pete entered and called out:

"Hey, Pete. Hey, me ole cock sparrer."

"I'll get some in, lads," he called back.

He liked Simon, who everyone called 'Yogi' because of his interest in yoga – or was it simply that he sat in the lotus position in the common room? He wasn't so sure about Stephen, who he hadn't quite weighed up to his satisfaction. He seemed all right, but he hadn't got a girlfriend and looked as though he should have one.

"How's the crumpet, lads?" he asked, as he straddled a chair at their table before placing the beers before them. They both thanked him, and he continued "I'm hoping to fix up a date to play here. I'll be teaching in Staffham next year, and this could be a regular gig. There's a big room above."

"You're not planning on staying in teaching then," enquired Stephen.

"Not if I can help it, old son. Do you know how much a teacher earns?"

"No, I've never really thought about it."

"Nor have most of them. Mind you, it doesn't matter so much for the women – they'll be leaving to have kids, anyway – but it's important for a bloke. He's the one who's going to have to bring home the rabbit, so to speak."

Stephen had never given the salary any thought at all. He'd wanted to teach, and that had been as far as he'd considered the matter.

"Besides," said Pete, suddenly, as though Stephen's remark had left a wound somewhere, "there's a lot happening on the folk scene at the moment. It aint all *My love is like a red, red rose* and coal mining songs. There's a lot of blues and rock getting' mixed in with it. Have you heard of Long John Baldry? And the Americans are going in for protest stuff – you know, Pete Seeger, Dylan – that kind of singer."

"How did you get started, Pete," asked Simon.

"I heard the Ian Campbell Folk Group, and I just knew that was what I wanted to do. I was only about sixteen at the time, and I bought this cheap guitar on the market. It cost me about three quid, but I couldn't even tune it, let alone play the bloody thing. It was my aunt who put me right. She sent me to a bloke down the street where we lived, and he got me going. He tuned the guitar and showed me a few strums. I played and played – that's the only way to get anywhere. There was an old second-hand record shop down the rough end of town, and I spent hours in there ferreting through the stuff they'd got – Hank Williams, Howlin' Wolf, Lightnin' Hopkins, Woody Guthrie, Alex Campbell. They had some sheet music, too, and so I was on my way ..."

As he spoke and Stephen and Simon listened, a commotion broke out at a nearby table where a group of lads, fresh from a football match, had been sitting around drinking. It had seemed peaceful enough until another group turned up and called out something from the bar; it was obviously a taunt of some kind. Stephen missed what was said, but Pete didn't. He stopped talking and looked up. Within seconds, one of the lads at the table flew across the room and landed a punch at the speaker who was too startled to duck. The blow landed on the youth's face and he struck back, but to no avail. The attacker, maddened with rage, landed thump after thump into his taunter's ribs, before he was pulled off by his mates.

"The bastard was calling me a queer. He's not getting away with it. I'll punch his bloody face in," he screamed, "You've gone too far, mate."

"Ease off, Jack. He didn't mean it."

"Didn't mean it? Then what's funny about it? Would you like to be called a queer?"

As his mates tried to calm the aggressive youth down, the landlord stepped in.

"I'm sorry, son," he said, calmly, "I'll get the wife to sponge your knuckles off. They're a bit bloody. Just sit down, while I see to it." Turning on the lad who had hurled the taunt, he said: "Out."

"Why? I int done nothing. I'm the one who got hit."

"Do you call saying someone is 'queer' nothing? I'm not having that sort of language in here. Bugger off."

"It was only a joke."

"Joke? Try it down the road in the Bear. Now out."

When the lads left and the quiet returned, Simon turned to Pete.

"What's this about the Bear," he asked.

"That's where the Nancy-boys hang out looking for a shag," replied Pete, "You want to steer clear of there unless you feel like some poof's dick up your arse. On the other hand, if you feel like a fight you can go and beat one of them up at turning out time on a Saturday night. Personally, I avoid the place; it might damage my hands – and I don't want that, do I, on the verge of a musical career?"

It was February 29, and the state prosecutors had completed their case. Nelson Mandela and his comrades now had a month in which to examine the evidence and present their defence. Right from the start, they had decided that the trial would be used as a platform for their beliefs. They would not deny that they had been responsible for acts of sabotage; they would not deny that they had turned away from a policy of non-violence; they would admit they had made plans for guerrilla warfare if sabotage failed.

Nelson did not want to be limited to giving evidence from the witness box in the form of question and answer; he had made it clear that he wanted to read a statement from the dock outlining their beliefs. He was not concerned with getting off the charges or of lessening his punishment, but with strengthening the cause for which they all struggled. He would dispute the state's contention that they had embarked on a guerrilla war; he would deny the claims of murder; he would deny that they had ever contemplated the intervention of foreign military forces.

He would be the first witness and set the tone of the defence; he would open the defence with a statement of their politics and beliefs. He began work on his statement, reading and writing quietly in his cell in the evenings.

CHAPTER 7

Kissing the lips of Baal

Kate Walsh was concerned for her friend. They were allowed one late pass a week, so that they could stay out until 11 o'clock, and one a month that allowed them to be out until one o'clock in the morning. Heather was now regularly abusing both privileges. Sister Maitland, who was in charge of the nurses' home, had made the position quite clear:

"Anyone infringing these rules will face instant dismissal. Is that understood?"

"Yes, Sister," they'd all replied.

"Oh, and no male visitors are allowed in the nurses' home under any circumstances ... We don't want a promising career blighted by one foolish act, do we, nurses?"

"No Sister."

They had, in fact, rarely infringed the rules; they'd usually been too damned tired for anything except sleep. There'd been, perhaps, a weekly trip to the cinema and, once a month, they'd dressed up and gone to the dance at Knutton Gardens, which was where Heather had met Barry Glover. Since then, she'd often been late and Kay or Joan had waited up for her, but not this late – not after midnight.

A high wall along the top of which was cemented

broken glass surrounded the nurses' home. The girls had found a way over this by placing a thick tarpaulin covered with a car blanket to cover the glass. If the boyfriend gave you a leg up from the pavement side, it was possible – by not placing too much weight directly onto any one point of the wall – to jump from the top to the home side. The drawback was, of course, that someone had to wait up ready with the tarpaulin and blanket, and then make their way down the stairs, out through the front door and round to the wall when the latecomer arrived and flashed her torch as a signal.

There had been one or two mildly twisted ankles but nothing serious enough to keep any of them off work after a furtive night out. Some of the girls would have nothing to do with the scheme but those with boyfriends, or simply a date, were only too pleased to take it in turns to wait up for each other. Kate had never had either – that is, a boyfriend or a date – but, anticipating that the day might come, she had willingly joined the watch scheme.

"I'm sorry," said Heather, when she did arrive, "I know you must be dog-tired and you're on duty tomorrow, aren't you? It might be easier if I stayed … you know."

"Are they allowed to have women in the blocks at the training college, then?"

"No, but there's no way of letting you know how late I might be, is there? And it's not fair on you – staying up 'til the early hours."

"Perhaps you should get in earlier."

"Oh, Kate!"

"How did you get back to town, anyway?"

"Barry came with me. Now, he's got the long walk back to college."

"Are you sure you know what you're doing, Heather?"

"No, perhaps I don't," she answered, giving her friend a brief hug, "but I know I love Barry, and I trust him."

Stephen Last tossed the paper onto his bed, lay back and stared at the ceiling. He'd just read the account of the Burton-Taylor wedding, and he wondered what love meant to people like them. Burton had betrayed his wife, and Liz Taylor had – as the newspaper put it – 'tied more knots than the average midshipman'. They'd married in Canada at the Ritz Carlton Hotel in Montreal. Burton had said he was "very, very happy". Liz Taylor had made no comment. Both had seemed aloof from those around them, rather like minor gods looking down on the people. Yet Burton was the son of a Welsh miner – a man of the working class. He'd come from a one of those valleys bedevilled by the Methodist church, where girls who got themselves in the pudding club were denounced from the pulpit and sent away from the village. Shame raged around such women who were seen as nothing more than sluts.

But how did the world look on Burton and his kind? As demigods! Stephen was angry. Somehow, it didn't seem fair. In one of Ian Fleming's Bond novels – *Goldfinger,* he thought it was – he'd come across the phrase 'money makes an effective winding sheet'. Was that the kind of cynicism that ruled the world? Would it be OK for Burton to return to his valley because he and Liz Taylor were wealthy: the same valley that turned away pregnant girls? He hoped it wouldn't, but thought it would.

It was a day of 'incessant rain and biting winds', but

Michael Ramsey did not regret his decision to join the St Patrick's Day pilgrimage. He had spoken about the closer links between Protestants and Catholics. He was aware that friendliness would need to precede unity and that time would be the master. He knew that he was unpopular in Northern Ireland, but he had a quiet determination to walk forward in the faith. He knew he threatened the gap that Protestants in the north had no desire to close: the gap between them and the Catholics in the south.

His declarations had further angered the orthodox.

"I expect to meet some present-day atheists in Heaven," he had said, and when asked about the Virgin Birth had proclaimed "I believe it is quite in order for a person to stand up in church and recite the creed even if he has scruples about the Virgin Birth provided he believes in the pattern of faith as a whole."

He had gone to Moscow, it was reported, in a purple cassock and a four-cornered hat and there had kissed the icon of St Elijah and knelt before the religious picture. A voice had roared from the north of Ireland:

"Dr Ramsey is a Baal-worshipper, his knees have bowed to the beast of Baal and his mouth has kissed Baal's lips."

Heather had been assigned to Casualty, and she loved it from the very first moment: the sheer chaos appealed to her orderly mind. 'To bring order out of chaos': some poet or other had said that, she was sure. Was it Milton? It didn't matter: her 'A' levels were done and dusted.

On the morning following her conversation with Kate, Heather arrived early in the department because she hadn't slept at all. Being wakeful, she'd washed

– remembering Sister Codsley's words "Cleanliness, nurses, is next to godliness" – and left the nurses' home quietly so as not to wake the others. Heather then walked to Staffham General along the river path. She relished the coming of spring, and it was in the air. Already, primroses were coming into flower and there were violets and a few coltsfoot flowers rising on their long stems. Around the stump of an old tree, two hedge-sparrows were flirting with each other. Heather knew only a smattering of what there was to know about the natural world; what she did know she owed to the nature walks they'd taken at school.

As soon as she arrived, Sister Godfrey, one of the two sisters on duty, called out to her "We've had a constant stream all night. Be quick, Nurse Burton, we can do with a hand. The young man in cubicle 4 has just been brought in. He's unconscious. Search his pockets for a wallet or something. We need to inform the relatives."

Although, technically, she was only supposed to observe, Heather had soon found herself drawn into "making herself useful", as one of the two sisters on duty expressed it

She removed the young man's wallet and wrote down what she'd discovered on a record card. Such procedures had soon become second nature to her, and she placed the card on the receptionist's desk.

"We'll have the regulars in soon. See to them when they arrive will you? They never seem to mess you about, Nurse Burton," Sister Godfrey pursued, with a smile.

It was true. A number of "regulars" always expected special treatment and would become quite grumpy if they were denied, but this was grist to Heather's mill.

She wound them up rather than pacified them, and they soon got to know that "Nurse Burton wouldn't stand for any nonsense". She took severed fingers and unruly children in her stride.

Heather took the check-in cards from the box on the wall, ran her eyes over the wounded and indicated to which cubicle they were to go so that one of the qualified nurses could make an assessment of the urgency. She moved quietly from cubicle to cubicle, assisting where she could: socks and slippers were removed from an elderly lady who'd poured boiling water over her foot, an open wound was cleaned to establish how deep it was, a nosebleed were stemmed with an ice pack, blood pressures were taken to save the doctor time.

Heather was soon fetching splints and crutches, applying bandages, making out appointment cards for the fracture clinic, accompanying patients to the x-ray department and administering injections.

"Don't forget to countersign any card if you carry out a treatment, Nurse Burton. Accountability is of paramount importance."

Malcolm X had always felt that the atmosphere of violence in the United States had been tolerated by the Kennedy administration, and that it was this atmosphere that had claimed the life of the President. He had spoken out, and been disciplined by Elijah Muhammad, who led the Nation of Islam, the religious-political organisation to which Malcolm X belonged. Malcolm X had accepted the discipline, which forbad him to speak publicly for ninety days, but felt hurt and betrayed.

His journey of faith had not been easy. Malcolm X had

seen, in black homes throughout the United States, that his people hung pictures of a white Jesus. Asian people, he learned, worshipped gods that looked like them – as did Africans and Europeans – but Malcolm X's people worshipped a god that was the very image of the people who had enslaved them. The Nation of Islam was a separatist movement, believing that its followers, who were mainly African-Americans, should create a nation of their own, either outside the United States or in some distant part of the country.

His falling out with Elijah Muhammad had been painful. Rumours had been floating around for some time: Elijah Muhammad had fathered children by women to whom he was not married, the Nation of Islam was seeking financial aid from people who could not even pay their rent and intimidation was suggested. Elijah Muhammad had asked him to tone down his speeches because of the "bad press" the organisation was receiving, but Malcolm X had been disinclined to accept such a restraint. He'd visited his leader and asked him about the reported infidelities, but come away unsatisfied. The assassination of Medgar Evers, head of the NAACP, in Mississippi in the summer of 1963 and the killing of the four little girls, when the 16th Street Baptist Church in Alabama was bombed, fuelled Malcolm X's anger and his antipathy towards "the white devils" even further. He felt the gulf widening between himself and the Nation of Islam, which had nurtured him. In New York, his comments about President Kennedy were seen as the last straw in his "betrayal" of Elijah Muhammad, and death threats were made.

Malcolm X was tired. Travelling the length and

breadth of the country, challenging debaters on television and college campuses, keeping his finger on the pulse of the civil rights movement and bringing the Nation of Islam from a small and loosely organised group to one of the most powerful political forces in America had worn him down both mentally and physically.

He announced his split from the Nation of Islam and announced the formation of the Muslim Mosque Incorporated.

It had been a busy month for the Beatles: their images were displayed in Madam Tussauds, Ringo was elected Honorary Vice-President of Leeds University, Paul McCartney denied that he and Jane Asher were married, the 'mop tops' – as the press liked to call the group – had begun filming *A Hard Day's Night* and they'd been named 'Show Business Personalities of the Year'.

For John, however, perhaps the biggest event had been the publication of his book, *In His Own Write*. In his spare moments, he'd written and doodled and scribbled, creating verses and caricatures as the group travelled by car and train and plane to their string of concerts. The book – published by Jonathan Cape and lauded by The Times Literary Supplement as being 'worth the attention of anyone who fears for the impoverishment of the English language' – was a collection of poetry and prose that delighted in surrealistic images and word-play.

"I love it, Cyn," he said, "The Goon Show was my inspiration. We used to take them off for hours when we were kids. And Lewis Carroll, of course – *Alice in Wonderland* is one of my favourite books. It's the off-beat humour that appeals to me – that and the satire. I love playing with words, turning them inside out, experimenting with their flexibility."

Cynthia – now recognised, publicly, as John's wife – watched him devour newspaper after magazine after novel, reading across a huge range of subjects: music, biography, history, design and mystery.

John's image as the intellectual Beatle grew and he was mobbed not only by his teenage fans but also the aristocracy who lined-up for his autograph. John was unimpressed by the establishment: officials from the embassies and the dowagers and debutantes. Behind the fixed smiles, the demands for autographs and "locks of hair for my daughter", these people saw John and his friends as nothing more than "working class yobs" that had happened to make it good. As often as not, they couldn't tell one Beatle from another. John realised this, and turned his back.

As Des Smith walked into the common room, he heard Stephen Last 'proselytising'. "... conversation is the junk and yet, at the same time, the currency of living," the exhausted voice was proclaiming.

A group of his student friends were sprawled around a table in the Red Room, some playing bridge, some flicking ash into one of the litter bins, all talking or chipping in on the conversations.

"It depends on how well educated you are," said Stella Aldridge, "You wouldn't expect a dustman to express himself with the same coherence as a lecturer. Not that I've got ..."

"... Anything against dustman," interrupted Des,

much to Stella's annoyance. "What makes you think dustman are incoherent? I assume you'd say the same about lorry drivers?"

"You wouldn't expect a lorry driver or a dustman to discuss morality, for example, with the same insight or in the same depth as a lecturer," snapped Stella, angry at this man's attempt to put her down.

"How many lorry drivers have you spoken to?" taunted Des.

"Well, at least one – my father."

The rest of the group looked up at Stella's declaration that cut Des off at the knees and created a tension in the group. Stephen, embarrassed at the anger between his friends, spoke up:

"We weren't discussing the cultural awareness of dustmen or lorry drivers," he reassured everyone, "but the nature of conversation."

"What – from your armchair? Safe here in Mother Culture's arms?"

"We were discussing exactly how it's relevant to forming opinions about real attitudes and real convictions – and the exchange between you and Stella illustrates that perfectly."

Des laughed; it was all he could do.

"Two diamonds," said Simon Wiseman.

"Two diamonds? Doubled," responded Mike Harrison.

"Doubled? I doubt it," replied Marguerite, who was Simon's partner.

"I'm not making myself too clear, am I?" apologised Stephen for no particular reason.

"Why not shut up altogether, Stevie," retorted Jenny, throwing him one of her coquettish glances.

"Look at it this way," Stephen persisted, "Conversation is very self-conscious. We speak to convey an impression of ourselves, and the impression we wish to convey depends upon the person to whom we're speaking ..."

"... to whom we're speaking? Christ, Last, you speak like a tome," laughed Simon, who was fond of Stephen.

Ignoring him and the laughter that surrounded the remark (Stephen's propensity for a certain pomposity of expression was always a joke among them), Stephen continued:

"But the impressions we create may not be of our real selves at all. They may only be true of the picture we have of ourselves; and the tension between these two things – our self-picture and our real-self – is always implicit in our conversation."

"But intellectual discussion ..." began Stella.

"... is no different," interspersed Stephen, "The seeking of truth is never free from the desire to create an impression.

"What's this load of cobblers, Last?" quizzed Paul Crisp, approaching the group.

"There you are," laughed Stephen, "Point made! Paul is nourishing his sense of herd solidarity at the expense of any truth my conversation might hold."

They all laughed at his remark; and it was a good feeling, sitting together, enjoying each other's company, comfortable in their comradeship, feeling free to take the mickey out of each other without reprisal and feeling free – at last – to speak their thoughts. 'Jokin' and talkin' about the world outside ... we thought we could sit forever in fun.' The words from *Bob Dylan's Dream* ran through Stephen's mind.

'Twenty-four hour a day, non-stop pop music,' thought Simon Wiseman, as he listened to Radio Caroline and the voice of DJ Simon Dee, who – his friends said – he rather resembled. Simon looked at himself in the small dressing table mirror in his room and ran a comb through his hair. '... and the thought never hit that the one road we travelled would either shatter or split.' Not yet: not for three more glorious years. The pirates were ruling the airwaves and sticking two fingers up at the establishment, the government and the BBC. Things were gonna change – and how! They'd moored the ship outside British territorial waters and there was nothing anyone could do about it. At last, young people could listen to the music they wanted to hear. Before the pirates, the only escape had been Radio Luxembourg.

Simon was home for the holidays, and he thought he'd sharpen-up his appearance and spin a few yarns to his old schoolmates at the pub.

Stella, too, was home, but she had few friends and was looking forward to returning to college after the Easter break. She'd been too bright to have many friends. She scared off the boys and didn't endear herself to many of the girls once it became clear that she was going places and they were staying in Manchester to work as clerks or waitresses. Grammar school had been the first step on her road to freedom; had she failed the 11+ that would have been the end for her, or the beginning of a life that revolved around a going-nowhere job until she met Mr Right, had his babies and cooked his dinner.

She'd been the 'brain-box' of her primary school: the one that always produced the stories or poems the teacher read out to the class, the one who got all her sums right, the one who was always top of the class at the end of the year. Her dad had taught her that much

"Get on, lass," he'd urged her, "I wasted my time and ended up as a lorry driver. I couldn't be bothered, see. I failed the 11+ and so they dumped me in a secondary school – under-funded, under-staffed, under-equipped and under-classed. The council put most of its money into the grammars, and that left the rest of us – eighty-eight percent of us – in the waste tip of the secondary moderns."

He'd always worried about how they'd afford to send her to college or university, but he need not have bothered. Nowadays, they had means-tested LEA grants. Bert Aldridge and his family qualified for the full grant.

Her dad had always been her hero – her dad and Che Guevara. She'd been fourteen when he and Castro had driven into Havana and freed their people from the yoke of American imperialism, from the gangsters who ran the casinos and from the likes of Hemingway who'd gone to live there because "Cuba had the most beautiful prostitutes in the world". Stella had been attracted by the glamorous excitement of the rebels, their women, the army uniforms and the fight for freedom. You could bring about change if you were prepared to fight for it, and the weapons didn't have to be guns: there was politics. Education, by itself, wasn't enough: it needed to be driven by a political force for change – change that would benefit everyone. Freedom was only a road away, a light shining in the distance.

She hadn't been ashamed of her dad, as Des Smith had supposed. It wasn't that at all. What she was aware of – what she had always been aware of since she first started to think for herself – was that her dad would have been more able to express his thoughts if he'd been better equipped with the words to do so. Orwell was right when he said '…to think clearly is a necessary first step towards political regeneration'.

It was her dad who'd put her off religion. "They'll never get anywhere, lass," he'd said, "They'll be arguing among themselves 'til the cows come home." She'd had experience of the viciousness of religious differences when she was a child and they'd played on the old bomb sites near her home. Although her dad had atheistic views, Stella's mum was a Roman Catholic. When they ganged up as kids, she was always a "Cathy Cat" and Stella would yell back "Prody Dog". She didn't know what it meant; it was just something you had to yell back.

He'd been heavy-handed, of course, with the strap – or, rather, the belt – but all parents were when she was a child, and she'd never really held it against him. It was intended for her own good. "Your dad's only concerned you should grow up decent," her mum had said as she wiped away the tears.

He'd always rationed how much TV they watched, as well. Not that she minded: most of the girls at the grammar school watched rubbish like *Six Five Special* where the likes of Cliff Richard, Billy Fury and Eden Kane thrust their pelvises at you. She could do without that: give her Francoise Hardy, any day. She'd played *Le temps de l'amour* over and over again on her Dansette. Stella had grown her hair long to look like her heroine. It certainly attracted the boys; it hung half-way down her back or was draped, brunette and lustrous, over her shoulders. Her hair certainly suited the folk singer look. She'd been years ahead of Marianne Faithfull and Mary Travers.

Apart from Che, her male heroes had been people like Bernard Levin and the crowd on *TW3*; there was a viciousness about the way they sailed into their targets that appealed to Stella. She hadn't had sex yet but wanted it; she needed to shed her virginity like an old skin. Just get rid of it – have done with it. Stella was certain that those intellectuals and singers on the Left Bank dispensed with their hang-ups somewhere on the banks of the Seine before they began discussing Proust in the evenings.

'The Wild Ones invaded a seaside town yesterday – 1,000 fighting, drinking, roaring, rampaging teenagers on scooters and motor-cycles. By last night, after a day of riots and battles with police, ninety of them had been arrested.

A desperate SOS went out from police at Clacton, Essex, as leather-clad youths and girls attacked people in the streets, turned over parked cars, broke into beach huts, smashed windows and fought with rival gangs.

Police reinforcements from other Essex towns raced to the shattered resort, where fearful residents had locked themselves indoors.

By this time, the centre of Clacton was jammed with screaming teenagers. Traffic was at a standstill.

The crowd was broken up by police and police dogs.

Several policemen were injured as the teenagers fought them.

A number of arrests had already been made. Addresses had been taken and messages sent to parents.

And worried mothers and fathers were beginning to arrive from the London area to bail out their sons and daughters.

The harassed police were glad to see them go. For the cells at Clacton police station were crammed with youngsters under arrest.

By last night the score of arrests and charges was:

Thirty for assaults on police and civilians; thirty for creating disturbances and fighting; ten for theft; and twenty for other offences, including drunk and disorderly, malicious damage and using abusive language.

The Wild Ones – this was the title of a Marlon Brando film in which teenaged motor-cyclists terrorised a town – have caused trouble in Clacton before. But not on this scale.

They began arriving on Friday and Saturday and many slept rough on the beach and pier and in promenade shelters.

Superintendent Norman Wood, the resort's police chief, who sent the call for help, said: "For some reason Clacton is attracting more than its fair share of these young thugs."

Mr James Malthouse, manager of a sea-front hotel, said: "I've seen riots in South America but this was almost mob rule."

(Daily Mirror; Monday, March 30, 1964)

Simon Wiseman, having downed his first pint in one,

offered his old school chum, Malcolm Reed, another, as he tossed yesterday's paper on the table at their local, the Mops and Brooms.

"What have you been up to, then?" he demanded of the leather-jacketed yobbo who sat opposite him.

"Nothin', Sime, honest, it wasn't like that," Malcolm replied, "They were pleased enough to see us when we got there. It was Bank Holiday weekend, for Christ's sake. We'd only gone to enjoy ourselves. The cafes were open, and the pubs, and the clubs. We were all havin' a good time. Most of 'em came on the train, anyway – not on motor-bikes. The Mods were all up one end – near the pier – and our lot, the Rockers, were down the other. It was a great evenin' – Saturday. There weren't many coppers about. Rock on, man!

All right, a few of us slept in unlocked beach huts and under the pier and that, but we didn't break in anywhere – and my girl insisted we went to a B and B she knew about."

"Are you telling me that this *Daily Mirror* story is a pack of lies?"

"Not exactly, me old mate, but it is a trifle exaggerated. After we'd had breakfast on the Sunday a few of us, throttlin' up to make a nice roar, did burn off down to the pier end – but only to annoy them poncy Mods. We parked up on the sea-front and strolled down towards 'em. And then they turned on us – hundreds of 'em. Punchin' and bloody kickin' they were. So we made a dash for it – to re-group like ... and get some reinforcements."

"Reinforcements?"

"Yeah. Word got about, see, and some of the lads

started to bike in from uver places – but they never got in. The police cordoned-off the town and wouldn't let 'em through."

"And they didn't try and break through?"

"No – Christ, you sound like a bleedin' copper, Sime."

"I'm just interested. Go on."

"We aint all yobs, Sime. There are some ex-servicemen among us Rockers, and they have a respect for law and order – so, no, we didn't break through the thin blue line. It was a stand-off between us and the coppers … Eventually, the police motor-cycle boys escorted those of us on bikes back to town."

"What happened to the Mods?"

"Most of 'em came in by train, so I hear, and the police commissioned another one and herded them back to Liverpool Street. And the ones on scooters were eased out of Clacton just like we'd been."

"So there were no arrests?"

"Not for fights between us and the Mods. A few people got pissed, but they were mainly Mods 'cause we can hold our beer better."

"And you've got more respect for law and order?"

"Right. Fancy anuver pint?"

As they spoke, Simon ruminated on the fact that he – unlike Malcolm and his girl – could not have afforded to go to Clacton, or anywhere else, and stay in a B and B for the weekend; neither could he have afforded a motor-bike or a scooter to get him there, and realised that that was how it would remain.

The post-war boom that was fuelling the prosperity of the 60s was not something from which he, as a teacher, would feel the benefit in his wallet. There were more jobs than workers to fill the vacancies, and employers had to put their hands more deeply into their pockets in order to keep people on-side. An employee who could walk out of one job in the morning and into another by the afternoon wasn't going to take any bullshit such as low pay. The teenager was now a force in the market place. Simon guessed that Malcolm would spend more money on clothes in a month than he had to spare for the year.

Chapter 8

A new message

Kate Walsh knew her mother's views well and was ashamed of them, but she couldn't disown her mother. Her views were, no doubt, in accord with popular feeling – particularly of her mother's generation. Not that her father agreed with the prejudice they expressed; he'd looked up over his copy of the *Daily Mail* and then looked down again when her mother began her outburst.

It had begun the previous evening when a letter to the *Wolverhampton Express and Star* had raised the issue of noisy West Indian parties.

"If they come over here, they should respect our ways," her mother had snarled, "or go back home where they belong."

"It was us who asked them to come, Flo," replied Maurice Walsh

"I can't think why," lied Kate's mother, who knew full well why post-war governments had encouraged people from the Commonwealth to emigrate, "They were better off where they were. At least they had the sunshine."

"But we didn't have the labour."

"You're not telling me that coloured people are good workers, surely? Everyone knows they're lazy."

"Not everyone," replied Kate's father, quietly, "fifty percent of the labour in some of our engineering firms is supplied by coloured workers, and they seem keener on overtime than their white brothers."

Kate smiled as she listened to her father, who was out to rile her mother rather than simply stand up for coloured workers. He had a post in the local branch of the Transport and General Workers Union, despite being a lifelong Tory voter, and did know his facts. Her mother did not dispute what he said, but tried another tack.

"They bring disease into the country. That's a well-known fact," she retorted.

"That's true," replied Kate's father, and then paused before adding – again, quietly, so as to aggravate her mother even more – "there has been one case of TB reported."

Her mother had left the table, then, to clear the dishes and wash-up; but next morning, at breakfast, irritated by what she saw as her husband's complacency, she had persisted in pursuing the conversation.

"Mrs Auden says she was followed down her street by a coloured man who stopped her five times before she reached her door."

"A coloured man stopped Maisie Auden? What for?" She must be all of fifty. I'd have thought he could have found someone a bit more ..."

"There's no need for that – Kate's having her breakfast. What I'm saying is it's well known that they can't get enough of you-know-what."

Kate spluttered over her mother's euphemism, and left the table to cough.

"Now see what you've done," continued Flo Walsh.

"I've done nothing."

"Exactly – and if it's left to people like you, the

situation will get worse, not better ... Mrs Auden's neighbour was driven out of her home by them."

"How did they manage that? I can't imagine anyone driving Maisie Auden out of anywhere."

"I said her neighbour, but Mrs Auden could be next."

"Well, as long as she doesn't come and live next door to us I don't mind," concluded Maurice Walsh, as he got up and left for work.

Kate, who'd come home for a couple of days to meet some old school friends, caught the bus from where they lived on the Codsall road and went into town. As she passed through Whitmore Reans and then Chapel Ash, Kate saw what had frightened her mother; there seemed to be more black faces than white living in these areas – and her parents had, when she was young, lived in Hordern Grove. There was a genuine fear among her mother's generation that these newcomers were driving out the whites and would, eventually, take their jobs.

At the same time, she wasn't inclined to believe the stories that were spread by the gossips. The immigrants were supposed to urinate and excrete in the street because they didn't know what toilets were for or because they were, intrinsically, filthy. Another story told of how they shoved this excrement through the letter boxes of white people, who'd lived in these areas for generations, in order to drive them out and buy up their property cheaply. She only knew a few coloured people – there were only a few at Wolverhampton Tech – but she couldn't imagine any of them behaving as described in the lurid tales brought home from the shops by her mother.

On Monday, April 20, Nelson Mandela stood in the dock and made his statement to the court.

"I am the first accused. I hold a bachelor's degree in Arts, and practised as an attorney in Johannesburg for a number of years. I am a convicted prisoner, serving five years for leaving the country without a permit and for inciting people to go on strike at the end of May 1961 ...

At the outset, I want to say that the suggestion made by the state ... that the struggle in South Africa is under the influence of foreigners or communists is wholly incorrect. I have done whatever I did, both as an individual and as a leader of my people, because of my experience in South Africa, and my own proudly felt African background, and not because of what any outsider might have said ... I hoped that life might offer me the opportunity to serve my people and make my own humble contribution to their freedom struggle ...

I do not deny that I planned sabotage ... I planned it as a result of a calm and sober assessment of the political situation that had arisen after many years of tyranny, exploitation, and oppression of my people by whites ... the hard facts were that fifty years of non-violence had brought the African people nothing but more repressive legislation, and fewer and fewer rights ...

The lack of human dignity experienced by Africans is the direct result of the policy of white supremacy. White supremacy implies black inferiority ... Menial tasks in South Africa are invariably performed by Africans ... children wander about the streets of the townships because they have no schools to go to ... both parents have to work to keep the family alive. This leads to a breakdown in moral standards ... and in growing violence ...

Africans want a just share in the whole of South Africa; they want security and a stake in society. Above all, we want political rights ... I know this sounds revolutionary to the whites in this country, because the majority of voters will be Africans. This is what makes the white man fear democracy ... This then is what the ANC is fighting for. Their struggle is a truly national one. It is a struggle of the African people, inspired by their own suffering and experience. It is a struggle for the right to live."

Nelson had been reading his speech, but now placed his papers on the defence table and turned to face the judge. The courtroom became extremely quiet, and he did not take his eyes from the judge's face as he spoke his final words.

"During my lifetime I have dedicated myself to this struggle of the African people. I have fought against white domination, and I have fought against black domination. I have cherished the ideal of a democratic and free society in which all persons live together in harmony and with equal opportunities. It is an ideal which I hope to live for and to achieve. But if needs be, it is an ideal for which I am prepared to die."

The silence in the courtroom was complete as Nelson sat down. He had spoken for over four hours. He felt that all eyes were upon him. A great sigh arose from the gallery followed by the cries of women.

Elizabeth Sturlson pulled the curtains back from her bedroom window, and the sun streamed onto her eiderdown, dappling the paisley pattern. It was Saturday, which meant no school; she was looking forward to seeing Des early and walking with him into Middlesbrough.

The town centre always bustled on a Saturday, and they'd just bump into friends without even making plans to meet.

The news coming out of South Africa had been bad for months. Nelson Mandela and his friends faced death by hanging if found guilty. They talked about it at school as part of their Liberal Studies. It seemed that blacks and whites were separated, and should never speak to each other. If a white person wanted a job done, they just told a black person to get on with it whether or not they employed the black person. 'Apartheid' wasn't just something that happened; it was government policy.

But it all seemed so far away. Soon she'd be holding onto Des's arm and making her way to their favourite coffee bar. She'd been a bit silly until she met Des. He'd introduced her to the Young Socialists and given her a direction. Before then it had been just been boys and silly talk – like blowing-up the Royal Family and the aristocracy so that socialism could become a reality. The talk had all been wild, too. One minute someone would be holding forth on Martin Luther King and black Americans having to ride on the back of the bus, and the next they'd be complaining that men were paid more than women for doing the same job. Focus: that's what Des had given her. Des had said that you could tell a person's politics by simple things like how they held a cup of tea. He always held his cup by the bowl with the handle pointing away.

At Young Socialist meetings, they'd sing The Red Flag – not that any of them were communists, but it sounded revolutionary. Her mother hadn't let her go on the Aldermaston march because she said she was too young, but she sang the songs. One, in particular, was her favourite.

"Last night I had the strangest dream I've ever dreamed before,

I dreamed the world had all agreed to put an end to war."

Des wasn't keen on coffee bars – especially the new one in the high street; he said they were bourgeois, and preferred a café – but he'd take her to The Gondolier if she asked him. Inside it was all black and red with round tables and tubular chairs. Des and his friends turned theirs round and sat leaning over the backs. They'd talk all the time about socialism and the next election, which they said Labour would win.

She wasn't sure about the Labour Party, and anyway she wasn't old enough to vote. Harold Wilson seemed a bit of a smart Alec, but he did talk about the need for a technological revolution and had to be better than the man from the grouse moors. If socialism did come it would mean a fairer society in which everyone would be happy and treated well. Sometimes, Des didn't seem so sure about that but you had to have principles and something to believe in or … or there would be no point in living.

She'd always enjoyed taking the leaflets round with Des and his friends. The people were never hostile to her even when they went to what were obviously Tory neighbourhoods. The kids there seemed freer, somehow – not all of them but some. That's where the beatniks tended to come from, with their sloppy sweaters, long hair and tight trousers. Des didn't like beatniks; he said they were pseudo-intellectuals with no commitment to anyone or anything but themselves.

The women were often ... promiscuous, as well; they slept around. She slept with Des, of course, but he was the only one, and always would be. Her mother didn't know, although Elizabeth sometimes wondered if she did but kept quiet. Anyway, she'd never caught them at it, and mustn't. Her mother wouldn't want to think her daughter was dirty and might turn out to be a prostitute. It was OK if the boy was going to marry you, and she was sure of Des.

Cliff Richard was thinking about God, and had been for a long time. He'd spent two years with the Jehovah's Witnesses, listening to them but never feeling he could commit himself to their way of thinking.

"It's a very personal thing to me," he said, "I've just been thinking a lot about God. That's all. It's very important to me. At one time, I felt I was a Jehovah's Witness, but held back from baptism in the faith. I've become dissatisfied with life, generally, and when that happens it pulls you down. It affects everything you do. There was always a Bible in our house, but I never heard my father speak about faith. I was baptized and brought up as an Anglican, but refused to go to confirmation classes. It seemed to me that I was being expected to pay lip service to the Christian code ... perhaps I didn't really give the faith a chance."

His friend, Hank Marvin had once said:

"I've always been a bit directionless and felt I didn't need a path, but would wonder what I was doing here ... I felt there had to be an answer. The Witnesses gave me that answer. They believe that there are things which are wrong – totally wrong. What they had to say took away the confusion you find in other churches."

What Hank said had got Cliff thinking.

Kate's old school friends had gathered in The Cellar, which was one of the new-style coffee bars in town and one of them had brought along a new friend. Kate recognised her as Glynis Hearn, an older girl from the Technical Grammar, who was now a teacher at Castleford, one of the local primary schools. Glynis had cast a scathing eye over the fish nets that hung from the ceiling and then sat quietly listening to the others chatting. In the background, Joan Baez was singing *Once I had a Sweetheart*, reminding Kate that she'd never had one. In the evenings, The Cellar sometimes doubled as a folk club, and they would gather round a guitarist and join in the singing, which consisted of many protest songs.

This morning the talk turned to coloured immigrants and the trouble the country would face if the problem wasn't sorted out. Most of her friends took a stance against what their parents were saying, but not necessarily always with real conviction. Kate had listened, once again, as the excrement stories were rolled out – this time with some derision – and had learned that the Indians were believed to be blocking the drains with rubbish because "they didn't have dustbins where they came from". Kate caught Glynis's eye and realized the older woman was amused or seething: the smile could have meant either emotion.

"They say that the West Indians hold all-night parties and use prostitutes," said Amelia Ball, "including the local white women."

"But that is rubbish, isn't it?" interposed Kate, "I mean none of the people who spread those stories actually know one way or the other, do they? And anyway, I don't believe that most white people believe any of it. We've had no racial trouble here."

"What we also ought to remember," Glynis Hearne cut in, suddenly, "is that people from India and the West Indies are citizens of this country." She paused as the ring of faces round the table turned to stare at her in amazement. "In fact," she continued, "so is everyone else who lives in the Commonwealth. Why do you think we had an empire – because we enjoyed foreign climes? The Commonwealth, or the Empire as it was then called, was opened up to provide markets for our goods and raw materials for our industries. The wealth of this country was built on that and the sweat of native labour. Everyone in our colonies is a British citizen, entitled under the law to come to this country, to settle here and raise their families here with full rights. What's more, we needed them after the war and encouraged them to come. We were short of labour, and needed to rebuild our wealth. A country can't dish out rights to people and then withdraw them when it becomes inconvenient ..." She paused and smiled, "Lecture over," she said with a laugh, "but all this silly talk is just that – silly. It's the talk of ignorant people and dishonest politicians who should know better. We have to find a way forwards, not backwards."

Simon Wiseman was glad the Stones were rolling. Sitting with his old mate, Malcolm Reed, in the Mops and Brooms and several pints into the evening, he wondered whether teaching was for him or whether he'd be better off "shakin' it abart a bit" and becoming a pop star. It would, of course, be handy if he could play a guitar.

They'd seen their favourite group at the Wembley Arena a few days before – up there with The Dave Clark Five, Billy J Kramer and The Dakotas, Manfred Mann, Cliff and The Shadows and – yeah, right! – The Beatles. "Well, yer can't have everyfing, can yer, me old mate?" *Not Fade Away* had dropped off the singles charts, but Mick had made his point with the way he held onto the 'f'.

They enjoyed themselves running down pop groups from the north – without actually meaning a word of it – when Malcolm turned the conversation, abruptly:

"What about this Smith bloke in Rhodesia, then?" he asked, "He's out for trouble isn't he?"

"He's a hard-liner," replied Simon, "His party, the Rhodesian Front, is dedicated to white supremacy. My dad's brother farms out there, funnily enough. He came over a couple of years ago, and brought a load of tea with him – Rhodesian tea, beautiful. I've never tasted tea like it: clean, fresh, crisp. It really woke your palate up in the morning. Not like the rubbish you buy here. He said that there was no way they were giving blacks the vote. If they did, it would be the end of civilized standards as we know them."

CHAPTER 9

A nigger for a neighbour

Spring had sprung when the sticker cards, printed with the slogan 'If you want a nigger for a neighbour, vote Labour' appeared in Smethwick. For the past two years, Peter Griffiths, the Conservative candidate, had run a campaign urging an almost complete ban on immigration. The word on the streets was that "even the coloured people want a ban because their own jobs are affected" and no one doubted the truth of this fear: more labour meant lower wages or a shortage of work.

At the same time, it was embarrassing to anyone who saw that the only way forward was not to create divisions between people of whatever colour who had lived and worked side by side since the 1950s. Conservative Central Office was particularly concerned to "keep the matter off the hustings in the forthcoming election campaign".

Maurice Walsh, sitting with a group of mates, while his wife cooked the Sunday roast, in The Woodman at Bilbrook listened with interest as Flo Walsh's prejudices were scythed down before him.

"The coloured people of Wolverhampton have shown themselves to be very law-abiding," said one councillor.

"That's not what they're saying in Smethwick, Arthur," provoked Maurice.

"They can say and do what they like in Smethwick, Maurice. We want nothing to do with immigration control. Let Smethwick approach the Home Office if they want to."

"I employ fifty or sixty coloured blokes in my factory," said the managing director of a firm in the town, "and there's no antipathy of any kind between them and my white employees."

"These people are very friendly, and are most anxious to come into our way of living and our way of life," replied a shopkeeper, in support.

"But they're not too fond of a hard day's graft, are they?" Kate's father persisted.

"Cut it out, Maurice. You're a union man. You know different," said the councillor, "Another round before we all go home to lunch?"

"You don't believe that, do you Maurice?" asked the shopkeeper, as the councillor went to the bar.

"It's what my missus believes."

"But she's a housewife, isn't she? Like a lot of them – with all due respect to your wife, Maurice – she never gets out and about in the workplace, does she? They don't know anything about the real world, and this gossip could be harmful."

Maurice Walsh laughed, imagining his wife's response had she been sitting with them.

"You're just a stirrer, Maurice. You want to be careful who's listening. It could be offensive. They work alongside my white men, and they put in just as much for a day's pay."

"That's as maybe," replied Maurice, "but – as Peter Griffiths has said – those posters sum up popular feeling."

"Do they – or are these people just fascists masquerading as Tory voters? We had a war not so long ago to stop that kind of thing."

Sheila Pratt drew back the curtain around the patient's bed and watched as her senior colleague folded down the bedclothes to expose the dressing. Sheila was on the surgical ward, and she was not 'bursting with confidence' as she stared at the red, puckered and swollen skin around the wound. The patient, a young woman, had had an appendectomy a few days before and complained that the wound still itched.

"It shows it's healing nicely," replied Sheila, and gained a smile from the senior nurse, as she moistened a swab with alcohol and wiped the wound from top to bottom.

"Always clean the wound from the top down and from the inside out, Nurse Pratt," she instructed, "and only use a swab once." She placed clean gauze over the wound and fastened it with tape. "Now, let's clear this away."

Once again they were in the sterilising room, emptying the dirty dressings and swabs, washing the bowls and instruments in soapy water before placing them in the steriliser and wiping the dressings trolley with carbolic. The routine – about which Joan Whiting complained so bitterly – was reassuring to Sheila, who liked to do things again and again; she found it gave her some confidence.

"It's your turn, Nurse Pratt. I've shown you how to remove stitches – now let's see you have a go."

Sheila looked at the elderly lady who was waiting for them with a ready smile, and felt awed by the woman's faith in her abilities. 'Oh my word,' Sheila thought, 'if only she knew how nervous I am.' She held the knot with the forceps and snipped the stitch with the scissors, pressing the flat of the scissors on the wound as she pulled out the stitch. She worked her way along the wound, removing each alternate stitch and trying to assess whether it was safe to remove them all. There was plenty of support, of course, and she was glad; Sister had told her to always consult before attempting anything about which she was unsure.

"You'll soon learn to judge properly for yourself but, until then, there's always one of the senior nurses or me."

Joan Whiting was unable to persuade any of the others to join her, but she was determined to go to Brighton. There was something about Brighton. Graham Greene had set his gangster novel, *Brighton Rock,* in the town and managed to convey an image of unparalleled seediness and violence; and Noel Coward had remarked "Ah dear Brighton – piers, queers and racketeers". Joan was well-read, but it wasn't the magnet of literature that was drawing her towards Brighton on that weekend: it was the excitement of potential violence.

The other girls always supposed that boarding school types were rather wet, rather cultured, awfully well-read snobs. This wasn't the case: many of the friends she'd made during her incarceration were as rough as they come. What made them different was that their parents had money. In order to shake off the boarding school image, some of the lads became Rockers. The smell of the leather gave them a potent sexuality: there's nothing quite as sensual as the smell of animal skin. Their parents' money also gave them access to motorbikes; to afford a Norton or Vincent, you needed to be either a working class lad sweating off his bollocks in a factory all week or the son of a well-heeled daddy.

Joan knew several from both sides of the social divide but it was a friend from boarding school who was taking her to Brighton; and the thought of 500ccs of Manx Norton throbbing away between her legs was attractive to say the least.

The weekend began well. She'd donned her Brando-style biker jacket, tight denim jeans, black leather boots, cotton T-shirt, studded belt and the white, silk scarf and roared off on William's pillion seat, her hair blowing in the wind. Arriving in Brighton, they made contact with friends at Jack's Café where William treated her to egg and chips plastered with tomato sauce – a touch of class Joan loved – accompanied by a cup of char. Soon they had Eddie Cochrane singing *Summertime Blues* on the juke box, with chat and laughter filling the air. Joan found the frenetic atmosphere intoxicating.

The lads would leave the café and burn up and down the road; occasionally, one of their girls would join them. Mostly, they sat around chatting and listening to rock 'n' roll music on the jukeboxes. One or two of the lads travelled further into town along the seafront, sussing out where the Mods might be gathering. Many had no scooters, Joan noticed when she joined William on one of the recces, and were arriving by train.

They passed the evening in the pubs and cafes, sometimes dancing but mainly drinking, chatting and listening to the music. Joan realised that she was getting bored; talking about joining the 'ton-up boys' had been one thing, but none of them, she felt, had much to say. Back at boarding school it had seemed exciting; sitting out the evening over a Coke it seemed less so. As the Saturday night rolled to its boisterous close, she and William found an un-locked beach hut and settled down. Both had the money for a B and B but the beach hut seemed more rebellious.

They were up by ten o'clock next morning and sauntering along the seafront looking for breakfast. Families were already settling themselves on the beach: the children with buckets and spades, the men sitting in deck chairs reading the paper while the women watched the children or joined them at the water's edge for a paddle. The small street cafes were doing a brisk trade. Joan noticed a large group of Rockers they'd been with the previous night swaggering along the beach. It was the first tremor of apprehension she'd felt. They weren't causing any trouble but there must have been a hundred or more of them; these were the ones who'd slept rough – under the pier and in the bus shelters. They'd obviously been up since sunrise.

What happened next happened quickly. One moment the beach was alive with the usual sounds – seaside music, waves on the shingle and the excited laughter of children – and the next it resounded with yells of anger and screams of pain. A swarm of Mods appeared and charged towards the Rockers who were ready. Coshes appeared, chains were swung and cudgels brandished in fists.

Joan saw one lad fall as he ran, and the next moment a boot went into his prone face. He looked up, bloodied and blinded, and the boot went in again. Behind them, inside the café where she and William had just been served breakfast, a window was smashed and glass shattered everywhere covering plates and floor. A group of Mods surged towards them, turning over tables and throwing chairs aside at the customers who'd failed to flee in time. Two of them grabbed William.

"You're the one, mate. You're the bloke we were looking for last night."

Joan stared in horror as the first fist went in, and William fell under a kicking of boots. The girls with the lads egged them on to further violence before turning to Joan and ripping her Brando jacket from here. As she went down under a series of kicks to her legs and groin, someone grabbed her hair and began to wrench it out. Looking up she saw the manageress of the café pile into the mob wielding a broom, which was torn from her hands before she was lifted and hurled across the counter.

As the old woman crashed into her own oven, Joan saw the police. A group of four, wielding truncheons, cleared the café and hauled William to his feet.

"It's all right," snapped Joan, realising her friend could be in trouble, "I'm a nurse. I'll see to these people."

"You've got a job on your hands then, love."

Joan looked up, blood streaming from her face and a sickening pain swelling in her legs and abdomen. In the café, several people had been shoved to the floor, cut and bleeding from the shattered glass. Through the wrecked window, Joan saw hordes of youngsters – dressed to kill in leathers or parkas – pitching into each other.

Terrified families, clutching their children, were attempting to reach the relative safety of the promenade before the screaming mob pounded them into the pebbles. Stones were flying through the air, thrown aimlessly and striking randomly. Other families, too far from the sea wall to flee for safety, were drawing their deckchairs around them in what resembled a wagon-train circle; but these were being pulled away and used as weapons.

A group of teenagers who'd been swimming were stripped and left naked, trying desperately to cover themselves with hands and towels. The mob stampeded over them, and injured Mods and Rockers staggered to their feet, blood pouring from mouths and noses.

As Joan watched, a second wave of Rockers crashed through the café intent on chasing the Mods across the promenade and into the town. Studded belts swung in the air. Staves drawn, a police cordon attempted to hold back the rampaging crowd. Screams and jeers filled the air. Bottles and broken chairs flew past.

Joan saw one of the constables fall, his helmet kicked from his head, as he tried to restrain a youth. He hit the promenade with a thud that made her feel sick. For less than a minute he lay stunned and then groped his way to his knees before helping a fellow officer to pin down one of the Mods. Four of them attempted to carry the youth to a waiting van, and then the cry went up "Mod! Mod! Mod!" Handfuls of pebbles showered over the constables from the beach, cutting into their faces. "Get them!" Joan felt repulsed as she listened. Were these louts really going to assault the police? For what seemed ages, indecision held sway, and then the mob dispersed into the town. She turned towards William and the other people injured in the café, and asked the manageress where her first aid kit was kept. The last Joan saw of the violence was two Rockers being tossed from the pier.

As the Pan Am flight from Paris took off for the States, Malcolm X's mind ran over, yet again, all that he had learned during his pilgrimage to Mecca. His hajj had been both a symbol of his break from the Nation of Islam and one of religious devotion. At first, he had been unsure of himself: he knew neither Arabic nor the Islamic rituals as they were practised in Saudi Arabia. Those who had shown him hospitality were Muslims, but they were white.

"One cannot be a true Muslim," they explained, "unless one wishes for his brother what he wishes for himself. Do you really feel that all white men are devils?"

"In America, the term 'white' is not merely a description of a person's colour. It reflects racial attitudes," replied Malcolm, "It implies the superiority of one race over another. A white man may ride at the front of a bus, but a black man must sit at the back."

He had been surprised at how well he was known throughout Europe and Saudi Arabia. He felt overwhelmed by the tens of thousands of Muslims from all over the world he encountered. 'They were all colours, from blue-eyed blonds to black-skinned Africans. But we were all participating in the same ritual, displaying a spirit of unity and brotherhood that my experiences in America had led me to believe never could exist between the white and the non-white'.

"I hope you will become a preacher of Islam in America," said the judge as he entered Malcolm's name in the Holy Register in Jedda.

On his pilgrimage he had met people of all kinds and races, many of whom had been fighters against oppression. He spoke to those in universities, to government officials, to King Faisal, to the ambassador from Mali, with Kwame Nkrumah, President of Ghana, where a state dinner was held in his honour by the Chinese ambassador.

Malcolm's trust in these people began to grow, and he saw them as individuals in the same way as he had always seen blacks. He came to see this as the way ahead, the road he must follow. Malcolm realised he had to change and he began with a new name – El Hajj Malik el Shabbaz.

On May 21st, his plane touched down at Kennedy Airport and he was met by his wife, Betty X, his daughters and a few of his followers.

Stephen Last was washing socks when Des Smith walked into his room. Papers lay scattered over the desk and, hands slithering with soap, Stephen bundled them into a pile.

"Your essay?" asked Des.

"Yes, it's coming on."

"I've been playing my guitar. I can't seem to make a start."

Stephen listened while his friend spoke of his difficulties. He had always admired Des, who he considered had lived a real life while he – Stephen – had sat 'twiddling his thumbs in the wings of life'. Des was from the north and had been engaged in politics ever since he could remember, while for Stephen such activities were something he'd only read about in the newspapers. Des believed that individual change could only come through social change and he approached the writing of his essays in that spirit.

They'd been set the task of 'relating theme and metaphor in Dickens's *Our Mutual Friend*, and Stephen had had no difficulty in linking the symbolism of the River Thames and Boffin's dust mounds with the central theme of the corrupting power of money. Des, however, had become bogged down by Dickens's social attitudes to characters like Eugene Wrayburn and Bradley Headstone, the former who he despised because of his moneyed idleness and the latter who he admired because of his earnest endeavour, a characteristic sneered at by Dickens. Des wondered what Dickens's attitude would have been had Lizzie Hexam been from a class above Wrayburn and it had been the man marrying up the social ladder rather than the woman. Who, then, would the laugh have been upon?

They talked far into the night, while Stephen's socks dried on the radiator (there were no adequate washing facilities at Collingwood Hall), digging deeply into the works of Orwell, with whom Des was very familiar, and Dickens himself, who Stephen had read widely. As the early hours of the morning beckoned them to sleep, with Stephen even more despairing of his academic views as contrasted to Des's real ones, Des asked, suddenly:

"Do you think our teaching certificate will raise our social status, Last?

"I've never really thought about it."

"Do you think if you took up with some middle-class bird here that she'd drop you as soon as you left college?"

Stephen looked at his friend and wondered who he was considering.

"Who would you place as middle-class in our Education group, for example?"

Susan Paget stroked the deodorant stick gently over her shaved underarms. 'Breasts a bit large,' she thought, 'tummy flat though.' She pulled on her pants and stretched the bra tight behind her back, smoothed down the rustling petticoat and watched her body's reflection in the long mirror her father had bought her to hang on the back of her door. Her skin shone and her hair, after twenty minutes brushing, glowed softly, as it dropped black to her shoulders, in the evening light. 'Cream dress, blue lace edging and blue sling-backs.'

The grass was soft under her feet as she crossed to Des's room. There was the soft humming of bees and the scent of hawthorn and, when she neared the open window, Susan heard the unfamiliar click of a typewriter. 'He must have borrowed Stephen's. No one else I know has one ... Am I really going after him? If Elizabeth were here, how would I feel then? How would I feel if I knew her? Silly putting it off. It's best settled for all our sakes.'

Des had seen her coming towards his window and his stomach turned over in one solid lump. 'She's *above* me, as Dickens would have said; she's above me just as – if Orwell was right – Estella was above Pip and Lucy Manette was above Sydney Carton. Mustn't lose my head, but I could do with a bloody good snog. She's one of the best looking birds in the place, and all these weeks we've been that close.'

Des hadn't got the book she wanted but he did fancy a walk and there they were again, brushing the dry moss on the stone wall and clutching at leaves.

"We've walked the whole length of this lane and said nothing."

"It's a quiet evening," Des replied.

"The foundry man falls in love with the countryside."

"I just said it's a quiet evening. I wasn't about to write an ode."

"Let's make a din," suggested Susan, with a laugh.

They crossed the little bridge under which Stephen had sat following Kennedy's assassination, and pitched some twigs into the brook. As they raced into the copse, the leaves hid them from the road and the spring sunshine cast the shadows of leaves and branches across them. Susan stopped at the water's edge and looked at herself in the slowly moving brook. Spurts of yellow and purple crossed the reflection of her face. She smiled down. Des reached up and shook the tree so that the white blossoms cascaded onto the surface of the brook and then drifted away. He shook the branch again and laughed. The fluttering blossoms rippled both their reflections. When they looked up, Susan tossed another twig in the brook, splashing his shoes.

"Up north," he said, "I'd ha' kicked thee doon stairs for tha'"

Susan threw another and he chased her back onto the lane. They paused on the bridge and he saw that she was panting, despite having run so short a distance. Her lips were parted and she drew the bottom one in under her top teeth. The look that passed between them was enough – at least for the moment.

"The Red Lion," muttered Des, looking aside from her, "it's not much further."

On May 27th, the third pirate radio station, Radio Sutch, began broadcasting from a disused War Department fort in the Thames estuary. Screaming Lord Sutch headed the venture in his own inimitable fashion. Radio Sutch joined the ranks of Radio Caroline and Radio Atlanta much to the delight of British pop fans. Simon Wiseman eased himself out of his lotus position with delight when he heard the news. 'A little anarchy,' he thought, 'goes a long way.' He made his way along the corridor of A House to Stephen Last's room.

"You've heard the news, have you?" he asked, bursting in, "I wonder what the establishment will make of this. You know – the BBC, the government, the telecommunication boys, the navy, the army … What a shame they've banned *TW3*. I can just imagine what David Frost and his lot would have to say."

Sister Talbot – her face twisted into what once, long ago, might have been the semblance of a smile – snapped "You use a pair of forceps only once, Nurse Pratt. Didn't they tell you that in PTS, or weren't you listening at the time?"

"Sorry, Sister," mumbled Sheila as she wiped the trolley one more time.

"And for goodness sake put some elbow grease into wiping that trolley."

"Yes, Sister."

Sheila had dreaded meeting Sister Talbot. She was the one sister on surgical who found fault with everybody. Sheila's dad would have said it was "constructive criticism"; Sheila found it anything but constructive.

"And you can't leave carbolic smears on the trolley, Nurse Pratt. You'll have to wipe it again."

Whenever Sheila looked over her shoulder, Sister Talbot was always there, it seemed, on the point of snarling. She was careful not to let the patients hear any of her chiding; the worst place was usually the sterilising room.

"You use sterile tongs to remove the bowls from the steriliser, Nurse Pratt, otherwise there's no point in them being sterile in the first place is there?"

Sheila, almost in tears, could not answer. She thought she had chosen sterile tongs; in fact, she was sure they were sterile.

"Is there, Nurse Pratt?"

"No Sister," Sheila managed to gulp.

"You do have a tongue in your head then?

"Yes, Sister."

"And the large bowls are placed on the top shelf of the trolley, Nurse Pratt. The bottom shelf is reserved for non-sterile items – namely …?"

"The blanket, the rolls of tape, the bandages … and … and …"

"And?"

Sheila knew – they'd been well-trained at PTS – but the simple words wouldn't come.

"And …," insisted Sister Talbot.

"The safety pins and …"

"I can't wait much longer, Nurse Pratt. Patients might be dying on the ward. The non-sterile bowl! What bowl, Nurse Pratt?"

"The non-sterile bowl …"

"The non-sterile bowl, Sister."

"The non-sterile bowl, Sister," repeated Sheila, her eyes almost full of tears, her mouth dry.

Her day continued on the same note of incessant criticism spiced with a biting sarcasm she had only previously received from her father and one or two schoolteachers who had made her life a misery during the year she was in their classes. Sister Talbot wondered why she'd ever considered nursing as a career: she was "clumsy removing the stitches", she "cleaned the wound in the wrong direction", she "failed to engage the patient in conversation" and she "held the knot with the forceps in the wrong hand". By the time her shift ended, Sheila knew she could take no more and decided to quit.

CHAPTER 10

The coal face

Joan Whiting was on a female medical ward and was not, she felt, "in her element". Not to put too fine a point on it, she was "a tad PO-ed with nursing". Going into one of the caring professions to annoy her father had seemed a good idea at the time, but not at the moment with "the awkward woman" calling out for a bedpan.

Joan provided it with barely a smile. She was going to let the lady concerned know that she, Joan Whiting, knew the lady was being deliberately demanding: she could have asked for it during the bedpan round. The 'bedpan round'! Was her life going to be circumscribed by 'the bedpan round'? She screened the bed, called for a colleague and they lifted the patient on and off the bedpan before wiping her with toilet paper and cleaning her bottom, using the small washbasin. Joan wondered whether she would ever get used to the smell of someone else's 'bowel movements'. Why call them 'bowel movements'? 'Shit' was so much more accurate as regards the smell and her feelings at having to perform something so personal on someone old enough to be her mother.

They were then back into the routine of emptying the bedpan, measuring the contents, washing and stacking the bedpan, cleaning the trolley using carbolic soap and taking off the pink gowns before returning to the ward – the female ward! Joan decided that she preferred the men's ward; somehow, she found it so much easier dealing with the men.

"What the hell are you crying about," asked Joan Whiting as soon as she entered Sheila's room and saw the other girl sprawled on her bed howling her eyes out. "I was looking for Kate."

Sheila didn't look up. She knew there'd be no sympathy forthcoming from Joan: of all the girls in training, it was Joan that Sheila feared most.

"Nothing," she replied, hoping Joan would go away.

"It must be something. Are you on surgical?"

"Yes."

"Talbot?"

"Yes," sniffed Sheila, trying to collect herself.

"For Christ's sake, Sheila, grow up. Talbot's a bitch – a Grade A bitch. Always has been and always will be. I expect her husband's gone off to find a bit of comfort elsewhere or he's divorced her. Good. Who could possibly blame him! If you can't deal with characters like her, you might as well give up nursing because you're going to meet a lot like her …"

"I'm leaving nursing."

"It's probably the best decision you've made. I might do the same. The smell of bedpans and dirty arses are putting me off my meals."

Sheila looked up, suddenly quiet and appalled. She'd never heard a woman swear before and deplored Joan's attitude. "They can't help it – these old people. That's what nursing is about – patient care."

"For you, maybe, but I'm not sure it's for me."

"What's wrong?" asked Kate Walsh from the open door.

"We're leaving nursing," snapped Joan, "Both of us – me because I can't stand the smell of shit and Sheila because she can't stand being bullied by a menopausal ward sister."

Kate laughed as she answered "Don't be silly – both of you will make fine nurses: Sheila because she has a natural talent for caring and you because you'll take no nonsense from junior nurses when you're a matron."

All three young women laughed at Kate's suggestion. There was something funny in visualising Joan as 'Matron'.

"Yes, Matron – No, Matron – Three bags full, Matron," continued Kate, as Joan snatched and hurled a pillow from Sheila's bed.

Martin Luther King's work kept him away from his family for much of the time, but today he was home. He opened the front door and called out:

"Where is everyone?"

His four children – Yoki, Marty, Dexter and Bunny – rushed from their rooms to greet him and soon he was chasing them all over the house, teasing and tickling and picking them up into his arms.

His wife, Coretta, fresh from a welcome home kiss, thought he was like a child himself and watched helplessly as Martin played one of the children's favourite games. Each of them took turns to stand halfway up the flight of stairs that went from the ground floor of their house; they would wait for Martin to open his arms before they leapt off into space towards him. He never failed to catch them; Coretta never failed to find her heart in her mouth.

When they eventually gathered in the kitchen, Martin tucked into pigs' feet and turnip greens – one of his favourite dishes.

"Eating is one of my major sins," he chuckled, "no doubt about it."

Pete Campbell looked around what had come to be called 'Pete's Room'. He'd taken up residence above the King's Head and some of his "fans from the Red Lion" had followed him, much to Pete's delight. The room was long and decoratively bare but its ambience suited the folk and protest scene; somehow, floorboards and tatty curtains fitted the image. Simon Wiseman loved the whole thing: the ringing scrape of the beer glasses, the smoke making its way down from the ceiling, the closeness of the students and young people from the town who crowded the tables.

"Pete's going to have to adjust his playing somewhat, unless he's going to strum his way through the music," commented Des Smith, "he's got a banjo player who plucks."

The remark was typical of Des, who held strumming a guitar in contempt; and that had been Pete's Red Lion style.

"It's Pete Seeger's song, isn't it," said Simon, "Doesn't he play banjo?"

"*Little Boxes*," cut in Susan, "I like that song."

"Do you live in a little box, Sue?" queried Stephen.

"No," she replied, guessing that Stephen was about to wind her up, "I live in a big, stockbroker box."

"With ticky-tacky people?" asked Des.

"No – with my stockbroker dad and mum," replied Sue.

"It's kept you warm and dry for nineteen years, has it, Sue?" Stephen persisted, "I find the song offensive myself – not the ticky-tacky houses because people deserve decent homes, but Seeger referring to people as 'ticky-tacky'. Who does he think he is?"

"He's not singing about everybody, Stephen – just a certain kind of person: the kind that's prepared to accept that kind of life – the 'ticky-tacky' life," Susan responded.

"Not everyone has the choice, pet," said Des, "Some people are glad of a home – even a ticky-tacky home. Better that than living in a slum with an outside toilet."

"Outside toilet?"

"It's true," explained Stephen, "Until I was thirteen – what, just over six years ago – and we moved to a new bungalow – one of Seeger's ticky-tacky places, no doubt – we only had an outside toilet."

"You mean you had to go outside to go to the toilet at night?" objected Jenny Pryce.

"No," replied Stephen, and paused.

Des laughed. He'd never actually had an outside toilet because he and his family lived in a council house but several of his school friends had lived in such houses.

"Don't tell us you had a piss pot under the bed, Steve," laughed Simon.

"Yes, that's exactly what we had. My mum emptied them in the morning."

"Uuuh," chorused the women at the table.

"We tried not to use them," Stephen said, quietly, "and I'd often just unlock the back door and go down the yard, but that's the way it was. It's why ticky-tacky people like me would much prefer a ticky-tacky house with an inside toilet. It's a move up the housing ladder."

Des was reminded again of why he liked Stephen Last. He had no real interest in politics – or, certainly, little experience of how the system worked – but he was a natural socialist.

> *"And the boys go into business, and marry and raise a family,*
> *And they all get put in boxes, little boxes all the same.*
> *There's a green one and a pink one and a blue one and a yellow one*
> *And they're all made out of ticky-tacky, and they all look just the same."*

Unaware of the dissension his song had roused, Pete Campbell brought it to a close. He looked around the room and saw Des Smith who, he knew, was a different kind of folk singer to him, and one who would take over the Red Room, if not the Red Lion, now that he was on the move. Pete knew, also, that he would have to extend his range and his style if he was to make it on the folk scene, and that he would need to attract the likes of Des to 'Pete's Room'.

"Des, how about a song from you?" he called.

"No, you carry on."

"Go on, Des," encouraged Susan.

"If he'll do it for anybody, he'll do it for you, Sue," murmured Jenny Pryce.

Des, flummoxed, looked at her and thought 'How did she guess? Is it that obvious?' A bead of sweat trickled from his hair.

"Hot, Des?' laughed Jenny.

"Depends who I'm with, pet."

He gripped his beer mug and drank slowly, keeping his eyes away from Susan, who was blushing to the roots of her hair. Des licked the foam from his lips and raised himself partway from his chair. He lifted his hands to the room in acknowledgement of the request. As he reached the raised platform on which the band played, he accepted the guitar Pete offered and began to tune the instrument.

"This is my favourite song," he said with a chuckle, "it's called tuning up." He'd heard the line from Tony Davis at a Spinners concert. The floor creaked under him as he wriggled the chair comfortable. He was calmer now "What does the landlord feed his woodworm on, Pete?" he asked, and the room laughed again. He looked across at the table where his friends sat and, from under his long eye lashes, saw that Susan had stopped blushing. He opened his mouth to sing and croaked. He laughed.

"I think I need a little biddy sup," he said, "Sue, would you?"

Susan smiled, picked up his beer mug and carried it over to him. Des grinned at her, and she recognised it as the grin he reserved for her. As she returned to their table, Des placed himself carefully in the chair and strummed a few chords. He talked to the room; he sparred with Simon, who was always good for a riposte, and wondered what to sing. 'A mining song? I feel like singing a love song. *Long Black Veil*?' Suddenly, he knew: it must be one they could all join in, and he sang:

"*The day we went to Blaydon, twas on the ninth of June.*

Eighteen hundred and sixty two on a summer's afternoon,
We took the bus from Balmbras, and she was heavy laden,
Away we went along Collingwood Street, that's on the road to Blaydon.
Oh me lads, you should've seen us gannin' . . . ."

On the chorus they all joined in, whether or not they understood the lyrics, and soon the room swelled with the sound of Northerners, Londoners, Midlanders, East Anglians and a Liverpudlian – Mike Harrison walked in as Des began – singing a traditional Geordie song.

Susan did not sing. She was quite choked, and sat watching Des, realising that they were now in the summer term of their first year, school practice was approaching fast and – even faster it seemed – the long summer holidays.

Michael Ramsey, Archbishop of Canterbury, could see the problem. Abortion was a criminal offence unless performed by the surgeon to save the life of the mother. On the other hand – and there always seemed to be another hand – this law led to back-street abortions where the mother's life was put at risk by criminals using un-sterilised tools. It was hard to accept – against a moral code that went back generations – that there might be reasons, other than the immediate danger to the mother's life, which justified abortion. Life was sacred; there was no escaping that belief. The human foetus had rights: thought of in this way, abortion was nothing less than murder.

The arguments for 'legalising abortion' – as the phrase went – usually took the line that one must consider the effects of another birth on the existing children, that an unwanted birth might have devastating consequences for the mother's mental health or that the baby might be unable to have a normal life. Yet, Michael had known people born severely handicapped who lived happy lives and families in the most adverse circumstances who produced some of the finest people he had known.

However, something had to be done; the issue would not go away. His bishops could not stand stubborn against change, and yet could not accept NHS abortions on demand.

Simon Wiseman was enjoying his first school practice; after all, it was only an observation. They were not expected to actually do any teaching, and it was only for two weeks. Watching the experts, taking some salutary notes, undertaking a few child studies and generally seeing how a school worked was all that was required. He knew he'd get on well with the staff: on the whole, he got on with everybody.

Mind you, the school had taken his breath away – just a bit. He'd come from Borehamwood and from a school that had been built in the 1950s: solid brick, wide corridors (in case another war broke out and they needed it for use as a hospital), individual classrooms with their own doors, a school hall, a library, a staff room and – oh yes, central heating.

He landed in a nice little country school in North Staffordshire – great staff, friendly children, pleasant atmosphere but few of the resources he and his school mates had taken for granted. To start with, there was no staff room; he and the other teachers had to crouch in what amounted to a broom cupboard under a flight of stairs for their breaks. It struck him that they must cut a comical image, crouched together – knee to knee, forehead to forehead – when the monitors came for the duty teacher's cup of tea or coffee. The staff seemed to accept their lot – just as they accepted that whoever arrived first on a winter's morning would have to check that the one stove which warmed the whole school was still alight after the caretaker had got it started.

Every morning, he was the first to arrive because the college bus left early in order to drop every student off at their placement school in time for the start of the day. On his first morning, Simon had come across a little girl in the playground. It seemed her mum always dropped her off before the staff arrived because she had to get to work, and the teachers usually let her sit in one of the classrooms.

"Don't you prefer playing out?"

"Not 'til the others get here and never in the winter," she replied, "It's freezing then."

"Can't your dad drop you off – or does he go to work early as well?"

"I haven't got a dad."

"I see," Simon replied, thoughtfully, "What's your name?"

"Ellie."

"Well, I can't get in myself. I've no key."

"The back door – the one by the toilets – will be unlocked. Mrs Crowden always leaves it unlocked."

From that day, Ellie had looked after Simon; she seemed to consider him her private property because she'd seen him first. She brought his tea to the playground, showed him where to hang his bag and found pencils and rubbers when he was working in her class. There was something about Ellie – perhaps her neediness –which made Simon understand what teaching was about.

The classrooms were bare enough with nowhere to display work: huge Victorian radiators and equally large pipes seemed to get in the way of everything. The children had tables at which they worked – Formica-topped in bright colours – but all the equipment was stored in large, wooden cupboards that dominated the room and circumscribed the space. The children in all rooms either faced the blackboard, he noticed, or had to turn round when the teacher was holding forth. There seemed no way in which the room might be re-organised into areas for science, maths, art, reading ... and so on; and yet, it should be and the children should be freer to move around.

He'd spent a long time with the head, Walter Rollins, who seemed to enjoy talking and was clearly proud of his school.

"The thing to remember, Mr Wiseman, is that you can't make a rose out of a cabbage seed, but you can make a wonderful cabbage."

Simon had to agree, but felt the cabbage was being compared unfavourably with the rose. Was one plant actually better than another? It might be argued that the cabbage was more use, mightn't it? 'You can't make a cabbage out of a rose seed, but you can make a wonderful rose.' It didn't sound quite right. When he'd expounded the philosophy of Walter Rollins to Stephen Last – he who had failed the 11 plus exam – Stephen had exploded. "We don't need to separate the roses and the cabbages at 11," he raged, "We need to have a better understanding of the nature of seeds." And yet, Simon could see that Mr Rollins's heart was in the right place.

The teacher, Mr Fennel, to whom Simon was assigned, was easy-going with the children, and yet he had a military air about him that would brook no nonsense. The children loved him. His lessons were quiet and purposeful. Any tensions the children brought with them – and Simon thought that children like Ellie must have difficult home lives – were soon dissipated in the calm atmosphere of the room.

"They don't need to be charging about to learn," Mr Fennel explained, diligently, "Some students we get from the training colleges think that unless the children are all over the room exploring there's no learning going on. Usually, it's the other way round ... Do you fancy taking a lesson? I've cleared it with the head. It's a nice class. They're lovely children, and it's a straightforward lesson on verbs. You can use the comprehension books. You'll enjoy it."

"Cool ...," began Simon in reply, before catching Mr Fennel's eye, "Yes, I'd like that ...Can I do it as a poetry lesson? I'll cover the verbs."

"Poetry?"

"Yes ... I can cover the verbs. I think the children will enjoy it."

"Very well ... yes ... but I don't think we've got a Wordsworth here," he laughed.

"You never know," riposted Simon, not to be outdone, "William had to start with *The Prelude* – and you've given me an idea."

The lesson had gone brilliantly, although not without consternation for the staff because Simon insisted on taking the class for a walk around their village.

"You're taking me," he insisted, "to your favourite places. I'm a stranger here. Show me your village."

Mr Fennel and one of the parents had come with him and the class had explored their favourite haunts – secret places of which even the mother was unaware. Simon had read to the children Wordsworth's account of his stealing the boat – gliding over or omitting the difficult bits that would have broken their concentration, and focussing on the narrative – before the jaunt. When they returned he set the class to work writing their own accounts, after reading *Skating*. "All shod with steel, we hissed along the polished ice." 'How they loved the sound!'

He collected the poems, displayed them on the back of the ugly cupboard on a backing of sugar paper and had the children who wanted to read theirs to the class. One boy called Christopher, who for the second week of Simon's teaching practice brought him a poem a day, wrote:

The Wreck
We play on the wreck
It's our special place that only we know about
Hidden holes in the ground covered in brambles
Are our secret places.
We make dens there and hide from our parents
When they call us in to tea.
The wreck goes down to Cole's farm
Where in the summer we pick peas
And hide in the golden corn
You can play all day in the wreck.

Mr Fennel was impressed, but worried about the verbs, and so Simon spent another lesson 'shod' and 'hissing', asking the children to find which words were "doing things" in their poems.

During his time at Leedham Primary, one topic of conversation that intrigued the staffroom was Christine Keeler's release from prison. To Simon's generation her nine months sentence had been an outrage: an act of retaliation by an establishment she'd shown up for what they were – hypocrites. The fact that she was released after six months did nothing to ameliorate their feelings of anger. Simon was surprised that most of the staff agreed.

What the likes of John Profumo did in his spare time wasn't just a matter for him, it was felt: as a politician and a member of the establishment, he had to set an example.

"When you're in a position of responsibility, you behave responsibly," said Walter Rollins, "Profumo met this girl at Lord Astor's, didn't he? He knew what she did for a living, and who she did it with. You don't go to bed with someone who's going to bed with a Russian spy – not if you're Secretary of State for War."

"He was a liar, too, wasn't he? Presumably he lied to his wife – or at least deceived her – and he certainly lied to Parliament," contributed the Deputy Head, Rosemary Civil, who was a member of the local church and sang lustily in the school assemblies.

"The whole lot need bringing down," said Simon's mentor, Mr Fennel, quietly, "Macmillan and all the toffs gathered round to protect one of their own set, and now they're going to suffer the consequences … Mind you," he added with a smile, "I can't say I blame Profumo. He's only a man, after all, and she was certainly a nice piece of crackling."

Simon laughed because most of his mates had agreed at the time: in fact, none of them actually blamed Profumo for what he did with Christine Keeler, or her for taking advantage of the Astor set.

"Personally," said Rosemary Civil, before leaving the crowded staffroom, "I can't see the difference between what they call a 'high-class call-girl' and a common prostitute. They're both doing the same thing. It's only that her customers pay more."

Simon thought, as she struggled past him in her tweed skirt, that 'it was a question of semantics – the words we use change our perception of the truth of things.'

In the Sunday Times of June 14, Enoch Powell wrote '…the immigrants who have come already, or who are admitted in the future, are part of the community. Their most rapid and effective integration is in the interests of all … Money is colour-blind, and economic forces will help the work of integration which must be done if a homogenous community, local and national, is to be restored'.

Nelson Mandela was ready for the death sentence. 'To be truly prepared,' he thought, 'one must actually expect it.' His companions, also, were prepared; they were not brave, but they were realistic. He thought of Shakespeare's line 'Be absolute for death; for either death or life will be the sweeter.'

The eyes of De Witt, the judge, were focussed on the middle distance, his face was pale and he was breathing heavily as he prepared to speak.

"... the function of this court," he said, "... is to enforce law and order ... The crime of which the accused have been convicted ... is one of high treason. The state has decided not to charge the crime in this form. Bearing this in mind and giving the matter very serious consideration I have decided not to impose the supreme penalty for the crime, but consistent with my duty that is the only leniency which I can show. The sentence in the case of all the accused will be one of life imprisonment."

Nelson and his companions looked at each other and smiled. There was a great gasp in the courtroom. Nelson turned and smiled broadly to the gallery, seeking out Winnie's face and the face of his mother, as the police hustled him out of the dock. He ducked through the door and was taken to the cells below.

CHAPTER 11

First Nights

"Thank goodness, for that," declared Kate's mum, "if he had said anything else I don't know what I'd have done."

Pope Paul V1 had condemned the use of the contraceptive pill; his encyclical had been read out from the pulpit of every Roman Catholic Church in the country. He had made it quite clear that birth control by any other means than abstinence was sinful. Catholicism had been a gentle thorn in the side of the family since Kate's childhood. Florence Walsh was a Roman Catholic, but practised her faith discreetly because Maurice Walsh was a sceptic and she didn't want any arguments in the house. Kate, herself, and her brother and sister had been baptised in the Catholic church, but none of them practised their faith except when accompanying their mother to special occasions at St Peter's and St Paul's Church in Wolverhampton.

Kate read much into her mother's outburst – not least the thought that abstinence as the only means of birth control had had no beneficial effect on her parents' marriage. As a child, she'd heard some talk about "the rhythm method", but had understood nothing at the time. It was only later, when the matter was discussed in muted terms in the newspapers, that Kate realised it was connected in some chancy way with the woman's ovulation cycle.

"There are a lot of unwanted children in the world, Flo," Maurice Walsh said quietly, with no attempt to introduce the usual bridling note into his comment.

"If it was right for us," replied Kate's mum, "it's right for future generations. Popes can't keep changing their minds about what is and what is not the Word of God. A Truth is a Truth. It's not to be changed for the sake of convenience."

Kate didn't often enter these discussions because she knew religion to be a raw spot between her parents, but she also knew – from the work they'd done at school regarding world population control and from her student involvement with raising money for Oxfam – that many Third World countries were producing more children than they could possibly feed. She also knew that there were Roman Catholics in almost every one of these countries, and that every hour a thousand children died of malnutrition.

"Do you know how many children will die today because their parents cannot feed them, mum?" she asked.

"There's enough food to go round," snapped her mother, in an uncustomary tone, "we just need to share it more fairly."

"That's as maybe," replied Kate, "but the fact is that by this time tomorrow thirty thousand children under the age of five will be dead. God surely cannot want that to happen, and as His voice on Earth neither can the Pope."

"People have the solution in their own hands. Don't have so many children."

Flo Walsh left the table abruptly, scooping up a handful of dishes as she went. Kate's father looked at his daughter and smiled.

"She knows what you're saying is true," he whispered, "but what can your mum or any other individual Catholic do about it? People need leaders. They need to be led in the interests of all."

"But many traditional Catholics like mum were against him allowing the use of the pill."

"As I said, they need to be led. They'd have come round in the end. They're all decent people at heart. People need leaders with the courage of their convictions. If you read about what went on behind the scenes, you'll find that ninety percent of the commission set up by Pope Paul favoured permitting some form of artificial birth control within marriage. Note that, Kate – *within marriage*. A handful of old men – cardinals in the Vatican – set their minds against the commission's report."

Birth control, in the form of a broken condom, was at the heart of Heather Burton's dilemma. She was pregnant. She knew when it had happened. It had been one of those nights in early March when she'd stayed over at the college with Barry. They'd risked it sometimes because they both hated using those horrible things, but she was sure that it was the night the condom had burst. She was about four months gone and knew that her nursing career was at an end. She'd have to hand in her resignation. A pregnant nurse on the wards wasn't something that the hospital would tolerate and, in any case, she would have to look after the baby when it was born. There was no one else; she couldn't ask her mother. She couldn't tell her mother, let alone ask for her help. Somehow, the baby would have to be kept secret.

"You must tell your mother," advised Kate, when Heather told her the news, "she may not like it, but you're her daughter."

"Would your mother understand? Can you imagine going home, sitting in the front room and announcing that you were pregnant – that you'd actually had sex with a man?"

"No."

"Exactly! Every opportunity my parents have worked to give me would be thrown back in their faces. My career, Kate, is at an end ... They'd invested so much into my becoming a nurse, and one foolish night has chucked it all in the dustbin. In addition, there's the shame my mum will feel. There are girls who do and girls who don't. My mum will still love me, but her daughter – and, by association, her – will be branded. An unmarried mother and an illegitimate grandchild – how can I land her with that just when things were looking so rosy?"

"Have you told Barry?"

"Not yet. I've guessed for a while, of course – after the missed periods – but he was into his finals and I didn't want him loaded with my worries."

"He'll have to know, Heather."

"I know, I know."

"Do you think he'll stand by you?"

Heather looked at Kate as she asked the question and raised an eyebrow. Kate wasn't sure whether it was quizzically or in contempt.

"I'll manage if he doesn't," she replied, "there's no reason why he should marry me if he doesn't want to, but I think he'll want to, although a baby so early in his career will be a financial burden he could do without."

Lyndon B Johnson had been as good as his word. On July 2nd, he fulfilled the promise made by John Kennedy to take the first steps in outlawing racial discrimination in the United States; the Civil Rights Act was signed in Washington. The act made discrimination illegal in hotels, parks and other public places such as libraries; it also made it illegal in matters of employment and the membership of trades unions.

As he signed the act, President Johnson shook hands with Dr Martin Luther King:

"Let us eliminate the last vestiges of injustice in America," he said, "Let us close the springs of racial poison."

"Amen," agreed Martin.

Sister Maitland, the Home Sister, on finding her rules had been infringed, was less than sympathetic.

"You girls never learn, do you? Why do you think we make the rules – hmm? Because we've all been through the same temptations! Now, the hospital has lost a damned good nurse and you'll be a social outcast, Nurse Burton – or should I say ex-Nurse Burton? An unmarried mother – is that what you wanted for yourself, is that what your parents wanted for you?"

"Is there any chance I might resume my training at a later date, Sister?" asked Heather, pragmatic as always and eager to turn the conversation in a positive direction.

"I shouldn't think so. Who will look after your baby, if

you do? ... Are you thinking of ... having the baby adopted?"

"Why would I do that?"

"You would then be free to re-start your training ... and you do have a responsibility towards the unborn child. Have you considered what sort of life you can give the baby? Have you considered how you will be seen by people?"

"Seen?"

"Some people will see you as ... little more than a street-walker. You'll have to learn to live with the gossip and the sneers."

"I'll have to put up with it, won't I?"

"If you're determined to do so, yes you will. You'd better tender your resignation to the hospital ... and, Nurse Burton, do consider the possibility of adoption. There are many childless couples out there who would give your baby all the love in the world."

John Lennon looked his wife over and approved:

"God, Cyn," he said, "you look fantastic."

It was the night of the Leicester Square premier of the Beatles' first film, *A Hard Day's Night*, and Cynthia had scoured London for days in search of something suitable to wear. Eventually, she'd come up with a silk, full-length tunic-style dress in black and beige; to go with it, she bought a Mary Quant coat in black chiffon.

The limousine in which she and John travelled with Paul, George, Ringo and Brian Epstein passed through streets paved with fans; ten thousand of them were there to greet the Beatles. When they stood on the red carpet with the press clamouring for their attention, Cynthia remembered that less than a year ago she had been on her own with Julian in a Hoylake bed-sit.

John had enjoyed making the film and was hoping it would show the public that the Beatles were more than just another pop group. A pop group might have a life span of merely two or three years; John wanted more and the excitement was running high.

Princess Margaret attended the premier, and even John was suitably over-awed by the presence of royalty. His anti-establishment views on hold for the night, he introduced Cynthia to the princess:

"Ma'am," he said, "this is my wife, Cynthia."

Princess Margaret glanced in Cynthia's direction.

"Oh," she said, "how nice."

Heather wasn't as sure of Barry as her answer to Kate had implied. After all, he had his whole career ahead of him. She felt that it was her who had messed things up. She should have been more ... more what – circumspect, morally responsible? The general view was that men couldn't help it, and it was up to the girl to say "no".

Barry hadn't even seemed aware of contraception when they'd first had sex. It wasn't something your parents talked to you about, and it was never mentioned at school. It was only because she was a nurse that the issue was raised at all, and after they'd slept together several times. Like most men, Barry felt that it would never happen to them, and it was she who had insisted that he bought some condoms. He'd baulked at that: it wasn't easy. "Anything for the weekend, sir?" his barber had asked with a grin, and Barry had been relieved. There was no way, he said, that he could have asked over the counter at a chemist's shop.

When she'd realised her predicament, Heather hadn't collapsed and cried. She was made of sterner stuff, she felt. Her parents wouldn't have expected her to "knuckle under", but she saw no way of supporting herself if Barry refused to marry her. Kate had been right, of course: she should have told her mother, but somehow that could not be faced – not yet, at any rate, not before she'd spoken to Barry.

When she did face Barry with the news, his response made her laugh despite the circumstances.

"Bloody hell!" he said.

"I'm sorry."

"It's not your fault, pet. It takes two to tango."

Nevertheless, despite his words, Barry had turned pale at the news. Another couple of years while Heather finished her training and he gained some experience in teaching had beckoned to them both. They would have been joyous years. He'd have taken a bed-sit in Staffham – he wouldn't have been able to afford much more on his salary – and Heather would have had her room at the nurses' home. They'd have managed like that while he saved up some money. Now, the prospect of being young and carefree had disappeared like the flash of a firework. He was to be a father and he was, as his dad would have said, "still wet behind the ears". But not wet enough to have got a girl in the pudding club or, on second thoughts, really wet enough to have got a girl in the pudding club. Why the hell did the threat of pregnancy have to take the joy out of sex?

Barry reached over, lifted Heather from her chair and took her in his arms.

"There's only one thing to do," he said, "We'll have to get married."

"There's no need."

"There's every need. We can't have our child born illegitimately. Have you ever heard such children called 'bastards' or heard them described as being 'born the wrong side of the blanket'? I don't think we want that do we, love?"

The sense of relief had flooded through her; everything seemed manageable when he spoke. If they were married, things would look better and her child would have a father as well as a mother. Once that was a given fact, she might be able to face her parents.

"Are you going to tell your parents?" she asked.

"No, not yet, not 'til things are hunky-dory. I'll just pay them a brief visit and say I've got a summer job down here. From September, I will have, anyway."

"I'll do the same, I think. I can't face mum yet ... We'll be a family, won't we, Barry?"

"Yes, I suppose we will, love," he answered, looking into her face, his arms still encircling her, "I'm sorry about your career, though. You'd have made a bloody fine nurse."

Miriam Davison was terrified. The mother stood in front of her holding the baby in her arms and begging Miriam to do something. It was Miriam's first night shift on the maternity ward and, until that moment, she had enjoyed the experience. She wanted children herself and intended to marry as soon as 'Mr Right', who she'd known since her schooldays, proposed. The mother screamed at her a second time and Miriam reached out for the baby who had turned blue. She was about to call out when the ward sister, starched and pale faced, took the child, gently, from her arms, crying:

"Fetch the duty houseman, now."

Miriam wasted no time. Within seconds needles and tubes had been inserted into the baby's arms, and resuscitation procedures took over. She watched spell-bound with remorse, fear and sorrow as the doctor and senior nurses struggled to save the child's life. It was to no avail; within half-an-hour it was clear that the baby was dead.

No one spoke as the needles were removed and the child's hair was combed and the ward sister placed him carefully against the pillow. The doctor nodded to the sister and left to break the appalling news to the mother who was being looked after by another senior nurse. The sister glanced at Miriam, smiled and nodded.

"Thank you," she responded, taking the smile to be one of understanding and acknowledging that she might need to leave.

In the sluice room, Miriam gripped the edge of one of the sinks and sobbed. There was nothing else she could do. Her commitment drained from her and Kennedy's words that had so inspired her only a few years before seemed hollow and unattainable. '...we were disciplined and purposeful and committed to change the world for the better, that we'd meet any hardship and bear any burden and support any friend to achieve that end ...' She hadn't expected hardship to be like this – not the death of a helpless, innocent child. 'Why?'

The ward sister touched her shoulder as gently as she had placed the dead child against the pillow ready for the mother.

"There are happier moments on maternity, Nurse Davison," she said, consolingly, "Dry your eyes and come back onto the ward. That will be best."

It seemed a long way from that special moment on Christmas Eve when she'd sat by the old lady who had squeezed her hand and asked for the ward choir to sing *Away in a manger*.

"It was the West End first night that had everything ... the film was Cliff Richard's latest and pretty well everybody was there ... Princess Alexander ... Robert Morley, eclectic as always ... the fans gathered to see their idol the fabulous Cliff Richard, a star in two hemispheres, world famous but boyish and unassuming ... Beautiful and regal, Princess Alexander riveted the attention of all ... the premier was in aid of the National Association of Youth Clubs ... the princess chatted with Cliff and his inseparable companions, The Shadows ... the good cause of youth clubs benefited from the presence of Her Royal Highness at a fine film ..."

'Good old Pathe News,' thought Stephen, as the item came to an end, 'it always catches the pulse of the nation.' He laughed to himself quietly in the comfort of the cinema. He and Simon Wiseman had come to watch *The Knack*, something neither of them felt they had quite attained.

The college year was over. Tomorrow, the porters would haul the student's large trunks from their rooms and, carrying their heavy suitcases or holdalls, everyone would make their way to the railway or coach station at Staffham, heading for home. Some would be picked up from college, but only those students whose parents could afford cars. For most it was either train or coach. Stephen and Simon were travelling down together as far as London, where their ways parted for the long summer break. Both of them had enjoyed their first year at college; both had gained so much in the way of companionship and freedom: Simon from his mother's tongue, Stephen from his father's constructive criticism. They wandered along the High Street and dropped into the King's Head for a pint of Joules bitter.

"Des and Sue are going to find the holidays a bit of a wrench, aren't they?" said Simon, out of the blue.

"Why?" asked Stephen, aware he'd missed something everybody else knew.

"I caught them saying goodbye tonight just before we went for the bus into town. They were in the porch of Sue's house when I passed."

"Go on," said Stephen, remembering a similar moment sometime earlier in the year.

"Sue was obviously distressed. I heard her say that she'd nothing to go home for. She was almost in tears. They both stood looking at each other but not wanting to make a move, like."

"Des was saying only the other day that he'd nothing to go back for in terms of work. There are no jobs going in Middlesbrough for students. It's as much as they can do to find work for family men."

Simon frowned: Stephen had a way of going off at a tangent, almost as though he wanted to avoid emotional subjects.

"You haven't noticed how they fancy each other, then?" he asked.

"Not really," replied Stephen.

"I would say that Sue was nearly hysterical with sadness. You could see it in her eyes and the hangdog way she stood. Des just looked embarrassed when I wished them both bon voyage."

"Des has a girlfriend at home, doesn't he," said Stephen, "and they're ... quite involved – if you see what I mean. It wouldn't be right for him to start a relationship with a girl at college."

"I wouldn't mind having a bird in both places," laughed Simon, "I wouldn't mind having a bird in one place, come to that. Another pint?"

Joan Whiting was more sympathetic than Miriam expected when she told her about the death of the baby. Kate was out, Miriam needed to talk to someone and Joan had walked in. She'd listened without interrupting while Miriam related her uncomprehending sadness over and over again. She actually squeezed Miriam's hand when the tears came. When she did speak what she said was unsettling but sincerely intended.

"Your religious beliefs are your problem, Miriam. Let them go, and find another road. Either your god is omnipotent, could have saved the child's life and chose not to do so (in which case, he isn't a god of love) or he isn't omnipotent and couldn't have saved the child's life (in which case he's hardly worth worshipping).

Your faith makes claims for him that cannot be sustained in a real world. There's horrendous suffering, and he lets us get on with it. Really? In the case of adults

– well, you could argue that they make their own beds and must lie on them, but that doesn't hold water, does it? No Jew chose Auschwitz.

But even if you accept that, how do you square a god of love allowing innocent children to suffer? They can't be held responsible for their own suffering. You can't justify it, can you?

Let him go and find another way … I'm not meaning to be unkind, Miriam. I have thought about these things. Your beliefs are shackling you to a way of thinking that makes it impossible for you to accept the facts of life as they are. Move on."

In a strange way, Joan's lack of faith only increased Miriam's. As she sat composed after Joan had left, Kennedy's words came back to her for a second time that day '… disciplined and purposeful and committed to change the world for the better …' It was our world, created for us by a loving God. He had placed it in our hands to change it for the better. It wasn't God that inflicted suffering on innocent children; it was the greed and ignorance of mankind.

Pete pushed his last shirt into the holdall and looked around his college room for the final time. It had been a good two years, and he was ready to move on. He was glad he didn't have to do a third year like the present bunch. He'd made some great friends, had some great times and had a job waiting in September at a local school. In the meantime, his group was going to play the folk clubs. It should be a great summer. He picked up his guitar and walked to the door. 'One last look and then on the road, man.'

In the common room – a place he would really miss – Simon asked:

"Are you taking Glenda with yer? Is she the groupie?"

"'course we are, Yogi, me old mate. We'll need someone ter make the coffee and keep our instruments polished … anyway, she's a great comfort is Glenda. She'll look after us lads – cooking and that sort of thing. We can't live off baked beans for a couple of months."

"How abart one last song, Pete?"

"OK fans," Pete replied, levelling his guitar, "I'm gonna lay down my sword and shield …"

"Yeah – down by the riverside, down by the riverside," chorused the common room.

Stephen should have left the room before the news came on at nine o'clock. He knew that and couldn't understand why he hadn't. Perhaps it was just that he wanted to see the news. As it was, he and his mother were now to be subjected to his father's views on one particular item, and where his father was concerned there was only one view – the right view, his father's view.

The first Brook Advisory Clinic had opened in London. The press build up had been virulent. Civilisation as we knew it would collapse, and any last vestiges of decency that might remain would be swept away on a tide of licentiousness. Lust would take over the world.

Stephen father was not religious in any way. He'd obliged his son to "get yourself confirmed" and told him that he was "Church of England until you're 21". Since Stephen had never expressed any religious views in the house, he'd always failed to understand why his father was so vehement that he should toe the line; there was no reason to suppose he wasn't. Perhaps, he thought, it was simply that his father valued tradition and saw any changes as being for the worst.

His line on the Brook clinic was simply that unmarried people shouldn't be having sex and that the clinic was encouraging them to do what was wrong in the first place. 'A licence to fornicate', was the phrase that occurred to Stephen as his father addressed the air somewhere in the corner of the room, his glare focussed between Stephen and his mother. Stephen's father never looked anyone in the eye when he spoke of these things.

He'd never actually told Stephen anything about sex except on one occasion Stephen remembered with vivid embarrassment. The *Sunday Mirror* had run a series of articles along the line that if fathers didn't talk to their sons about these things boys might grow up to become homosexuals. Appalled by such a fear, Stephen's father had asked for his help finding something in the loft. In the dark, he'd said:

"Do you know where babies come from?"

"Yes," Stephen had replied, hurriedly, eager for his father not to pursue the subject, "we learned about it at school."

"Good," gasped his father, relieved, "Well, if you want to know anything don't be afraid to bloody well ask."

Stephen's answer had been true up to a point. A series of BBC radio broadcasts with an accompanying black and white booklet, had explained sexual reproduction in some detail. He remembered, with a smile, that even the least able child in his class had gained a 95% pass in that end of term's science test; but he wasn't sure that any of them knew too much about sex itself.

Pete Campbell's Appalachian Four took to the road in late July, making their way north to the folk clubs of Leeds, Bradford, Middlesbrough, Liverpool or anywhere that would offer them a gig. Pete had assembled the group and chosen its name. He realised that he had to embrace the folk scene as it was – "the purists", as he put it to the group – but he wanted to retain the popular American connection; he wanted his group to sing songs that were popular as well as those that were "ethnic". He had little patience with the "real ale drinking, brown bread, yoga and sandals brigade"; he felt Lonnie Donegan's *Cumberland Gap* had as much right to be included as *Caller Herrin'*, and actually preferred it. He thought the name would capture for the purists the sense of "folkiness", giving them access to the clubs as well as the pubs, where all people wanted was a good sing-song.

He was the only singer in the group, as far as he knew, and played lead guitar. He'd also found a banjo player (something considered "authentic" by the folkies) and a bass guitar player (something not approved of but which he favoured to risk since it gave the group a good back-beat). The fourth member played just about everything – penny whistle, Jews harp and harmonica included – and was Pete's "ace in the hole", since he also had a wide knowledge of folk music. Moreover, he owned a Mini Clubman – not ideal, but better than hitching.

Their first gig, in Leeds, was in a large, bare room above a pub. The local folk society hired it on a weekly basis and people just turned up to play. When Pete Campbell's Appalachian Four took to the small, raised platform at one end of the room they took over – other singers joining them as well as they could. Pete began with

Dylan's *Blowin' in the Wind*, which caught the air of protest, and immediately following the applause went into a series of songs made popular by The Spinners – *Dirty old town, The foggy, foggy dew, Whiskey in the jar,* and *The last thing on my mind* – before risking Buddy Holly's *Peggy Sue* and Lonnie Donegan's *Rock Island Line, John Henry* and *Frankie and Johnny*. When time ran out and the evening came to a close, Pete rounded off with *We shall not be moved*.

As the group finished their beers and packed away their instruments, the landlord offered them £10 to return and play on the Sunday night.

Chapter 12

Clashes

Barry Glover was more depressed than he'd ever been. Looking at the only room they could afford only deepened that feeling of desolation. Stuck up some back alley and entered only through a communal door, the bed-sit consisted of an unlit hallway, a bathroom with no window and two other rooms – well, one room, really, where you lived and slept. The kitchen was little more than an elongated broom cupboard: as you stood at the cooker, your backside rested on the wall.

The walls worried him: they were papered with what appeared to be tinfoil, and there could only be one reason for that – damp. At the moment, it was high summer but what the hell was the place going to be like in winter? It would be October or November when the baby was born, with the cold weather settling in for the season.

He barely noticed the furniture, but Heather had taken it in at a glance: one single bed, one decrepit armchair, a foldaway table that didn't foldaway but collapsed and a couple of non-matching chairs. The gas fire looked as ancient as the landlord who had stood beaming in the doorway, a badly-rolled cigarette hanging from his bottom lip, dropping ash onto the very threadbare, very dirty carpet.

The place was going to cost them £5 a week – about half what he would earn as a teacher. Life looked grim. They took it and paid a month's rent in advance – money he'd borrowed from his dad. Barry was glad that the LEA had offered him a few weeks work at the school prior to the holidays: that meant he'd be paid over the summer. There was going to be so much they'd need. He was glad he'd managed to get a summer job. Once the term was over, he'd start work in the local brewery.

"You all right, pet?" he'd asked, seeking some reassurance that he was doing his best.

"It'll be fine. We'll paint it up. I'll buy some material cheaply and make some curtains and throws. You'll see," she smiled, and he realised what it was he'd loved about her from the beginning.

Nelson Mandela was imprisoned on Robben Island and, by August, winter had closed in. Each morning, ever since they'd arrived, he and the other prisoners had been assembled at the entrance to the courtyard, where a pile of stones awaited them. Using wheelbarrows, the prisoners moved the stones to the centre of the yard and began crushing them into gravel. They did the work sitting cross-legged on the ground, while the warders walked between them enforcing the silence. Nelson reflected each minute of each day on the tedium of the work. The temperature rarely rose more than a few degrees above freezing, and neither the work nor their clothes kept him and his fellow prisoners warm.

From those first days, life had begun to settle into a pattern. The routine, as well as signifying a well-run prison for the authorities, also brought comfort to the prisoners because it seemed to make the time go faster. Nelson did not want to lose track of time; he feared losing his grip and so, with each day and each week resembling the one before, Nelson decided to make a calendar on the wall of his cell.

He knew that prison was designed to break his spirit and crush his resolve. He could not let this happen; he knew that within the confines imposed upon him he must, together with the other prisoners, create a life of his own. He had to remain true to his ideals, even if no one else was aware of them. The fight would be different to the one they'd fought outside but it would be against the same enemies – racism and repression. Above all, he knew that he must hold on to his dignity as a man – as a human being. He knew he could do that – knew that under no circumstances would he allow anyone to rob him of his pride.

Desmond Smith stood by the railing of the park. 'Elizabeth can wait a few minutes,' he thought. He watched the children sucking dirty thumbs, and listened to their voices shrieking as they played on the swings and slide. He could remember doing these things himself, and he wondered. What did these children want from life? A few of them were busy tormenting a stray dog, offering it crusts of bread, which they thrust in front of its nose while it sniffed and then snatched away, stuffing the food into their own mouths and laughing. By the shops, women in rollers chatted. 'Saturday night ballroom beauties with their white legs and factory-pasted faces,' he thought, and then regretted it. 'Education has to be more than a migrant's ticket to suburbia. I don't want Shaw's hand-me-down socialism. Let's dip into the lives of the working class and watch them perform like puppets on a string.'

He crossed the road and made his way towards Elizabeth's house. 'I've gone too far with Elizabeth to pull back. I liked the look of her the first time she walked into the club with her friends, straight from the sixth form with their political clichés and folk songs. She kissed me like an aunt at first but now ...' He laughed to himself, but knew he didn't want to go on. Des turned, stuffed his hands deep down into his trouser pockets, walked back passed the shops and kicked a tin can into the road.

When Elizabeth arrived at his home, Des was hunched over his guitar. She watched him through the window and knocked on the pane.

"I thought you were coming round," she said.

"No, I've been kicking tin cans."

"What?"

"Nothing. Well, are you just going to stand there?" he snapped. "Sorry."

As soon as the door clicked to, she was in his arms and they were kissing. He was home again and the rest melted away.

"I bet you've had no breakfast," suggested Elizabeth, "I'll cook you some."

"You'll be lucky to find anything in the larder."

"I'll buy it."

When she returned and stood cracking eggs into a bowl, Elizabeth thought that this was just like being married. 'Yet, there's so much I want to do first ... He'll be a good father. He's family minded ... he likes his potato scallops crisp on the outside and soft in the centre – crackling in the mouth.'

Des picked at his bacon carefully, cutting away the fat and putting the rind to the edge of the plate. He broke the skin of the egg gently and dipped the meat.

"Would you say people here played down their emotions," he asked.

"You ought to have heard our neighbour when the kids broke her prop and the washing came down," laughed Elizabeth.

"I mean our deeper emotions. I've never seen my parents, especially my mother, break down in front of strangers."

Elizabeth remained silent, wondering what was going through his mind.

"Some of the people I live with at college seem to thrive on it."

After the breakfast, Des went back to his guitar and Elizabeth, having washed up, sat watching him. 'The strings picked lightly, the bony fingers spatulated on the steel wires. He's playing a tune that trickles into sadness. His flicking fingers dropped forward, the thumb down and across the bass string.'

Seeing her in the chair, her feet stretched onto the hearth, Des placed his guitar aside and dropped to the cushion beside her, his legs straddling the arm. He placed his hand under her hips and lifted Elizabeth across his knees. They kissed and sighed into each other's necks. 'When you're with a woman,' he thought, 'you lose your own identity. You're a couple, and there are expectations. All marriages are shotgun marriages, in a way.'

Lyndon B Johnson was determined to bring the war in Vietnam to an end; he was equally determined that the

South Vietnamese should not be placed under the yoke of North Vietnamese communism. He was on the horns of a dilemma.

A torpedo boat of Russian origin had attacked a US destroyer in the Gulf of Tonkin and Lyndon received almost full approval in Congress when he asked for permission to authorise an air strike in reprisal. 'Almost' was the key word for there were rumblings of concern lest more US troops should be committed.

His words were strong in defence of his action; they had to be if he was to carry the country with him.

"There is no threat to any peaceful power from the United States, but there can be no peace by aggression and no immunity from reply ... That is why we answered aggression with action."

Des Smith, standing outside the cookhouse door breathed in the sharp, foetid bite of sheep's dung. The long, purple-flecked stretches of Dartmoor were spread out before him. He thought he preferred the dark, satanic factories and smoke-filled air of Teesside, 'but thank God Stephen's letter came.' He'd told Elizabeth that he might have to get a holiday job away from home, and Stephen, who had one lined up with a restaurateur who catered for the territorial army, had suggested he might be able fix Des up as well. Des felt great; the burden had dropped from his shoulders as soon as he caught the train south to Suffolk, where Stephen lived.

He'd been amazed and uncomfortable at Stephen's home, where he'd spent one night before meeting up with the caterer's van that drove them down to Devon. He'd disliked the father immediately, sizing him up as what he called 'a silent bully'. More than that, however, he'd been surprised at the three-bedroom bungalow, which was Stephen's home on the edge of the golf course. It hadn't struck him as 'working class' anymore than had Stephen's parents. The following day, as they made their way to Stowmarket, where the caterer had his restaurant, he'd said so.

"... Not, like, that you've ever made a big thing about being working class, Stephen – I'm not saying that."

"I've never thought about it much, but I clearly come from working class stock. One of my grandfathers worked on the railway and the other was a farm labourer. When he died, he lived in a tied farm cottage and left one shilling and sixpence – enough to buy a pint of beer. My father is a cabinet maker – he served a five year apprenticeship to become one – and my mum, before becoming a full-time housewife, was an upholsteress. They met where they both worked at Tibbenham's in Ipswich. I should think that's as working class as you get, isn't it?"

Des couldn't deny the truth of what his friend said, but evidently southern working class wasn't the same as northern working class. There was no suggestion of poverty in the home – far from it: it had every comfort imaginable.

"My father's always had work, you see. We moved to the bungalow when I was thirteen. Until then, we'd lived in a terraced house near the docks. I know where my roots are, Des. I know why I want to teach."

"Why's that?"

"My big chance came when a Labour council built the Ipswich Civic College, where I was able to get my 'O' and 'A' levels. But for that, I'd have been on the educational scrap heap. When I was at secondary school, I even considered having to learn a trade, despite the fact that I knew I'd be no good at it – I haven't a practical bone in my body. Then the chance came to further my education and I was lucky enough to be in a position to do so. I took it, and it opened new worlds for me. We shouldn't throw children aside. No child should be allowed to fail, and education is the only way – I repeat, the only way – forward for most of us. When I qualify as a teacher, no child will leave one of my classes unable to read and write. Give someone words and they can think."

Des had heard his friend say as much before, but not in this situation and not with as much vehemence. Stephen's home had placed a momentary gulf between them, but it was a gulf of circumstance rather than intent and Des realised that they shared the same road.

Simon Wiseman tossed the newspaper aside. The International Olympic Committee had decided to impose a ban on any South African athletes taking part the next Olympic Games in Tokyo, and Simon was pleased. It seemed a move in the right direction, and had the support of Nelson Mandela's party, the ANC. With Mandela languishing on Robben Island, most African states had threatened to boycott the Games if South Africa was allowed to participate.

Stephen Last tensed his shoulders and heaved the large colander of cabbage onto the draining board. He grinned at the cook.

"Thanks, Stephen. Just tip the cabbage in the boiler, will you, and then help Margaret with the dishes."

He dried a large pudding tin and placed it on the shelf above the sink. He gazed down the length of the kitchen. 'Cold when you get here in the morning, but by midday the steam has soaked you through to the skin. Sweat drips from your armpits and catches the elastic of your pants. Aprons are filthy with vegetables, dirt and blood from the meat. The things that go through the mincer: scraps of bacon and other meat, bits of veg and a load of fat. Cottage pie never tasted so good.'

Tossing the last piece of cutlery in a drawer, he turned to Margaret who was sitting at the table resting her feet; by midday, having been up since 6.30 to cook the breakfasts, they were singing. Margaret was a young woman, Stephen guessed, probably in her early thirties. This month in the summer was necessary extra money for her; to earn it, she'd left her family behind.

"Do you mind if I stroll outside for a moment, Maggie …," he began.

"Don't call me Maggie," she snapped.

"Sorry?" he replied, stunned, watching her looking at him blush.

"I don't like 'Maggie'," she laughed, "My name's Margaret."

He couldn't recall a woman ever snapping at him before except his mother when she was in a certain mood; that was when you kept out of her way or got a slap round the head. He wondered why Margaret had laughed at his embarrassment. His question had only been out of courtesy since he was helping her prepare lunch; he'd no intention of not going outside for a breath of fresh air.

He strolled across to the moor that bordered the army huts and listened to the skylarks singing. He knew them from the heath near his home. His father had told him that they fly vertically as high as possible and sing their beautiful song to draw you away from their nests, which are on the ground. He loved the song with its vigorous phrasing, and watched the birds hover. He thought he could hear the sea, but perhaps that was just memory. 'I love the sound of the sea thudding on the shore. It's so … so … so resonant … I could write here. At home the pencil blunts on the paper, but I could write here all day.' He walked away from the kitchen. A slight breeze took the sweat slowly from his skin and he shivered in the warm summer air. The apron flapped round his legs.

Later that evening, Stephen and Des sat opposite each other in a local pub. They'd finished in the kitchen by nine o'clock and strolled down to the nearby village. The pub was noisy and cramped; a low-beamed ceiling was hung with brass lanterns, and horse brasses were squashed along the beams.

"It's horrible," remarked Stephen, "but the synthetic charm of these places works, doesn't it?"

"Hmm. Sorry, I wasn't listening … the synthetic charm of country pubs isn't top of my concerns list at present," was Des's moody response; and then he continued, "you believe all women are naturally possessive, don't you Stephen?"

"Yes, I suppose I do, but I'm not sure why since my experience of them is severely limited … Watching other couples, I suppose … and thinking about it. A mother will defend her children against criticism in a way that a father will not, a mother will fight to the death to protect her young, and girls always have a 'this is mine' expression on when they've got a boyfriend. Yes, I'd say women were naturally possessive."

"Once you're 'theirs', you become a possession like a new hat or a bag," remarked Des.

"I've never been in that position," Stephen laughed, "but I can imagine. Have you ever seen women going for a bargain at the sales? It's a fearsome sight. I've got it, it's mine and I'm going to keep it …"

"And then they start to re-create you in their own image by suggesting what you should wear …

"… and, eventually, how you should think, perhaps?

"A girl will see a flower growing in a wood," mused Des, "and she'll *have* to pick it – not just smell it and feel it and leave it where it is to carry on growing. She'll have to pick it and carry it home and place it in a vase of water and tend it carefully each day until it dies."

"You're a poet, Des, and you know it, hope you don't blow it."

They both laughed at Stephen's recall of Bob Dylan's lyric from *I shall be free no 10*. Des looked at his friend and thought 'I can't tell him about Susan. Christ, I admire his detachment. He's almost cold-blooded. What I wouldn't give for a no complications woman at this moment.'

As they talked, two of the girls who worked at the camp wandered into the pub, smiled and moved towards their table. Des had flirted with the tall blonde before, and was sure that the dark-haired girl had eyed-up Stephen. Des knew the pattern; the women would have decided which bloke each of them was going for before they arrived. He was also sure that he and Stephen had been followed down to the village.

Stephen dropped into conversation with them immediately, and Des smiled as they responded to his rather dry, Suffolk wit. He wasn't a natural chatter, but once Stephen got going he was funny; and it was clear the girls wanted to keep him going.

It turned the evening round for them. In the toilet, as the pub was about to close, Des said:

"You realise they've got us marked down, don't you?"

"Have they?"

"Of course they have. What shall we do? It's all right for you, you're free. I've got Elizabeth to think about."

"Short of hopping over the wall and making our way back, I don't see we've got much choice but to go along with them. We can't hurt their feelings."

Coming from anyone else, Stephen's comments would have sounded salacious, but Des had the direct impression that his friend was talking straight.

Marianne Faithfull was staggeringly beautiful, everyone agreed, and her big hit, written by Keith Richards and Mick Jagger, had taken the pop charts by storm. *As Tears Go By* – not a number the Stones would have been heard singing dead – was on everyone's lips that August. Apart from her beauty, and that tumbling mane of hair framing her face so wonderfully, she had an air of decadence about her. She was convent-educated, of course, and convent girls weren't expected to fraternise with the likes of the Rolling Stones, who were dubbed 'the bad boys of pop'; but there was more to it than errant Catholicism. She had a way of looking at the camera which conjured images of Brigitte Bardot and, perhaps, Francoise Hardy. Marianne was exotic – or, maybe, erotic.

Stephen, once more in the dormitory shared by the male kitchen workers, opened his diary and wrote by the light of his torch.

I don't want to write this, but I have to clear my head or I'll be awake all night thinking about it. I've just upheld my whole ethical outlook and achieved nothing more than hurt the feelings of a lovely girl. Des and I met two of the girls who work in the kitchens at the pub and they'd paired us off long before they got there. When we left, the slim blonde had Des moving well ahead of me and the short, dark girl and she was dead keen. She had been all night. She'd teased me with her thighs and bedroom eyes and I wanted to get her on the back porch.

She wasted no time in steering us towards a hedge and running her hands up under my shirt. She then kissed me like the clappers and, after that, clung to my mouth all the way back to the camp. I enjoyed her passion; it was probably the first time in my life I'd really been kissed in that way. I was pounding at my trousers, but I only wanted a bloody good snog. Back at the camp we went straight for the potato store. She told me she'd fancied me since we arrived at the camp, that she could always tell with a lad, that she was genuinely keen on me – and then she slipped her hand between my thighs.

After that, it's not all clear. She wasn't a virgin, I could tell that she'd been around by the way she handled things. She was so serious. I had my tongue down her throat and her skirt pulled up and then she was fiddling with her tights and her roll-on and my trousers. I must have realised what I was doing as I eased her away from me. She was stretched back over the potato sacks, gurgling and moaning, but I couldn't allow myself to do a bloody thing. Sex before marriage was something I'd always been taught, and thought, was wrong.

Stephen stopped writing and sank back on the iron bed. 'She meant nothing to me. I would have been using her, as she was using me. There was nothing even really sexual about it … not in the way I've always thought about sex as a spiritual link between two people in love. She wanted it as much as me. She'd had sex before. She enjoyed it and good luck to her … But I couldn't. It was as though I would have incurred a responsibility towards her.'

"It was horrible," said Joan Whiting to Kate and Sheila as they sat in the Café Noir after seeing *A Hard Day's Night*, "but it was blown up by the press."

She was referring to her experience at Brighton in May when she'd gone down "for a bit of fun" with her Rocker friend. Sheila had expressed how "appalled" she was at the Mods and Rockers violence in Hastings over the August Bank Holiday, and Joan always found Sheila being outraged very amusing. There was just something about her friend's attitude that was "so working class": she couldn't think of a better description. The working classes always seemed to be "outraged" or "definitely disgusted" at the behaviour of the young – most of them young working class!

"It said in the papers that the police had to be flown in by aeroplane," Sheila persisted, "and they've now established a special Riot Squad."

"Did the Daily Mirror print that with capital letters," teased Joan.

"As a matter of fact, it did, and with good reason,

Joan. We don't want this kind of thing in Britain," Kate cut in.

"I know, I know – it's what we fought a war to prevent. But these youngsters don't give a stuff about the war – it's in the past, it's part of their parents' generation ... and, anyway, as I said, when you read below the headlines, you find that three youths and a couple of girls were arrested and charged with 'threatening behaviour'. It'll all fade away when they press stops talking about it."

"You a student, are yer?" asked the lorry driver of Des, as they sat in the transport café tucking into a huge plate of bacon and eggs. The lorry driver had picked Des up as he made his way home from Devon, and insisted on paying for both meals.

"Yes."

"Thought so. You can always tell. I mean it's yer manner. You wouldn't mistake me for a student, would yer?"

"No," I suppose not," replied Des, embarrassed at the acknowledgement. 'Why shouldn't a lorry driver be a student?'

"'Course not. I never had much education myself. In my day there was none to have ... you think it's important, do yer? My kids are going straight to work when they leave school. Look at it like this – they'll be earning twice as much as you."

"That's true enough."

"It's a fact. I'm not sayin' anything against it, you understand. You've got ter have yer David Frosts and yer Malcolm Muggeridges, but that aint fer us."

He shoved a newspaper across the table towards Des.

"Cor, she's all right int she?"

Des saw a picture of a blonde Swedish-looking girl leaning over the bows of a boat. Her body was twisted at an uncomfortable angle so that her breasts hung solidly in the bikini. Behind her in the boat was a pair of water skis. The caption below read 'Sexy Svelt Stars on Skis'.

"That's what yer want when yer get home, mate. Somefin' like that. Not a pile of bleedin' books," he suggested, subsiding into a rattling cough and heaving chokes of laughter through the phlegm, "You could de yerself a bit of all right with that, eh?"

Nelson Mandela waited anxiously. He'd been on the island for nearly three months when he was told that his wife, Winnie, could visit. He sat in a chair looking through the smudged glass in which a few holes had been drilled to permit conversation. It was intolerable not being able to touch her and share a private moment together.

When she arrived, dressed elegantly as always, he spoke tenderly; it was the only way he could express his love. He saw immediately that she was under enormous strain: the difficulties of getting to the island, the indignities of her treatment by the authorities and the frustration of not being able to hold him all told on his wife.

They spoke awkwardly, watched closely by the warders who were there to observe and intimidate, and they could discuss only family matters. Nelson was aware that he was powerless to comfort his wife or care for his children. Speaking only in English, he talked about his family: his mother, his sisters, Winnie's family and his children.

"Time up! Time up!" cried the warder.

It was not possible, Nelson thought, that half an hour had passed. He and Winnie were rushed from their chairs. They waved a quick goodbye and then she was gone and he was left with only the memory of where she had sat.

Miriam Davison was enjoying her time on the maternity ward, and determined that she would, when the time came, do midwifery training. She wasn't at all fazed by the "discomfits of giving birth" – in the words of the senior nurse. There was something about the need to remain calm under what could be very trying circumstances that appealed to Miriam.

This was never more apparent than the night on which the teenage girl was admitted in an advanced stage of labour. The girl was on the point of giving birth when her parents had rushed her to casualty. The father, apparently unaware that his daughter had been pregnant, was raving:

"I'll kill the bastard. Show me him. I'll kill the bastard ..." endlessly.

Miriam surprised herself by taking him aside and saying:

"Be quiet. You're doing no good and may even be doing harm. Sit down, be quiet and do something useful such as looking after your wife."

The man stared for a moment and then sat in the nearest chair, while Miriam helped the senior nurse push the trolley, on which the girl was writhing, to maternity.

"Do not bear down, do not bear down."

Doctors arrived and the baby was delivered – broad-shouldered and as clean as a whistle – into the world. They'd calmed the girl with a little oxygen and within minutes of the birth she was sitting up nursing her child.

"The practice of whipping the baby away is not right, Nurse Davison. Mothers should be encouraged to nurse their babies."

It was not customary, and the senior nurse was flying in the face of tradition but she knew what she was doing, and Miriam realised she had set eyes on a quiet revolutionary.

"By the way, Nurse Davison, you handled the girl's father out of the way very efficiently. The parents were obviously unaware of what was happening. Well done."

Afterwards, Miriam was shocked to find that the mother was only nineteen – more or less the same age as herself and unmarried. It offended her principles – her sense of what was right and how people should behave, but she hadn't thought about that at the time.

CHAPTER 13

Crossroads

Heather Burton was desperate not to be overcome by their present circumstances. Barry had done his best: he couldn't afford more on £11 a week and she wasn't in a position to earn. Her parents would have been appalled at the quality of the home Barry had provided and, to be fair, they would have helped, but she couldn't tell them for all the reasons she'd been through a hundred times. Whatever way you looked at it, she – Heather Burton – was an unmarried mother, and that meant one thing and thing only: she was a slut. Nice girls didn't have sex before marriage, and there was no way that her mother could explain to the neighbours that her daughter was a nice girl really.

There were married, of course. Barry had obtained a licence without too much fuss and they'd gone to Staffham registry office, where the registrar had looked her up and down to see if he could detect the bump. They'd been no one at the ceremony except Kate Walsh, who'd been kind enough to offer herself as a witness, and a college friend of Barry's; it hadn't felt like a wedding at all – at least not how she'd imagined a wedding. Afterwards, they'd all gone to a pub in the High Street and had a drink "to celebrate". Heather laughed as soon as the word entered her head. Celebrate – what was there to celebrate? It had been no different from the many times they'd "popped into the boozer" after the pictures.

Barry's job was going well: that was one good thing. He'd enjoyed it from the first day, but there was no money to show for it yet. He'd been told that the two weeks he'd done in July would come in his September pay packet. Pay packet! It was a term he used deliberately. It kept him in touch with his working class roots, he said. It would actually be paid into his bank account; he was a salaried professional! It couldn't come too soon. There were so many things to buy; the list the hospital had given her was as long as your arm: that list had produced their first row. When he saw it, Barry turned white at the thought of how much it was going to cost, and Heather sensed his fear. It had made her angry. After all, the baby was his as well!

Afterwards, they'd made up and she'd cuddled down into his arms while he stroked her bump. It would only be another couple of months before the baby was born; already she could feel it kicking, gently. The thought of the child within her absorbed Heather more and more: so much so that she felt herself drifting away from Barry. The intimacy they'd once shared was no longer so intense. The baby was consuming her every emotion and Barry was falling into second place. Heather knew he was aware of her feelings, but she wasn't bothered. He'd be there when he was needed.

She walked a lot; it took up her time, and it was time that hung so heavily on Heather's hands. Never before in her life had she been alone for so much of the day. School friends and nursing friends were replaced by the baby. She would talk to it quietly as she strolled by the river bank, and the people she met regularly on her walks soon became part of her life – her new life. It was strange, but an old people she met seemed drawn to her now, realising she was pregnant, and they were a comfort. One old man insisted on offering her chocolate. "You're eating for two, now," he always said with a smile as he shared his daily bar.

The nurse at the hospital had, at first, been less than sympathetic, as though she was handling someone with a disease, but Heather had won her over with her diligence at the pre-natal classes. She'd been told that the exercises and breathing techniques would help when it came to the delivery. Enjoying sports, she'd always been fit and had no difficulty locating the right muscles, whereas some of the other women struggled to find their diaphragm let alone their pelvic girdle. Heather smiled quietly at this little triumph, especially when the instructress suggested she might have made a good nurse herself. In fact, she enjoyed the classes. They gave her somewhere to go and provided structure to her day and the company of other women.

The only person she saw from her past life – it was funny to think of her recent student nursing time as a 'past life' – was Kate Walsh, who had been sweetly supportive all along. When Kate was off-duty, they would meet for a drink in The Gondoliers – the new coffee bar in the High Street. Heather sensed both disapproval and supportiveness in Kate's manner and said as much.

"I can't disapprove of you, Heather," she replied, "and your baby will be brought up in a loving home with a mother and father – you and Barry – but that isn't always the case. Miriam was telling me about a young girl – only nineteen – who'd been rushed into hospital with what

Miriam called 'an unexpected pregnancy'. It can't be right – to bring a child into the world with no means of supporting it. It's selfish."

"At least, I know where I stand with you, Kate," Heather replied with a smile, "but it does happen, you know – even to the nicest people."

"It doesn't have to happen. You're just lucky that Barry stood by you."

Alec Douglas-Home knew that he had to call an election and the thought rather appalled him. He knew that he would not present an appealing image on 'the box'. A make-up girl had once told him that she couldn't make him look any better on television because he had "a head like a skull".

Moreover, he resented the whole idea that Prime Ministers – or, indeed, any politician – should have to be concerned with their 'image'. It struck him as a trivial consideration; after all was said and done, he wasn't an actor and the ability to give a performance should not be a pre-requisite for success in governing the country.

The cartoonists had had a field day with his half-moon glasses, and already the public perceived him as being somewhere between a lunatic and a clown, although incurably dull – thanks to a closing comment on that programme, which tried to pass itself off as satire, by an over-grown under-graduate called David Frost.

Stella Aldridge dumped her briefcase on the long, library table and sighed. Her eyes swept faces and she saw Stephen Last leaning on one of the windowsills carefully examining the pages of three books he had propped against the pane. Further along the table she'd chosen, Des Smith was poring through a heavy volume.

"You don't know anyone who wants to hitch to London to look at an exhibition of psychiatric art, do you?" she asked.

"Yes," replied Stephen, "I'd like to do that."

"You?"

"Yes. I'm interested in that sort of thing."

"It's in two weeks' time," Stella informed him, with a frown.

"Fine."

"You'll come?"

"You want someone to hitch with?"

"Yes."

"I'll come."

Stella smiled and turned to her briefcase. Des looked up and caught her eye, aware of what was going through her mind. She hadn't intended the comment for Stephen, but for him.

"Hello," he said, "working?"

"Yes, French students have translations …"

"And the English department just read books?"

"All right, all right," Stella laughed, "I give in."

'I wish you would', thought Des, 'with those heavy breast swinging against my chest, I'd come like a rocket … mind you, she'd tie your balls in knots and give them a flick as she slammed the door.'

"You're in digs this year, aren't you?" asked Stella.

"Yes, with Stephen … What's your translation about?"

"Marriage in France."

"Oh, and who are more unfaithful – men or women?"

"The men are just more … indiscriminate," replied

Stella, having almost said "promiscuous" but not quite liking to do so. She continued "Perhaps women are unfaithful only when they commit themselves?"

"So it's OK as long as you're sincere, and women are more sincere about sex?"

"If you say so, Des."

Stephen looked at them as they talked and, once again, envied Des his ease with women. He glanced around the library to take his mind off the enormity of what he'd done in offering to join Stella on a hike to London: students were bent over books, ball pens scurried notes into files. There was a 'conscious silence'. He noticed that some students wrote frantically, précising each paragraph, 'banging themselves into dumbness', he thought, knowing he'd heard or read the phrase somewhere. Others pored over a single page many times and then turned their eyes to the ceiling, fixing their eyes on a focus beyond the words – 'a point indefinable.'

David Frost, on returning to London with his girlfriend, Janette Scott, was accosted by reporters. The pair had just holidayed in Hawaii and booked into their holiday bungalow as Mr and Mrs Frost. In was customary for unmarried couples to book separate rooms, or – as would have been the case this time – separate bungalows, but they had defied the convention and booked in together.

The press were fascinated and wanted to explore David's attitude to marriage. "What about marriage?" they asked, over and over again, to which David replied "Marriage. What's that?" As the son of a Methodist minister, he was expected to give a more fulsome and conventional answer.

When the couple arrived home, they turned on the television to find that his off-the-cuff remark was "the quote of the day" and considered to be a "fearless analysis of the state of modern marriage". David Frost was considered to have shown great courage in saying what he did.

Watching the programme, Simon Wiseman laughed rather bitterly to himself, remembering Yevtushenko's lines '… our descendants will burn with shame … remembering that most peculiar time when plain honesty was labelled courage'.

David himself was more concerned with the forthcoming General Election. It had been assumed that the Tories would receive a trouncing but polls suggested that this might not be the case. The general public seemed hesitant to give themselves over to Labour rule, perhaps preferring Dull Alec to Smart Alec and his technological revolution.

Kate Walsh wasn't enjoying her time on the ENT ward as much as she had her training on the other wards; the turnover of patients was so rapid that it was impossible to get to know them properly, and for Kate this familiarity with each patient was one of the joys of the work. The procedures were of a minor nature: tonsillectomies, ear operations and sinus washouts. It was, however, a very sociable ward; the patients might only spend the day of their operation in bed, and after that would wander about chatting or playing cards or dominoes.

One young man, admitted with facial injuries, had fallen from the top to bottom of his stairs.

"I don't know what happened, nurse," he said, "One

minute I was at the top of the stairs perfectly all right, and the next I was in a heap at the bottom. My missus had to call the ambulance."

"Had you been drinking?" asked Kate.

"Well of course."

"How many pints had you had?"

"I don't know … about seven or eight, I suppose."

"Well, you were obviously drunk," suggested Kate, in all innocence.

As his fellow domino player laughed, the young man leapt to his feet. Kate thought for a moment that he was going to strike her.

"What do you mean – drunk? I'm never drunk. I can drink myself sober," he roared, his face convulsed in anger.

"That's a myth," replied Kate, standing her ground, "You're lucky you didn't break your neck in the fall."

The anger in the young man's face doubled. Kate smiled, fully aware that she had this person on the run. She'd never handled a young man with quite as much authority before and it did her good to know she could do so when necessary.

"You'll certainly be off the booze for a bit," she continued, "you're on analgesics to relieve the pain and antibiotics to cope with any possible infection, and alcohol is forbidden with both medications. We'll have to make sure your wife doesn't smuggle any in for you this evening."

The General Election, which Sir Alec Douglas-Home had decided he must call if he were to have any chance of being elected as Prime Minister in his own right, was not the only problem he faced as autumn approached. Ian

Smith, the newly-elected Prime Minister of Southern Rhodesia, had arrived in London for talks, and he had made his position abundantly clear; he knew, he said, how to spell the word 'compromise' but it had no place in his political dictionary. If Britain insisted on the black majority being given the vote, the whites would break away from the Commonwealth and make a unilateral declaration of independence.

Alec was aware that whenever Great Britain had handed over power to another government it had always been on the basis of a majority vote. If there was to be an exception, he felt that scrupulous care would need to be taken to ensure that the minority would be pledged to helping the majority along the road towards a shared political rule. Alec could see that whatever decision was taken there was almost certainly going to be a time of deep trouble ahead for Rhodesia – evolutionary progress or bloody revolution.

Sheila Pratt knew that as part of her training she would be required to take responsibility for monitoring the complete care of an individual patient; this would form part of one of the compulsory assessments for her state finals.

Her friendship with Kate Walsh, in particular, had given Sheila more faith in herself; she no longer felt that she was "out of the bottom drawer", which was a favourite phrase of her parents and aunts. The indoctrination of childhood, however, can never be completely erased, and Sheila knew that she would need to proceed step by little step if any of her fragile, newly-found confidence was to flower. So, she chose her individual with care.

"The children's ward, Nurse Pratt? My, you're brave," Sister O'Malley re-joined when Sheila made her suggestion.

"I feel I know something about children, Sister."

"Well, I wish you luck," replied Sister O'Malley, pausing before adding, "I'm sure you'll be fine. Which child in particular did you have in mind?"

"Raymond."

"Ah, yes – the pyloric stenosis. It's quite common, you know, and frightens the hell out of parents. He's down for the theatre, tomorrow. We'll have to prep him. It should be an interesting experience. Have you had to wash out a baby's stomach before?"

"I have assisted."

"Well, now you're in charge … Don't worry, we'll be watching!"

As soon as Sheila had taken the first child into her arms, she'd felt the wonder of its little body squirming against her. She took the tiny hand and felt the little fingers curl around hers; she nuzzled her chin against the tiny head and sniffed.

Sheila washed and dried the small bottom with a wad of cotton wool before placing the little boy gently on the triangle of nappy and bringing the central flap up between his legs. She held the three corners with her hand against his tummy so that there was no chance of the safety pin pricking him.

When she fed the little boy, Sheila wanted to get married and have a child of her own. Warming the bottle, testing the temperature of the milk on her forearm, nursing him against her breast, feeling the child guzzling the milk and hearing him burp loudly on her shoulder were more than acts of nursing; they were acts of love. Sheila needed to feel those acts; they lifted her from the dowdiness of her upbringing and took her into a special place where she was important and useful and ... revolutionary. She didn't know where that word had come from – perhaps something Kate had said.

The following day, the "pyloric stenosis" had to be prepared for theatre. Only, he wasn't "the pyloric stenosis" and he wasn't just Raymond; in some strange way, the little boy was every child who ever was or ever would be. At that realisation, Sheila experienced the wonder of nursing.

She'd injected saline under his skin in order to keep him hydrated, and now she passed the tube through his mouth to wash out his stomach. She knew it was a terrifying moment for the patient, and she accomplished the procedure neatly, quickly and quietly. That was, perhaps, the worst part of the preparation, but Sheila knew, without even hearing the result that she'd passed her assessment.

When she returned to the Nurses Home, Sheila found not Kate, who she'd wanted to tell about the assessment, but Joan Whiting, who was watching *Crossroads* on their little television set.

"I know," yelled Joan, "it is rubbish – the sets wobble, the plots don't hold water and the acting is wooden – but it's relaxing, and I need that after a day on women's surgical."

"I passed my assessment," replied Sheila, "I'm sure I did."

"Monitoring the complete care of an individual patient?" asked Joan.

"Yes. I've been looking after a little boy."

"Well done."

Somehow, that "well done" from Joan Whiting meant more than if it had come from Kate.

"Has Meg sorted out her problem?" asked Sheila.

"Meg?"

"Meg Richardson. Has she sorted out her problem with the rude guest?"

"Yes," replied Joan with a laugh, "flinty Meg of the Crossroads Motel always sorts out her problems. It pays to be flinty in life."

"Oh, I don't know," answered Sheila, "I'm not sure that's true at all."

Kate was home for the weekend. Greeting her at the front door, and placing her suitcase in the small hallway, her father said:

"You wait 'til you read the Express and Star."

The *Express and Star* was Wolverhampton's key newspaper, and Maurice Walsh read each edition from cover to cover, not missing a word or sparing his wife a provocative detail. It transpired that the 'If you want a nigger for a neighbour, vote Labour' posters, which had appeared in Smethwick during the spring, had now turned up in Wolverhampton, phrased slightly differently but with the same offensive, unhelpful message 'Vote Labour for more nigger-type neighbours'. Renee Short, the Labour candidate for Wolverhampton North East, had condemned them outright:

"These are fascist tactics," she'd said.

Renee Short didn't hold much credence for Florence Walsh, who was a dyed-in-the-wool Conservative, because it was generally believed that Renee Short changed the fur coat she usually wore for a plain raincoat when she visited her constituency. The truth of this assertion had never been tested, but Florrie Walsh's belief that it was so enabled her to ignore any opinions uttered by the Labour candidate.

Enoch Powell, who was the prospective Conservative candidate for Wolverhampton South West, had taken a more cautious approach when asked about the posters.

"I have not seen or heard of them," he said, "I have not started my campaign yet ... and so I am not making any comment or observation on anything at this stage."

Kate's father smiled as his daughter finished reading the article and sipped the tea her mother had placed on the little side table by the settee.

"Your father's just trying to provoke me," she sniffed, "He agrees with me about immigration. It's got to be stopped. There won't be enough jobs for our own people if it carries on, and Enoch Powell needs to speak out if he's to get my vote."

"He'll get your vote anyway, Florrie," laughed Maurice Walsh, "he's the only one you've got to vote for."

"Nevertheless ..." began Florrie Walsh, and then subsided into silence.

Enoch Powell was aware of the feelings running riot in the town. He had attended a meeting with the Conservative candidate for the Bilston ward, at which the candidate, John Oxford, had spelled out what he saw – and what he thought his constituents saw – as a serious problem.

"I can take you down to Stow Heath," he said, "and what will you see? Fifty or sixty cars pulling up, a juke box blaring out music until three in the morning, and gambling and prostitution will be in evidence."

Enoch had remained quiet throughout John Oxford's rant and made no reference to immigration in his own speech. He was aware that control of immigration was essential not only for the people of Britain but for the immigrants themselves; he was convinced that strict control must continue if the evils of a colour question in the country was to be avoided for his own generation and that of his children; but, for the moment, he was keeping his own council. It was a time for caution.

Amanda Harrelson arrived as a first year student as Stephen Last's year returned for their second time, and she immediately latched on to the group that drifted around Des Smith and the emerging folk scene at college. This group included Paul Crisp, who – with Mike Harrison – had enjoyed the freedom bestowed on a group of men in a college where the male-female ratio was one-to-ten. Neither Paul nor Mike had, necessarily, 'gone the whole way' with any, or even some, of the girls they'd taken out, but they'd had a free hand.

When the new intake arrived, Paul and Mike looked them over for "potential totty" and lost no time in taking them out and "showing them the ropes". They were both attractive lads. Paul, in particular, had 'a way with women', and Mike had a clapped-out old car that, nevertheless, went places.

One evening, Paul found himself sitting in the Wong Gon restaurant in Newcastle-under-Lyme with Amanda. Paul's attractive features included his knack of being a good listener, and Amanda enjoyed talking. As the steaming char sui slid from the basin onto his fried rice, Paul smiled encouragingly. Since it was the beginning of term, he'd splashed out and bought a bottle of wine with the meal. The waiter poured a taster into his glass and Paul sniffed and swilled it with a show of expertise. When he'd finished, Paul smiled at the waiter and nodded approvingly.

"I've often wondered what would happen if someone sent one back," said Amanda.

"They'd have to change the bottle."

"Would they?"

"Of course. You couldn't drink corked wine."

He smiled rather smugly at his show of knowledge, realising he'd made an impression. He knew that most people assumed the waiter was asking you to approve the wine whereas, in fact, they were giving you the chance to check that it wasn't corked. He'd picked that little titbit of information up when he'd taken out a girl from the French department, and recalled his embarrassment at his own ignorance at the time.

Amanda talked throughout the meal, except when she was actually chewing or laughing. 'She's like a TV jingle,' he thought, 'so alive. It doesn't matter what she's saying. It's just exciting listening to her.'

"I'm from Preston," she offered as information about her background, "You should have seen my mum and dad on the night I left. Dad felt obliged to say something but he didn't know what. He was pacing up and down for hours. He kept coming into the living room, sitting for a minute watching the telly and then he'd get up and go out. We heard him hammering – he's making a kitchen cabinet, see – and then he'd come in for a cup of tea. My mum kept saying 'for goodness sake, sit down, Bill' but he wouldn't. Anyway, eventually, my eldest brother came down – he's studying at the local tech – and asked dad to go for a drink. Well, he put on his coat and cap and came in and said 'Well, our 'Manda, I suppose you'll be abed before I get back' – why I don't know because he knew I wouldn't – 'so I'll wish you luck and ... well, be careful. Some of those lads will ...' and then my mum told him to shut up and my brother dragged him off."

As she talked, Paul listened and watched. He was fascinated by her every movement. She was thin and angular but every inch of the surface of her body seemed to tingle with nervous energy. If ever anybody could be said to be electrically charged, it was Amanda. Her eyes never left his face as she talked and it seemed to Paul as if he was the only person in the world who mattered at that moment. He had never felt so enveloped by a girl. Amanda's hair was cut in the Rita Tushingham style from *The Knack ... and how to get it* and she made him feel more like Ray Brooks than Michael Crawford. Her eyes sparkled. The pupils were placed quite centrally in her eyes so that a rim of white could be seen all round the blue orbs.

"You're friendly with Des Smith, aren't you, Paul?"

"Yes."

"What's that club of his?"

"It's a folk club. There wasn't much chance to get it going last year but he's hoping to, this – in the Red Room and, maybe, the Red Lion."

"Some of us girls though of joining ... Are you in it?"

"You just turn up ... we sort of gather and sing. Des plays guitar and other people turn up with harmonica or banjo or whatever. Anyone who wants to can sing. Do you sing?"

"A little."

The waiter, his greased hair shining black in the concealed lighting of the restaurant, helped Amanda on with her coat as she left, and Paul tipped him – not ostentatiously but ostentatiously enough for Amanda to notice and approve.

"Nice to see you again, sir," said the waiter, with a fawning smile.

Paul returned the gesture with thanks, as the look in the waiter's eyes suggested a familiarity that was not warranted.

"We'll look forward to next time," he replied.

Mike Harrison was waiting with a girl called Sue, who'd made up the original foursome, and drove them back to college in his lime green banger. When the car pulled up and Mike and Sue's mouths locked in the obligatory snog, Paul hesitated, not wanting this girl to feel that she was taken for granted. Amanda, sensing his hesitation, wasted no time. She slid a slender arm along his neck, tickling him behind the ear, and drew his head down to her mouth. It was too soon in the relationship for a French kiss, and so she brushed his lips gently with hers, encouraging them to cling together. Paul responded and felt that his fingers had never stroked a more beautifully tapered neck. Both closed their eyes, and were looking at each other when they re-opened them. Amanda smiled. It was captivating.

Outside, it was drizzling and Paul raised a black umbrella over Amanda's head as she stepped from the car, swinging her legs onto the wet gravel. She raised the collar of her coat, nestled into him for a second and then slid her arm though his so that the umbrella covered them both as Paul walked her back to block.

Chapter 14

A victory for Labour

One o'clock in the morning. Thin reeds of rain fell continuously. In the darkness frequent gusts of fierce wind swept the reeds into a living, twirling sheet of wet. Like a rag, it whipped their faces until Stella's was raw and shining; she could barely open her eyes. Stephen's shoulders shivered against his neck. He leaned forward and rubbed the dangling wet hair against the sodden collar of his coat. Stella looked away along the shining road. Yellow headlights shone in the dark. A car passed, spraying their legs. Stella dropped her thumb.

"You'd think they ... My god isn't it bloody. You'd think one of them would stop," she yelled.

"We've certainly had no luck tonight. Can I take your bag?" he asked, instinctively knowing that when a woman is in a bad mood it pays to offer some comfort.

"Thanks."

Stephen took up the hitching, waving his finger in the air in a whirling cone of streaming rain. Dark hedges spiked the roadside, black against the grey, thudding sky. The water hit the pavement, splashing upward between their legs. The rain fell so intensely that the branches of the trees could not hold it; they hung loosely, washed clean of the grit and dust from the road. The brown, gruntled bark shone like copper in the headlights.

Stella stooped under the storm, back bowed, hanging almost from the waist. Her feet slid through the puddles. 'If only we could find a motel somewhere,' she thought, 'but, anyway, we couldn't afford it.'

"The thought of marriage appals me," she said, suddenly, blinking water from her eyes as she looked up at Stephen and saw him laugh. "Why are you laughing?"

"Nothing was further from my mind, at this particular moment, than marriage," he replied, chuckling, delighted that she should even want to discuss it. "You don't want to get married?"

"I can't ever see myself succumbing to anyone. People try to swamp you with their own personality. I don't want to lose my individuality ... Not that anyone would want to live with me, anyway."

"Oh, I don't know. You ..."

"You don't know me," she snapped, "I'm wonderful at mixing my problems," she continued, wanting him to ask what they were, and disappointed when he remained quiet.

'I should solve her problems,' he thought, 'grab hold of them as though they were some lout who'd accosted her, grab them by the arm and twist them out of the room. I'd be her saviour. She'd love me then, and I could ease away her fear of marriage: a loving hand, a tender touch. Two people entwined in the throes of love.' He didn't laugh at his thoughts; they embarrassed him.

Stella was huddled in the corner of the seat, cushioned wet on the upholstery. Stephen sat beside her, hanging on to the front seat, talking to the driver.

"See this car," the man was saying, "how much do you think it cost?

"I've no idea," replied Stephen.

"Nar, go on, have a guess."

"I don't know. I've no idea. Don't ..."

"Seventy five nicker," said the driver, proudly, pausing and then laughing, "Mind you, I had to knock the geezer down. He was a university type. Smart suit and everything but he didn't know nothin' about cars. I could tell that right away. I mean he was all dressed up in his fancy suit, but he didn't know nothin' about cars. Knocked him down ..." He paused to light a cigarette.

"Some friends are expecting us," Stephen interposed, "but we don't like to knock them up tonight."

"You don't want to worry, mate. They probably aint in bed yet. We don't go ter bed early round here. The day's just beginnin' in London. People round here are night people ..."

"It's nearly three in the morning."

"Early days. What's the name of the road? I'll take you there."

'He did it out of sheer kindness,' thought Stephen, 'this man who has the world by the balls.' He and Stella were standing on the pavement outside the parents of a friend's house, not liking to knock at the door. The day might just be beginning where the driver lived, but the great city had gone to bed long ago in Radlett.

"What are we going to do?" asked Stella.

The house was in darkness, surrounded by darkness and stillness. A neat hedge separated the concrete and flower beds from the pavement.

"We can't knock them up at this time of night, can we?" replied Stephen.

Stella shrugged. Stephen looked at his watch.

"Well," he continued, "do you think they'd mind? Have you met them?"

"I told you. Pat wrote and told them to expect us."

"But not at this hour," Stephen persisted.

Stella swung the duffle bag backwards and forwards between her legs.

"We've got no money for a hotel," she said, "We can't stand here all night."

"No, I suppose not," responded Stephen, hoping that a light would go on in the house, "Actually, I was thinking. We passed a station at the top of the road. We could spend the night in the waiting room."

"Are you allowed …?"

"It wouldn't do any harm."

Stella looked at the house once more and then followed Stephen.

The station foyer was strewn with empty packets, cartons and strips of torn poster. Everything, but particularly the litter, was smeared with grey dirt. The paintwork, damp to the touch, flaked from the wood panelling that covered the outer wall. The short corridor leading to the station steps wound by a lift, rusted and chipped. The platform looked lonely.

"That must be the waiting room with the light," said Stephen.

As he spoke, a man appeared from the waiting room and jumped down onto the rail. He ran across the tracks, pulled himself onto the opposite platform and disappeared into one of the rooms. Stella jerked back, pulling Stephen with her.

"Don't let him see you. He's a loony. I don't want to get mixed up with him."

"We can discuss the exhibition of psychiatric art," laughed Stephen.

Stella glared at him. They waited. Minutes went by, while she tugged at Stephen's arm, trying to get him to leave the station.

"He's probably drunk," said Stephen, in a tone he hoped was reassuring, "he's probably settled down."

"I'm not going down there with a loony."

"We can bar the door. There'll be no need to open it until the station gets busy later in the morning."

The man appeared on the platform as Stephen spoke, looking along the line, his head twisting furiously from side to side. Again, he jumped onto the line and leapt unevenly from sleeper to sleeper, eventually disappearing into the darkness. 'He'll get killed,' thought Stella. The man re-appeared, panting heavily, mouth wide, his face drained of any trace of colour. They watched as he hared across the rails to the far platform. He ran up and down, his body solid on the concrete, his feet seeming to hardly leave the ground. Suddenly, he turned and vanished into the waiting room.

"What did I tell you," said Stella.

"Come on," urged Stephen, "let's go to the foyer."

"He may come up here."

"I don't think so. He's more likely to stay in the waiting room where it's warmer."

"You can't tell with loonies. I once worked in a mental hospital."

In the corner of the foyer, Stephen thumped his bag into softness and pushed it behind Stella's back where she sat on the dusty floor.

"You say you worked in a mental hospital?" he asked.

"It was a holiday job. I helped out with the cleaning and so on."

"Did you have much to do with the patients?"

"It's horrible. Once you get in there, you never get out." Stella pulled a cigarette from her duffle bag and lit it. "Most of the patients return again and again. They never really leave. There's no cure, except one. They open your head and cut a central nerve. You're never any trouble after that; they cut out your spirit. You become a vegetable. You just sit there day after day, wanting nothing and feeling nothing."

There was a rustle of paper from the corridor. Stephen tensed. Stella reached for him and then withdrew her hand. Stephen ventured round the corner of the stairs before she realised what he was doing. Stella jabbed out her cigarette on the wall, saw the damp patch on Stephen's bag and realised she was very wet and cold. 'Stephen's no match for him,' she thought, and then he returned, 'having left me.'

"Wind," Stephen offered by way of explanation. "It was a piece of paper. He's in the waiting room asleep."

"What's the time?"

"About four o'clock. There was a timetable down there and I took a look. We can get a train into the city at six … yes, I know, it's a couple of hours, but we are in the dry. We can get some breakfast in a café, hope the sun is out tomorrow and have a doze in the park until the exhibition opens."

"Assuming it doesn't rain and there's a café open."

"I can't promise dry weather, but there will be a café

open on one of the markets," he said, realising he had adopted his father's sarcastic tone.

"I'm not moaning. I know we can't afford a hotel. I'm tired, that's all, and the loony's got the waiting room while we're stuck up here."

The early train was almost empty and drizzled into London through a grey fog. In the market, crates of vegetables were split open on the pavements, and they dodged their way round to, first, the toilets and then the café. Traders in white overalls heaved load after load from the backs of trucks and lorries.

The café was marked by scraps of uneaten food left on the tables, and this repulsed Stella, although Stephen barely noticed the mess and tucked into his breakfast ravenously. 'Chips with everything,' thought Stella.

The park was green and the weather dry. 'Green as it never is in summer,' thought Stephen. The pond threw up the image of its surroundings: evergreen bushes and the swaying branches of beeches, dark against the blue sky. Their clothes began to dry.

They found chairs and sat together during the morning, and 'talked of Pope and Proust and Plato,' thought Stephen, smiling to himself. It was true and seemed the most natural of things. He had always found the company of women stimulating. At the tech college, it was the women as much as his mates who had opened his thoughts to infinite possibilities. As coffee time approached, he looked at his watch.

"Time to make tracks for the exhibition," he suggested.

They walked through London in the crisp October air,

her breasts heavy against his side, and he thought he'd never been so happy.

Harold Wilson faced the forthcoming General Election with a degree of quiet confidence: the polls were favourable, his plans were in place and there was evidence that the country had had enough of Conservative rule. The sixties were a time of change, and the people were ready for change. He thought through his strategy with care; he was determined that the Treasury should be cut down to size, he decided to set up a Ministry of Technology to capitalise on the forthcoming scientific advances and he was committed to setting up a 'University of the Air' to "bring higher education to those who had not or could not find the time to attend a full university course".

Harold, himself a Christian, recognized that "from the Party's earliest days a great number of converts had joined Labour because they believed that socialism was a way of making a reality of Christian principles in everyday life". It was this belief that gave him his positive approach to politics.

Alec Douglas-Home presided over an intelligently planned campaign, one facet of which was the decision that he should tour the country, speaking in towns and villages, making himself known to as many people as possible.

He was distressed to find that Labour was determined to undermine his attempts to reach the people. At his open-air meetings hundreds of young Labour supporters were packed immediately below the platform from which he intended to speak. These "hooligans", as Alec thought of them, would bawl as loudly as possible below the microphone, drowning out his words until he lost track of what he was saying. His inability to hear his own voice and hence follow his own coherent arguments produced a strain that he was unable to conceal from the television cameras, and he appeared to be on the defensive.

In the Rag Market at Birmingham, Labours tactics were well organised. A disorderly crowd of ten thousand had been augmented by young socialists grouped in hundreds. As one bunch ran out of breath with its bawling, another took up the shout. No one in the crowd could hear a word, and pandemonium broke out. As Alec left the hall, a lout kicked out at him. Alec avoided the blow and the lout's hob-nailed boot collided with his neighbour's knee-cap. Looking back over his shoulder, Alec saw the two of them had come to blows.

Barbara Castle, a member of Labour's National Executive Council, admired Harold Wilson's skilful handling of the election campaign as much as she had admired his conference speech in 1963. She'd sat spellbound as he talked of "the white heat of the technological revolution" and pointed out that the Tories had no idea such a revolution was fermenting. Harold explained his concern that these advances in technology should be harnessed for the public good. He pointed out that we were not training enough scientists and that 12% of new PhDs were going abroad to work.

She could not believe her party's luck when Lord Home – now Sir Alec Douglas-Home – became Prime Minister: his grouse moors image was, she knew, political suicide for the Tories, and yet they seemed unaware of the fact. Harold was up in front with the scientists and economists;

Alec was an aristocratic amateur. She was filled with delight as the bright grammar-school boy pitched into the effete landowner.

Michael Ramsey, Archbishop of Canterbury, looked on with the detachment proper to his position as head of the Church of England. He and Alec were old friends, and Michael admired his integrity and ability. He found Harold friendly and easy to talk to; they were both dons, and talked liked dons. Though a non-conformist, Harold 'had religion in him', and Michael found this to be a bond.

Maurice Walsh folded his copy of the Wolverhampton *Express and Star*, placed it on the arm of his chair and rolled another cigarette. As he puffed away, much to his wife's annoyance and to the detriment of the living room ceiling, he pondered on Enoch Powell's attitude to immigration. The politician's utterances had been mild enough to date, but the local paper reported him saying in his election address *'For years now, since the late 1950s in fact, discussions with people, whether about education, housing, pensions, employment, or other things always comes round to this topic – immigration ...' It will be Mr Powell's business to show that the Conservative Government's action and policy on this has been the only sound and humane policy which is available..*

Maurice, an avid reader of the local paper, recalled another article by Enoch along the lines that *'there is an inescapable obligation of humanity to permit the wives and young children of immigrants already here to join them; it follows that the rate of all other new admissions must be reduced further still'*. It seemed to make sense: if the country could only absorb so many newcomers, the wives and children must come first.

The General Election campaign seemed far away to Kate Walsh. Still working on men's surgical she was preparing for the afternoon visiting hour. That same morning they had admitted an Irishman, Patrick Adams, who was involved in a pub brawl, which resulted in a broken arm.

"We need to be ready for this one," said Sister Hall, "I know the family, and they're a law unto themselves."

She'd said no more and wandered off to the sluice room. When visiting time arrived, what the ward sister had indicated materialised. Mrs Adams walked in to visit her husband accompanied by two of their children.

"I had nowhere else to leave them, nurse. I had to bring the two. The others are at home with my eldest daughter."

Kate smiled, sure that no one would object despite the strict rule that visitors must be limited to two people at a time. This seemed reasonable to her, but there were times when even the most reasonable of rules needed to be broken – or bent a little.

As Kate was going off-duty that night, Sister Hall called her into her office.

"Nurse Walsh, why did you allow the Irish family to have more than the regulation number of visitors without saying a word to them? I did indicate, quite subtly, that they were a law unto themselves."

"Mrs Adams had nowhere else to leave the young ones, Sister. She did explain."

"Mrs Adams's young ones, Nurse Walsh, are Mrs Adams's problem – not ours. If she chooses to have a tribe of children, that's her business. If we break the rules for one, we must be prepared to break the rules for all, and then where would we be?"

"It just seemed sensible …"

"Sensible? Rules are made for a good reason, Nurse Walsh. It's not for us to reason why …"

"Oh, but – with due respect, Sister – it is. That's what the sixties are all about."

Sister Hall raised an eyebrow and almost smiled.

"Sister Hall almost smiled," laughed Joan Whiting, when Kate relayed the incident to her the next morning, "You must have shocked her into silence. We had teachers like her at the boarding school. Ex-army: everything was done by the rule book. It's what got us through the war. My father's a bit like that …"

"But they did get us through the war," Kate remonstrated, quietly.

"Time to move on, Kate. You said so yourself."

"Yes, but I wouldn't have wanted to upset Sister Hall. She's a good sort."

Michael Ramsey, pondering the possible outcome of the General Election, was reflecting on how a Labour government might view the abolition of the death penalty. The case was clear to Michael: life is sacred and the state ought not to take it away, too many miscarriages of justices had resulted in the hanging of innocent people and statistics showed that the death penalty protected society no better than long terms of imprisonment. Despite his conviction of these truths, Michael – in his maiden speech when Archbishop of York – had been unsuccessful in persuading the House of Lords to support the proposal; they had thrown it out by 238 votes to 95 in 1956. They had supported the feelings of the vast majority of the British public rather than the opinion of the House of Commons. Even his predecessor as Archbishop of Canterbury, Geoffrey Fisher, had spoken in favour of keeping the hangman.

The public saw helpless old ladies brutally murdered for no more than a few pounds and they wanted retribution; they also wanted to feel safe in their beds. There had never been any call from the majority of the public for abolition, but attitudes were changing within the church.

"The death penalty is a denial of the gospel, and by practising it the state takes on the prerogative of God," stormed Mervyn Stockwood, Bishop of Southwark.

In January 1962, he had brought to the Convocation of Canterbury a motion that the death penalty should be abolished for an experimental period; every bishop had voted for abolition. The *Daily Mail* had suggested that, perhaps, the bishops had dozed during the debate; but the vote had given a new impetus to ardent abolitionists such as the Labour MP, Sydney Silverman, and it did look – given a Labour victory – as if times might, indeed, be changing.

Sitting in the Fitzwilliam Arms, which was situated in the village of Swynnerton, a short walk from the college, Stephen Last was more or less enjoying a pint with Des Smith, Marguerite Banister, Jenny Pryce and Susan Paget: more or less enjoying only because they were discussing his "excursion" with Stella Aldridge. Stephen had considered their visit to the psychiatric art exhibition to have been a success, but the word round college was that he had proved rather inept.

"Like babes in the wood" was the expression Des had used.

Stephen usually remained silent under any kind of attack – he'd learned that was the best defence when being assailed by advice from his father – and, with Marguerite, at least, he felt he was in sympathetic company.

"Never mind, Steve," she said, in that comforting way of hers, "you did your best, and no harm was done."

Stephen smiled a thanks, still perplexed and annoyed that Stella should have talked unfavourably about their trip. His eyes caught the whitewashed walls, and he saw the landlord disappearing into the cellar. Marguerite reached out and helped herself to some of the bread and cheese they'd ordered. From somewhere in the village, he thought he could hear a clanging sound. The landlady appeared in the doorway.

"Smith's shoeing a horse," she said, by way of information.

'It would be warm work and welcome on a day like this,' thought Stephen. He saw the sweat parting the smith's hair in black streaks, the blue dungarees and the leather apron, sweat-sodden in the red heat of the furnace; he saw the fire glowing on the working muscles of the smith, watched the man's eyes set deep in their sockets, and felt inadequate.

"Penny for them, Stevie," suggested Jenny, smiling with that curve of a mouth he'd always wanted to kiss.

"I was wondering what we were supposed to do that we didn't do," he said.

"Not 'we', Stephen, 'you'," replied Des, "It's the man

who's supposed to sort these things out. Hadn't you noticed?"

As Des spoke, Stephen saw Susan start and stiffen. He wondered what stage their thwarted friendship had reached, glimpsing only half the story but detecting the spite in Des's comment.

"You should have knocked them up, Stevie," urged Jenny, "they would have expected it."

"At three in the morning?"

"It would have given you and Stella a chance to dry out and clean up. She'd have preferred that to walking about London in wet, day-old clothes ... only the brave shall inherit the fair, Stevie."

"Or those rude enough to wake perfect strangers in the middle of the night," he replied, with a laugh, taking her jibe in friendship, knowing what she actually thought of Stella.

"Wake up! Get up!"

The night warder's cry woke Nelson Mandela as it had woken him every morning since he had been imprisoned on Robben Island. It was 5.30, but he had always been an early riser and the hour was no trouble to him.

He cleaned his cell and rolled up his blanket and mats. He used the water in the concave lid of the iron sanitary bucket to wash and shave. He took his time. There was no need to hurry because they would be in their cells until 6.45.

When the time came, Nelson went and emptied his sanitary bucket, which was known as a 'ballie'. He washed and cleansed it thoroughly; otherwise the stench in the cells would have been unbearable. Even this odious task had its pleasant aspect: it was the one moment of the day when the prisoners could pass a whispered word with each other because the warders did not linger.

The common room of A House at Collingwood Hall was ready for the results of the General Election. Those students – like Stephen and Des – who were in digs for their second year had arranged to bunk down somewhere in house for the night. The tables were strewn with cards and dominoes outplayed by what was happening on the television; darts hung idly from the board. Occasionally a student would slope off to the kitchen and heat something or other; otherwise, there was little or no movement: beer glasses were refilled, cigarettes were handed round, ash trays were emptied as necessary but that was all.

What dominated the room was talk. It was thirteen years since a Labour government had run an instinctively conservative country. The young men gathered round the television set had high hopes that times were about to change; the "natural party of government", as the Tories liked to think of themselves, was going to be ousted. The Profumo affair, followed by the appearance of Alec Douglas-Home as the unelected, grouse moor prime minister had shown the old-boy network up for what it was: a self-serving group of men, all friends from their public school days, all of whom trotted easily into universities that denied places to equally intelligent but indifferently educated working class people.

At least, that was the way that Stephen Last, Desmond Smith, Simon Wiseman and others of their generation saw the situation. Being under 21, they had no voting rights, of course, but the mood of the country was in their favour.

Those who had fought for them in the Second World War (their fathers and uncles and mothers and aunts) had not reaped the rewards promised (not since Atlee's Labour government had been ousted in 1951) and it was they, and the young just old enough to vote, who would force the change.

It was a change that they felt would be far-reaching. Those, like Stephen, lucky enough to have come from towns where Labour councils had established technical colleges to educate properly those rejected under the discredited 11+ system, were determined to change society for the better for all, and not just for the favoured few. Education was the road to freedom. It wasn't enough that the working classes should only be educated far enough for them to be of use to the ruling classes; the right to be educated was a right in itself. The 'array of talent' at Oxford and Cambridge needed to be widened beyond the members of the establishment; and the 'redbrick' universities – so sneered at by anyone lucky enough to have parents rich enough or connected enough to get them into the "top two" – needed to receive their fair share of government funding to attract the best students and teachers.

The talk – at times angry, at times full of rough humour – dominated A House far into the early hours, taking many through to breakfast time. As each 'Labour gain' was flashed onto the screen, a roar of approval echoed along the tatty corridors of the old building that was considered good enough to be a training college for the country's future teachers.

On screen, BBC stalwarts such as Robin Day, Ian Trethowan, Kenneth Harris and Bob McKenzie with his swingometer, kept a rapturous house and nation informed and the politicians on their toes. Towards the end of the evening, with George Brown, Deputy Leader of the Labour Party, in his most ebullient mood, Robin Day asked him if he felt that Labour could govern with what turned out to be an overall majority of only four:

"Can you govern without a clear majority?"

"We shall govern. The country has given us power. We shall proceed to govern accordingly," replied George, "I should not worry yourself about that ... You are interviewing a member of what looks like the new administration ...We shall govern according to the policies we have put to the people ... We shall govern and do our best to put the nation back on its feet."

George Brown – viewed always as erratic and headstrong but a favourite of the Labour Left – was virtually bouncing with joy. Stephen Last noted the phrase "You are interviewing a member of what looks like the new administration". There was something, he felt, almost childlike in the man's demeanour.

"... Goodness gracious, Robin, you don't seem to listen ...," he continued.

"Mr Brown, may I call you brother?" intervened Robin Day.

"I would be delighted."

"Goodbye, Brother Brown."

"Goodbye, Brother Day."

It was a great end to a great night. The laughter at Collingwood Hall rang out afresh from voices already hoarse with laughter and applause. Labour was in, a new age was dawning, times really were a-changin' and a road to freedom was opening for everyone.

Chapter 15

Concord

Martin Luther King with his wife, Coretta, had flown to Norway to accept the Nobel Peace Prize for 1964. He now sat on the stage looking out over the huge auditorium. Before him in the audience sat the King of Norway, who rose to his feet, slowly and began to clap. Others followed suit, and soon the whole auditorium was applauding the Baptist preacher who had advocated and pursued the peaceful road to integration.

Martin was aware of himself as the little boy who had no longer been able to play with his white friends once they were all old enough to start school, the little boy who wasn't allowed to sit in the front of the shoe store in his own town, the man who had to ride on the back of the bus and who had been arrested for sitting next to a white man at a lunch counter.

Dr Gunnar Jahn introduced him as "the first person in the western world to have shown us that a struggle can be waged without violence." Martin stepped forward to accept his prize. Trumpets blared, pomp and ceremony was all around but he could see only the millions of Negroes in the United States who "were part of the battle to end the long night of racial injustice". He accepted the award on their behalf.

"One day," he said, "we will have a finer land, a better people, a more noble civilization because these humble children of God were willing to suffer."

Susan Paget walked across the playing fields, windswept under a grey-clouded sky. A day that had promised snow was now left a little wet and raw. She held the collar of her coat around her ears and watched the rise and slip of the skyline as she walked. Dark trees, obscured by the brown earth and the dull sky, looked so brittle with winter that a touch would crack them.

She heard his footsteps behind her on the ground, and hardly dared to look back – hardly dared to wonder if his face was smiling that smile or whether it was racked with indecision. He was so close and so silent. She half-turned and he touched her arm. Susan ached with the fear of what she might have lost, and yet it was something she had never gained. The phrase 'smiling through a graveyard' came into her head.

"You understand,' he asked, coming alongside her, "I couldn't let myself fall in love with you. There's Elizabeth."

"I understand, Des. I know how you must feel."

He kissed her cold lips under the grey sky, standing there, apparently alone, in the middle of what seemed the vast expanse of the playing field. 'His lips were warm and soft, and I rested in his arms, and he was kissing me gently … with relief.' Susan brushed her gloved hand at the tears on her cheek. She wanted to sob until the ground at her feet was sodden with her tears.

"I knew why you were picking on me," she whispered, "You've been doing it since we got back in September."

"I'm sorry."

"Don't be. I understand."

'I don't want anybody else,' she thought, 'not now, not after this. I knew he could love me.'

They walked slowly on until they reached H House, where Susan had her room.

"Would you like a coffee?" she asked, and Des nodded.

The hall lights dimmed. A circle of students sat under the apron of the stage, books in hand. One or two others cavorted at different points in the hall. Paul Crisp, his Monmouthshire Welshness to the fore, spoke Dylan Thomas's lines from the stage. Several people laughed.

"Can we get started," snapped Stella Aldridge, "or do we have to sit here listening to Paul projecting his Welsh manhood from the stage?"

"Have you no soul, Stella. This is the Welsh bard at his most lyrical."

"Where's Stephen?" asked a pale, thin girl sitting next to Stella, "I thought you were going to persuade him to join us."

"How?" replied Stella.

"How?

"How … do you persuade … the dead?" asked Stella, flicking her eyelids without moving her head.

A youth next to her laughed, used to Stella's style of conversation when taken by such a mood. There was a mumble and a scraping of chairs. The youth who was to direct the play, *Under Milk Wood*, glanced at Stella and pretended to make a note on his pad. Paul Crisp climbed down from the stage and sat next to Amanda, who he'd persuaded to join the drama group – or had she persuaded him? Paul wasn't sure.

"Is Stella Aldridge here?" called a voice from the door, "Telephone."

"Who is it?"

"Didn't say. It's a fella."

"It must be your Stephen, Stella," taunted a Welsh youth who was known to be eager for the part of First Voice, "the lyrical Stephen. You should have heard him reading Eliot's *Wasteland* in English. Quite a turn of phrase he has, and a classical cadence to the voice ..."

"Shut up."

"Now don't be ... you brood too much, Stella. You need to take life on the cusp ..."

"Shut up, you Welsh pig. You're wonderful with other people's verse, aren't you? Anyway, you mean 'at the flood'. It's Shakespeare – *Macbeth* ..."

Several of the men laughed, and Stella rose to the occasion.

"If that's Stephen Last, tell him the sun has set. Tell him there's a cold, bare mountainside waiting for him somewhere. Tell him to take a walk." Her voice caught the pitch of the roof and rolled across the hall. "Tell him ..." She paused, struggling to remember Lawrence's words. "Tell him ... there's a black rock blown bare of snow ... a vague shadow of something higher. Always higher ... on the crest where the wind will overpower him with a sleep-heavy iciness ... he'll come to a hollow basin of snow. It's the reflection of his soul."

A few students blushed, and all were silent. Paul moved in his seat. Amanda reached for his hand. There were quick glances around the circle, with scarcely a movement of the eyelids. All were listening. Someone clapped. Stella dropped her book and reached for her coat. She walked from the hall fumbling in the coat pocket for a cigarette, which she stuck between her lips.

"Isn't our Stella a great actress?" said one of the girls as the hall doors slithered together.

"It could be that she's actually upset," said Amanda.

"Yes, but isn't she a great actress?"

Simon Wiseman, who'd managed to keep a room in college during his second year, was listening to the Stones' *Little Red Rooster*. It had gone straight to number one, and deservedly so. It was the sort of thing that only the Stones could have done. Simon was a big fan of Keith Richards, in particular. He reckoned he was the best lead guitarist on the pop scene – on any scene for that matter. Keith Richards didn't believe in learning what he called "all that classical stuff". He reckoned it killed any talent stone dead – nice one, Keith – and Simon felt the same about the way they were obliged to study literature in college: all that literary analysis. Why not just read the book and enjoy it? Simon reckoned the Stones had soul – all right, rhythm and blues-fed soul, but soul. They weren't confined to Tin Pan Alley numbers. What they needed to do now was bring out an LP with some of their own compositions; they needed to shake up the hit parade with some rock 'n' soul. Simon laughed, stood and did his Mick Jagger impression, just as Mike Harrison tapped on his door and opened it at the same time.

"You at a loose end this weekend, Yogi?" he asked.

"Why? What have you got in mind?"

"Crispy and I are going up to my home town

– Liverpool. We wondered if you'd like to make a threesome."

"Rock on," said Simon, with a chortle.

Dick Crossman, Minister of Housing in the new Labour government, went up to town on the morning train. He was to attend a meeting of the Economic Development Committee. They were to discuss Concorde – the Anglo-French project to develop a supersonic aircraft. He knew that something dramatic had to be done; the economic crisis – Harold Wilson estimated that the Tories had left the country with an £800 million deficit – demanded that Concorde should be scrapped.

They were warned by the Attorney-General, however, that this would be tantamount to tearing up our treaty with the French who would be delighted to receive the compensation. While the Chancellor and the First Secretary – both economic ministers – were determined to cancel the project at any price, Douglas Jay, President of the Board of Trade, was appalled at the consequences of breaking a treaty. George Brown, Deputy Leader, seemed rather 'free and easy' in his attitude to the idea of cancellation, Dick thought, while Dick himself was inclined to a more moderate view. The Cabinet Committee seemed to be in an impossible position from which to negotiate a compromise.

Barbara Castle, now Minister of Overseas Development, was beginning to realise just how completely the civil service was in control of the government; something that had not occurred to her before she took office, despite nearly twenty years in politics.

Nothing had prepared her for the inter-departmental intrigues that obviously preceded every Cabinet meeting. She had expected to discuss policy decisions that were then passed on to her department to carry out. What she hadn't expected was that bargains had already been struck between the various civil service departments – bargains designed to protect the interests of each department – and that ministers would be briefed accordingly. It seemed to her that the civil service existed not to carry out government policy but rather to protect the interests of the civil service.

Why, why, she asked herself couldn't the Cabinet meet first, decide on policies in the interest of the country and pass these down to the civil service to carry out?

The three girls waved, silhouetted against the yellow light from the doorway of their hall of residence in St Catherine's College, Liverpool. Simon, Paul and Mike stood for a moment watching the darkness, Paul nudging the others with his elbow. Picking the girls up had been easy. Mike had simply drawn up to the kerb in his car and invited them to the Jacaranda Club that evening. The girls hadn't demurred.

The club had been packed with the youth of Liverpool, all keen on a good night out. The lads' inability to dance any particular sequence of steps had been masked by the fact that no one on the dance floor could move anyway; this had the additional, beneficial effect, of pushing you tightly up against your girl for the evening. Simon remembered that his – the pretty, reserved one – had worn what seemed to be a bra with rather a thick strap, as though she was armoured against assault. 'Chance would have been a fine thing,' he thought, echoing a phrase of his mother's.

"How about that, then, lads?" chuckled Mike as he re-started the car.

"I must admit I feel bloody marvellous," replied Paul.

"It's just a matter of knowing the places to pick them up," laughed Mike, "the St Catherine's girls always walk into town, on a Saturday afternoon, along the road where we found them. They can always say 'no', but they never do."

"I did enjoy it. No harm done," added Paul.

"I thought you and Amanda were getting serious, Crispy," said Simon.

"We'll have to get this one down in our little black book, Paul. Give it a couple of stars," said Mike, "We did well last year, Yogi. It was a bird a week, wasn't it Paul?"

"Yes, but I didn't have a regular bird at college then."

"Oh come on, you're too young to get serious. You've got a bird at home, haven't you Yogi?"

"Sort of," Simon replied with some hesitation.

"But you're at college now," Mike said, persuasively, "Remember the song we sang on the way back from the pub last year? 'And then while I'm away, I'll have sex every day, and I'll send all my spare ones to you …'" he sang to the tune of the Beatles *All My Loving*.

The other two joined him on abusing the chorus "All my spare ones, I will send to you-oo-oo All my spare ones; darling, I'll be true," with more bravado, realised Simon, than truth.

"Hah, hah, they were gagging for it, weren't they? It's

always the same with these all-women colleges," laughed Mike.

"Did you notice," Paul mused, "how they fumbled about on the pavement when we picked them up this evening? They were waiting to see where we were going to sit in the car."

"What do you mean?" Mike asked.

"After we chatted them up this afternoon, they decided who each of them was going for. I got the thin bird, you got the raunchy one and Simon got Miss Prim. The girls decided who got who."

"You're a philosopher, Crispy," cut in Simon, "all I know is we had a bloody good snog, and I feel all the better for it."

As Mike's car drifted into town, they passed two girls walking along the pavement, and Mike pulled up beside them.

"Cut it out, Mike," said Paul, realising what his friend was up to.

"Hey, want a lift?" called Mike.

"Knock it off," Paul insisted, laughing.

"Want a lift?" repeated Mike, "Where are you going? Can we help? We're going to town ... come on."

"Cut it out, Mike," laughed Simon.

"Come on – a lift to town. We're student teachers. Are you going our way? We're harmless."

The two young women hadn't broken step as the car cruised alongside them.

"We're harmless," Mike insisted.

"That's what we're afraid of," replied one of the girls, and they both laughed.

Mike wound up the window, turned the car from the

pavement and drove on. It had been a great evening and had ended on a chuckle.

Dick Crossman had found the civil service to be incredibly helpful in dealing with correspondence, which was so vast that no politician could hope to handle it satisfactorily and do their job properly.

On almost his first day in office it had been explained to him that there were three ways of dealing with correspondence: he could draft a personal reply in his own handwriting, his department could draft a 'personal' reply for him to sign or his department could draft an official reply. Seeing that Dick was still puzzled, his Private Secretary had gone on to say that he could simply put his in-tray into his out-tray, without leaving a mark on it, and then Dick would never have to see any of the correspondence again.

In this way, the department could ensure that routines were not disturbed and that the Minister's life was conducted correctly.

The threat of Southern Rhodesia making a unilateral declaration of independence hung over the new Labour government. Harold Wilson made it clear that such a move would be treasonable, and he'd bent over backwards to find a solution with Ian Smith, Southern Rhodesia's Prime Minister, sending British emissaries scurrying round to reach an acceptable compromise. Harold could see in his heart, however, that this was not achievable because a referendum had shown full support for Ian Smith in his own country.

Southern Rhodesia was on the verge of joining its

neighbour, South Africa, in becoming an international outcast: white supremacy was to dominate both countries, and civil war threatened as the black majority fought to gain what was seen to be theirs by right.

Miriam Davison had known her boyfriend since they were at school. She remembered him as he was on their first day – a rather snotty-nosed little boy who had snubbed her offer of a handkerchief; but their mothers knew each other and so, that night and every night for the next six years, they'd walked home together and, eventually, played together.

Just before puberty reared its initially ugly head, they'd played doctors and nurses in the outside toilet of her house. Her mother had discovered them – Patrick stripped to the waist and Miriam washing him with a flannel and a bowl of soapy water. Wise beyond all her daughter's understanding, at the time, Miriam's mother had stopped the game, but taken them indoors for squash and biscuits. She hadn't mentioned the game to Patrick's mother – at least as far as Miriam knew – but the incident took the children into her confidence, and a warmth had existed between them ever since.

Throughout secondary school – he at the boy's grammar and she at the girl's – they had met in town after school and travelled home together. They had gone through the religious phase together and been confirmed in the same church. When puberty came, at about the age of eleven for her and thirteen for him, he had kissed Miriam and stroked her breasts, but Patrick never groped. Without speaking, she'd made it clear that sex came after marriage, and he had never pressured her or tried to persuade her otherwise. In the circles in which they moved this was seen as 'respecting the woman', and was something expected of a man.

They had their own private language – the language of lovers – and used this when together; it was a blend of childlike talk and romantically-charged words. On holiday together one summer – camping in Italy, in fact – they'd discussed their futures, and used their special language to talk about the children they both desired.

"I've spoken to your father," said Patrick, one Saturday in Staffham after they'd watched *Goldfinger* and were sitting in a small, Italian restaurant by the river, "and asked for your hand in marriage."

He dropped to his knees beside her at the table – much to her embarrassment but accompanied by the applause of the waiters – and proposed, opening the box that contained the engagement ring as he did so.

"Will you marry me?"

"Yes," she replied, "I'd love to, but get up!"

Miriam guessed it must have taken him all summer to save up for the ring, which she knew would have cost about £40 – almost four weeks wages. He'd said nothing to her; the surprise had been total. He walked her home along the river path. She was snuggled under his right arm, which rested across her shoulder, and he held her left hand, ring uppermost, in his. Miriam felt she had never been happier or felt stronger.

Harold Wilson's Labour government set up the National Committee for Commonwealth Immigrants and offered Michael Ramsey, Archbishop of Canterbury, the chairmanship.

"We are faced, not just with a political difficulty but with a moral need," said Harold, attuned as he was to the need for action and pleased to think that his stroke was an imaginative one.

Harold was aware of the issues raised in places such as Smethwick and Wolverhampton by the 'nigger for a neighbour' campaign and of the rising tide of pamphlets exhibiting a distinctive racist tone; the term 'Black Country' had taken on a different meaning from its original, industrial one. It was essential to secure justice and fair treatment for all citizens irrespective of their colour, race or creed

Michael was appalled at the number of blatant racists who claimed to be so on Christian grounds. Two clergymen in Sussex had set up an organisation whose aim was to offer repatriation to West Indians by paying them to "go home"; such an organisation, however well intended, was bound to attract followers who simply disliked black people living in Britain.

Michael began to make speeches, gathering both support and recrimination from all colours, creeds and races as he did so. It was essential not only to persuade reluctant whites to welcome a multiracial society but to prevent blacks, disillusioned with the attempts of the government to secure them equality, from disappearing into black power organisations.

Des could see that Jenny Pryce, who had a sweet and gentle voice, was reluctant to sing at the folk event he'd arranged. The song he'd chosen for her was *The Water is Wide* – a sad lament of faithless love – but she was nervous, and he knew the reason was Stella. Marguerite had told him.

"She puts you off, Des," answered Jenny, in response to his question, "Once she's finished her song she sits and stares, afraid you'll outshine her. It'd be all right if she'd clear off to the back of the room, but you can feel her watching you with those hard eyes of hers."

"OK, she's a bitch, but if I promise to keep her to the back of the room, will you sing? You won't have to look at her face. John will play for you and I'll occupy Stella elsewhere."

Jenny laughed up at him in that flirtatious way of hers.

"I bet you will," she said, as he smiled that smile, "All right, I'll sing, but only for you."

Students crowded the Red Room as Des entered with Jenny. She looked round and shivered with nervousness. Stella came up to them, immediately.

"Where have you been, Des? We're all waiting," she snapped, ignoring Jenny, who wanted to crawl back into her shell.

"I had something to sort out," replied Des.

Streaks of cigarette smoke curled to the ceiling. Seats were full. Student Union officials ran for more. Some students lolled on the floor, while others sat on windowsills.

"I needed to run it through, Des," insisted Stella, "I can't sing it now."

"Right, then scrap it."

"What? There's no need to be like that, Des. If you'd rehearsed me, I wouldn't have minded. Jenny …"

"I haven't been rehearsing with Jenny," he replied, turning away from Stella and addressing Cliff Jenkins, who stood plucking his banjo, "Are you right, Cliff? Let's go."

With Des accompanying him on guitar, Cliff burst into *Foggy Mountain Breakdown* and the evening was off to a flying start.

Back in their digs, Des was in a good mood; the evening had been a great success. Stella had, eventually, sung the Lorna Campbell number, *The Sun is Burning in the Sky*, and followed it, later in the evening, with *La Vie D'amour*. Des had kept her out of the way for Jenny's songs which included the Joan Baez number, *Once I had a Sweetheart*. The evening had also included a number of songs from Des's own stomping ground in the north-east – *Down in the Coalmine*. A lad from Norfolk had sung *The Lincolnshire Poacher* and some Londoners, led by Simon Wiseman, insisted on including *Down at the Old Bull and Bush*, although Des had his doubts as to whether it really fitted the folk tradition.

After he had talked for a while, Des noticed Stephen's quietness and asked about Stella, but found Stephen hard work. He said little and appeared to be indifferent. Des hoped he'd shout it from the hills if something like it happened to him, but admired Stephen's rectitude at the same time. 'He has rigorous self-control. Everything is strapped in. At the moment, I feel like an island in the sea of life, a centre of calm in the pent-up, stretched-out, hung-down, strung-up and just plain twisted. I don't know why – there's a storm brewing for me, and it'll be coming in on two fronts.'

"You've not had much experience with women, have you?"

"No," replied Stephen, "At the tech college, we tended to go about in groups. Apart from the girl I told you about

– and I was only in my early teens at that time – there's been no one."

"It puzzles some of the lads, you know."

"In what way?"

"Well, let's put it like this. We spent a lot of time together in the first year and then shared these digs. I reckon some of them thought you might be queer."

"But not you," laughed Stephen.

"Well, they knew I had Elizabeth at home."

"I don't want people thinking badly of you, Des. I assume you're happy that I'm not queer. You weren't expecting to keep your back to the wall, were you?"

Des roared with laughter. He admired the directness of Stephen's humour.

"No, I didn't have any worries in that direction, but it does puzzle me that you haven't had a woman – except Stella," he tempted.

"I went to an art exhibition with Stella. That's all."

"But she hoped for more?"

"I don't think so. She was just narked that I wasn't man enough to knock up her friends at three o'clock in the morning."

"It was more than that, Stephen. Like most of them, she's looking for a bloke."

"That wasn't the agreement."

"She's an attractive bird, and I bet she'd go like the clappers."

"Once you get involved with a woman you lose your freedom, Des – unless ... unless you can love them and leave them ... and I couldn't do that. I'm not the sort of bloke who'd be any good at casual relationships. Once I knew I loved a woman, the sexual side – which is what we're really talking about – would be a spiritual journey lasting a lifetime."

"You've been reading too much D H Lawrence. It isn't like that at all, and most – if not all – women know it. Sex for them is a means to an end. Any bloke who's had any experience of women soon learns that truth. They use it, and that's why some of the men round here behave as they do. Take it up while it's on offer."

"You don't believe that once you're sexually involved with a woman that you've made a commitment?"

"I wouldn't say that exactly, but you need to be realistic about these things."

'One cannot be a true Muslim unless one wishes for his brother what he wishes for himself. Do you really feel that all white men are devils?'

Working with whites as well as blacks since returning from his Hajj, Malcolm X – now Al Hajj Malik al Shabbazz – had travelled widely and met eleven heads of state across the world. He had gathered support for an appeal to the United Nations; he claimed that the United States had violated the human rights of African-Americans.

He had made many enemies among his old friends in the Nation of Islam and among militant groups who resented Malcolm's willingness to work with whites. The word on the streets of Harlem was that Malcolm had been marked for death.

CHAPTER 16

Christmas Spirit

"You're engaged. Ooh, let's see the ring, Miriam," cried Sheila Pratt, "Oh I can't ever see myself being engaged."

"You're a bit young, aren't you, to commit yourself to one man," teased Joan Whiting, "there are plenty of fish in the sea, you know."

"You try catching one," remarked Kate Walsh, "I envy you, Miriam – nicely, of course, but I'd love to feel that there was one man – just one man – who cared more for me than anyone else in the world."

"Dreamer!"

"Don't be cynical, Joan. My dad and mum were young when they married, and they're still in love."

"How do you know?"

"Stop it, stop it. Let's be happy for Miriam," pleaded Sheila.

They were getting ready for the Christmas dance at Knutton Gardens, and it was the first time their off-duties had coincided since Miriam's engagement. Sheila was happy for Miriam in an unworldly way. She didn't ever expect to attract a man for long and accepted that this was to be her lot in life; accepting this notion about herself left no purpose in envy, and so jealousy was not part of her make-up.

At Knutton Gardens, where she knew she'd at least dance with her friends, Sheila enjoyed the company of the young men but expected to be the last one they'd ask to dance. They tended to drift towards the group of men they'd met before, and one of them had attracted her: the one called Stephen, who also seemed shy. They hadn't spoken much – not privately – but Kate, noticing her friend's interest, nudged her towards Stephen on that particular night.

There was something old about him, Sheila thought: he listened, rather like her granddad listened, but didn't say much. There was something about him that said "I'm not special", and this attracted Sheila.

"You're very easy to talk to," she said, "I usually feel that if I open my mouth, I'll say the wrong thing."

"It's the way we were brought up," he reassured her, "my father always said that 'little children should be seen and not heard'".

"Did he mean it?"

"It made no difference whether he did or not. I believed it, and the belief lingers on."

"Even if you've got something interesting to say?" she asked, pursuing the point.

"Especially if I've got something interesting to say because then the fear that no one will listen is even more intense."

"But you're very intelligent, aren't you?" Sheila responded, "You've read a lot."

"I was a late reader, but once I learned I never stopped. I used to walk across town to school reading a book as I went."

"I never went to grammar school. I failed the 11+," Sheila confided, feeling safe with this man.

"Neither did I," he replied.

"You never went to grammar school?"

"No … There's no need to feel ashamed."

"Well I am."

"I passed the IQ tests in the November, "continued Stephen, "and then failed the attainment tests in the February. So my primary school had a pupil bright enough to go to grammar school but who'd failed to attain the necessary standards. Whose fault was that – mine or the schools? Obviously, it was the school's fault – unless you're going to dismiss me as lazy, which I wasn't."

Sheila realised she'd touched a sore point and was about to retreat when Stephen continued in a quiet voice:

"Besides, where I came from – Ipswich in Suffolk – only 12% of children went to grammar school, even if 25% would have benefitted from a grammar school education. In places like Monmouthshire, there were grammar school places for 40% of children, even if only 25% were likely to benefit from a grammar school education."

"So it wasn't fair?"

"More than that – it's questionable as to whether all children are ready to be selected at 11. The result is that people like you and me are cut off from learning a foreign language or studying science properly forever … Besides you can be sure that an inordinate proportion of the available money goes to the grammar schools and the secondary schools are left under-funded."

"I never knew that …"

"Neither did I until a lecturer at the training college was arguing the case for comprehensive schools. He explained all that to us."

"I always felt … stupid."

"There's no need, Sheila. The stupidity lies in the waste of talent, in the laps of those who design and perpetuate the 11+ system. The times they are a changin'. Watch the papers."

Sheila had never felt so relieved in her life. The burden of ignorance and of feeling so inadequate dropped from her shoulders like a heavy rucksack at the end of a long walk.

"Thank you," she said, looking Stephen in the face.

"Glad to be of service," he laughed.

At that moment, Mike Harrison lurched over, the worse for drink.

"You're not talking shop again, are you Last?" he joked, "Don't you know how to treat a girl? Fancy a dance, sweetheart."

Sheila smiled at Stephen, feeling reluctant to leave, but Mike tugged her to her feet.

"Enjoy yourself," laughed Stephen, disappointed, "Don't breathe on the lady, Mike. She might pass out."

It wasn't the birth that had troubled Heather; it was bringing the baby back to their grotty flat.

The birth had been easy enough, considering everything she'd expected from conversations with girlfriends in the playground. There'd been a lot of probing she could have done without and she'd heard herself swear at least once and several voices insisting that she "bear down" and "remember her exercises". The nurse had offered her gas and air, but Heather had said "no" without the "thanks", unsure as to why she'd refused. When her labour had reached a certain stage, bearing down had been painful beyond anything she'd imagined, but then it had dispersed suddenly and the baby – a boy – was there in her arms, as clean as a whistle and with Barry's broad shoulders. She'd cried at that moment, with relief and joy and asked to see "her husband" who was waiting in the corridor. It seemed archaic that he couldn't have been with her, but there you are, regulations are regulations and, as the nurse assured her, "men only get in the way". She'd looked at Barry as he was looking at the baby, and all the difficulties that had surrounded them until that moment seemed to vanish in the fog. Somehow the baby – that little, enormous presence – focussed her mind in a way that nothing else could have done.

No, it was the flat – that horrible little grotty shithole that took up nearly half of Barry's salary every month – which depressed Heather. Looking round, with the baby – they were going to call him Charles because they both liked the shortened version 'Chas' – asleep in his very second-hand cot, Heather wondered how they were ever going to invite friends "back home" to admire the little treasure, and he was a little treasure.

Heather never got tired of looking at his tiny hands or feeling them curl around her fingers. Breast feeding hadn't been recommended, and so he'd gone straight on to Carnation milk from a bottle. Heather felt cheated at that decision, which seemed to have been taken from her; she'd rather liked the idea of the little boy suckling on her nipples – but the doctor and nurses knew best, or did they? Wasn't that why she'd gone into nursing – to be a bloody nuisance and challenge accepted practice? But at least it meant that Barry could be involved, and Barry had been very good. Despite having to get up for work next day, he had covered the middle of the night feed from the moment – ten days after the birth – they'd brought Chas home.

No, it was that bloody flat that got on her nerves, and the way the landlord was always round for his rent the moment it became due, as though they'd ever been behind with their payments.

When she and Barry walked the baby in the extremely second, or even third, hand pram, her husband was always proud to be seen pushing it. Once or twice, she'd pushed Chas round to the school to meet her husband when he came out of work, and the other staff had gathered round – the women cooing and aahing, the men giving Barry knowing nudges as though he'd done something extremely clever. Barry's staff obviously saw them as a married couple, which they were: married young, of course, which is always a bit suspect, but respectably married nonetheless. They didn't seem to view her as "the kind of girl who, you know, dropped her knickers at the drop of a hat", and she wasn't. Sex, anyway, had disappeared from their relationship at least for a while, and that was a relief: if it wasn't there, they couldn't be looked down for enjoying it, could they?

No, it was the flat that got on her nerves. They were going to have to do something about where they lived. Somehow, with Christmas coming up the place seemed worse than ever. Christmas was a family time, wasn't it?

Des Smith held Elizabeth's letter in his hand, reading as he walked.

'... *and don't worry about the money, Des. You never have before. As long as I get you back for Christmas, I don't mind not going anywhere. I never have. Running after dance tickets isn't in my line. It will be a nice Christmas – just you and me. Oh, Des, I can hardly wait. The last few days always seem so long. I will meet you on the station and then we'll be together. See you soon, then ..."*

Des sighed. It wasn't the money; it was going back and having to meet her again.

The coming of a Labour government had brought an early Christmas present to those murderers facing the death penalty: their sentence would be commuted to one of life imprisonment. The House of Commons had voted and two thirds of its MPs had supported the motion that the gallows be abolished. The new legislation was likely to be supported by the House of Lords, but Michael Ramsey knew that the fight for total abolition was by no means over: there were those who felt that certain caveats, such as the killing of a police officer or killing for a second time, should apply. Hanging, as the ultimate punishment, was merely shelved for a trial period.

Stephen's father was horrified at the idea of abolition.

"They've devalued the seriousness of murder," he said, "If you kill someone, you deserve to die. You wait and see. They'll be shooting people as a matter of course when they do a robbery, now."

Stephen didn't argue; it wasn't worth it.

"Those buggers aren't going to spend their lives in prison. They'll be out on parole before you know it, free to kill again. I don't know what the world's coming to. We fight a war to keep our families free, and the next thing we know is we're living next door to a murderer."

Stephen smiled as he rose from the settee to leave. He'd

secured a job "on the Post" for a third Christmas and was thoroughly enjoying it. Working inside the sorting office was tedious but delivering the post outside on the streets was a delight. He usually timed it so that he picked up a last round just before 5 o'clock; this gave him overtime and another area of the town to visit. He loved the total feel of Christmas – the lights, the bustle, the steamed-up windows, the cards through the letter box – and he loved the privilege of jumping on and off the trolley buses with impunity. Conductors never bothered to ask for your card, after a while; the post bag, bulging with cards, was proof enough of your entitlement to ride free of charge.

Kate Walsh hadn't realised just how irregular things were on the wards at Christmas. Miriam had relayed her feelings of awe last year when the ward choir had sung for the old lady, but this hadn't prepared Kate for the mayhem of celebration. Christmas trees had been donated by local businesses, and the wards were decorated with balloons, tinsel and – inevitably – mistletoe in the doorways; even the ward windows were painted to give the effect of snow caught on the frames. Greetings cards were strung above the patients' lockers, which were decorated with holly and ivy.

Visitors were asked to bring presents in by Christmas Eve and these were distributed on Christmas morning by a consultant dressed as Father Christmas and paraded around the wards on a wheelchair as a sledge.

"You must have some mistletoe on your cap, Nurse Walsh," one of the young doctors had said before kissing her firmly on the mouth, "I can't be sure of catching you in a doorway."

Over a year into her training, Kate felt that she was, at last, growing up, becoming a woman, establishing her place in the world. She and Miriam had gone to the pictures on the previous night and the *Pathe News* man had been full of it: the Variety Club, with the likes of Sid James (as Father Christmas), Charley Drake and Stanley Baker distributing presents to "underprivileged children in homes and hospitals". He'd talked of "unmistakeably proclaiming the Christmas message" and "emptying our pockets", of "being free to make merry and having the money to do it", of "showing our best side" and of "the Christmas spirit in the Free World" as though that, itself, was an actual place.

1965

Chapter 17

The Magic Circle

"We needed and bastard, and we got one," said Des, emphatically, talking of Winston Churchill, who had died on January 24th.

Stephen Last looked at his friend, and the expression on his face was one of shock and dismay. His father and uncles had served in the forces during the war and, while they had never talked much about what happened, none had shown any disrespect to Churchill. If they had any reservations, they kept quiet. Stephen had been brought up, throughout his school years, to see Churchill as the saviour of the nation. The man had been an inspirational leader throughout the war years and had anticipated the Nazi threat while others had trusted Hitler and even considered collaboration. More than any other human being, Churchill had been responsible for saving the world from German and Japanese domination.

"I don't think you can dismiss him quite as easily as that, Des."

"You're sentimental about the man because of his public image," replied Des, "He was one of the moneyed classes, steeped in privilege like the rest. During what they call his 'wilderness years' he sat around painting and writing. He didn't have to work. People like him – and, to

an extent, you and me – coast along on the backs of the
workers, especially people like coal miners. Has Churchill
or any of his class ever spent the best part of their working
day bent double while they hacked at a coal face?
Remember what Orwell had to say – 'it is only because
miners sweat their guts out that superior persons can
remain superior'. It was only because tens of thousands of
ordinary soldiers were prepared to have their bollocks
shot away that we can wax lyrical about the likes of
Churchill."

"That may be the case," replied Stephen, "but the
country needed leadership and he gave it. You get nowhere
without principled leadership."

"Stephen – what we need is principled socialist
leadership. The more we wax sentimental about the likes
of Churchill, the less we're likely to become a real
democracy. Churchill, Macmillan, Douglas-Home –
they're all of a class. They're toffs, and toffs have ruled
this country for centuries. They consider themselves to be
the rightful rulers, and they arrange everything to suit
their own convenience and feather their own nests and the
nests of their kind. Get focussed on what matters.
Churchill is a distraction – a diversion on the road to a
socialist state."

Kate Walsh stared, open-mouthed, at the consultant as he
balled-out patient after patient. She'd met tension before
– working in a hospital where life and death was a real
issue and so much depended on your care for the patients
this was inevitable – but never outright rudeness. What
seemed to make it worse was that the man was clearly
enjoying himself.

"Sit down, woman," he bawled at one lady who'd come about a problem she had with her throat, "and put that handbag out of the way. How the hell can I examine you if there's a left luggage compartment between us? Now, what's the problem?"

"I'm finding that ... that I'm ... snuffling rather at night and ..."

"You mean you're snoring? Why not say so? And it's getting on your husband's bloody nerves, and he's told you to sort it out? Why not say so? How old are you?"

"Fifty ..."

"Well," he snapped, before the lady could reply, "Don't be shy. You're obviously no spring chicken," he added with a laugh.

"Fifty four," she almost snapped.

"Well, what do you expect at your age? Everything moves south after you reach forty, and you've been moving south for over a decade now – your breasts, your belly, your bottom and your throat muscles. They're getting slack like everything else about you. Tell your husband that if he wants a woman who doesn't snore to find himself a younger model, and to stop wasting my time. Good morning."

The woman looked at Kate, who exchanged glances with the regular staff nurse and smiled sheepishly. The consultant caught Kate's eye as she did so, and he smiled; it was obvious to her that he thought he was being funny – even reassuring, perhaps.

"Buck up, Nurse. Show the old lady out and bring in the next patient," he chortled, giving her a wink.

The next patient was a boy of about eleven, Kate surmised, whose mother thought he was going deaf.

"All boys go deaf when they don't want to hear something," roared the consultant. Now, you clear off to the waiting room while I talk to your son."

The woman hesitated only for a moment, glanced at the nurses to assure herself that somebody other than the consultant would be in the room with her son and walked away without a murmur.

"Now, let's look in your earhole, son, and see what's up. Didn't you want to help with the washing-up or something, eh? Telling your mother you were deaf! Boys of your age don't go deaf," he continued, inserting his otoscope into the boy's ear, "My God, you've enough muck in there to grow a field of cabbages. Nurse, take the lad next door and ask the registrar to syringe his lugholes out."

"Next," he yelled, scribbling a few notes on the medical record, as the boy left, laughing.

When the out-patients' clinic was wound up for that morning, the consultant caught Kate watching him and said:

"You don't approve of me, do you?"

"I don't see the need to shout at patients," replied Kate, firmly, "They come here concerned about their health and it's our job to help them."

"It's our job, Nurse, to reassure them, to convince them we know what we're doing, even when we don't. The voice of authority is always assertive. If you talk loudly enough, you must know what you're doing."

"I don't see the need for rudeness ..." Kate began.

"Patients expect it, Nurse. They enjoy a little rough humour. The lad left laughing, didn't he? Tell it as it is. Give it to them straight, and then the patients know where they are ... By the way, you did well this morning: very calm and efficient. Are you in your second year of training?"

"Yes."

"Think about ENT work when you're qualified, Nurse Walsh. We select our nurses very carefully for the ENT ward and clinic. We can't have fools around here. You need to know what you're doing," he concluded as he left, his coat flapping in the breeze from the abruptly-opened door.

'At least,' thought Kate, 'he knew my name.'

Barbara Castle was finding that she, being a woman minister, posed problems for the civil service. Clearly, a number of those who ran her department found it difficult to cope with a woman. There was one senior civil servant who felt it was his role to decide which of her instructions should be passed on to the officials concerned. This irritated her but she found it difficult, despite the convention whereby a minister is allowed to choose their close staff, to have him removed.

However, there was always a lighter side to the civil servant's predicament, and this came when she required a ladies' lavatory: there wasn't one. It appeared that such an eventuality had never raised its head. The problem was solved by requisitioning a gentlemen's toilet – thereby inconveniencing those who had used it previously. Barbara found herself washing her hands beside the urinals and smiling. 'It would have been much easier for everyone,' she thought, 'if we'd lost the election and things could have carried on as normal. There's no place, yet, for women in politics.'

"You don't see much of Paul these days, do you Mike?" asked Jenny Pryce, in that mildly waspish voice she adopted when teasing a man.

She knew full well that Paul had been hooked, very effectively, by a first year student called Amanda Harrelson. Jenny had watched as Amanda's grip tightened on Paul. As she put it to Marguerite Bannister:

"I've watched her sharpening her claws. Paul won't be playing the field for much longer."

"Don't be bitchy, Jenny," remonstrated Marguerite.

"I'm not. I'm just envious. Even those falsies I wore when we came back in September didn't entice anyone."

"They looked good, though. The trouble with you is you flirt with everyone. None of the men quite know where they are."

Jenny had made no reply. She enjoyed flirting, it was true. If you liked that kind of thing, you couldn't help it. She looked up at Mike, who she didn't fancy.

"Couldn't you find two together, Mike?"

He laughed, ignored her and wandered off to the bar where he clumped down his empty glass. There were few students in the pub, but a welcoming fire blazed in the grate, where Stella Aldridge and a friend sat, occasionally drawing back from the heat.

Jenny listened to the faint but insistent chords coming from Des's guitar as he tuned-up. She saw Susan chatting to Mike, and wondered how her relationship with Des was progressing. Susan had gone through the usual ploy of inviting friends to tea in her room in H block, and Jenny noticed that Des had stayed on. She'd quite fancied Des herself, but he hadn't responded to her flirting. Perhaps Marguerite was right: perhaps she needed to focus on just one bloke, but she couldn't do that – not just yet.

Stella's voice began to sing, and Des – quick to catch the moment to move the evening on – picked a few chords and began to accompany her. 'Plaintive,' thought Jenny, 'like a crying cat … the bitch! The bitch is singing my song.' It was true.

> *"If I were a tiny sparrow, and I had wings, and I could fly,*
> *I'd fly right back to my false love and all he asked I would deny …"*

Des realised, too, but Stella's voice was powerful, and well-capable of holding a line without the music. Des had no choice but to play on.

Other students wandered in, shivering, breathing steel from the cold night into the warm air. Girls huddled under the arms of the men. The blood-gouted face of the landlord peered over the bar, pulling pints. Unsmiling, he shoved the drawer back into the till. The Red Lion had taken on a different tone since the new boy – the north-easterner from Middlesbrough – had started to play from time to time. The heavy, amplified rock of Pete Campbell had been replaced with a gentler, more folksy, sound. People could hear themselves talk; and locals – just a few – had returned to the pub.

The door slammed-to in the wind and Stephen Last walked in with Simon Wiseman.

"Two pints of bitter, please,' he said to the landlord.

"At the beginning of term, Last, you mean bugger. I'll have a vodka and lime, as you're paying," Simon riposted with his usual chortle.

Stephen grinned at his friend; they were back after Christmas, and the feeling of camaraderie was great. Simon took the drink from Stephen's hand and sauntered over to the fireplace.

"Very nice, Stella," he said, encouragingly, "We could hear you halfway up the road."

She smiled. A compliment from Simon was OK, but not as important as if it had come from Des, and he was annoyed that she'd commandeered Jenny's song.

"Can you get me some fags, Stephen," Simon called across to the bar.

"Fags?"

"*Consulate*."

Simon smoked *Consulate* – the cool smoke with the taste of menthol. Stephen laughed at his friend who liked to be up-to-date. You couldn't take offence at Simon; it wasn't possible. Stephen glanced over his shoulder. Several of the women were watching him, aware of what was considered his faux pas with Stella, and he blushed. Keeping his eyes on the bar, and avoiding the landlord's glance, Stephen paid for the drinks and cigarettes and dug his nails into his palms. The slight pain was enough to distract him and hide his embarrassment before he turned.

As Stephen did so, Des handed his guitar to Marguerite and walked over to his friend. He didn't see why his room-mate should be embarrassed by the likes of Stella Aldridge.

"If you're buying a round, Last, I'll have a pint too," he laughed, "After all, we do share digs."

Pints in hand they made their way to the group settling around the fire.

"There's a song we used to sing in school," Stephen suggested, "It's Welsh, originally, I think …"

"You did folk singing in school?" Des queried.

"Yes. The head used to play the tunes on the piano, of course – I can't imagine Mr Baldry playing the guitar – but all of us enjoyed the singing. It had a nice tune – the one I'm talking about. It would suit your voice, Jenny, if you happen to know the song."

"What's the tune?" asked Des, "And what's it called."

"The Ash Grove – yes, I know, it lacks your northern grit but it's a nice song."

"I know it," said Jenny, "We sang it, too."

"How's the tune go?"

Stephen began, without much confidence, to hum the melody he recalled but could not sing. Within a few bars, another student, Maurice, who was from Ireland, had drawn an harmonica from his pocket and taken over the tune. Des captured it and was soon accompanying on the guitar. Stephen could only admire their skill. Jenny picked up the words she remembered from her schooldays. 'It was a magical moment,' thought Stephen, as he listened, 'just magical. This is what being away from home at college is all about.'

Dick Crossman, Minister of Housing, sat on the front bench, squashed between Barbara Castle and Tony Crosland, and sighed. The House was packed and Winston Churchill's old seat was left vacant. The tributes to Churchill were proceeding endlessly, led by the party leaders – Harold Wilson, Alec Douglas-Home and Jo Grimond. Dick considered that enough tributes had already been paid and found the process lugubrious. He dozed off into a quiet slumber. Even Harold's comment "There is a stillness and in that stillness each has his memories" failed to stir him.

Nelson Mandela stood up and stretched the pain from his back. It had been nearly a month since they'd been brought to the lime quarry, where the work was far more strenuous than they'd experienced in the courtyard. No explanation had been given as to why the political prisoners had been moved to work elsewhere, but Nelson considered it to be just another means by which the authorities put them in their place, reminding Nelson and his colleagues that they were no different from normal prisoners and must pay for their crimes. The prison officers were asserting discipline.

The first day they'd fallen asleep in their cells straight after supper at 4.30. Mining lime wasn't easy. The lime quarry was an enormous, white crater. With a pick and shovel, the prisoners had to break open the rock containing the lime and then shovel it out.

If, as Nelson suspected, it was an attempt to crush the prisoner's spirits, then the authorities had failed. Despite their bleeding hands, the prisoners were invigorated by being in the open air with the sun on their backs and the sea wind on their faces. It was good to use all one's muscles, to watch the birds flying overhead and see springboks grazing in the distance.

Kate Walsh felt exhilarated despite her run-in with the "coarse consultant", as she explained the man's bad manners to her friends. She'd borrowed a deposit from her dad and secured the rest of the money on hire purchase to buy a Honda 50, which she now rode home.

'Home' – well more like home than the Nurses Home had been! She, Joan, Sheila and a new student nurse they'd met called Christine had taken a flat together. It was only £6 a week, which meant that each of them only had to find £1 50 shillings. It meant freedom. Freedom from what, or for what, Kate wasn't sure, but it meant freedom. Miriam had declined the invitation to come with them, and Kate thought that this decision had something to do with Miriam being engaged and not eager to embrace the new found freedom!

The flat was the ground floor of a large house with bay windows in what must once have been a posh area of Staffham. It had stained glass in the front door. Kate thought it must have been Victorian, but she didn't know anything about architecture and so wasn't sure.

There were only two bedrooms, but they were big ones. Kate shared with Joan because she was more acute in dealing with Joan's spiky nature, and Sheila and the new girl shared the other room. They also had a living room, which was huge and lit only by a gas fire. The ceiling was high with fancy plasterwork and a picture rail that had clearly been designed for large pictures because the ones they had disappeared in the space on the wall. The kitchen, which was also big, opened onto a back garden.

They'd decided to share expenses and take turns in cooking the meals they had together, but they ate mostly at the hospital. Having done domestic science at school, they could all cook, more or less, and 'at-home' nights were proving to be fun.

'It was good,' thought Kate, 'to be independent and earning some money.'

Joan had surprised her when they first made arrangements about sharing the house together; she talked about "coming to an agreement about visitors". Kate listened, open-mouthed, as her friend discussed the need to "accommodate boyfriends".

"You don't mean you'd invite a boy into the bedroom?" she asked, bewildered.

"What choices have we? You can't invite one into the living room – not if you want a bit of privacy – and that only leaves the bedroom."

"But he might get the wrong idea."

"… or the right one," laughed Joan, "Where did you 'entertain' boyfriends when you lived at home?"

"I didn't have any, really … but if a lad from school came round we sat in the front room … Have you someone in mind, then, Joan?"

"There's someone at the riding stables I might be interested in. It depends."

"On what?"

"On whether he's got anything about him when it comes down to it. Some of these boys who come from what mummy calls the 'county set' can be rather wet."

Listening to her friend, Kate realised just how far apart were their worlds, despite both of them being in the same profession. She had been only vaguely aware that Joan went riding (something she'd only dreamed about), wasn't sure who the 'county set' were and had never before heard anyone called their mother "mummy". Unable to resist the temptation, although she felt it would make her sound silly, she asked:

"You don't mean you'd go the whole way?"

"I'd have to be sure of him first," replied Joan, "He wouldn't be getting something for nothing, but … I might … if he was worth it and I trusted him."

'Freedom,' thought Kate, 'what ... enticements do you hold?'

Alec Douglas-Home was not as downcast as he might have been, seeing that his Party had lost the General Election in October. The fact remained that the Party was, he felt, regaining confidence, and its reputation was on the rise. There was also a very good chance that the Socialist Government, with its very small majority, might be thrown out

There were, as one might expect, some reservations. One of these concerned the way he had been chosen as leader. This had come about through what was termed the 'Magic Circle'. They were experienced Conservative Parliamentarians who knew 'the form of every runner in the field' and could act quickly and decisively in electing a new leader. However, some members of the Party felt that 'candidates favourable to the establishment' might have an edge over someone who had proved rebellious, or that the 'Magic Circle' might even rig the results. Alec had, therefore, decided to initiate a new system for electing the Party leader.

Other discontents were also reverberating through some sections of the party: some of the younger Conservatives were restless. They were unhappy with his decision to support the Opposition where their policies were in the national interest and only oppose them when they were not. This was felt to be weak if not actually wet. They desired what was termed a 'more dynamic leadership'.

This popular view was gaining ground, and Alec wondered whether it was time for him to consider handing over to a successor.

Chapter 18

'Out of our heads'

Martin Luther King had, he felt, been on the mountaintop long enough. It was time to go back down to the valley where his people didn't have jobs and were starving and couldn't vote themselves a better, fairer life. Selma, Alabama, was calling to him.

It was less than two months since he had received the Nobel Peace Prize in Oslo. He knew electoral reforms were not being implemented. Sixty per cent of Alabama's population was black, but less than one in every hundred had dared to add their names to the electoral register. Officials used every excuse to bar them from their democratic rights: tests designed to make them fail and prove themselves ineligible, tricks, threats and bureaucracy. One man had been refuse because he failed to cross a 't' on his registration form!

"Our cry is a simple one," he stormed from Browns Chapel Church, "Give us the ballot! We're not on our knees begging for the ballot. We are demanding the ballot! If Negroes could vote, our children would not be crippled by segregated schools and there would be no oppressive poverty."

When they marched on the courthouse, Sheriff Jim

Clark was waiting for them. He knew the law: no more than twenty people could march together at a time.

"I've been keeping blacks in their place for years," he boasted, "and I don't aim to stop now."

That night, Martin and several hundred protesters found themselves behind bars in a Southern jail.

Stella Aldridge took the razor blade from her toilet bag and placed it on the window ledge. Water splashed and steamed into the bath. She looked at the door, and then sat on the edge of the bath, watching the swirling heat, her legs tensed against the side, her toes pointing to the floor. Stella closed her eyes very slowly, and breathed deeply. 'So warm ... the last time, so gentle ... watching it drain slowly into the water. Gradually sleeping ... peaceful ...' She opened her eyes, reached for the toilet bag and took out the flannel, dropping it into the water. She leaned towards the cold tap, and began to whirl the water with her hand. 'Deep and warm.'

Stella stood, stretched to the taps and turned them off. She listened to the voices in the showers, and looked at the door again before sliding the housecoat from her shoulders. Through the window she could see the moon. 'The cold moon shining from the darkness of the sky,' she thought, laughing to herself. She looked down into the gently steaming water, and then at her naked body. Her eyes were still and her shoulders slumped. Outside the door, she could hear giggling.

Stella stepped over the edge of the bath and lowered herself into the water. She stretched out, fully, watching the water lap around her breasts, shoulders and feet. When the water receded with her breathing, it left her breasts chalky-white.

She reached for the blade, sliding it from the ledge and holding it under the water. She looked at her left wrist as though it belonged to another person, leaned over slightly and pushed the blade into her vein. She dropped the blade and sank back in the warm bath. Misty-red, the blood flowed slowly and drifted. Stella's eyes watched the meandering blood for a while and then closed.

The Rolling Stones were doing well: Keith had just bought a 2.4 Jaguar and they'd released *The Last Time*. Judging by the fan's reaction, it wouldn't be long before it was rocketing up the charts. There were good feelings, too, about the way things were going. Some had said Keith was just a 'hit and miss guitarist' but it was now clear that there was talent there, and that he'd 'built up an instinctive feel for what was right or wrong'.

He didn't believe in marriage, he'd said, and didn't think about the future. He thought today was what counted. He liked his cars well-upholstered and they had to have a record player. He and Mick had amassed one of the biggest R & B collections ever, but he acknowledged that American R & B artists – who were one of their biggest influences – didn't do well in Britain.

"No, they don't make it big over here," he said, "I reckon there's three reasons why they don't click with the British teenager fans. One, they're old. Two, they're black. Three, they're ugly. This image bit is very important – though I must say it doesn't matter to us. But the Americans have helped get things going over here ... their influence is big if their popularity isn't."

Mike Harrison laughed and slid across the pathway. Des

tried to grip his flailing arms, supporting him as well as he could. Stephen Last propped up Simon in the same way, while Simon chortled in his ear. His drunken friend hung and swayed from Stephen's neck. Mike fell to the ground, overcome with the beer he'd consumed at The Red Lion.

"If you can get this idiot off my neck, Des, I'll help you to pick Mike up."

As Des tried to disentangle the two of them, Simon gave vent to a steam of alliteration:

"Let go Smith – you ponce. You're a ... prick, a poof, a pontificated pansy, a pervert, a prostitute, a procurer, a pimp, a pixillated purveyor of porn ... a pander, a ..."

"No one's perfect," replied Des, twisting Simon's arm partway up his back as he eased him from Stephen's shoulder and sat him on the ground.

Somehow, Stephen and Des managed to lift Mike onto his feet and found themselves supporting different burdens on their way back to the college: Simon was now chortling in Des's ear as Mike expressed his appreciation to Stephen.

"You're a wonderful fellow, Last ... you realise that, don't you? You've a heart of ... a heart of ... Consideration ... Here, you put your arm round me. You ... you're good friend ... Here ... you have a rest on Michael's shoulder."

As they approached the residential blocks, Simon and Mike whistling at every girl who passed, the quartet met several couples and groups who had arrived on the last bus from Staffham; among them were Paul and Amanda. Mike staggered towards Paul, who grinned with his mouth closed.

"Paul, me old mate, how are yer?" he enquired, slapping Paul on the shoulder, "Where yer bin?"

"A meal – we've been for a meal."

"Great, great," replied Mike, before he turned to Amanda and pretended to peer into her face, "Whosh shish en? ... Hey? A lil dolly? Hey? ... Whosh yer name? I'm Mike. Everyone knowsh Mike. Goo', ole Mike ... ushed to be Paul's mate ... You've enshoyed yershelf have yer? ... Hey?"

"Yes," said Paul, hurriedly.

"Great. Great. Ash long ash you've enshoyed yershelf. Thash the main thing innit? Ash long ash you had a goo' time."

His smile at Amanda, as he spoke, was not returned.

"He's drunk," explained Stephen, foolishly.

Amanda looked at him as though he'd arrived from another world, before tugging Paul off along the pathway to her block.

"Come up and she ush, Paul mate. We'll make yer a cup of coffee."

"Har! Yeah. OK," replied Paul, looking back over his shoulder, "Get him to bed, lads."

"I doan need bed, Paul mate. Ash long ash you've enshoyed yershelf. Thash the main thing."

Pete Campbell looked at Hughie Spragg, his banjo player, with a mixture of contempt and disbelief. They'd just finished their final gig and were enjoying a beer at the landlord's expense in 'Pete's Room' above the King's Head in Staffham. It had been a good evening, but with the usual crowd and Pete felt that he was still going nowhere. It was difficult, if not impossible, to teach all week and find satisfying gigs at the weekend. Beside, who wanted to live just for the weekend? And yet, he couldn't see his way clear to giving up teaching so that he could travel round in his mate's Mini Clubman with the Appalachian Four. He'd said as much to Hughie, not for the first time.

"You wanna drop out," answered Hughie, "like I said. Why should you put up with being paid fuck all for teaching, when you could travel round the country doing what you want?"

"Mind your language, sunshine," called out the landlord, who was stacking chairs to one side ready for the cleaner who came in the morning.

"There's no one here," complained Hughie.

"I'm here," replied the landlord, "and if I want to hear the language of the gutter I'll go and live there. Besides, my wife might walk in, and what would she think?"

Hughie didn't actually give a stuff what the landlord's wife thought, but modified his language as he continued:

"The trouble with people like you, Pete, is that you feel you have this duty to work. Why? This is a rich country. Super Macmillan told us that. 'You've never had it so good,' he said. Well f ... blow him. If he and his mates weren't keeping their grip on 85% of that wealth, life would be a lot easier for all of us. Let's share it round a bit. The dole, as they call it – as though their doing us a favour by *doling* out a little cash each week to those who need it – is a way of spreading the wealth around, and it keeps everyone happy. The bosses don't have to pay so much in wages if the dole queues are long: the higher the unemployment, the lower the wages. Quit your job and take to the road."

"The country still needs teachers and nurses and

firemen and policemen and doctors and dustbin men and
... Need I go on?"

"You're missing the point. You're subscribing to the
establishment's way of thinking. Why should all those
people you mention work their arses off for bugger all to
keep the country going when 85% of the wealth is stuffed
into 15% of the pockets?"

"Because we want a better world?" suggested Pete,
who was quite angry by this time.

"For who? For ..."

"For our children," suggested Pete, quietly.

"So you're prepared to be screwed for the sake of
future generations who will still be slaving away in fifty
years' time to keep the establishment classes in clover? ...
No answer to that, is there?" Hughie continued after a
pause, "If we're going to change the system, we have to
refuse to comply with the current one. We have to bring
the 'ruling classes', as they call themselves, to their knees,
and we're not going to do that by cleaning out their toilets
... The system stinks, Pete, but, at present, there's plenty
of money around, so why not drop out and do what you
want until the bosses see sense?"

Pete knew nothing of Hughie except that he played the
banjo well and the 'folkies' liked a banjo. He imagined
himself putting his colleague's arguments to Glenda when
he got back to their flat.

"You mean you live off the dole?" he asked.

"I always have since I dropped out. I couldn't see the
point of sweating my guts out at university for a degree I
didn't want. And I'm buggered if I'm going to sweep the
streets so that the politicians have somewhere clean to
walk all over us. So, now they pay me to do what I want.

I don't live by their rules; I live by mine. If I feel like doing a day's work for a little extra cash-in-hand, I do – and the tax man, collecting my hard-earned money for the bosses, can bugger off. If I feel like lolling around all day, I do. No rules and no expectations. No one, but no one, is going to exploit me so they can sit back in their country estate."

"Where do you live?" asked Pete, drawn into this man's life.

"There always some bird who'll put you up. Otherwise, you can find a squat with some like-minded people."

"A squat?"

"Yeah. They're plenty of empty houses around. Why should anyone go homeless? We pool our resources, help each other out, share what we have. Hell, man, some nights we're out of our heads – you know."

Pete didn't know. Despite having come across people like Hughie before, he hadn't entered into their way of life. Like his parents before him (his father had been a postman), Pete's life had centred round school and, now, work. Dropping out had never been a consideration, but it would free him up to take to the road and make for himself the career he wanted.

Dick Crossman, Minister of Housing, had been asked to produce a hand-out on immigration when he went to Stoke at the weekend. He knew immigration was the 'hottest potato in politics'. Ever since the Smethwick election it had been clear that it could be a real vote-loser for Labour: letting a flood of new immigrants in would be seen to be casting a blight on the city centres, imposing too tight a control would be seen as a dereliction of Labour's traditional stance. As a Midland MP, Dick had taken the line that some controls must be imposed for the benefit of existing immigrants, while ensuring that those already here were integrated properly into the community.

He worked frantically during his lunch hour drafting the speech he intended to make, and then sent copies to Harold Wilson and Frank Soskice, the Home Secretary.

Stephen strode into the market place and became one with the crowd. He disliked crowds, but felt comfortable – inconspicuous might have been a better word – among the throng. People pushed and shoved, making their way between the stalls, intent on their purchases. Unpleasant though the smells were, Stephen enjoyed the mustiness of the clothing stalls and the pungent odour of the vegetables. 'The stall-holders are blue with cold,' he thought, 'not like me, just wandering. They have to stand all day. These are people with real problems. All I have to do is make sure I get my English essay done within two weeks. How we moaned about that in class.'

The stalls rattled under the force of the dull, persistent wind. Awnings flapped, tugging at the ropes. A little girl, a dirty finger wet in her mouth, pressed herself behind a coat rack, eyeing her mother thrusting handbags into place.

"You might well grin, my girl – and take that dirty finger out of your mouth. It's all right for your father driving round in the van after the stuff ... Handbag for your girlfriend, sir," she called to Stephen.

"I ... er haven't got one," he replied, smiling.

"Haven't got one! What's wrong with you? You're not one of them, are you?"

"No," he answered with a laugh, and then added because he knew he wasn't and realised it would make the woman laugh for some reason, "At least, I don't think so."

She laughed and he lowered his head and thrust his hands in his jacket pockets. He glanced up at the clock tower in the square. 'Free like a bird on the wind.' The crowd surged him forward. Brawny arms held out tomatoes, parsnips, cabbages:

"Lovely firm hearts, dear," cried the stall-holder, with a chuckle.

'The vegetables of winter,' he thought. 'The wind-aching stalls … the gossip … the old ladies, their faces shrivelled with time, squeezing their way through the alleys of the market, their bags bulging.' He looked towards the hot-dog stall; steam rose from the onions, and he felt hungry. 'I do enjoy being alone. How awful it must be never to be alone, always to have someone bullying you into doing something.'

It was too early for lunch, and he made his way, through a littered alley, towards the park, passing the pensioners gathered on the benches, passing the pavilion from where, in the summer, they came out for cricket. On the other side of the park, he found the railway cuttings and followed the line until it brought him back to the town centre. 'High gutters smeared with industrial dirt, cigarette packets, posters fluttering … the stench of old beer rising from the cellar of a pub. White dust settling on the houses, the rumbling thunder of goods trucks overhead, paint peeling from shop fronts … the grease-gobbed river sludging to the sea …' He stopped his train of thought, feeling it was pretentious, realising that he was hiding from life. 'Words,' he thought, 'should help us to access life, not hide from it.'

He arrived back at the market, crossed the road, narrowly missing being run down by a car, and made his way towards a café he knew well; it was time for lunch.

"Stephen."

It was the voice of Marguerite. He looked up and saw her standing in front of the café with Jenny Pryce.

"You haven't heard about Stella?"

"Go on. What?"

"She tried to commit suicide last night."

"Tried? Where is she?"

"In sick bay."

"What happened?"

"She slit her wrists in the bath. One of the other girls found her and called Sister."

"I'd better go and see her ... Thanks, Marguerite. I'll see you."

"It may just upset her ... there's no need. It's not your fault. I just thought you ought to know."

Stephen ran to the corner and disappeared around it; he then slowed and walked.

"It was November, wasn't it?" said Des, shoving the cup of tea into Stephen's hand.

"You sound like Marguerite."

"So what? Marguerite may not be your intellectual calibre, Last, but she's no fool. Why don't you do us all a favour and trust someone? It's not your fault."

"It's not a matter of trust. Stella's a strung-up girl. It seems to me, perhaps knowing her better than you ..."

"I got Stella's picture the first week we were here."

"Clever."

"No – I'm just interested in people, Last ... You're attaching too much importance to yourself. Stella would have done this, anyway."

"That's what Jenny said."

"Jenny?"

"I bumped into her and Marguerite when I came out of the sick bay. They'd come back on the next bus. And you're right – it did no good seeing Stella. She just said she was sick of talk, talk, talk. She said she thought ... she really thought I had something."

Michael Ramsey, Archbishop of Canterbury, knew he was not qualified to undertake Sydney Silverman's request. Silverman, an MP, was an ardent campaigner against capital punishment and with a Labour government now in power he saw success beckoning.

"It is quite certain that with the bill in your hands the chances of ultimate success would be so much greater," he said.

"I am only an amateur Parliamentarian," pleaded Michael.

He felt it his duty to stand up to the rudeness of those who would oppose the bill, but it would mean spending many hours in the House of Lords and the cancelling of his other engagements. He pondered the matter for two days.

"I know that I can count upon considerable help from the Lord Chancellor and others," he said, finally, "and it is in that knowledge that I feel it to be a duty and a privilege to accept what you ask of me."

Within a week, Lord Dilhorne, who was horrified that Michael had offered to pilot the bill to which he and many others were strongly opposed, wrote to Michael begging him to re-consider.

'... *frankly I do feel it would be most unwise and inappropriate for the Head of our Church to move a second reading of this bill. It is a most controversial measure on which feelings run high ... a very great number of Church people will think it inappropriate ... I mentioned this rumour to an old and distinguished member of the House whom we all respect. He made the comment that if the rumour were true, it was both shocking and unwise ... I have no doubt that if you do it, it will give rise to very strong criticism both in the House and outside which is bound to impair your position and that of the Church.'*

Jenny Pryce rose from one of the chairs towards the back of the Red Room as Stephen made for the door. She'd sung her song – in fact she'd sung three and was feeling pleased with herself. She reached the door first and opened it for him, with a smile.

"Are you all right, Stevie?" she asked.

He smiled at her and her cheek: it was just like Jenny Pryce to open the door for a man, and he guessed that was why she was amused. Outside, they walked closely together for the warmth. The February wind was bitingly cold.

"Do you feel like a drink?" she asked.

"Do you mean the pub?" he replied, not relishing the idea of even a short walk on such a night.

"Well, we're allowed to have men in our rooms until

ten o'clock," she sauced him, fluttering her eyes, "Can I trust you? I do make a really nice coffee."

The coffee was nice, and he said so, sitting on the edge of her bed while she watched him from the chair that stood by what might have been intended as a desk but looked more like a dressing table.

"We travelled a lot in France when we were children. Mum and dad love France and everything French. He says the French are the only people in the world who can really make coffee. He always brewed it at home and saw it as his duty to teach us children."

Listening to her, Stephen realised how little he knew about Jenny Pryce, despite having been in her company on and off for over a year. He'd never before met anyone who'd been to France; the furthest his family ever went on holiday – apart from visits to relatives – was a day trip to Felixstowe, which was about twelve miles down the road from his home in Ipswich.

"Dad is a chemist," she said, reading the puzzled look on Stephen's face, "Do you know how much grant I get … £1 a term!"

"I'm on £44," said Stephen, "Not the top rate, but nearly. How on earth do you survive on a £1 a term?"

"I'm reliant on dad, aren't I?" replied Jenny, "and any work I get during the holidays. But, as Des says, it's good of the LEA to give us beer and book money."

It was true: everything else – food and accommodation – was provided by the college, and you could claim any travel expenses back at the end of the year.

"Stevie," she said, suddenly cutting into their conversation, "you shouldn't blame yourself over Stella, you know. She didn't intend to kill herself. Anyone who wants to really do that always succeeds. Stella was just drawing attention to Stella. She knew one of the girls would find her in time, or else she'd have come running from the bath. There's no such thing as 'attempted' suicide."

"You're a bit hard-nosed about it, aren't you, Jenny?"

"Women know women," she answered, with a hard chuckle, "Someone like Stella – she's well-named, isn't she? There's only one star in her life – will drag you down."

"Thanks for your concern, Jenny. You've talked this over with Marguerite, I take it?"

"It's the talk of the house."

"Do you think she'll get sent down?"

"No. She's also the star of the French group, and one of the select ones chosen for the French exchange. There's no way the principal, Miss Mauldon, is going to let Stella fade away." Jenny chuckled at her witticism. "This exchange, which is coming up, is one of the feathers in her cap. It's a very progressive move on the college's part."

She walked over to the bed and sat beside him, resting one hand on Stephen's leg, while the other stroked his cheek.

"Cheer up," she urged, "You take things too seriously. You need to play it a little cooler."

"I am what I am," he replied, standing as though to leave.

"There's always room for change," murmured Jenny, rising from the bed to stand facing him.

She continued stroking his cheek and kissed him with those soft lips of hers that fluttered against his own. He'd 'never been kissed like that before' – the words of an old song entered his head as Jenny looked into his eyes with those pale blue ones of hers and with that smile flickering on her face. She put her arms round his shoulders and drew him close. 'Never been kissed like that before, and with intent,' he thought, taking her in his arms and holding tight.

Malcolm X – now called El Hajj Malik el Shabbazz – thought back to the night his house had been fire-bombed. He had been asleep when he heard the sound of shattered glass. He'd immediately thought of his daughters asleep in their rooms, and he called to his wife, who was pregnant with twin girls, to wake. They gathered their sleepy family together and made for the back door. The living room was on fire. Gasoline had been used and there was a bottle of the liquid in the back room where Malcolm's eldest daughter slept. Broken bottles littered various parts of the house.

With his temperament and his principles, Malcolm did not expect to live long. Now, he waited at Brown University to talk to the students. He was to give his talk in the Audubon Ballroom. It was a mild February afternoon. On the streets he had seen black women, their Bibles under their arms, dressed in their wide Sunday hats, heading home from church.

He paced up and down in the backstage dressing room, pondering his words. He heard the audience file in and sit on the folding chairs that covered the dance floor. He noticed the women wearing long Islamic dresses as he walked out onto the stage and faced his audience.

"Brothers and sisters," he began, calmly.

"Get your hand out of my pocket!" yelled a man in the audience as he leapt to his feet.

Security guards rushed towards the two men who were arguing. The one who had stood pulled something from inside his coat.

"Watch out! Watch out!"

Pandemonium broke out in the ballroom. Chairs were hurled through the air. Women – including Betty Shabbazz – pulled their children to the ground and tried to cover them with their bodies. The air was filled with screams. One man standing in front of Malcolm was firing a pistol, while two others fired from the side – one with a sawn-off shotgun. One of Malcolm's bodyguards fired at the man who had caused the disturbance and hit him in the leg.

Outside the ballroom a man was wrestled to the ground; he was punched and kicked as the police tried to protect him. The fleeing crowd jostled with reporters, keen to phone in their stories.

Malcolm was prone on the ground, his head nursed by a Japanese woman who had brought her son to hear him speak. Someone called for an ambulance. Betty Shabbazz approached the still body of her husband, and saw the dark bloodstains spreading across his white shirt. Hope may have lingered for a moment but only for a moment. It was terribly clear that Malcolm was dead – assassinated.

CHAPTER 19

Bloody Sunday

"He doesn't know what's happening to him, Jenny," said Des.

"I'll treat him nicely, Des, since he's a friend of yours," she replied.

They smiled at each other, conspiratorially, as though they shared a secret and a concern. Stephen had said nothing to Des, despite their sharing digs, but news had trickled around college that he and Jenny were "going out together". Des was pleased for his friend; he'd always thought that Stephen needed a girlfriend to "humanise" him. Stephen, he felt, "lived in his head too much". He also knew that it could spell if not the end then certainly a change in their relationship. There'd be no more wandering casually to the pub or cinema together as mates; Stephen would have other claims and other considerations.

Des was also concerned about Marguerite. He liked her – she being from the North East like him – and thought Jenny was a good influence. He didn't like to admit, but had to acknowledge, that girls from the south – or Midlands in Jenny's case – were more liberated, and Marguerite needed liberating. Her boyfriend, Bobby, who she'd known since her schooldays, was a typical North-easterner; he was a nice lad – Des had met him several times over the summer – but he saw women in a certain role, and that meant, however unconsciously, they were at a bloke's beck and call; not exactly subservient but near enough to make Des feel uncomfortable for Marguerite.

Des could see her returning from college as a qualified teacher and slipping in to the role of housewife. She'd do the cleaning, the washing, the cooking and the shopping without any help from Bobby because that was the way things had been for their mothers' generation. Even after they had children, Bobby would feel it quite all right to pop off to the football match on a Saturday, leaving Marguerite to cope; he'd also have his "nights out with the lads". He'd expect his shirt ironed ready for work, his meal on the table when he arrived home, his slippers warming by the fire and might even put his shoes out in the kitchen for Marguerite to clean.

Des knew this because it had been that way for his own mother and it was settling down like that between him and Elizabeth. If ever she was round his house and they were alone, it was Elizabeth who did the cooking while he sat back playing his guitar. There was nothing deliberately selfish in either him or Bobby; it was simply the habits of the culture. Both he and Bobby would see to the garden, mend a bike or put up a shelf – and be insulted if their woman tried to do so – but the house and the children and the domestic chores were strictly a female reserve. Marguerite had to be equipped to break the chain before she returned home, and he told Jenny as much.

"You have great faith in me, Des," she prompted.

"You'll look after yourself in marriage, pet – I've no doubt of that – but Marguerite is a softer touch and she deserves more." He paid the compliment, even if it was back-handed.

"More than Bobby?"

"No – more than the life our mothers had: she doesn't need to be taken for granted."

"And you think I'll make a man of our Stephen," she quipped, emphasising the northern 'our' with a laugh.

"I think he's man enough, but you'll soften him up," replied Des, not wanting to equate manhood so narrowly with sex.

Sheila Pratt enjoyed living out more than she'd thought possible; moving from the Nurses' Home was like throwing off the last shackles of her upbringing, and her confidence grew. Now, the three of them with the new girl, Christine, were able to decide where they went and when and how long they stayed out at night.

Since her talk with Stephen Last, she'd even felt less stupid and begun to see that she wasn't just becoming a nurse; she was part of what her dad might have called ' a bigger picture'. She thought of the four of them as the four musketeers; there was solidarity in the group, and the future opened up. Like Kate, she now believed that their generation was building a new world, but one that would enable her to do justice to her roots.

Alerted to unspecified dangers by her mother, she'd always been wary of men but being with Kate and Joan had pushed her doubts aside – or, at least, to the back of her mind. She wasn't ready to go as far as Joan looked like going, but she was keen to find a boyfriend; only, he had to be from her class – someone with whom she could feel comfortable.

"You're not keen on that Stephen, are you?" asked Kate.

"He's the only person I've met who has ever explained my lack of education so clearly. Until he said what he did, I'd always felt a failure."

"Being grateful to someone isn't the same as fancying them …"

"I didn't say I fancied him!"

"But?"

"I might," laughed Sheila, "I've never felt free to fancy a boy before. It's such a relief."

"My mum always said that 'Mr Right' would come along when the time was ripe," laughed Kate, "She said I wouldn't need to go looking for him."

"Do you believe that, Kate? It would be nice to think that might happen."

"No, not really. I think mum said it to keep me clear of boys."

"I was never expected to attract anyone – anymore than I was expected to become a nurse – but I don't feel that now."

"'Respect yourself, and others will respect you'. My dad said that, and he's right. You've come a long way since you started, Sheila. I heard one of the tutors mention you as being an exceptional student the other day. You were asked to insert one of those awful tubes down into a patient's stomach, weren't you?"

"Yes, but I was supervised."

"But you did it efficiently and without distressing the patient?"

"Yes, I suppose I did. We needed to aspirate a patient's stomach and I had to insert the tube through her nose.

The knack is to get the patient to swallow hard at the critical moment, which the lady did and I pushed the tube quickly down."

"Well, as I said, your tutor was most impressed."

Sheila blushed and wondered whether she'd impress boys in the same way.

The Selma marches had taken their toll. As they spread to nearby towns and more blacks made their presence felt, so the opposition became more aggressive. On one of the marches, a teenage boy – Jimmie Lee Jackson – was shot and killed. When he heard of the youth's death, Martin Luther King called for another march; this time, he wanted to take the protest from Selma to the state capital, Montgomery.

"I can't promise you that it won't get your house bombed. I can't promise you that it won't get you beaten up. But we must stand up for what is right."

Governor George Wallace didn't agree; his view of what was right rested on the law. He issued an order that the march was to be stopped at any cost, that his state police were to "enforce the law any way you have to".

It was on a Sunday that the marchers arrived at the Edmund Pettus Bridge on the edge of Selma; they saw state troopers on the far side donning gas masks.

"Halt! You have two minutes to turn round and go back to your church."

Nobody moved.

"Troopers advance!"

They did: some hurling tear gas, some wielding batons, others on horseback whipping their way through the peaceful crowd. All but seventy of the five hundred were forced back to Browns Chapel Church; the seventy who didn't make it ended up in hospital, instead. It was a day they called 'Bloody Sunday'.

Mike Harrison wondered whether he'd bitten off more than he could chew after only his first week at what he and the other student teachers had come to call Mob Lane Secondary. The school, a post-war building with enormous and noisy corridors, was somewhere on the edge of Birmingham. He'd chosen a junior/ secondary course, and Mob Lane was his secondary practice.

Some of the classes were all right, but only a few. The worst of all was 2B. Secondary education being subject-based there was no such person as the 'class teacher', although the children did have the same person for registration each morning, which gave them a point of contact with at least one particular adult each day. Mike wondered how personal a relationship a teacher could build with any group of children under these circumstances. On his first morning, he'd watched 2B's registration teacher, Christine Riches, call the register, and listened as her voice rose almost to a shriek so that she could be heard above the din.

The children treated him in the same way when he took an English lesson later in the morning. He'd chosen an extract from *Dracula*, hoping it would hold their attention. Afterwards, Christine had commented:

"When you read that extract from the story, your voice was wonderful. Try to keep it like that, and not shout to be heard. You were almost shrieking by the end of the lesson."

'The pot calling the kettle black,' he thought, but

decided the thought was unkind. 'Perhaps she's not even aware she shrieks, anymore.'

The set play text was *Romeo and Jennyt*, which Mike thought a good choice since it dealt with teenage love and bigotry. He thought both subjects offered something of immediate interest to the children and a starting point for several fruitful discussions. He was disappointed to find that the children in 4A had never actually seen the play – anywhere at any time, either on stage or on film. The play had been read round the class several times and their regular teacher had given them notes on the key themes, which they'd discussed.

"It's the language, sir. We don't understand it. People don't speak like that, do they? I mean what's *'her vestal livery'* and why is it *'sick and green'*?"

"But you understand that Romeo is in love with Jennyt and wants … to … to be with her," Mike replied, ignoring the question: he'd never worked out, himself, what Romeo meant by that phrase.

There was silence in the class save for a few titters, which he also chose to ignore.

"Have any of you seen *West Side Story*?"

They had, and loved it. Did they realise that the film was an updated version of Shakespeare's play? No: no one had told them. As the lesson meandered on, Mike decided that he'd take his next lesson with 4A in the hall; Shakespeare needed to be acted. It was a simple decision thwarted by the lack of hall time and the fact that 4A's following lesson was on the other side of the school in the science lab.

"They'll never get there in time, Mr Harrison, and, besides, it wouldn't be a good idea to get them wound up before a physics lesson. They're better off in class sitting down," exhorted 'Dusty' Miller, who taught maths and physics.

Mike, therefore, cleared the classroom before the children arrived, stacking the chairs and tables against the wall.

"We're going to act out part of the story," he exclaimed, as excited as the children. "Get into groups of four or five and choose which part of the play you want to act out. You know the story by now."

Hurriedly, the children huddled together in groups – all of the same sex; there seemed no way that they were going to act out any of the love scenes. The lesson was rowdy and a complete failure. Unleashed into an unfamiliar situation, the children were unable to cope. Mike's assurance that they could use "ordinary language" didn't help. The tense fight scene between the houses of Montague and Capulet deteriorated into a wordless brawl and the scenes between Lady Capulet, Jennyt and the Nurse never left the ground. Some children sat speechless, while others talked so loudly and so endlessly that each group had to shout to be heard. Mike wondered whether he could get hold of a copy of a filmed stage version and how much it would cost. He wasn't a drama teacher: his subject was English. 'Perhaps,' he thought, as the lesson subsided into chaos, 'I should leave acting to the actors. Thank God, I wasn't being observed.' To close the lesson down and re-establish some order, he sat the class in front of him and picked up the text.

"Listen," he said, "you need to get inside the characters. You need to see the world through their eyes. A father worries about his son, Romeo. We can all understand what it is to worry about someone we love – yes? Romeo wants to hide away from the world – we can all understand that – yes?"

There was no response, except rows of blank stares. Mike flicked through the book to Lord Montague's speech that followed the fight.

> *"... Away from light steals home my heavy son*
> *And private in his chamber pens himself,*
> *Shuts up his windows, locks fair daylight out,*
> *And makes himself an artificial night.*
> *Black and portentous must this humour prove*
> *Unless good counsel may the cause remove."*

There had been no sound, not even a fidget, while he read and every eye was on him as though the children saw him as a figure from another world: perhaps they did.

"It was the way you read it, sir," said one of the girls, "You can understand it when you hear it that way."

How, he wondered, was he to take these children into this other world? The thought remained with Mike during his first week, throughout lessons that had not even a moment's joy.

Geography was his other main subject, and one which he enjoyed. His lesson with 2B concerned glaciation: in particular, glaciated river valleys. He recalled his own excitement when drawing these for his 'O' level notes: the steep sided river valleys carved into a 'U' by the encroaching glaciers. Mike entered the classroom full of enthusiasm. 'Enthusiasm, they say, is infectious,' he thought.

He turned from the board – having drawn, swiftly and decoratively, the steep-sided 'V' of his river valley – and held up an enlarged photograph of a local beauty spot.

"How many of you have been here?" he asked, and named a beauty spot along the valley of the River Trent.

They had all been to Stone, spent their younger years splashing in the river and would soon walk the banks with their lovers. 'Start from the known and move to the unknown' had been the advice of his teaching practice tutor, and it must be good advice. A room of blank faces stared back at him. Somewhere in the background, Mike heard the taunting chant of "stu-dent, stu-dent", but it was a whisper from the playground rather than a muttering in the room.

"Come on," he entreated, "where did you go for your picnics? Where did you play?"

He knew they had no intention of answering. Five minutes into the lesson, his desperation suddenly reached shrieking point. What if his tutor came in? What if Christine Riches decided to monitor this lesson? A grin spread across the face of one boy. They knew he'd lost control. Children had no respect for a teacher who couldn't control their class. They'd start to play about in a moment, and no work would get done. There must be some of them who wanted to learn – mustn't there? They were waiting for him to lose his temper and pounce on one of them for doing nothing wrong: then, they'd have him – guilt and all. Perhaps he was the one out of line? Was he treating them as children rather than as young adults?

Later, in the staffroom, in what was called a 'free period', Mike collapsed over a mug of insipid coffee and looked up to see 'Dusty' Miller watching him.

"Don't let it get you down, son. You've just had 2B for geography, haven't you? That lot have broken experienced teachers. A brilliant piece of foresight by the powers-that-be put too many rotten apples into the one barrel. The decent kids daren't show any interest because they'd have it taken out on them in the playground. So you get a roomful of sullen stares for forty minutes. Just thank God it wasn't a double period. We had one supply teacher walk out at coffee time. It was that or a nervous breakdown, he said …"

"They were completely ignoring me after ten minutes," said Mike, "they were talking among themselves and even chasing each other around the room. One boy blew a bubble with his gum …"

"They were waiting for you to lose your temper. Did you?"

"No."

"Good – at least you kept your dignity. What they resent – among other grievances inherited from their parents – is their belief that you are better than them … I suppose, in a sense, we are, but realising that doesn't get you far. Keep your head down, grit your teeth, face out the forty minutes and look forward to the decent classes … there are some … and the weekend to come."

'Dusty' Miller went on like that for forty minutes. Mike knew that he hadn't gone into teaching just to get through the day, but he also knew he couldn't stand too many lessons like the last one – not if he was to keep his sanity and pass his teaching practice.

As the coach picked the students up after school and began the long trek back to college on that first Friday night, Mike found himself sitting next to Bryn Edwards

– he who had advised Stephen Last to "dip his wick" before he got married because the girls enjoyed it, but after marriage, it wouldn't be fair on his wife. Mike laughed quietly as he recalled Stephen passing on Bryn's advice. Mike unloaded the grief of his week onto the Welshman.

"Of course, it's easier for me, isn't it? All the kids love PE, don't they? And, if they don't, you can soon find a niche for them," Bryn exploded, cheerily, into the conversation. "The only person I've had any trouble with is Keith Taylor, the PE teacher. One of these ex-army types, isn't he? I met them when I was at school. People like him are one of the reasons I went into teaching. They seem to think physical education is a mixture of Swedish drill, football on a cold afternoon and bullying. The idea of enjoyment doesn't come into it. He gave me a list of the best boys and told me to send the rest to kick around on the bottom field. Bugger that, I thought. I'm here to coach enjoyment into the game and develop the lads' skills. Any boy can enjoy a sport if someone takes the trouble to show him what to do. You haven't got to be good at it to enjoy it."

"Taylor is the bloke who goes out with Christine Riches, isn't he?"

"They're engaged, man. Nice bit of crumpet, she is. I wouldn't mind having a fling there, myself. I heard that she and Taylor were caught canoodling. Got a dressing down from the Head, didn't they? Quite right, too: you can't have that sort of thing going on in school. It gives the wrong impression. Mind you, he spoke well of me when my tutor turned up: gave me a glowing report."

"You've had a good week then?" suggested Mike, half-sarcastically.

"I can't complain ...' he began, and paused before continuing, a frown crossing his otherwise serene brow, "Mind you, there was one thing troubled me. Nothing to do with Keith Taylor – it was the boys. I was chatting to 3D in the changing rooms after the lesson and they came out with these comments about 'wogs'. I listened for a bit. I couldn't believe my ears. They were going on about 'sending them back home where they belong' and how they 'live like pigs' ... and so on. I interrupted. I felt I had too. I said 'you can't say that'. The strange thing was that one of the lads was obviously of West Indian extraction, and he was laughing. Albert, his name: Albert Theophilus McGregor. They called him 'Chocolate' and he loved it."

"They were expressing their parents' views, weren't they?" said Mike.

"Oh, I know. I gave them a few things to take home, I can tell you. We can't have that kind of thing in this country, can we?"

Enoch Powell was aware of the stirrings of discontent within his constituency. He had thrown his weight behind 'periodic and precise' controls on immigration, alongside Sir Alec Douglas-Home and the new Leader of the Conservative Party, Edward Heath; but he had been unprepared to commit himself further.

However, the report of the Medical Officer for Health for West Bromwich, Dr Bryant, had pointed out that the immigrant birth rate was high. He explained that this was to be expected since the immigrants were young and of child-bearing age. However, together with an earlier report by Dr Galloway, the Medical Officer of Health for Wolverhampton, Dr Bryant's report was seized upon to suggest that there would soon be a 'black majority' in Wolverhampton. Mr Powell's attention was drawn to the concern of his constituency party. There were fears that within twenty-five years whites could find themselves in a minority in the Black Country.

Sheila Pratt had a boyfriend. They'd thrown a party in their flat on the third Saturday in the month and this student had asked her out; she could hardly wait for Easter when he'd promised to take her to the theatre. Sheila had never been to the theatre.

"What shall I wear?" she asked Kate Walsh.

"Anything you like, sweetie," interjected Joan Whiting, "These days, anything goes. Mummy hates it. She says that the theatre has been taken over by the scruffs, whereas when she and Daddy were our age it was a social occasion and people dressed up for a night out."

Sheila stared, dazed, and looked to Kate for an explanation, but her closest friend looked as clueless as she did. Joan smiled at them both, indulgently.

"Anyway, who is the lucky boy?" she continued, deliberately avoiding offering any help.

"Julian ..."

"Julian! Oh, that one ..."

"I thought he was very nice," interrupted Kate, determined that Sheila should not be put down.

"So did I, so did I," Joan cut in, hurriedly, "He was an English student from the university, wasn't he? What's the play?"

"It's by someone called Harold Pinter."

"Oh God – you're in for an evening then. Mummy hates Pinter. She says he writes plays about unreal people doing nothing. Still, at least he's not boring. You'll have a good laugh. Which one is it? I didn't know they were putting Pinter on in Staffham."

"It's in London," said Sheila.

"Julian's taking you to London?"

"That's what Sheila said, Joan."

"He must be serious about you."

"What do you mean?" asked Sheila.

"Just that any boy who's asked me out has never suggested London. Not the students, anyway. They simply couldn't afford it. Is he well-healed?"

"I don't know. He was nicely dressed."

"Yes he was, wasn't he? I remember now," Joan pondered, "Well, enjoy yourself. If it's London, you'd better not be too casual. Try a smart dress. You can borrow one of mine if you like. And it may be a good idea to bone-up on who Pinter is before you go. Mummy preferred Noel Coward. She always said he ensured a good evening out ... Anyway, I must go. I've got a lecture coming up on tropical diseases."

When she'd gone, Sheila bit her bottom lip. 'She was kind to offer me one of her dresses, knowing I have nothing suitable, but she's left me feeling so inadequate. I've never been to the theatre, I don't know how to behave when I get there, I'm not really sure what to wear and I don't want to let myself down, Julian sounds as if he might be posh and out of my class and I haven't got a clue who Harold Pinter is.' She looked up at Kate who read her thoughts and smiled.

"It'll be all right," she reassured her, and Sheila burst into tears.

Michael Ramsey looked thoughtfully at the message he'd received from his chief of staff. Two civil servants, experts in the passage of bills through Parliament, had advised him that if the archbishop agreed to pilot the death penalty abolition bill it would increase tension in the House and produce a ruinous atmosphere. There was no certainty, they said, that the bill would pass successfully and they did not like the idea of their archbishop opening himself up to what would be merciless criticism.

CHAPTER 20

Acquitted

"The black people of Selma will struggle on for the soul of America," Martin Luther King proclaimed on his arrival back in that city, "but it is fitting that all Americans help to bear the burden."

Over the next few days, nuns and priests and rabbis and ministers – almost all of them white – gathered in Selma, drawn by Martin's call to "bear the burden". By the day on which the march was timed to begin, there were over three thousand people, blacks and whites, waiting at Browns Chapel Church. Three of the white ministers had been attacked by other whites as they left a 'blacks only' restaurant; one of them, the Rev James Reeb of Boston, having died from a club blow to the head. His death had drawn more to the cause.

"The real hero of this struggle is the American Negro," said President Johnson, "His actions and protests, his courage to risk safety, and even to risk his life, have awakened the conscience of the nation."

Martin marched in the front line as they approached the Edmund Pettus Bridge; beside him marched a rabbi, a priest, a nun and a representative of the United Nations. The marchers headed down Highway 80 towards Montgomery. Members of the United States Army, on the orders of the president, lined the route to protect the marchers.

They marched through small, dusty Negro townships; they camped at night along the route; they were met by the young outside their schools and by those who could walk only a short distance in support. On the morning of the fifth day, their journey ended with Martin and Coretta leading twenty-five thousand people into the state capital.

"They told us we wouldn't get here," said Martin, from the steps of the Capitol, "There were those who said that we would get here only over their dead bodies. But all the world today knows that we are here, and standing before the forces of power in the State of Alabama saying 'We ain't goin' to let *nobody* turn us around'. So I stand before you today with the conviction that segregation is on its death bed."

Hands were linked among the twenty-five thousand and voices were joined:

> *"We* have *overcome, we* have *overcome,*
> *We* have *overcome today*
> *Deep in our hearts, we do believe*
> *That we* have *overcome today."*

"You'll come round tonight, won't you?" urged Susan Paget, as she watched Des Smith stretch his long legs.

"Yes, sure," he replied, uncertain as to where their relationship stood.

It was a summer's day in early spring and, rather like a drunken man, everyone was deceiving themselves that tomorrow would also be great. Stephen Last sat on a chair next to Des and they were talking in whispers for no particular reason. The lawn on which they sat faced the tennis courts of the new college – Coseley College of Education – that was to replace Staffham Training College; here, they would be accommodated for their final year. The tennis courts were bordered by rose beds, and a gardener was bent double over the flowers, his brown, weathered arms flexed in the unexpected heat. Students lounged around the lawn, many of them reading. It was quiet, very quiet. Only the sound of women on the tennis courts disturbed the air – the sound of their excited voices and the occasional screech of a nesting blackbird.

'I'll rush over to Susan's room, bang the arse off her and then piss off,' thought Des, not sharing the thought with Stephen, 'Elizabeth will be waiting for me down the road.' He thought it with a sense of disgust for himself. He had been drawn into a love affair that he desired but knew he shouldn't want. It was also a love affair of which he was, if he admitted the truth, frightened. Susan had asked him home several times but he'd always declined. What he'd heard of her family disturbed him; he couldn't see himself being able to cope with the leafy suburbs, the private schools, the dinner parties, shopping at Habitat, passing the time of day with people who "worked in the City". How could anyone 'work' in the City? Work involved toil and sweat. The gardener crouched in front of them was working; people who commuted to the City were on a pleasure trip. You didn't 'work' sitting at a desk.

Susan rose, smiled at them both 'because she's like that' thought Des, and wandered off to play her game on one of the courts. She was a PE student, and this afternoon was, for her, lesson time.

"There's an element of aggression in all intercourse, isn't there?" questioned Des, when Susan was out of earshot.

"I hadn't thought of it like that," replied Stephen, for whom it had seemed more like a leisurely walk down a summer lane.

"I'm randy as hell," replied Des, "It must be the heat."

"You're in season," Stephen replied, and they both laughed.

"It's OK for you, you lucky bastard. You've been almost human since you got together with Jenny."

Stephen didn't reply, but removed his sports jacket while watching Des, who had leaned forward on his seat, deep in troubled thought.

"It hurts, sometimes, just to be alive," Des sighed, "What's the point of living, if you can't enjoy life?"

"You still don't know where you stand, then," Stephen pursued, wondering how far his friend wanted to commit his views to words.

They talked for a long while, but Des didn't acknowledge his fears, only repeating what he'd already said about wanting Susan and not wanting to hurt Elizabeth. When they moved, eventually, the courts had cleared and the sun was dipping behind the new buildings but it was no cooler. In silence they walked towards the dining hall. A clear blue sky, scudded with a few white clouds, stretched over them like the skin of a drum.

Paul squeezed Amanda's waist as they walked, and she nuzzled her chin into the cleft between his chin and neck. 'Warm hair tickling my nose. All her movements so definite.'

"Do you think you should stay in the folk club?" she asked, bringing her head up and round so that she looked him in the face from below.

"What do you mean?" Paul replied, sensing – if not actually knowing – her drift.

"Well, I've been thinking. We do waste a lot of time, don't we?"

"In what way?"

"I was just thinking … that … perhaps … you know … you needed more time at your work this year … that's all."

But it wasn't 'all', and Paul knew it. His final year was months away, and there was no pressure on him to produce any more work than usual. He said nothing.

"I mean you do have a lot of work to get through, don't you, love," Amanda persisted. "The more you can do now the easier it will be in your final year, won't it?"

"I can't do next year's work now," replied Paul.

"No but … I'm not saying. I was just thinking about your work, love."

"Anyway, we've said we'll be there tomorrow. Des's got a group coming, and we can't let him down."

"All right, love. I was just thinking about your work. That's all."

'It wasn't all. It wasn't 'all' at all, but she's got a right, now, I suppose, to worry about me. After all, we are … a twosome,' he thought.

Ronnie Kray was delighted. Despite running a gang that controlled the London docklands using torture and murder, he and his brother, Reggie, had been acquitted of charges that they ran a protection racket. Moreover, he was getting married, and East End showbiz celebrities were attending his wedding; he had even received good-will telegrams from Judy Garland and Barbara Windsor. Their publicity machine had gone into overdrive, projecting a glamorous, caring image for the Kray brothers; life was good and the champagne corks were popping.

"Come on, mate, you're late. Your coffee will be cold. Where have you been?"

Mike's voice was excited, expectant. Paul glanced over his shoulder and saw several of their mates sitting in Mike's room, all chatting over mugs of coffee.

"I ... er ... had some coffee with Amanda."

"Well, come and have another one."

"What's up, Crispy?" demanded Simon Wiseman from somewhere in Mike's room, "You gone off us or something?"

"Come and have your coffee, man."

"I'm a bit tired, lads."

"Come on in, man," urged Mike, desperate to link-up with his first year friend again.

Paul grinned. It was the old, familiar grin. As he entered the room a great cheer went up.

Joan Whiting looked at the white-gloved finger of her Nurse Tutor and saw the smear of dust on the finger tip. She was really pissed-off and this might just be the last straw. The tutor, a certain Sister Daley, raised an eyebrow without saying a word. She didn't have to say anything: she was fully aware that Joan's success when her formal practical assessment came round depended on such moments of evidence.

The tutors arrived occasionally, always unannounced, and spent the day with you on your current ward. It didn't matter whether you'd got your period or just had a row with your boyfriend: everything still had to be perfect. In Joan's case, both strictures applied; and her periods were always painful, but it was no good telling Sister Daley about how she felt. Sister Daley either didn't have periods or had them under strict control.

Joan had spent a long time scrubbing down the bed and locker of a discharged patient. She thought she'd covered every inch of the bed frame. The bloody thing reeked of Stericol, for heaven's sake! It was just as she was finishing that Sister Daley approached the bed and crawled underneath it. Yes, crawled underneath the bloody thing and found the only specks of dust remaining. Joan had grown used to having her bed inspected at boarding school, but this was different. It wasn't just the smear of dust; it was the disappointment that she'd failed to secure the high standards of cleanliness expected.

"She was right," said Kate with an unfamiliar lack of sympathy, when Joan told the story on her arrival back in their flat.

"I know she was bloody right," yelled Joan, "That's what's so annoying ... Do you know, I almost threw my cap at her. I'm on the verge of giving up nursing, Kate."

"Don't do that, Joan. You'll make a good nurse, as I've said before, and you'll probably be a Tartar yourself."

Joan laughed. The moment of anger passed.

"Are you coming to the Rag Week Ball?" she asked.

"I don't know. I haven't got a boyfriend."

"Nor have some of the other girls. Come on. If we're not quick, the tickets will be gone."

Jenny Pryce was having a similar conversation with Marguerite Bannister, and receiving a similar answer.

"It's all right for you, Jenny. You've got Stephen now. My Bobby is hundreds of miles away."

"We've been through all that, Mo. I won't let Stevie get in the way."

Marguerite laughed and replied:

"You shouldn't say that. I like Stephen. He's nice."

"I know, but you can't let a boyfriend get in the way of a friendship, can you? Come on, Mo, you'll enjoy it. We'll all be together. We've got to get the tickets if we are going."

Jenny Andrews triumphed at the Oscars, winning the Best Actress Award for her performance as Mary Poppins. The film had eventually arrived in Staffham and Sheila Pratt had been taken to see it by Julian. This helped to mask his embarrassment at not being able to take her to London because he'd got the opening date of the Pinter play wrong: it was June, not April. Sheila had enjoyed the film – although she wasn't sure about Julian – and came away feeling comfortably warm; it was a nice sensation.

She'd also found out who Harold Pinter was, although quite why he was so important Sheila had not really understood. Julian had described one of the plays, which was about an old man, Stanley, who lived in a boarding house with a strange couple and who is taken away by two men who might be going to kill him. When she asked why, Julian explained that Pinter kept this a secret.

"The play is about politics," he explained, "McCann and Goldberg, who might be hired killers but who might not, represent the state and religion. Stanley has done something in the past to upset someone in power, and the time has come for him to be called to account."

"I thought you said the play was a comedy."

"It's called a 'comedy of menace'. It is very funny in parts."

"But Stanley does try to rape the girl, Lulu?"

"Yes."

"So he isn't a very nice person? So why should we care what happens to him?"

"He represents the individual in all of us struggling to retain our identity in a repressive regime."

"Then why didn't Pinter make him a sympathetic character? You told me that he also tries to strangle his landlady. Isn't he better locked up?"

"You shouldn't try to understand the play at its face value. What's important is not Stanley's character but what he represents."

"The individual and their need to resist the state … or anyone who tries to impose their values upon you?" questioned Sheila.

"Yes."

"Like parents and schools?" she persisted, wondering when she would get her first chance to see a Pinter play and seeing, albeit dimly at first, how her own life had been moulded in ways she found destructive. Realising she wasn't stupid – just discarded by the school system and downtrodden by her parents – Sheila saw a door somewhere far away through which, one day, she might pass.

Mike Harrison's voice stopped Paul in his tracks as he and Amanda walked by the main block.

"Over here, man," he called, "you're in good time."

"We're going through, love," urged Amanda, "I want to see ..."

"You've got your tickets, haven't you?" asked Mike, fearing the worst.

"No we haven't," said Amanda, before Paul could attempt an apology.

"For heaven's sake man: this group is famous! We're lucky we had them booked before they were signed up by Phillips. They're from Liverpool. It's The Spinners."

"This is a chance we'll not get again, Paul," cut in Des, emerging from the hall, where he'd been setting out chairs and getting things ready for the group.

"We just don't think it's worth it, do we love?" insisted Amanda, feeling somewhat out-gunned with the appearance of Des.

"Well ... you know ... we'd planned to go somewhere else," pleaded Paul.

"Can't it wait? Does it have to be tonight?"

"Come on, Paul," urged Amanda.

"Probably ... we'll see ..." began Paul.

"We had arranged ..." interrupted Amanda.

"OK," snapped Paul, "We'll see ..." He knew they should go to the concert, and wondered whether Amanda thought he was going to run off. Didn't she trust him?

"Shall we go, love?"

"Just a minute."

"We said ..."

'No *we* didn't say. *You* said ... and I agreed,' he thought, squeezing her arm gently.

"Are there any tickets left?" he asked, expecting a negative answer.

"You're not bloody kidding there are," replied Des, "I can't believe we're having to drum up support for this group at the last minute. Everyone says they like folk music, don't they? Why aren't they here?"

Students from the college, Keele University and the hospital began to drift in as Des spoke and Paul eased Amanda in ahead of him, knowing that he would hear about this afterwards, wondering if it was to be a wedge driven into their love.

Among the students came Pete Campbell with his girlfriend, Glenda, and Hughie Spragg. Hughie, a charismatic figure among the students, soon had a group around him as he talked.

"Broken dreams, man," he began, drawing attention to his latest thoughts, "Nothing adds up. Capitalism has failed, communism has failed. All we have left is the individual. Everything must be centred on the individual and their right to be free. Governments make false promises to get elected and leave us betrayed. What we need is a radical ideology based on the needs of the individual. We need to be liberated. We need a revolution that compels."

Stephen Last (who had no time for the likes of Hughie) caught Des Smith's eye and smiled. Des was fuming quietly and said:

"Personal liberation won't lead to anything other than a society that's selfish in a different kind of way. Whoever leads that society will themselves become corrupt. Social revolution is the way forward and education is the road. People have to come to understand that governments and bosses sort things out to suit themselves. Money rules and labour counts for nothing, but labour is the bedrock on which society is built. Once people grasp that piece of knowledge, they will want to elect governments that serve the interests of society as a whole rather than the interests of the select few."

"Hey man, you're talking my language," Hughie enthused.

"No, I'm not," cut in Des, "you're talking about individuals doing what they want – what you call personal liberation. I'm talking about society finding a way forward for itself. Your way leads to people 'doing their own thing', whatever that might mean. The socialist way leads to people engaging with politics and changing the way we live as a society."

As the talk drifted on, Stephen moved off to find Jenny and Marguerite, who had grabbed a front row seat.

"Des on his soapbox again, is he?" laughed Jenny.

"He's tackling one of the counter-culture types – you know, 'let's all loll about while someone else brings home the bread' brigade," replied Stephen.

"Doesn't he need your help then, Stevie?"

"To Des, socialism is a way of life. He's immersed in it – lock, stock and barrel. To me, it's a possible light on the horizon. He knows more about the political imperative than I've ever known ..."

"You've got a great respect for Des, haven't you, Stephen," suggested Marguerite.

"Yes ... but I'm not sure I see politics as the road to individual freedom. In some respects, I find myself agreeing with Hughie, and it makes me angry."

"You agree with Hughie?" cried Marguerite, not believing her ears.

"Not as a lifestyle. It's just that I doubt whether politics will ever free the individual. I think the only road to that kind of freedom is education, but individual freedom has to take place within a fair society. Thinking that through is where Des is years ahead of me ..." Stephen laughed to lighten the moment; he didn't want to bore anybody. "I think Des can handle Hughie," he concluded.

The house lights dimmed as he spoke and the audience took their seats rapidly. When the stage lights went up, The Spinners were there – uniformly dressed, much to the annoyance of the pure folkies – and the evening roared off with *The Irish Rover*. Everyone in the hall knew the song (or, at least, part of it), which had been sung in the Red Room many times, and all joined when they could:

"There was Slugger O'Toole, who was drunk as a rule,
And fighting Bill Tracey from Dover
And your man Mick McCann from the banks of the
   Bann
Was the skipper of The Irish Rover."

The evening continued with the likes of *The Blaydon Races, Waters of the Tyne, The Foggy Dew, To Be a Farmer's Boy, Colliers' Rant, Banks of the Ohio, Bucket of the Mountain Dew, Jamaica Farewell* and *We Shall Not Be Moved*; their songs came from all parts of the country, as did the students in the hall, and from places abroad most of the students had never seen. They were all delivered in The Spinners' inimitable style – basement-bred, genial, true in spirit, sensitive to the time and delivered on acoustic guitars. There was a feeling of camaraderie among the group – Tony Davis, Mick

Groves, Hughie Jones and Cliff Hall – that spilt over into the hall.

It was a comfort to Stephen that up there on the stage was a well-known group whose collective heart seemed to be in the right place. They'd given traditional folk a new voice, and yet the integrity of the tradition was not thrown overboard. It was the road forward for the individual and for society: shaping the traditional to meet new challenges, taking the best of the old forward with the new. He wasn't one for tearing up the past and starting completely afresh.

The Spinners finished their evening with *The Leaving of Liverpool*. Mike Harrison's voice, cracked but joyous, could be heard above the rest, but the Collingwood Hall Training College for Teachers was filled with song that evening. Suddenly, it seemed as if Liverpool was everyone's home.

"Have your lot been at it again, then?" asked Simon Wiseman, downing his first pint of the evening with his old school mate, Malcolm Reed.

"It's rubbish, Sime. It's the newspapers building up a few scuffles into a range war."

Simon, who was drinking at Malcolm's expense since his spring term grant had been spent, smiled inwardly at his friend's use of the term 'range war'; it showed the good that could come out of reading cowboy comics when young.

"So all this stuff I'm reading about is inaccurate, is it? 'Renewed hostilities', 'walking wounded', 'police cells overflowing with the scum of the earth', 'running battles' …"

"There were a few scuffles ... OK it was a little rougher than at Brighton, but nothing like the papers are going on about ... Anyway, which one used the phrase 'scum of the earth'?"

"I forget ... it's time you grew up, Malc. It's time to put the leathers away and become respectable."

"I'll never do that, Sime – never. When I'm old and grey, I'll still be rockin'. Give me a break. You can't expect us to have respect for kids who ponce around on Italian scooters and wear Italian clothes, can yer? Do you know what those pricks listen to? The Small Faces – The Who – the Yardbirds! Come on! Be serious!"

"I rather like The Who."

"Look, Sime – it was just a ripple on the pond of life ..."

"'Ripple on the pond of life'? Where the hell did you get a phrase like that?"

"Don't know – perhaps I've got the soul of a poet. But come on, this Mods and Rockers stuff is over – believe me. The papers will have to find something else to write about over the bank holidays. Things are changin', Sime. You gotta move with the times."

CHAPTER 21

Mandate

Ian Smith had won his mandate; his road towards a declaration of unilateral independence was clear; the blacks in Southern Rhodesia were to be denied the vote. Ian's party – the Rhodesian Front Party – had won all 50 of the 'European' seats. The political alliance, funded by wealthy cattlemen and tobacco farmers, had ousted the liberal whites in the government.

Barbara Castle, dismayed at the Prime Minister's attempts to find a compromise solution, could see the dangers of a racialist Southern Rhodesia; an alliance with South Africa would produce a "stranglehold on black governments". If a Unilateral Declaration of Independence (UDI) was proclaimed by Ian Smith then the lifelines of surrounding African states would be severed: road and rail links across the continent would be the first casualties with all that implied for the economic development of many countries. She was determined to make Harold see that the British government must not sell out to Southern Rhodesia.

'Returning to college is always great,' thought Simon Wiseman, as they staggered back from the Red Lion. 'A night for crying, joyfully – whatever that may mean.' His neck felt as though it was cracking under the weight of

Mike Harrison's arm. Stephen Last and Des Smith tottered beside them, talking inanely of nothing much, when Stephen said, suddenly, in that way he had of coming out with the thoughts of others:

"How many drunken copulations are there tonight?"

"How many drunks are copulating tonight," responded Simon.

"I wonder if Crispy's copulating?" suggested Des, knowing that would rouse Mike's indignation – not so much at the thought Paul might be enjoying himself but because, somehow, Amanda seemed to be denying him the pleasures of drinking with his mates.

"Copulating Crispy," said Simon, "What a title for a song!"

"Ha! Ha!"

"Ha! Ha! Ha!"

"Haaah!"

Their laughter rocked them back to the residential blocks, mingling with that of other dark shapes that swayed in the night: shapes that trod, gingerly but noisily, to their rooms. There was no moon and the blackness became even more immediate as the campus lights flickered off. The grass was dry and unyielding. As they approached the block, the light in Paul's room died.

"See that," said Mike, "he must have heard us coming."

He lurched forward and banged on Paul's window with his knuckles. He yelled with the pain as they struck the glass.

"Hey, Crispy, it's us – the lads," he continued.

"Come on, Crispy," chortled Simon, "We know you're in there."

"Knock it off, lads." urged Stephen, "He might have his girl in there."

"No, he hasn't," said Des, "We know he hasn't."

Stephen was the first to look at Des, followed by Simon and Mike. Des was perspicacious in these matters in a way that the others were not, and they knew he was right. Paul had, quite simply, gone to bed, whereas, only a few months before he would have joined them at the pub, his voice raised in song, the lustiest of them all. Suddenly, Mike began to sing, in a low, light baritone; the tune was *Shenandoah*, which the others recognised as they picked up on his words and joined in the singing, their voices slurred with pints of Joules.

"Oh, Crispy Boy, we long to see you,
Away with grasping women,
Oh Crispy Boy, we long to hear you,
But away you're bound to go, cross the wide Missouri."

As Des and Stephen sat round the low table in Simon's room waiting for coffee, Des turned to Mike, who was reclining on the bed, and asked:

"What made you sing that?"

"I don't know, really. It came from somewhere, I suppose."

"Have I ever given you my image of women and love," said Des.

"Probably, but tell me again."

"Picture love – a man's love that is – as a wild flower growing in a wood. The woman sees the flower and wants it. So what does she do? She picks it, takes it home and puts it in a vase of water …"

"… and watches it die?" questioned Stephen, on Des's pause.

"You northern types shouldn't have that problem, Smith," said Simon, coming down from the block kitchen with four, steaming coffees.

"Why not?"

"Well, you rule your women with a rod of iron, don't you? Darn here, in the sarth, we have ter behave in a more civilised manner."

"You Cockney git," laughed Des, lunging at Simon and spilling coffee down his shirt front.

"Poor old Paul's really under the thumb, isn't he?" said Mike, sadly, from the bed, as Simon placed the cup on his chest.

"Perhaps any man is under the thumb," teased Des.

"Come off it – you get what you ask for," quipped Simon, as he tossed a cushion on the floor and took up the lotus position.

"You mean Crispy should have put his foot down?" said Mike.

"Maybe, it's what he wanted," suggested Des, "Maybe he's happier than when he was playing the field."

"Come on – at our age?" said Mike.

"You tell us what a man wants, Last," said Des, turning waspishly on Stephen.

"It's not that easy …"

"No, come on, Steve, tell us," yelled Mike, "You seem to have cracked it."

"It's not a matter of having got anything," replied Stephen, aware that it was the drink talking in all of them and not wishing to continue, "If you …"

"Go on – if you what?" Des persisted.

"She's a right bitch," interrupted Mike.

"Come on, lads, we don't know what we're saying. It's all beer talk," said Stephen, laughing to cut the conversation.

"She's probably afraid of losing him, Mike. You and Crispy had a right reputation in our first year," said Simon.

"It was a great year. Cor – the birds we took out!"

"You were, one might say, a collector of hymens," suggested Stephen.

"A hymenologist," continued Simon.

Des did not smile, and Simon caught his eye, seeing disapproval for what reason he could not fathom.

"Come on, Smith, it had a certain wit about it … anyway, how's Sue-Sue these days?"

"Knock it off, Yogi," suggested Stephen.

Simon, however, was beyond remonstrance. He lurched from where he'd been sitting on the floor, took Des in his arms and began to dance around the small room, singing as he did to the tune of the north-eastern song *I went and lost me penka*.

"Oh, Sue-Sue is a nice girl,
Oh, Sue-Sue is a nice girl,
Oh, Sue-Sue is a nice girl
… make her yours today."

Des pushed him off, roughly, and Simon collided with the chest of drawers, knocking a pile of washing off the top.

"Shut up, you Cockney bastard."

They were all laughing, even Des, as he and Simon fell in a heap on the clothes. Mike helped them both from the floor and he a Des pummelled Simon down onto the bed where more coffee was spilt. Cries rent the air, a chair crashed backwards. Stephen grasped the table. Eventually, Simon wriggled free.

"I'll make some more coffee," he said and made for the door as Stephen picked up his washing from the floor. 'A great night,' thought Stephen, 'a great night, and a silly one.'

"Why do we always get drunk?" asked Mike, chuckling away from where he was stretched on the bed.

"You talk such rot, when you are, don't you?" said Des.

"I'm swimming. The debris of my life is floating before me," Mike continued in the same vein.

"A drowning man – 'death by water ... forget the cry of girls ... and the profit and loss ... the stages of our ... youth ... and enter the whirlpool ...' suggested Stephen, scrambling Eliot's poem.

"What the hell are you talking about, Last?" asked Des, relieved that he had not made a fool of himself when he shoved Simon away so angrily, relieved that his ill-temper had been scooped up in the camaraderie, "It's not death that bothers me, but bloody living. After having to live, who can worry about death?"

"Have you ever drifted away on the current of your drunkenness," continued Stephen, "at a time when you've been really depressed – just drifted away like Ophelia in the river to the point when you might have drowned, and then woken, just in time, to find your mind has cleared – that suddenly you see things clearly?"

"You can't change circumstances," said Des.

"No, but you can live outside them, as though they were once part of something or somebody else."

"What the hell are you idiots babbling about?" said Simon, coming into the room with their second tray of coffees.

"I just don't want to think," said Des, ignoring him, "that my years here will have been wasted."

Dick Crossman, Minister of Housing, was pleased with the outcome of the debate on racial discrimination at London University; he had won by two to one. Afterwards, he offered to take Iain Macleod, the Conservative politician who had also spoken on the motion – which was a vote of no confidence in the Labour Party's policy on racialism – back to his St James's Street flat.

"I cannot express adequately how much I enjoy being a minister," he said to Iain as the ministerial car drove them home.

"Of course you do," replied Iain, "Being a minister is the only thing worth doing in the whole world."

"I wouldn't go so far as that, but it is enjoyable."

"You and I are politicians," explained Iain, "A minister's life is the only thing in the world worth having."

Dick realized what he meant.

Michael Ramsey, Archbishop of Canterbury, heard the advice coming out of Rhodesia; the government of Ian Smith was not to be trusted. Already, it had initiated imprisonment without trial, suppressed the *African Daily News* and slowed the pace of African education. The Churches in Rhodesia had close links with those in

Britain, and the advice of the bishops was unequivocal. Moreover, some members of the Rhodesian Front wanted the introduction of a system of apartheid similar to the one that operated in South Africa, where Nelson Mandela was imprisoned.

It was assumed to be certain that the government would declare independence from the mother country, and if Britain did nothing then she would be seen as an accomplice in the setting up of a racialist state. The Rhodesian government had to be resisted – if necessary, by force. Michael knew that Rhodesia possessed an army and an air force, but wondered whether the servicemen would be prepared to fight against the British, who would represent the Queen. He wondered whether, likewise, British soldiers would be prepared to fight against the Rhodesian forces; after all, many would have families in that country.

Harold Wilson and his Labour government were opposed to all that Ian Smith represented, but they had publicly declared themselves to be against the use of force, also. They looked weak and their very vacillation was likely, Michael thought, to provoke rebellion by the Rhodesians. Perhaps, he thought, the Churches could provide the much-needed backbone.

Christine Dixon – the flatmate of Kate, Joan and Sheila – was looking forward to night duty. Despite Kate Walsh's assertions to the contrary, Chris was convinced that it would be a doddle. The patients would be sleeping – having been settled down ridiculously early by the day staff – and she was looking forward to tea, biscuits and a cosy chat with the other nurses. She'd heard tales of

Matron's unscheduled calls but surely, she thought, the jungle drums would beat out a warning somehow.

"You won't find it cushy at all," Kate had said, "to start with there is never enough staff. You'll probably find one sister covering up to four wards, aided by you and an auxiliary. Just pray that nobody falls out of bed, that there are no emergency admissions and that the auxiliary is good ... they usually are."

But then Kate was a fusspot: one of those people who were just too conscientious to be true – nice and a really good nurse, but a bit of a Goody Two-shoes.

The shift started quietly enough. When the day staff had briefed them on the patients – whose details they were expected to know off by heart – Chris checked drips, tubes and drains which, she'd been warned, had the habit of becoming detached. She then toured the wards handing out medication and drinks.

She didn't enjoy cleaning and sterilising bedpans and wondered why the hell they couldn't use the disposable ones she'd seen in films set in American hospitals: but that was Britain – twenty years behind the States. However, it was part of the job and Chris saw to it rapidly.

She also went and chatted to an old lady who seemed disorientated and kept asking for her husband who had been dead for some years; Chris knew this from the patient's notes. The old girl kept on waking from a dream that clearly unsettled her, and so Chris spent time listening and talking in what, she hoped, was her most soothing voice.

She also checked, regularly, another elderly lady whose blood pressure and pulse were very weak. She was unlikely to toss and turn very much, Chris thought, but if she did and managed to yank out one of her drips it might prove fatal.

After a final check on every other patient, who all appeared to be dozing, Chris decided it was time to settle down to tea and biscuits and a cosy chat with the auxiliary who had worked on the same wards for many years and had stories to tell. They were, in fact, chatting quite comfortably when the Matron walked into the ward. Since the Ward Sister had been called away to help in Casualty, Chris stood, quickly, to welcome Mrs Hack, who smiled discreetly and returned the "Good Evening, Matron" in a voice so quiet it was scarcely audible. Either she didn't notice the tea and biscuits or she was saving that knowledge for her report.

Chris accompanied her on the tour of the wards and was amazed at how well she knew each and every patient: names and relevant family members, diagnoses, prognoses, treatments, whether an operation was planned and each person's particular idiosyncrasies (if any). Once or twice she paused at what Chris had to say and looked her straight in the eye with a 'are you sure that is correct, Nurse' expression; always, a smile, which could have been either condemnatory or reassuring (depending upon how confident you felt), played about her lips. There was sternness about Mrs Hack that suggested she would brook no mistake, and yet a kindliness that indicated she realised the difficulties faced by nursing staff. At least, that's how Chris saw her and, although she felt in awe of the lady and her ability to recall so many details of each patient, she never felt threatened.

When the tour came to an end, Matron paused at the ward door and said, without a smile:

"I'm afraid I disturbed your tea-break, Nurse Dixon. It will be stone cold by now: so do make yourselves another cup after you've checked the adjustment on Mrs Youngs's catheter. *Otherwise*, it was nice to see a ward all ship-shape and Bristol fashion."

It was the 'otherwise' and the slight emphasis Matron placed on it which upset Chris the most: not because she felt criticised but because she felt she'd let down someone of Mrs Hack's quality: a real professional for whom nothing but the best was good enough for her patients.

The second reading of Lord Arran's bill to legalise homosexual acts between consenting adults – that is, anyone over the age of twenty-one – received its second reading in the House of Lords and was carried by ninety four votes to forty nine. Michael Ramsey had supported the bill, and had no doubts about his decision despite the abuse to which he was subjected.

Michael's view was that homosexuality was neither a fault nor a disease: it was something with which some people were born. He considered that the sexual instinct expressed itself in various ways, and that homosexuality was one of them. He believed that we could not change men's basic desires any more than we could replace an arthritic leg, but that we must do our best to correct, by psychiatric medicine, that which was deviant. The existing state of affairs had prevented homosexuals seeking help in this way because of the fear of the consequences; to legalize the condition would not only allow such people to seek help but also prevent them being blackmailed. He accepted the Churches view that lust was a sin and that the homosexual relationship, if physical, was a form of lust. What was needed, therefore, was pastoral care.

The opposition had been formidable. There was a great deal of ignorance about the condition among the public at large and MPs had been loath to back the bill for fear of antagonising their constituents. Youth leaders felt that if Parliament did not take a firm stand on the matter it would make the protection of young people more difficult. Viscount Montgomery of Alamein – a man held high in the esteem of the general public because of his contribution during the war – had declared "One might just as well condone the devil and all his works," and begged the peers to "knock the bill for six". Viscounts Dilhorne and Kilmuir, both lawyers and trained as devastating speakers, declared that they did not understand how anyone who cared for the moral welfare of the country could condone acts of immorality.

Michael had never faced such men before in his public or private life, but he made every effort to persuade other bishops to support the bill and five or six did so. So, the bill was passed and went into the committee stage. Letters of complaint poured into Lambeth Palace. He was accused of promoting pornography, sanctioning sodomy and portrayed as debauched in the *Daily Mail*. Even supporters of the bill thought it 'imprudent' that the Archbishop of Canterbury should appear to know so much about the subject of homosexuality and considered his knowledge about such details as anal and oral intercourse to be 'unedifying' and 'beneath the dignity of his office'.

But Michael considered the passing of the bill in the House of Lords to be a moral gain for the State.

Glenda, who had been Pete Campbell's 'girl' since they met during their first year at Collingwood Hall, was dismayed by the influence Hughie Spragg was having on her love. Ever since their folk tour of the previous summer, Pete had been hankering to quit teaching and go on the road; it went against the grain.

She'd noticed it first when Pete changed his style of dress. It had usually been jeans and a check shirt, but now these were embellished with a long corduroy jacket and a variety of daft hats. She didn't mind the Bob Dylan so much, but a scarecrow hat! He'd also started to grow his hair longer, whereas he'd always kept it short and neat. He wanted to be noticed as a strolling minstrel, playing wherever the music called. Pete wanted to become an item on the folk road. He was spending more and more of his spare time with Hughie Spragg; they'd sit around for hours just plucking away at guitar and banjo.

She'd never been possessive. She was sure of that fact and she didn't want to tie him down, but she was afraid of him taking a road that led nowhere. Few of the hopefuls made it big. Even those folk singers who had hits only managed one or two. Teaching was a safer bet, and, besides, it was a vocation, not a self-indulgent trip.

"You worried I'll go off, are you babe?" he said, laughing, when she tackled him.

"No. I'm worried you'll lose your way and end up going nowhere."

"If you don't take the first step on the road, babe, you ain't ever going to know whether you'd have made it to the end."

"You've had good evenings at what everyone calls

'Pete's Room'. The audiences are growing and staying with you."

"It's not exactly the London Palladium though is it, babe?"

"You always said that 'entertaining' took second place to 'teaching'. What was that you said 'Those who can *teach*, those who can't just *do*'.

Pete laughed. He'd been having a go at that smug bastard Shaw – the armchair socialist windbag – who'd had a sneer at teachers.

"You used to say that you wanted to open up the world of music to thousands of children. You can't do that if you give up teaching."

"What makes you think I'm giving up teaching?"

"I can read you like a book, Pete. I love you. I know what's going through your mind. It's May, and you need to get your resignation in before the end of the month if you don't want to go back in September."

He walked over and sat by her on the old sofa they'd found in the market. He put his arms round her and kissed her and drew her down into the cushions. She didn't resist – she never had – although she knew what he was up to: he was diverting the conversation.

When they'd made love, she continued the conversation as though it had never been disturbed.

"You are yourself, Pete. You don't have to dress like Hughie Spragg ..."

"Hughie's a great banjo player."

"Hughie is a waster. Hughie thinks only of himself. He just wants to be noticed – hence the daft get-ups. You have already touched the lives of hundreds of children, Pete. You're an inspired teacher, whereas Hughie is a second rate banjo player just as Shaw was a second rate playwright – give or take the odd play or two," she ended with a laugh.

"Are you getting broody, babe …?"

"Don't patronise me, Pete – and don't call me babe."

"I've always called you 'babe'."

"That was before you met Hughie Spragg. He uses the word quite differently. Women are just conveniences to him, and when they become inconvenient he shoves off."

"You don't like Hughie, do you?"

"I'm happy with him as your banjo player, but I don't like what he's doing to you."

Pete knew she loved him. He'd always been attractive to women, but once he and Glenda got together there'd never been anyone else; being faithful was his way of returning her love. He also knew she was right about Hughie, but Hughie offered a road to … to somewhere. He wasn't sure where, but there were hit records, theatre stages, appearances on chat shows and … yes, fame, if he took the road with Hughie. Glenda was right about his changing mode of dress, of course; he was getting dressed for his journey. He saw himself wandering the road, dropping off somewhere at night, sitting on a rocking chair, drinking, smoking and talking folk philosophy with the locals. A crowd would gather to listen to his strumming, and then he'd begin to sing.

"You can do all that, Pete, without taking to the road," said Glenda.

Enoch Powell, speaking to a group of Conservative ladies in his constituency, touched a new note, which was certainly not Conservative Party policy.

"The Government is fiddling with irrelevancies about the ownership of steel and land, while the urgent necessity of a change in the Immigration law remains unattended to," he said, "It is wholly absurd that while entry of aliens from France or China is controlled and policed with utmost efficiency, and permission to work and, even more, to settle is granted only with the greatest care and circumspection, Commonwealth immigrants still stream in with little surveillance and an absolute right to bring or fetch an unlimited number of dependants ... These immigrants from the Commonwealth should be subject to the same considerations, controls and conditions as people from anywhere else."

"He's right," insisted Kate Walsh's mum after she'd heard what Enoch had said from a friend who'd attended the meeting.

"It's not what he was saying a year ago," taunted Maurice Walsh, "He said then that the dependants of people already living and working here had an absolute right of entry. I think the term he used was that we had 'an inescapable obligation' to allow dependants in."

"You would say that – anything to contradict me."

"It's the truth. I remember the conversation in The Woodman at Bilbrook. Besides, it's written into law in the Commonwealth Immigrants Act of 1962."

Florence Walsh looked at her husband, wondering for a second whether he was pulling her leg, but knowing he read the papers from cover to cover, missing not an item.

"Laws are made to be changed," she responded, rather lamely she thought.

"It was brought in by your lot, Florrie," he said, smiling quietly to himself.

CHAPTER 22

Permission to study

Heather Burton sat back in the chair and swallowed, in one gulp, her vodka and lime. It had gone badly but not in the way she'd expected. She and Barry had at last decided that they must tell both sets of parents.

His parents had been fine. His father, Stan, had welcomed them and the baby with open arms, sitting them down in a comfortable living room with tea and cakes.

"Ee, lass, he's picked a right good looker in you. Never seen a lovelier face. And is this the bairn? If he takes after Barry, he'll be a nice lad. Sit you down. Mother will be in with a cup of tea shortly."

Heather felt as if she'd known them all her life and been sitting having a chat with them for as long. Barry's mother came in quietly and looked her up and down for a moment or two, but that was what Heather had expected. The old lady would be wondering whether had son had been hijacked by a tarty piece, trapped into a marriage he didn't want by a slut with an eye for a decent lad.

She got up to shake hands with Barry's mother as soon as she sensed her presence, and caught the change of expression in the woman's eyes. Instantly, she could tell that the woman liked her, saw her as a decent girl who'd make a good wife for Barry.

"Sit down, lass," she said, "Our Barry should have brought you home sooner. What must you think of us … and is this Charles, is it? Isn't he beautiful? May I …"

"Of course."

Before Heather had time to help her, Muriel Glover had picked the baby from the pram and was cuddling him and humming a tune.

"Aren't they a blessing? We do feel bad – not having given him anything. You must let us know what we can do …"

It went on like that for the whole afternoon; and before they left, Barry's brothers and sisters, aunts and uncles, cousins and in-laws had all been round. If Heather wanted an 'instant' family she certainly received one.

The reception at her own home had been different – not unfriendly (far from it) but it carried an air of disappointment, and Heather felt she only had herself to blame. Her father, William, had opened the hall door with a broad smile, kissed her on the cheek – something that she'd noticed was unusual among fathers but which he'd always done – and helped her in with the pram. He'd parked it carefully in front of the grandmother clock, and then turned to Barry, who was standing nervously in the open doorway.

Heather was aware that her home was what Barry would consider 'southern posh', although they lived in the Midlands, and she knew he was as much on edge as she felt. The hallway smelt of beeswax; her mother was house-proud. The carpet floored the whole hall, and they sank into the pile. It wasn't that her parents were rich; it was, quite simply, that her father, who was in local government, had never been out of a job and her mother worked in a local department store and knew everything there was to know about home furnishings. Two regular incomes had arrived without a doubt every month, and her parents had been careful with money.

"Hello, son, pleased to meet you."

"Hello, Mr Burton."

"Call me Bill – everyone does. Come in, come in."

"Is mum here?" asked Heather.

"In the kitchen. She's ... er ... getting lunch."

Heather didn't like to leave Barry alone with her father, but wanted to breast her mother before she introduced her husband. Charles was sleeping soundly, and she didn't want to disturb him. Unsure what to do, she looked first at Barry and then at her father.

"A drink," said William, catching her indecision, "would you like a sherry, Barry?"

A sherry: she couldn't imagine Barry wanting anything less than a sherry.

"Thanks," replied her husband, "that would be great."

Heather laughed, still uneasy that her mother had not appeared but amused at Barry's enthusiastic reception of the offer of a sherry. It broke the ice.

"Perhaps a beer is more to your taste?" suggested William, "I think I'll join you."

All three of them laughed, and Heather's father led Barry into the lounge, while she turned to the kitchen and her mother. As she did so, Sybil Burton emerged from the hall. Heather knew her mother would strike an elegant note: she'd always done so and scared off early boyfriends. There's something about the poise of beautiful women in their mid-forties that alarms and attracts young men, and Barry was no exception: normally forthright, he stood quite tongue-tied. She was slim, attired in a sheath dress belted exactly on the waist that emphasised her slender figure and there wasn't a hair out of place. Heather thought she must have removed her apron before appearing in the hall because there was no way her mother would have stood at the cooker without one; she was determined, Heather knew, to make an impression.

"Aren't you going to introduce me, Heather?"

"Mum – Barry, Barry – mum," Heather responded, annoyed at the very moment she should have been calm.

"I'm sorry we have to meet like this, Mrs Burton ..." began Barry.

"Yes ... where is Charles – or 'Chas' as I think you like to call him?"

Charles, or Chas, was introduced and Heather noticed that her mother's face relaxed and then tightened. She knew exactly what was going through her mother's mind: the baby was lovely – and he was – but he represented a missed opportunity.

"Lunch will be ready in about twenty minutes. Has Bill offered you a drink, Barry?"

"Yes ..."

"Then if you'll excuse me, I'll see to the meal. Heather, perhaps you could give me a hand?"

Heather learned afterwards that her father had been "as friendly as you like" with Barry, asking how his first year in teaching was going, commenting on the new Labour government, enquiring about his hobbies and wondering if he could be of any help "because things must be a little tight".

Heather's experience with her mother had been somewhat frostier: not because of the baby, but because Heather hadn't confided in them as soon as she discovered she was pregnant.

"How could I, mum? After all you and dad have done for me, after all the hopes you vested in me and my future in nursing, how could I confess I'd let you down?"

"It isn't your dad and me you've let down, Heather ..." She paused at that point, quite deliberately Heather thought, before continuing, "Had we known earlier, we might have been of more help to you and Barry. What kind of flat have you got on what Barry must earn as a teacher?"

"We manage ..."

"You don't have to just manage ... I take it the pram is second-hand?"

"Off the market – probably third or fourth hand."

Sybil Burton's left eyebrow shot up her forehead, and Heather apologised.

"Sorry, mum, I didn't mean to be flip ... I didn't come to you because I knew the embarrassment it would cause with the neighbours. Nice girls don't get pregnant before they're married, do they? There's a word for girls like that, isn't there?"

"They didn't in our day. As I expect you've surmised, I was 'intact' when your dad and I married. It's true that our generation thought ... sex was for married people and that somehow you should 'save' yourself for your husband. There was something coarse about girls who ... you know ... but times change ..."

"I'm sorry ..."

"It's too late for sorrow, Heather. Your dad and I just

hope that Barry makes a good husband … he certainly seems a nice young man … Now, if you'd take the plates through … careful they're hot."

Her mother hadn't stopped cooking while she spoke and the final tour de force, the gravy imbued with the juice of the beef, was now poured into the gravy boat.

The meal went well. Once she'd spoken her mind to Heather, Sybil Burton relaxed and seemed to bear no grudge against Barry at all; her attitude seemed to be that it had been up to Heather to preserve her chastity, and that ' the man' couldn't be held at fault. Heather wasn't sure whether her mother had arrived at that conclusion herself or whether her father had advised calm and "no recriminations". She could hear him saying the words.

By the time the meal ended, late into the afternoon, and Charles had been fed and passed from hand to hand and crooned to sleep by Sybil, a great deal had been achieved. If Heather didn't like the present flat they would help them find another or help with the deposit on a first house, and they would like to "buy something for the baby. He'd soon need a pushchair, and there were some nice ones in the shops", and "perhaps we could go shopping one day when Barry is at work. I'll come up to Staffham, if that will help". Her mother meant shopping for clothes for all of them, and Heather appreciated her kindness.

"The other thing is, both of you," continued her father, "we'd like to offer our help with Chas. I know Heather had set her mind on qualifying as a nurse, and your mum and I see no reason why this should stand in your way. It might prove a trifle difficult at first, but I'm sure we can manage something …"

"But you both work …"

"I don't have to work …," Sybil began to say.

"But you love your job."

"Yes, but your qualifying seems more important. I can talk to my manager about going part time. I'm sure we can arrange something. It's a question of flexibility – that's all."

"If you think about it, Barry and Heather – about the future, I mean – it will be much easier for you if two professional salaries were coming in, and that can only happen if you, Heather, complete your nursing training. Will they take you back?" asked Bill.

Sitting with the vodka and lime, bought by her father, Heather pondered that question. Her mum was right – it wouldn't be easy in more ways than one – but if she could get back into nursing it would help to secure their future. She'd always wanted to nurse; it was her contribution to society. Her parents had always emphasised the importance of that when she was young. 'Ask not what your country can do for you, but what you can do for your country.' Somehow, it would put everything back on track.

Nelson Mandela and his fellow prisoners had permission to study, but their road to learning was obstructed as much as possible by the authorities. Certain subjects, such as history and politics, were banned. They were always short of funds because they were not permitted to receive money from their families, and they were not allowed to share books. The authorities often regarded some of the recommended books as unsuitable and these were banned. The vagaries of the postal system, the remoteness of the prison and the deliberate slowness of the censors meant that the books would often reach the prisoners after the date on which they were due to be returned; in such a case a prisoner might receive a fine without having received the book. There were no desks and chairs fit for studying; the prison offered only a wooden board that jutted out from the wall at chest height and nothing on which to sit.

Although every Saturday morning the chief warder arrived crying out "complaints and request, complaints and requests," these were largely ignored. The chief warder would nod his head, say "Ja" and pass on to the next prisoner without writing anything down.

Dick Crossman was frustrated with the way in which the Prime Minister, Harold Wilson, was running the government. He had not grown up, Dick thought, since entering No 10. Even the house itself was a spitting image of Harold's own little house in Hampstead. The Treasury had forced him to let Jim Callaghan become Chancellor and George Brown was allowed to 'go a-whoring' after his incomes policy rather than form a strategic plan. What was needed, Dick thought, was an 'inner Cabinet' to formulate a consistent policy.

The new Labour government was drifting along, allowing the various departments of the Civil Service to make the real decisions. 'He sees his job as carrying out the manifesto ... and yet from the point of view of the electorate this technical promise-keeping is quite unimportant,' Dick thought.

John Lennon knew that they should not accept the MBE; his whole instinct was against the idea. He had no time for the aristocracy and had parodied the previous premier, Sir Alec Douglas-Home as Sir Alec Doubtless-Whom.

Lords, ladies and debutantes who would previously have turned up their noses at four lads from Liverpool were fawning all over them; the Beatles, he felt were on the point of being canonized.

Brian Epstein, their manager, however, insisted that the Beatles must accept the medal.

"John – to refuse it would do great harm to the group. Paul, George and Ringo all feel honoured. You must accept."

'It'll be a sell-out,' thought John, while knowing that his great respect for Brian would oblige him to compromise his ideals.

Harold Wilson expected the storm and smiled to himself as he sat back, lit his pipe and read the papers. Old soldiers and statesmen were threatening to return their medals. One already had, claiming 'the British royal house has put me on the same level as a bunch of vulgar nincompoops.' Harold was unabashed.

"Some of the heavyweights in the press ... don't understand the role the Beatles have come to play in young people's lives. I see them as having a transforming effect on the minds of youth, mostly for the good. It keeps a lot of kids off the streets," he said to his wife, Mary, "They introduce many young people to music, which in itself is a good thing ... the Mersey sound is new and important. That is why they deserve recognition ... Besides which they have brought millions of pounds worth of trade into Britain."

"Not going?" questioned Christine Dixon when she found Sheila Pratt in tears on her arrival back at their flat, "But you were looking forward to it so much."

"Julian thinks I'd be bored by the play."

"Has he chucked you?"

"Yes."

"I'm sorry ... You hadn't gone all the way with him, had you?"

"No, of course not – we've only known each other a few months. What sort of girl do you think I am?"

"No offence, Sheila. I just didn't want to think the bastard had had his way with you and then given you the shove, that's all."

"He wrote me this letter," said Sheila, half handing it to Christine.

"I don't want to read it, Sheila. I can guess what it says ... These university types are all the bloody same. They're being *educated* and we nurses are being *trained*. They don't consider us quite up to their mark, do they? I expect it was because you liked *Mary Poppins* that put him off – the bloody snob. Anyone who likes *Mary Poppins* can't appreciate Harold Bloody Pinter."

"I'm not stupid."

"No one said you were you. He wouldn't have been attracted to you in the first place unless you'd struck him as intelligent ... I went out with a university student once. I'd attended one of their medical lectures. He thought I was training as a doctor. When he found out that I was 'only a nurse', he didn't want to know ... Which Pinter play was it?"

"*The Homecoming*. It's opening at the Aldwych Theatre this month. I was really looking forward to going."

"Right – let's see if we can get tickets. We might even meet the bastard there ... In the meantime. Let's go to The

Café Blanc and have a coffee and some cake. That'll cheer you up."

Des, who had not been looking forward to Rag Week, considering it one of the more childish aspects of student life, was ecstatic. It had not only gone well; it had gone well with Susan. Their relationship, always delicately balanced between a sense of should and should not (on both sides), had blossomed. They'd enjoyed each other's company and he'd come to a decision regarding Elizabeth.

The first day of the week had started conventionally enough. Students all over the college were racing up and down corridors attired artily or in fancy dress. Des wondered how long it had taken some of the women to get themselves up so casually and to such effect. Mike Harrison had been beside himself, and Paul Crisp – reclaimed – had been stripping beds. Des wondered whether or not he should report him to Amanda.

At the climactic moment of leaving for Staffham, Mike's car refused to start. Dressed as a clown and carrying his Rag box, he was pulling the starter and cursing the engine while four of the six or seven students he was going to pack into the car were pushing. Des remained on the back seat squashed between Marguerite and a first year girl with big breasts he didn't know. Mike's make-up ran in the heat as he got out with the starting handle.

When they rattled into town, Staffham was alive with streamers strung from the lampposts and confetti was everywhere. As they could only move slowly down the main street behind the procession, Mike decided to take a side street. It was one-way, and Mike took the wrong direction. When the bobby approached them, Mike offered to do some acrobatics as a penance rather than pay the fine. The policeman was sweating in his blue serge uniform but took Mike's antics in good part.

"All right, sir, if you'll just move along," he said with a smile.

Unperturbed and immune to the copper's relaxed attitude, Mike continued to pull faces and crack jokes until the others pulled him into the car. Des realized that he would never have dared behave like that to a bobby, but where he came from bobbies were not looked upon as friendly.

As they got out of the car a group of girls rushed over and covered them with confetti. The symbolism wasn't missed on either Susan or Des and they smiled at each other, Susan giving that little giggle for which she was well-known.

When they'd managed to struggle through the crowds to the bridge, they saw two blokes from the university swinging a girl out over the river. On the far bank, two others were waiting to catch her. A crowd of townsfolk were watching them, their faces nearly expressionless. Were these the educational elite? Were these worth ratepayers' money? When the crowd was large enough, students pushed in among them with charity collection boxes. Just for a moment, perhaps, everyone wondered whether the lads intended to throw the girl or not, but doubt vanished the instant they let go and she sailed through the air to be caught by the two on the other side. The crowd roared their approval.

The crowd dispersed and they found themselves being shoved towards the town centre. Des was keen to get

Susan alone and suggested a coffee. She didn't demur as the others, caught up in the surge of bodies, followed the floats. Alone in the throng, they felt, yet again, that something had been settled between them. They'd tried to keep their relationship platonic, 'but can a friendship between a man and a woman ever be platonic?' wondered Des.

When they left the café, they wandered down the main street looking for their friends. Mike and the others were rattling tins alongside the procession. Simon called out "The Stuffed Pig" as they passed. He was dressed as a jester, and Des thought his yoga exercises must be doing some good because he was cartwheeling and somersaulting quite easily, much to the amusement of the crowd.

The Stuffed Pig was along a side street, and Des and Susan found Stephen and Jenny sitting there, holding hands across the table, when they arrived. Jenny Pryce had fostered a huge change in Stephen Last, Des thought. The coldness had gone, and Des enjoyed his company even more than he had in the first year. Next year – their last at college – they were both in hall at the new Coseley College of Education, which was situated in the village of Coseley on the edge of the Potteries. The only thing that troubled Des regarding Stephen was that his friend was 'all or nothing'. He'd once said that if he committed himself to a girl it would be totally, and Des wondered whether or not Jenny saw the relationship in those terms.

The others arrived, led by Simon and Mike, and the clown and the jester began to work the tables. Mike, safe behind the mask, took the mick out of anyone who refused to contribute, while Simon chortled and forward-rolled his way to the counter. People were not sure whether they were joking or were really frolicking for money, and so the proprietor stepped in, offered a decent sum and asked them to leave. Jenny and Susan were shaking with laughter in the corner.

When they left – the girls to get a bus back to college and Stephen and Des to return to their digs – they saw two students standing back to back in the road, holding up traffic from either end. They were dressed in top hat and tails and each held a flintlock pistol to their shoulder. They walked away from each other, while a second counted to ten, and then turned and fired; both dropped to the road. Four more students rushed towards them holding stretchers. They rolled the duellists onto the stretchers and carried the bodies away.

Cynthia Lennon was over the moon. Brian Epstein, the Beatles manager, had always said that the group would be "bigger than Elvis", and they were: nothing in the world approached the phenomenon of Beatlemania.

With the fame came the money. She could remember the time when she'd been confined to a bedsit with just one set of sheets; now, she and a friend would drive down to Walton-on-Thames and 'run amok', snapping up high-quality sheets, pillowcases and bed-covers. She could afford as many as she wanted, and the feeling was wonderful.

On the London scene, the Beatles with their wives and girlfriends were the hippest crowd in town. Whereas once chicken and chips at a local café or curry at the nearby Indian constituted a night out, they now dined at the capital's coolest restaurants and nightclubs. Life was one long party – and could they party! They adorned celebrity soirees and designer boutiques; they were on everybody's 'most wanted' list. The atmosphere wherever they went was plush: brocade drapes, candlelit corners, deep sofas, cushioned benches, French menus. They were the hottest crowd in the hottest spots. Wherever they went, other famous faces greeted them: Freddie and the Dreamers, Gerry and the Pacemakers, the Rolling Stones, The Who, Georgie Fame.

Along the way, they were introduced to cannabis. The Beatles had first tried the drug when they met Bob Dylan; they'd never used it before their trip to America, and Bob soon had them stoned – rolling and giggling round the hotel room. The 'boys' enjoyed the dope and used it regularly, but Cynthia never took to it. She didn't like anything that made her feel she'd lost control of herself.

Chapter 23

'The gesture of a maverick'

John Lennon was looking forward to the publication of his second book, *A Spaniard in the Works*, despite having had one or two annoying experiences when his first book, *In His Own Write*, had come out the year before. George Melly, the jazz musician and Observer columnist, had written a glowing review, and then met John at a launch party. John thought the man was patronizing, but they were both drunk, and that may have explained his manner.

"I hate trad jazz," John had said, "it blocked me and my friends from the Cavern. You're one of the blockers."

"Did you like my review," replied George in his most soothing voice.

"I didn't read it."

"I said how much I enjoyed your book and mentioned what I thought were your James Joyce influences."

"I don't know what you're talking about. I've never heard of him. Who the hell's James Joyce?"

The conversation – if you could call it that – had wandered on, with George struggling to find a point of common agreement, until they came to musical influences.

"Of course, you must feel, as I feel in my sphere," George had said, "that one's real debt is to black singers like Muddy Waters and Chuck Berry, who invented the idiom in which we both sing."

"I accept nothing of the sort. I refute all influencers. I could eat them for breakfast," roared John in reply.

"Oh come on! Your music is as derivative as mine."

"They don't make anything like I make," John had raged, almost coming to blows with George, who was pleased he hadn't since he felt John might have won.

Sir Alec Douglas-Home had prepared the ground for the democratic election of a new Leader for the Conservative Party, and felt that the time was now right for him to resign from that position. He, therefore, approached the July meeting of the 1922 Committee with that in mind.

"I have to tell you," he said, "that, having weighed to my best ability all the considerations, I have asked our Chairman – Sir William Anstruther-Gray – to set in motion the new procedure. I myself set up the machinery for this change, and I myself have chosen the time to use it. It is up to you to see that it is completed swiftly and efficiently and with dignity and calm. I do not intend to stand for election."

He resigned the Leadership of his party in the belief that it was in a position to secure "victory at a General Election".

Dick Crossman found that the resignation had taken the House by surprise and was 'the only topic of conversation'. A friend rang to say that she thought Harold Wilson had been instrumental in bringing the resignation about by saying that Alec Douglas-Home was his greatest asset. Dick thought Alec to be 'a funny man', and wondered whether there was any truth in what was being said: that Harold's remark had forced the issue for the Tory Leader.

Des put pen to paper and wrote his letter to Elizabeth.

Hello Pet,

Another year collapses with a whimper, and I can't say I'm not looking forward to the end. But I am depressed at the moment because I'll have to take work with Stephen's restaurateur at the holiday camp if I'm to earn any money for when I get back home. Stephen's coming this year, too, which has quite surprised me now that he and Jenny are close, but I suppose he needs the money. He can't find a job here anymore than I can in the north-east, although I'd have thought it was a bit easier in the Midlands.

You must get tired of hearing me go on about this place but it does take up three years of our lives. Our emotional relationships are supposed to switch off at the beginning of term and then switch on again at the end. All computerised, see – on/off, on/off – binary maths for the personal life. It's an artificial existence. In the case of people who meet here they have to postpone their personal lives until the holidays are over – unless they can afford the train fare to go backwards and forwards or have the money to stay in digs.

Stephen is torn between going home to see his parents after he's finished at the camp or coming straight back up to the Midlands to see Jenny, but he's got nowhere to stay here, anyway, unless he can get a mate to put him up. I don't think he's at the stage when he'd be able to stay at Jenny's. Anyway, he feels he owes it to his parents to see them sometime over the summer.

Even Paul Crisp is breaking free from Amanda for a few weeks, which is something none of us can quite believe. If ever a man has changed, it's Paul. I can't understand it. He was such an outgoing chap, and now he's shackled like a prisoner to the cell wall. If she loved what he was, how can she love what he's become since they met? Why do people find it necessary to change each other? Do they have to mould what they love in their own image – God and the clay? Why, eventually, are they anything but themselves with each other?

I didn't mean to say any of that, but I'll leave it because I know you'll write back having made sense of it. I do miss our chats.

All my love,
Des

Enoch Powell decided to stand as a candidate in the Leadership election. Many in the press described this as 'the gesture of a maverick', and Enoch relished the description. He was a maverick, and that was exactly what the party needed. He had, quite deliberately, set out to make speeches and write articles that would re-kindle the flames of the old Conservatism. He was a man who spoke his mind, and he knew it was for this for that his constituents admired him. He had appealed for industrialists not to cooperate with the Labour government, he had called for "fresh ideas" for Tory policy, he had spoken out against "restrictionism" in the labour market and he had derided Labour's export drive. His decision to stand was supported by his Midland colleagues; his time had come.

Christine Dixon had failed to get tickets for the new Pinter play; it was sold out.

"No doubt to wealthy Londoners," she said to a group of them who sat in The King's Head.

"There's nothing wrong with wealth," said Joan Whiting.

"You went to public school, didn't you?" suggested Christine, "I'd expect you to think that …"

"Was there a hint of sarcasm in that remark, Chris?" snapped Joan, "You should feel sorry for us public school types. Being shut off from my parents for most of the year wasn't my idea of fun."

"Sorry. I can appreciate what you're saying. I'd have hated it. But public school did guarantee you a good education, didn't it? And you can't buck that asset, and it shouldn't be a privilege of the wealthy."

"I agree. I agree. So improve the education in the state sector."

Christine sat subdued. She was aware of her own educational shortcomings, and had found an ally in Sheila, but she had no idea how state schools could do better.

"We had smaller classes and less distractions," continued Joan, "There was bugger all else to do a lot of the time but read, and reading improves the mind."

"I did read a lot," said Sheila Pratt, who had watched in silence while her two friends cut at each other, "but I didn't know what to read."

"That was my problem, too," continued Christine, "although with a large family you don't get much private time. I did my homework on the table mum used for her ironing."

"You come from a large family?" asked Joan.

"There were seven of us."

"Are you Catholics?"

"No! Everyone asks that. Mum and dad just liked children ... but, of course, there wasn't much money to spare ..."

"I bet," said Joan.

"I'm not so much against public schools, by the way," continued Christine, suddenly returning to their previous subject, "but they do perpetuate the class divide, don't they?"

"I'm sitting here with you," replied Joan, laughing.

"Yes ... but you needn't be. You have other choices that your education and old school network provide."

"Yes, that's true ... and you're right. Public schools do perpetuate the class divide, and I don't like that anymore than you do."

"I believe you," said Kate Walsh, speaking for the first time, "A lot of the issues facing this country aren't about race or creed or colour. They're about class."

"Well, you've got a grammar school boy in charge of the Labour Party, and another – Ted Heath – about to become Tory Leader."

"You think he'll win?"

"Daddy has no doubt about it. He's a rank Tory and keeps his eye on what's happening in politics. He says that Heath will hold the centre ground of the Party – and he's pleased. Heath stands for technology and for the state guiding what he calls 'modern capitalism'. Daddy has no time for the old Tories like Macmillan and Douglas-Home. He says a 'modern economy cannot be run by the toffs' but neither can we leave it to the socialists who will just nationalise everything, which will lead to stagnation."

"Stagnation?" queried Kate.

"Nationalisation takes away the profit motive, Kate. If people aren't working to make a profit – that is, if they get paid anyway – then they won't put their heart and soul into what they're doing."

"I don't think that's true," replied Kate, "I'm not going to be any less good as a nurse because the pay is relatively poor. It's a matter of professional pride – of doing the job well because ..."

"A job worth doing is worth doing well. I know, I know, but not everyone looks at work in that way."

Sheila Pratt sat almost dumbfounded. She understood what her friends were talking about, but it was all new to her; not once in her childhood had she ever heard her parents or any of their friends talk in this way. Conversation around the table had always been about everyday matters: never politics, economics, class, labour disputes.

Michael Ramsey spoke for the bill to abolish the death penalty on the second day of its second reading in the House of Lords. He acknowledged that a "terrible crime deserved a terrible punishment" but pointed out that this should not be motivated by a desire for vengeance.

"The taking of a life," he said, "devalues life."

He pointed out that there was no convincing evidence that the death penalty deterred criminals, and said that a life sentence was, in itself, "a terrible deterrent". What we needed was a "wise, stern and human penology", not a system that punished killing by further killing, albeit at the hands of the state.

The debate was carried by two hundred and four votes to one hundred and four. All the bishops voted for abolition of the death penalty, and it was abolished subject to a review after seven years.

Help! – the Beatles second movie – premiered and was looking to be a great success, but John Lennon wasn't happy. Constant touring had worn him out and he needed to rest.

He'd enjoyed working with the people he met while making the film. He and Eleanor Bron had sat for hours in the hotel bar during filming in Austria and talked about philosophy and politics.

"Deep down," he'd said, "I'm Labour. Politics is a state of mind, but you've got to protect your money, haven't you?"

Materialism was gnawing away at John. He liked the money but he was being swept along on a tide not of his choosing. He sat in his music room at Weybridge amidst the mass of recording machinery, smoking marijuana, feeling euphoric but getting nowhere. Nagging away at him was the thought that the Beatles had changed from the group he'd envisaged. He didn't regret their popularity; he regretted that they were no longer a rock 'n' roll group.

"I wanted the Beatles to be *the* biggest thing. It's like gold. The more you get the more you want ... I don't want to sound as if we don't like being liked. We appreciate it, but you can't spend your life being dictated to ... People pay six shillings and eight pence for a record and we have to do what they say ... I don't like that side of being a pop star."

The trappings of fame were becoming stale, and his life shallow. He and Cynthia enjoyed fine wines, expensive restaurants, celebrity friends, the wit of people like Peter Cook whose home John visited, trendy discotheques, posh hotels, spending money on decorating his home; but he didn't like touring.

Live performances meant that the group were treated like monkeys; they were shoved on and off the stage for the screams of the fans. Performing had lost its creativity. John wanted to spend more time writing and recording in the studio. Moreover, he wanted to spend time with his son, Julian: on one occasion, he couldn't even remember the boy's age!

John confided to his wife before going to Germany that he was looking forward to being at home for longer periods where he could work in peace. Cynthia just wanted 'the old John back' and for them to be together as a family again. She hoped that this might lead to him cutting back on his drug taking and give him the chance to be a proper dad to Julian.

CHAPTER 24

The floating pound

"It's irresponsible to have more children than you can afford," insisted Joan Whiting, either to annoy or in complete disregard of Christine Dixon's feelings.

"Having children is one of the great joys of life," responded Miriam Davison, "It's not a question of *whether* you can afford it but of *how* you afford it. It's a question of a family's priorities."

Christine Dixon smiled to herself. She liked both her friends for quite different reasons. At the present moment she wasn't so much put out by Joan's outspokenness as by Miriam's priggishness. Christine *wanted* a large family; Miriam felt that to have one was her *duty*. Miriam had this conviction that having as many children as possible was a religious obligation. Their mutual desire gave them a bond, but Christine wondered how Miriam would cope with having a large family and fulfilling her responsibility to society.

The bond between Miriam and Joan was quite different, and it was a difference that set them apart from the others. Miriam, she'd discovered, had gone to grammar school, while Joan had been educated privately, and yet they had something in common; they were both from the middle class. Joan's father was a diplomat of some kind, and Miriam's was a lawyer. Both had a confidence that that did not come naturally to her or Sheila. Christine felt that it was this lack of confidence that, sometimes, made her sound aggressive.

Listening to her friends arguing, she remained silent, remembering the joys of a large family rather than the tribulations. Her parents had been happy, and she thought that was the key to the family's 'togetherness'. Their wedding picture had always stood on the mantelpiece, and Christine must have looked at it every time she passed through the living room. It showed a couple in the doorway of a country church: her dad short and stocky, her mum slim and neat. They were looking into each other's eyes in a way that set them apart from the melee of wedding guests who were throwing confetti and laughing. Ever since she'd seen them as people – as distinct from being, simply, mum and dad – Christine had noticed they always looked at each other in that way.

Later, when she and her mother talked of these things, Christine realized every outfit in the photograph, including the bride's and bridesmaids' dresses, had been scraped together from borrowed materials and the clothing coupons of generous friends and family. It was a poverty that was to follow her through her childhood years. School uniform was supposed to be the great leveller, but there was her uniform (and those of her brothers and sisters) and there were the uniforms of those children from wealthier homes: children like Miriam and, she supposed, Joan. Neither, she felt, had ever worn hand-me-down clothes: clothes handed down not only from brothers and sisters but also from cousins and next door neighbours. Christine accepted this without resentment, but thought Miriam might be in for a shock when she and her husband came to clothe a large family.

"Say something, Chris," demanded Joan, "What are you thinking?"

"My thoughts were drifting," Chris replied, "but they were around the joys and tribulations of having a large family ... and what it is that binds we six nurses together."

"Are we bound together?" asked Joan.

"Oh yes," replied Chris, "we are on the cusp of a revolution."

"Cusp?" enquired Sheila Pratt, not afraid, momentarily, to show her ignorance.

"A cusp is point of balance between one state and another. We are about to leap off into a new world."

"What on earth are you talking about?" asked Joan.

"I was thinking how different we all are, and yet how similar. All six of us are driven by a desire to improve our society. Utopia is within our grasp."

"What's that got to do with large families?" Joan asked, in that sharp way of hers.

"Nothing especially ..."

"Everything," interrupted Miriam, "The world is a large family and as the world gets smaller – that is, as we come to know more about each other – we are going to have to learn to live together just like a large family with all its individual differences."

"Kennedy, again?" snapped Joan, looking at Miriam.

"I think I acquired my beliefs at my mother's knee," laughed Chris, "It's all this 50s stuff. You know, building a better society after the horrors of the war. Our parents have begun that revolution, and it's our obligation to continue the ... fight."

"You chose the right word, at least – 'fight'. It will be a fight. I didn't come from a large family, but I did live among a lot of other children in a large boarding school. I didn't experience this … this sense of being together you talk about. Believe me, it was always a matter of resolving our differences that mattered."

Christine didn't want to pursue the argument. She knew her thoughts had "rambled on", as her father used to say, but what she had thought held a truth – or several truths – and she wanted to think about these quietly, away from Joan's derogatory comments.

"What good does it do to be able to sit at a lunch counter, if you don't have the money to buy a hamburger?" asked Martin Luther King, thinking how poverty crippled the lives of black people right across America.

He thought of the slums he'd seen across the land: tumbledown homes where blacks lived, unable to find work and with the pangs of hunger gnawing at them. These people knew there was a better life and that it was beyond their reach: anger was the consequence.

In Watts – a poverty-stricken black neighbourhood amidst the wealth of Los Angeles – a white policeman tried to arrest a black man, and the man fought back. A crowd gathered, and someone threw a bottle. Some-one else set fire to a car. It was a riot, and it had to be crushed.

When the news reached Martin, he flew to Watts and walked the streets. Thirty four people had been killed, and thousands injured. Homes and stores had been destroyed. The cry on the streets was "Burn, baby, burn!"

"Violence only leads to violence. Hate cannot drive

out hate. Only love can do that," Martin remonstrated with the mobs.

"We won. People are listening to us now."

"Thirty four of your people are dead, your community has been destroyed and you can say that you've won? How can you say that?"

"If America doesn't come around, we're going to burn it down. We're not for this non-violent stuff anymore. The time for peaceful marches is over."

"If every Negro in the United States turns to violence, I will be the lone voice preaching that this is the wrong way. We must continue to work towards first-class citizenship, but we must not use second-class methods ... I'm tired of marching for something that should have been mine by rights at birth ... I'm tired of living every day under the threat of death ... I don't march because I like it. I march because I must."

Labour's White Paper on 'Immigration from the Commonwealth' sent shock waves through society; nobody who had supported the Labour Party could believe that they were proposing to tighten up immigration controls. The number of work vouchers each year was to be limited and all immigrants would be expected to come to a job or possess a skill of use to the country. The measures proposed, although within the scope of the Commonwealth Immigrants Act, were against its spirit, which extolled the right of every Commonwealth citizen to come to the Mother Country. Moreover, when in Opposition, the Labour Party had objected to any suggestion that controls might be tightened.

Dick Crossman, sitting in Cabinet, considered that the

Government had done the right thing, unpleasant though it had been. The Labour Party in government had become 'illiberal and lowered the quotas when they was an acute shortage of labour', but not to have done so would have meant almost certain electoral defeat in the West Midlands. With a Commons majority of only four, this eventuality could not have been accepted with any equanimity. Dick felt that 'the fear of immigration was the most powerful underflow in politics'. He also felt that they had 'out-trumped the Tories' by doing what they would have done in power. Racialism, he thought, was endemic and had to be dealt with by controlling immigration when it got beyond a certain level.

The Conservative Party silenced its supporters who wanted tighter controls, and the more liberal-minded members began to talk about 'integration'. Young Conservatives produced a national policy for integration of existing immigrants and spoke out against racial prejudice and discrimination. Leading members of the party, who had earlier called for tighter controls, began to attack Labour's White Paper for having 'a greater increase of restrictions than the Conservatives wanted'.

Harold Wilson was on the horns of a dilemma. The balance of payments deficit – the difference between what we were earning and what we were spending – was such that the country was facing severe economic difficulties. He was being advised that it was necessary to devalue the pound, or – to use the preferred term – that the pound should be 'floated': this would make exports more competitive and bring much-needed wealth into the country. The alternative was to 'defend the pound' by making cuts in public services, and this was unthinkable. Harold was committed to defending the pound and maintaining social services. How could a socialist Prime Minister think otherwise?

The Rolling Stones were facing no such difficulties. Together with their manager, Andrew Oldham, the Stones were dissatisfied with the deal that had been struck with Decca Records, and so Andrew brought in Allen Klein to improve the band's royalties situation.

The Stones were quite taken with Allen. Keith Richards described him as a "little, fat American geezer, smoking a pipe and wearing the most diabolical clothes", but he made them laugh. More than that, Allen knew the legal side of things.

"We have a killer on our side," said Andrew, "who can handle Decca."

Allen did. His tough negotiations guaranteed the Stones a $3 million contract over the next five years.

"He did a good job," said Keith.

More than that, however, *I Can't Get No Satisfaction* – the Stones latest release with a fantastic new riff by Keith that he'd thought of in his sleep – was storming its way to the top of the charts. It was the ultimate, teenage anthem.

Pete Campbell had come to a decision, and handed his resignation in on time; from the end of August he would no longer be a teacher but Ramblin' Pete Campbell, leader of The Appalachian Four. Hughie was over the moon and Doug Green, their man-of-many-instruments, was also going along, which was good because he was the only one with transport. The bass guitarist, who called himself 'Nat' Stewart, was OK for the summer but was returning to teaching in September. Pete had phoned round the clubs and pubs who'd offered them gigs the previous summer and so they had the first few fixed up by the end of term.

In the end, it had been an easy decision. One of the other teachers, a man in his forties who might have been a sculptor, had scared the life out of him.

"Do it now or you'll never do it. Look at me. I'm a sculptor, but I just didn't have the guts to chance my arm. I'll be stuck here teaching these kids until I pick up my pension after forty years, and I know I'll feel a complete failure. If you don't get out now, everything will close in around you. Your woman will want to marry and have kids, you'll have a mortgage round your neck and you'll actually get to like teaching. But you'll never know what you might have been if you'd got out there and used your talent."

Pete had shared this view with Glenda, who was unimpressed but saw the wisdom of the man's words.

"Teaching is full of people like him – people who think they should be writers or painters or singers or instrumentalists or poets or ... anything but teachers. And we don't need them. Teaching is a vocation, Pete – you had it once, but if you've lost it, you're best to get out altogether. Get it out of your system, and then perhaps you can put your mind to the job."

Glenda was disappointed. She'd thought about marriage and children and building a home. Pete's decision would put her plans back years but she didn't want to hold on to him against his will. No, she wouldn't be coming with them this summer. She'd stay in their flat, recuperate after her absolutely knackering first year's teaching and prepare for the next one, which she was anticipating with pleasure. She'd also try and round up some groups to keep 'Pete's Room' on the folk map, and if he was unfaithful to her while on the road with Hughie Bloody Spragg she'd cut off his balls when he got back and fry them for him for supper.

CHAPTER 25

Racial Harmony

"What do you think of Dylan going all electric, then?" Simon Wiseman asked Stephen Last on their return to college.

"Bob Dylan is about the words," replied Stephen, resting the cup of coffee Simon had made on his friend's desk, "If you can't hear those, it's a shame and a waste of time."

They were sitting in Simon's room at the new Coseley College of Education, chatting and waiting for the others to arrive. All seven had managed to get a room on the ground floor, which had been an achievement since there were only seven rooms. They were beautifully and purposefully furnished, and a far cry from those at Collingwood Hall, which – it was claimed – were held together only by the sticky tape on the walls.

Simon's reference was to Bob Dylan's Newport Folk Festival appearance when he'd been booed by the folk purists who bewailed and begrudged Dylan's move into the rock field.

"But we all listened over and over again to The Byrds version of *Mr Tambourine Man*, didn't we?" insisted Simon, "I expected Bob got a bit pissed off with other groups having hits with his songs."

"I remember one of the girls in the first year saying that Dylan ruined *Blowin' in the Wind* when he sang it. She was hooked on the Peter, Paul and Mary version. But I still preferred Dylan's and I think his *Mr Tambourine Man* has a conscience – a heart beating at its centre – which you don't hear when The Byrds sing it."

Heather Burton – or Glover, to use her married name – was back on the wards. Her parents had come up trumps. It was a mixed blessing, but Heather was pleased overall. Her youth had gone; those careless days of laughter with the girls would not return. She was a mother now and a married woman: that was the way her life was orientated. She was in a year group below Kate and the others and so their paths seldom crossed – but she was back on the wards. Focus on that opportunity, she told herself, and get on with training.

She felt little kinship with the other student nurses. They were only a year younger but seemed almost childish. What's more, they irritated Heather and she knew that to be annoyed by your colleagues was unprofessional. 'The patients come first, last and everywhere. Only the patients matter,' she told herself, over and over again.

The two she was working with today – in the theatre of all places – were two of the clumsiest she'd met. Maybe it was her feelings, though, and they weren't clumsy but simply inexperienced? Heather smiled, and the two younger students smiled back, obviously nervous of her. She found them hanging round the junction of two corridors, uncertain what to do.

"We've been waiting for someone to tell us," explained the blonde one, who would have looked more in place on the cover of a fashion mag, Heather thought. The corridors were bustling with people who took no notice of them. Patients were being wheeled by on trolleys, accompanied by nurses in white dresses and wearing masks.

"We shall need to go to the locker room," urged Heather, "it won't show much initiative if the Theatre Superintendent finds us standing here."

In the locker room, there were toilets and showers at one end and a rack of white theatre dresses at the other. The dresses were short-sleeved with V-necks. Along the top of the rack was a selection of white plimsolls, scrubbed clean.

"We shall need to shower and then change into one of these," Heather explained, "and don't wear your suspender belts or stockings under them. There's a locker for your uniforms."

There were only four sizes of dresses but Heather found one that nearly fitted and tied it with the belt. She was pleased to have shelved the stiff, white collar of her uniform. She looked at the other girls and all three were laughing at how ridiculous they looked when Sister Stephenson walked in. She stared, open-mouthed for a moment, gathered herself together and frowned.

"Hmm," she said, "it's not often I find you young girls actually ready ... Ah, Nurse Burton ... yes, of course, you know the ropes, don't you?"

"Yes, Sister," replied Heather, "but it's Glover, now, not Burton."

"Yes, yes ... of course. I do apologise."

Sister Stephenson was doubly embarrassed – at Heather's condition and the fact she'd used the wrong name. Here she was speaking to someone young enough to be her daughter who had been an unmarried mother and actually had a child of her own. Heather's mother had been embarrassed, too, but had swallowed her pride and got on with the job of returning Heather to her training. The two women smiled at each other, knowing they had more in common with each other than with the younger students despite the age difference.

Striding ahead of the students, Sister Stephenson pointed out the theatres, which were numbered one to six. Each pair had a sponge room. Heather peered into one: the sterilising machines ran down one side and sinks for scrubbing instruments down the other.

The instrument room was lined with glass-shelved cupboards. Sister Stephenson placed a set of instruments on the table.

"You'll need to memorise the name of each instrument and the order in which they go into the set if you're to be any good in theatre. I'll give you an hour or two, and then come back and test you."

When she had gone, the two younger students looked at Heather. She wondered why she felt so confident. It wasn't because she'd done this before. 'It's surprising what a difference a year and a baby make,' she thought.

"Rampley sponge forceps, Parker clamps, Mayo's needle holders, Kocher's assistant scissors, Moynihan clamps," she laughed. "They sound like the incantation for a magic ritual, don't they?"

Neither girl smiled back at Heather.

"Oh come on, you've covered all this in PTS, haven't you?"

"It's one thing to know the names. It's quite another to have to remember them in theatre."

"We will. I don't know why I'm so confident, but I know we will."

Harold Wilson, too, was feeling confident despite the small majority his party held in the House of Commons. It was his view that they should soldier on for another session, although the advice of Dick Crossman and others had been "to hold an election this autumn, with the trade and gold figures good and with the Opposition ill-prepared, is the right time." The current wisdom was that it was either an early election or a pact with the Liberals.

"I have no plans to talk to the Liberals about a pact," he said. "If I wanted one I couldn't persuade the Party to deliver. I am not going to meet Heath or Grimond about it. It is a House of Commons matter. If the Tories want to do some political manoeuvring, let them discredit themselves. The Labour party should leave it to negotiations between the Whips and we should keep our hands clean."

Dick Crossman listened with dismay. He knew Harold saw himself as the gritty Yorkshireman, the British fighter who never gives in but hangs on to the bitter end. He felt that to carry on with a majority of only two would be to miss a golden opportunity.

"Why not travel up to the Conference with me by sleeper?" suggested Harold, "we will talk on the way."

Paul Crisp picked his way through the muddle of suitcases, rucksacks and duffle bags that littered the corridor to the kitchen. Fresh bottles of coffee, packets of tea, bags of sugar, loose oranges, apples and bunches of grapes with opened packets of biscuits were scattered on the worktop.

He pushed them to one side and arranged his two cups. As the kettle boiled, Des and Mike came into the kitchen.

"Making coffee, Crispy?" asked Des, "let's have a cup."

"I've only got the two cups, lads. Sorry ... the water's hot."

"Enjoy your holiday, did you?" asked Mike, "How were the hostels in France?"

"OK, lads."

"I thought they were supposed to be grotty over there."

"No, they were OK."

Des thought it was like speaking to a dead man: no comeback, no camaraderie, no interest in the rest of us, so unlike Paul Crisp.

"You better run along, Crispy," he suggested, "Amanda's coffee might get cold."

'Very bloody funny, Smith,' thought Paul, and left with the drinks. Balancing the cups in one hand, he pushed open the door with the other. The new air piston was powerful and jammed him as he went through; hot coffee spilled over his hands.

"Are you going to keep this, love?" asked Amanda, holding up a photograph album he'd started at college in the first year, when he returned to his room, "Only I thought you said ... you know ..."

She sidled up to him, looked down at his feet and ran his tie through her fingers.

"I thought we were going to start a new album from when we met."

Paul took the album from her, tugged at the clips, removed and ripped each page singly, dropping faces, beaches, rag days ... into the waste bin. 'It's best,' he

thought, 'Amanda's right ... a fresh start ... I've matured.
I love Amanda. She loves me.'

> *"I'm a-thinkin' and a-wonderin' walking down the*
>   *road,*
> *I once loved a woman, a child I am told,*
> *I gave her my heart but she wanted my soul,*
> *But don't think twice, it's all right."*

As he relaxed in the comfort of his new college room,
Stephen sat listening to Dylan's words, and thinking about
Paul Crisp. He'd never approved of Crisp's 'womanising'
in the first year. It seemed to him that either you loved a
woman and went with her or you waited for your time to
come. Nevertheless, he liked Paul, and didn't like what
was happening to him since he'd met Amanda. She was
sucking the joy out of the lad. Once the life and soul of
any gathering, Paul was now a misery, unable to connect
with anyone except Amanda. It wasn't right. Inexperienced
though he was with women, Stephen felt that there was a
morality to relationships. But perhaps it was the other
way around? Had he had more experience with women,
would he have realised that there was no morality to such
relationships?

Enoch Powell had not responded to the invitation
extended to him by the Council for Racial Harmony – a
group founded by Wolverhampton councillors, members
of the Fabian Society and other liberal-minded people.

"We might have expected some leadership from Mr
Powell," commented George Costley, a Labour councillor,
"but it appears not to be forthcoming. His weight behind
us would have been a great help.

Kate had met Bill, while out clubbing with the others. Clubbing formed much of the basis of her social life until Bill came along. He'd been one of a group of lads they'd met at what was called The Grosvenor Club. It sounded posh, but was really only a sort of night club where they over-charged you for the drinks. Bill and his friend had seemed all right – quite good-looking and well-behaved. The other lad had tagged onto Sheila Pratt, and Kate felt pleased for her friend. The only thing was – it separated you from the others. Somehow, Joan and Christine seemed to be dropping away; they were no longer a foursome.

Exams were taking over, too, and this meant that even more of the fun was draining from their lives. Kate had done well; she knew it was true and that her parents would be proud. She'd been through every ward in Staffham General and had loved every minute of her training. Now, with success in sight, she turned to her books with a vengeance. Only Miriam Davison outshone her in assiduousness. What Kate wanted was to absorb the theory so fully that the practical exams would fall naturally into place; she didn't want to stand by a patient's bed wondering what the hell she was doing and why! The final assessment would see her in charge of a ward for a day and, boy, was she going to do well.

Dick Crossman had spent the morning reading the first draft for Harold Wilson's Conference speech. He was troubled by a passage towards the end of the speech in which Harold had more or less said that the Labour Party had "stepped forward and introduced the New Britain".

"But we haven't done it. That's the trouble. And people know we haven't. We haven't even got across the image of a new era. Don't pretend. Let's say instead that we have only built up to the skirting, and ask people to give us the chance to build the whole house," insisted Dick.

"That's a fine idea," replied Harold, lighting his pipe.

"You know, any idea of us being a Kennedy regime is absurd," Dick continued.

Harold looked at him, contemplatively, puffing away quietly for a while before delivering his self-effacing smile.

"I suppose you're right, Dick. You can't really sell a Yorkshire terrier as a borzoi hound."

"In Britain, we prefer a terrier to a borzoi as our leader. It's a clear electoral asset."

The door of Des Smith's room burst open and Mike Harrison stumbled in, much to the surprise and amusement of his friends who were sitting around chatting and drinking coffee. Mike tottered in the doorway, one hand tenderly pressing a bleeding lip. With the other, he slammed the door shut.

"She bit me …It's all right for you to laugh. Knock it off, Yogi, and get me a plaster or something. Blimey, I thought she was going to eat me."

Simon struggled, laughing, to his feet and made for the first aid box in the kitchen, while Stephen and Des gathered round Mike. He'd arrived back in house about half-an-hour before accompanied by a girl with a moustache, who'd poked her head round the door and said hello. Mike had introduced her as Doris. He'd borrowed some coffee and shot off to his room.

"Where the hell did you find her?" asked Des.

"In a pub in Hanley."

"Christ, you can certainly pick them."

Before Mike could reply, Simon returned with the plaster.

"I can't put that on."

"You said to get a plaster."

"Let's have a look," suggested Mike, more or less to himself, as he walked over to the curtained sink area in Des's room. He looked at himself in the mirror, dabbing at his face with water. "She's not coming, is she?"

He walked over to the door and turned the key, before returning to the mirror.

"I'll have to go in a minute," he said, plaintively.

Des laughed with the chuckle that always attracted the girls.

"Is it worth it, lads," he said, "look at us. What the hell are we really after?"

In the background, Bob Dylan was down on *Maggie's Farm*.

Miriam Davison was despondent over the death of Albert Schweitzer. He had been held up to them at school as a person to emulate. "He is one of the most remarkable men of this century," they'd been told. "He is a philosopher, a theologian, a gifted musician, a missionary and a doctor. He gave up all he loved to serve those less fortunate than himself – the lepers of French Equatorial Africa. Like Jesus, he loved the outcasts of this world."

She and Patrick, her fiancé, sat quietly together as they finished their meal at the Won Gon in Newcastle-under-Lyme.

"He was a gifted musician, you know," said Miriam, "His interpretation of Bach's organ works is considered to be unsurpassed by anyone."

"He also lectured in theology at Strasbourg University. You wonder, sometimes, why he gave all that up, don't you."

"To look after those people who had been rejected by their own society, Patrick ... Do you ever think you might be attracted to missionary work?"

"I knew you were thinking that."

"Did you?"

"Yes ... it's what drew you into nursing, isn't it?"

"Well, not the thought of becoming a missionary, but I was drawn by a sense of religious duty ... yes."

"It'll need careful thought, Mimi ... having a large family, which is what you said you wanted, wouldn't be easy in equatorial Africa – not for a white couple who weren't native to the area. You'd have to consider the children's education and everything ..."

"Yes, yes, I know that, Patrick ... trust you to be ... practical. But it is worth thinking about, isn't it?"

CHAPTER 26

'The way to encourage rebellion'

The Beatles were nervous as their Rolls-Royce arrived at Buckingham Palace, but John had tucked something to soothe them inside one of his black boots.

Thousands of fans crowded the gates, struggling for a glimpse of the Fab Four as they stepped from the limousine, immaculately dressed and with their mop-tops suitably coiffured. It was the ultimate accolade, the seal of approval, to be the first pop group ever to be awarded the MBE.

John, Paul, George and Ringo looked around, apparently suitably impressed with their surroundings. They were kings of the pop world attending an investiture with their Queen. After the initial fuss – the usual explosion of old colonels – it was generally agreed that they deserved the award, if only for the millions of pounds worth of trade they'd brought to Britain.

Just before the actual investiture was about to start, the Beatles adjourned to a small toilet inside the palace and passed one marijuana joint around.

Stephen Last thrust forward across the lawn against the gusts of wind, the autumn leaves swirling about his legs.

The trees were being ripped to skeletons, and he gripped the pile of books he carried closely against his chest. As he reached the path, Des Smith appeared from round the corner of the college, white-faced, the grey shaving marks texturing his cheeks. Stephen thought he'd never seen his friend look so ghastly. Des stopped as he saw Stephen, and they watched each other for a moment across the boisterous leaves.

"Working?" asked Des.

"Like hell. I'm burning my guts out over this one."

'This one' was Stephen's English special study, and he'd chosen to chase the incidence of black comedy across English and European literature; partway through and with no chance of turning back, he wished he hadn't.

"I've hardly started mine," complained Des, who'd chosen to examine Orwell's literary criticism in terms of the writer's political agenda. "Apart from the reading, that is. I'm finding it difficult to pick out an angle of attack ... Coffee?"

The coffee was scolding hot, but both gulped and swallowed.

"You're a lucky bugger, you are," said Des, with a heartless laugh, thinking not so much of Stephen's 'luck' with Jenny Pryce as with his own lack of it with Susan Paget.

"Are you and Elizabeth still not settled?" asked Stephen, evading the 'Susan issue', which he knew troubled Des endlessly.

"Not as we were before ... I've really been through it with Susan. I'll never be able to give myself to a woman again."

"You can hardly lay the blame at Elizabeth's feet."

"Last summer, Elizabeth was quite narked when I spent time playing my guitar. I could have understood her attitude if it had been a short holiday, but we had all summer – all day to see each other … 'I gave her my heart, but she wanted my soul' …"

Stephen smiled at the quote from Dylan. He'd benefitted from his friendship with Des. He'd come to view women in a different light; they had suddenly seemed more accessible.

"Elizabeth means less to me now. I can't take love seriously anymore … You can be making love with a woman and working out the symmetry of the wallpaper …"

Stephen's intimacy with Jenny Pryce hadn't reached that stage. They hadn't 'gone the whole way', but he was totally absorbed in his love for her when they were together. Further down the road there was a promised land. He and Jenny would get there when they were ready.

"People do things because they're frightened not to do them," he said, without knowing why or from where the thought had come.

Des looked at his friend, about to protest that he and Elizabeth hadn't got that involved because they'd followed whatever everyone else was doing. In fact, none of his mates had had sex before that summer – the summer before he left home for college. He couldn't help wondering, now, what had motivated Elizabeth. Was it the belief that if she 'gave herself' she would be more likely to hold on to him? Was he letting her down if he didn't marry her?

His desire for Susan had been overwhelming, and she'd surely got something from him, hadn't she? And yet, somehow, he couldn't quite commit himself. It was the thought of her background, the thought of where she'd come from and to where she'd return. Somehow, he didn't feel he could cope with being middle class.

Harold Wilson had already made the decision to travel to Rhodesia himself and negotiate directly with Ian Smith. He was quite committed to the task, despite the risk it might involve with regard to his own safety, before he spoke to Cabinet. Those who knew and admired him saw Harold's predicament: he was dreadfully concerned to avoid a state of war with the Smith regime. Many of the white settlers in Rhodesia had relatives in Britain and the British public, while acknowledging the need to stand up to Smith's racist policies, would not tolerate the government sending in troops against fellow whites. Besides, Edward Heath, Leader of the Opposition, would exploit such a move with ruthlessness; white Rhodesians had a powerful lobby in the British Parliament.

The Cabinet could see that Harold was right to be doing everything possible to avoid a Unilateral Declaration of Independence by the Smith regime, but doubted the wisdom of Harold going personally to Salisbury. UDI was coming, Dick Crossman thought, whatever Harold attempted to achieve as an alternative; Ian Smith had made that 'insultingly clear'.

"Could not a delegation be sent out? Might it not include Alec Douglas-Home, the Shadow Foreign Secretary? You risk not only your life but your reputation."

It was clear to Barbara Castle that Ian Smith was enjoying 'playing cat and mouse' with Harold: one moment he would hint at concessions to the idea of majority rule and, at another, withdraw them. She passed a note along to one of her colleagues; it read 'if we sold out on this I should resign'. She was all for sending in the troops to suppress what amounted to a colonial rebellion. It had been done in the past – why not now?

Seizing the chance – and she was never nothing if not dogged – Barbara collared Harold in his study at Number 10.

"You do realize, Harold, that if the Rhodesian negotiations go the wrong way I shall have to resign?" she stipulated.

"I would resign myself," he replied, bouncing her threat back with typical cheerfulness.

"I see the Pope has exonerated the Jews from any blame attached to the death of Jesus," remarked Joan Whiting, "That must be a tremendous relief for them all."

"You'll not rouse me, Joan," laughed Kate Walsh, "We've had a nice evening. Let's keep it that way."

The four of them – Joan and Kate with Sheila Pratt and Christine Dixon – had taken advantage of the fact that they all had the same night off, and gone to see *Help!* They were now sitting in the Coach and Horses, enjoying a drink. Joan, not one to let the conversation lapse into trivialities, decided to goad Kate about Pope Paul VI's latest gesture.

"Joan has a point though, doesn't she?" insisted Christine, "Who the hell is the Vatican Council or the Pope, who's supposed to lead them, to condemn a whole race for something that happened nearly two thousand years ago."

"I agree, I agree," said Kate, soothingly.

"For centuries, the Roman Catholic Church has preached that all Jews were, and are, guilty of complicity in the crucifixion of Christ. So, it's OK to torture, murder and persecute Jews with impunity," continued Christine.

"Leave it, Chris. You can't blame Kate for what a group of old men in the Vatican have done," pleaded Sheila.

"I'm not – we're not," said Joan, "We're just talking about it. It's in today's paper, Sheila. It's news. It's taken the Catholic Church centuries to undo an injustice. Why?"

"You don't go along with all that stuff, do you Kate?" asked Christine, quietly.

"No ... I'm not a practising Catholic – except when we go to special services with mum ..."

"So would you use birth control?" Joan asked.

"I don't know ... I've never thought about it from a personal point of view, but I do agree with birth control. In the Third World, it's the only way to prevent children being born who can't be fed."

"Isn't there ... I don't know ... an hypocrisy there, somewhere? I mean, can you just pick and choose what you believe and what you will or won't do from your faith?" asked Joan.

"You sound like mum – 'a Truth is a Truth, it's not to be changed for the sake of convenience' – but life's not like that, is it? I look to the Church for spiritual guidance, but I'm not to be bullied by a group of old men who make up rules to suit the church rather than ... rather than the people the church serves ... I've never thought about it like that before, but it's what I feel."

"But the Pope is in direct communion with your God, isn't he? These 'rules' are divinely inspired, aren't they?"

Christine badgered Kate, pleased to be involved in the kind of argument they'd always – as a large family – enjoyed at home.

"Mum's generation believes that to be true, but I'm not sure mine does. The Vatican must have a spiritual authority as far as Catholics are concerned, but I'm not sure that all their decisions are inspired by God or made for the right reasons. Some are made from expediency and others simply for the benefit of the Church rather than in deference to the teachings of the Bible."

"Kate – they'd have burnt you at the stake for saying that, three hundred years ago. It's heresy! Are you sure you're not an atheist?" said Joan, with a laugh.

"Oh yes. I'm not sure that God is the old man in the sky with the long, white beard but I'm aware of a spiritual dimension to our lives. We just mustn't let ourselves be bullied by the priests – men who have little or no experience of the world, and certainly have no experience of the marriage bed."

Sheila stared 'gob-smacked' at Kate, who seemed to be off-loading the stifled thoughts of a Catholic childhood.

"I respect your views, Kate," said Christine, "but I've no time for any of this religious twaddle. It's time we looked at man – and woman – as the centre of the world, and found a way forward based on our common humanity. Religion divides people more than it unites."

"It doesn't have to ..."

"But it does, Kate. Look at Northern Ireland: a country divided by one thing – religion."

"There are bigots on both sides ..." began Kate.

"... and some of the worst bigots have no faith at all," continued Christine, "There was no spiritual dimension to Fascism ... I see that, but I think mankind is the centre, not religion ... Are you religious, Sheila?"

"We never talked about it at home," replied Sheila, "It was never discussed. I know nothing about it except what we were taught at school – ooh, and Sunday school."

"You went to Sunday school?"

"Dad made us. He said it gave him and mum a bit of peace."

Michael Ramsey, Archbishop of Canterbury, sat down to write his letter to Harold Wilson. As President of the British Council of Churches, he had listened carefully to the views of many people. At its meeting in Aberdeen, the council resolved to sanction the use of force in Rhodesia as the last resort.

Rhodesia possessed a modern army and air force – British trained and British led – and it was doubtful, Michael thought, that such a force would be willing to fire on the Queen's men; likewise, any force sent by Britain would think twice before firing on those they regarded as British. He knew that the Labour government was against such a move, but he knew, also, that there were those who considered the threat of force would be sufficient to end the rebellion before it began. One such person was Kenneth Skelton, Bishop of Matabeleland in Rhodesia.

Renouncing the use of force as an option was a way to encourage rebellion. If the Churches supported it as a last resort it might help to put some backbone into Harold Wilson's negotiations with Ian Smith. Otherwise, Michael was convinced that the government would find itself involved in the establishment of a racialist state. Christian morality was never on the side of conflict, but morality demanded the use of force if all else failed.

Michael put pen to paper.

Pete Campbell was pleased with the progress of the Appalachian Four so far – at least he was pleased with reservations. They weren't making enough money to live on but Glenda always sent him a postal order and, as Hughie Spragg pointed out, "there was always a chick somewhere who'd give you a meal if you played your cards right." Pete had no desire to shuffle his cards. He wasn't there to be unfaithful to Glenda by "grabbing a piece of arse", as Hughie put the notion, but if some of the folk groupie birds wouldn't take 'no' for an answer it made life difficult.

What Pete wanted was a recording contract. He didn't agree that folk couldn't be electric. Dylan had led the way at Newport, but the British folk scene was dead set against the idea; and Pete was wise enough to know that whereas Dylan might get away with it (and hadn't *Bringing It All Back Home* shown that to be true?) he – Pete – would have a fight on his hands. The labels that mattered – like Transatlantic – were signing up the ethnic types: those with violins and penny whistles. He wasn't rooted in that tradition. His father had been a market trader, and not a steelworker, a coalminer or a farmer's boy. He was more comfortable with *The John B Sails* than the *Foggy, Foggy Dew*. Also, he wasn't a writer of songs – he was no Ewan MaColl, but more the Lonnie Donegan of folk.

It was three months into their rather ragged tour that Pete Campbell's Appalachian Four met Ken Parkes, who offered to manage the group. Hughie disliked the man on sight – he didn't see how a taxi driver could know anything about folk music – but the other two members of the group thought they had nothing to lose by accepting Ken's offer.

"These taxi drivers get around," explained Doug Green, their man-of-many-instruments, he with the transport, "This guy may look as shifty as a Cockney barrow boy, but he'll know the clubs as well as the pubs."

"And he's a persuasive little sod," continued Penny Grove, a girl who'd dropped out of school and into the group when 'Nat' Stewart, the bass player, had returned to teaching at the start of term, "We might start to earn some real money."

Penny wasn't as good a bass player as Nat, but she was learning; moreover, despite describing herself as a "drop-out", she had her head screwed on, and Pete respected her opinion.

"How much are you getting in the pubs?" asked Ken, "As much as you can drink and a tenner in your hand at the end of the night? The clubs and the universities will pay you a hundred pound a time. How long would it take you to earn that much teaching?"

As Pete had been on forty pound a month working in school, it didn't take long to work that one out; he agreed that the group should play Manchester University the following Saturday, when Ken said he was sure he could fix it.

Michael Ramsey looked at the high altar in Canterbury Cathedral with dismay. The word PEACE had been sprayed on the altar using an aerosol paint gun. Red and blue paint smothered the chairs and a Bible open on the lectern. The tomb of the Black Prince and St Augustine's chair had been similarly treated.

Michael's letter supporting the use of force as a last resort in Rhodesia had shown him who his allies were: he had been supported by the Communist Party and a group of Oxford atheists. A quiet smile crossed his face as the thought occurred to him. It was true, of course, that some in the House had also proved to be allies: Michael Foot, Shirley Williams and David Steel and, privately, Edward Heath among them.

Overall, however, the public outrage had been hostile: the *Daily Sketch* and the *Daily Telegraph* had blazoned correct, but possibly misleading, headlines to the effect that he supported force, while the *Daily Express* and the *Daily Mail* had been appalled and shocked, indulging in cartoons of the archbishop armed to the teeth and wearing a grenade instead of a cross around his neck.

He had also offended Canon John Collins of CND fame and Lord Soper, a leading pacifist, as well as the Rhodesian Front in England that was allied to the right wing of the Conservative Party. The Earl of Southesk had invited him to resign. Worst of all, perhaps, was the deafening silence from his own clergy: only a few – notably Mervyn Stockwood, Bishop of Southwark – came out in his support.

Outwardly, he remained serene, apparently tolerant of the storm of abuse that raged about him, but inwardly he was facing his "most grievous trial". He felt frightened, fearing that if he approached a former friend he might be repulsed. He was called a "bloody bugger" by a once-courteous peer in the corridors of Parliament and attacked by friends in the press. The police gave him protection at Sunday services in Canterbury Cathedral. It was a sore trail for a shy man.

Marguerite Bannister passed the newspaper across to Jenny Pryce and pointed to the one article that had dominated conversation in so many homes across the land. There were tears in her eyes and hate in her usually gentle heart.

Ian Brady, a twenty-seven year old clerk, and his twenty-three year old typist girlfriend, Myra Hindley, had been charged with the murder of ten year old Lesley Anne Downey, whose body had been found in a shallow grave on Saddleworth Moor.

The couple had also been linked with the disappearance of twelve year old John Kilbride, whose body had also been found buried on the moor. A third body, that of seventeen year old Edward Evans, was found in Brady's house wrapped in a blanket.

The article went on to talk of the nation's 'universal disgust' at the crimes and of the crowd of two hundred who screamed abuse when the couple appeared in court to be remanded in custody while the police carried out further investigations.

"You realise what's happening today, don't you?" said Marguerite, quietly. "Parliament is passing that bill which will abolish the death penalty. When this pair are found guilty – and they will be – they won't hang for what they've done ... they'll lose their freedom, hopefully forever, but they won't hang … There's at least two other children missing as well, you know … but Hindley and Brady won't hang for their horrible crimes … It isn't right …It can't be right."

CHAPTER 27

'You stay in the stadiums, Billy'

During the long summer of 1965, Billy Graham had been sickened by the wanton violence and widespread destruction in the Watts neighbourhood of Los Angeles. As he toured the area accompanied by Dr E V Hill, a respected black pastor in Watts, Billy realised there were no easy answers, and had no doubt that extremists on both sides exploited the situation for their own ends. He was sure there would be no solution to the problem of racism without spiritual renewal. 'Hatred and racism are fundamentally moral and spiritual problems', he thought. During that summer he held several rallies.

"You stay in the stadiums, Billy," said Martin Luther King, "because you will have far more impact on the white establishment there than you would if you marched in the streets. Besides that, you have a constituency that will listen to you, especially among white people, who may not listen so much to me. But if a leader gets too far out in front of his people, they will lose sight of him and not follow him any longer."

Pete Campbell's Appalachian Four had a rough ride at the first gig arranged by Ken Parkes; the students at

Manchester University booed as soon as the group plugged in their equipment. Pete was appalled. He'd expected a similar welcome to that enjoyed by The Spinners at Collingwood Hall. Students might not like electric folk; he'd quite expected not to be asked to return but not outright hostility.

"They've become a mob," said Doug Green, as the four rested from their first set, "They're taking their cue from what happened to Dylan at the Newport Folk Festival. We can do without this sort of thing."

"It's only a few," pleaded the union rep who joined them in the Green Room, "we're sorting them out."

"It's a few too many," snapped Penny Grove, "If we get any more of that when we go out for the second set, I'll tell them to fuck off."

Hughie laughed and Pete looked at her in amazement. He'd never heard a woman swear like that before; in fact, come to think of it, he'd never heard a woman swear. On the odd occasion he'd let a 'bloody' drop from his lips, Glenda had picked him up on his "bad language".

But the gig brought them their first lengthy bookings. The publican father of one of the students offered them six weeks work in two Irish bars that he owned – one in Liverpool and the other in Manchester.

"You'll need to include some Irish numbers in your repertoire," he said, "*The Irish Rover, The Black Velvet Band, Whiskey in the Jar* ... songs like that. You'll go down a treat."

"We could even manage *The Wearing of the Green*, if you wanted it," said Penny, giving him a sly look.

"No, I think you'd best leave that one," replied the publican, "Unless, of course ..."

"Leave it to us," interrupted Ken Parkes, "We'll come up with something suitable."

Pete smiled at the "us" and the "we". Ken's knowledge of folk music could be written on a postage stamp, but he had brought them the contact by mingling with the audience and Pete was grateful. Moreover, this promised to be his kind of music: folk with a punch.

Sitting in the Fairfield Arms afterwards, Penny said:

"We need to re-shape the show for these venues. We're going to be playing several nights in the one place. We're going to need a helluver lot of material and a different slant each night. We're also going to need to break up the singing with some chat – just to keep down on the number of songs …"

"And to engage the audience," agreed Pete, "I can see that, and I can see that we shall need to follow-through on songs so that similar ones fall together …"

"A satirical section followed by a humorous one followed by a sentimental one, you mean?" asked Doug.

"Yes – you're not going to follow *John Henry* with *The Unicorn*, are you? We need to control the mood of the audience."

Pete could feel the excitement rising in him. He'd get Glenda up over the weekends. He'd missed her in more ways than one: she wasn't just a good cook. If Ken could get a rep from one of the record companies in one night, they might start to get somewhere.

People in Britain were sick to death of the smut, permissiveness, innuendo, foul language and blatant sexuality in television programmes and films; it was time for a clean-up, and the country had found a crusader.

Mary Whitehouse announced the formation of the National Viewers' and Listeners' Association.

The moral slide had started with *TW3* in 1962 and careered downhill ever since. Mary had the support of over half a million people – a sizeable proportion of the population considering that most people who moan are reluctant to actually do anything about their complaints.

Kate's mother, Florence Walsh, was one of those reluctant to rise from her armchair but had signed up to Mary's organisation, pleased that, at last, she and people like her had a voice. It was clear that Mary was prepared to face ridicule and abuse to promote a cleaner country, and Florence was behind her all the way.

Maurice Walsh was also relieved. He felt that his wife might berate him less if she perceived a spokesman out there in the public domain. He would encourage his wife to write letters to Mrs Whitehouse rather than lecture him from the fireside.

"There's no doubt you have a real crusader in Mrs Whitehouse," he said to his wife, passing a glance to Kate from behind the *Daily Mail*.

Kate wondered whether to respond. She'd brought Bill home for the weekend and didn't want a scene, but she knew her father could be quite good fun in his present mood and that he and Bill got on well.

"Times move on, Mum," she said, "We don't want to go back to the days when the Lord Chamberlain told us what we could and could not watch."

"Better that than have children subjected to filth in their living rooms."

"People can always turn off what they don't want to see,"

"Hmm! Do you really think that will happen? And anyway, we don't want it on the screen in the first place. I don't pay my television licence to have people put smut on the screen. Why should I turn it off? I pay my licence fee. I want to watch something decent – not what some dirty little tyke at the BBC thinks I should watch."

"I think what your mum is saying, Kate, is that someone, somewhere, will decide what we watch. It won't be us, and she'd rather it was the Lord Chamberlain than some smutty script writer or producer at the BBC. Programmes like *'Til Death Us Do Part* and *TW3* will only lead to worse. They'll start a downhill slide into the cesspit. We'll soon be watching people having you-know-what on the screen," reasoned Bill

Kate looked at Bill, open-mouthed. Was he taking her mother's side? And was he as old-fashioned as he sounded?

"At least Bill's got some sense," said Florence Walsh, "at least he can see what I mean."

"He can also see what I mean," replied Kate, giving Bill a look that suggested she might continue the argument elsewhere.

"You've got a fellow traveller there, Florrie," interjected Maurice Walsh, "It's not often someone in the family agrees with you so whole-heartedly. Do you fancy going down The Woodman, Bill?"

Bill did, leaving Kate to help her mother prepare the Sunday lunch and argue out the rights and wrongs of censorship.

Ian Smith had issued his Unilateral Declaration of Independence: all the dashing about and the last minute talks by British politicians with the Smith regime had failed to achieve any measure of agreement. Dick Crossman had always known this would happen, and so, he thought, had everyone else. Rhodesia's ties with Britain, the Commonwealth and all of black Africa were broken. There couldn't have been more than a quarter of a million whites in the country, but they were now the ones to decide its future.

Britain was under pressure to punish Rhodesia for this illegal act; the government was under pressure from most African states and many international powers. 'Harold could never accept that there was an alternative to a negotiated settlement,' thought Dick, 'and now he's unprepared to act.'

"I didn't sleep well last night, Dick," said Harold, "and it's quite unlike me."

"What are your plans?" asked Dick, with some hesitation because he'd previously been reluctant to press Harold for a decision. "What are you organising?"

Dick had the impression that Harold saw no choice between 'conventional military action and conventional diplomatic action', and yet there had to be a third course. Could he not consider the use of black subversive action to put pressure on Smith?

"UDI is seen as succeeding in the short run, isn't it?" pursued Dick, "Sanctions – if they work at all – are unlikely to have any immediate effect?"

His tone was a questioning one because he was still reluctant to push Harold further, and sensed that the Prime Minister felt he could do nothing about the matter once UDI was declared. During negotiations, Harold had dominated the scene. He had even taken on a 'more portentous, statesmanlike appearance', but he now had no plans to crush the rebellion, no way of enforcing law and order.

Stephen Last rested his back against the wall and stretched his legs sideways across Jenny's bed. She handed him a cup of her excellent coffee and sat beside him. They'd got on well together since they'd taken up with each other in the spring, and were easy in each other's company. The sexual restraint hadn't been a real impediment to their friendship; both had been brought up in a world where the man respected the woman's wishes. When she was ready, Jenny would make her desires clear.

"Would you like me to cook something tonight?" she asked, "I've got the ingredients for a nice curry."

The kitchens in the new residential blocks were well equipped, and Jenny worked wonders on the new cooker.

"It'll be great," he replied, "I'd like that. Thanks."

"You're always so appreciative, aren't you, Stevie? I don't think I've ever met a man who says 'thanks' so often."

"Breeding," he replied with a laugh, not meaning what he said but knowing it to be true.

"You're quiet tonight. You've got something on your mind, haven't you?"

"Yes, I have ... The Ipswich pool interviews are taking place next term and I've got an application form."

"You're going back home when we finish our course?"

"I feel I owe it to my parents. They've supported me through O levels, A levels and this three years at teacher training college. I think they'd appreciate me going home for a year as a way of saying 'thank you'."

"I see. I thought you'd be coming to Wolverhampton and ... perhaps finding a flat somewhere."

"It's not that I want to go, you understand."

"But you do, don't you Stevie?"

"I don't like ... thinking of not being with you next year but ..."

"But what?"

"There's no chance you can come down to Ipswich, is there? It's a nice town."

He hadn't meant to ask the question; he didn't suppose that Jenny felt less need than he did to return home.

"So is Wolverhampton, and we know the Midlands ... perhaps I feel the same about going home for a year."

"Yes, of course ... I didn't mean ... I just meant that I don't want you to feel I think any less of you because I'm returning home. I just see it as my duty."

After their conversation, Jenny decided she didn't feel like cooking a meal and so they walked silently, hand in hand, through the village of Coseley. It was an evening cold but gently coloured by a purple sky. They gazed into private houses and watched people passing, as they made their way towards The Offley Arms. There was gentleness between, but also a sudden realization that they must bring their relationship to a moment of decision. If they were engaged, the year apart would have a point: it would be saving towards the wedding. If they remained just boyfriend and girlfriend, they would drift away from each other.

"If you were in my position with Jenny, you'd stick close wouldn't you?" Stephen asked Des when they returned from the pub, where they'd met and the tension between Jenny and Stephen had subsided for a while.

"You're not kidding."

"You wouldn't be tempted to leave her, even for a while?"

"Christ – what are you driving at? I thought there was something funny going on between Jenny and you tonight."

"I'm happy with Jenny – don't get me wrong – but I feel I owe it to my parents to go back home for a year. My mother, in particular ..."

"Stephen, if you leave Jenny for any reason – real or imaginary – you're mad. It's not any of my business, but if things between you are as they seem ... then it would be callous and pointless. Christ – you amaze me, Last! Are you really as hard as nails – the tight little bugger who came here over two years ago, knowing nothing about women at all? Why think of doing anything like leaving her for a year? Why even consider it? God – you depress me."

"I shouldn't have shared my problems. Sorry. A problem shared is a problem doubled."

"This is no time for stale wit," snapped Des.

At the monthly National Executive Committee meeting, Ian Mikardo suddenly leapt to his feet. Dick Crossman was astonished, but used to Ian's imperious style.

"We have to make a decision about votes for eighteen year olds. If we don't do it this very morning, the Speaker's Conference on electoral reform will reach the item without Labour members submitting a view to paper. I would like your views."

Dick offered his strong supported, followed by Tony Wedgwood Benn, and no one who sat round the table spoke against the idea. 'The funny thing is,' thought Dick, 'none of the prominent members of the Government are here – Harold, George Brown, James Callaghan or Michael Stewart – and yet the NEC has taken its collective decision. It must be good for the Labour Party that the Executive acts on its own."

Miriam Davison was very busy on the gynaecological ward. It was an efficient ward run by Sister McKechnie, and it suited Miriam's temperament. It was only a small ward situated in the old wing of the hospital but the very intimacy, thought Miriam, suited the needs of the patients. She liked the high Victorian windows; no one could see out very easily, but no one could peer in, and that was right. There were sixteen patients. They were admitted for scrapes, hysterectomies, vaginal repairs and ... 'terminations'.

Miriam hated the very word. A termination was an abortion; it was the taking of a life, whichever way you looked at it. It was one part of her nursing she saw as a contradiction; you couldn't nurse an abortion. An abortion was dead. You could nurse the ... mother. Well no, you couldn't nurse the mother because she wasn't going to be one.

She knew she should never have brought the subject up with Joan Whiting, but Miriam felt the need to challenge someone's moral stance on the issue. It was the reluctant desire for such an argument that took her round to the ground floor flat shared by her friends. Joan listened to Miriam with that implacable face of hers, but remained thoughtful when Miriam outlined her objections. It was Christine Dixon who spoke first.

"I can see what you're saying, Miriam, but I can't agree with you."

"I thought you were all for large families."

"I am. There are seven of us, but we were all wanted. Can you imagine what it's like for an unwanted child in this world?"

"That argument doesn't justify abortions. People should think before they create a child they don't want," retaliated Miriam.

"But they don't. We're not all guided by your fine moral sense, Miriam."

"Heather's baby was the result of a broken condom," said Kate, "but she wouldn't be without Chas now."

"Heather was fit to be a mother. Some of these girls aren't. They don't want the child, and the child is condemned to a loveless life. Far better that the life should not be started in the first place," said Joan, coming into the conversation at last.

"This isn't a moral issue, Miriam. It's a practical one."

"That makes no sense at all, Christine. Morality should inform all we do. We're moral beings, not animals."

"But it doesn't. Morality, as you put it, doesn't have any place in some people's lives. They just do what they want to do, and an unwanted child is the result ..."

"Whoa – just a minute," Joan interjected, "There is such a thing as being carried away by the moment. Not all women who find themselves pregnant are sluts, Chris. You don't know Heather, but if you did you wouldn't describe her as promiscuous."

"I'm not saying you would. I'm sorry. I didn't mean to insult your friend."

"It's not a simple issue, is it?" said Sheila Pratt, "People have different views of what's right and wrong. I do think that it's down to the individual conscience of the two people concerned. I don't think anyone can impose their own moral standards on everyone else."

They all looked at Sheila, who only spoke when she had considered an issue fully. Joan found it amusing that Sheila liked to prepare all her arguments in advance in case she was wrong-footed.

"Why – you're not having it away, are you Sheila?" she suggested, spitefully.

Kate led the laughter; she felt it would ease Sheila's embarrassment, and it did. Sheila laughed with her friends.

"No, I'm not," she replied to Joan, "I've just been thinking about it, that's all."

"We're all a little ahead of the times, aren't we?" Kate continued, "Despite what's being talked about in the papers at the moment, hospitals only do terminations if there's a risk to the health of the mother or the child, and that risk has to be certified by two doctors."

"Abortions on demand will come," said Joan, "You can see it a mile off."

"Exactly," insisted Miriam, "and that's my point. We should be encouraging a moral attitude to life, not an expedient one. One of the consultants was talking about it today, and he said he'd never carry out an abortion unless it was absolutely necessary. He said that we were moving in the wrong direction."

"He'll have no choice," replied Joan, "Legally he'll be bound to abort if there is any chance of a risk of any kind to what they'll call 'the wellbeing of the mother'."

"But surely, that's better than these girls going to a backstreet abortionist, isn't it?" asked Christine, "Dirty old women operating in unhygienic conditions, causing infection and haemorrhaging."

"No one has to go to such people," insisted Miriam.

"But they do go, Miriam, they do go. Right or wrong, they do go. If I had to vote on the matter, I'd vote for hygienic terminations in a nice clean hospital ward," insisted Christine, "But we're back to square one, aren't we? This is where we all came in ... let's go out and enjoy ourselves. There's a new film on – Julie Christie in *Darling*. If you want to witness moral turpitude, Miriam, come and watch Julie."

"Dirk Bogarde's in it, isn't he?" asked Kate, "I've always fancied him."

"I'm meeting Patrick, later," said Miriam, "Enjoy yourselves."

It could have been an excuse, but they all knew Miriam wouldn't have made any excuse that involved a lie, however small. Waving her goodbye, they all knew that she was really going to meet her fiancé.

"What's going on?" whispered Mike, pulling Simon into the shadow of the wall.

Returning from the Offley Arms, they'd entered the college grounds and crossed to their residential block, where they'd seen torches flashing and heard sliding windows and the sound of singing voices. A figure was pacing between the two men's blocks with a torch in its right hand. The figure would turn at the sound of a window or voice and flash the torch towards it; at which point another window would slide up or another voice start singing.

"Torchy, Torchy, the battery boy."

The figure twitched and turned in the darkness responding foolishly to the taunting sound of the television jingle. Soon, torches also appeared at the windows and flashed on and off at the lone figure, picking it out for a moment and then shutting it back into darkness.

"Torchy, Torchy, the battery boy."

When one of the torches lit the figure's face, Simon realised that it was Andy McGregor, the Geography tutor and titular housemaster of their block. It was his role to keep order in much the same way that order had been kept at Collingwood Hall, where each house had a housemaster living with his family. The wisest of these turned a blind eye, but Andy was not among the wisest – or it may have been deemed that he took his role seriously.

"We should have been in by eleven," whispered Mike, "He'd better not see us. He won't be in the best of humours."

"Torchy, Torchy, the battery boy," sang several voices from several windows simultaneously and in a rough harmony

Among them Simon thought he heard the Welsh tenor of Bryn Edwards.

"The revolution starts here," laughed Simon, as they crept carefully along the wall to the shadow of Stephen Last's unlit window on which they tapped lightly.

CHAPTER 28

An absolute promise to work for peace

Elizabeth Sturlson, Des's girlfriend, was aware that his feelings for her were on the wane; she had sensed it that first summer when he returned from teacher training college only to leave within a short time to find work down south. She wasn't sure whether there was anybody else, but she didn't think so; it wouldn't be like Des to be unfaithful. Her friends had warned her that it might happen – that their relationship would be under strain when he went to college, but she'd laughed it off; she'd thought they were too close for anything to come between them.

University hadn't dulled her love for Des. She was in her second year at Leicester, and loving every minute of it. Philosophy and political studies hadn't been her first choice, but you couldn't read English unless you had Latin at O level and Latin hadn't been offered as a subject at their grammar school. She'd made stacks of friends and was enjoying herself without feeling the need to have a special boyfriend. They'd tried it on, but she'd laughed the lads off and the friendships were good.

Des remained special to Elizabeth. They hadn't met until the sixth form when he'd been in his final year and she'd just started. He'd been the good-looking boy with the guitar and she'd been the envy of her friends, but there was more to their friendship than a boy-girl romance. They shared a similar background: ink-stained desks fixed to the floor of classrooms by metal runners, pens with steel nibs that needed dipping incessantly (the new biros were barred), classrooms stuffed with forty children so the teacher never got round to see you because you were bright and didn't need the help, the boys and girls in separate playgrounds, cod-liver oil and orange juice ladled down your throat like medicine, food rationing until you were eight or nine, green lino on every floor and "making do because you don't know when the hard times will return" (one of her mother's oft-repeated warnings), Monday wash days with huge sheets flapping on the garden line, terraced housing and back alleys, having your hair plaited every morning or cut "short back and sides", your father "laid-off" at a moment's notice, the hard graft of the allotment at the end of a week's work, steam trains and arriving at your destination covered in smuts, having your aunts spit on their handkerchiefs and rub your face clean, the cream and brown paint of the council houses when you were moved from the back alleys, walking a mile to school and back four times a day (only the poor kids had school dinners), the only green being the town's park a mile away (there was not a tree or blade of grass in sight where they lived), Friday bath night when all the children shared the same bath one after the other (mum and dad, she knew, stripped washed at the kitchen sink), the house always freezing cold with ice on the inside of the windows in winter.

None of this made you bear a grudge, but it forged your attitude towards society. Before Des, it was always a feeling; after Des, it became a thought. After Des ... and yet before!

It was before Des that she became aware of communists and socialists. Her dad talked about the Workers' Educational Association and knew a man in the NUR, which she later learned meant the National Union of Railwaymen. This man could "make trouble for the bosses", but Elizabeth wasn't sure what this meant. She'd heard of strikes, but they just inconvenienced everybody; she remembered one strike when the family went hungry for what seemed weeks on end.

She knew, too, that her dad was in the Labour Party and was suspicious of the Communist Party. Communists wanted to dominate people, and not free them. One of her friends at grammar school had a father who was a Labour MP and was going to "change society through Socialism", which she understood to be "taking over the means of production". It was all about workers having a share in the future of their society, and only people like her mum and dad and herself could make that happen. You couldn't trust the Tories; only Labour politicians would bring change that would benefit everyone.

Parliament, too, was removed from the people; the politicians down there fostered the north south divide. In the south people were richer and had better houses with bathrooms. People needed to feel more involved, and yet no one seemed to understand what went on so far away. Parliament was remote from the people.

These were vague ideas that formed her mind before she met Des and through him became involved in folk music and the Young Socialists. Des got on well with her dad.

"Education frees people to think," he said, when he realised Des was to become a teacher, "If you're going to become a teacher, son, that's good news. It's time teachers came from the working classes rather than the middle. Education is the way forward."

Elizabeth agreed with her father and with Des, but university had made her ask whether teachers in the classroom could do it all, whether changing people's attitudes was enough, whether it wasn't in politics that the real power resided. Didn't education need a political arm? She was beginning to wonder whether life had more in store for her than the role of mother, housewife and … whatever work she decided to do when she completed university.

Yet she saw none of this without Des. She'd given herself to him as only a girl in love can and the idea that it might not be forever was not to be considered.

Marguerite Bannister had no such doubts about her future. She was looking forward to leaving college the following July and settling down to work as a teacher in the local secondary modern school; they didn't teach Home Economics in the grammar as far as she knew, but she wouldn't have worked there among the privileged if they did. Her role was to raise the expectations of the underprivileged: the children who wouldn't make grammar school even if they were bright enough because they hadn't the background to support them through higher education.

She and Bobby would save up until they had enough

deposit to put down on a house, and then they'd get married. When that happened, she'd be a housewife and then – perhaps a few years down the road – a mother.

"… and yes, he can put his boots out to be cleaned every night, and I'll do them gladly," she taunted Jenny Pryce.

"Really?"

"Really – and why not? I love him, and Bobby will see that as a sign that I do."

"But you'll be holding down a job, as well as him. Can't he clean his own boots?"

"Why should he? I'll be the housewife and see to the housework and the children. He'll see to the garden and the allotment and the decorating and everything else a man does. He'll even put out the rubbish!" she laughed.

"I don't think I could clean a man's boots," replied Jenny, coping with a mental image of Stephen placing his shoes by the kitchen stove each night.

"Could you cope with digging a vegetable plot? Your man will have to. And, when you leave off work to bring up the children, he'll have to bring in enough to keep the house going. What would you rather do – go to work or be a mother?"

"I'd like to do both, I think."

"You can't – not properly: being a housewife is a fulltime job. But you can always return to teaching when the children reach school age. You'll have the best of both worlds."

"You're really going to be content with your Bobby, aren't you?"

"I love him. I'll have a worthwhile job and a good man. What more can a girl ask for?"

Jenny didn't see herself in that way. She wanted a husband, eventually, but she wanted a career as well. Not to rise to the top or anything of the sort, but to have somewhere interesting to go each day.

Her dad was a chemist and her mum worked as a typist in an insurance office. Between them they brought in good money and the family was able to go on holidays abroad. France had been a favourite place, and she and her brothers spoke the language quite well and she – the eldest – had got a grade 1 at O level. They'd tried to persuade her to read French at college, but Jenny hadn't wanted to make the effort. Home Economics was fun and easy enough; swatting French grammar would have been a real bind.

Because both her parents worked, she'd been a "latchkey" child after she went to primary school, and there had been a lot of worries about her turning into a "juvenile delinquent" because of it, but she hadn't, and neither had she come from a "broken home".

She'd been quite relieved when Stephen said he wanted to go home for his first year teaching. It would give them both a breathing space. She liked him. He was considerate and kind and gentle, and he had a sharp wit in company when the mood took him. She liked his brand of sarcasm, but he could be a bit of a bore. Sometimes he was just too intense. Thinking was all right as long as you didn't take it too far. Life was to enjoy. There was only so much good you could do in the world, only so many wrongs you could right.

Harold Wilson returned from America with an absolute promise from President Johnson that he would be allowed to work for peace and not send British troops to Vietnam. He was hoping to achieve a similar success with regards to Rhodesia. The Sunday papers had got hold of a story that he 'was preparing a peace offensive': truth to tell, he would be prepared to negotiate with Ian Smith. His strategy was to leave as many lines open to the illegal regime in Rhodesia as possible. Barbara Castle and her friends in Cabinet had put him under pressure to seek a military solution, but his whole instinct was against the idea. Barbara had pushed him for an answer as to his intentions but he'd managed to wriggle out of giving any commitment not to negotiate a way forward.

Mike Harrison knew that teaching would never provide him with sufficient salary to finance the life-style he envisaged for himself. Already, as college days were about to move into their final two terms, he was supplementing his grant by delivering cars for companies around the country. His studies were suffering, but only slightly and his wallet was full. If you weren't naturally attractive to birds, you could always seed the ground with money; there was nothing a bint liked more than being treated to whatever she fancied.

It had been a real blow when Paul had taken up with the Amanda bitch. They'd been great mates during the first year and the next two had looked really promising: plenty of crackling but no commitment. Now, Paul was tied down hands and feet. There was no rescuing him. Mike had tried, but the engagement ring was going on the finger during this year. You could bet on it. Some of the lads had, although the odds were poor.

He still couldn't understand why Paul had committed

himself so fully to just the one woman when there were so many out there gagging for it. What's more, they had the advantage of the car! Mike was one of the few blokes who could drive and had a car in college. The good life was stretching out before them both, and Paul had to go and settle on Amanda.

Still, there was Sue – one of the new first years – who seemed to fancy him. Next year, back in Liverpool, he'd settle into a local school during the day, deliver cars at weekends and overnight for the contacts he'd built up, find some crumpet locally and have Sue as his link back to college when he had a spare weekend. That way, he'd keep his options open. Life could be looking worse.

Like Mike, Christine Dixon was having no real luck with the opposite sex. She knew it was because she was too outspoken. She'd found that men didn't really fancy women with opinions. She was also mildly annoyed with herself that this gap in her life troubled her. Chris felt that she ought to have better things to do than worry about men – or the lack of them.

Nursing had seemed to present an opportunity to get involved with life – and it did, up to a point. What it didn't do was to provide you with a social life. Joan, she felt, would leave nursing, Sheila would go on getting higher and higher qualifications just to prove that she could, Kate would simply find a man and become a mum and Miriam would establish a mission hospital in darkest Africa. What Christine didn't know was what she would do before that big family came along to occupy her time.

Life had never been dull at home. You simply didn't have a minute to yourself with six brothers and sisters. There was never a problem finding something to do. Now, there was her three days off-duty to fill, and home was a thing of the past. She went back regularly, but that was what it was – the way back; what she wanted was the way forward.

She had no huge political fixations. She had opinions, but no great desire to change the world by traipsing round doorsteps with leaflets. Yet, talking with the others had made her think she should do something.

Kate obviously came from a family where politics was a football: her family were driven by the news of the day, by what was in the papers. From what Kate had said, Chris judged that both parents were Conservative voters despite the father being a trade union official. Kate, she thought, would react against her parents' views.

Sheila's family had never discussed politics, and Sheila had no views at all. Chris thought Sheila might end up on the fence voting Liberal, but the party had the reputation for harbouring poofs, and Sheila wouldn't support queers.

Miriam was a righteous rather than a political socialist. Her views really came from her religious beliefs rather than the dogma of any party. Miriam would steer her own path through life, regardless of the cut and thrust of parliamentary debate. The truth was self-evident to the believer.

Joan, whether she liked it or not, was going to be a Tory voter all her life. Seeing himself as a realist, her father had settled the family's opinions. Like him, Joan had no time for socialism, which simply squandered national resources, and saw conservatism – "with a small 'c'", to use Joan's expression – as the only way forward, provided the toffs were kept to one side.

She, Christine, had views that had suppurated from family chat, but no commitment. She might just be old enough to vote at the next election, depending on when that came; she'd be twenty-one in 1966. She felt she'd vote for the Labour Party because they seemed to represent the way forward.

In that outspoken way of hers, she said as much one evening when she and Joan sat in The Stuffed Pig. Joan laughed and agreed without too much reluctance. It always surprised Chris that Joan, who could be so prickly at times, didn't seem to give a stuff what people thought of her or her views.

"You should join a drama group," Joan said, "Most of the arty types are as woolly-minded as you. You'll bump into plenty of chaps there as well, all keen to get your knickers down while they discuss Marx with you."

"I've never acted in my life."

"There's always a first time. You're bright, and there's nothing to it, really. We did a lot at boarding school, of course. It relieved the boredom. You just pretend to be somebody else. One of the local groups is doing *Roots* in the spring. I'll take you along. You'll make a good Beattie …"

"*Roots*?"

"It's a play by Arnold Wesker. He's one of the kitchen sink dramatists. You'll like it. It's about a family of Norfolk yokels who get upset when their daughter arrives home full of socialist ideas she's picked up from her boyfriend. Although God knows what their Norfolk accents will sound like in Staffham."

"What's kitchen sink drama?"

"They didn't teach you much at your state secondary modern, did they?"

"We weren't considered bright enough to appreciate plays – but what is kitchen sink drama? I'll need to know."

"No you won't. You'll just learn the part and get on with it, but – if you must know – kitchen sink drama is the kind of play that features working class people. There's a lot of shouting and the men go off to drink in grubby pubs, while the women stay at home and scrub the floor. It's supposed to be more realistic than the type of working class people portrayed by Noel Coward and Terence Rattigan in their plays. You know, everyone is angry most the time and drop their aitches."

"Working class people aren't like that."

"That's what daddy says, but the middle class critics and theatre directors think they are. It's all the rage. You've seen *Saturday Night and Sunday Morning* haven't you? And *A Taste of Honey*? Well, that was a play before it was a film. Everyone is all very radical and is going to change society for the better."

"I'm not being condescended to."

"No, no – most of this stuff is written by working class people. Arnold Wesker is from the East End and Shelagh Delaney, who wrote *A Taste of Honey*, is from Manchester, as far as I remember. You'll enjoy acting, Chris, and there is a lot of socialist politics in these plays. It'll suit you. Take Sheila along … Come to think of it, she'd make a good Beattie if she had your confidence. I'll take you along and introduce you after Christmas."

"Are you in this drama group?"

"God no, but I know someone who is. He was at boarding school with me. I think they've even got a kitchen sink in this one."

Dick Crossman, exhausted by yet another Cabinet meeting on Rhodesia, was looking forward to Christmas. He found his Ministry eager to wind down on Thursday, although Christmas Eve wasn't until the Friday, but he said that was impossible. He was determined to clear his desk before the Christmas recess. Eventually, following a solid day's work, he arrived home late on the evening of the 23rd.

The new college buildings at Coseley had all the mod-cons any student could need; it was a world away from the communal troughs in the old buildings at Collingwood Hall. Stephen walked into the huge laundry room one Saturday morning to find one of the first year girls surrounded by a heap of shirts. It was strange to see a girl there at any time because they had their own laundry facilities on the ground floor of their residential blocks. Being a creature of habit, he always did his week's laundry early on Saturday and might easily, he thought, have wandered in wearing his dressing gown.

"What are you doing here?" he asked, abruptly but not intending to be rude.

"I'm going out with the captain of the rugby team," answered the girl, nervously.

"Sorry – I didn't mean to sound sharp. It's just unusual and I wondered why you were here."

"There are plenty of machines."

"I know. It wasn't that … what has going out with the captain of the rugby team got to do with it?"

"You get to wash the team's shirts."

"You what? Wouldn't it be easier if each of them washed their own shirt instead of asking you to wash the lot?"

"It's something you do," snapped the girl, her eyes flashing in anger.

"Right," he replied, and began to load his own washing.

He smiled at the girl and wondered at her ... docility ... was that the word? Why the hell should someone be expected to wash twenty odd shirts, and what kind of lout would expect them to do it?

"It's one of the privileges of going out with the rugby captain, I suppose," he said, hoping that somehow a point had been made.

Heather Glover was really looking forward to Christmas. The hospital had been kind enough to see that she was off-duty for both days and she and Barry were going to her parents' house. Chas was just over a year old and walking quite comfortably. He was going to enjoy himself unwrapping his presents as much as they were going to enjoy watching him.

Her mother was looking after everything, and so Heather would have absolutely nothing to do. It had been hard working as a student nurse and looking after Chas, and she felt the rest was essential. Barry had been good and done his bit, but much of the traditional housework seemed to fall on her shoulders.

She was aware of how tired she was most of the time and of how married life with Barry wasn't what they might have expected. The freedom of those days in his room at college seemed to have disappeared forever. They didn't make love as much as she would have liked. Once Chas was in bed and asleep they didn't like to wake him and, besides, they were glad to flop back on the old settee. They were still in the flat because Barry had put his foot down at accepting the offer of help with the deposit for a new house from her parents, saying that they'd "find it sooner or later" and "didn't want to be in debt in two directions" when they finally secured a mortgage. That had been that!

Her parents had come up trumps in looking after Chas – or Charles, as her mother insisted on calling the baby. Sybil Burton turned up as regular as clockwork on the days they had pre-arranged, and always declined the offer to "stay the night", which was a relief to Heather.

When they arrived on Christmas Eve, the new stove, which had replaced the log fire in the open grate, was burning brightly and Sybil's traditional decorations were all in their usual position; not a holly leaf was out of place. The sherry was on the sideboard and Barry's beer was cooling in the fridge. The tree glistened with bells and bows and chocolate treats and the fairy lights with the nursery rhymes Heather remembered from her childhood. Chas's eyes sparkled as he watched the tinsel flicker in the glow from the stove or looked up and saw the streamers meticulously placed from the central light shade to each corner. The presents for the grown-ups nestled against the log her father always used to secure the tree. Artificial snow curled symmetrically into the corner of each window pane in her mother's annual attempt to emulate Dickens.

It was all still a little stiff, but not as before and Heather realised that the feeling could be in her mind alone. Certainly, Barry seemed to make himself at home, dropping into her father's usual chair on the right hand side of the fireplace. He had a mug of Newcastle Brown Ale in his hand and a dash of foam on his lips.

The Christmas cake stood on the sideboard by the bottles of sherry, port and red wine. Heather went with her mother into the kitchen to admire the turkey, stuffed and waiting, alongside the precisely sliced carrots, Brussels sprouts, parsnips and potatoes ready for roasting. Balls of stuffing resided in the usual blue dish.

Somehow, as she looked at Chas, her teenage reservations about the replication of Christmas year after year faded. There was continuity in the tradition that bound them together as a family from the past and into the future. Heather looked across at Barry, as she and her mother re-entered the lounge, and smiled. The next few years were going to be difficult but in the end it would all, she was sure, come together.

1966

CHAPTER 29

As stable as a case of dynamite

Simon Wiseman sat in the bar of The Red Lion and sank his second pint of Joules bitter. He and Cliff Jenkins had buddied up in the second year, as others of their mates drifted into the arms of various women, and were now on their Professional Art course; their chosen assignment was to study and paint the various pub signs in the vicinity of Coseley College of Education – or, indeed, any pub signs they could reach on their professional studies day. This morning they'd cadged a lift on the one of the college coaches that still ferried students backwards and forwards between the new college and the County of Staffham Training College at Cotes Heath.

It was a bitterly cold January lunchtime but since their assignment involved more drinking than drawing this wasn't going to be a problem for either lad. The idea had been Cliff's, who was determined to emulate his hero, his fellow Welshman, the hard-drinking Richard Burton. One of Burton's boasts was that he could sink two pints in under thirty seconds, and Stephen Last had asked Cliff what took Burton so long, whereupon he'd downed one in ten. Cliff didn't see how this could be beaten.

"Stephen's like that," said Simon, "He once did forty press-ups in the common room because one of the PE lads

– your countryman, Bryn Edwards – was claiming that he'd just made thirty. With Stephen, it's simply a matter of willpower, mind over matter. He's no stronger than Bryn – certainly weaker – but he's determined. And as far as drinking is concerned he'd be under the table after six pints. He couldn't drink through the night like your hero."

"Richard Burton is a hero to us Welsh lads, you know. He's everything the lads from the valleys ever dream off …"

"'Make love to Elizabeth Taylor, catch hell from Richard Burton'", laughed Simon, quoting the lines from Dylan's *I shall be free*.

"No, no! Lovely lady, but she's a side issue. It's what he represents that matters. He got away from the valleys, didn't he? Through sheer talent. All of us would like to do that, see. It's an enclosed world, Yogi. You wouldn't believe how narrow it is. I'm not just talking about the chapel – although that's tight enough, like a noose about your neck – but down there you think Cardiff is the capital of the British Isles. It doesn't matter how you get away – football, boxing, acting or, in my case, teaching – as long as you do, so that you can widen your world. As a kid, I didn't know who Emlyn Williams, the Welsh playwright, was, let alone people like Noel Coward and Laurie Lee and John Steinbeck and …"

"Anyone else who's written a book or a play or …"

"Right! You get the picture. Burton snapped the bonds and with one leap he was free … it's a hard life, you know, for those who stay. The pits are only romantic for those who don't have to go down one. Can you imagine being bent double at the coal face, ankle deep in freezing water hacking away with your pick? My parents were both glad I went in for teaching, and the thing is it's not until someone like Richard Burton shows the way that you realise it's possible. It's all too easy to be drawn into a way of life that goes back generations. Education's the answer, see. It widens your horizons in more ways than one."

Simon looked at his friend as Cliff spoke, and felt humbled. He'd grown up in a council house in Borehamwood. It wasn't the lap of luxury, but it was free from any kind of hard graft. He couldn't imagine what it was like to spend your whole working day hewing ton after ton of coal from a seam in intolerable heat and darkness, lit only by the lamp on your helmet, surrounded by stale air, muscles cracking with the strain of the work and never able to straighten your body. His father had worked in an office; his mother had been a housewife. Both had been free to wander out at lunchtime and look up at the sky. Compared to Cliff's people they sounded like the idle rich.

"So you won't be going back to teach in Wales, then bach?"

"Oh yes I shall, Yogi. There are kids there who need a nudge. There's nothing wrong with a miner's life if that's what you want, but kids need the opportunity to choose … Do you fancy another pint? Then, we'd better at least try to make a quick sketch of the pub sign and make a note of the colours. I'll do that while you have a chat to the landlord about the history of the place. We'll have done a good morning's work then."

Dick Crossman had changed his mind about Harold Wilson's tactics in coping with the problem of Rhodesia.

He had to admit to himself that the Prime Minister had been successful in carrying public opinion with him as the situation deteriorated.

"It's my Cuba," he said, referring to Kennedy's crisis in 1962.

"I must say, Harold, you've played it with astonishing tactical skill. First, negotiations to try to prevent UDI; then, mild sanctions that didn't upset people and now, I understand, you're moving forward with more serious sanctions. You've certainly caught the opposition on the hop."

Harold chuckled and lit his pipe.

"The newspapers seem to have accepted our line. They're talking about Rhodesia as a 'success story for the government'. Certainly, the public have been with us, step by step," he said, smiling through the tobacco haze before adding, "and, as you say, we are showing up the lack of leadership qualities in Ted Heath."

Stella Aldridge folded the sheets across her breasts and looked down at Edward French's back. He was a PE student in her year and rumour had it that he'd "put it around a bit" ever since he came. Not that Stella minded: she wasn't making a lifetime commitment with him. He'd done what she wanted and done it most efficiently; he taken her virginity and it was well out of the way. There'd be a few more like her around desperate not to return home as virgins once their course was finished; Edward should have a nice couple of terms.

She moved slightly, adjusting the cigarette between her fingers, and he stirred, woken by her movement.

"I'd better be off," he grunted, "we've a cross-country run this morning and I need to warm up."

"I thought you'd have done all the warming up you needed," she laughed.

He looked embarrassed, as though she'd accused him of using her; she'd noticed before how he trailed a little guilt each time he left. She laughed again, watching him pull on the pants over his tight, large buttocks. 'God, he is fit,' she thought with a sigh, 'There's no spare flesh on him ... wide shoulders tapering to a narrow waist ... sinewy thighs and those muscular buttocks. I could use another dose of him before he goes, but I'd better not. Don't want to show too much need. I can always get a man. I know that now.'

"You intend to go out with honours, don't you?" she asked, intending the implication.

Edward looked up from the mirror where he was straightening his tie.

"I should get good grades," he replied, There's no point in not, if all that's needed is a little extra work. I imagine it'll count in the secondary school."

He seemed so focussed, and Stella wondered, not for the first time, where she was going. She wondered whether teaching would offer her the intellectual outlets she craved. 'Everything he does, every movement he makes has a purpose ... even screwing me had a purpose ... all done without wasting too much feeling ... all down to technique ... all worked out in advance. He doesn't talk much about ... about abstract things like Art. He doesn't talk round and round a subject. He just gets on with it ... whatever it is.' She laughed. It was a hard sound and Edward looked across at her as he brushed his hair and made for the door.

"I'll be back later, "he said, "and we'll go down the pub."

The door clicked shut. Stella looked across at the files and books on her desk. 'It ends for him with a click, but I can't work now, damn him. How can I put my mind to a French essay?' She lit another cigarette and sat up, pulling the sheets round her legs and leaning forward on her knees. 'Last was no good, but he could talk and make you think. Blast him! Why can't you find everything you want in the same man? Stephen had a feeling for what he was doing, writing, saying, but Edward ... He has the right words, he uses the expected language, he knows the jargon that moves them but it's all without feeling ... mechanical. He's just a ... functionary.' She laughed at the word as it occurred to her.

"Functionary," she said aloud, "Let's func ..."

Riding back on the college coach to Coseley, Simon turned to Cliff Jenkins and said through a deepening alcoholic haze:

"Did you see George Brown on *The Frost Programme* making an arsehole of himself?"

"Yes but we love him, don't we? He's about as stable as a case of dynamite, and that's what makes him attractive, man. No one wants their politicians perfect. You want characters: people who'll give you a good laugh. ... As long as they keep him on a leash, he's an asset to the Party. He said himself he didn't want to be Prime Minister."

"Thank God," replied Simon "You wouldn't want his finger on the nuclear button, would you?"

George Brown, Foreign Secretary and Deputy Leader of the Labour Party, had appeared on David Frost's programme and taken everyone's breath away with his honesty. The newspapers could only praise him. No one expected a politician to be honest. When his colleagues thought of George they did so with trepidation. Within the space of seconds he could turn from capricious to stable, touchy to affable, pompous to humble or peevish to genial.

"Some see him as a visionary," persisted Cliff, "The kind of bloke who, if you lit his fuse at the right moment and pointed him in the right direction, might take us far along the road to a real Socialist country …"

"While others consider him a mad dog that's best kept chained in the backyard," replied Simon, laughing.

"Time and tide, man: brush up your Shakespeare."

Cliff's remark caught the usually genial Simon slightly off-guard. His own English studies left a lot to be desired: he was in no position to take his affairs at the flood and had serious doubts whether they would 'lead on to greater things'.

George had 'confided' to David Frost – publicly and before millions of viewers – that he didn't believe he had what was needed to be Prime Minister:

"I think I've many other things to give and I'll give of them. But I never thought … that that's anywhere on my menu."

"Why do you feel the Prime Minister wouldn't be ideal for you?" asked David Frost.

"Oh … for very many reasons. I'm much too … aggressive, you might say assertive … I like to get things out, get them out quickly, get them done; whereas I think a Prime Minister needs – he's got to ride the team. He needs different qualities than the qualities I've got."

Back in his room, Simon listened to the radio with growing horror. A US Air Force B-52 bomber carrying an H-bomb had collided in mid-air with a refuelling plane, and crashed into the Atlantic off the coast of Spain. US military chiefs were mounting an immediate hunt to locate the wreckage and the H-bomb. Fears of a nuclear explosion and an outpouring of radiation were rampant. 'When will they ever learn?' thought Simon, echoing the words of *Where have all the flowers gone?*

He'd been on every Aldermaston march since he was sixteen in 1961. He'd listened to the public row between Bertrand Russell and John Collins over the philosopher becoming involved in the Committee of 100 and resigning from the CND; he'd ranted at the British government's decision to allow the Americans to use Holy Loch in Scotland as a base for their Polaris submarines and joined the protest in Parliament Square when over eight hundred people had been arrested including Lord Russell and Arnold Wesker; he'd watched the Russians build the Berlin Wall and end a moratorium on nuclear tests, the French commence nuclear tests and the West Germans use nuclear-powered submarines.

In 1962, he'd joined the youth wing of the CND and sung folk songs as they marched. 'YOUTH AGAINST THE BOMB' their placard had said and their anger had infused each song with a particular bitterness. There were similar movements among sane people in every country – Germany, France, Yugoslavia, America and even Russia among them – but still the bastards wouldn't listen to the voice of the people.

Eminent politicians now in power had been involved, including Michael Foot and Barbara Castle. Simon had stamped his feet, rubbed his hands and chaffed his aching limbs with the most illustrious in the land. He'd distributed the Spies for Peace leaflets in 1963 and helped expose the RSGs: the shelters where those who had caused the nuclear war would find refuge and prepare to start another one, no doubt.

CND had brought about the 1963 treaty whereby a partial ban on nuclear testing was signed by the Russians, the Americans and the British, but still they were manufacturing nuclear weapons and still they were carting the bloody things round the world, irresponsible to the last.

'Perhaps, after all', thought Simon, 'there are good and abiding reasons for my decision to become a teacher. I'd better brush up my Shakespeare … and Eliot … and Swift …and the bloody lot.'

Joan Whiting approached the young, female doctor cautiously but quite determined to sort her out.

"Excuse me," she said, "May I have a word?"

The young woman did look rather amazed, and Joan wasn't surprised: there was what she considered to be a contemptible hierarchical system in the hospital, unspoken but present. It was unusual for a nurse to approach a doctor directly, especially a student nurse: the expectation would be that the nurse spoke to the ward sister who might speak to the matron who might consider speaking to the doctor. The doctor smiled, quite condescendingly thought Joan, and that made her more determined.

She'd been working on the gynaecological ward for a week and had watched with dismay whenever Dr Claire Hewitt approached a patient. They would invariably scud up the bed and grip the headrest, tightening every muscle in their body as they did so; their lips would purse as their eyes glazed over. Joan had actually seen the knuckles of several patients turn white in an effort to resist what they feared. Dr Hewitt would grab the legs of the patient and lift their knees before opening them to begin an internal. She then carried out what should have been a sensitive examination of a woman's most delicate part with less care than Joan's mother showed stuffing the Christmas turkey. In as many words, Joan said so.

"I beg your pardon!"

"The patients actually fear you coming onto the ward."

"Do you know who I am, Nurse … Nurse …"

"Joan Whiting. I realise I should have addressed the issue through Matron …"

"Indeed you …"

"But I considered you'd appreciate a more direct approach."

"It's hardly your place to correct a doctor, Nurse Whiting."

"A nurse's prime duty is to alleviate patient suffering, and that is what I am attempting to do."

Joan was aware that Dr Hewitt had not expected a mere nurse to be quite as confident in dealing with authority, but Joan had had plenty of experience at boarding school in dealing with adults. Moreover, both her parents were no-nonsense people; her father's diplomacy had always been forthright. The doctor looked her up and down for a moment or two, and gave her a look that suggested she would be taking the matter further. Joan knew she wouldn't: she had too much to lose.

Barbara Castle was unperturbed when the backlash descended upon her: she had expected as much when she introduced the breathalyser. Road deaths caused by drunken drivers had been rising alarmingly. She abandoned the idea of random testing previously suggested and opted instead for its use only when the police considered what was termed 'a moving traffic offence' had been committed. The police were entitled to test only if the driver had been stopped for another offence or, if when stopped, the police suspected the driver had been drinking.

She knew that fining was not enough. The penalty had to be tougher, and so she introduced automatic disqualification if the alcohol level in the blood exceeded 80 milligrams per 100 millilitres of blood.

It would be a year before the bill became law. In the meantime she listened, stoically, to calls for "leniency for first time offenders", "leniency if the vehicle was used for the driver's livelihood" and accusations by motoring organisations that "the proposed law constitutes an infringement of civil liberties".

"I'm not going to let anyone have a first go at trying to kill someone," she said, pursing her thin lips, stubbornly, "or a magistrate take the line of 'there but for the grace of God go I'."

CHAPTER 30

Coming together

Susan Paget was looking forward to her twenty-first, but knew it was a risk inviting her college friends down to her home; there was the ever-present fear that the two groups would not mingle. Des had always put off going when she asked, but Susan felt that if he did come with a group of friends it might make him less anxious about the idea of coming alone. Their relationship had been passionate, and her desire for him was adamant. He possessed what she most admired in a man: drive and purpose.

There had always been something soft and easy in her life with her friends at home. She'd not realised this when growing up through her childhood and the years of the early teens, but it had become very apparent to her once she met the kind of men who went to the training college. All of them – well, most of them – possessed a kind of anger; within each was a desire to improve society, and she sensed that nothing would stop them achieving that ambition. She'd never met this kind of drive before; beside such men, people like Rodney seemed no more than dilettantes – dabblers on the edge of the real world. When they'd all gone up to Des's for his twenty-first – she on the edge of the group and close in the company of Marguerite

– his friends had only emphasised further their sense of mission.

In Middlesbrough, Susan had entered an unfamiliar world: a world where poverty was apparent. Des's mother had served them a welcome meal: the occasional piece of meat was to be found amongst the potatoes and a few vegetables. At home and in the homes of her friends, meat had been the centre of the dish, and it had never occurred to Susan that there were people in 1960s Britain who could not afford meat. The experience had humbled her, and made her begin to understand the huge class divide in her country.

On their return to college, Des's attitude amongst their friends had changed from one of playful banter to one of embarrassment and anger. "I was a bit disappointed," he'd said, "that my college friends didn't mix more with my mates at home." Stephen, she remembered, had been both saddened and annoyed by this comment, believing it to be more "a reflection of Des's insecurity than an expression of the truth". She agreed, and – once college had exerted its influence – their mutual attraction reasserted itself.

Her friends were travelling down either in the cars of Mike Harrison and Robert Davis or Clive Fencott's van. Nobody else had transport, and only Mike had bought his own vehicle; Clive was the son of a grocer from Grantham and Robert's dad was a publican in Dudley. Susan didn't like to think how many might be crammed into the back of the van as she waited in her parent's porch. She'd come down early by train and everything was ready for her party.

It began well: her parents welcomed Susan's guests and

then disappeared discreetly, explaining that they were too old for parties, were spending the evening with friends and would probably stay the night.

As the crab and avocado sandwiches, herring and apple on rye, ham and asparagus slices, olive and anchovy bites, smoked salmon pancakes with pesto, cheese and potato scones, savoury parmesan puffs, leek and onion tartlets, quiche Lorraine, and caramelized onion tarts – so lovingly and proudly prepared by her mother – were consumed and the drink flowed most people loosened up, mingled and chatted.

Only Des seemed on edge, picking, somewhat churlishly Susan thought, at the food as though it offended his socialist principles. She decided to humour him and enjoy herself: a few more pints and he would share the laughter, bring out his guitar and gather them all around him.

She saw Stephen, squashed against the Chesterfield, chatting with Rodney and drifted towards them. She remembered Rodney's comments about Stephen's sports jacket in December 1963 when they'd met on the station as they both went home for their first Christmas after leaving for college.

"I can't imagine anyone wanting to teach," Rodney was proclaiming, "Why would you wish to spend your life trying to bang some culture into the heads of oiks?"

"For precisely that reason," Stephen replied in his enigmatic way.

"Hmm?"

"What's the difference between an oik – as you put it – and you?"

"Hmm?" asked Rodney again, largely through his nose.

"Education," said Susan laughing at his discomfort and Stephen's refusal to be specific, as she arrived on the settee and put her arms round Stephen, "Education is Stephen's road to freedom for us all."

"And you're happy to be paid bugger all for doing it?"

"To be honest, I haven't given the money a thought," replied Stephen.

"I can understand a woman doing it. After all, it's just pin money. But the husband has to bring home the bacon, as they say. How the hell do you hope to raise a family on a teacher's wage?"

"I haven't given it any thought."

"Well perhaps you should, old boy. It'll be your responsibility when the time comes. My father said that love flies out of the window when the wolf howls at the door – if you get what I mean."

"Rodney, it's what Stephen wants to do!"

"I'm not offended, Sue," Stephen assured her, tapping Susan's wrist lightly, "Anyone who marries me will have to be prepared to live on a teacher's salary. If they're not, they'll need to find someone else."

Rodney stared at Stephen as though he was some creature from another world. The gulf between the two men was so wide as to be unbridgeable. Susan wondered whether they held each other in mutual contempt. For Rodney, the key to success was money and he would choose his career – or have it chosen for him by his father – with that consideration in mind. Watching him, she was struck by the similarity between Rodney and her father – not in character because her dad was a much nicer person, but in their understanding of the world. Were people like Stephen living in cloud cuckoo land? She lived in one stream of thought at college and in quite another when she was at home; eventually, to embrace one she must leave the other.

"But the man's a bloody terrorist," cried a voice from across the room. Susan looked at Rodney and smiled at Stephen. It was Alistair locked in combat with Simon Wiseman, who was clearly enjoying the tussle.

"I must go," laughed Susan, "before Alistair becomes too strident. He's obviously enjoying himself, and Yogi's winding him up."

"Who the hell are they talking about?" asked Rodney.

"I think I heard Nelson Mandela's name mentioned," said Stephen.

"You stay out of this, Stephen. Alistair doesn't need you and Yogi against him."

"A freedom fighter," Simon was explaining as Susan came up to them.

"Put your friend right, Sue-Sue," pleaded Alistair, "Nelson Mandela is a terrorist. The man said so himself at his trial. He didn't deny he'd planned sabotage ..."

"After fifty years of non-violence had brought his people nothing," continued Simon.

"And so he turned away from a policy of non-violence and made plans for guerrilla warfare ..."

"If sabotage failed," Simon persisted.

"So he was a terrorist. No state can tolerate that kind of behaviour. He has himself to blame for his imprisonment."

"No state can continue to pursue a policy that rests on the belief that one race is superior to another. Africans just want a stake in their society. They want political rights ..."

"And educational opportunities," said Susan, siding with Simon, "Come on, Ally, you agree, really."

"No, no I don't. We don't have terrorists in this country. We don't have little groups of people planning to blow things up. People like that are bloody nuisances. There are ways of doing things ... Ghandi in India, Martin Luther King in America ..."

"Ghandi always said that he pursued his policy of non-violence because he knew it would work against the British," said Simon, "Nelson Mandela is up against a different mind-set ..."

"There's diplomacy – the British way. Jaw, jaw rather than war, war – if you see what I mean?" asked Alistair, as though Simon might have some difficulty understanding what was meant by diplomacy.

"Yes, I grasp your general meaning," laughed Simon, "It hasn't been too successful in Rhodesia, though, has it. Diplomacy only works if you're talking to someone who'll be ready to compromise and the mentality of the regime in South Africa is very similar to that in Rhodesia."

"Diplomacy hasn't worked in Rhodesia because it's being handled by bloody socialists who have absolutely no understanding whatsoever of the nature of the beast. Had Sir Alec Douglas-Home won the last election – as he bloody well should have done – the Rhodesian problem wouldn't be a problem. Savvy?"

Susan could see that Alistair, having drawn a crowd around him, was about to take off. She wondered whether to distract him or let him fly. One look at Simon's face and the faces of Stephen, Mike, Marguerite and Des determined her to wait; everyone looked as though they were enjoying the crossfire. There was every chance that Alistair would make a fool of himself or that at least two of her college friends – Robert and Clive – might come in on his side, leaving the argument nicely balanced between her friends. Susan wanted that to happen.

"What have they done since they've been in – hmm – except bang out endless bloody policy statements. The cost of living is rising, their incomes policy isn't working, inflation is soaring, productivity is stagnant, every decision the government makes – if you can call it a government – has to be approved by the unions. They won the election, anyway, by the smallest of majorities and the greatest of luck. The British public has little faith in the socialists – and they know it. That's why they're frightened to go to the country to obtain a decent majority so that they can govern properly. In the meantime, the money markets are all of a jitter and the pound is suffering ..."

Susan looked at Des; she didn't want him to think that these were her views, and was both relieved and surprised to find him smiling. Political dissent was in the marrow of his bones, she supposed, and people like Alistair were fair game.

"If all this is true," Des said suddenly, "then you'll expect to win the general election when it comes?"

"Without a doubt, replied Alistair, "The Party has been transformed since '64 by Sir Alec and under Edward Heath. The organisation has been strengthened, we've re-thought our policies to meet the needs of all the country (not just those who vote socialist), we've proved to be an effective opposition, public opinion is turning back to us, we are united which is more than can be said for Labour, our status with regard to foreign affairs is unmatched by the socialists who flounder embarrassingly whenever they meet another country's diplomats and we are the only Party likely to make headway in Europe which is vital if we are to remain economically viable ..."

"... and you read the *Daily Mail*," queried Des with a laugh.

Susan had seen Des deflate opponents before, but never with quite the effect it had on Alistair, who collapsed like a pricked balloon. Even his friends laughed.

"You'll see," he yelled, "you'll bloody well see at the ballot box." Then, he laughed too, and with the point scored Des rallied. Later in the evening, Alistair took Susan aside and whispered "I only let your friend off the hook for your sake, Sue-Sue. I could have roasted him had I wanted, but didn't like to spoil your party." Strangely, she believed him; it was just the kind of diplomacy Alistair would have found so attractive.

Dancing carried the evening forward, dancing and drink, as the differences descended into clichés and the British propensity for mocking each other smoothed the evening.

"Watney's Red Barrel," crowed Mike, "It's the stuff we water daisies with up north."

"Youngs Tartan Bitter is what the men drink," agreed Marguerite.

Des seemed to feel at home, and that was what Susan wanted.

"You've changed, Sue," said her friend, Anna, when Susan brushed into her with her latest boyfriend on the stairs. Sue's parents had locked the doors of all the bedrooms except Sue's and the snogging was taking place on the stairs, the landings and in the hallway.

"That's what college is supposed to do for you, Anna."

"Are you coming home to teach?"

"I don't know," replied Susan, and it was true. She'd given the matter no thought at all, since there would be a job somewhere. "Anyway, how have I changed?"

The boyfriend drifted away as the women spoke.

"You always used to be so relaxed. Now, you seem on edge."

Trust another woman to notice what she'd been trying to hide – successfully she thought – all evening.

"Is it him – the slim, good-looking one with the guitar?"

"Yes," said Susan, since there was no use in denying it, "I'm in love with him, and he with me, but we can't carry it forward. There seems no future in the relationship."

She hadn't meant to admit all that – not to Anna and not at a party; it was the drink talking, the vodka and limes loosening her thoughts and her tongue.

"You can't stop thinking about him? He is dishy. I'd snap him up. Men only need a shove in the right direction."

"It's our backgrounds. They're so different. Des looks on this as 'the stockbroker belt'."

"Is that why you let Ally make a fool of himself – to show that you weren't on his side?"

"Yes."

"You went down-market, darling, when you went into teaching. Why not go all the way?" suggested Anna, laughing, and then continued "I didn't mean it. I think it's a noble profession. That's what they say, isn't it?"

"What are you doing?"

"I've gone into banking, and daddy insisted I started on the shop-floor."

"Are you enjoying it?"

"Yes … it's power, Sue, power. I know it's not popular to say so, but money is power. You can make things happen with money. Without it, you're going nowhere."

"There has to be more to life than the pursuit of wealth. The men I've met at college – not only Des but nearly all of them – want to change society. That's why they're going into teaching, and I want to be part of their world."

"At the end of the day, Sue, it comes down to money. He who pays the piper calls the tune?"

"If that's true and can't be changed, it would be very depressing."

Susan wanted to move away but her good manners, her very breeding, made that impossible. When the boyfriend eventually returned, however, she made for Des who was singing in the conservatory surrounded by a group. She went over and leaned her head on his shoulder, and it was clear he liked her gesture.

Des had been singing *Cushie Butterfield* when Susan came over. The song, about a northern lass who enjoyed her beer, was well known to the college crowd and seemed a particular favourite of Marguerite's to whom Des always addressed it. As it finished, someone – and Susan thought it was Stephen – began playing Dylan's *To Ramona* on the harmonica. Des looked across to the sound, his eyes not without anger at first, and then picked out the chords on his guitar.

"Ramona come closer, shut softly your watery eyes
The pangs of your sadness will pass as your senses they
rise"

Susan found the sadness of the song almost unbearable and yet it wasn't without hope; it wasn't without a road forward.

"From fixtures and forces and friends your sorrow just
stems
They'll hype you and type you and make you feel that
you've gotta be just like them"

One song led to another of the same kind and the evening for a while became Dylan's: *Blowin' in the wind* followed and then *A hard rain's a-gonna fall,* and they were all back on the Aldermaston marches, with Des looking contemptuous of what he considered the phoniness of protesting in the comfort of a middle-class home. He changed the tone with *Honey, just allow me one more chance* and *It's all over now, baby blue* through *Mr Tambourine Man,* but was dragged by the group back to *The times they are a changin'* and, finally – Des decided it was going to be final because he could see most of Susan's friends as the future establishment who would be dead against changing too much – *Maggie's Farm.* As he said to Stephen when they talked on the way back in Clive's van:

"I couldn't see the chimes of freedom flashin' too long for any of them."

Stephen had been quiet all evening. He disliked dancing, feeling awkward as they twitched around, and had sat on the edge of groups listening. Susan joined him when Marcus arrived with Anita, expecting that someone like Marcus might prove fair game for Stephen.

"Love," Marcus began, fondling Anita's breasts by wrapping his arms around her from where he sat, cross-legged, behind his wife, "is a duty for us all. Love is the force that must drive us forward. Love is society's only redemption. Love is all we need to make the world perfect. Love one another. Love is the promise of mankind. It is the one genuine force that drives the universe. Without love we are pale shadows on the face of the moon. Love is divinity linking gods and men."

Stephen caught Simon's eye and smiled, but was silent. Simon's favoured sitting position – the lotus – was always done with a touch of irony, as though he was taking the mickey out of himself and those who vouchsafed eastern mysticism as the only saviour of the world.

"Love is a net," continued Marcus, as Anita began a solemn chant, seemingly half-humming, half-buzzing two words over and over again in various orders. Stephen was reminded of psalm singing at his secondary school, which had once been a church school. Back then, the words had had some meaning, however obscure to him as a schoolboy in his teens, whereas Anita's chanting verged not only on the monotonous but also on the meaningless.

"Love is a net thrown by the gods to link the many strands of mankind in one harmonious … harmonious creation," faltered Marcus, as though he'd lost track of any sense in his words, "Love … love is the golden lining to man's grey cloud …"

Rodney, crouched behind Susan, snorted quietly in her ear, but she ignored him.

"Love gives shape to the shapeless, form to the nebulous, understanding to the ignorant …"

Aware that this might continue far into the next morning, Stephen rose and walked across to where the beer waited. He found Simon at his side smiling.

"Tell me, Yogi," he said, "why this eastern mysticism of yours should take us any further forward than traditional religion?"

"It puts man at the centre, man. The person standing next to you is a god. The man down the road is a god. The thug on the corner of the next street is a god. Love is all you need to bring us all together. Where there is love, hate cannot survive."

"Do you think there are people who really believe all that stuff? Or is it simply another way of persuading people to accept the status quo, to accept their poverty with a smile while the priest and the rich man look on benevolently?"

Simon laughed. He and Stephen had had such a discussion many times before. They sat together on the stairs and talked, joined by others as the various groups sort places to sleep or doze. Susan's mother had left sleeping bags and blankets in the airing cupboard and some took advantage of these, while others slept where they sat or lounged. Some continued to talk or dance or sing through the night, while others went to the kitchen and prepared an early breakfast from a fully-laden refrigerator. Only Susan's local friends with cars – the likes of Rodney and Alistair – drove home as dawn broke, sozzled by a night's drinking and shattered.

Dick Crossman felt privileged that he was one of those close associates with whom Harold Wilson could discuss the future. Sitting round the dinner table with Harold's wife, Mary, his personal assistant, Marcia Williams, MPs of the calibre of Tony Wedgwood Benn, Peter Shore, Gerald Kaufman and Harold's financial adviser, Tommy Balogh, Dick listened intently as the Prime Minister spoke.

"I have been reading *The Making of the President*," he said, "Theodore White's book on the recent American presidential election, and it has made me think of my own role. I am not a father figure, you know. I am a doctor figure. That's what Mr White tells me – I am a doctor figure ... I have been thinking about how the election will be won. I want you, Dick, to stay behind in London when we begin the fight. You, Tony, I would like to run the television shows ... As for me, I have got to be at No 10 most of the time ..."

"Well, for God's sake," interrupted Dick, "don't rush off to your own constituency, Huyton, for the last five days as you did last time."

"I agree," replied Harold, "that is something I absolutely mustn't do."

Emboldened by Harold's agreement, Dick continued:

"I was speaking with the Chancellor only last Thursday ..."

"And what did James have to say?" enquired Harold.

"That he didn't want to be Chancellor in the next Government ...I said to him in that case he should be Leader of the House if we return with a big majority – inspiring the back-benchers, controlling the House of Commons, planning the legislative programme."

Harold chuckled but said nothing; it was something he really would like. Dick considered it a 'delightful evening'. It was the first time he felt that as a group they could do some good because Harold trusted them.

CHAPTER 31

Breakfast with the PM

Kate Walsh was aware that Joan Whiting had always been on the edge of giving up nursing and was deeply concerned that the NHS might lose a potentially first-class matron. She could see that Joan, once she had the bit between her teeth, was the kind of person who might well be radical enough to move the service forward, while still holding to the basic tenets of the faith.

"'Tenets of the faith'," laughed Joan, "What the bloody hell are you talking about?"

"You know exactly what I'm talking about," insisted Kate, "so stop pretending otherwise. I'm talking about the basic principles on which the NHS was founded: that everyone, from the cradle to the grave, should have free access to first class nursing services twenty four hours a day, three hundred and sixty five days of the year."

"Yes, all right. It's just that I get so bored sometimes with all the routine stuff."

"It's the routine stuff handled professionally that makes nursing what it is. There's nothing boring about basic nursing procedures. They're what keep people alive and well."

"All right, all right, I give in. Can we go for a ride on

your scooter? There's a nice pub in Eccleshall. It's a shame to waste such a nice evening, especially in March."

"I shan't stop bullying you."

"I know, I know, but at least I'll have a beer in my hand."

The ride exhilarated both of them. Riding along the A5013 at 40 miles per hour (the most Kate could coax from her Honda 40), the wind blowing through their hair, gave both young women a liberated feeling.

The Royal Oak was a traditional country pub with log fires, beer locally brewed by Joules of Stone (which was just up the road), wooden beams, bars and floor – and a snug.

"We can pretend to be Ena Sharples and Minnie Caldwell," suggested Joan as Kate parked her scooter.

"How do you know this pub?" asked Kate.

"Young farmers," Joan replied with a laugh, twitching her nose in a suggestive fashion, "They meet here. There are some big boys among them, I'll tell you."

'Young farmers' suggested another world to Kate: the county set, gymkhanas, fox hunting, gin and tonics, posh accents, money to spare. It was Joan's world, but not hers.

"Can you ride?" she asked.

"Of course," replied Joan, "naturally … oh dear, have we ruffled the working classes again? There's nothing stand-offish about these people, Kate. They may vote Tory, but they're quite human."

"I've never imagined riding a horse," mused Kate, "It's just something that people like us never did."

Joan hugged her as they entered the pub. Several men turned to look when the door opened, and one or two eyebrows were raised.

"The lounge is the other door, ladies," said one of the drinkers, trying to be helpful.

"Really," replied Joan, laughing, "We prefer the bar, but we've no objection to you going next door ... if you don't want our company."

The landlady smiled to herself at the banter, but was ready to intervene. This wasn't a student pub and the local women rarely, if ever, used the bar. There was always a chance that any woman who did so might be taken for a tart.

"There are a couple of students from the training college in the snug, girls. If you'd like to join them, I'm sure they'd appreciate the company ..."

"If they're not queer," laughed one of the men at the bar, to a round of raucous laughter from his mates.

"Ignore him. He's ignorant," continued Ida, the landlady, "What can I get you ladies?"

"I'll have a pint of your best bitter, please," replied Joan, "Kate?"

"A vodka and lime, please."

"Oh, we've got the rough and the smooth here, boys."

Joan smiled as she paid for the drinks and she and Kate made their way to a seat. 'There's still a long way to go,' she thought, 'Women don't use the bar or drink pints, and any man who chooses the snug must be queer.' She looked at Kate, who read her thoughts, and they both laughed.

"I wonder who the lads in the snug are," Joan whispered.

"Drink your beer. I'm not interested in pursuing men. I've got Bill to think about."

"I'm surprised you see much of him. All we seem to do is work and sleep."

"I don't, and it is a problem. When I'm not working I'm too tired to want to go anywhere … but he's very patient."

"Is it love?"

"Maybe … but love needs time to grow, doesn't it, and time is what we don't get."

"I don't know how you even think of having a steady boyfriend, Kate – at least until we finish our training in a year's time. I make do with the occasional snog with a young farmer," said Joan, raising her voice on the last sentence, "Mind you, I sometimes get a weekend away with one of my old school friends – especially if he's a biker."

"Shut up, Joan. Do you fancy a packet of crisps?"

Kate brought the two packets of Smith's crisps from the bar, smiling at the drinkers who obviously found the presence of women in the bar to be intrusive. They opened the little blue packet and shook the salt in the bag.

"We need to be careful, though, don't we? We could become a couple of old maids or one of those battle-axe sisters who take out their sexual frustration on the students. Do you remember Sister Talbot – the one who almost drove Sheila out of nursing?"

"Chris, of course, has joined that theatre group, hasn't she?" said Kate, whose thoughts had moved rapidly from Sheila to the drama group and Chris.

"And, according to my friend, Adrian, is knocking them all for six. She didn't get the role of Beattie – that'd already been snapped up – but she's playing Pearl, the one who can't see further than the next meal and will never leave Norfolk … God, fancy that – never leaving Norfolk … It's a good part for Chris, though – playing against type."

"You think she'll go far?"

"Oh yes … she's bright. No background, and so no social advantages, but that won't stop Chris, and good luck to her."

"Do you think I could learn to ride, Joan?"

"What? I mean pardon … Of course you can. You think that might give you a social advantage, Kate?"

"I want to be a really good nurse," replied Kate, elbowing her friend in the ribs, "but meeting you has shown me there's more to life than work. I don't mean I want to go off for the weekend with ex-public schoolboys on their motorbikes, but there's a world out there that people like me only ever come across in Enid Blyton stories."

"Christianity will go," said John Lennon, "It will vanish and shrink. I needn't argue with that; I'm right and I will be proved right. We're more popular than Jesus now; I don't know which will go first – rock 'n' roll or Christianity. Jesus was all right but his disciples were thick and ordinary. It's them twisting it that ruins it for me."

John was reading extensively about religion. He was seen by the public as a restless iconoclast. His image as the 'deep-thinking Beatle' was projected throughout the media.

When Michael Ramsey, Archbishop of Canterbury, heard about the comment, which had been published in the *London Evening Standard*, he was not unduly offended. He smiled quietly to himself, thinking that perhaps the young man had a point: attendance at Evensong was certainly on the decline.

Besides, he had more pressing matters that required his attention. The splendour of Michelangelo's Sistine Chapel was awaiting him; the four hundred year break with the Roman Catholic Church was showing signs of healing. An attempt at Christian unity was essential if the Church of Christ was to move forward as it should, and Pope Paul's invitation was to be welcomed. The Vatican had recently lifted the ban on marriage between Catholics and Protestants by announcing the ending of ex-communication for those who offended.

There would be Anglican priests who would condemn him, of course. Michael expected such a reaction. He would no doubt be condemned as a traitor to the Protestant cause, but there was no charity in such a view; reconciliation and mutual respect must take the day.

Dr Ian Paisley with four of his colleagues had booked themselves on the same flight to Rome and attempted to invade the first-class compartment where Michael and his party were seated. Fortunately, security guards had prevented what would have amounted to a very unpleasant scene. At Fiumicino airport, Michael's party had been whisked away in a Mercedes provided by the Vatican before any of the other passengers were allowed off the plane. Dr Paisley had been refused entry to the country – on what grounds Michael was unsure – and his supporters who had been allowed in were booed by the Italians when they tried to disrupt a service at the Anglican church of St Paul's.

Soon, he would be face to face with Pope Paul V1 in the Sistine Chapel beneath Michelangelo's painting of the Last Judgement where they would exchange their messages of greeting. Once that sacramental moment was completed, they would exchange gifts and turn to the nub of their meeting: their common spirituality, a joint commission of theologians and the Roman Catholic doctrine that deemed the ordination of Anglican ministers to be invalid.

When Dick Crossman arrived for breakfast with the Prime Minister, he found that he was not expected and that Harold was still in his bath, although he'd eaten previously. When Harold did come down he launched immediately into his main concern: he wanted to become more involved in the election campaign.

"You've made your decision, Harold," begged Dick, "to stay out at least until the week before polling day. Don't go back on it now."

"I feel I need to speak about the trade unions."

"For God's sake, don't do that. Keep out of it for at least two days longer."

There had been talk in the press of a kangaroo trial by shop stewards at the BMC plant in Cowley, where two workers had been tried and fined; during the proceedings, a noose was, reportedly, suspended over the 'court'. Dick felt that there was something in the story and was desperately concerned that Harold should not become involved personally.

Joan Whiting ordered her second pint – largely to impress the drinkers at the bar – and returned with it and Kate's second vodka and lime to their table in the corner.

"Do you fancy going into the snug?" she asked, "It might be fun, and we've sufficiently impressed these blokes. I might pick up a student teacher to take home with me."

The two students were Stephen Last and Simon Wiseman, who both stood immediately the women entered: the snug was small and usually reserved for women.

"Don't go," said Joan, "there's four chairs. Are you the two queers?"

"Queer enough, no doubt," replied Stephen, guessing what had been said in the bar.

"But not that queer," laughed Joan, "I'm Joan and this is Kate."

"Cool," replied Simon, "I'm Yogi and this is Steve."

"Yogi?" queried Kate, which gave Simon the chance he needed to launch into his transcendental meditation spiel.

Stephen listened to all he'd heard before, pleased that his friend had an attentive audience in Kate but sceptical: sceptical about whether Simon really thought yoga had anything to give the western world, sceptical about whether his friend saw it as anything more than a laugh. He caught Joan's eye and smiled; he could see he'd found a fellow sceptic. Given that India, where the practice developed, was riddled with poverty and whose children were dying in their thousands through hunger, Stephen didn't see that transcendental meditation had got them very far; except, that it conditioned the poor majority to accept their lot while the Indian rich became richer. The development of every human faculty to raise an individual to a state of heightened consciousness was all very well, but only if you'd a full belly in the first place. He doubted, too, whether, the emphasis on self was any way to deal with what were usually described as "the stressful and nerve-wracking conditions of life in the West".

"You're not a convert, Steve?" asked Joan, when Simon had finished.

"No, I'm not," replied Stephen, "I don't see the point of running away from one religious outlook into the arms of another."

"There's no harm in trying the techniques," snapped Kate, shocked at his bluntness, "If it offers a way forward, it can only do good in the world.

"Or blind us to the truth."

"Which is?"

"That the only way man is going to move towards a fairer world is by picking himself up by his own bootstraps."

"Man or woman," offered Joan.

"Or woman," conceded Stephen.

"Would you girls like a drink," asked Simon, "it's my round and Steve and I have time for another before we catch the bus."

"The bus?" questioned Kate.

"We catch the Staffham bus back to Collingwood Hall and then the last college coach to Coseley," said Simon.

"Why come all this way for a drink?"

"We've been in Staffham for the day and thought we'd drop off here."

"Do you often go to Staffham for a day out?"

"*Alfie* was on at the flicks."

"Did you enjoy the film?" asked Kate.

"It was a laugh," Simon responded, "Michael Caine is great. It's got something for everyone, really. If you want a bit fun it's there, but underneath it's serious. Right, Steve?"

"Yeah … it blends the two well."

"Steering a delicate course between charm and corruption," suggested Joan, with a glance at Stephen.

"If you say so … Do you want that pint? Simon's tongue is hanging out."

"I'll have a half – no you'd better make it a pint," replied Joan.

"Kate?"

"I'd better not – I'm driving."

"How many have you had?"

"Just the two … I suppose a third won't hurt. Thank you …I don't see how promiscuity can be charming," mused Kate, returning to the film.

"It's the way it's done," said Stephen, "Comments like 'it'll round off the tea nicely' or 'it's surprising what you can get on the National Health these days.' You can't help but laugh, but the film's got its heart in the right place. It's on the side of the women he messes about."

Kate looked at Stephen as he spoke, and when the time came to leave Joan said:

"You fancied him, didn't you?"

"Who?"

"You know who."

"I've got Bill to think about," answered Kate as she mounted her scooter.

"I know, but you fancied him didn't you?" insisted Joan, climbing on behind.

"Talking to men is so different from talking to a group of women, isn't it?" replied Kate, skirting away from Joan's suggestion.

"It's called sex," laughed Joan.

"No it's not. It's just that the conversation wouldn't

have been so serious if it had been the four of us in the pub."

"Depends on the men you're with."

"I wouldn't want it all the while, I suppose, but it was nice for a change. We spend most of our time in the company of women, don't we, and it's nice to get a change of perspective – a bit of variety in your life."

In Kate's home town of Wolverhampton, a debate had been arranged at St Luke's School by Mr Joe Holland who had been chairman of the Wolverhampton branch of the British Immigration Control Association. His opponent was Alderman Lane, leader of the Labour group on the council. The local paper, the Wolverhampton *Express and Star*, reported the meeting as being 'crowded and often rowdy', predicting that immigration control would 'be one of the major issues in this month's elections'.

On March 17th, Mr Holland stood as an anti-immigration Independent candidate in the local borough elections and polled twenty-seven per cent of the votes, being beaten by the Conservative candidate by only four hundred votes. 'There are still plenty of votes to be won by taking a firm line on immigration' reported the *Express and Star*.

"What do you think of that then, Florrie?" asked Mr Walsh, Kate's dad, lowering his paper carefully to his lap so that he could see his wife's face.

"It's time someone made a stand," replied Mrs Walsh, "before we're overrun by blacks."

CHAPTER 32

A move in the right direction

There was still a week to go before polling day and Dick Crossman had another idea to promote Labour's chance for a really significant victory. He was walking across the park for another breakfast with Harold when it occurred to him that it would rack up tension in the campaign if the Prime Minister was reported to be ill and confined to bed. A stink bomb had caught him in the eye at Slough causing a slight injury, and the suspense certain to be engendered in the press would give his Birmingham meeting a fillip.

"But suppose I don't go to Norwich today, how shall I spend the afternoon?" enquired Harold.

"Well, you can govern the country."

"No, there are no boxes coming upstairs now in No 10. There is no work for me. I should just sit about," he replied with a laugh.

"You being you, Harold, that's something you can't do. If you really feel at a loose end this afternoon I can't stop you going to Norwich."

It was gratifying to Dick, watching the ITN news in the evening, that Harold made one of his best speeches of the campaign. He'd had every excuse to take at least a day off, and yet felt he couldn't let down those people waiting in Norwich.

Kate Walsh, working in Casualty, thought back to the night in Eccleshall when she'd said OK to her third vodka. Four people had been wheeled in, one with a serious head injury and three with minor cuts and bruises. One of these was a boy whose leg was badly cut and who had a large piece of skin flapping. One of the men – the driver – smelt of alcohol, and Kate wondered whether, after all, Barbara Castle hadn't been right to introduce the breathalyser; if it could prevent accidents like this, it would be worthwhile.

While the doctor saw to the head injury with the help of the sister, Kate turned her attention to the boy. He was in a state of shock and so she saw to it that he was kept warm and had a supply of oxygen before she administered a local anaesthetic prior to stitching the wound. She talked to the boy as she worked, distracting him with questions about his hobbies. When she'd finished, Kate looked at the wound and saw that it was a neat job – not unlike stitching the hem of a skirt; she was pleased with the result.

Billy Graham was in the throes of planning what would come to be called Berlin '66. Its theme was to be 'One Race, One Gospel, One Task' and it was to be held in the city's Kongresshalle. Holding the congress in Berlin would remind the world that only twenty years had passed since the Holocaust. Billy wrote to the chairman of the board of trustees of the Jewish Information Society of America 'I cannot possibly believe that a true Christian would ever be involved in anything anti-Semitic'.

It was not Billy's intention to be political, and others shared this view: notably, the reverend E L Golonka, a native of Poland, who understood Eastern Europe very well.

"I warn you, strongly, not to give the impression that any evangelistic and missionary activities are connected with the official policies of the United States and West German governments."

Who should Billy invite?

He felt that Oral Roberts, a long-time friend and a renowned proponent of the growing charismatic movement, should come, but as an individual and not as a representative of the movement; Billy had reservations about the "ecstatic manifestations" of this movement – manifestations that some evangelicals found disruptive.

He also wanted observers who were not necessarily even Christians. One of these might be Rabbi Arthur Gilbert. He had written to Billy, following the World Evangelical Congress, 'I want to tell you ... particularly during this Blessed Season, how meaningful it was for me to attend the Congress. I was moved by the depth of spirit demonstrated by the participants, and I was particularly delighted to see that a sensitivity for man's social needs accompanied a commitment to the proclamation of the Gospel'.

Two attendees he especially wanted were members of the Auca Indian tribe from Ecuador who in 1956 had speared to death five young American missionaries who ventured into their forest to bring them the Gospel. Through the witness of Rachel Saint, sister of one of the martyrs, and Elisabeth Elliot, widow of another, several members of the tribe had come to faith in Christ. These men would be "vivid reminders of God's transforming power".

Pete Campbell's Appalachian Four were disappointed. Sure, Ken Parkes had them working in clubs and pubs throughout the north but the recording contract was yet to show results. They'd had interviews on local radio stations, and made one or two television appearances but what they really needed was a recording contract with an organisation like Transatlantic Records.

"If you can't get this for us, Ken, you might as well bugger off," said Penny Grove after yet another university appearance, "and I'll manage the group. I'm bloody sure I can get one of those recording executives to see things from my point of view."

"They're flooded out with folk singers, and you're neither protest singers like Dylan or traditional folk like the Ian Campbell Four... or whimsical like Donovan. It's difficult ..."

"Donovan!" she snapped, scathingly, "Donovan isn't a folk singer. He's a Bob Dylan look-a-like and nothing more."

"He's developing his own style."

"Aren't we? Can't you market us as the English Peter, Paul and Mary? You know, The Spinners with feminine sex appeal?"

Pete had always been the lead singer, with Penny and Doug sometimes harmonising on the vocals. It had never occurred to them before Ken and Penny's spat to try her as a vocalist.

"Can you sing?" asked Pete.

"Can't anyone sing folk music?" replied Penny, laughing.

"It's an idea," said Pete, quietly, dubious about the changes it would bring.

"It's a selling point. What we need are some suitable songs," cut in Ken, "We could put in some Joan Baez numbers …"

"Like?" asked Pete, not wanting to get involved in protest songs.

"Like *Railroad Bill, Long Black Veil* … some of Dylan's songs that she sings … *Don't Think Twice It's All Right, Farewell Angelina* …the universities would love it …"

"Yes," said Pete, sensing a move for the group that might be in the right direction so long as they stayed within the American folk tradition, at least.

"No need to worry, Pete," Penny assured him, reaching up to put an arm round his shoulder, "we'll not lose sight of where you came from."

Labour had romped home with a majority of a hundred seats, as compared with their four in the '64 election. The new common room at Coseley College of Education lacked the intimacy of the old one at Collingwood Hall; rows of new, upright chairs glued to a television set failed to give the companionship of the tatty old ones interspersed between card tables and the dart board in A House. There was, simply, no sense of slobbing out with your mates. Nevertheless, the accustomed roars went up as 'Labour gain' after 'Labour gain' hit the screen.

In The Offley Arms on the following night the student teachers toasted another Labour victory. Only Des showed any reservations about the outcome, annoyed by what he considered the inappropriate jingoism attached to the celebrations.

"They've kept unemployment down," he said,

philosophically, "but how long will that continue? If they devalue the pound …"

"Devalue the pound?" queried Jenny Pryce.

"Make it worth less, so it costs you more to live," explained Des, "If they devalue the pound to make us more competitive, unemployment's going to rise isn't it?"

"Is it?" asked Jenny with a smile.

Stephen looked at her and also smiled: hers was inspired by the usual desire to be flirtatious, his to hide ignorance. He wondered how many of those listening to Des actually understood the economics involved in the points he was making. Stephen could only admire Des's grip on the political realities.

"Wages are already high from the bosses' point of view – way above price rises – and so they'll start to lay people off. The public won't be so cheerful when that happens."

"Cheer up, Des. It's your party that's won."

"Not yet – not until the first working class lad sits in No 10."

"Isn't Harold working class enough for you, Des?" laughed Simon.

"He isn't working class at all, Yogi: he's a bright lad from the lower middle classes. It's a move in the right direction – at least he's got where he is by virtue of his own abilities rather than because his daddy sent him to the right school – but we've a way to go yet."

'The middle classes really wanted us to win,' thought Dick Crossman, 'and Harold's personality has been a great help.'

"Yes," said Harold, when Dick mentioned it to him, "the middle classes – not the professional or upper classes but the middle classes. They think they've got a PM like them."

"One of their own kind?" suggested Dick, "A man whom they are proud to have at No 10. They feel they have a competent government and voted for it."

Kate Walsh looked dubiously at the horse; she hadn't imagined they were quite so big.

"You wanted to learn to ride," laughed Joan, and then added in a whisper, "and Virginia is the girl to teach you. She may not have as much brain as one of her horses but she's been in the saddle since she was born. When it was obvious she wasn't going to get many O Levels let alone make it to university, daddy set her up with a riding stable and she's making a fortune."

"You went to school with her?"

"We're old chums. She taught me to ride at boarding school. Thick as a plank but very good at two things, and both of them involve riding."

Virginia – "call me Ginny" – was a big, healthy girl who looked as though she'd been fed, Kate thought, on the fat of the land. She had one of those voices that Kate's mother said "sounded as though she'd got a plum in her mouth". It was the kind of voice that made Kate cringe both with embarrassment and a sense of inferiority.

"Never ever ridden before – at all?" exclaimed Ginny, her voice filled with incredulity.

"I've never been this close to a horse before," replied Kate, too defiantly she thought.

"Good God. I can't imagine never having ridden." She looked at Joan and laughed, uproariously. "It's damned good practise for what lies ahead. Well, we'd better see what your seat is like. Daisy's a nice little mare. A bit frisky if you give her too much head, but nice all the same. Unlike Freddy – if you don't keep a good grip on him with your knees, he'd be off at the gallop in no time. We don't want that, do we? Joan – I think you can manage him. He won't be your first stallion, will he?" She laughed again, as though she and Joan shared some secret knowledge, which – thought Kate – they probably did.

Ginny led her at first, and Kate was pleased because she felt anything but easy perched over six feet above the ground on an animal that jolted and tossed her around like a sack of potatoes. When the hack – as Ginny called it – got under way, however, Kate was at the mercy of Daisy.

"Rise in the saddle with her," screamed Ginny – as though such a piece of advice meant something to a non-rider, "Don't just sit there – she'll throw you all over the place."

The gallop was better – somehow there was less up and down and more forward movement – but at the end of the ride Kate felt as though her legs had been stretched open on the rack and she ached in every muscle of her body.

"If your backside is sore, I can give you some horse liniment," advised Ginny as she took their pound notes and shut the gate of the stable yard behind them

"Did you enjoy that?" asked Joan as they mounted Kate's Honda with difficulty.

"No," replied Kate, "and I'm one pound lighter."

"Have you heard The Stones latest, Steve?" asked Simon Wiseman, his tongue firmly in his cheek.

"Am I likely to have heard The Stones latest, Yogi?"

"You ought to open up, man. 'Turn on, tune in, drop out'."

"They've arrested that bugger, haven't they?" asked Stephen, bitterly.

"Leary? Yeah. Possession of narcotics. They're mind expanding drugs, man. He's a leader in the field."

"Maybe, but only in the right hands. Do you think youngsters are going to produce songs like Bob Dylan because they take Leary's advice? Drugs are just going to scramble their brains. People like Leary have a duty to the youngsters in their care, and advocating drug use isn't good advice. Psychedelic drugs! It's a dangerous craze – and you know it."

"To get back to The Stones, me old mate – *Aftermath* is really great. Mick and Keith have written all the songs on this one. You ought to listen to it. There's more to life than folk music, but don't tell Des ... Seriously, just listen to *Mother's Little Helper*. It'll turn you on – even you, Steve."

Simon insisted on playing the LP, and Stephen listened. He had little respect for pop music and no appreciation of its value. It was forty five minutes of agony, but he conceded he liked *Lady Jane*.

"What's the other instrument they're using on that?" he asked.

"That's Brian experimenting with a dulcimer."

"He's clever, isn't he? I like the sound. It's a bit like adding a violin to a folk song. 'There was an Abyssinian maid, and on a dulcimer she played'"

"Coleridge took drugs."

"Yeah, but he wrote *The Rime of the Ancient Mariner.* What has Leary written that's worth reading? Anyway, despite his few great poems, Coleridge wasn't in the same class as his friend Wordsworth, who never touched drugs."

"Leary is founder of the League of Spiritual Discovery."

"You don't need drugs to undertake spiritual discovery. You just need imagination and the time to read and think. Anyway, what spiritual discovery is Leary into?"

"Hinduism."

"Great – and he thinks adopting the religious beliefs of the East is likely to take us forward in the West?"

"You're a cynic, Steve."

"Look for real solutions. Stop hiding away, Yogi."

"It must be true, then?" said Christine Dixon, tossing the magazine over to Kate Walsh. "If the Americans tell us it's true, who can hold any doubts?"

Kate picked up the copy of *Time* from where she lounged on the settee, nursing her aching buttocks. '... in a decade dominated by youth, London has burst into bloom. It swings, it is the scene.'

"London is the fashion capital of the world is it?"

"If you happen to live there, and if you happen to have the money to spend in Carnaby Street or on the King's Road," replied Chris, scornfully, "Something we'll never have as nurses."

"Do you resent that, Chris?"

"Not really. I'd rather be doing something useful with my life than earning enough money to be doing something trivial. It just annoys me that the papers convey this image of our generation as representing this 'explosion of youthful freedom'. If you believed everything you read you'd think we were all 'dedicated followers of fashion'. It's rubbish. Most of us have a hard enough time finding the money to pay the rent. Look at us. Look at your friend, Heather, and her husband, Barry. We're being manipulated by people who want what little money we do have spare into conforming to an image that's false. All right, we wear miniskirts and go to discos and like the Beatles but this stuff about 'our own style and culture' and 'having money to spare'. It's bullshit."

"Chris!"

"I come from a large family," she laughed, "I have brothers. Besides, Joan has opened my eyes – Joan and the theatre group she got me into ..."

"How's that going?"

"Fine – you must come and see the play. It's on next month ... I like Joan, despite our differences. Why is it that people of her class always see things so clearly – especially where money is concerned?"

"Because they're brought up with it?"

"Maybe. I don't know. But she's sees through all this media crap – just like that! She doesn't get carried away with all the nonsense."

"But she does dress fashionably?"

"Yes. I suppose she can afford to. I expect her parents help her out. Mine would never have the money."

"Nor mine," replied Kate.

"They're doing what?" asked Stephen when Des waylaid him in the corridor with the news.

"The Education staff are doing a series of lectures called 'The Philosophy of Education' when we get back after Easter. It won't be in the education rooms. We're all to assemble in the hall."

"What the hell for? They'd be better off telling us how to teach reading. We'll all be in schools in six months. We need to see Tom about this."

"It won't make any difference, Last. They're working towards this college providing a degree course. It's the aim to have teaching an all degree profession, and so the course will become more theoretical."

"I'm all for that – it'll improve our status in the eye of the public, but we need the practical courses. Apart from PE and your own subjects what do you actually feel able to teach?"

"See Tom if you like. He's a decent bloke and the best Education lecturer in the place, but it won't make any difference … Mark my words, they'll change the title to something like 'The Philosophy of Education in the Classroom' and trot out what they'd planned to do, anyway."

CHAPTER 33

Where have all the flowers gone?

Hughie Spragg was going through "another of his periods of disenchantment with life", as Penny Grove put it to Pete Campbell.

"He'll always be a pain in the arse, Pete, because he only wants to do what Hughie wants to do – and that isn't work. When the going gets tough, Hughie gets going – in the opposite direction."

"I take it you don't like him?"

"He's a good – a great – banjo player, but that's all. You always know he'll let you down just when you need him."

With Penny coming to the fore on the vocals, the group's fortunes seemed about to improve but Hughie was late at the recording studio yet again. When he did eventually arrive, sauntering along as though only looking cool mattered Penny said nothing but gave Pete a meaningful look. The session went well, although it involved several takes on the tracks that involved Hughie and he lost it on *Foggy Mountain Breakdown* altogether.

Afterwards, sitting in The Fairfield Arms, Penny let rip.

"It's not good enough, Hughie. Professional recording

engineers aren't going to want to fuck around while you get over the drugs you took the night before."

"Steady, steady," urged Pete, eager not to upset the other clientele or antagonise Hughie.

"I am steady," replied Penny, "It's the Banjo Boy who's got the shakes. Look at him."

"Cool it, man, cool it," simpered Hughie.

"I'm not a man, man, and I'd be incredibly cool if you did your job properly and on time."

"You'll miss me when I'm gone," answered Hughie, attempting to turn on what he thought of as charm.

"No we wouldn't. We may not find another banjo player as *great*" (she emphasised the word as though it constituted an insult) "as you, but we would find one who turned up on time and was actually fit to play. We've got to go back now and do part of that demo tape again because you've been on the marijuana all bloody night. Look at yourself. You're sweating like an old man with the ague, your feet can't find the floor and hold your body in place for more than a couple of seconds, your voice is on the other side of nowhere, your fingers can hardly find their place on the frets and I bet your head feels as though it's stuffed with cotton wool. Doesn't it?"

Pete listened, watched by the fourth member of the group, Dougie Green, who looked as though he felt their leader should intervene. Pete didn't: he sat and waited, thinking that this would be 'kill or cure', as Ian Fleming put it on the back of one of the Bond novels.

Hughie placed his beer glass unsteadily on the table.

"So you think you might not miss me?" asked Hughie, his voice a blend of threat and pleading but mingled almost with relief.

"I doubt it."

"Right. We'll see."

"That's right – bugger off. Is that going to be your answer to everything, Hughie, until the drugs take hold of you and dump you by the side of the road?"

"I'm not taking this – not from anyone. If you don't want me, I'll be ramblin' on."

"No you won't, Hughie. You'll drop off at the nearest squat and cadge some drug or other off one of your mates. You're not going anywhere."

"We'll see. You do your thing and I'll do mine."

"You have to work at life, Hughie – at jobs, at relationships. They don't fall at your feet. It needs guts and effort. Have you got the guts, Hughie? Can you be bothered to make the effort?"

"I don't call this fun. This aint bringing me no pleasure," he said, wearily, draining his glass to the dregs.

They watched him drift from the bar, dragging his banjo case behind him. For a moment, Penny almost went after him but thought better of it.

"Well done," said Pete, "now all we need to do is find ourselves a banjo player."

"You're pleased, really," replied Penny, "You know as well as I do that he'd have let us down at every turn. We'd never know whether he was going to turn up for a recording session or a concert."

The elation of Labour's election victory was fading for Dick Crossman. In Cabinet they were faced with a new problem: the seamen's strike. It was absolutely necessary to impose a Prices and Incomes Policy and this could not be done if they gave way to the demands of the seamen.

Already wages were outstripping prices and yet the seamen were demanding what amounted to a further seventeen per cent pay rise. Harold had met forty eight of the seamen's leaders at No 10, along with Ray Gunter, whose union affiliations were strong. It was all to no avail: the National Union of Seamen turned down any offers, demanding that any time worked over the forty hour week should be considered as overtime.

"We've assumed the necessary powers to control the ports, dock labour, food prices and transport services to and from the docks," said Harold, "and we've declared a state of emergency. The line I have taken in my television broadcasts has proposed this as the only reasonable line."

"We cannot possibly give way now," said James Callaghan, Chancellor of the Exchequer, "whatever damages the strike may be doing, any backtracking on our part would damage the pound even further."

"We could achieve a settlement at any time," intervened Ray Gunter, Minister of Labour, "The employers have offered to put up the money. It is the government that is preventing the settlement because of the Prices and Incomes Policy."

"The fact that the employers have offered to meet the demands of the seamen is neither here nor there. We must fight it out," replied James.

Dick was aware that those who were for fighting it out also realised that standing firm was going to ruin the country: our balance of trade was suffering.

"I've sat here for hours. I feel like a boiler," said Paul Crisp, dangling his legs from the edge of Mike's bed and watching Mike pacing the room, cigarette in mouth.

"Two days back. It's like years," said Mike.

"It's the last term," replied, Paul, "Forever!"

"That's some consolation, considering all the work I've got to get in – not to mention teaching practice."

Paul shifted his buttocks on the bed, thinking of the Easter holiday. 'It was a great break,' he thought, 'walking in the park with Amanda, watching the swan. It took you away from work. It's wonderful when she doesn't fret about me. She's so concerned she might lose me – as though that would happen!' He looked up at Mike, who was staring out of the window at the sky, dark with rain and thunder.

"Mike … you and the lads … you think Amanda henpecks me, don't you? You all dislike her."

"It's not that Paul," replied Mike, not taking his eyes from the sky, "You've changed, that's all. Anyway, it's none of our business."

"Didn't you expect me to change when I got a steady girl?"

Mike shrugged, but said nothing.

"You and the lads have never given Amanda a chance. You've always thought I was under the thumb … but I like it like that. It doesn't bother me."

"It's just that you cut yourself off, Paul. We were trying to shake you up a bit."

"She resented your attitude … She felt a bit insecure."

"She thought I was your bad angel, did she Paul? That was no reason to cut yourself off."

"I told you – I didn't want her to feel … uncertain."

"What are you doing next year?"

"I'm going straight into teaching," answered Paul.

"Why don't you get your diploma, first? It's worth so much more."

"It'll put off for another year any chance of Amanda and me getting married. I want to save as much as I can next year, and so I'm getting digs in Staffham. Amanda's year is the first degree course year. By the time she finishes we should have enough for a deposit on a house – with what we've saved already by working in the holidays. If we tighten our belts we shall have a house – mortgaged up to the hilt, like, and with no furniture, but we should have a house."

Mike laughed quietly to himself. 'Poor sod,' he thought.

'Ian Brady and Myra Hindley, the infamous couple known as the Moors Murderers, were sentenced to life imprisonment in London's Old Bailey today …'

Miriam Davison on a visit to her friends' 'apartment' – as Christine liked to call the ground floor flat they shared – was cooking a meal for all of them, or at least for those who were off-duty. She was setting the table when her eye caught the headlines on the paper Chris Dixon was reading.

"Are you with the 'bring back hanging' brigade, Chris?"

"Only if there is absolutely no doubt whatsoever," replied Chris, "Too many innocent people, convicted on grounds of 'beyond reasonable doubt', have been hanged by the neck until dead for me to want it back completely."

"The taking of any life is wrong – even Brady's and Hindley's."

"I'm not with you there. In their case there is no doubt

that they killed at least three young people – two children and a teenager. They tortured them, they took pictures of their ordeal, they recorded the children's pleas for mercy on tape and then they killed them. They've shown no remorse, and I don't think they ever will."

"Would the threat of the death sentence have stopped them?" asked Miriam.

"It didn't, did it? That was in force when they committed their atrocities …"

"So what would hanging achieve? The threat of it was no deterrent. The children would still have died horribly."

"It would be a punishment for their crimes."

"God will punish them. It's not for us to do His work."

"Oh Miriam, not all of us believe that to be true … and even if it is, your God might forgive them, mightn't he? 'One sinner who repents': isn't that the way you think? We can't forgive a crime like this, Miriam – not us ordinary human beings. We need to see Brady and Hindley punished. We need to see their awful lives ended."

Paul Crisp's final teaching practice – in a primary school with a class of ten to eleven year olds – convinced him beyond any shadow of doubt that a teacher's life was the one for him. He remembered being taught science by being required to take notes while sitting at his desk or, if he and his friends were lucky, watch the teacher carry out an experiment. 'It shouldn't be like this,' he thought at the time, 'we should be finding out for ourselves.'

He recalled an interview with Barnes Wallis, the inventor of the bouncing bomb. The great man had been asked how the idea came to him, and he'd explained that at school his teachers had taught the principles of science by giving the pupils time to experiment. He learned to observe and make deductions; he hadn't been told, but had discovered for himself.

"Our job, Mr Crisp, is to prepare these children for the 11+. They don't have time for finding out; they need to know," explained Melanie Hooper, the class teacher.

"But the exam was taken last February, Mrs Hooper, and the children aren't tested for the 11+ in science. Surely, we can ease up a little now? It's May, the weather is wonderful and we can make a mess on the grass – not in the classroom. You'll be welcome to join us."

Melanie Hooper had her personal problems, and the young man's manner had its appeal. Paul smiled and turned on his easy charm; he wasn't a Welshman – well, a Welshman from Monmouthshire – for nothing. She joined her class on a sunny afternoon while they wondered how water could be transferred from one pail to another using a piece of plastic tubing.

"You should have a word with the Head, Mrs Hooper. There's a drastic shortage of pails in the science cupboard. I had to borrow four from the caretakers and steal another four from college – goodness knows what the cleaners will say. Even so, the children are obliged to work in groups of four, and that's too many. We don't want that, do we?"

"Are you pulling my leg, Mr Crisp?"

"We need more buckets, Mrs Cooper."

She laughed, felt young again and knelt among the groups of children.

"Air pressure – or, to be precise, atmospheric pressure: remember what I told you," said Paul, offering advice but no solution.

The lesson continued into playtime and beyond. Other children gathered around, wondering what was happening, and Mrs Hooper shooed them away. It was a lovely afternoon she thought. She had never seen the children so relaxed and keen to learn. Paul asked the children to write up their findings in class. Even those who had not understood the science had seen their siphons work and wondered.

"It mustn't seem like magic, Mr Crisp."

"It must, Mrs Hooper. Science must seem like magic – in the beginning and always. It's the sense of wonder that makes us ask the question 'why?' If I'd told them the answers, the magic would have disappeared. One afternoon – on my last teaching practice – I sat with a group of children doing nothing – nothing, that is, except watching a butterfly hatch from its pupa. The class had set up the vivarium with their teacher and waited for nature to take its course. We sat and watched – watched and wondered, Mrs Hooper – as the caterpillar which had become the pupa emerged as a butterfly. Can you imagine the children ever forgetting that moment?"

"You have quite a poetic turn of mind, Mr Crisp."

A turn of mind that saw Paul emerge from his teaching practice with a distinction. He'd had it easy, of course, and he knew that: it was the summer term and the school was within a few weeks of breaking up for the long holiday, sports day was staring them in the face and he'd offered to return and help, the children were out on the playing field each day at play and dinner times.

Amanda had been ecstatic. She'd kissed him more fervently than usual before they went to celebrate at the

Chinese restaurant in Hanley and before her conversation had turned to his education special study.

"Did it turn out all right after all that work?"

"Yes" he replied, "thanks to Stephen. It was his suggestion that turned it from something ordinary into something special."

"Don't put yourself down, love."

"I'm not. I'd done five straightforward case studies. His idea to carry out those simple sociometric tests in the classes of the children concerned made my study special. I was able to place the five children within their class social groups and relate their position to their personalities."

"But it was you did the work, love – not Stephen Last."

"I wouldn't say that exactly. He guided me through the testing and helped me construct the sociograms that plotted the children within their peer group structure."

For a moment, Amanda thought her fiancé was returning to his mates, but perhaps it was only him being fair. She didn't like Stephen Last particularly but he had helped Paul and that was a point in his favour.

Heather Burton was enjoying the struggle, but it was a struggle. She'd looked forward to working in the theatre. She felt that surgery was at the heart of medicine – the "cutting edge" as she put it to Barry – but now there was Chas, and she saw him in every patient. Nursing had become more than just a worthwhile profession, more even than a vocation; it had become personal in a way she could not have anticipated before becoming a mother.

The first incision of every operation held a fascination and, now, almost a fear. The peeling back of the layers of skin to reveal the internal organs improved her knowledge of anatomy, but infused her with trepidation. The internal organs – and once she had watched a heart beating – looked so red and raw, and Heather wondered at the fragility of the human body. The first time a severed breast slopped into the dish she held ready, Heather closed her eyes and felt like puking. When the first amputated leg hit the floor beside her, she thought of her own father who suffered from diabetes and was always complaining about the coldness in his feet.

The small talk and dark humour of the operating theatre – so necessary "to keep everyone sane", she was told – sounded a trivial note. Heather saw only eyes behind the surgical masks, and was reminded of gangsters planning a raid; and yet these men and women were artists and commanded her respect and admiration.

She didn't talk to Barry of these things; they had an agreement that work was left in the workplace otherwise their snatched times together – and her shifts made these times particularly difficult to secure – were wasted. Home-time had to be for them and for Chas.

It was a relief, therefore, to be able to chat with Kate on the rare occasions when they were able to meet. She found her old friend quite unchanged – almost a girl still and almost serene. They sat over coffee and Heather was able to dissect the theatre staff, personality by personality.

"I find them a race apart," she said, "Even the sisters are prima donnas."

"They have to be, Heather. You can't get emotionally involved with life and death. The more detached you are, the more focussed you are and the more focussed you the less likely you are to make a mistake."

"Have you ever made one?"

"Once. I dropped a swab onto a tray of sterile instruments, and they all stood around umming an aahring while the theatre sister and I went to replace them. It happens … but there's great camaraderie, too. We all sat around afterwards eating a huge breakfast."

"Do you think you'd like to specialise in theatre work, Kate?"

"I don't know. Some of the surgeons are so difficult you'd have to have a strong personality to survive, but if you clicked it would be very satisfying work. In the best teams, they get to know each other well and the patients benefit. There's no doubt about that. I've even heard a surgeon ask a sister for advice during an operation. There's great respect there, but you have to earn it."

CHAPTER 34

Swinging London

David Frost was sceptical about the idea of London as 'the swinging city'. He recalled *Esquire* calling it 'the fun machine', but it had been the article in *Time* magazine that coined the phrase 'the swinging city'; this was the phrase to capture the popular imagination and ignite the tourist industry. He was uncertain whether London's influence was 'spreading around the globe' and creating rock groups 'with English names' in such places as Prague; he was even more uncertain whether comparing the modern city with that of Shakespeare's London was valid.

He noted the emphasis on fashion (ruffled blouses, patent leather shoes and bell-bottomed trousers), cocktail bars, discotheques, art galleries, the film world and youth. Youth was the word and flip jargon was in: "fab", "gear", "groovy", "with it" held the linguistic stage.

David – despite 'jet-setting' as part of his work in the States – felt that the London scene had 'passed him by' but done him some good. On the strength of the excitement generated, he had persuaded ABC Television to finance his show 'David Frost's Night Out in London' and he'd booked Lulu, Danny La Rue and the pop group called Dave, Dee, Dozy, Beaky, Mick and Titch.

He still faced one huge problem, however. He had to find at least three people from a 'list of mega-names': Laurence Olivier, Peter Ustinov, Peter O'Toole, Albert Finney, Peter Sellers and Sean Connery.

It wasn't swinging for Stephen Last either. He was well ahead with his work. His study of the use of sociometric testing so that children could be placed in suitable class groups that drew in the isolates to mingle with the stars had been well-researched, thoroughly tested in one of the schools to which he was attached and well-received by his Education tutor; but he still had to face those final exams and those unknown questions.

Everyone, he noticed, was a trifle "scratchy" – as he expressed it to Jenny Pryce when they sat in her college room one afternoon.

"Are you referring to me?" she asked, sitting up suddenly.

"No, it's pretty general ... and you are the least 'scratchy' of all. In fact, I can't recall you ever being in anything but a good mood."

"Sugar tongue," she laughed, kissing him gently with those soft lips of hers.

"No, I mean it ..."

"But you're still going home for a year?"

"I have to, Jenny. I feel I owe it to my parents."

"Yes, OK," was the answer that bypassed her feelings.

She'd refused to make an issue of Stephen's decision, but she hadn't liked it – not one little bit. They couldn't afford to rent a flat together – not if they were to save up to ... for what might happen. She knew that but thought he might have, at least, wanted to find some cheap digs in

Wolverhampton so that they could be together. She didn't think her parents would offer him a room; they wouldn't have liked to … to "encourage anything", as her mother would have said if she'd asked; but he could have found digs.

She didn't have this feeling of his that it was a duty to go home and give your parents a year before you moved on. Jenny simply wanted to meet up with her old school friends, and living at home would save her a lot of money and give her at least a year free and with something to spend.

She wasn't sure about Stephen's motive, either: was it that he didn't love her and was this his way of easing out of what had been a comfortable relationship?

Susan Paget, whose parents lived in Woodford, a leafy suburb on the edge of London, felt that the city wasn't going to swing for her either: not without Des and not on a tenner a week.

She was sick with anxiety that this was to be their last term together – ever: all the friends she'd made – not only Des, but all of them – would soon go their separate ways and Susan felt that they'd never meet again. Somehow, it was more than she could bear.

She pushed the file away, rose from her desk and walked to the window of her room. She stared at the empty campus, watching lights burning in rooms. 'Everyone is alone, all poring over books; all that passion burning itself away to leave us with nothing – nothing. In a few weeks now it will be less than nothing. The chance we had will be extinguished forever. How I've tortured myself longing for him. Now: hollowness and loneliness.

How could it all come to nothing? How could all that feeling I had come to nothing? I made a fool of myself and all for nothing. Could we have made it work? Yes, yes we could. I won't know myself when I get home. Home! London!'

Susan looked at herself in the wall mirror over the sink in the vanity unit and wondered at her reflection. She flicked her hair into place, fluffing the top. Shaking her head furiously from side to side she walked from her room.

Des was going home to Middlesbrough, or was he? The 'swinging city' held no attraction for him; in fact, he found the very idea repulsive; but he wasn't sure about returning home. He hadn't secured a teaching post as yet – he'd deliberately put it off – but there were plenty of jobs around, everywhere. Did he want to go back home? There was Elizabeth. Yes, there was Elizabeth. Perhaps he should go back. She was a good lass and she was expecting him.

In Cabinet, the atmosphere was slightly better: the seamen's strike was almost certainly coming to an end since the seamen were prepared for some kind of settlement. Harold had delivered a statement to the House making it quite clear that he knew the names of the active communists who had been responsible for starting the strike and alleged that "a tightly knit group of politically motivated men" were working to prolong it. Despite the consternation his statement caused on the Labour back benches, Harold showed no signs of repentance and demanded to know, by asking round the Cabinet table, exactly where everyone stood on the issue. Dick Crossman and Barbara Castle were both critical of his actions, and Dick noticed that the Cabinet was finely balanced on the issue and that Harold's position was 'not too strong'.

What was bedevilling them all, of course, was the proposal to re-introduce the Prices and Incomes Bill, which had been dropped when the general election was announced. With wages outstripping prices something had to be done but there was no agreement within Cabinet on what that something should be.

Frank Cousins, the Minister of Technology, considered the proposals to be "poppycock": legislation was not the way, he felt, to deal with the problem.

"What we need," he said, "is voluntary cooperation between both sides of industry. Giving a government power to require wage or price increases to be submitted to a statutory Prices and Incomes Board is not the way forward ... You ought to remember that the Minister of Technology is first for Questions on the day after the Second Reading of the Prices and Incomes Bill. He ought to be warned of this, you know."

Dick realised that this was Frank's way of threatening to resign and lead a revolt on the day the Bill was debated in Parliament. He said:

"Such a policy is not an adequate socialist alternative to the customary strategy of deflation. What I want to know is how we propose to stop this drift into unemployment. I have no objection to an incomes policy, but I do not want to see us using such a policy in isolation."

Barbara Castle wanted a policy with two levels of award; she also suggested that ministers should show a lead by cutting their own salaries.

"We need a two-norm policy: one that copes with the lot of the lower-paid worker while holding down the higher salaries. I would also urge you to consider the introduction of a national minimum wage. If the policy is to be applied fairly it should apply to dividends as well as wages."

Jim Callaghan wanted a complete wages freeze.

Cynthia Lennon – like her friend Maureen, Ringo's wife – had been brought up in a home where the women did the caring and nurturing and the men did the providing. She admired Maureen, who was so devoted to Ringo that she would stay up until four in the morning to greet him with a home-cooked meal when he arrived home.

They would visit each other's homes because John was always at his most relaxed with Ringo, who was 'gregarious and fun-loving'. In Ringo's replica pub, The Flying Cow, which he'd had built in their front room, Maureen kept them all supplied with 'endless plates of food'. In the large grounds, Ringo had built a go-cart track and there was a TV in every room: the 'ultimate luxury'. The four of them usually socialized with the other Beatles, George and Paul, and their girlfriends. They would holiday together and spend Christmas in each other's homes.

That summer – the summer of 66 – they were at the heart of swinging London: hip restaurants, nightclubs, designer boutiques, film premieres and celebrity parties were the order of the day and night. The candle was well and truly burned at both ends. One night, while John and Cynthia were out with George and Patti, someone slipped LSD into their drinks.

For John, it was the beginning of a new enchantment: the drug's ability to lift him out of this world, to expand his mind and discover himself was an answer to his prayers. Attending fashionable art galleries in London, he soon discovered where the best LSD could be bought. His tensions and bad temper were replaced by understanding and love. When John arrived home in his Rolls-Royce at dawn, after a night of clubbing and hard drinking, he was accompanied by a retinue of hangers-on and drug pushers.

Cynthia was appalled. Despite John's desire that she should try the drug, she'd never taken to it; she'd found her one trip to be "horrifying". This angered John and the rift between them widened.

"It upset John but I couldn't handle it," she said to Maureen, "Suddenly there's this new mental barrier between us. I've told him that I'm worried about Julian growing up in this kind of environment, but he won't listen."

Outside Earls Court thousands of fans screamed to gain admittance, but the venue was already full. Inside, the object of their attentions, Cliff Richard, stood beside the American evangelist, Billy Graham, and gave his testimony. He was thrilled to be giving his testimony but had approached the lectern scared to death. He gripped it tightly, realising he couldn't move his arms; he had "pins and needles". He was dressed casually in a brown corduroy jacket and he looked out over the arena of twenty five thousand people.

"I have never had the opportunity to speak to an audience as big as this before but it is a great privilege to be able to tell so many people that I am a Christian," he said, "I can only say to people who are not Christians that until you have taken the step of asking Christ into your life, your life is really not worthwhile. It works – it works for me."

He spoke of Christianity as a "moral way of life". He explained his desire to always be moral, and not be ashamed of it. He talked of reading the Bible nightly and of the trips he had taken with his Crusader group to such places as Whipsnade Zoo and the Norfolk Broads.

He had come into show business when he was seventeen and "lost his childhood immediately". He had never done "youthful things" and felt dissatisfied. He felt he could do more with his life. He wanted to leave show business after his Christmas pantomime commitments had finished and embark on a three year divinity course.

When Cliff had finished his testimony he sang *It is no secret (what God can do)*.

As Miriam Davison arrived for her shift the next morning, she had the day's newspaper under her arm and her eyes were wide. When she bumped into Sheila Pratt, who was on the same ward, Miriam could no longer contain her excitement.

"Have you read about Cliff Richard at Earls Court with Billy Graham?"

"I don't believe he's going to stop singing," replied Sheila, "He'd never do that: he wouldn't want to disappoint his fans."

"He would if he felt God had called him. He's said that Jesus is his personal saviour. He would heed the call."

"Is that what you believe, Miriam – that Jesus has saved you?"

"Yes – oh, yes."

"From what? Why did you need to be saved?"

"It saves you from sin – from leading an immoral life. Once you take Jesus into your life, you follow Him and His teachings."

Sheila had never thought much about religion. Her father had told her that she was "Church of England until you're twenty one". She took it that he meant she was to cause no fuss by questioning things, and she'd never done so.

"We never talked about religion at home," she replied, "and we didn't go to church."

"Going to church doesn't make you a Christian, Sheila."

"I believe in God."

"Believing in God doesn't make you a Christian. To be a Christian you must give testimony in front of witnesses. In that way you commit yourself to Christ. You pledge to put time aside each day to read the Bible. You do Christian things. You find the true purpose of life. You turn aside from the permissive society, from lust, greed, pride and the other sins."

Sheila had always admired Miriam's calm. Listening to her, she felt that it came from her faith.

"Is that why you and your fiancé are going to work abroad when you're qualified?"

"Once I've got my midwifery, yes."

"Isn't there a need for nurses in our own country? That's the reason I've gone into nursing – because it's a worthwhile job and will help other people. Good nurses – people who really care and know what they're doing – will make this country a better, healthier place."

"You can serve God anywhere. Patrick and I feel called to Africa. The church has missions out there and the people live in appalling, unsanitary conditions. There is widespread disease. There is a great need, and we feel we'd be doing good."

Not for the first time in her life, Sheila felt inadequate. Everyone else always seemed either more intelligent or better educated or filled with purpose. She shook herself. It wasn't like that: she was motivated and within the year would be a qualified staff nurse.

Mary Quant's boutique, Bazaar, had come of age. Opened in Chelsea in 1955, it was now at the very heart of Swinging London. In 1964, Mary had introduced that iconic fashion item, the mini-skirt, and her use of bold colours and geometric designs had taken the world of fashion by storm. The geographical centre of the fashion world had shifted from Paris to London; it was London that set the scene and pace for the rest of civilisation. Mary had played a huge part in this transformation, bringing youth culture to the high street.

In the Queen's Birthday Honours List, Mary was awarded the Order of the British Empire. She was the toast of the town, a trailblazer, the creator of the 'London Look'.

Paul Crisp was leaving the stage, where they'd been rehearsing *The Crucible* when his English tutor, Keith Pritchett, collared him.

"Paul, could you do me a favour – round up a few likely people for a going-down party at my place – bring your girl, of course – oh, and Stella and … well, you know

... people who are going to enjoy themselves – we don't often get the chance to do anything like this – informal, you know – all right?"

"Fine, thanks," replied Paul, wondering who the hell to invite without upsetting Amanda. The English group – yes. The Education group – probably.

"Thought I'd mention it now, otherwise I'd have forgotten completely – we'd better make it after the exams – say, Thursday next? Oh, bring Des along with his guitar. You know, third year English people – anyone who's likely to make things swing," continued Keith, grinning and swinging his first in a small arc before patting Paul's arm in a matey fashion and disappearing, rather breathless, through the swing doors.

"Who are you going to invite, love?" asked Amanda, anxiously.

"Pritchett said the third year English group and any others who might be hip."

"You won't ask everyone from the English group, though, will you, love? Did he definitely mention Des Smith?"

"Yes – and inviting Des means inviting Stephen and Mike and Yogi ... I can't offend old mates, Amanda."

CHAPTER 35

"Schoolmasters are always trying to change children"

Stephen Last was reading a novel. He had a passion for Dickens, who hadn't been one of the set authors, and was, once again, partway through *Our Mutual Friend*. He was sitting on the lower flight of stairs that led down to the foyer at Coseley College of Education. Beside him stood a rubber plant, which looked ungainly and was coated with a fine dust. The foyer was absolutely silent save for a faint hum of voices coming from the common room. His body, despite the angularity forced on it by the fall of the stair, was relaxed to the point of exhaustion.

Des, guitar in hand, walking across the forecourt from the music department, watched his friend. 'Tired but easy,' he thought, 'it is finished.' He forced back the stiff swing doors, paused for a moment, approached the steps and tapped Stephen on the knee with the neck of his guitar.

"You asleep?"

"Reading a novel for the sake of it, and not because I have to. Where're you going?"

"Pritchett's party. Aren't you coming?"

"I didn't know about it."

"Funny – they must have asked me for my guitar. Are you going out with Jenny tonight?"

"No – she's off to see a friend in Wolverhampton. She's pregnant."

"What? Christ!"

"Not Jenny, nuncle – her friend."

It was the first time Stephen realised that Des had not appreciated the platonic nature of his friendship with Jenny. Well, not entirely platonic, but they hadn't gone the whole way.

"Why not come to the party, then. I could do with some good company, and it might annoy Amanda – you being one of those who led Crispy astray," Des suggested with a laugh.

"I don't know …"

"Come on, you miserable bugger. You can't leave me defenceless among the Drama Club crowd, the pseudo-intellectuals, the paper Marxists, the readers of the hip poets or Kerouac or Dos Passos …"

"I don't think you'd be exactly defenceless, Des. All right – I'm in."

The earth was wet, soaked by the thunderous rain of the past week. Soil-scented wisps rose from the earth, tarmac gleamed like a dolphin's back, grass trickled with water and the blue sky reflected the last light of the sinking sun as Des, Stephen and several others fell from Mike Harrison's old car. Realising he'd been snubbed by Amanda's influence on Paul, Mike had been only too pleased to offer a lift and gate-crash the party. Stephen roamed his eyes along the flower beds and sniffed the air as Keith Pritchett opened the door.

"Come in, come in," he chortled.

Keith was dressed in slacks and a sweat shirt and looked so different from the be-suited tutor who lectured them on the virtues of Jonathan Swift and others.

"Toilets – if you want them – are down the hall. You can tell from the pictures on the doors – better than labels – so ordinary …"

He seemed to wait for an answer, perhaps one of appreciation, but no one spoke. Stephen wondered how Pritchett had managed to secure a flat with two toilets. He noticed Rodin's *Thinker* and Botticelli's *Venus* on the toilet doors as Keith ushered them by and into the kitchen.

Plate upon plate of food was crammed on the draining board. Several girls buttered thin wafers of brown bread, assisted by Clive Ralston. He lectured on drama and Stephen admired him: just listening to the man talk with enthusiasm on his subject was infectious. As they entered, Clive was patting a petite girl with a ferret-like face and very clear blue eyes on the hips, gently. She was Margaret Cornley, a member of the other English group. In the first year, he'd rather fancied her in a quiet kind of way. Margaret giggled, sucked in her bottom lip and waved her eyelashes.

"Here it is – help yourselves," said Keith, cheerily.

Plates stacked full, they wandered into the lounge, which was crammed with students and some lecturers. Groups, crushed against the walls, spilled into the centre of the room. In one corner there was a record player and an untidy pile of LPs, EPs and singles. A woman sat by these, thumbing through them. Her eyes were puffy and batting up and down behind thick-lensed glasses. 'She looks as though she's trying not to cry,' thought Stephen, 'She's sexy in an intellectual sort of way.' He didn't know what that thought meant, but he understood it. Stephen had met her once before on a trip to the Belgrade Theatre in Coventry where they'd wasted an evening watching Henry Livings's *Eh?* It was Mrs Ralston.

"Hello, Stephen,"

"Hello, Mrs Ralston," he replied, daunted by the fact that she even knew, let alone remembered, his name.

"Emma – for God's sake call me Emma tonight."

At that moment, Cliff Jenkins – banjo player with Des and pub sign artist with Simon – ambled across and smiled at Emma Ralston.

"Ah, here's our tame Welshman, Stephen …"

"No Welshman's tame, Mrs Ralston. We come from the hills, see – 'the wild hills, rich with the spilled blood of our ancestors …'"

"'… an impotent people, sick with inbreeding, worrying the carcase of an old song'", continued Stephen, continuing Cliff's misquote from R S Thomas's poem.

"Might have known only Stephen Last could be so offensive without anybody taking offence," laughed Keith, leaning over his shoulder and smiling at Emma.

"There's no malice in Stephen," said Emma, "That's why. And a joke's a joke. However it might sound, if it's humorous it simply isn't racist … I read your special study on black humour, Stephen. It was brilliant."

"Thank you," said Stephen, thinking 'even if nothing else happens tonight the evening will stay in my memory forever', and realising he was falling in love with a lecturer's wife.

"He's a bright boyo, is our Stephen – no offence taken."

"I should think not. It was a Welshman who said it. I was merely quoting."

"Are you going to play for us, Des?" asked Emma, watching the lad from Middlesbrough poring through the records.

"I think it's the only reason I've been asked."

"Don't say that – anything – play anything you like," urged Keith, handing them all a glass of beer.

As they drank, not quite sure what to say next, another of the lecturers walked in. Stephen noticed his hair was exceedingly dry and that large flakes of scalp were sprinkled on the shoulders of his dark lounge suit. He offered cigarettes all round and drew deeply on his own. He looked as though he'd just come from delivering a lecture on something or someone controversial, but Stephen decided this could not be the case – not at 8.00 o'clock in the evening. It was the suit that made him stand out, Stephen thought, glancing down at his own sports jacket, which he'd worn ever since arriving. 'Fashion and Last occasionally bump into one another' Des had said soon after they met. Everyone had laughed, and Stephen remembered feeling that he'd been accepted for himself.

"Sorry I'm late: had to run the family over to the in-laws. Where's your husband, Emma. I've been looking for him," asked the newcomer, whose name was Roy Bunn.

"I've no idea, Roy. I suppose he must be around somewhere. Perhaps he's in the kitchen. I heard sounds of mirth from there some while ago."

"He's spreading bread," said Stephen.

"Sounds rather jolly. I'll grab a knife."

As he spoke a great bay of laughter came from the kitchen.

"My husband," suggested Emma with a sound somewhere between a sniff and a laugh.

Clive Ralston juggled a roll-mop as it slithered in his hands. Shrieks of laughter came from the women when it plopped into the darkness of his mouth.

"Go on, try another," urged Margaret Cornley.

"Do you mind ... I think you're trying to choke me."

More shrieks accompanied his second effort. Keith and Roy rushed into the kitchen.

"What! Showing them how to eat roll-mops," yelled Keith.

He picked one from the dish and straightened his throat. The women hustled him into the lounge, followed by Clive and Roy, the dish of roll-mops in hand.

"Demonstration! Demonstration!"

Clive half-climbed and was half-pushed onto a chair that someone placed, hurriedly, in the centre of the room. He glanced at his wife and dropped the fish down his throat. The dish, slopping salt, was passed across the press of heads and waving arms.

"Another! Have another!" yelled Paul.

He grabbed one himself and stood by Clive's chair, mouth open. Clive smiled, tilted back his head and gulped down the roll-mop before dropping another into Paul's mouth. Shrieks of laughter filled the room. A melee of hands and heads stretched towards the dish, swallowing, coughing, spluttering and choking.

Chill air wafted along the hall as the door opened and dancers spilled out onto the lawn from the cramped lounge. Des swilled the beer from his glass, watching the foam cling to the sides. Stephen was in the midst of a small group, gesticulating. Knots of students sat talking, occasionally calling across the room. A few couples smooched in the hall or in one of the side rooms. Keith Pritchett knelt by the record player, cursing and trying to fix an extension speaker. Sweat stains seeped across his shirt. He waddled backwards, balancing the speaker, leading the tangled flex into the hall. Edward French released Stella's hand

"Can I give you a hand?" asked Edward, easing Stella from his knees.

"Thanks Ed ... If you could unwind the flex, while I back out with the speaker, I'd be grateful."

Stella stood, looked round and tottered. She was breathing heavily when Amanda caught her eye.

"You've got to hold on for a while yet," said Amanda, smiling, "The night is still young."

Don't you worry about me, Mandy. I'll be there at the end ... Look at your boyfriend."

Paul was twirling about and waving his arms high above his head opposite Simon, who mimicked his every movement.

"Hey, Rob Roy," called Stella, "Why don't you go and toss your caber?"

Paul laughed and Simon rushed from the room, only to return with a mop, which he proceeded to toss between himself and Paul.

"Toss yourself over the boiler room," laughed Stella, swaying slightly.

"How much have you had, Stella?" asked Amanda, eager to stop Paul making more of a fool of himself.

"Don't you worry about me, Mandy. How mush hash Pauly had?" replied Stella, slurring her voice deliberately, "Doan you think he'd look nish toshing hish caber?"

Amanda glanced at Paul and then looked for Edward. She called along the hallway:

"Hey, Eddy, Stella needs some air."

"Doan you worry about me, Mandy Sweety, I can drink you under the table any goddam day I please ..."

"There isn't an abomination award going that you ...," began Des.

"Very good, Des," purred Stella, pleased that he'd been listening and had picked up the quote from Albee's play.

She clapped as Cliff Jenkins came across. Laughing, she fell into his arms, watched by Edward who'd returned with Keith.

"Come on, my dove," chuckled Cliff, winking at Edward, "Everybody dance! There'll be dancing on the hillside, there'll be dancing in the vales ..."

"The land you know will still be dancing" continued Edward, making a grab for Amanda,

"When you dance home again to Wales," sang Paul in his best Monmouthshire Welsh, pulling a girl with him across the room.

The six of them danced along the hallway, colliding with the walls and the smooching couples.

"Is he always like that?" asked Emma Ralston.

"Except in Wales," replied Des, and was pleased she laughed at his cutting remark.

Des plucked the strings, gently, holding the faintest echo of the chords. An harmonica joined him, plaintively playing *The Streets of Laredo*. Slowly, caressing the melody, Des sang. Several people hummed, and one or two sang softly. Stella reached for a low stool, and sat taut and upright. Songs they all knew brought them together: songs they had shared during the past three years. Voices as rough as grit, voices straining for the note, laughing voices and sad voices that rumbled in the crowd.

Outside it was dark and the dancers were tired. Keith had turned down the lights and the room was illuminated only by the bright moon. A thick haze of smoke had built itself down from the ceiling. It was warm in the room, and the bodies were crammed close together: bodies stretched, bodies pressed, arms and legs jutting at odd angles across the carpet. Empty beer crates provide seats for those who wished to sing, and many did, especially Stella, who sang *Where have all the flowers gone?* She followed this with *We shall overcome.*

"How about a song from the tutors?"

Cliff's voice called, his banjo resting across his knees. Yells and cheers irresistible, laughter and tears. Keith was on his feet, kicking the beer crates to one side. Clive and Roy joined him, while the other tutors hid among the students. Clive and Roy stood, arms linked, lighting each other's cigarettes and tossing others into the crowd.

"What will it be?" demanded Keith.

"Something classical," said Emma, "Something from the Elizabethan songbook."

"*Where the bee sucks? Drink to me only? …*"

"Last – you bugger. You sang that for a dare once in a counter-tenor voice during an RE lesson," yelled Des.

"Is that right, Stephen?" asked Emma.

"Sort of … I can't sing and I don't really have a voice – counter-tenor or otherwise – it's just a knack of catching the sound. I only did it to see whether everyone else could keep a straight face while Miss Hunt listened."

"Come on, come on," urged Cliff, "Let's not let the tutors off the hook. What's it to be?"

"*Peg-o-Ramsey*," said Emma.

"*Peg-o-Ramsey* it is," agreed Clive, "And then our counter-tenor."

Cracked falsettos and trembling bases – accompanied by Cliff on banjo with Keith, insistently rhythmic, forcing the words and Clive and Roy guessing at the odd phrase – led into the song Stephen had been obliged to contribute. He was relieved to find Emma singing with him backed by Des's strumming on his guitar.

Standing at the gate, Stephen could see the surrounding hills lit by the full moon. His shirt was open to the cooling air. It was very quiet. Under his hand the gate was hard and unyielding. He opened and closed it, walking out on to the road. He stood quite still and thrust his hands deep into his pockets. He looked up at the hills, seeming to discern green patches of fields and the dark shadows of farmhouses.

"I thought I'd find you here."

Des stood behind him leaning on the gate.

"Is this it, then, Des?

Des shrugged and shook his head upwards. Together they stood without speaking for a long time, watching the faint, drizzling mist thicken on the hillsides. After a while, they went back to the party.

Nelson Mandela had been on Robben Island for over two years when he learned that he was to receive the second visit from Winnie, his wife. She had been under constant harassment since her first: he would sometimes find newspaper clippings about Winnie placed on his cell bed by the warders. In this way he learned of the police persecution of her and her brother and sisters.

Nelson missed his wife enormously and needed the 'reassurance of seeing her'; besides, there were family matters to discuss. She arrived agitated, having had to travel in the hold of a ferry where the fumes made her ill. Despite having dressed to look her best, she looked ill and drawn when Nelson clapped eyes on her.

Watched closely by the warder they discussed their financial situation, the education of their daughters who Winnie had placed – illegally according to the authorities – in an Indian school and the health of Nelson's mother who had not been well.

Nelson was worried about his wife: he knew she would be prey to people who wished to undermine her, and she would be lonely.

"How is the church?" asked Nelson, wishing to find out how the ANC was faring but knowing he could not ask questions outside family matters; and he would listen as she answered in the same coded language.

"How are the priests? Are there any new sermons?" he continued, and learned in this way much of what was happening in the outside world.

"Time up!" yelled the warder after half-an-hour.

Nelson refrained from meeting his wife's lips on the glass barrier that separated them. 'I want her to leave first,' he thought, 'In that way she will not see me led away by the warders.'

Winnie whispered a goodbye and left, hiding her pain.

"Did you see *The Frost Programme* last night?" demanded Roger Turl, headmaster of Castleford Primary School, "The man ought to be frogmarched out of the country. We'd be a lot better off if he went back to America. He was always a waste of good television time here."

Stephen Last sat in one corner of the staffroom, listening quietly and trying to assess the dynamics of his first posting. Suffolk LEA was a considerate authority and allowed newly qualified teachers to take up their post in July thus securing them an August pay packet: much appreciated after three years at training college.

Mr Turl was raging about the programme in which David Frost had used the actor, Robert Morley, to send up the teaching profession. Morley was well-loved by the British public because he was what was known affectionately as 'a character'. In conversation with David Frost, he'd commented with displeasure that schoolmasters were always trying to change children. David – eager to have audience involvement in his new programme so that it 'broke the hermetic seal between the studio and the public' – saw his chance when a spokesman from the National Association of Schoolmasters in pursuit of a pay claim had said "People seem to forget that schoolmasters are probably the most valuable members of the community." Subsequently, David and his team had invited an audience of 'schoolmasters and schoolmistresses' to the programme on which Robert was to appear.

"Schoolmasters are always trying to change children," said Robert, after David had warmed him to the subject, "Somebody years ago told some schoolmaster ... that his job was not only to teach, but to mould the character of children. I don't want them to alter my child, nor do I want them to go on this lunatic tack that every child must be an eager child, no child must be a lazy child, no child must be a fat child. I know that the lazy and fat are the salt of the earth! And if you don't have children who run slowly, what fun is it for the children who run fast?"

"We've got some teachers in the audience ...," began David.

"Oh, that's a great mistake," interposed Robert, popping his eyes in characteristic fashion, "I don't think you want anyone who knows about it! I thought the whole object of this programme was for people to talk, like you do, on a subject about which they know nothing whatever."

"Robert Morley was very modest – not to say self-effacing – about his comments," suggested Raymond Burrell, the teacher to whose class Stephen had been attached.

"I'm not talking about Morley," blustered Mr Turl, "he was good enough to acknowledge that he was fat and lazy! I'm talking about Frost. He sets himself up as some sort of social campaigner and then sets about maligning the very profession that might do something to improve society. The man's an entertainer – pure and simple. Why pretend otherwise?"

"He certainly isn't admired by everyone at the BBC," said Emily Farrow, who ran the infant department, "His

TW3 may have been popular with the public but it cut across the principles of good journalism ..."

"Well said Miss Farrow," applauded Mr Turl, "It debased political argument and brought schoolboy humour to our screens. I don't think that's what we pay our licence fee for, do you? Who needs a glimpse into Mr Frost's lavatory?"

He looked around the staffroom for support, laughing at his own stab at humour. Raymond Burrell looked at Stephen and gave an advisory smile. 'It's best,' thought Stephen, 'to say nothing. I can see what Mr Turl is saying but ...'

"Robert Morley did make some good points, didn't he?" Stephen said when school had finished for that day, "It is better that children should be taught how to use an atlas and consult a travel agent rather than learn, parrot fashion, the name of every capital city in the world."

"Don't let Roger Turl hear you say that," laughed Raymond, as they stood talking in the classroom, "The curriculum here is a watered-down version of the one Roger had in his secondary school."

"What's a secondary school teacher doing as head of a primary school?"

"Bloody hell, lad, are you a revolutionary? You need to chum up with Bill Richardson. You and he will make a right team. Next year should be fun. Watch what you say in the staffroom. Some of them will take it right back to Roger. You'll soon learn who you can trust. You don't want to queer the pitch in your probationary year."

Stephen was on the coach travelling to Wolverhampton to see Jenny when he realised that England were on the verge of winning the World Cup. The coach was alive with expectation and national fervour. He'd bumped into Alf Ramsey on Ipswich station when the England maestro had been manager of Ipswich Town; he remembered the man's quiet smile as they passed on the platform. He'd admired the man without knowing precisely why. Somehow, Ramsey had seemed so unassuming and so purposeful: a man of action rather than a talker, a man who would, quite simply, get the job done.

Now, the emphasis was on the players, however, and Geoff Hurst in particular, during extra time. There was an element of jingoism – about that there was no doubt: it was essential that our team did beat the Germans. Their questioning the third goal was deplorable, not just because we wanted to win but because they had no right to ask such a question about an English team. When Geoff's third goal hit the net, putting any dispute beyond discussion, those on the coach exploded with joy: men cried, women screamed, strangers shook each other by the hand and the driver gripped the wheel more tightly.

The radio commentator described the scenes of hysteria on the pitch and Bobby Moore's smile as he accepted the Jules Rimer Trophy from the Queen. It had been a great team and a well-deserved victory.

Chapter 36

'Failed to live'

Sheila Pratt stood at the back of the crowd by the graveside, listening to the priest as he committed the child's body to the earth. "'For it will not do to hiss humanity because ... one baby failed to live"'

'Why?' thought Sheila, 'What does he mean? Who is this D J Enright and what's he talking about?' She'd never heard of the poet and the traditional words "dust to dust, ashes to ashes" brought her no comfort. She had seen the little boy and watched him die, and the shock was overwhelming.

Sheila was working on the infants ward and had come across the little boy, Nathaniel, suddenly. There he was, lying in the cot, his head so huge he looked like some creature from a film about aliens.

"Hydrocephalus, Nurse Pratt," said Sister Magnusson, "It's a mercy he'll not be with us for long."

"It doesn't seem right," replied Sheila, hardly knowing what she was saying.

"No – the death of a child never does. I've told the parents to go home to rest, and to come back later. Nathaniel will die – probably sometime tonight."

Sheila found herself in the sluice room crying. It was there she was found by Sister Magnusson.

"I'm sorry. I know nurses shouldn't."

"Nurses should, Nurse Pratt. It's why we do the job. The day you can turn a dark joke on a child's death will be the day you need to leave the profession, but he needs us now. Later is the time to cry it out."

Sheila gasped in some air. She'd heard the dark jokes; she'd seen them laughing in theatre when they amputated a leg, and she understood the reason: you had to get it out of you. Sister Magnusson's attitude was different: perhaps dealing with children you never got used to premature death.

As she stood listening to the priest, Sheila remembered laying out the little boy: washing his little body, putting him in a clean nightshirt and placing a flower from the ward table in his hands before wrapping Nathaniel in a white sheet. It was the last act of love a nurse could do for anyone but especially, it seemed, for a child.

'Lenny Bruce, the American comedian, whose risqué act featured jokes about racial prejudice and religious tensions and was banned in Britain as well as America, died today at the age of 39 as the result of a heroin overdose …'

"And serves the bugger right," said Christine Dixon, "I've no time for these druggies. If they can't perform without drugs, they're better not to perform at all."

"Feeling a tad intolerant today, are we Chris?" mocked Joan.

"Maybe, but who wants to listen to the views of a junkie?"

"You like Dylan. His lyrics are drug-inspired."

"A song is different, and Dylan has never wanted to be thought of as a messiah. 'It's no use talking to me. It's the same as talking to you'. Didn't he say that? But these modern comedians stand up there as though they were high priests putting the world to rights."

Martin Luther King, together with his friend and ally Ralph Abernathy, had moved north to Chicago. They were living for a time at 1550 S Hamlin Avenue on the west side of the city to show their support for the poor of that city. This was an area of slum buildings.

Martin had heard that "racial steering" was operating in the housing market. During the previous months housing agencies had been checked and it was clear that preference was given to whites.

"If a white and black couple apply for housing and that couple are identical in income, background and the number of children they have the house goes to the white couple," said Martin, "If we now have the right to sit at the same counter as the white man, we must also have the right to live next door to him."

Fearful that the marches might turn violent, Martin approached Mayor Daley.

"I will not lead a violent march. I would rather arrange with you that the march be called off," he said, concerned that looting might occur as it had when the garbage men marched in Memphis.

Later he said to Ralph:

"I want there to be no excuse for the police to move in."

"You may find yourself less welcome here than you were in the South, Martin," Ralph replied.

His words turned out to be true. During the march through Marquette Park, the mob gathered. Abuse was hurled and bottles thrown. Equality might be a legal right, but it wasn't welcome in Chicago. Martin was hit by a brick as the march continued. He had always known how dangerous his work could be and he'd told his staff that if anything happened to him they must continue the non-violent struggle. 'I'm not going to live a long life,' he thought; it was something he'd always known.

Hughie Spragg had made it to the festival. He wasn't sure how, but some chick had been involved, and he'd arrived in a truck. He hadn't seen the chick since, and couldn't remember what she looked like. She'd cleared off when she found him on a trip.

He'd seen flowers dancing in the air, but after a while claustrophobia had set in and he'd wanted to get outside into the fresh air. He crawled about among the bodies for a while trying to find a bush to hide in. It was while he was crawling around that he'd felt the acid coming on. Suddenly he felt less than human, but braver than ever. He was a monster and could do anything: leap walls, fly above trees, soar to the moon. He was terrified. His eyes rolled in their sockets and he wanted to vomit. So he did.

When he came round, everyone was laid out, sprawled on their backs, side by side, heads to feet, waiting for the music to begin. It was going to be three days of free love and rock music: right up Hughie's street. It was all happening. The bloke next to him was snoring, and so Hughie gave him a shove.

"What you doing, man?"

"Painting the revolution," the snorer answered, "What's with you?"

"Writing a novel," replied Hughie, unsure what else to say and not wanting to remember Penny Grove throwing him out of the Appalachian Four.

"That's cool, man. Everyone should do their own thing. Know what I mean."

It wasn't a question: just a statement of belief. Hughie found he could think – not clearly but with one word following the other.

"Shame about Bob," he said, suddenly, surprised by his own words.

"Bob?"

"Dylan. He crashed his motorbike. He's broken his neck, man. He aint gonna sing again."

The snorer, silent now, looked at Hughie for a while and then turned over and went back to sleep. Hughie stared into space for a while. His head still felt as though the skull was about to crack open like a boiled eggshell. A shadow passed over him and a girl stood, legs akimbo, looking down at him. He wondered who she was.

"How much you got in the kitty?" she asked.

"Bread?" asked Hughie.

"Yeah, bread. We got to have bread."

Hughie pulled his wallet from the pocket of his jeans and gave it to the girl. He knew there was nothing in it.

"Fuck you," she said and stormed off.

Later in the day, he found himself sitting by a tent with some drumsticks in his hand. He was beating on the drum watched by several girls. Another man was keeping in time with him. Night was drawing on, and Hughie wanted some conversation. He was also hungry – very hungry – and didn't quite know when the food was coming. He wandered away in search of something to eat and found a group sitting in a circle chanting.

"We're chanting for peace," muttered a girl in answer to his question, "We're thinking of marching to stop the war in Vietnam."

Hughie wondered what it had got to do with them. Wasn't it the Americans?

"We should get arrested for civil disobedience," the girl persisted, "The police are fascists."

A girl merged from one of the tents holding a banner that said 'STOP the war in VIETNAM'. The chanting began again as she held the banner above her friends.

"In the States, students are sitting in front of trains to protest. The fascist bastards are throwing them into vans and locking them up in cells."

"Has anyone got anything to eat?" asked Hughie.

Sister Magnusson had told Sheila that Matron wanted to see her, and so she stood, her knees trembling, waiting. When Mrs Hack opened her office door, Sheila nearly passed out.

"Come in, Nurse Pratt."

When Matron had re-seated herself, she held out a letter.

"This is from Nathaniel Moyes's parents," she said, "I understand that you went to the child's funeral."

"Yes, Matron."

"Why?"

"I felt I wanted to, Matron. I felt it showed Mr and Mrs Moyes that we cared, that the hospital isn't just somewhere you come when you're ill."

"We wouldn't want too many healthy people obstructing the corridors, Nurse Pratt."

"No Matron."

Mrs Hack stared at Sheila for a while, and Sheila couldn't make out whether she was intimidating her prior to a disciplining. She had gone to the funeral for the reason she gave, and she had plucked up the courage to speak to Mr and Mrs Moyes afterwards. Mrs Moyes had been in tears and Mr Moyes had spoken to her:

"You mustn't fret yourself, Nurse. The little lad would have had one helluver life if he'd lived. It's all for the best. Thanks for all you've done."

"And thanks for coming to pay your respects," Mrs Moyes had added.

"It is difficult not to become emotionally involved, Nurse Pratt, but we can't go to every funeral we might be tempted to attend. We have to preserve a certain detachment if only for our own sanity ... but Mr Moyes has written to thank us for all that was done for Nathaniel on the infants ward and he mentioned you in particular ... I think what you did has bestowed considerable credit on Staffham General, and I would like to pass on my congratulations ... and thanks."

Sheila noticed the pause before Matron said "thanks"; it wasn't, she thought, a word that Matrons used a great deal.

"Are you thinking of working at Staffham when you're qualified at the end of the year, Nurse Pratt?"

"I hadn't given it any thought, Matron. I don't like to … presume …"

"Presume?"

"I mean I don't like to think I might be lucky enough to qualify."

"It's not a question of luck, Nurse Pratt, but of dedication, study and hard work."

"Yes, Matron."

"Should you 'be lucky enough to qualify'," continued Matron, pausing as she emphasised Sheila's own words, "we should look most favourably upon any application you might make for a post at Staffham General. Sister Magnusson speaks highly of your work and would welcome you as a permanent staff nurse … Well done."

"Thank you, Matron."

When Sheila left Mrs Hack's office she was, as she later told the girls, "walking on air". It wasn't just that she thought she might now qualify if she continued to work hard; it was more that she was now her own person. She had broken free of all those constraints her childhood had placed upon her; she was free of the sense of her own inadequacy.

CHAPTER 37

What must I believe to be a Christian?

Stephen Last sat in the corner of the staffroom at Castleford Primary, on the day before term was due to start, listening to Roger Turl, the headmaster, holding forth. He seemed to be talking to the new staff but was obviously targeting his remarks towards everyone.

"It's important that we all stick to the same rules," he said, "because otherwise the little blighters will play us off one against the other. They're all in the little booklet I've given everyone, but I'll go through the main ones just in case."

'Just in case,' thought Stephen, 'no one bothers to read the booklet.'

"First of all, the children *must* walk in single file on the right hand side of the corridors – *always*. There's no point in some teachers insisting on that and others ignoring it."

The school was a modern one built to take children from the council estate in which it was situated. The corridors dominated the building: they were wide enough to allow two hospital trolleys carrying stretchers to pass each other comfortably. Stephen remembered a similar building from one of his teaching practices; evidently, schools in the 1950s had been built to serve as hospitals should another war break out.

"Secondly, no child is to enter their classroom until the teacher arrives. They are to wait *quietly* in the corridor. Thirdly, when the whistle goes at playtime, they are to line up, double file, in their classes and no one moves until every child is silent. If they enter the building silently and walk to their classrooms in an orderly manner then lessons can begin purposefully."

Stephen glanced at Raymond Burrell, who he'd come to respect during his two weeks at the school in July, and saw the older teacher suppress a smile. Raymond had rock-solid discipline but an easy manner with the children. Roger Turl's quasi-military style must fit uncomfortably with Raymond's view of how children should be handled. On the other hand, Stephen had taken classes that were uncontrollable; one of these had been that of Gwyn Tucker, who was known as a disciplinarian, while another had been Samantha Wood's class who were all over the place. She seemed to have no discipline at all. 'It's a poser,' thought Stephen as he listened to Roger Turl, 'but one I'll have to sort out or sink.'

Kate Walsh was surprised that she felt no tension at all as she and Sheila Pratt waited in the corridor looking at the notice on the double doors of the hall. It read 'Silence: examination in progress.' Several other student nurses were also hanging about, and they all exchanged sheepish smiles, wondering how they would be paired. It didn't seem fair that they'd have to work with someone they didn't know, that their success or failure depended on the knowledge and skill of a stranger, but that is how it would be when they were qualified.

Sheila was white with apprehension. Failure now meant failure forever: there would be no second chance. She would only hear the voices of her parents saying "I told you so. A nurse! People of our class don't become nurses.' She'd had this all out with Kate the night before – relentlessly – and Kate now took her hand and gave it a squeeze.

"I wouldn't mind if I was paired with you, but it will be a stranger …"

"… Who will be just as keen as you to pass her practical finals. Remember Sister Magnusson said she was so impressed with your ability she'd take you on at Staffham General."

The doors opened and a starchy-faced Sister appeared, beckoning them into the examination hall. It was lined with trestle tables crowded with hundreds of different types of medical instruments and equipment. Kate gave Sheila a final squeeze as they were both paired and followed their respective examiner to the waiting 'patient'. Kate smiled at her partner and read the instruction card detailing their nursing task. They were to set up a trolley for a patient who had just been admitted in an unconscious condition; they had just ten minutes. Kate smiled at the other girl who she recognised from having worked with her in theatre and after a brief discussion their trolley was ready: oxygen, airways, suction and catheter. Without speaking, they placed the patient in the coma position and waited for the questioning to start. When it came, Kate found herself explaining the purpose of every piece of equipment, why she had selected "that particular position" and "what else might you have needed to consider, Nurse?"

The morning wore on with Kate and her unknown colleague setting up trolleys for various operations, explaining the order in which the instruments would be required and how each might be sterilised. The whole morning passed with Kate in a trance-like state: her world seemed to fade away into another sphere of activity. Nothing existed but the instruments, equipment, task notes, patients and examiners. Afterwards, she remembered looking up once or twice and seeing everything she'd known disappearing into the grey, autumn sky beyond the metal-framed windows of the great hall. Somewhere out there were her friends, her parents and Bill; somewhere out there were pubs and clubs she'd visited, walks she'd taken, holidays she'd enjoyed and moments of friendship and delight. None of them had any meaning during that morning; all were a vague and distant memory.

"I've rarely seen anyone as focussed as you, Nurse Walsh. Good luck. I think you'd better go and comfort your friend."

The Stones, back from their successful American tour, were exhausted.

"Hawaii was my scene," proclaimed Keith Richards, "all those gorgeous sun-tanned girls with grass skirts and flowers in their hair. When we arrived at the airport they all put garlands around our necks and started kissing us. It was just like an Elvis Presley film!"

They were working on their next single *Have You Seen Your Mother, Baby, Standing in the Shadows?* It was about the attitude that existed between parents and children. On the publicity photograph, they were all dressed in drag: Mick as a maiden aunt, Brian as an air hostess and Keith in RAF uniform. Things were changing: clothes were more way out, eyes were large and glazed.

"Don't get too friendly with the children to begin with, Stephen. Establish discipline first, and then you can ease off. Once they know where you've drawn the line in the sand, class life will settle down into a steady routine. The children will know where they stand and so will you, and they'll be grateful that you've established a quiet, working environment for them. All my children look forward to coming to school, and some of them *really* look forward to coming. It gets them out of homes where people spend their time arguing the toss and shouting at each other. These are nice children – some are difficult but they're all nice. They just need to know where they stand. Start off as you mean to go on and you'll have a great year ... oh, and call me Ray." Raymond Burrell smiled as he spoke, patted Stephen's arm and walked off along the corridor to his room.

Stephen waited for his class as they came in from the playground, all sheepish and subdued until they'd got his measure. He'd broken up the straight lines of wooden desks and arranged them in groups of four or six. This created more space and, with forty children in a room built for thirty, space was of the essence. This had also allowed him to create an art area by the door that led outside to a lawn and a space for displaying some science models he'd planned the children should make. His was a third year junior class and so the children were aged between nine and ten.

"Hello," he said with a smile, "I'm Mr Last and I'm the new boy here. I don't know the way around as well as you, and so I'm going to need your help for the first week or so. You know my name but I don't know yours and so I'm going to call the register very slowly so that I can put a face to a name … and I promise you this – by lunchtime, I'll know every one of you by name."

Kate Walsh did all she could to soothe Sheila's worries but was relieved when they went into town to meet Christine and Miriam, both of whom had faced the same practical that day. Their plan was to go and see *Blow Up*, Antonioni's new film, "if only to avoid dissecting endlessly every question each of us has been asked and every answer we've given", as Christine said in that pithy way of hers.

"What a dreadful film," said Miriam, as they gathered in the Café Blanc afterwards, "It portrayed a world without any kind of morality: a godless world."

"The world is godless for many people these days," replied Christine, "We don't all have your faith, Miriam. It's hard to believe in your kind of god when there's so much suffering."

"God has given us the freedom to choose. Suffering is man's doing – because of his greed."

"But many people have no choice. Where you're going – Africa – there's disease, famine, lack of water, unhygienic housing, and no education … those people don't choose to live in those conditions."

"But we can learn from suffering – by accepting it as a fact of our human existence and approaching it creatively, by showing love and sympathy and by making sacrifices.

It is out of suffering that the greatest human achievements have arisen."

Kate, whose own parents had never agreed on religious issues, listened, almost appalled, to what sounded to her to be rather a cold approach to human suffering. How long could one tolerate babies dying of hunger, despite the Christians showing love and sympathy? Perhaps the longer they continued in that vein the longer the suffering would continue? What was needed, surely, was for someone, somewhere, to *do* something! She said so.

"We live in a world of moral choices," urged Miriam, "If everything was pre-arranged by God, giving us no choice at all, where would you find virtue? We'd be like those people in Wells's *The Time Machine*. We'd just go about our lives giving no heed or thought to anyone, even ourselves. We'd be little more than automatons – not living, sensate creatures with the capacity to care for our fellow human beings. Is that the kind of world you want? Is that why you are training as a nurse? Making the world a better place is in our hands – not God's. There's no good blaming him if we've made a mess of things. We need to do something about it. My inspiration, as a Christian, is my belief that Jesus was the Son of God and that by following His teachings I can attain eternal salvation ..."

"By doing good deeds?"

"No – and there's no need to adopt that tone with me, Chris – not just by doing good deeds, but I can hardly claim to be a follower of Jesus if I ignore his central teaching – Love your neighbour as yourself – and I can hardly do that just by sitting at home thinking about

Jesus." Miriam laughed as she spoke and added, "You're inspired by Christian principles, Chris, whether you like it or not."

"I'm a humanist," said Chris, "I believe that man can improve his world through scientific achievement and education. I don't see that god – any god – comes into it."

"But science doesn't give you the values that inspire you to improve the world. Only faith can do that."

"And education," replied Chris.

At lunchtime, Stephen dismissed his class one by one and by name. He felt he'd made a good start as he walked with two of his girls who'd offered to show him the way to the dining hall.

He'd told his class that he was going to re-arrange their desks so that they were able to sit and work with people they liked. His final education study on sociometric testing had convinced him of the value of friendship groups and the two girls with him were not only 'stars' within the class but formed a 'cluster' that attracted others – a cluster that would draw in the isolates who lingered, forlornly, on the edges both in class and on the playground and, later, in life.

They passed the main hall where that morning Mr Turl held his assembly and exhorted the children to "live well and learn well in the coming year". Challenge was in the air, and Stephen felt good to be part of the endeavour. He sat in the dining hall with the children and ate his school dinner, wondering whether this vast space was used other than when the children were eating. He'd already discovered that the main hall was over-timetabled, and this space, if vacant for most of the day, offered opportunities for drama.

"Do you believe in God?" asked Sheila when Miriam's fiancé had picked her up and the other three were walking back to their ground floor 'apartment'.

"I think so," replied Kate, "My mum is a Catholic, but we've never been brought up to go to church regularly although she does. It created too many arguments with dad. But I think there must be a creator."

"And the virgin birth and all that?"

"If there's a God, I don't see why there shouldn't be a virgin birth and a resurrection."

"I saw David Frost's programme with the Archbishop of Canterbury. He said that St Luke's gospel made it clear that there was a virgin birth; but that it wasn't necessary to believe that to be a Christian," Sheila continued.

"So what was it necessary to believe? Can you simply make up your own mind and pick and choose as you fancy?" snapped Chris.

"The archbishop said what Miriam said – that you had to believe that Jesus was the son of God, that he was divine."

"But he also said that he didn't go along with the Bishop of Woolwich saying that God was within us. He saw God as a separate being – someone a Christian could have a personal relationship with – and that's the fudge, isn't it? If God is a separate being and not just an idea within each of us then he could intervene in the suffering of the world."

"Miriam says that he does – through us," replied Sheila.

Kate had lived through these arguments many times as a child, caught between her mother's religion and her father's agnosticism. She looked at Sheila as her friend spoke and then glanced at Chris, who smiled.

Motoring through the Grampians on his way to see the Queen at Balmoral, Dick Crossman was charmed by the perfectly windless autumn day in the valley of the Dee. He was due to have a Privy Council meeting with the Queen and had travelled to Aberdeen on the ten o'clock sleeper the day before. The mountain slopes were beautifully forested and Balmoral itself, which he considered a 'typical Scottish baronial house', was fronted by a 'nice conventional rose garden'.

Dick was Lord President of the Privy Council and it was his duty to meet with the Queen and read aloud the fifty or sixty 'Titles of the Orders in Council' for Her Majesty to agree. This he did, pausing after every five or six for the Queen to say:

"Agreed."

He concluded with the words:

"So the business of the Privy Council is concluded."

The whole procedure took exactly two and a half minutes and Dick reflected that it was 'the best example of mumbo-jumbo you can find'. He and three other ministers had all taken a night and a day to travel to Scotland to stand for two and a half minutes while the titles were read out. He wondered whether it might not have been simpler for the Queen to travel down to Buckingham Palace.

"I watched a little boy die," Sheila persisted, her worries over possibly having failed her practical forgotten as she thought about what Miriam had said, "and he had no choice. He had no chance to choose the right way, no chance to show he was or wasn't greedy. He was not even aware he was alive. He lay in a cot in one of the side wards and he just died. I went to the funeral, and his parents accepted the death as the best thing that could have happened. 'It was all for the best', his dad said. Nathaniel was his name and he died of hydrocephalus. Why did Miriam's god allow that? Why was that little boy brought into the world just to die so horribly? Surely he can't have been there just to make those who cared for him feel virtuous?"

Kate could only listen while Chris made them all some coffee. When she placed the drinks and some biscuits on the low table in the lounge they all shared, she said:

"I worked on a cancer ward during our training, and the nurses who do that fulltime are special, believe me. I don't believe in Miriam's god ... Some of the nurses may have been Christians – I don't know – but whether they were or not, they were special, and what made them special wasn't their faith but the work they do. While I was there, I helped to nurse a man who was dying of lung cancer. He'd reached the stage where he could no longer cough. The phlegm was rattling away in his chest and he was struggling to breathe. We used suction to draw some of the liquid off his lungs, but it only ameliorated his distress; breathing was a huge burden for him.

We'd moved him to a side ward so as not to distress the other men in the main ward, and one of us was always there, holding his hand and talking to him. He'd been aware of the others in the ward a couple of days before but now he was barely conscious. It was as though he'd made the choice to pass on. He was absolutely weary with the struggle to live.

I was left alone with him on several occasions, while the senior nurses fetched drugs and oxygen and so on, and I listened to him drowning in the fluid discharged from his cancer. I didn't want to be there. Who would? But I stayed with him and was pleased to do so – if you understand what I mean. If I hadn't been a nurse ... if I'd simply have been a relative ... I'd probably have left the room, but I was a nurse and my presence – even though the man was often unconscious – was a comfort to him when, for brief moments, he became aware.

I'm not saying I'm virtuous because I stayed with a dying man; I'm saying that my work lifted me beyond myself. I put another's care before my natural feelings of fear and revulsion. Because of the work we do – nursing – we become better people. And it must be true of other work as well. What we are, what we become, doesn't depend on some vague notions of a creator god; it depends on what we choose to do with our lives.

I was with this one man when he actually passed on. He suddenly seemed awake, and he gripped my fingers and I swear he spoke (although I may have imagined that), but we held hands and were aware of each other, and then he was gone and I let him depart, peacefully and dreamlike at the very end ... It was what Miriam would call a spiritual experience, but it had nothing to do with religion. It was one human being to another ... drink your coffees. They're getting cold."

"Do you fancy a drink this evening?" asked Bill Richardson, as he and Stephen walked to the bus stop.

Stephen didn't: he'd rather fancied a quiet night at home reading in his bedroom. Living with his parents after three years at college, he'd suddenly lost his social life but found it didn't bother him a great deal; he'd discovered 'the bliss of solitude'. But Bill Richardson, who – like himself – was a new teacher at Castleford, was having problems with discipline already – after only three weeks – and Stephen felt obliged to help a comrade. He agreed, and eight o'clock found them sitting in The Cricketers, which was in the town centre and convenient for both of them.

"You need to scrunch them," said Stephen, borrowing an inappropriate phrase from his favourite Dickens novel, hoping to set Bill back on his heels.

"You sound like Turl."

"Not in the least. I received some good advice from Ray when I started – set the boundaries and everyone's happy. You've failed to do that and now the lout element is running your class. It's not fair on the other children: thirty-six decent kids having their classroom disrupted by four louts. You need to take control now or you and your class are in for one helluver year."

"So you go along with this control business, do you? 'Get a grip on the kids!' 'Sort them out!'"

"Who's in control of your class at the moment – hmm? The disruptive element: Martin Spall, Luke Rogers ... and their mates. Wouldn't it be better for the other children if you were?"

"But I don't want to control them. I want them to learn the value of self-control."

"Which you consider they're doing in an atmosphere of mayhem?"

Bill seemed cowed by Stephen's attitude (as well he might) and changed tack.

"It was OK for the first week, but three weeks on, they're all over the place ... I heard Martin Spall boasting that we were the worst behaved class in the school ... but I don't want to impose these awful house points ... That isn't what education is about – beating the next man down. It's about co-operation, and they're not going to learn that by having someone control them ... they need to value what they're doing for itself ..."

He floundered off, and looked at Stephen, who smiled but said nothing. Without a word, Bill left the table and bought two more pints of Tolly bitter.

"We had a particularly bad lesson last week, but it was after Tucker had taken them for music. He always screws them down tight and when they arrive back in class they're ready to burst with exasperation. They hate his lessons. They find no joy in them. No joy in music! Come on – that isn't the way to teach ... They seem unable to understand my attitude to teaching. It's almost as if they want me to punish them ... Some of them have done almost no writing at all since the beginning of term ... and their handwriting! But is that important? Is that what education is about? When they do write something, it's unbelievable. Look at this."

Bill took a scruffy sheet of paper, which he'd folded in four, from his wallet and handed it to Stephen. The poem was entitled *Darkness*, and Stephen read it out:

"Darkness is the night
And the ending of life
When the spirit leaves the body

And flies into the infinity of space
Beyond the stars and the galaxies
To rest in peace with the beginning of worlds."

"Isn't that great?" asked Bill, "and can you get writing of that quality when you're insisting on children putting capital letters, full stops and commas in the right places?"

"You don't have to insist on any such thing," Stephen replied, "or have your classroom disrupted by bad behaviour to obtain writing of quality. Children don't work best in a noise. I don't know why there's the lunatic idea that quality comes from chaos, why if a child is sitting still they are 'passive'. Running round the classroom doesn't make them 'active learners', just noisy ones ... Take a look at the writing on my classroom wall sometime – particularly the poems by Katie Burns and Megan Spall. Yes, that's right, Martin's sister ... You'll have to get a grip on them, Bill, or they'll run you out of the school."

"Did you realise that Tucker uses a slipper?"

"Have you seen him?"

"No, but the children have told me it's true."

"I'd be surprised if it were – a hand maybe, but not a slipper ... but I think Tucker is more a voice man, and he has a certain manner about him that's intimidating. The children are frightened of him, I agree ... you don't have to instil fear to gain the children's respect, but you do need to gain control," laughed Stephen, to break the tension between them.

"Control – that bloody word again!" answered Bill.

Stephen put aside the newspaper and sat back in his chair. It was very dark outside and the intense glare of the desk lamp bounced back from the page. He could hear his parents locking the doors and fastening the windows. When he'd bid them goodnight, he'd felt free of them for the first time in his life. He'd seen them as people apart; he'd felt free of those demands they placed upon him. However unconscious that placing had been, it had happened; their moral world had guided his behaviour. He'd never 'broken free' of his parents as teenagers are said to do. He felt they no longer had the right to make claims on his behaviour. Perhaps that was why he'd come home: not out of a sense of duty as he'd told Jenny, but because he needed to free himself from the constraints of his childhood.

Uncomfortable with the way he was thinking, Stephen turned to the paper again. Joan Baez was a free spirit and an active one. She'd just walked a group of black children to an all-white school in Mississippi. Martin Luther King had focussed the world's attention on the southern state because of its unjust education policies. Stephen smiled as he remembered Dylan's satirical song '*a can of black paint fell on my head, I had to sit on the back of the bus, cost me a quarter*'. Black humour if ever humour was black. The paper went on to say that police had watched without intervening when a 'white mob' attacked a group of blacks who were trying to integrate themselves in a school in Mississippi.

He felt small: a little man in a big world. Would he ever make a difference?

The Black Horse Inn was a spit and sawdust public house, painted black and white and cramped on the edge of a narrow pavement that was cracked and mossy. It was poked into a side lane along which the sickly smell of the slaughterhouse wafted. This part of the town was gloomy, leading to the waterfront and old docks. Rows of terraced houses that had seen better times now shared their lives with wasteland and scrap-metal yards.

Stephen looked up at the gaps of sky between the houses, glancing occasionally at William who was trying to avoid the gutters, which were littered with rusty tins and cigarette packets swept along by the rain that bounced and splashed from the rooftops. It struck the walls as it fell and then tumbled onto the street.

Stephen had been to school with William. They'd attended St Margaret's Church of England Boys' School from the age of eleven, failures of the 11+ system and children of parents who were determined they should not be condemned to Tower Ramparts Secondary Modern School for Boys, which was considered too rough. They'd met up on Stephen's return to Ipswich, both having completed their training as teachers.

William held traditional views about more or less everything. On his return home, he had moved back in with his parents who lived in the village of Westerfield where William's mother had already infiltrated the local church and WI.

"It's an organic community" he'd said to Stephen, "the old boys in the pub – they're real characters, and the place has a real village spirit: whist drives, darts matches, jumble sales … and the school, of course. You've never finished your work there, have you? I'm pretty much settled here in Suffolk, really."

Their talk had drifted towards old friends, and Dave and Mark had been foremost in both their minds. Mark, in particular, had moved Stephen's intellectual development forward rapidly: he'd moved from novels to philosophy, history, logic, art and politics. They'd all been new worlds to him at the age of seventeen.

"I met Mark in town," William had said, "They'd like to meet up at The Black Horse next Friday evening."

"How is Mark?" Stephen had enquired.

"Still bumming around. He refused to do a fulltime job and so he got the sack. They've both been fruit picking – or were. Dave's got some place out in the country … Mark's painting, of course," and added with a laugh, "Houses, I think."

"You don't approve of Mark, do you?" Stephen had asked.

"I think it's hypocritical to live off the state so that you can get on with your painting, and then spend your time criticising the very system that puts food in your mouth and clothes on your back," William had replied, "He despises the very things that allow him time to paint – the money-makers, the industrial rat race, as he calls it."

As they made their sodden way to The Black Horse, Stephen remembered that he'd not challenged William's objections.

Mark was sitting over a pint of bitter with several friends, including Dave. They both smiled as William and Stephen walked in. The landlord, his freshly-shaved face shining in the light of a yellow bulb, said "Evening gents" with a smile that closed one eye in what Stephen supposed was intended as a knowing wink. At the word 'gents', the locals, who seemed to have accepted Mark and his friends as regulars, looked up with a degree of what Stephen considered to be hostility. He grinned and looked down at his clothes – a new sports jacket and trousers he'd had to buy for the job – and realised that, by the hand-me-down traditions of these people, he and William would look posh. 'Silly,' he thought, 'I was born and bred a few streets from here.'

He sat opposite his old friend, Mark, while William got the drinks in, and looked him over. 'Long, curly hair, and a thick beard: every inch the struggling artist.' The flow of the conversation was unnatural but only for seconds, and then Dave said:

"You surprised us all. We never thought you'd turn out to be respectable ... I suppose teaching is the only justifiable job left – the only one worth doing. But we never thought you'd settle."

One of Dave's friends – a girl – murmured her assent, and the youth sitting next to her grunted in what might have been disapproval or agreement.

"What did you expect me to do?" asked Stephen.

Dave grinned, pushed his spectacles onto the bridge of his nose and sniffed but gave no answer. He was an anarchist when Stephen had known him at Ipswich Civic College where they took their A levels. 'Anarchy: a political theory, which would dispense with all laws, founding authority on the individual conscience.' Stephen had looked up the definition in his *Collins Westminster Desk Companion*, which had been his 17th birthday present from his mum and dad; until he met Dave, Stephen had supposed that anarchy was lawless disorder in a society where people did what they liked without compunction. Dave had put him right on that one.

"You gave up the idea of going to university," he suggested to Mark.

"After a year of getting by on odd jobs, it seemed to suit. I had time to do what I wanted to do."

"That's the important thing," said Dave, and his friend's grunted approval.

"How's the painting going?"

"The main problem is getting your work exhibited," Mark replied slowly, "Art galleries want twenty-five percent if the painting sells."

"They have to make a living," said William, sitting next to Stephen with the beers.

"On the backs of the artist?" asked Dave.

"Whose backs is the artist living on?" replied William.

"You've always been a bit smug, haven't you, Will? Content with the world as it is?"

"How would you set about improving it, Dave? Protest marches?"

"We're organising one next Saturday, funnily enough. Would you care to come?"

Stephen laughed, and Mark joined him. William looked at Stephen and grinned, his round, sunny face lighting up as he tackled Dave's view of society.

"I'm afraid not. I've promised to help my mother with her cake stall at the church jumble sale. We're raising funds to refurnish the vestry."

Stephen roared with laughter, unsure whether William was serious or whether he'd picked on those qualities of social life that would most annoy Dave. Dave's friends looked at both Stephen and William as though they were an alien species.

"You're raising funds to refurnish the vestry when people are dying of hunger?"

"Do you think rattling a tin in the high street or marching with your friends is going to stop hunger?"

"The church is supposed to give a moral lead," snapped Dave, "but all it does is bolster the complacency of the establishment. This country spends more on defence than it does on housing. What does your church have to say about that? Love your neighbour? How many of your Christians would refuse to fight in a war? How many protested about the bomb? What do you believe in, Will? What are you alive for? What are you going to change?"

"I believe that you have to live and work – and protest – within the framework of the state. I believe that democratic representation is the most effective means of effecting change and, on the whole, that things tend to work out for the best. I also believe that there are things only the experts really understand – disarmament being one of them. The Nuclear Test Ban Treaty wasn't signed because you marched to and from Aldermaston; it was signed because the Americans and Russians realised the folly of continuing the Cold War. I also believe that people have the right to hold their own opinions."

Stephen thought that it was going to be a good evening. He gave Mark a smile, which was returned.

Chapter 38

'In that silence …'

Susan's letter arrived as Stephen was leaving to catch the bus:

… This old biddy must have looked through the window at my lesson. 'What these children want,' she said, 'is the three Rs!' I'm getting really depressed. These old teachers are frightened. They want to hold on to what they know like grim death – 'anything provided it doesn't move', as Des used to say.

You'll be surprised to know that I've seen Rodney a few times since I've been back. He has changed a lot since THEN and, perhaps, I have too. We met at the youth club – you know I ran one at the church – and when I got back they asked me to help out again. So that's two weeks a night filled! Five to go! No seriously, I enjoy it really. Sometimes it seems as if the last three years haven't existed at all.

You know you are welcome anytime. I could do with a chat. Why not come down? Have you heard from the others? Des? Marguerite? Anyone? ….

He'd read it twice before the bus left Ipswich and was thinking about it all the way to Newbourne. He got off, in a cloud of dust, at the village pub where Mark had arranged to meet him. The late summer heat was intense.

Dust settled on Stephen's shoes and he shuffled his feet. The village street was quiet; there was no sign of any movement from the houses staggered along the roadside. He walked to the bench outside The Fox and waited for Mark.

After a while, he saw his old friend's stooped figure ambling towards him. Mark's head had always seemed too large for his body and as he walked it nodded; his legs seemed not quite able to manage the weight of the body and the head. As he drew closer, Stephen noticed the watery-blue eyes blinking at him in the sunlight. Mark smiled by pulling down and then flexing the corners of his mouth.

They sat quietly, comfortable in each other's company, over two pints in the cool of the bar. Scrubbed clean, the table had a faint tang of soda; the cement between the red tiles on the floor was as white as the pristine walls.

"Does Dave own this place, then?" asked Stephen.

"No, we're squatters," replied Mark, chortling into his pint mug, "We can't find the landlord. Dave wants to rent it."

"Just the two of you, is there?"

"Well, we get a few of the pseudo-intellectual, Marxist agitators and some of the arties at the weekends ... Dave is busy painting placards with a crowd of them at the moment."

"Is that why you arranged to meet me?"

"You sceptical sod, Last."

"You're no more convinced by protests than I am, are you?"

"You can't just sit around watching what's going wrong in the world without doing something about it, and protest marches are a way of bringing the public's attention to what governments are up to – often behind our backs. We weren't aware of RSGs until Aldermaston, were we?"

'RSGs – Regional Seats of Government – where those whose ineptitude had brought about the nuclear war could scurry off to when the bombs started falling, while the rest of us fried in the heat and radiation.' Stephen remembered Simon's exhilaration at being on that particular Aldermaston march.

"I take your point."

"You just don't like crowds, Last."

"If everyone is thinking it, it must be wrong – the mob mentality."

"You think the march on Washington was a waste of time?"

"No, no! I respect marches of that kind. Marches like that will change the world ... but not on their own."

Mark had made his point and didn't pursue the issue. He bought a second round and they discussed his up and coming art exhibition.

"Art is the paring of wood when the real work of the day is done," said Mark.

"Are you putting that in your brochure?"

"It's one of my key themes. You must come."

They walked to Dave's squat, dropping down into the wide, flat valley and passing under arches of deep green trees shafted by the dusty rays of sunlight. Giant roots were gnarled and twisted at peculiar angles from the crumbling, sandy banks. The low, running hedges dived and curled to the banks that were layered with coarse, withered grass. Turning from the steep of the hillside,

Stephen could see in the distance the mirrored shine of the river as it lumbered across the low flood plain to the sea. 'It's quite easy,' thought Stephen, 'to live in the world without being part of the world.'

"I have no intention of being part of this world, Stephen," said Mark, catching his friend's thoughts, "I'll earn my living in ways I consider uncorrupted by capitalism, but I won't contribute to a society based on greed and materialism."

"On a practical note, how does Dave expect to pay the rent if you find the landlord?"

"His parents died when he was young, and he was brought up by an aunt, but they left him well-provided for – or, at least, comfortable."

The squat, which was approached along a wide driveway, lorded over by high trees, looked Spanish in style. It was whitewashed plaster – great lumps of which had fallen away to reveal the wood beneath – and the arches of the doors and the windows were round. In front of the house, Dave had cleared a patch of land and was growing vegetables. He smiled when he saw them and rested from jerking the handle of a rusted pump; yellow water dribbled from the spout. The well was deep and the wall around it was decaying like the house.

"How do you like it?" he asked.

"Close to the earth," replied Stephen, "and closer to Heaven?"

Several chickens came scurrying across the veranda and pecked the ground around Stephen's feet. Inside the house, holes appeared at odd places in the walls and skirting boards and doors flagged from one hinge, but the creepers had been cut away from the rooms that were used. 'Brown paint and washed dirt,' thought Stephen, ' nettles at the kitchen window, a musty smell, peeling paint, dark and lowering woods, desolation ... and the sense of someone who used to live here.'

In one room several of Mark's arties were painting placards: 'HANDS OFF!' 'LIFE NOT DEATH!' 'LOVE' 'THE PRICE OF A NATION'S PRIDE'. He wondered what the protest was about. In one corner he saw a hurricane lamp; candles were stuck in wax on the mantelpiece above the open grate.

"We have a fire here in winter," explained Dave, "it's quite cosy."

Among the placard painters, Stephen noticed the pregnant girl he'd seen in The Black Horse. She wore the same plum-coloured, velvet dress; it pulled tight where she was swollen with her child. Stephen wondered what chance the child would have in life. The girl cast him a vicious look from between the rats' tails of her blonde hair.

"Are you sight-seeing?" she asked.

"Stephen was one of us but now he's settled down," explained Dave with a laugh.

"What have you settled down to do?" asked the boy with the girl.

"I'm a teacher," replied Stephen.

"Could be worse, I suppose. I'm an engineer by trade – served my apprenticeship – but I'm here by inclination."

"And you'll be able to support your child by following your inclination?"

"What's it got to do with you?" snapped the girl, "We aren't on the dole! We don't ask for hand-outs!"

"I'm sorry. I didn't mean to suggest you were."

"You'll be conditioning children to conform," said Dave, "That's what education is about – getting children to conform to the rules of society. You're simply an instrument of the ruling classes."

"I don't think so," replied Stephen, "I think we'll be educating them to ask the question 'why'. You can't change society by opting out. You have to get in there and do something. Education is the greatest agent of change we have. The world in forty years' time won't be the world we know now – not if we're successful."

Dave opened his mouth, closed it and then opened it again.

"Whatever we become is the result of social pressure," he said with great urgency, "The moment a child is born pressure is brought to bear by parents, friends and teachers. By the time the child is old enough to think, its character is formed. The child is conditioned by the society in which it lives – by the morality of that society. What you are now, Last, is the sum total of your experiences – you're conditioned from birth. You can never make a decision that you can call your own. Everything you say and do is a reflection of your past ..."

The talk staggered on through the afternoon until dusk arrived with spaghetti, tinned meat and coffee. As they crouched in the damp kitchen, Stephen looked up at a scratching sound that came from the ceiling.

"Rats," explained Dave, "I woke up one night to find one watching me from the doorway. It was big and gave me a start, but after a while it shuffled off. They leave us alone, but we do have to lock the chickens up at night ... You can stay the night, if you like."

"No. My parents will be worried. I'd better get back."

"Still not free of your upbringing?" asked Dave.

Later, as he made his way to the last bus, Stephen thought about Dave's remark; it had not been said unkindly, and it was true. He wasn't free of his parents' morality.

John Robinson, Bishop of Woolwich and bestselling author of *Honest to God*, read the report and smiled to himself. The report had been commissioned by the British Council of Churches. He thought that it went straight to the fundamentals, and knew he would be required to say so.

What the report had to say about sex was going to be the main problem. It was the one field in which the church had always had absolutes. Elsewhere – in areas such as stealing and lying, for example – the church had held the view that the rules were only guidelines: it acknowledged that there might be times when the rules were broken. There might be an occasion when it was necessary to lie to save a friend's life; there might be an occasion when someone stole to feed their family. The church had always seen this to be the case, but never where sex was concerned.

John ran the arguments and counter arguments through his head. He had been invited to speak for the report's conclusions on *The Frost Programme*, and he knew where David Frost was likely to home in: he wasn't a man to allow an inconsistency to walk on by. He was to be up against the Right Reverend Graham Leonard, Bishop of Willesden, who had just sent a letter to his clergy expressing opposition to all the principles of the report.

It was the disappearance of these 'absolute' truths that concerned people. Sex outside marriage had always been viewed as wrong: adultery and fornication had always been seen as lust, and viewed in the same light as such things as pride, covetousness, greed and hate. John could understand that many people found the disappearance of the old, simple 'truths' to be threatening: they had, after all, built decent lives around them. At the same time, he felt the report to be 'balanced and conservative', representing a very large body of opinion within the church.

Bill Richardson had ignored the headmaster's stipulation that the children were to wait in the corridor until their teacher arrived: Bill had allowed them to go into the classroom. He'd heard that Raymond Burrell, Stephen's mentor, always allowed his children to do so, and Stephen had permitted his monitors to be in class, going about their business without supervision, during break.

When Bill arrived, peace had been restored from bedlam by Gwyn Tucker.

"I caught them, Mr Richardson, in flagrant breach of the headmaster's rules. All over the place they were: running round the desks, fighting with rulers, flicking ink pellets. I saw Taylor using ink pens as darts! Spall and Rogers were standing on the art table, fighting like pirates. Even the girls were at it – pulling each other's hair and screaming like banshees."

Tucker turned to the class who now sat silent and thoroughly subdued at their desks.

"Who do you think you are? You have a nice teacher like Mr Richardson who allows you all sorts of freedoms, and what do you do? You abuse them! What kind of adults are you going to grow up into: hooligans and ... wild women. You're not a crowd of gypsies; you should know how to behave. Do you want your own children to behave like that? Well? Sharon Spratt – you were one of the hair pullers. Stand up! What have you to say for yourself? Do you want your children to behave like louts? Do you?"

"No, sir."

"I should think not indeed. Well, let me tell you – they'll take their example from you. If you can't behave, neither will they! I think lines might be the best punishment here, Mr Richardson – and plenty of them. I'll leave them to your tender mercies."

Tucker left leaving Bill standing with his children, sick at heart and physically sick in the stomach. For two pins, he'd have walked out and never returned. They had let him down. You couldn't be their friend: not if you wanted them to behave. But he wasn't going to end up like Tucker: bawling and shouting his way to success. 'Success': there was no doubt that Tucker was successful. His fourth year class, his 10 to 11 year olds, always had the best reading and maths results and the writing on his walls was immaculate; the italic hand had never looked better. But it wasn't the way. It wasn't the way.

Dick Crossman found himself part of the 'Club': one of the few selected by Harold Wilson to 'stay to dinner' and discuss defence and foreign policy. Dick wanted the discussion to take place during the meal but George Brown was too drunk. So it wasn't until their 'uproarious dinner' was completed and they'd retired to the long gallery that the discussion began. Even then, George wasn't fit to take part.

Denis Healey began by saying that he could reduce the defence budget considerably by reducing our expenditure East of Suez, cutting our costs in Germany and winding up our commitments in the Middle East.

"Wouldn't it be better if we made a basic change to our foreign policy," asked Dick, "rather than attempt to meet commitments while whittling away our ability to do so?"

"That might be true intellectually," replied Denis in a rather superior voice, "but practically it is impossible."

"But you just said something different to me last time, Denis," shouted George, "What do you really mean? How can you make such an enormous cut without demanding something of me as Foreign Secretary?"

"We shall end up with token forces in the Far East, the Middle East and Germany that are quite unable to meet our obligations," Dick insisted.

He felt that it was no business of a Labour government to assume huge responsibilities abroad and then leave our troops without the weapons to meet them; he saw it as a futile attempt to remain 'Great' Britain, one of the three world powers. He realized Harold was trying to stop him speaking and that he was alone among the seven of them.

Afterwards, when the others had retired to bed, Harold took him aside:

"I brought you into this club. Do you still want to be a member? Because if you do, you know, your behaviour has got to be very different. You mustn't go on talking to Barbara, least of all about the things we discuss here. You've got to be a member of this club – an insider – along with us. Otherwise it won't work … It's not only a matter of military security; it's a matter of a relationship with other members of this inner group now that I've brought you right in."

'So why has he brought me in when he knows I'm a Little Englander?' thought Dick, 'Why take the risk of me as a jarring element? Does he feel a need to have unconventional people close to him because he knows his own extremely conventional nature?'

'Timothy Evans, the 25 year old truck driver who was convicted and hanged for the murder of his wife and child in 1950, was today granted a free pardon by the Queen ...'

Des Smith turned off the radio in disgust. Timothy Evans was someone they discussed at college whenever the question of capital punishment was raised. Evans was the classic example of the wrongness of capital punishment. It had become evident – after a long campaign initiated by Ludovic Kennedy's book, *10 Rillington Place* – that John Christie, who was himself hanged for the murder of several women, was the more likely killer of Evans's wife and child. Christie had been their lodger at the notorious address.

For Timothy Evans, justice had come too late – a point made nicely on *The Frost Programme* when Alexander Lovegrove, the prison warder who had spent two months with Evans in the death cell, appeared on the programme.

"What he kept on saying was it was Christie ... All the weeks before the end, he said it was Christie. Every time he had a visit, he'd tell his mother and father it was Christie. But he seemed to give up hope after his appeal ... On the last night up to half past twelve we were playing cards and he mentioned Christie once or twice, but he knew he had to go in the morning ... at seven a.m. he shook hands with me with tears in his eyes ... he wanted me to go in there with him, but the authorities didn't allow it ... about three years later, I looked at the paper one morning and right on the front page it had a story about a mass murderer – Christie. And I said to myself, 'Where have I heard that name before?'"

In his opening address at Berlin '66, whose theme was 'One Race, One Gospel, One Task', Billy Graham said:

"The evangelistic harvest is always urgent. The destiny of men and of nations is always being decided. Every generation is crucial; every generation is strategic. But we are not responsible for the past generation, and we cannot bear full responsibility for the next one. However, we do have *our* generation. God will hold us responsible at the Judgement Seat of Christ for how well we fulfilled our responsibilities and took advantage of our opportunities."

Joan Whiting sat with Kate, Christine and Sheila watching the news. It was Joan's 21st and they'd all managed to get the evening off. It was to be a simple enough do: Joan had persuaded the landlord of the King's Head to let them use the upstairs room.

"After all", she'd said, "we've spent enough money here listening to Pete Campbell."

"You might get Pete if you're quick. They're back here, but off to America soon."

"We couldn't afford ..."

"Pete won't charge you. Not if I know Pete."

And Pete hadn't: he'd agreed to play for nothing "as

long as the beer and food is free," he'd said. The landlord was to provide the crockery and cutlery "from a mate who owns a restaurant," and Joan and her friends had spent the day preparing the food: sandwiches, vol-au-vents and the like. There were loads of people coming – medical students, nurses, student nurses, student teachers – but, suddenly, Joan was thinking of calling the whole thing off. 'How could we eat and dance and drink tonight, after watching this.'

After several days of heavy rain, the colliery slag heap had slid downhill at an alarming speed. The tipping gang working on the mountain saw the debris begin to move but its speed was such that they were unable to raise the alarm in time. Forty thousand cubic metres of slurry smashed into the village of Aberfan. On its way it destroyed a farm and mowed down twenty terraced houses.

It was the last day of school at Pantglas Primary before the half-term holiday and the children were leaving their assembly hall where they'd been singing *All Things Bright and Beautiful*. They heard the roar.

"It was a tremendous rumbling sound and all the school went dead. You could hear a pin drop. Everyone just froze ... the sound got louder and louder, until I could see the black out of the window," Gaynor Minett said afterwards.

One teacher ordered her class to hide under their desks. Some thought it was a jet about to crash. The slurry slammed into the northern side of the school, filling the classrooms with thick mud and rubble.

A thick fog covered the village and no one was able to see the landslide, but everyone could hear it. Frantic parents rushed to the school, digging and clawing through the rubble and debris, trying to uncover their buried children and teachers. A few children were pulled out alive in the first hour.

As miners arrived from neighbouring collieries on the back of open lorries with their shovels in their hands, the police from Merthyr Tydfil organised the search-and-rescue operation. Hundreds of people drove into the village to help, but their efforts were hampered by the vast amount of water and mud that continued to pour into the village. There was little they could do, and after 11 o'clock that morning no child or teacher was found alive. One hundred and forty-four children died with five of their teachers.

As the news continued to come in, the four nurses listened. Joan Whiting moved away from the others and looked out of the window. Not normally a woman to cry, Joan felt the tears running down her cheeks. They were mixed with anger. 'Someone was responsible for this awful catastrophe,' she thought quietly to herself, 'There must be legislation dealing with the dumping of mining waste. If what the reporters are saying is correct, this slag was dumped above known springs on the hillside. There must have been officials or engineers responsible for the safety of the mines. What were they doing to allow that to happen?'

She turned back from the window when she felt Kate approach.

"I think I might cancel tonight," she said, "I don't see how …"

"No Joan. It's your 21st and cancelling the party won't help those children or their parents. It's something … it's something that cannot be borne … something we must learn to live with always."

"It shouldn't have happened."

"Apportioning blame …"

"I'm not apportioning blame, but catastrophes like this can, and must, be avoided. We need laws and people who are fit for their jobs. Someone or many were not."

CHAPTER 39

Making it happen

Joan sailed through her written finals; she completed the answers in only two hours and left the hall, leaving her friends sweating for their remaining hour. She'd shown none of the natural nerves in full view in the others because she'd felt none. It wasn't so much supreme confidence as supreme indifference. She'd decided that nursing wasn't for her; she'd work out her first year because the experience might come in useful, but felt she'd go no further in nursing as a career. Certainly, the idea of becoming a matron held no appeal. Joan had known this for some time, but it was the tragedy at Aberfan that made her decide, finally, to study law at university. There were people out there who needed to be held to account, and that was something only the law could achieve. Her father would be pleased with her decision. In that quiet way of his he'd be talking at his club about his daughter "showing some sense at last".

"Returning to your background, Joan?" asked Christine Dixon, as they talked over their prospects afterwards in the Café Blanc.

"And you?" replied Joan, ignoring Chris's intended jibe at her middle class upbringing and boarding school education.

"I've applied for a job at the Royal in Wolverhampton. I did some community work there and the circumstances of some of those people are appalling. I came across streets where several Jamaican families were all crammed together in one house. However careful and clean they are, these families have a real fight to stay healthy and free of infection. Those people came over here to work in our car factories, and they deserve better health care."

"Good luck. You've a long fight ahead. Nursing in the community, you're going to come up against some tough characters, Chris. The last three years will seem like a doddle when you look back."

Cynthia Lennon was worried sick about John's health. Drugs had taken away his appetite for food and were now consuming his appetite for life – at least, for family life. She and their son, Julian, were becoming more and more isolated from the world her husband sought to inhabit. She was content to draw and paint or do her needlework in the evenings, and John often went out alone.

He was becoming more and more addicted to the drugs, and hid marijuana and LSD in the family garden, fearing a police raid. He had left the Beatles – the "four wax dummies" as he called them when asked to do another tour – far behind. Swinging London, with its boutiques and art galleries, was the lure.

There was one in particular he favoured – the Indica in Piccadilly. It was the hang out of Mick Jagger and Marianne Faithfull among others. Here a particular exhibition was to take place, and John was invited to a preview. He was promised a "happening"; it was to be "off-beat", "freaky" and "weird".

'... what art can offer is an absence of complexity, a vacuum through which you are led to a complete relaxation of the mind...' 'What is real? Is anything real? A thing becomes real to us when it is functional and necessary to us'. 'As long as we strive for truth we live in self-induced misery ...' John read the words in the beautifully printed brochure. He was about to shake hands with another world.

Mark and Stephen stood in the doorway of the Ipswich Library in Northgate Street whispering. Occasionally, the woman at the desk looked up at them, hitched her skirt, compressed her lips and sniffed. Dave approached the desk, several books tucked under his arm. He placed the books on the desk and poked his nose. The librarian did not look up as she stamped his books. He strolled over and leaned on the shelf over the radiator. People working in the library looked up at the studded message on the back of his leather jacket; some sneered, while others blushed or looked away when he caught them watching.

"Look at this lot," he said, "All this knowledge. Cram it in and what have you achieved? Nothing. We need a new outlook – not more, dead knowledge. Anarchy. A democratic anarchy."

"Herbs and yoga," suggested Mark, laughing.

"You'll have to start off creating little camps throughout the country," said Stephen, "like the nudists."

Mark laughed and Dave followed suit – just.

"I'm quite serious, Last," he said.

"Your dream ignores the very nature of people," Stephen insisted, "At least, people in large groups ..."

"Civilized man, you mean – kept in order by a frightened authority?"

"Will you keep your voices down, please?"

The librarian stood beside them, fiddling with her black fountain pen.

"Pardon?" said Dave.

"Would you keep your voices down, please? You're disturbing the other users."

"They can join our discussion," said Dave.

"The library is hardly the place …"

"The library is exactly the place to hold a discussion," interrupted Dave, "Where can we raise our voices in protest against oppression if not in a public library? Where else can the common voice be heard? You are a pawn of authority masquerading as a servant of the people. Look to yourself. Look to yourselves," he cried, addressing the other library users, "Mark my words! See the truth of my words!"

He turned and the dusty, yellow light filtering down from high in the old ceiling caught the pattern of studs on the back of his jacket. 'WHERE THERE IS AUTHORITY THERE IS NO FREEDOM'. The doors swung unevenly to as he passed through, and Mark and Stephen found him leaning against the outside wall laughing and excited.

Bill Richardson had been obliged to take the football team to the inter-school match. He enjoyed cricket, and was considered a good player but hated the cold, wet, winter days of football. None of the other staff had seemed eager to accompany the boys; besides, he was the one who took games. He'd been offered the job on the recommendation of his former headmaster who had remembered his prowess on the cricket pitch and assumed it to be the same on the football field. Roger Turl would brook no refusal.

"Wet?" he'd asked, apparently astounded at Bill's suggestion that the match should be called off, "They love the wet. It does them good. There's nothing, nothing like haring up and down a soccer pitch in the pouring rain. It'll make men of them."

"There's a strong wind, Mr Turl. It'll be very cold out there. We don't …"

"Moore's Acre have phoned through to say that the pitch is playable, and they are dead keen not to let the chance slip by: it's often difficult to fit in a missed match later in the year … Mind you, Moore's Acre is expecting to win the league again this year. They usually do. Let's get out there and see if we can't tweak their noses – eh, Mr Richardson?"

Standing on the edge of the field, watching the match, Bill could imagine nothing worse than having his red, raw, nose tweaked by anyone, especially the gym master at Moore's Acre Primary who had shaken his hand with such ferocity that the tears had come to Bill's eyes. As the cold crept through him and he stamped his feet to keep warm, Bill sneaked several glances at his watch, hoping that time would fly. It didn't. He saw the fathers who'd turned up to watch their boys play peering at him. These were Ipswich supporters and memories of becoming Champions of the Football League in 1962 were still strong: never mind their current, temporary position in the Second Division. On that pitch might be a lad who would restore Town's fortunes.

They lost, miserably, and back on the coach Bill huddled against the steaming window hoping he wouldn't face the question 'why' from Turl. All he wanted to do was go home, clutch a hot cup of tea and eat the hot stew and dumplings that he knew his mother was preparing. On the coach, the boys were depressed by their defeat and quarrelsome. Several scuffles broke out. Bill tried to ignore these but was forced to intervene when the coach driver complained.

Roger Turl had already left school when the coach returned, but vented his ire the following morning in assembly when he gave a blow by blow account of the team's defeat, and wondered whether they knew what football "was all about".

"Ignore him, Bill," said Emily Farrow, one of the infant teachers, when they bumped into each other in the staffroom at playtime, "He's always like that when we lose. He thinks it's funny to run the boys – and the staff – down."

"He seemed to know a lot about the match. Who told him?"

"One of the disappointed fathers, I expect, Bill. He always listens to the parents. Sport isn't about taking part: it's about winning."

"We're not a professional team. This is school football. It's meant to be enjoyable and teach co-operation."

"Really? You've a lot to learn."

Along with his imprisonment on Robben Island, Nelson Mandela's harassment by the state continued. The Transvaal Law Society was now moving to have him struck off the role of practising attorneys; the society was attempting to punish him at a time when they believed he would be in no position to offer a defence.

Nelson told the authorities that he would contest the action.

"I shall need to prepare adequately: that means I must be excused from my work at the quarry. It also means that I shall need a proper table, a chair and a reading light in order to be able to prepare my brief. I shall also require access to the law library in Pretoria."

"Mandela, why don't you retain a lawyer for your defence? He will be able to handle the case properly."

He knew they were frightened of the publicity his appearance would attract; besides, he would be seen to be fighting for the same values for which he was imprisoned.

'I shall require certain documents and books, records from the Supreme Court, a list of the state's witnesses and summaries of their prospective testimonies.' Nelson began a spate of correspondence with the registrar and the state attorney. They demanded to know the nature of his defence; he refused, saying that they would discover that in court. He refused to yield his rights; the authorities refused him a table, chair, reading light, exemption from quarry work and permission to travel to Pretoria.

Many letters later, he heard that the case had been dropped. Imprisoned, they had supposed him helpless; they were mistaken.

"I don't talk the same language, Steve," Bill moaned as they sat in the staffroom alone one night.

The building was empty except for the caretakers who were busy cleaning and keen that the staff should have gone home. Stephen had been setting up a science lesson for the following morning much to the annoyance of

Mr Nunn, the senior caretaker, who was eager that he should vacate his classroom.

"I thought they did sums and English in the mornings," he said.

"Not if I'm doing a science lesson and need time to set it up," replied Stephen.

He'd borrowed as many wooden blocks as Emily Farrow and her colleagues in the Infant Department had been ready to relinquish.

"I want them back," she'd insisted, "I shall count every one. You have no idea how much persuasion it took to convince Mr Turl that they were not a waste of money."

"I can see his point, Emily. They are wasted down here in Infants. All your children do is play around with them. Up in the juniors we do science."

"Then why haven't you got any?" she asked, laughing.

"I don't think Turl has much sympathy for practical science;" answered Stephen, "Just tell them: it's quicker, and you can stuff more facts in that way."

He recounted the story to Bill as the besieged young teacher puffed away on his third after-school cigarette.

"Turl's attraction in education circles is that he represents 'standards', and 'standards' mean children learning as many facts as their brains can hold. Many of them will understand these facts, but many more won't. There's a lot to be said for the Chinese proverb – the one Emily loves. 'I hear, and I forget; I see, and I remember; I do, and I understand.' Those are the lines along which she organises her infants, and Turl leaves her alone – more or less – because he believes that the real learning starts in the juniors. If he walked into my science lesson tomorrow morning, he'd go nuts. What is the point of children playing around with blocks and slopes and weights when you can tell them or show them that the steeper the slope the more weight it requires to raise a block along it?"

"But he should be concerned with improving education. He and the older staff just seem content with things as they are."

"That isn't fair. None of the infant staff think that way. Nor do Ray and Anne and …"

"OK, I take your point. Actually, Anne has been very kind to me. I think she knows what I'm going through."

Anne Smallman was the Deputy Headteacher. She was charged with doing what Roger Turl did not want to do: directly challenge new teachers who he feared might not be toeing the line. The fact that she was a naturally kindly person was a great help to her and a comfort to the teacher concerned.

"What happened?" asked Stephen.

"Turl sent her to see me about my discipline problems. He'd 'mentioned' to her that my classes were noisy, but she was eager to assure me that he wasn't 'worried'. He was sure I would 'get on top of the situation'. She offered to 'sit in' on one of my lessons 'if it would help' She didn't want me to think 'she was interfering'. She kept repeating that Turl 'wasn't worried' and that she only 'wanted to help'. She was very nice, but it was disconcerting."

"She's a bloody good teacher, Bill. You don't hear a sound from her classes and I've never heard Anne raise her voice. Some of the lads play her up a bit, I believe, but the girls – who love her – keep them in order."

"You like the children, don't you Steve?"

"Naturally."

"Do you ever use corporal punishment?"

"A soft hand slap on the backside with some of the lads. It's just a signal to say they've gone too far. The lads prefer that to a lecture about their behaviour."

"But never the girls?"

"No, no," replied Stephen, "I'd never strike a girl, however softly, any more than I'd strike a woman. It's unmanly in itself and it would set a bad example to the lads."

John Silkin, the Chief Whip, listened quietly while the arguments for and against a new disciplinary code were tossed back and forth across the table at the Party meeting. He knew there was no point in interrupting until the steam had been released from various boilers: members were not going to "give up their principles", and nor were they going to lose the chance to expel the ringleaders of the group who had defied the Whip.

When he was, at last, called to speak he made what Dick Crossman considered to be a 'deeply moving, simple speech on how conscience couldn't be limited to temperance or pacifism'. His arguments were based on the assumption that every member of the Party may on occasions have to abstain as a matter of conscience; this must be accepted as the right of every Member. He emphasised that when a Government did things that were not in the Party manifesto then members had the right to challenge the Government and, if they felt it necessary, to abstain from voting for the measure.

Dick felt that it was the only way to run a modern left-wing party.

"I would point out," concluded John, "that I have no intention of allowing collective group decisions to be called 'decisions of conscience', and I would define an organized group as one whose intention were known to the press before the Whip knew it."

"Do you like Twiggy, sir?" asked Katie Burns, during Stephen's practical science lesson.

It was the kind of cheek that Stephen had come to expect of Katie Burns and one or two others in the class.

"I would *like* you to get on with your science experiments, Katie Burns," he replied with a smile, and moved on to the next group.

His sociometric testing had put the children in friendly work groups and the more able were placed to help the less: he'd found that those children who had difficulty learning often picked up understanding from their friends.

At lunchtime, as the class was dismissed, Katie repeated her question.

"To be honest, Katie, I don't know who Twiggy is," he replied.

"Don't know, sir!" she replied looking round at her assembled friends who were equally astonished, "Don't know who Twiggy is?"

"I have no idea."

"She's a model, sir."

"A model what?"

"A fashion model, sir."

"Ah! Why is she called Twiggy?"

"Because she's thin. Her legs are like matchsticks."

"Is she ill, Katie."

"She's setting the scene, Mr Last," said Janet Martin, interrupting the flow of the conversation, eager to contribute.

"You mean the London Scene, Janet – the Swinging City?"

"Yes, Mr Last – Carnaby Street."

Janet Martin was one of Stephen's success stories. Dressed in a washed-out uniform, with hair that reminded him of Chaucer's pardoner and laughed at by some other children because they liked to accuse her of having fleas, Janet had been the classic isolate; that is, until Stephen put his arm round her while she stood at his desk having some sums marked, made a fuss of her generally and placed her among the star cluster of Katie Burns and Megan Spall. Janet's image among the other children changed overnight as did the image she had of herself and as did her work.

"Come on," he said, "let's go for lunch and you can tell me all about Twiggy."

They did, and he learned that she was "only seventeen", had bobbed hair, thick eyelashes, and slim legs and weighed just over six stone. They even knew how much she earned, which was ten pounds an hour. 'More or less,' thought Stephen, 'what I earn in a week.' The group of girls furnished him with information about the Kings Road as well as Carnaby Street, which this Twiggy was said to 'epitomize', and someone called Mary Quant.

He was amazed but not surprised. Knowledge is more relevant to a child if you start from where they are and what they want to know – or what you can interest them in knowing. When he enquired what 'epitomize' meant, Megan Spall laughed, raised her eyebrows in surprise and said "typical".

Michael Ramsey had to make his speech in the House of Lords. It was on the report, *Putting Asunder*, which he had commissioned. He had chosen Bishop Mortimer to lead the commission. Mortimer was not only a well-respected moral theologian but also a conservative man. The recommendations of the report had, therefore, been startling.

The number of divorces had continued to rise and the idea of a man and woman living together without marriage had become socially acceptable, whereas the Church stood for family life and abstinence from sexual intercourse outside marriage. Something had to be done, and the Church must offer a lead.

It had to be accepted that divorce was a fact of life, even though the Church still held the view that marriage was 'until death do us part' in an ideal world. The Church had always refused to marry a person who had been divorced but was also ready to accept a remarried couple back into the fold in order that they might receive pastoral care.

Michael thought that society was heading in the wrong direction: it was abandoning the belief in the sacredness of family life and sanctioning what he considered to be 'illicit unions' both before and after marriage. He welcomed the new openness with which sex could be discussed but thought that people were becoming 'undisciplined' in their attitude and overly preoccupied with sex for its own sake. While deploring this casualness, Michael could also accept that a couple living together and intending to do so for all of their lives did not fall into the same category as promiscuity.

The law on divorce was also deplorable: the only grounds being 'an offence against marriage', which might be adultery, cruelty, desertion, insanity or bestiality.

Michael could see that this hunt to establish the 'guilty party' was unacceptable: evidence often had to be fabricated – as when an hotel room and a woman were hired to 'prove' adultery.

When his commission suggested, therefore, that this should be put aside and the sole grounds for divorce be 'the irretrievable breakdown of the marriage', Michael was prepared to accept the recommendation. His only caveat was that he did not agree with the idea of 'divorce by consent': the breakdown must be shown to be 'irretrievable', and must carry the consent of both husband and wife. The Church had a very real interest in retaining the stability of marriage and family life.

Stephen's half-term break had not gone well, although he'd said nothing; he was not close enough to anyone to whom he could speak freely. When Des's letter arrived it only made him feel worse:

'I suppose you spent the half-term with Jenny, you lucky bastard – or have you more pressing things to attend to? ... I've not settled here yet. Most of my mates have moved away and Elizabeth is still at university ... We travel to see each other when we've got the cash, but you know how it is ... I went to see Mike at half-term. He'd lined up six birds for us – all going in different directions, of course ... It ended up with me sorting out two reasonable ones at this dive we went to ... He says that Crisp and Amanda are getting married as soon as she leaves college next year. So Crisp will be the first one hitched ...Have you heard from anyone? I wrote to Susan but no reply. We were a little shaky again towards the end, but I would like to see her really. I'm thinking of

coming down south sometime. I might even call on you,
you bastard ...

Since they'd left college, everything seemed to have
gone adrift. They'd enjoyed the friendship there but
hadn't appreciated it – hadn't valued it for what it
represented, and now they were alone in a new world ...
and Jenny had given him the old heave-ho.

They'd been walking the lanes near her parents' home
and he'd felt closer to her than ever when she said,
suddenly:

"I don't know whether I want to continue our
relationship, Stevie."

"What, now – this year – or for good," he'd replied,
not really knowing what he, or she, meant.

"For good," Jenny had replied, and then added, "No, I
don't mean that."

However, she had, and when they said goodbye at the
bus stop (she never offered to go with him to the railway
station), Stephen accepted that it was the end of what he'd
found to be a tender friendship. They'd talked, of course,
following her rejection, but got nowhere. Eventually –
long into the afternoon – she'd said, quite simply:

"I find you too serious."

"Boring?"

"No – just too serious."

CHAPTER 40

Christmas broadcast

"What's up, lad?"

"I'm going home, sir."

"What for?

"My football kit, sir. Mr Tucker says I can't do games unless I've got my kit, sir."

"Just a minute, Lenny, just a minute. Mr Tucker wouldn't have sent you home mid-morning to get your PE kit."

Bill Richardson, passing across the playground with a group of his lads to check the Stevenson screen, stopped Lenny Rance in his tracks. He knew Lenny, and he knew he was lying. Lenny never had his PE kit because he hadn't got one; either his mother couldn't afford it or couldn't be bothered to kit the boy out. Bill also knew that Tucker had no sympathy for the plight of children like Lenny, who always came to school looking as though he'd fallen out of bed already dressed in the clothes he was wearing yesterday. Lenny was running away because he was frightened of Tucker, who would have stood and lectured him in front of the other boys.

"Come with me, son, and we'll see if Mrs Bird has a spare kit," he said, and then turned to his own lads, "Can

I trust you lot to check the weather instruments without messing about?"

"Yes, sir," was the unanimous reply, and, somehow, Bill knew that he could despite their generally poor behaviour. There was sympathy among the other children for someone like Lenny; in their heart of hearts they knew he was always at a disadvantage and that it wasn't his fault.

Mrs Bird, the school secretary, made a tut-tut sound because she felt that school secretaries were always being imposed upon but she found Lenny a kit.

"You bring it back, mind," she said, "Don't you go and lose it – again!"

"Yes, miss," replied Lenny, his face lighting up.

'The boy is disorganised,' thought Bill as he made his way back to the playground, 'but it's hardly surprising: his whole house must be like that – his whole house! His whole life! What chance has he got to make anything of himself?'

The Cabinet was in turmoil. Harold Wilson had staked everything on the success of the talks on HMS Tiger where he and Ian Smith, the rebel Prime Minister of Rhodesia, had met thirteen months after the Unilateral Declaration of Independence by the African state. Harold's conditions for a settlement had been very clear in his own mind: the abandonment of UDI, the relinquishment of Mr Smith's control of Rhodesia's armed forces and black African representation in the Rhodesian Cabinet.

After two days of intense talks, Mr Smith had signed the agreement and returned to seek the support of his Cabinet.

"I saw no reason for signing the agreement", said Ian,

"but Mr Wilson seemed keen for me to do so and I obliged. It did not commit me ... the African is not interested in our democratic government. The Africans are highly susceptible to intimidation – by witchcraft, for example. We cannot lower our standards ... There's no use spending money to teach Africans ..."

The Rhodesian Cabinet rejected the British government's terms for a settlement.

Harold had entered the talks hopefully. His problem now was how to present the failure on HMS Tiger to the British public. He was beginning to feel a deep indignation towards Ian Smith, personally. It had been impossible to negotiate with the man: he would blur the known facts, take up in-trenched positions and express 'thoughts' that appeared absolutely meaningless when examined in the minutes of their meeting.

"How idiotic it is that Smith should be going for this will-o'-the-wisp notion of Rhodesian independence," he said

"For heaven's sake, let's get a grip on reality," interjected Dick Crossman, "this 'will-o'-the-wisp' government of Smith's is likely to be a reality long after this Labour government is thrown out of office."

Kate Walsh danced around the apartment, waving the letter in her hand.

Dear Madam,

I have much pleasure in informing you that your application for registration has been approved and your name has now been entered on the Register of Nurses maintained by the General Nursing Council for England

and Wales. Your registration number is ... and you are now entitled to call yourself a Registered Nurse ...

Your State Registered Badge will be sent straight from the manufacturers ... When you receive your badge great care should be taken of it ...

'Great care, great care!' They needn't worry about her not taking care of it: the badge had been hard-earned.

"We've got to celebrate," she shouted, "We've got to celebrate."

They'd all been successful: Joan, Chris, Sheila and Miriam – all of them who'd started training together three years before. It had been five long years for Kate, who had also spent two years as a cadet nurse. They'd all got jobs to go to when their registration dates became effective in the New Year. There was just Heather Burton, who'd got herself pregnant and was now lagging a year behind them. 'If only,' thought Kate, 'if only ...'

"Are you thinking about Heather?" asked Joan.

"Yes."

"She's doing all right," said Sheila, "It's just a struggle with the baby to look after as well ... but she's got Barry as a consolation."

"We're qualified nurses now. Staff Nurse Dixon, no less," laughed Chris, "It might be us lagging behind Heather in a year's time. We need to find husbands. Well, some of us at any rate. Miriam's engaged and Kate's got Bill but there're three of us still on the lookout."

"Speak for yourself, Chris," replied Joan with a smile, "I'll find Mr Right when I want him, but he can bide his time at the moment."

'... *It'll be great, man. We can celebrate our first Christmas in real work. Des is up for it. He came over to Liverpool the other weekend and we had a great time. He's been in touch with Sue, and I'm seeing if I can get Crispy interested ... Have you been in touch with Yogi?*'

The tone of the letter was such that Stephen could feel Mike's excitement. He wanted a get-together at some time over the Christmas break. Stephen could almost feel himself being pummelled by his college friend. 'College friend? Do friendships end so abruptly? We spent three great years together. Is it all over now?' The words of Bob Dylan's song came back to him. '...*our choices they were few so the thought never hit, that the one road we travelled would either shatter or split.*' As he read the letter, Stephen would have given much to be with Mike. He would even have drunk a cup of his foul coffee.

'...*How's it going down there? How's your love life? Is it true that you've split up from Jenny?*'

So the news had spread along the grapevine. Stephen found he didn't really mind. Throughout his childhood, he'd worried about what people might think, but such things no longer concerned him. Working in the real world had taken him out of himself; you couldn't deal with the Martin Spalls and Lenny Rances of this world – and all they had to cope with – and be too worried about what people might say about you behind your back. Let them get on with it.

All the same, he missed her pressing against him, her wavy hair tumbling over his chest. Perhaps he should have pushed the relationship further? It was just that she seemed disinclined to go the whole way.

Mike had always been out to grab whatever he could.

He wasn't particularly attractive to look at, and Stephen had always sensed that Mike wasn't rated too highly among the girls at college. He and Jenny had sat one sunny afternoon in the middle of the village of Coseley watching other students traipse back from the pub. In particular, they'd watched the couples, and Jenny had commented that a grade A girl (as she put it) usually seemed to get a grade A boy.

"It's not often that you see a really attractive girl with an ugly bloke, is it?" she'd commented.

They'd gone on to categorise the couples as they walked by until the conversation had become quite technical, taking into account not only appearance but social class. Stephen had thought of Des. Both he and Susan had been 'grade A' as far as looks were concerned. It was the class issue that had spooked Des: he being from the industrial north with an out-of-work father, and she being from the stockbroker belt around London.

Thinking about it as he read Mike's letter, Stephen wondered whether that had been a factor in Jenny chucking him: she being the daughter of a chemist, and he being the son of a cabinet maker. It hadn't occurred to him at the time.

Michael Ramsey placed aside the copy of the *Daily Express* that his aide had shown him. His chairmanship of the National Committee for Commonwealth Immigrants had never been a comfortable position, and now Robert Pitman had maligned him in the newspaper, accusing him of presiding over a sloppy committee, encouraging complaints against racial prejudice and being ' the most dangerous man of all' as far as the question of race was concerned. On the other side of the fence, immigrant leaders suspected him of being a government stooge, hiding rather than exposing the discrimination they faced.

His earlier fear of black power organisations rising from the discontent of their people in the face of the ineffectiveness of government was still with Michael. He had also witnessed an upsurge of white racialist groups.

He recommended to the Home Secretary that more members of immigrant communities should be recruited into the police force; he helped television companies plan religious programmes for people of different faiths.

But there was still far, so far, to go. As the Lord Chancellor, Lord Gardiner said:

"It only needs for a coloured bus conductor to be promoted to an inspector, and trouble follows."

"Mr Last," said Roger Turl, walking into Stephen's classroom just as he dismissed the class at lunchtime, "I'm concerned that the standard of writing in your class may be slipping – the standard of grammar, I mean, not handwriting."

Without more ado, Roger Turl began opening desks and flicking through the children's writing books. Stephen watched, a trifle amazed, as the headmaster went from desk to desk, apparently seeking a bad example. There were children who had difficulty with spelling and grammar but Roger had no idea where to look since he was not known for frequenting the classrooms at all; but Stephen was fairly sure that no child's work had worsened during the time in his care.

The headmaster seemed frustrated as book after book

appeared to offer no cause for complaint. Katie Burns and Megan Spall – always the last to leave and still hovering when Roger had entered – watched with what Stephen thought was a smile on their faces.

"Where does Eva Rush sit?"

"There, Mr Turl"' cut in Katie, quickly, as she opened Eva's desk for inspection.

"Are you still here?"

"Yes, Mr Turl. We were waiting for Mr Last to come to dinner.

"Well run along. Mr Last will be there in a minute."

Both Katie and Megan looked at Stephen as though seeking his permission. He smiled and nodded.

"Of course, Eva's a bright girl," said Roger after the girls had left and he was flicking through her English book.

"Have you found any cause for concern, Mr Turl?"

"She's a bright girl … you wouldn't expect …Are you teaching grammar, Mr Last? Do the children know their parts of speech? Can they distinguish a pronoun from a noun? Would they recognise an adverbial clause? Do you use the comprehension books?"

"They are nine to ten year olds, Mr Turl …"

"It's in the syllabus."

"… and grammar cannot be taught in isolation from the practice of writing. They'll know their verbs from their nouns from their adjectives by the end of the year, but I'll teach such things from the children's own work – not from a text book."

Roger Turl looked at Stephen evenly for a few moments and seemed to wonder. Having found nothing in half a dozen desks to complain about, the headmaster smiled at

Stephen as though some victory had been achieved and walked from the room. What he'd left behind was a very bad taste in Stephen's mouth. Lunch was the last thing he felt like, but the children were expecting him and he didn't like to disappoint them.

In the corridor, as he made his way to the dining hall, Anne Smallman, the Deputy Headteacher, collared him.

"A word," she requested, "Has Mr Turl been hassling you?"

"He walked into my classroom without a by your leave and started ferreting through the children's books. He seemed to be looking for examples of bad English and was somewhat aggrieved to find none."

"I thought as much. He'd probably had a parent on the phone. Someone who's been asking their child what a verb is ... or a noun ... or anything ... and the child couldn't say. He's always like that when a parent has complained."

"He'd be better off backing his staff."

"Mr Turl likes the quiet life ... but what I'm saying is, Stephen, don't let it worry or upset you. We all get hauled over the coals from time to time – whenever a parent complains."

"He'd be better off getting us together to devise an appropriate curriculum. Do you know that the History syllabus starts with the Stone Age for the seven year olds and ends with the – I quote – 'Establishment of the Parliamentary System' with the eleven year olds?"

"Mr Turl has a secondary background."

"It's hardly appropriate though is it, Anne?"

"No, but change is slow in the educational world, Stephen. Don't be in too much of a hurry. I guessed what had happened because he was approaching your room with that 'I'll catch someone out' smile on his face, and I didn't want you to be upset."

"Thanks, Anne, you're very kind. I'll be all right."

Dick Crossman put the proposal to the Queen that the BBC and ITV should alternate in presenting her Christmas broadcasts.

"It would be very selfish of me not to allow this," she replied.

"It's not a question of selfishness, Ma'am; you must do exactly what you want."

"I think I would prefer to keep the BBC camera team. I have got to know them so well. I don't really want to face a new team from ITV."

"For heaven's sake, don't do anything you don't want. You must do exactly what you feel like. That's what the BBC and ITV want you to do."

The private audience lasted six minutes, and when Dick went outside the ministers waiting wondered what on earth had been going on.

"I wanted the chance to speak with you alone," said Des to Stephen as they strolled through the wet streets of Staffham, "I'm going out with another girl."

Mike's idea had brought some of them together. Susan had declined, saying she felt obliged to spend Christmas with her family, as had Marguerite, who was with her Bobby, and Paul and Amanda. In fact, it was the unattached – or, in Des's case, the awkwardly attached – who had arrived in Staffham the day after Boxing Day: Mike, Des, Stephen, Simon, Cliff Jenkins and a few others.

Stephen and Des were now making their way to the King's Head where Pete Campbell was doing his last British gig before the American tour.

Stephen looked up at his friend and did not approve. He saw Des's eyes upon him and his soul shrank to its puritan roots. Des had been intimate with Elizabeth. Surely that meant something with regards to commitment, didn't it, or did the act of love-making mean no more than a kiss on the cheek or a shake of the hand?

"She knows I'm engaged."

Stephen hadn't realized that Des's relationship with Elizabeth had actually reached the engagement stage. 'When did that happen? After we finished college? Elizabeth must have … What must she have thought, expected, anticipated?'

"Where did you meet her?"

"At the folk club. Her name's Moira. She's a side-line. We meet when we can."

"It's a bit risky, isn't it?" asked Stephen, not knowing what else to say since voicing his disapproval wasn't on the cards.

"Oh no – we've got it planned perfectly. Moira gets the train to somewhere along the coast. I get the same train but a different carriage … Elizabeth doesn't know about her and need never know. The last thing I want to do is hurt her … Moira knows how things stand. She says we'll both probably feel hurt when it ends but that's part of the price … It was dead up there, back home, before Moira. Great until I finished work and then nothing with Elizabeth still at university. When I met Moira it gave me something to live for. She has given me back some interest in life. Yet I still love Elizabeth … I don't think of them as one and the other, but as two people who in different ways are important to me …"

He paused for what seemed a long time, but Stephen remained silent, not knowing what to say and realising that Des wanted to get things off his chest.

"When that business with Susan occurred I realised – and it was a bloody shock I can tell you – that you could love two women at the same time. Moira is important to me in a different way to Elizabeth … I suppose one woman isn't enough for me … I'm sorry if I'm going on a bit. I'm not trying to justify anything. It makes a change to have someone to talk to."

Stephen couldn't but think that Des was blinding himself, and yet his friend had always been so perceptive, especially where women were concerned. It was a relief when they reached the pub, opened the double swing doors and heard the music from the upstairs room.

Christine Dixon flitted across the room with plates of food.

"Please help yourselves," she said as they entered, "we're celebrating our success."

"Success," queried Stephen.

"We – that is Kate and Miriam and Sheila and Joan and …ooh, several more of us have qualified as nurses and … and we're celebrating."

She flashed a smile and offered them the plates of food.

"We're not gate-crashing are we?" asked Stephen.

"No – you're Mike's friends, aren't you? We've met before. Remember Knutton Gardens? … Sheila's over there. Sheila remembers you very well."

Sheila did remember Stephen.

"I felt so much better after what you said about being an 11+ failure," she said.

"Thanks."

"No – you know what I mean. I'd never looked at it like that before: that it was a question of how many grammar school places might be available rather than how many children might benefit from a grammar school education."

"Stevie – Baby!"

Simon Wiseman launched himself at them, his face broken by its usual broad grin. It all came back to Stephen as he saw Simon: 'it' being those three years of easy camaraderie at college.

"Yogi! Hi! It's good to see you again. You couldn't persuade Susan to come up?"

"No – she's otherwise engaged. I'll tell you later after a few beers."

"Oh, this is Sheila. Sheila – Simon called Yogi because of the way he sits."

"Do you really do yoga," asked Sheila.

"He's a black belt," said Des, who'd come in on the conversation.

Sheila looked at Des, quite taken by his charm, but then turned to Simon.

"You really do yoga? Be serious."

Leaving Simon to expostulate on the teachings of Patanjali and the wisdom contained in his *Yoga Sutras*, Stephen and Des moved across to the Appalachian Four who were setting up. Des had always disliked electronic folk, but felt a decided envy that Pete Campbell was actually on the verge of an American tour; his own playing seemed limited to the folk clubs of the north. Besides, music offered another way of life and he was finding that teaching was so demanding: all he wanted to do at night was sleep.

Pete was effusive. They'd had a good year touring the country and their manager had persuaded Transatlantic Records to produce their first album. They'd even found a banjo player to replace Hughie Spragg: not as good as Hughie, perhaps, but more reliable. Pete Spencer was also more amiable and an ex-boyfriend of Penny's. Penny Grove had taken on more and more of the singing, and this pleased the crowds "who liked a bit of crumpet to front the group" and their style had become what Pete described as "British Country and Western". Des wondered what the Americans might make of the description.

"We've only got small venues," said Pete, laughing, "but it's a start, and it'll set us up for a return home. Having an American tour behind you can't do your cred any harm."

Pete started with The Spinners' *All Day Singing* and the room was with them all the way. Stephen and Des – both of whom disliked dancing and crowd music – moved away from the band and sat with a beer.

"What about the long term future of the Labour Party then, Des?"

"Bloody hell, Last, *this* is supposed to be a party."

"Never mind that. Someone will drag us up too soon and you're the only person I know who has any really sensible views on politics."

"I don't know where Wilson is heading. It could become a real Socialist party that represents the working classes – you know, the vast majority of the people in this country, the ones who actually do the work, the back breaking work on which the rest of us rely for our food and the fuel that drives our industries and heats our homes – or it could follow the right wing of the party."

"Which is?"

"The Gaitskellites. In that case it'll become more like the American Democratic Party, which is run by people like the Kennedys."

"Wilson has moral convictions. He may be a pragmatist, but there are certain things he wouldn't do, certain actions to which he wouldn't stoop …"

"Because he's a Methodist," snapped Des with his usual sneer at religion.

"Yes. There's no harm in a conventional morality based on religious teachings."

"I've often wondered about you, Last. You say you're an atheist but you claim so much for religion."

"Many people are in the Labour Party because …"

"… they see it as a way of fulfilling their religious beliefs in the political life of the country."

"There's nothing wrong in that."

"No, but if the Labour Party is to get anywhere, the leadership must be prepared to make radical changes to the way the country is run. It has to be run for the benefit of the majority – not the minority, not in the interests of those who simply do not work but make their money on the backs of the rest of us. Wilson is rather conventional, as you say, and I'm not convinced that such a man can be a radical …"

A woman's voice broke into their friendly rant.

"Do you remember me? I'm …"

"Kate – and we met in the pub in The Royal Oak in Eccleshall. You were drinking vodka and lime, and your friend was knocking back the pints ... ooh, and you had a scooter."

"You've got a good memory."

"I never forget a face."

Des laughed as Stephen spoke and Stephen realised he'd missed another chance. Des had taught him that women loved flattery, and that flirting with them was a way of flattering. He should have made his rejoinder special to Kate: her face, not just any face, but he lacked the knack or the charm or something.

"This is Chris. I don't think you've met," she said, laughing and remembering she'd quite fancied Stephen when they'd met at the pub. "You'll like Chris. She can never quite find the right phrase either."

"Shut up," retorted Chris, giving her friend a nudge, "and go and dance with your boyfriend. Kate and Bill have been going out together for ... what – it must be two years, mustn't it? I just wanted to say that there's more food on the table in the side room."

She looked at Stephen Last. There was something about the hunch of his shoulders and the way he stood up when they'd approached the table, and the way he had of looking right into your eyes, and a kind of lost dog appearance. One of her brothers had been like him as had one of their Labradors: in need of looking after.

1967

CHAPTER 41

Draft Dodge

Stephen was amazed to receive Simon's letter, but realized he shouldn't have been: it accounted for Simon's absence from the group who sat in the bar of the King's Head after closing time. The landlord had closed the doors and put up the shutters; they were all able to settle down to a comfortable drinking session without upsetting the local constabulary.

They'd dispersed as the evening came to an end. Stephen had no clear memory of how the dispersal had taken place, except that he found himself sitting around a large table with Des, Mike, Cliff Jenkins, the Appalachian Four, Glenda, Joan Whiting and Christine Dixon. He had wondered where Simon might be and it was Christine Dixon who told him – sometime in the small hours – that "your friend, Simon, said he'd walk Sheila home. They've been chatty all evening". Stephen had then offered to walk Christine back to the 'apartment', Joan Whiting having disappeared from the table earlier. She'd accepted.

Simon's letter made it clear that he and Sheila had 'got on rather well' and he wondered if Stephen 'felt like a weekend in Staffham' where the two of them 'could make up a foursome with Sheila and the girl called Christine something-or-other'. Stephen wrote back to say he'd go and was free any weekend. He could hear Des laughing at what he would construe as some very neat manoeuvres on the part of the two women.

Mark's exhibition had opened and Stephen had an invitation to the private view. Standing in the large, bare, hollow and grey hall, with the skylight high in the roof, he nodded at the sketch of a nude.

"Who was the model?"

"Art school," replied Mark, "fleshy piece. I don't know how much she was paid."

"They don't fall over themselves to pose for you, then?"

"No, it's not quite like it is in the films ... an unattractive bloke is an unattractive bloke whether he's an artist or not."

Stephen felt awkward at what he saw as a confession from his friend. He'd never thought of Mark as being either attractive or unattractive to women any more than he'd considered how he might appear. The consideration had never occurred to him. Mark chewed his bottom lips for a while and then said:

"Sometimes I wonder what it would be like with a woman; at others I feel grateful that I'm emotionally free. Nevertheless, being emotionally free does mean that you're emotionally deprived – immature, if you like ... On the whole, I suppose I'm glad I don't have to compromise. Which is what it entails, doesn't it?"

"Probably ... for her happiness, yes."

Stephen thought of Dylan's lines '*You say you're looking for someone, Who'll pick you up each time you fall, To gather flowers constantly, And to come each time you call, A lover for your life and nothin' more, But it ain't me, babe, no no no, it ain't me babe, It ain't me you're looking for, babe.'*

"Exactly," said Mark, "harnessed by another's echoes. How you conduct yourself should be your concern, but it obviously can't be if you're responsible for another's happiness ... I don't want to sound ruthless but my work comes first ... Still, I can see what I'm missing ... and I'm missing a lot."

"Frustration is creative?"

"When it doesn't distract," replied Mark, laughing and blowing down his nose.

Dear Stephen,

Tell me it's not true. Tell me it's not true. It's happening again. I've just had a letter from Susan asking me about Rodney. He seems to be up to his old games again – insisting that it'll hurt him not to have sex. They've been seeing a lot of each other and things are getting heavy ... Could I send my shoulder to cry on by registered letter? I don't think she's actually frightened of him. She doesn't feel he's likely to take her out into the country and rape her ... It seems almost indecent for Susan to be asking me about Rodney, don't you think? I begin to wonder whether I shouldn't go down and see her. What do you think?

Stephen didn't want to think. He liked them both; he'd been fond of Susan and Des had been a good friend – an intellect that sharpened his own. The Susan-Des relationship had been on and off at college, and Stephen had never been sure how far it had gone; only that Des had felt unable to cope with being part of the stockbroker set that was Susan's home ground.

Roger Turl had no doubt that Cassius Clay, the heavyweight boxing champion, had joined the Black Muslims and changed his name to Muhammad Ali to dodge the draft.

"The man's a complete and utter coward," he said from the chair he always used in one corner of the staffroom: the chair that Anne Smallman had warned Stephen never to use when he first joined the staff in July and had, inadvertently, sat in.

"I agree with you, Headmaster," replied Gwyn Tucker, looking round the staffroom for anyone who might dissent.

"Anyone has the right to refuse to fight," said Bill Richardson, quietly.

"Are you a pacifist?" asked Gwyn.

"As a matter of fact, I am."

"Really? But you're no doubt grateful that we took the trouble to go to war against Germany in 1939? Otherwise, you'd be under the heel of the Nazi jackboot by now, boy – and drinking lager!"

"I don't like lager," Bill answered.

"It wouldn't matter whether you liked it or not. Ve haf vays of making you drink!"

Roger and Gwyn exploded with laughter. Stephen said nothing. He accepted that Nazi Germany had to be stopped and that war was the only option in 1939. He was no pacifist, but could see as clearly as anyone that the war being fought in Vietnam by the Americans to prevent the spread of communism could not be won. Cassius Clay had claimed that he "had no quarrel with them Vietcongs". But was that really the point? Weren't there times when the individual conscience had to come second to your country's commitments, pointless or otherwise?

Billy Graham remembered with gratitude Cliff Richard's stand for Jesus Christ at a small dinner party Billy had given in London. The guests had included Sir Alec Douglas-Home and 'a prominent member of the royal family and her husband'. The conversation had revolved around Christianity and, in particular, the deity of Jesus Christ. One of the guests, 'reared in a sect on the fringes of Christianity', could not accept the full divinity of Jesus Christ. Cliff, in arguing against this view, had shown a great knowledge of the Bible and his exposition on the message of the scriptures had been vigorous.

"He's too soft with them, Mr Last," said Megan Spall, "My brother needs a firm hand."

Martin Spall, Megan's brother, had been sent into Stephen's class by Roger Turl, who had been called to Bill Richardson's class by Samuel Morris to quell the riot. Samuel had been "unable to teach because of the noise coming from next door". Samuel had been very patient with Bill, offering him both advice and assistance during his first term, but now felt that something needed doing urgently: Bill's noisy classes were "disturbing the whole school". Samuel occasionally resorted to "a light tap with the gym shoe if a particular boy was recalcitrant and not amenable to normal discipline", but he was not by any means a bully like Tucker: he never raised his voice or spoke abusively to the children. He simply couldn't abide rudeness and felt it harmful to the "quiet working atmosphere of a good school". His children liked him, and that was enough for Stephen.

Stephen wasn't sure that he should discuss another teacher's discipline with one of his children, but Megan was actually talking about her brother.

"Mr Richardson doesn't believe in what you call a firm hand, Megan. He believes that children need to discipline themselves."

"But that's no good if it doesn't work, Mr Last. If Martin gets out of hand at home, dad gives him a belt."

"Home isn't school, Megan … Does it work at home?"

Megan laughed. She knew Stephen liked and trusted her, and this gave her the freedom to speak.

"Not always, Mr Last, but dad says if you spare the rod you spoil the child."

"Does he hit you?"

"No, Mr Last. He'd never do that."

"And does Martin mind? Does he think it unfair?"

"No, Mr Last. He gets on well with dad but he's a boy and I'm a girl. Martin goes fishing with him. I don't."

Stephen thought what a complicated world it was: every home had its own standards. But schools couldn't operate like that: you did need a consensus of opinion. The recent Plowden report, whose recommendations had already been leaked prior to its publication, had suggested the abolition of corporal punishment in primary schools. This had caused the expected uproar in the staffroom.

"Martin," he called to the lad who sat quietly at the back of the classroom, "What were you doing?"

"Running around, sir, and hitting other kids with a ruler."

"Why?"

"I was showing off, sir. The other kids expect it. It's what I'm known for."

"Is it what you want to be known for?"

"Everyone wants to be known, sir."

"He likes fighting, Mr Last," said Megan, helpfully.

"But in class?"

Martin shrugged his shoulders.

"I take it you're quite a bright lad – you find work easy, if you're anything like your sister?"

"Yes, sir."

"Then why not be known for being clever?"

Martin looked at Stephen in bewilderment, and Stephen realised he'd missed the point altogether.

"The other kids would laugh at me, sir."

"Yes, OK, I get the message," replied Stephen, hurriedly.

The boy was a leader within his class group and within the school as a whole – as was his sister, Megan – but he was trapped within the image he'd created for himself: the gang would not respect Martin Spall if he suddenly became the class swot, and status was everything.

The Cuckoo
The cuckoo is the bully bird
It lays its egg in another birds nest
And tosses out the other birds own egg
It always picks on smaller birds
So the young cuckoo
Can throw out the other chicks when it hatches.

Stephen was pleased with the poem, and left the punctuation alone. Mr Turl might not approve, but

Megan Spall's sensitivities were more important at that moment. She'd been pleased with the poem, and Stephen didn't question her too far about any underlying significance. Perhaps there was none: after all, they'd been discussing winter and the coming of spring.

Nursing from the Wolverhampton Royal, Christine Dixon found her work in the community to be as challenging as she had expected; it was an eye-opener. One of the first families she met was from Pakistan, and they ran a corner shop in Whitmore Reans. It was open all hours. The elderly grandmother of the family had been having trouble with her legs and needed her varicose veins stripped out.

"You'll find the women reluctant to talk at first," said Sister Davey, who introduced Chris to the family, "but they do come round once you've gained their confidence. We need to persuade Grandmother Patel to spend some time in hospital. The idea of two weeks away from her family is frightening for her, but those legs are only going to get worse if she refuses treatment."

The room above the shop was sparsely but neatly furnished. There were no chairs or settees and the family seemed content to sit on cushions. This puzzled Chris, but in a room so small the arrangement had considerable advantage, although not for Grandmother Patel's legs. Mr Patel – who, eventually, Chris learned was called Kamal – seemed reluctant to show them upstairs, but Barbara Davey wouldn't take no for an answer.

"They're protective of their women", she later told Chris, "where they come from the women aren't allowed out into the streets, but they work them like donkeys – the women, I mean. Grandmother Patel still serves in the shop, though she can barely stand comfortably."

The old lady smiled discreetly at Barbara but looked with suspicion at Chris the first time they met. Beside her sat a young girl, Munni, who Chris took to be a granddaughter; she was there to translate.

"I learned to speak English at school," said the girl, "very quickly – from the teachers and from the other children, but my grandmother speaks no English at all."

Barbara Davey nodded to Chris, indicating that she was to do the talking.

"We need to persuade your grandmother to come into hospital. If she doesn't her legs will only get worse, and she may find that she cannot walk at all. It is only a minor operation but it will be necessary for her to stay in for about two weeks. She will then need to take it easy at home for another fortnight."

"My grandmother will not want to be away from home for so long."

"You will be able to visit her. There are specified ..."

As soon as she'd used the word, Chris felt uncomfortable. Specified! What comfort did it give to know you could see your loved ones for an hour a day? Especially in the case of this old lady who could speak no word of English.

The young girl spoke to her grandmother and Chris watched the old lady's eyes glisten with tears of fear. Here she was – an old stranger in a foreign land faced with two official-looking women in uniform who were dead set on taking her from the bosom of her family. She bowed her head as the urgency of her granddaughter's appeal drove home.

As they left, the girl spoke hopefully:

"She will come to understand. I will speak with my mother and she will know what to do. Grandmother is very precious to us, and we will look after her."

Keith Richard had 'turned on to a wide range of drugs' on the Stones' American tour – pot, amphetamines, uppers, downers, some smoke – but it was acid that 'blew the world apart'.

"I was never that dedicated to it. If I knew it was good stuff I'd have a few good trips. I never got into an evangelical thing about it, like this is the beginning of a new world. I was like 'Wow, I'll take this if I've got a couple of days off'."

Bill Richardson had to admit to himself that something was wrong. He would wake at night sweating profusely from a dream he could not remember, and when four o'clock arrived on a Sunday afternoon he would get the shakes. He hated his job at Castleford Primary. He knew that when he arrived at school on the Monday morning he would be greeted by cheek of a kind unknown to the other staff, even the mild-mannered Emily Farrow in Infants; when they spoke to him, the children had a grin on their faces. It was a grin that told him they had the upper hand.

In class the children would ignore him, chatting and giggling among themselves or playing some silly game on the desk as he tried to get their attention. His classes would push scraps of work at him expecting a compliment, while knowing what they presented was rubbish.

He was not used to failure or being a witness to it in

others. His teachers at the private school he'd attended always had something of interest to offer, and he and his classmates had listened; they'd listened to stories and snatches of stories that had drawn them into reading more. Moreover, the atmosphere of the classroom had been relaxed. He recalled teachers sitting on desks, their legs swinging back and forth as they read, sharing a joke with the pupils; no one seemed to take advantage of the casualness.

He was 'off sick' and ashamed to return. It was a drama lesson that had been the final straw: bad language, bad behaviour and Roger Turl coming into the lesson bringing immediate silence – immediate silence and the end of creativity. What creativity? He was kidding himself.

The Church's stance on abortion was clear: even if the report of the 1964 commission had denied that abortion was the same as murder, the official position was still that the foetus was sacred and 'capable of being God's child for all eternity'. It had a right to reverence and a right to life. Nevertheless, so had the mother whose life should not be imperilled or her health wrecked.

On January 17, Michael Ramsey addressed the Convocation of Canterbury. He upheld the commission's view but raised questions. Might the health of the mother include consideration of the effect a birth would have on the rest of the family? Might the birth have detrimental psychological effects for the mother? Would the child be able to live a normal life? He disliked the idea of handing over any such decisions to the doctors: he had known families where the handicapped child flourished, and large families that produced 'some of the best of humanity'.

Michael was totally opposed to what was termed 'abortion on demand', and yet it was clear that the current law was inadequate. The line was a fine one to draw. Concessions would have to be made. Abortion might be countenanced out of consideration for the overall health of the mother, the risk of the birth of a deformed or defective child, a child conceived following rape and circumstances where the mother would be incapable of looking after the child.

Whatever was decided, something must be 'got through Parliament'.

Stephen was in Staffham for the foursome night out with Simon, Sheila and Christine. He and Simon had travelled up together on the train from Euston, and had bumped into Paul Crisp and Amanda Harrelson in the High Street. They were now sitting on a settee in what was otherwise a bare room. Opposite them sat Paul on an upturned crate and behind him Amanda hovered with a tray of tea things.

'She is talking, loudly, about the house, as though an invisible audience has gathered to listen to her diatribe,' thought Stephen, unkindly.

Paul thumped his knees occasionally, whenever Amanda mentioned how unfurnished it all was and how their voices echoed on the stairs. Stephen listened with a quiet sense of foreboding especially when Paul mentioned how they "settled the mortgage" and hoped to "pay it off over a reduced period at reduced interest rates" if Amanda managed to "stay at work for five years before having the first baby". By the end of this period they "will be about forty and Paul should have secured a good position". With this financial boost they "will be able to sell the present house at a decent profit, assuming the value of property continues to rise at the present rate, and settle a second mortgage on a larger house" which "will see us through to our old age".

Simon and Stephen were shown each room and each was accompanied by an exhaustive description. As they discussed furnishings, a feeling of warmth ran through Stephen. 'Setting up home is a splendid notion,' he thought, 'as long as it remains in proportion to living. Forty years on a mortgage seems to upset the scales.'

Paul bounced around the kitchen, pulling clean saucepans from the cupboards and tapping the tiles with his foot. Amanda discussed the financial value of growing your own cabbages.

"It's great, really great, setting up your own home. You'd never guess the number of things you have to get. We're trying to buy as much as possible: cash. By the time Amanda moves in I'll have things growing in the garden."

"We're having to save really hard this year. We never go out to the pictures or anything like that, do we Paul? Paul's got to paint the back of the coal shed this weekend."

"Amanda's making a rug at night between writing her essays."

"When we've got the main furniture we'll start to get the carpets for each room. I'll have to polish the arms of the settee, Paul. I only did it a few days ago. The dust!"

When they waved goodbye, Stephen saw Amanda pointing at the ragged edge of the grass.

"What a gas!" said Simon.

Van Rensburg was one of the warders who considered it his job to make the prisoners 'lives as wretched as possible'; he 'pursued that goal with great enthusiasm'. One morning he informed Nelson and the other prisoners that there was to be no more talking while they worked in the quarry or on their walks to work.

"From now on, silence!" he roared.

Discussion was the only thing that made life bearable, and so this order was met with dismay. During that lunch hour, when Nelson and other leaders of the ANC were discussing what to do, Major Kellerman – who, according to Van Rensburg, had issued the order – walked into the shed that served as their dining room. He coughed, obviously with embarrassment, and announced that the order was rescinded.

Nelson and his colleagues were pleased but suspicious; even more so, when the usual charges made against the prisoners as a daily routine were dropped.

On returning to his cell, Nelson found that he had been moved from No 4, which was near the entrance, to No 18 at the end of the passage. It was the prisoners' guess that they were to receive a visitor and that Nelson had been moved to the end of the row so that his complaints might be heard last of all – if at all because time would probably have run out. They agreed that each of them should say that the prisoner in cell 18 would speak for everyone.

The following morning, Major Kellerman appeared and introduced Helen Suzman, a member of the liberal Progressive Party in Parliament, who was a lone voice against the Nationalists. In turn, she was introduced to each prisoner who passed her on to Nelson. She shook his hand firmly and introduced herself. Many stories were at large about the plight of the prisoners on Robben Island, and Mrs Suzman had come to investigate.

Nelson complained about the food and the poor quality of their clothing. He also demanded the right to receive newspapers, access to information and the facilities for proper study. He also complained about Van Rensburg. It was unusual to complain about an individual warder, but Van Rensburg was in a class of his own when it came to the harsh treatment of prisoners.

Mrs Suzman listened carefully, made notes and promised to take the issues to the minister of justice. She then examined each of the cells, talked to the other men and strolled around their courtyard.

Within a few weeks of her Helen Suzman's visit, Van Rensburg was transferred. Nelson remembered, with admiration, this little woman (she was five feet two inches tall) and the courageous way she had conducted herself in the unfamiliar surroundings of the prison. She was the only woman ever to 'grace' their cells.

CHAPTER 42

Strawberry Fields

John's *Strawberry Fields Forever* and Paul's *Penny Lane* had failed to go straight to the top of the hit parade; it was the first record to fail to do so since *Please Please Me*. It had been released as a double A side single and was about the area in which they'd lived in their home town, Liverpool. Penny Lane was where George, Paul and John had met, shopped and caught the bus; Strawberry Fields was the name of a children's home, close to the home of John's aunt. He had passed its red sandstone walls many times.

'Were they slipping? Were the fans disappointed at the Beatles decision to cease touring?' Simon Wiseman didn't give a stuff one way or the other: he was a Stones fan, as they came from the 'sarf' and the Beatles came from the 'norf'. He smiled to himself, recalling the fun they'd had at college pitting one against the other: region or pop group.

He thought Lennon was a bit way out – probably drugs. 'Nothing is real'? He needed to face 2B in the morning: get a real job. He'd soon know what was real and what wasn't.

He was getting on well with Sheila Pratt. It was just his bloody luck that they'd met up *after* he'd left college:

three years in the Midlands and not a bird in sight, and now he was travelling backwards and forwards, whenever he could afford it on a teacher's salary, to see her. He was due up at the weekend. Sheila wanted to take him round to see where she lived. He wasn't quite sure about that, but why not. Nothing is real.

Stephen, stopping off at Susan's on his way to see Christine Dixon, sat uncomfortably on the edge of her parents' settee. It wasn't the expensively furnished room but the glass of sherry that he found uncomfortable; that and Rodney standing over him, his own glass idling in his big, white hands. Susan's nervous giggle – something that had marked her out and that he'd found rather attractive at college – had, if anything, intensified and gained an edginess. Stephen recalled Rodney's earlier comments regarding the salary of teachers being "pin money" and how he (Stephen) ought to give some thought to what he would be earning. "… the husband has to bring home the bacon … It'll be your responsibility when the time comes." People like Rodney always seemed to have everything under control. Stephen found that he was admiring and disliking him at the same time.

"Stay, Stephen. It would be nice to have a chat with you again. We can always get away early. It's just that we have to go."

"I'm sure Stephen understands, Dido," said Rodney, and Susan blushed at the nickname.

'Who the hell does he think he is,' thought Stephen, 'he has no business being sure of what I may understand.'

"We'd have cancelled the dinner if we'd known, but it's too late now."

Stephen knew nothing about fashion – designer or high street – but even he could see that Susan's evening dress was a cut above the rest. He smiled to himself at the aptness of the old phrase. Her hair was in ringlets; she'd obviously been to a hairdresser to acquire such a look. She was made up in a way he'd never seen at college. The picture she made standing by Rodney in his dinner jacket placed her in another world.

"Look Rodney, phone and say we've been held up. We'll have a drink with Stephen before we go."

"Udders will have the meal ready for eight, Dido. We can't very well …" Rodney spoke quietly but paused with a grimace, drawing back his lips and sucking through his teeth.

"I shouldn't have come on spec," said Stephen, helpfully, draining his sherry and swilling off the taste with saliva.

Kate Walsh had tried to keep in touch with Heather Burton as often as possible, although this had proved extremely difficult with Kate in her final year, Heather picking up the nursing course in her second year and looking after the baby.

"How's Chas?" asked Kate, as they sat drinking cappuccinos in the Café Blanc one rare morning when both were free.

"Chas is fine," said Heather with her customary good humour, "It's Barry and me who are absolutely shattered. Sometimes, Kate, I don't think I can go on with this course."

"Don't say that."

"You say that to everyone, Kate. I had a letter from Joan only the other day complaining about you."

"Complaining about me?" Kate laughed and said "Trust Joan to land a job in one of the London hospitals!"

"Well, she would with her connections, wouldn't she?" replied Heather, without a trace of envy, "but she isn't enjoying it one little bit."

"It's the Queen Charlotte, isn't it?"

"Yes. Evidently, they're worked like navvies and the sisters are unbearable. Joan says you wouldn't think the new nurses were actually qualified professional people. She says that even at boarding school she wasn't spoken to in the way some of the sisters at Queen Charlotte's speak to her."

"Joan once called a lady doctor to heel. If I had to guess who's going to come out on top, it wouldn't be the sisters! Anyway, how are you?"

"I'm all right really, but everything is such hard work. Barry and I haven't … you know … for weeks. We're both absolutely knackered when we get in at night. Once we've played with Chas and got him to bed, all we do is fall asleep."

"Still, it must be nice to have a home."

"Yes … it's just that it was sex that got us into this … situation in the first place, and now it's the last thing on the agenda."

Kate wondered what it must be like sleeping next to a man. She'd wanted to wait until they'd got married, and Bill was so nice he hadn't quibbled. Saving herself for marriage was how she saw it: saving herself for the one man who would mean everything in the world.

The Vietnam War had dragged on with enormous casualties on both sides and no sign of any negotiated peace merging from the conflict. Dick Crossman felt that the visit of the Russian president, Mr Kosygin, to Britain had been a 'series of dinners with nothing going on', but eventually decided that something had been going on: there had been a British attempt to get in on the peace negotiations. Britain had not been drawn into the war, and Harold Wilson saw himself in a strong position to influence both the Russians and the Americans. He felt he had the 'absolute confidence of LBJ' and had 'won the confidence' of Kosygin. Discussions had been 'on the very edge of success' and then 'dashed away'. There was no point, he felt, in being either anti-American or anti-North Vietnam; the 'mechanism for peace negotiations had been established'.

"Look," said Dick, "if you really were on the edge of peace on Friday and then again on Saturday, didn't the bombing start again rather rapidly on Monday? Isn't the explanation that the Americans thought peace might be breaking out?"

Harold denied this but conceded that no actual contact had been made with North Vietnam.

As they left the room, James Callaghan, Chancellor of the Exchequer, said to Dick:

"You have an irresistible temptation to say what people don't like to hear. You certainly satisfied it by your behaviour in Cabinet."

Christine Dixon had rather fancied Stephen Last when he and his friend had appeared at the King's Head. She wasn't quite sure why: it wasn't the way he dressed, which was just like a schoolteacher, but something about his manner and the reassurance he'd given Sheila – and how he listened! It wasn't so much that he didn't say anything – he wasn't quiet by any means – but he actually listened to what you had to say. Chris hadn't come across that before – not in men, or for that matter in many women. It had been her idea to get him up for a Saturday night out with Sheila and Simon. Sheila wasn't sure about the arrangement for either of them, but she did like Simon.

Now, she and Stephen had seen each other a couple of times and were sitting in the Bishop's Mitre on Tettenhall Lower Green, having watched *Poor Cow*.

"All she wanted was a man and a baby," said Chris about the film's heroine, Joy. "I don't think that applies to many women these days, do you?"

"Probably not," said Stephen, not knowing too much about what women wanted or having given the matter much thought. He was hung up on Joy's comment that she needed 'different men to satisfy her different moods'. "I wondered whether Joy would have been different in a different environment, or whether what happened to her was simply the result of being the kind of person she was."

"You mean she was a slut," asked Chris.

"She behaved like one, but her choices were few …"

He paused, reminding Chris of her dad when he took them for walks on a Sunday. Her father would suddenly stop in the middle of a sentence as though a thought had struck him. When he was like that, she and her brothers and sisters had learned to be quiet. She watched Stephen and realised she might love him.

"Underlying her predicament," he continued, "was the grinding poverty they faced and the lack of opportunities, and money. It's hard to carve out a life for yourself on a fiver a week and no education."

"Did you notice how they harped on about her figure?" said Chris, "36-24-36? It's the same in all the newspapers. Whenever you see a photograph of a film star, they always give her ..."

"... vital statistics," he laughed.

"Are they so vital?" asked Chris, laughing with him.

It was good to share a similar sense of humour – a sense of the ridiculous. Walking Chris home to her flat on the Upper Green, Stephen suddenly had a memory of her flitting across the room with plates of food, her mane of golden blonde hair caught in the rush, and his heart seemed to turn over. Chris caught his eye at that moment and some understanding passed between them.

The flat was approached through an archway, beyond which was a small courtyard; rough slabs paved the entrance. Had there been a horse-drawn hansom cab in sight this might have been attractive. However, to one side of the archway was a dry cleaners shop and the courtyard was littered with junk: mainly worn-out electrical items that no one had bothered to dump. There were also beer crates, an old tin bath and numerous plastic tubs. Beneath the arch, the door to the left led to the landlord's house and the door to the right to Chris's flat.

"Would you like to come up?"

"Will your friend mind?"

"She's away for the weekend ... but I mean come up for a drink."

Stephen laughed. She'd made things clear without offence and left him with no sense of rejection: quite the contrary, in fact.

They climbed a set of stairs the walls of which were papered with foil, as were the hallway and bathroom. There were two single beds in the living room: one under the window and the other along the wall that separated the living room from the kitchen.

"Snug," said Stephen.

"It costs us five pounds a week – two pounds, ten shillings each. A fiver is about half of what I earn. It's OK and we're free. I come from a large family. There are seven of us and so I'm used to sharing and even slumming-it a bit. Mum and dad never seemed to want to spend money on the house, but we were happy."

"Do you want a large family yourself?"

"Yes, I think I do, but not yet. I've some nursing to do first. If you take a look you'll find some red wine in the kitchen, and some glasses – well, two glasses – in the cupboard."

The kitchen was perhaps eight feet long and no more than three feet wide. The walls were not lined with foil, but the paper looked ancient. The wine was called *Corrida*, and had a bull's head on the label. When Stephen returned to the living room, Chris had pushed the stray clothes somewhere and cleared the little dining table, which was pushed into the back corner by the small window that overlooked the rooftops of the courtyard outhouses, of papers and books. She caught his look and smiled.

"You're a very tidy person, aren't you?" she said.

"Excruciatingly so! When I start work, my desk isn't only cleared of trivia: everything I'm going to use is placed in a precise position."

"I'm very tidy at work. It's part of the training and we

have to be for the sake of the patients, but at home ..." She threw her hands in the air and laughed. "Are you hungry? I'm suddenly starving."

"I suppose I am. We didn't eat before we went to the cinema, did we?"

"I'm good with the pans and food. Shall I rustle something up?"

"That would be nice. Thank you."

While Chris cooked – and it looked like being sausage and mash with onion gravy – Stephen sat at the table in the corner that gave him a view of the kitchen. It had been that mane of blonde hair that first caught his attention, but now he saw how well built she was: not fat, but what his mother and aunts would call "well-covered". She had high cheek bones and huge, blue eyes. Her lips, without a touch of makeup, were the reddest he'd ever seen and the skin of her face was flawless.

They talked while Chris cooked, and talked on through the bottle of Spanish wine, while the darkness outside deepened and a February fog, cold and clutching, closed in. It was personal talk: the kind one shares only with trusted friends. It was the talk of dreams – personal and public. They were each attracted by the other's plans for the future. He was fascinated by her large, sprawling family; she, by his ordered existence. Her bluntness was a model for him; his circumspection a magnet for her. After she'd expressed her humanism, Chris asked:

"Are you religious?"

"I went to a church school but considered myself an atheist when I went to college, although one of my closest friends there thought me to be dangerously religious."

"Why?"

"He said that I had a notion of perfection that was out of this world. He wasn't being sarcastic. He was just commenting on how men and women create their own gods. He was a socialist, and concerned with the here and now."

They both sat quietly after he'd said that, but were not uncomfortable in each other's company. Had they known each other better, their hands would have touched across the table.

"Where had you planned to sleep tonight?" asked Chris, eventually.

"I've a college friend called Robert. His father is a publican in Dudley. I'd planned to catch the bus there."

"You'll never get to Dudley tonight. Even if you catch the last bus from here, you won't be in time for the last bus to Dudley."

"It'll be all right. Robert was one of the few at college with a car. He said he'd pick me up from Wolverhampton town centre at any time."

"He must be a good friend."

"We were all good friends at college. They were special years. 'Our choices were few, so the thought never hit that the one road we travelled would either shatter or split'."

"Dylan?"

"Yes."

"One of my brothers was mad on him ... You can stay, if you like. I mean, you can use my bed – it's clean – and I'll use Pauline's. She won't mind. It's dark and foggy outside."

"That's very kind of you, Chris, but I promised Robert I'd spend some time with him. He wants to talk. He's got girlfriend troubles."

"And you always keep your promises?"

"Yes," he answered, with a slight frown.

"Everyone's important to you, aren't they, Stephen?"

"Well, I imagine your friends are important to you, aren't they?"

"Yes ... but sometimes you put yourself first."

She seemed to be hinting at something beyond his understanding. Not that she wanted to sleep with him: she'd made that clear. It was something else about relationships and their relative importance.

Outside in the fog, he found a phone box and called Robert, telling him he'd be walking down the Tettenhall Road and through Chapel Ash to the town centre. Would Robert be kind enough to pick him up somewhere along that that route?

Emrys Hughes, the Labour MP for South Ayrshire, was hoping to take his private member's bill through Parliament; it was the Abolition of Titles Bill. Dick Crossman had already advised the Queen that Mr Hughes was considered a jester, and that the bill should be allowed to proceed.

"No one is going to take it seriously, and we should only be misunderstood if we stopped it," said Dick in his role as a member of the Privy Council.

It was obvious, however, that the Court felt 'rather differently'. The Prime Minister had been approached and wanted it stopped. The Lord Chancellor and the Chief Whip had been notified.

Later that morning, when Dick arrived at the Palace, the Queen and he discussed stomach upsets but didn't touch on the issue of the Bill; he had been advised 'not to raise the matter'.

Sheila Pratt stood watching her childhood home. Simon had agreed to travel with her to Leeds because she wanted to show him where she'd spent her childhood. She needed, she said, to stand outside and look, and would he come? Simon had shrugged, grinned, said "What a gas!" and they'd caught the train from Staffham.

It was a terraced house, one of twenty-two along one side of the street with a further twenty-two on the other. Her family's house was number four, and next to the corner shop. They stood on the far corner because Sheila didn't want to be disturbed by her family. She'd dressed in new clothes and had a hat pulled down over her face; she also clung onto Simon's arm because no one would recognise her with a boyfriend, especially one dressed in skin-tight black jeans and winkle-picker boots.

She had already confided to Simon all she'd told her friends – particularly Kate in whom she'd put her trust early on in their friendship: her sense of worthlessness, the low expectations her family had of her, the ways in which they'd resisted her attempts to enter nursing. He never asked questions; he just smiled and cheered her up, saying – only half in jest – that "if Stephen had said it, it must be true". Simon had made grammar school where he'd nearly wasted his time: he had no 11+ hang-ups, no feeling that he must catch up.

The back passageway was a gritted path leading past a variety of gates and fences, all in an immaculate state of repair. Her people were working class poor, but proud like everyone else on the street. In most back gardens stood a shed – the reserve of the man of the house. One man kept pigeons, which circled regularly over the adjoining streets; another kept rabbits for their pelts, which his wife made into treasured gloves. The kitchen ran out from the rear of the house and attached to this were the coal shed and then the toilet. Simon, who came from a council estate in Borehamwood, had never seen anything like it.

"I didn't know anyone had outside toilets," he joked, "not after Victorian times."

"We had a chamber pot under the bed for night use," replied Sheila, "but no one like to use it and so we crept outside, winter and summer alike."

Backing onto the toilet was a small covered area that housed the dustbin. From there you could look over the fence into the backyard of the shop, where boxes and crates were neatly stacked.

Sheila was overwhelmed by how ordinary her house looked. It wasn't simply that it looked the same as all the others because in their own way each was unique; it was more that each home imposed the same constraints on its inhabitants – constraints passed down through the generations. She said as much to Simon.

"'God bless the squire and his relations, and keep us in our proper stations"', he said with a laugh.

"Where does that come from?"

"I think it was Dickens, but he may have got it from someone else."

"You see, I don't know things like that ..."

"... and it makes you feel stupid?"

"Yes."

"It shouldn't. I'm well-read because I was given the chance and took it. It was easier than working on an essay. You've got your whole life ahead to read, whereas I'll never know the difference between a catheter and a stethoscope, couldn't lay out a theatre trolley, bring a baby into the world or nurse a sick old lady."

"Don't be silly."

"I'm not. Value what you are, have learned and can do. Look at it this way. If there was a catastrophe along this street now – say a gas main blew up and there was rubble and bodies everywhere – who could do something about it – you or the squire and his relations?"

Sheila tucked in her bottom lip and hugged him. In life, it was good to have someone value you. At the same time, it wasn't the squire and his relations who had held her back; it was the limited aspirations of her own family.

"Do you want to meet my parents," she asked, "I can't not see them, having come all this way. I just needed to know that I was free. I'm ready now."

"An SRN is ready for anything," chuckled Simon, "Were they proud of you when you qualified?"

"I think so. Mum didn't say anything and dad went out to the working men's. I think they were too surprised to say much."

Keith Richards and his friends were recovering from an LSD trip, sitting in front of the telly and listening to Bob Dylan's *Blonde on Blonde*. His house guests were the rich and famous: Mick Jagger with his girlfriend, Marianne Faithfull, among them. Marianne was sitting wrapped only in a fur rug when the police arrived.

The officers set about searching for the drugs they suspected would be in the house. They found some incense sticks, sachets of mustard, four amphetamine tablets and a bottle of heroin pills; they missed the heroin stuffed down the couch and overlooked the hash in Mick's pocket as well as the case of drugs on which David Schneiderman, the drug supplier, was sitting.

The next day, to avoid the press, the Stones took the road to Morocco.

CHAPTER 43

Squat

Stephen opened his parents' door and found Des Smith, wet and bedraggled, facing him in the sullen rain. He was pale, and his coal-grit chin so defined that he seemed a spectre in the bleak light of the porch. Behind and around him the night was as black as tar with an occasional sheet of rain flashing the light from a distant car or house. Des stepped inside, grinning and dripping rain onto the carpet.

Stephen's parents had been in bed a long time. He took Des's coat, trousers, shoes and socks, stuffing and hanging them behind and around the kitchen boiler. Soon Des was seated in the lounge, wearing a pair of Stephen's pyjamas, rubbing his wet head with a towel and gulping tea from a large mug.

"You can still brew, then," he said, pulling his chair towards the open fire, leaning his gaunt face to the flames. "I didn't know they still had these down here."

"You just caught it. Uneconomical: we're having a gas fire put in."

"I felt like getting away," said Des, "just for the weekend, couldn't think where to go. Anyway, I knew you'd be in. Couldn't be sure of Mike but I knew you'd be in."

Stephen knew his friend wanted someone to talk to but couldn't admit it. Stephen didn't feel like going into his breakup with Jenny or talking about Christine; he remained silent and waited.

"Elizabeth is working hard at the moment, even when she makes it home for a weekend and so things are a bit … Sometimes it's a relief to say goodnight," Des said, eventually, chewing on his words as though he suspected them of lying. "In some ways, it's better when she stays at university for the weekends … It's easier with Moira … Moira's important to me in quite another way …"

"How come you asked her out in the first place?"

"I didn't. As I said at Christmas, we met at a folk club. She was part of a … crowd. She said she didn't like me at first … but we kept meeting up. You do … at these places. We sort of drifted into each other's company, really."

"And you think it won't hurt Elizabeth?"

Stephen realised he must have spoken sharply because Des looked up. This was what he wanted to chew over.

"Let's have your view, Sigmund. You know mine."

"Don't you think that business with you and Susan affected you and Elizabeth?"

"That was different. Between Moira and me it's honest. I started off by just trying to help Susan. She said she needed someone to talk to, and then it led to more. We never knew where we stood."

"But you felt guilty?"

"It's different with Moira."

"And you're trying to convince yourself that it won't affect you and Elizabeth?"

"She need never know. I don't want to hurt her."

"You were pretty bloody, Des, while that business with Susan was going on – hypersensitive about what your friends thought or said …"

"You think Elizabeth knows?"

"Who's going to pay the price?"

"You think I'm manipulating Moira? How much of my life do I have to justify?"

"Another?" replied Stephen, taking Des's empty mug.

It was chill in the kitchen. The white tiles seemed to have a calming effect as Stephen brewed two more mugs of tea. When he returned to the lounge, Des was still staring into the fire. He began talking immediately.

"Anyway, I'm moving down south next year – maybe to London. The extra allowance will help us to save up and get married."

"You're moving south!" Stephen laughed.

"Yes," responded Des with a grin, "It might civilise me."

"And what does Elizabeth think about that?"

"That it'll be better having a happy Des every now and then rather than a miserable one more often … I can't stay up there, Stephen. It was not having Elizabeth about and my mates all being away or caught up with their own lives that made me take up with Moira in the first place … Anyway, it's not fixed yet … I can't go on as I have this year … I've a mate who lives in London. It'll be easier all round."

He gulped at his tea. Neither one nor the other said much more. They sat gazing at the burning logs. After a while, Stephen gave his friend some blankets and a sheet, and went to bed, leaving Des on the settee in front of the fire. He set the alarm to make sure he woke earlier than his parents, neither of whom would want to find a stranger asleep in their lounge when morning came.

Harold Wilson and George Brown were back from their tour of Europe. It was a shared view that General de Gaulle had been impressed by their attitude, and that much had been achieved by their meeting with him.

"The record you've given us doesn't convince me that we have the remotest chance of getting in," said Denis Healey, "It would not be advisable to enter without first negotiating the terms."

Dick Crossman agreed with Denis, but thought what an advantage it would be to have gained entry before the impending agricultural review; against that advantage, of course, had to be set the facts that we would be entering with our economy flat, our growth rate low and our capital seeping into the European economy. He could also see that our factories would move on to the continent where labour costs were lower.

Bill Richardson had had enough. He knew his lessons were chaotic; he didn't need Tucker to rub it in his face. Their confrontation had occurred after the meeting about discipline. Tucker had insisted that the key problem with discipline was that everyone was not following the rules "laid down quite clearly by the headmaster".

"It's obvious that the children will take advantage of any apparent *softness* on the part of any teacher," he pointed out, dwelling on the word 'softness' as though it was almost an obscenity. "Why can't we all obey the rules? That's what I want to know."

None of the other staff spoke, feeling quite uncomfortable for Bill. Roger Turl listened with a quiet smile on his face; he needed the Gwyn Tuckers of this world to speak up for him. Feeling that he had gained the high ground, Tucker continued:

"The problem is that some teachers allow their children into the classrooms before they arrive to establish order. And what do the children do? Play up, of course. They throw things around. There're papers, books and pencils all over the floor and the children running round. They must be made to wait in the corridor until the teacher arrives!"

"I don't agree with that, at all," said Stephen, quietly, "My children always go into class, sit down and wait for me – *if I'm not already there.*" He added the last phrase very softly; making a point about staff lingering too long in the staffroom after the bell had gone.

"And I suppose you've never had any trouble spilling over from the playground should you arrive late, Mr Last?" Gwyn cut in. "Experience may, perhaps, show the folly of your ways and the risks you are taking with the children's safety."

"It happened once," acknowledged Stephen, "and I sorted the two lads out in no uncertain terms. I don't see why a whole class should be penalised because you get the occasional clown who has to be disciplined."

"But there's no need for them to be in the classroom until you arrive. Mr Turl's instructions are based on years of experience, which ..." Gwyn raised his hands in a resigned fashion.

"I have to say that I agree with Stephen up to a point," interrupted Raymond Burrell, "I allow those I can trust in at playtimes and lunchtimes. They respect the room because it's theirs, and the less reliable ones come to respect it, too ... I always encourage them to be in class seated and ready for the next lesson when I arrive."

"But with the greatest respect, Mr Burrell, it doesn't work with all the classes and it makes it easier on everyone if we all obey the same rules."

"I agree with Mr Tucker," said Jane Trentham, whose class, Stephen had noted, was always immaculately behaved although they tended to ask permission to do anything – even sharpen a pencil, "These modern methods are all very well in the leafy suburban schools, but Castleford Primary isn't like that: we serve a catchment area that is largely council housing and we get the kind of children who come from those homes ... I don't mean to sound snobbish ..."

She didn't, and Stephen realised that to be true. Jane Trentham – whose husband was a solicitor and who lived in one of the large houses on the old ring road and who moved in social circles where Stephen would have felt coarse – did not look down on any child or any parent; she did not regard them as being her social inferiors, but simply as being "different" and "needing handling in a different manner", as she'd once told Stephen. Few teachers at the school were held in greater respect by the parents than Jane Trentham.

"You have only to walk through the estate to see that they have little respect for property. Their own homes testify to that fact as do the state of their gardens and the abundance of litter everywhere. If we are to ever improve their lot then we must show them a better way whilst they are at school. The children are victims of their environment as are many of their parents. Would you want to live on this estate? Of course not, but they have no choice. It's up to us to show them that life doesn't have to be that way: that we can all pull ourselves up by our own bootstraps. That's what education is about, but we won't get anywhere unless the children first learn respect … I do apologise, Roger, I didn't mean to go on, but this is why we teach, isn't it?"

"Not at all, Jane, not at all: what you have to say makes a great deal of sense."

The debate seemed to fizzle out at that point, but Gwyn followed Bill back to his classroom.

"Mr Richardson, a word if I may? The way you teach and discipline your children is no concern of mine. If you like them all over the room, stacking their desks to one side for your *free drama lessons*, that is up to you. But *please, please* will you keep the noise down? For those of us on either side of you, attempting to *instil some knowledge* into our children in the hope that it may one day be useful to them, the noise is disruptive, you see, *disruptive*. Obey the rules! They're there for all our sakes."

As he read the letter, Stephen felt subdued but was not surprised by Susan's decision; everything he had seen when he paid his 'on-spec' visit was confirmed in what she said:

Dear Stephen,

At last yours truly has taken the plunge! I bet you never thought I'd make it! Rodney and I have discovered how much we have in common since I've been home again and, well, the past is past and best forgotten. We can have a good life together here. I feel sure of that now.

What with one thing and another it's the first time I have really felt certain and settled in a long time, as you know.

I hope you can come to the wedding. I am trying to get as many of my college friends as possible to liven things up a bit. You know what relatives are like! We're trying to keep the guest list equal and Rodney seems to know so many more people than I do down here. We decided rather on the spur of the moment in the end. There are so many things to do, it's unbelievable. Mum insisted on our getting the invitations out by Easter so that she can arrange the reception. You have to book so much in advance round here. And then there's the business of finding a house! That will be one of the Easter holiday pleasures.

I did hear that you had broken up from Jenny, but do bring a friend along if you want. The formal invitations will follow so do let me know. Oh well, down to it!

Love,

Susan

Closing the letter quietly and replacing it in the scented envelope, Stephen felt that life was closing in rather too quickly.

When he arrived at No 10, Dick Crossman found Harold Wilson pacing up and down in a restless fashion. He'd never seen him so rattled. It was the impending failure of the Prices and Incomes Policy, of course. Labour was attempting to establish a statutory policy that would link the two because for one to outstrip the other was a recipe for disaster; but the unions were having nothing to do with it. The trade-union group of backbenchers had listened to Dick's speech not comprehending what he was trying to explain, and Jack Jones of the Transport and General Workers Union had threatened to disaffiliate his union if Labour persisted with the idea.

"I am even attracted to the idea of forming a Labour Party that would be independent of the unions," said Harold, "rather along the lines of the American Democratic Party. Only it wouldn't be like that, would it? We would end up like that miserable French socialist party.

"We missed our chance last October," said Dick, "You should have handled the unions yourself. Only you could have swung it."

"Ah, Barbara might have done so, but certainly Michael Stewart didn't."

"I think the only course we can take now is to prepare ourselves for a virtually voluntary system, while warning the public that if it fails we shall have to take other measures," suggested Dick.

"We couldn't impose a wage freeze. That's quite impossible. What we should have to do is cut public expenditure. If they take too much in real wages we shall have to cut their schools, their hospitals and their housing. This is what we've got to tell them."

"If that's what you want to tell them, the great thing is to get it out in the open as soon as possible."

Hughie Spragg was in his element: he'd found that his banjo playing opened many doors. Back home, peddling dope had brought him in enough money to make the trip to America. He didn't like selling the stuff, but a living had to be made somehow. Now he was in New York, "a stranger in a strange land" (as he kept saying to the chicks), he made enough cash just playing. He'd found friends as soon as he arrived; they'd picked him up at the docks, his banjo strapped to his back.

"Look after your banjo, man. It opens doors."

Platt had said that, and it was Platt who'd found him a place to doss. It was a junkyard, but you couldn't have everything – not 'til he found a chick to take him in, anyway. They slept there at night and got out before the workers arrived in the morning. The boss knew they were there but didn't seem to mind. He even put them on to an Italian restaurant where they could help themselves to the waste. There were always good pickings from the bins once the place had closed at night. As Hughie said:

"We're performing a public service. We're benefactors."

The chicks seemed to like that word; it wasn't one they used in New York, and Hughie made sure that he spoke with as posh an English accent as he could manage. It went down a treat. The thing was that the food was always fresh – well, as fresh as it comes off someone's plate. But at least it wasn't the mouldy stuff they found behind the supermarkets; you had to scrape the rind off the cheese before that was eatable.

When his mind was clear and he could think, Hughie allowed himself to be appalled at the waste. It was something he hadn't noticed at home where everyone felt obliged to 'clear your plate'. He'd been brought up on that mantra; it was nice to break free.

It was the same with clothes; you never needed to buy any. He'd even found a pair of cowboy boots. Everyone seemed to wear those. They'd just been dumped in the junkyard, and so Hughie helped himself. Nobody seemed to mind – not even the blokes who ran the yard. It was cool in New York. There was plenty for everyone, and Hughie was helping to share it around. What you might call 'a social activist' or 'active socialist'. He liked the phrase when it occurred to him as he came out of a marijuana haze one afternoon.

They were all getting ready for the 'be-in', and the women were taking a lot of trouble. Despite the fact that no one worked there always seemed to be money from somewhere. Hughie decided that the chicks must come from rich homes and had just dropped out for a while. Their parents must be supporting them, and he couldn't see why; it wouldn't have happened back home. Back home you got a job.

The be-in was to take place in Central Park during the Easter Day Parade. Platt said that they expected thousands to turn up from towns along the east coast alone. Excitement was high. There would be poetry and songs and painting. Hughie tuned his banjo and adjusted his boots, which were on the large side. He began singing:

"*I'm a rambler, I'm a gambler; I'm a long way from home*
And if people don't like me, they can leave me alone."

As he sang he watched the women getting ready. They were serious, really serious: the daisies in their hair, the badges proclaiming LOVE and PEACE, the bodies painted to recall images seen on the LSD trips, the feathers in their headbands.

"It's a spiritual quest, man," said Platt, "we're gonna

change society. Soon the whole of America is gonna be like us."

Stephen Last had agreed to sit in as part of the ring around Mark's squat. The letter Mark had received made it clear that 'unless you and your friends move out by the weekend we'll burn you out'. Its tone was unequivocal.

The squatters had hacked down the nettles on two sides of the house, making an area to sit, and had placed lines of dry wood and undergrowth from the house to the trees.

"If they burn the house, they'll have to take the forest too," Mark proclaimed.

Posters had been hammered into the ground declaring SQUATTERS RIGHTS and WE BORE FRUIT IN THE WILDERNESS. There was an atmosphere of suppressed excitement mingled with fear and anger.

As the darkness closed in, Mark and his friends heard the crackling of branches and the rustling of old leaves in the forest. Mark had placed the women to the rear of the house where they were protected by a hawthorn hedge and nettles.

"If there's a fire," he whispered, "grab a beater, flatten the nettles and run towards the hill."

Lanterns clanked and a few of the men who were approaching laughed. Dave's ring stood holding hands, arms outstretched. Stephen found himself holding the left hand of the pregnant girl; it was warm with sweat. He squeezed it gently and she looked at him.

From somewhere, a chicken squawked. There was a scuffle among the men at the edge of the forest and their faces could be seen in the paraffin flares of the lamps. One of the men stepped forward, beef-red face above a heavy, lumbering body.

"Ar right, now yew go. Yew go orf uppa road and there'll be no trouble. Gew arn."

The flames wavered in the darkness. Beside Stephen and to his left, Dave was shaking with laughter. Mark, hurricane lamp in hand, stepped forward.

"We don't want trouble either," he said, "What have you got against us?"

"Never yew moind. Gew."

Dave's laughter could now be heard, and Mark glanced back angrily. Another flare stepped from the trees and a voice called:

"What Jack means is that you have no right here. It is not your land and you pose a fire risk. This is an agricultural area. A neglected fire could burn down whole fields of wheat."

"We cultivated the land. Before we came it was neglected."

"I'm not arguing with you. We are concerned for our crops ..."

"We'll help you harvest them when summer comes."

"Yew int gonna be here for summer," called Jack, "We doan want yew here."

There were cries of "scum", "filth" and "rabble" as several lanterns emerged from the forest.

"We're not scum: we care. We're not filth: we wash. We're not rabble: we think," replied Dave in a voice suppressing his laughter.

"Bloody clever dicks. Come on, let's get them out. There're only twenty of them."

The gaggle of men moved forward. As they stepped

into the light from their own and Mark's lanterns, Stephen could see that they were big men – probably farm labourers used to heavy work. There must have been about ten of them altogether, he thought, and they would have no trouble shifting Mark's commune.

"There are women here," he called, "and one, at least, is pregnant. Avoid …"

"What did oi tell yer? They got wimen in there."

"Steady Jack. We'll give you ten minutes to get your belongings together and then you must go. There's time to catch the last bus into town."

"We're not going," said Mark, "This is passive resistance."

Several of the men rushed towards him as he spoke and one pinned Mark's arms to his side, picking him up as a child might lift a doll.

"Into the house," Mark yelled, "Get into the house!"

There was a rush for the house, the squatters trying to gain access before the villagers could block their way. Bodies tripped and stumbled across the veranda as the advancing line of lanterns ran towards them. Stephen heard someone scream; it was the art student. There were tears in her eyes. Beater poles were raised as barriers. The lanterns leapt and jerked in the dark. Faces gleamed with sweat and eyes dilated. Suddenly, Stephen heard cries from the back of the house and heard his name called, but nothing made sense; all was consumed in the scramble of bodies and the sound of cursing. A window was smashed and the front door slammed open against the broken shutter.

"In here," urged Mark's voice.

Stephen turned to look as he reached the door and saw

the frail body of the art student jumping up and down on the veranda.

"It isn't what you think," she screamed, "There are no women living here – not all the time ... You're wrong about the women."

Her voice was hoarse, and she paused as though considering the import of her untruth. Stephen smiled. 'Even in these circumstances,' he thought, 'as she struggles to turn the tide of the inevitable, she considers the truth of her words.' He felt joyful and turned to the girl.

"I'm sorry, miss – here," said one of the villagers as he lifted the girl from the ground, kicking and struggling, and carried her away from the house towards the edge of the forest before Stephen could reach her. He turned and went through the front door. Mark slammed it shut behind them both.

Stephen noticed that the front room was crowded with members of the commune, as he heard an axe thud into the door.

"Don't resist," shouted Mark, "this is peaceful protest. Just sit."

A hand reached in to remove the door bar, and one by one the squatters were lifted from the house. Dave thought it frightening how easily the men asserted their assumed authority. One by one, Mark's supporters were placed on the bracken at the forest's edge until the house had been cleared.

Dave smiled at Stephen and nodded. Stephen caught his intention, and the others followed the two of them back into the house; and so a peculiar scene developed that he remembered long after. Men holding lanterns crowded the doors and windows while others lifted the squatters to the woods, repeating the procedure over and over again as the commune members scrambled back, climbing through broken windows and smashed doors. Flames flickered, tempers rose, lanterns died and were relit until one of the men slung a lantern into the thatch.

Stephen picked himself up from the ground and watched the flames shoot across the dry roof. Within seconds the ugly crackling and the roar of the flames were all that could be heard. Several of the villagers and squatters were still in the house. Burning thatch drifted through the air, dropping to the forest. People rushed towards these outbreaks of fire with beaters; others watched, transfixed by the dark figures that jerked and twisted like marionettes in the glowing room. Black shapes spilled from the windows and doors. Hands reached out, dragging them clear. One voice yelled when the roof crumbled, smouldering between the walls; lathe and plaster, quickly devoured, keeled over.

It was a tomb-like crowd that gathered by the forest when the smaller fires had been beaten to the ground and the counting began; it was a crowd still subdued, apart from one or two who laughed towards the burned-out ruin, when it was discovered that none was missing.

"It had to be – that's all. I'll call the fire brigade. They'll need to see to this ... I should get away," said the man who had dragged the art student clear, and the villagers dispersed rapidly with barely a murmur.

Mark collected a canvas bag from where he'd placed it behind the hedge and they walked sullenly towards the road, following the sound of breaking twigs.

CHAPTER 44

Going Black

Miriam Davison was just sixteen when the two ideas came to her: she would train as a nurse and then devote her life to missionary work. She remembered the moment precisely, and was able to recall its every detail: the taste of the tea, her fat uncle standing legs akimbo, her father's dislike of the man, her mother fetching the best china tea service from the cabinet in the front room and the look she gave Miriam's father, the green cake stand with its collection of freshly baked cakes (oat and date slices, fudge fingers, cornflake cakes and farmhouse fruit cake), the lace tablecloth and the floral wallpaper.

Her uncle (her mother's brother) was on a visit from Rhodesia where he farmed "using cheap black labour", as her father expressed the situation. He was wealthy. There was no doubt about the fact; he oozed wealth. Whereas the cakes would have lasted Miriam's family a week (they would only have been allowed one before being required to eat another slice of bread with a thin spreading of one of her mother's conserves), Uncle Jack wolfed through them as only the rich and vulgar can: with no regard for the appetite of others.

His farm was near somewhere called Mount Darwin, and he talked of his "spread" and there was mention of "livestock". She got the impression of the farm being somewhere high up and there was talk of hills. Miriam supposed that the large bag of tea he'd brought was also from his farm: certainly, they all felt obliged to drink it, and she'd never sipped any tea so clean and crisp and so full of that English Breakfast flavour before. The taste of that tea remained on her palate ever afterwards; no other cup was ever quite the same again.

What also remained with her was a sense of injustice and need: as Uncle Jack strode their sitting room, she imagined him riding the hills bullwhip in hand. He talked endlessly and boastfully and mentioned Karanda and a new hospital that was being built there by the missionaries. He seemed to approve of this venture if not of the missionaries. Suddenly, an image came to her of an open courtyard in which stood a huge tree, its leaves and branches shading those who sat in the sun, and across the courtyard walked nurses in the white and blue uniforms.

The next Sunday, Miriam asked at the church and she was told about the Evangelical Alliance Mission "serving God, serving others". It was enough for Miriam.

"And you're really going out there?" asked Joan Whiting, as they sat in The Anglesea Arms, Joan with a gin and tonic and Miriam with a grapefruit juice and tonic.

"Oh yes, it's going to be a busy year. I've got this midwifery course to finish, Patrick and I get married in July and then we're off in September."

"To spread the word of your god," said Joan, but not in a questioning tone.

"No: to work as a nurse where I am needed."

"But it's your god calling you?"

"You have a problem with God, Joan, because you cannot give yourself to Him."

"I wasn't being sarcastic – surprisingly, perhaps. I think what you're doing is admirable, Miriam. I …"

"Go on," urged Miriam, as Joan hesitated.

"I wonder whether the bigger picture isn't a little more complex, that's all. You are going out there to spread the word of your god through good works and preaching. Whatever you might say, that is true. And I don't doubt that the world will be a better place for your having been in it – just as it will because Kate and Chris and Sheila and the others have all impacted on their little patch … *but* it's the politicians who make the key decisions. They're the people we have to influence, and what clout does a nurse or a teacher or anyone else possess when those decisions are made? … One of those student teachers Kate and I met in the pub at Eccleshall said much the same thing – something like 'democracy gives you the right to choose who will kick you around for the next five years' He was right. If we're to change society, we have to be in at the top.

Daddy knew that when he insisted I studied the subjects I did at 'A' level. He humoured me when I tried to break the mould and train for something 'useful' like nursing, but he knew where the real decisions are made. He hadn't been a diplomat since the war for nothing … and, of course, his generation had fought the war, hadn't they? Throughout my childhood, I could taste the war. It was always present in my father's thinking. He said in the 50s that our future was with Europe, that the Commonwealth would go its own way and that trading with Europe was the only means we had of maintaining our economy ... He also said that economic links would mean political links, and he was comfortable with the idea: political links would mean less chance of another war breaking out in Europe ..."

Miriam listened to what seemed to be a voice from another world. She had never thought of these things. Politics took place in London and were not part of her everyday life or the life of her family or the life of her local Baptist church. It was from here she had drawn her faith and seen the road ahead.

"You're leaving nursing?" she asked.

"Oh yes, I've a place at Oxford in the autumn. I'm reading Law, and European law will be high on my agenda. I'll work as a lawyer when I'm qualified ... I might even go into politics when the time comes ... I will become indispensable where and when the real decisions are made."

Miriam thought of her own father. He had been a lawyer, but nothing like Joan imagined: a small man looking after people's legal interests in a small town.

"Well, I shall finish my midwifery training at Queen Charlotte's and then it's Africa for me and for Patrick," she said, smiling.

Sitting in the Koh-I-Noor in Temple Street polishing off his chicken madras, Stephen Last said, with a laugh, to Christine Dixon:

"What's all this about Wolverhampton 'going black', then?"

"Enoch Powell?"

"Yes, it was in an article he wrote in *The Telegraph* a

couple of months ago. He said something about streets being struck with terror whenever a 'for sale' notice went up because the street would 'go black'."

"It happens. In parts of the city where I work – places in Powell's constituency – there are whole streets where you won't see a white face. When immigrants move here they tend to congregate together, which is natural enough I suppose."

"He was saying that the white population are being driven from their homes and that property values are going down. He lives here, doesn't he?"

"I believe so. People in the town hold him in great respect. He's seen as understanding the problems of the locals, and they also argue against more immigration."

"What, even the West Indians?"

"And the Asians. They see it as a threat to their own jobs."

"It's no way forward, though, is it? You can't stop relatives coming in. It wouldn't be right."

"They can go back home," said Chris, "That's something you sometimes hear said."

"But you don't believe that, Chris, do you? It's no answer, is it?"

"I don't find that attitude acceptable – no, but there are intelligent people who do."

They paid their bill, both relieved that it only came to 17/6 for a meal for two with drinks, passed a word or two with the Indian waiter, while he helped Christine on with her coat, and walked back across the town. In Chapel Ash, the Saturday night was peaceful; people, usually couples, were returning from a cinema, a theatre or a restaurant.

"Let me take you down here," said Chris, as they came to Compton Road, "it's where some of my work takes me. Here and the little side roads that run off the main one. This is what scares the local whites."

Stephen could see what she meant; in almost every house along some of the streets a black face could be seen at the window or standing, usually smiling, in the doorway of their home. Children – mostly, he supposed, of West Indian origin – were playing in the streets or being called in to bed by their mothers. A group of men stood chatting and smoking on several of the corners. When they turned into Merridale Road, Chris was hailed by a large woman holding a baby against her shoulder.

"Nurse Dixon, hello."

"Mrs Brown? Hello ... oh, this is my ... my ...friend."

Mrs Brown laughed, shifting the baby to the other shoulder so that she could shake Stephen's outstretched hand. The laugh was complicit, thought Stephen, as the two women shared a single thought.

"He's a nice looking boy," said Mrs Brown, and laughed again as Chris blushed, "My husband is home now. You tell him off, Nurse. He smokes too much and sets a bad example to the children."

"How's Eugene?" asked Chris, nodding towards the baby.

"It was only a cough, Nurse. She is much better."

As she spoke a man appeared on the doorstep with a boy of six who ran out to greet Chris. He flung his arms around her legs, looked up and grinned.

"This is Albert. He is my oldest. He suffers from asthma, and they are talking of sending him to the special school at Kingswood. I don't want him to go, Nurse."

"It is for the boy's good, Charmaine. They will be able to treat him better there," called the father as he stepped onto the pavement and smiled at Chris. "She is a great worrier, my wife, Nurse Dixon. Tell her it will be alright."

"It may not come to that, Mr Brown. Let's wait and see."

It was the first time that Stephen had seen Chris in working mode; it was in distinct contrast to the opinionated firebrand he'd come to know. Although she said little, her voice was both knowledgeable and reassuring. He saw both parents relax.

"Theophilus worries about nothing. He leaves all the worrying to me," complained Charmaine Brown in tones of mock-grievance, "I should worry less if he would stop his smoking."

The banter continued for a while, until Chris made her excuses and she and Stephen cut back to the Tettenhall Road and began the walk to her flat.

"Some of these houses are quite insanitary," she said, "and that's a large part of the problem. My flat is bad enough but I do, at least, have an indoor toilet. Many of these people still have to go down the back yard at night or … you know. Some of the walls are damp with mould. The landlords should be required to bring these properties up to an acceptable standard."

She talked on about her work as a nurse in the community, and Stephen listened with one ear, but his thoughts were stirred by Charmaine Brown's laugh and his sudden, first-hand knowledge of the work Chris did daily. The student days were over – as if he didn't already know – and their adult life had begun: he, teaching and she, nursing. He and she: and all the others who had left school only a few years before. Life had suddenly become serious. It was time to talk, but Stephen didn't feel ready for that moment – not yet, not so soon.

"I happen to be a Christian," said Cliff Richard, "and I wouldn't live with someone to whom I wasn't married. If you throw marriage out what do you put in its place? The whole point of marriage is that it keeps people stable. Marriage is binding and living with someone isn't … If you're a Christian like I am you need a spiritual affinity with someone … marriage is the public commitment of two people who are free to marry, who want to live together, who cannot live without each other and who want to cement their relationship."

He would know when the right girl came along.

"You're leaving?" said Stephen, looking closely at Bill Richardson as they sat over their pints of Tolly bitter in The Cricketers.

"A job's come up at my old private school. I can't turn it down … don't look at me like that, Stephen. It'll be a relief to get out of Castleford."

"I can believe that in your case," replied Stephen, "but will Castleford be any better for you teaching in a public school?"

"The atmosphere is more purposeful. When I was a kid I knew why I went to school. I went to learn – to come out at the other end better than when I went in. Do you understand? It isn't like that at Castleford. The children there don't seem to care either way."

"That only applies to some, and with some teachers, and it isn't the children's fault."

"We are obliged to teach classes of forty – and no one complains, not even the teachers. We just accept that state education is done on the cheap and we manage as best we can … You don't have to cope with classes of forty in a private school."

"I bet," said Stephen, "I suppose you have to struggle along with groups of fifteen or so, don't you – preparing the next generation who will go on to public school and then into the civil service so that they can continue running the state education system of this country in total ignorance?"

"Yes," replied Bill, and they both laughed.

"What you choose to do, Bill, is none of my business – I know that – but unless the establishment take a real interest in state education nothing is going to change, and they won't take an interest because their children aren't involved."

"You'd ban private and public schools?"

"I don't see how you can do that in a democracy, but we need people in power who've been through the state system and whose children will go through the state system. That's the only way that the necessary money is going to be generated."

"It isn't just a question of money, Stephen."

"No, I can see that's true, although there's only so much you can do on the amount they allow for each child to be educated … but put the right people in charge and you'll achieve a different attitude to the value of education."

"And you think that me continuing to teach at Castleford Primary is going to achieve what you want to see, Stephen."

"No, of course not, Bill," Stephen replied, lamely.

The docks

I was born down by the docks, where the green river laps against the wooden beams and where my Nana lives in one of the big houses with a basement. The houses along Bath Street were flooded in 1953 when the water came all the way up the street and poured into the houses. But my Nana was all right because she lives at the top of the road next to the pub and the dirty water only reached her doorstep. In the summer the River Lady takes people on trips along the River Orwell. You sit on a seat and watch the fields and woods as you go by. The river is very dirty. It is full of mud and waste from the docks. Sometimes on Sundays when we go for tea I walk along the docks with my Granddad and he talks about the ships and the birds. There is a special bridge by the docks. It has a concrete slope and when he was a boy my Granddad used to walk over the slope. It was safe then because there was no traffic but now it isn't.

We sometimes walk right up into the town and go to Christchurch Park where he buys me an ice cream and we watch the ducks on the pond but I like the docks best. Sometimes me and my friends go down and play by the river. My mum says she learned to swim in the river but we go to Fore Street swimming pool near the docks or Broome Hill in the summer. There are steps leading down to the river and we play dares to see who can go down the furthest. It is dangerous because the river splashes right up the steps ...

Stephen watched Janet Martin as she wrote about the docks and her grandparents. Afterwards he helped her to put in the full stops. The girl, once the confidence was in her, could have gone on and on. He was reminded of Joyce's stream-of-consciousness technique and Molly Bloom's long soliloquy at the end of *Ulysses*. Punctuation was important, of course, but it did tend to stifle the natural flow of a child's imagination and their recall of events. He couldn't remember having written anything half as good when he was at school.

Simon Wiseman was in a quandary; indeed, it seemed as if he faced several. In the first place, he was quite obviously on the verge of failing his probationary year. 2B had been his nemesis – although 'nemesis' was hardly a fair word to use: no one – certainly not 2B – had any reason to seek retribution as far as he was concerned – far from it. But let's face it – he had been a crap teacher and nearly every class he took had been all over him to the detriment of their education and his career. He should have done what Stephen Last did: having had a bad secondary school practice in his second year at college, he should have gone in for primary teaching. It was just that he rather fancied teaching teenagers: he felt he understood them – being an overgrown one himself – and might do some good. It hadn't worked out like that, however, and he was struggling badly and sometimes felt on the edge of a nervous breakdown.

If only he knew how near the head was to failing him,

Simon could have made a snap decision: just quit, there and then, and bugger off, leaving the little bastards to educate themselves. It's just that there might be a chance he would pass the year successfully; in which case, he could find another, kindlier school in which to work and earn a living next year. They might, of course, let him re-take the probationary year in another school; it seemed a shame to have wasted three years at teacher training college and another actually doing the job he'd wanted to love. If there was a chance of either of those options then he thought he might face Hell for the one last term.

The other aspect of his quandary was Sheila. Travelling back and forth between London and Staffham every weekend was more than he or she could afford on their teaching and nursing salaries, and yet they were getting on so well. She wanted to move to Borehamwood because it was near to London but was working so successfully at Staffham General, particularly under the kindly guidance of Sister Magnusson, and she was reluctant to move.

Simon had enjoyed his student days in Staffham and the Potteries and was happy enough to move back to the Midlands, but he would need a job. They couldn't live on fresh air and Sheila's salary – not that he'd have even considered living off his girlfriend, anyway.

The crux of the matter was whether or not he gave in his notice to the head. This had to be in by the end of May, since they had to allow three months in the summer term, and that was only six weeks away. Would receiving it sway the head's decision? Would it be a matter of him thinking 'why should I pass Wiseman when he is clearing off?' Teachers weren't easy to come by and a bad one was better than no teacher at all: at least it was a body in front of a class. If he simply quit now, no other school would take him on; and, anyway, he couldn't quit without another job. However cool you were, you needed money. 'And now abideth faith, hope and money, these three; but the greatest of these is money'. He laughed at his recollection of Orwell's corruption of the Bible text. Laughter was the best medicine. Where had he read that one?

CHAPTER 45

The teacher's nightmare

Anne Smallman, the Deputy Head, had done all she humanly could to help Bill Richardson. She'd sat discretely with his class while he taught them, she'd offered gentle advice as they strolled to the staffroom during breaks, she'd listened while he listed his woes, she'd waited patiently with his class in the corridor keeping them quiet until he arrived, she'd made polite suggestions about structuring his lessons in such a way that noisy interaction between the more disruptive pupils was reduced: all to no avail. Not only had his relationship with his own children crumbled, but the knowledge among the children that he couldn't control his class was widespread and having an adverse effect on his work with other classes. Even when he picked up on her suggestions – like dividing up the troublemakers before they entered the classroom and making the children enter one by one, which had worked wonderfully – he let the idea slide within days.

Now, Roger Turl was on her back, worried about the reading and maths test results. The school had always prided itself on these being the best in the county at 7+, 9+ and 11+. This year – rather late in the day Anne thought, since the children were about to be tested – Roger felt that "Mr Richardson might let the school down". Anne knew that he might, but what could she do about it at this late stage? Evidently, the children had already told him that it would be his fault if they didn't do well; even at 11 they were cunning! They also knew that Mr Turl came round to each class with the results and discussed them in general terms with the children while the teacher listened. Perhaps they were looking forward to Mr Richardson's discomfort? Children had no mercy for "soft" teachers who had let them down.

Anne took Bill aside and offered to conduct the tests herself, hoping that she might complete them in a calm and purposeful atmosphere. It was the most she could do to make something of a bad situation.

"I'm failing, aren't I?" he said, almost in tears, "I do nothing but talk about school all the time. It's driving my friends mad, but I can't get away from it. I wake in the night worrying about the next day. However long I spend preparing my lessons each one ends up in the same mess. Every day is a battle."

It was no good her saying that everyone had tried to help him. There were times when sympathy was exasperating to the listener. Whatever suggestions were made, they never seemed to impinge on the exact problems the poor teacher faced. There – she'd said it! She'd admitted to herself that she thought him a poor teacher. She hadn't meant it: in many ways Bill could have been inspirational, she thought – but he wasn't.

"I just don't seem to get on with my class," he continued, "they're all over the place. When you come in – or Mr Tucker intervenes – they settle immediately, but the peace doesn't last long. And I don't want to be like … you know. With the greatest of respect, I don't think you get the best from the children teaching in that way. You can't be down on them all the time."

"I think you will just have to struggle through the rest of this year, Bill. There's no way that you're going to regain control of them now …"

"Control! You see – that word again!"

"The problem is that the younger children in the school already have an expectation that they can do what they like when they come into your class next year. Unless you start as you mean to go on in September …"

"Do you think I'll be here in September?"

Anne didn't know Roger's thoughts on Bill's chances of passing his probationary year, but she almost hoped that he might be moved out if only to another school.

"I almost hope I'll fail," Bill said, quietly, "it's a bit like committing suicide, really. Once you've put your mind to it, once the act is all but accomplished there's a sense of relief."

When they entered Sweden for the start of their European tour, the Stones were strip-searched for drugs 'down to their Y-fronts'. News of the bust at Keith's house was front-page news. The gigs were a riot: fireworks, bottles, smoke bombs, police with truncheons and dogs, tear gas and batons were the order of the day.

When they returned to Britain, Keith and Mick appeared in Chichester Crown Court on May 10 charged with drug offences and were remanded on bail of £100 each to appear at the West Sussex Quarter Sessions on June 27.

They began work on their next album, *Their Satanic Majesties Request*, the next week. Mick wanted to out-do the psychedelic success of the Beatles' *Sergeant Pepper*, while Keith wanted to stick to the Stones rock 'n' roll roots and Brian wanted to go back to a pure blues style; it was a time wracked with tension within the group.

The album was produced amid the pressure of the drugs busts, Mick's experiments with LSD and the ever-present media.

Barbara Castle, Minister of Overseas Development, knew where she stood on the question of Europe. Both Harold Wilson and Ted Heath had refused to allow their parties a free vote on May 10, when the government's motion that Britain apply to join the Common Market was passed by 488 votes to 62, but her views were quite decided.

When Harold Macmillan had made his application, Barbara had immediately launched an Anti-Common Market Committee and she had contributed her piece to the *Daily Herald* when that paper ran a two-day debate on the subject of entry. She argued that the Common Market 'did not help world trade or the development of backward economies'. Britain, she argued, would 'have to put tariffs on food and other imports that, previously, Commonwealth countries had been able to send duty free'. There would, she felt, be 'a fundamental shift of loyalties'. France wanted Britain only as a market for her high-priced food: there would be no concessions for the Commonwealth. Failure to agree to de Gaulle's demands would leave us standing, humiliated once more, on the doorstep.

Moreover, she had cheered when Hugh Gaitskell declared:

"It does mean the end of Britain as an independent

European state. ... It means the end of a thousand years of history."

Barbara had also warmed to de Gaulle's comments directed at Britain:

"You who eat the cheap wheat of Canada, the lamb of New Zealand, the beef and potatoes of Ireland, the butter, fruit and vegetables of Australia, the sugar of Jamaica – would you consent to feed on French produce, which would cost more?"

Harold Wilson's view was less charitable. He saw de Gaulle's "non" as a reflection of the Frenchman's desire to have his own way in Europe, to create an economic structure of which he, and he alone, was the head. He resented Britain's role as a world power and the efficiency of Britain's, and Australia's and New Zealand's, agricultural policies compared with those of the French.

Kate Walsh's reputation for efficiency had landed her in a difficult situation. A sister from men's medical had gone off sick and Kate was coerced into being a replacement. It would have been bad enough at any time, but she and Bill were in the midst of planning their wedding and that seemed fraught with unexpected difficulties. "One thing at a time," Bill had said, but he always said things like that and she always felt irritated.

Her parents were not wealthy, and were having to cash in some war bonds to help pay for the wedding. Kate and Bill had begun saving relentlessly, foregoing the usual pleasures of going out with friends, towards some day in the future, but the budget was still tight. She hadn't really expected Bill to propose when he did, and now everything was being done in rather a hurry; on the other hand, Kate was rather pleased because Miriam was definitely getting married and both Sheila and Chris seemed to be courting seriously, and since she had been the first to have a boyfriend she didn't want to be the last to get hitched.

It was work that was causing most of her problems. She was what amounted to an Acting Sister and was in charge of staff nurses whose experience was up to hers; the only difference being that she was a permanent member of staff. Kate couldn't abide sloppiness and had reprimanded both nurses and orderlies on several occasions. She'd seen one SEN serving breakfasts to patients without even passing the time of day; on another occasion, she'd caught a staff nurse having a quick cigarette in the sluice room; and the orderly had been chatting to one of the nurses while he helped to strip and wash a patient. The dignity of the patient who had to listen to their banter while he was being cleaned seemed to count for nothing. The nurses had taken her rebukes quite professionally but the orderly had reported her on the grounds that she was not directly in charge of him and had no business reprimanding him in public; evidently, he'd complained to his union who had reported the matter to the hospital. When Kate was herself rebuked by the Matron she couldn't believe her ears.

"Am I to understand that we must tolerate such behaviour?" she asked.

"We do our best not to upset the unions, Staff Nurse Walsh."

"We do our best to nurse the patients in a professional manner. This man had no business to be in a nursing situation at all, let alone chatting up a nurse at the same time."

"The patient first and last?" replied the Matron, wearily.

"Yes."

"You might well be right, Staff Nurse Walsh. I only hope that you manage to survive in your chosen profession without putting too many backs up."

Thinking about the discussion afterwards, Kate realized that Matron was very tired and carrying out her duty in an almost somnambulistic state. She was probably in her fifties and found the workload wearisome: nursing, after all, was a very physical occupation.

Back on the ward, she'd given the orderly a look that "paralysed him on the spot" (as she told Bill that night) and rolled up her sleeves ready for the consultants' rounds. She enjoyed the rounds. There wasn't one consultant who didn't seem to respect her opinion. One in particular, a Mr Marks, who had listened to his registrar's reading of a patient's chart and questioned her in detail regarding the patient's chest condition, his fluids, his appetite and the progress and nature of his treatment had actually referred her observations to a group of medical students as being "sufficient to arrive at a reliable diagnosis".

The auxiliaries also seemed to appreciate her orderliness: the patient's care was the foremost and – during difficult times, when staff were rushed off their feet – the main concern of everyone. Several of them told her that they "knew where they were when she was on the ward". The registrars, eager to impress their chiefs, could sometimes be difficult – demanding immediate access to test results for which the ward was still waiting was a common bone of contention – but Kate's reputation among the consultants stood her in good stead.

Talking to Bill one night, as they sat writing out wedding invitations, she said:

"My enthusiasm for wanting everything just so is either going to make or break me."

"Yes," he said, very quietly, "you can't be working at full throttle all the time. You need to learn when to turn off."

Somehow, Kate thought she never would.

Standing in the cathedral in Limerick, Michael Ramsey thought again about his lecture in Dublin on Rome and Canterbury. In it he had, yet again, sought to move people's thinking nearer to a day when Protestants and Catholics might achieve unity. He was here to dedicate a window in the cathedral and he was surprised at the number of Irish Anglicans who turned up for what was a family occasion.

"The Church of Ireland boils up in the most unexpected of places, doesn't it?" he said with a smile, thinking back to the times when he had been vilified by the newspapers in Northern Ireland for his trip to Moscow, when he wore a purple cassock and "kissed Baal's lips".

Nelson Mandela had never imagined that the struggle for equality would be 'short or easy'. Much of the ANC's underground organisation had been dismantled: members were on the run, exiled or imprisoned. The state had strengthened its stranglehold: the police were more ruthless, the 'economy was stable', the government had powerful friends in Britain and the United States.

In other parts of Africa, however, the struggle continued: in South West Africa, in Mozambique, in Angola and in Rhodesia fierce battles were being fought. Nelson learned of these struggles from fellow prisoners who had been involved in the fighting. Political education and military training were marching forward. What concerned Nelson most was that the various organisations should, whatever their differences, remain united in what was a common task – the ending of white imperialism.

Pete Campbell's Appalachian Four had not had an easy time in America. Playing at high school hops and in what amounted to village halls was not what he'd had in mind; and it had been a freezing winter.

He was tired of arriving, stone cold, and tuning up, while watched by a bohemian crowd who were obviously wondering what these English types were doing. They seemed to have no sympathy for the traditional British folk songs (unless they'd been sung already by an American performer) even if they touched on the same themes: the rail men, the seamen, the farm workers, or the forlorn maiden. It wasn't what he'd expected. After all (he thought), Bob Dylan, Joan Baez and Paul Simon had all been influenced by British folk music; they'd even sung some of our songs!

The air of the village halls would always be thick with smoke and the smell of American beer – some were even pervaded by the sweet smell of pot – but they lacked the ambience of the British pub. The crowd would be bohemian, but in a careful, 'Americanised' way. He wasn't sure where that thought came from – 'Americanised' – but it came and must have had to do with the fact that the crowds were self-consciously rebellious. It was the self-consciousness he found disturbing.

Some of the blokes tried to make out with Penny, but otherwise she seemed to offend rather than attract the audience: almost as if she was intruding on their song territory. It didn't bother her, however; rather it spurred her on to put them out, and it was Penny's cheerfulness that kept the group together and moving. She delighted in 'stealing' some of the songs of Peter, Paul and Mary, particularly *Lemon Tree* to which she added a particular poignancy. Another of her favourites, if she thought the crowd was hostile, was to sing the "*original* (she stressed the word) English version of *Scarborough Fair*", much as she admired Paul Simon's.

All the while they travelled by the wonderful American trains and coaches through Kentucky, Tennessee, the Carolinas and Virginia, it was New York that was pulling them – or rather, Greenwich Village. They had little hope of meeting Dylan, but there was always the chance; and they all wanted to meet him. When they arrived, they were surprised to see people sleeping in alleyways. Much as Dick Whittington had considered London's streets to be paved with gold, so the British had always thought of America as the land of the free and rich. At least Ken Parkes had arranged decent accommodation: cheap but clean.

It was in the Village in a club along a narrow passage-way that Penny sang *Barbara Allen* because someone in a bar had mentioned that Dylan had sung it. It certainly caught the imagination of the crowd; hearing a woman's voice singing about a hard-hearted woman somehow made the lyrics even more distressing.

"Coming together in death," said one listener "is no coming together at all."

That line in itself, thought Pete, could be a lyric.

Ken Parkes seemed to know several of the Village locals and one of them, a man called Mike, promised to get them a spot at Gerde's Folk City. This was a club usually reserved for well-known folk singers but Mike said that on Monday nights unknowns were welcome to perform. Pete and Penny put their heads together to choose a selection of songs that they thought might go down well. It was their first real disagreement: Penny insisted that they stay with typically British folk, while Pete said he felt more comfortable with a variety of songs – protest, skiffle and rock.

"You're not at The King's Head, now, Pete, belting out American songs for a British audience. This *is* America. They don't want us singing their songs to them."

"The high schools haven't exactly welcomed British folk, though, have they?"

"These people are different. They're hip folksters. They know their songs. They know what's ethnic and what's commercial – and commercial isn't what they want."

"She's right, Pete," said Dougie Green, "We're different or we're nothing."

Pete had to respect Dougie's knowledge of folk music and so he left them to it. What they chose was a collection of British folk that allowed Dougie full rein to add some blue notes on his harmonica, Pete to occasionally rock the melody with his guitar playing and Penny to deliver some of her most plaintive and sexy lyrics. Their banjo player (who they called Spence to avoid any clash with Pete) doubled on bass guitar when Penny was singing and added his own frills to the collection. *Maggie May, All Day Singing, North Country Maid, Gypsy Rover, A-roving, Cherry Ripe, Once I Had a Sweetheart, Scarborough Fair* and *Early One Morning* went down well; and Penny finished with *Barbara Allen*, which raised a few eyebrows as though she was poaching on their reserve.

Nevertheless, despite their success, Pete was uneasy. He liked British folk but it wasn't his natural choice; it wasn't really his kind of music. He was more influenced, as Lonnie Donegan had been, by the American tradition. There were artists far better than he was at singing authentic folk songs; and he didn't want to be second best to anyone. The idea of being a British Country and Western group now seemed more of a dream than ever. When he turned in that night, Glenda seemed far away and 'Appalachian Four' a rather ridiculous name for a British group.

CHAPTER 46

Flower Power

It had been a difficult decision but Stephen Last had made it: he'd handed in his resignation to Roger Turl at Castleford Primary. It hadn't been well-received by Roger but that wasn't what worried Stephen; he felt, quite simply, that he'd let the children down. Not his present class, of course – they'd move on to their fourth year in September – but those he'd come to know and who had hoped to be in his class next year.

The problem was Christine Dixon. He and she and been getting along quite nicely. Nothing much had been said, and there'd been no commitment from either of them, but both knew that there was a possibility of ... well, whatever. Neither he nor she could keep travelling backwards and forwards between Ipswich and Wolverhampton – well, he'd done all of the travelling since she had a shared flat and he still lived with his parents, but that wasn't the point; they liked each other's company and wanted to be together at weekends.

If he didn't retire before the end of term, Stephen would feel obliged to stay on for another year rather than leave a class partway through one; somehow, he felt – rather than thought – that wouldn't be a satisfactory arrangement.

Wedding bells were ringing – not for them, but they were ringing.

He'd been at Aldeburgh with Mark when he made the decision, stretched out on the beach while Mark painted with difficulty. It was a bleak day and the light was right but the wind wasn't. It came in squalls, cutting through their philosophising with keenness. Sitting on the edge of the world gazing into the infinity of the seas was pleasant enough, and there was no point in Mark wrapping his canvasses until a pub opened at seven o'clock. When the time came, cold and hungry they made their way towards a drink, scrambling over the stretches of marram grass and along a narrow, crumbling track. The rank marshes stretched before them, reed-sprouted, leading towards the village. Between the gusts of wind, they could hear the stillness and the rush of the sea as it rolled onto the beach and clinked together the pebbles.

Stephen's last sight of the view that had held him all day were the dark clouds oozing over the horizon; rolling upon each other, they seemed to fall and spread across the grey, eastern sea. As he watched, more appeared clambering over the back of the forerunners, streaked with a red light. They were heavy, exhausted and moving nearer.

A log fire roared in the grate, the landlord served them two pints of Adnams' bitter, and Stephen wished, not for the first time, that pubs served food as they had in the old days. Later, they'd have to walk along to the fish and chip shop, famed for its frying and fresh-caught fish. An old man who seemed to know Mark nodded and began to talk. He spoke not so much to them as to the air between their tables. He spoke of past storms, rising seas, the fish crying out for light and boats on the blackening sea. As he talked, the night grew colder, the wind rushed under the door and howled up the chimney. The landlord switched on the lights when he could no longer see their faces. Several men – some with their wives – hurried in, pushing the coconut mat up against the door. Stephen had the impression that the impending storm would lift the bar and whirl them all away. The room shrank, drawing them together.

"I'm going down to the beach," said Stephen, after their second pint.

"Yer friend, mad, is he?" asked the old man, laughing.

Mark laughed with him, listening to the phlegm rattling in the old man's throat. More warnings followed him out, all friendly enough and without strident concern.

Stephen enjoyed the struggle to the beach, and knew he'd achieved something when he collapsed in the shelter of a fishing boat. Above him the black clouds shuddered with spasmodic light, lurching drunkenly over the village. The wind tore every loose object from the beach and hurled it at the houses, chasing cork, driftwood, seaweed and shingle down the streets. A lobster pot rolled towards him and veered in under the shelter of the boat. Pebbles clattered back under the waves.

He made his way along the seawall until he reached a point beyond the village. Shivering in the first drop of rain, solid as lead, he made his way to the dunes. The rain fell in vertical planes, grasped and twisted by the wind, and glistened on the rooftops he could see as he peered out beyond the wall. He was sodden and exhilarated.

The falling waves, trapping and crushing each other in their haste to reach the shore, were flecked with shattered foam. The salt spray, flung skywards, mingled with the falling rain. The cowering and retreating lower waves sucked at the beach. Stephen looked beyond the immediate fury of the storm to the rise and dip of the dark waters. It was then, across the broiling sea, that he heard the cry of a gull.

It was being forced inland by the storm but seemed to be trying to settle on the waters. Again and again it swooped, was caught by the wind and tossed away. When it finally reached land and attempted to alight on a boulder or breakwater, the wind swept it up again. It would cry, raucously, at the turmoil – the slashing rain, the billowing wind-throbbed clouds, the tumultuous sea – as the storm curled in over the dunes, eating away at the cliffs and descending into the village, drawing earth and sky together in a churning, wailing darkness.

It seemed determined to settle and unable to embrace the fury that raged around it and ran through the night. Stephen could not help but admire the gull with its determination to impose itself on the storm. When he returned to the pub his mind was settled.

At the launch party for *Sergeant Pepper's Lonely Hearts Club Band*, John Lennon was high on drugs and alcohol; he was also smoking heavily, and looked haggard. His eyes were glazed and his speech was slurred.

The party was held in Brian Epstein's Belgravia house at the centre of Swinging London: psychedelia was the order of the day together with Carnaby Street fashions, miniskirts, flower power, kaftans, bells, and joss sticks.

The tables at the party groaned under the weight of gourmet food, and love and peace were in the air.

"Will they buy it," asked John, "I like it. We all feel it's another step up, but will it sell?"

Cynthia was worried about his health and his state of mind. She feared he might kill himself. She'd never understood his attraction to drugs, but wondered whether it was a means of escaping from the fame and idolizing. What she did know was that the gulf between them was widening. John was restless, seeking a new direction in his life, and his addiction (Cynthia was in no doubt that he was addicted) was keeping him away from her and from their son, Julian.

"Don't worry." said Brian, "He's a survivor."

George Martin wondered whether the album would have come out as it did, with its multi-layered nuances, if he had not orchestrated the production. It was an incredible achievement, a change of direction for pop music and he didn't think it would have been formed as it was had the Beatles not been on drugs. He'd been patient, finding it impossible to deal with 'the boys' when they were giggling all the time, and thought that his contribution had given the album coherence.

Dick Crossman saw the news in the early edition of the evening paper; Israel had launched its attack on Egypt. The Israeli's had been provoked into doing so when President Nasser had ordered a shipping blockade which denied Israel access to its only port on the Gulf of Aqaba. The Israeli's had struck at Arab airfields, destroying four hundred Egyptian, Syrian and Jordanian planes.

Moshe Dayan, the Israeli Defence Minister, was directing the attacks, driving deep into the Sinai Peninsula and pressing west as far as the Suez Canal and the strategic fortress of Sharm el Sheikh.

"What are your government's intentions with regard to Jordan?" Dick asked the Israeli Ambassador.

"We intend to occupy the hills of Samaria," he replied.

Britain, Dick knew, would remain neutral. George Brown had said so, quite categorically, to the House. Harold also made it clear that he had been in touch with President Johnson who had no intention of helping the Israelis in any way.

Des Smith felt impelled to join the Israeli forces as a volunteer in the same way that George Orwell had become involved in the Spanish Civil War, but time ran out on him: by the third day of the war, it was clear that the Israelis needed no outside assistance, voluntary or otherwise.

The pro-Israeli feeling in the country was running high. It was a case of David against Goliath, but the giant of Egypt stood no chance. Jericho, Bethlehem and Jerusalem were all in Israeli hands; devout Jews were now able to worship at the Wailing Wall.

Bill Richardson gathered together as many newspapers as he could and handed them round to his class.

"Sort out what you think about this Arab-Israeli War," he said, "Take sides if you want, but have reasons for your attitude."

It would be a good lesson, he thought, provided the head didn't walk in: newspapers always kept them quiet even if they only read the bits that interested them.

The 'eyes of the world' were on Keith Richard and Mick Jagger when they appeared before Judge Block in Chichester; Keith was charged with allowing cannabis to be smoked on his premises, and he faced a £1000 fine or ten years in prison. It was his biggest gig so far and he dressed for the part: dark frock coat, lacy shirt and fag in mouth. Mick was charged with possession of amphetamines.

The jury were only out for a few minutes before finding the two Stones guilty. Mick was given three months in Lewes prison with £100 costs, while Keith got a year in Wormwood Scrubs with £500 costs.

Keith made light of it when his legal team – expensive, high-powered lawyers – got him out next day on appeal:

"The food's awful, the wine list is terribly limited and the library is abysmal," he said.

Mick said he'd written poetry and signed autographs; they both received a 'hero's welcome from fellow inmates'.

"I'm free to do what I want," said Keith, "any old time."

Bill Richardson was dismayed when he heard that Stephen was leaving. They'd had their differences, but he respected the other's integrity: never once had Stephen kow-towed to the accepted view of education. He was, if anything, a little too earnest, too keen to keep the children "on track" and he had no tolerance at all for rudeness or indiscipline, but he was liked by the children and so Bill supposed he must be kind.

He did fit rather too well the schoolmaster look: sports jacket and flannels with pens in pocket and untidy in appearance – but his tie was always loosened at the neck!

He seemed to have few interests outside school: his preparation when he arrived on Monday mornings showed that he'd given little time to himself. The age-old virtues seemed embodied in Stephen: self-denial, perseverance, order.

Bill didn't consider that to be a good thing; teachers needed to get away from the job and from their school-selves, and to forget work at the weekends. He played the violin in various musical ensembles, and he felt that his hobbies added to what he had to offer the children. He didn't want teaching to be a battle: perseverance wasn't one of his strong points – and yes, it sometimes led to him losing his temper with the class.

What they both had, however, was idealism. Stephen because he thought the system had let him down and disputed any school's right to fail any child; Bill because he wanted to upset the apple cart, and get children to question their values and society's values. Stephen going would mean he'd have no one to back him in the staffroom if he challenged any of Turl's edicts, and no one on whom he could off-load his worries.

Anne Smallman had come to see him – probably sent by Turl – to check that he was staying on next year.

"Stephen's decision has come as a bit of a shock," she said.

"I think he has a girlfriend in Wolverhampton," answered Bill.

"Nevertheless," replied Anne, "He's only been here a year."

Bill liked Anne – she'd always been helpful in the face of Turl's dismissiveness – but occasionally she showed that ... prissiness, that ...small-mindedness so typical of teachers. Perhaps that's what happened to a basically nice person after years in the profession? Perhaps that's what came of trying to be the expected role model for the children? It was certainly how other professions – people he met outside school – saw teachers; the moral conscience of the nation, out of touch with real life.

On June 22nd, members of the Ascot Action group of the Committee of 100 held a banner in front of the royal procession on Ladies' Day at Ascot. It was a gesture reminiscent of Emily Davidson's action when she threw herself in front of the king's horse on Derby Day 1913 in support of the suffragette movement. The Committee of 100's banner read YOU ARE BACKING DEATH IN VIETNAM. Feelings against the American's intervention on behalf of South Vietnam against the communist-inspired invasion by the North were growing in the country.

Simon Wiseman read the article in *The Guardian* and remembered the glory days of the CND. Membership had declined with people's apparent acceptance of nuclear weapons and the signing of the test ban treaty. Crowds at demonstrations had dwindled from the 100,000 who packed Trafalgar Square in 1963 to a few hundred. 1963 seemed a long time ago, as did Bertrand Russell sitting in Trafalgar Square protesting against American Polaris submarines in Holy Loch, Arnold Wesker and others from the 100 going to prison, Simon and a girlfriend protesting against the building of the Berlin Wall with the rich and famous outside the Soviet Embassy in '61, the Cuban Missile Crisis in '62, the 'Spies for Peace' pamphlet that unmasked the RSGs ... It had been great fun, but it was all over now.

On June 12, the US Supreme Court had ruled that no individual state could ban interracial marriage. It was an attempt to curb racist legislation, which had provoked riots in New York, riots on the campus of Texas Southern University and seen the National Guard ordered into Mississippi. Feelings were running high in minority communities; non-violent protest was being scorned by many blacks who felt that the time for peaceful marches was over.

Martin Luther King remained adamant that violence was the wrong way.

"Darkness cannot drive out darkness," he said, "only light can do that."

Sometimes he felt he was a lone voice, and he knew his work was dangerous. One day, he gave Coretta some red carnations. She kissed him, thanked him and said:

"They're beautiful … and they're plastic."

There was a question in her voice because he'd never given her artificial flowers before.

"Yes," he replied, "I wanted to give you something you could always keep."

Chapter 47

Censorship

Nelson Mandela was dismayed at what Neville Alexander of the Non-European Unity Movement had to say at the memorial service the prisoners on Robben Island held for Chief Luthuli.

The news of the chief's death had shocked them all. Apparently, he had been hit by a train while walking near his farm. Chief Luthuli had been president of the Natal ANC, and his death left a 'great vacuum in the organisation'. Chief Luthuli was a Nobel Prize winner, a well-known figure on the international stage, and a man who was held in esteem by both blacks and whites; he was articulate, confident and humble.

At the memorial service, held in section B of the prison, everyone was allowed to pay their respects. When Neville Alexander spoke, however, it was clear that he had come to condemn the chief; he accused him of being a white man's stooge, mainly on the grounds that he had accepted the Nobel Peace Prize, and made no attempt to offer even perfunctory condolences.

Nelson considered it 'wrong-headed' and 'entirely contrary to the climate of cooperation the prisoners were trying to create'. Uniting the black organisations was essential in the struggle for liberation.

"Have you read this, Florrie?" asked Maurice Walsh, looking up from the *Sunday Express*, and knowing his wife – who was just clearing away the Sunday lunch she'd cooked with Kate and Bill's help – had had no time to read the paper. "It's your Enoch again."

"Dad!" warned Kate.

"I'm only saying ..."

"You're stirring!"

Bill laughed as he cleared away the last of the dishes. He liked Kate's father who was always the devil's advocate.

"What's he saying this time?" asked Bill.

"CAN WE AFFORD TO LET OUR RACE PROBLEM EXPLODE? That's the headline," answered Maurice.

"We ignore him at our peril," insisted Florrie Walsh.

"What does he go on to say?"

"That's enough, Bill. You're encouraging him," said Kate.

"He's arguing that the time has come to turn off the tap. Listen, this is what he says – 'when the consequences of an unrestricted right of entry for dependents are so grave, it is reasonable to point out that families can also be reunited by immigrants returning home'."

"And good riddance," exclaimed Florrie.

"Mum – no! These people have made their homes here. They came over in the 50s to work in our car factories. They're part of Harold Macmillan's 'you've never had it so good' society."

"That's no reason why we should look after their families. If they want to see them, they can go home ... We'll be having mixed marriages next. Do you want to see loads of little half-castes running around the town?" snapped Florrie.

"Yes," said Bill in that rather timid way of his that annoyed Kate so much, "I must say I do … It's the way forward to a mixed-race society."

"You mean you think it's all right for a white woman to marry a black man? I don't believe it," answered Florrie in a tone one of obvious, genuine bewilderment.

"It's unusual, I know …"

"Unusual! There's only one kind of white woman who gets mixed up with the coloureds – and we know what sort they are!"

"What would you have done, mum, if I'd come home with a coloured boyfriend?"

Kate's anger came through in the quiet question, and Florrie Walsh looked up at her daughter. There would have been no question of her throwing Kate out had such a thing happened, anymore more than if Kate had arrived home pregnant – an unmarried mother! Quite simply, it was something that Florrie would not have anticipated.

"I would have been surprised if you'd done that," Florrie replied, "I would have expected you to show more respect for your father and for me."

Later that evening, as they walked back from The Bentlands, where they were planning to hold their wedding reception, Kate turned to Bill.

"Mum isn't a racist, you know."

"I know. Anyone hearing her would suppose she was a rabid one, but I don't believe for a moment that she'd join the Ku Klux Klan …"

"It's not funny, Bill."

"I'm not making a joke of it. The fact that normally she's a decent person is what makes it worse."

Silence prevailed as Kate turned over what was on her mind.

"What do you think of mixed marriages?" she asked, eventually.

"As I said, it's strange. It hasn't happened – at least, not very often …"

"And people do stare if a white woman is seen with a coloured man, don't they?"

"Yes … and I've done so myself. You can't help thinking that the children of such a marriage would be … misfits – and it shouldn't be like that."

Barbara Castle's expectation that there would be a backlash when her legislation to introduce the breathalyser actually became law proved to be accurate. Her postbag was full of anonymous, abusive letters: one accused her of having 'ballsed our darts matches up … you wicked old B', another showed a dagger dripping with blood over the words 'We'll get you yet, you old cow'.

One weekend, while walking on the Berkshire Downs with her husband, Ted, she dropped into the little village pub at Woolmer. Barbara found a corner seat while Ted went to the bar to order the drinks.

"I had Barbara Castle in here the other day," proclaimed the landlord as he topped the bitter with some lemonade to make the shandies Ted had ordered.

"Really?" said Ted, with a smile.

"Oh yes, but we don't want that woman setting foot in here do we? Oh no! So I refused to serve her."

Back in the corner seat, Ted suppressed his laughter when he caught his wife's eye.

"He's s decent enough chap," whispered Barbara, "He's just caught up in the general wave of prejudice, but it's a government's business to lead opinion."

"I'm sorry you're off, Steve," said Bill as they enjoyed a final pint together, "I'm not sure I can survive in that place without your support – even though we haven't always seen eye to eye. It's the petty rules that get to me – like that business of the children waiting in line until the teacher arrives."

"It's a sensible rule. It's for the children's safety. You can't have them charging about the classroom without supervision."

"But you're the one who ignores it – you and Ray Burrell."

"Our classes are well-disciplined … "

"Discipline – that word again!"

"Ray and I drew the line in the sand when we started last September and I quickly sorted out the lads who messed me about. I know I can trust my children and so they get the freedom of the classroom when they arrive and at break and lunchtimes … But it's not just a matter of trust, Bill – it's also a matter of teachers getting to their classrooms to greet the children *at all times*. It's not good enough to stroll up five minutes after the children arrive."

"All right, all right – but I'm not the only one."

"That's no excuse. Gulp down your coffee and get out of the staffroom!"

"You'll make a good head," said Bill with a laugh, "a real bastard but a good one."

"I've never given it a thought," replied Stephen, and it hadn't occurred to him that someone like him might even be considered.

Bill rather envied Stephen his ease with his children. There had been days with his own class when he'd been glad that the key troublemakers were off sick and there had been days when he had been off 'sick'. Bill despaired of the whole educational setup: the hierarchical structure, the unsuitable buildings, the passive acceptance of the status quo by the teachers, trying to deliver a modern curriculum using modern methods to classes of forty, tatty staff facilities (there were only two staff toilets), the isolation of teachers within their own classrooms. Stephen, on the other hand, looked pragmatically on such things.

"If the only classroom available is so damp that mushrooms are growing on the ceiling," he said, "that's where you teach."

"You're referring to the mobiles?"

"Mobiles that haven't moved since the 50s – yes."

"Children shouldn't be taught in such conditions."

"I know but I'm not wearing myself out worrying about it. That's the head's job. My concern is the children and what I can teach them."

Mr Last is very strict but very kind. He doesn't like people messing about, but if you hurt yourself he always puts his arm round you and puts a plaster on the cut. Also, he always listens to what you have to say and he never tells you off for coming to school in the wrong clothes. He is very good at telling stories and drama. In drama we put all the desks and chairs against the wall if we can't get into the hall and he lets us do what we like when we are acting

*after he has told us what he wants. He is very nice to
lonely children and always puts them in a friendly group.
He never tells you off if you get work wrong but he always
says how well you have done when it is right. He is very
patient when he explains things. In the dinner hall he
usually sits with the children. Once he told the cooks off
because they put salt in the custard by mistake. Mr Last
told us we didn't have to eat it. He puts our work on the
wall. When we come in the next day it is good to see it up.
Mr Last is also good at science. He lets us do experiments
so that we find out for ourselves. I wasn't any good at
maths until I came into Mr Last's class but now I am and
I have more friends. One of my friends couldn't read and
Mr Last taught her how. Now she is a very good reader.
He doesn't get cross if your handwriting is bad when you
write a story but he likes long stories. He reads some of
them to the class.*

Anne Smallman said she'd asked the children to write
him a testimonial for his new job and the one she'd chosen
was written by Janet Smith. She'd corrected some spellings
and punctuation, she said, and Janet had been happy to
stay in and write her piece out again. Stephen was almost
in tears when he read it and, once again, felt bad about
leaving. He considered Janet to be one of his major
successes: she arrived friendless and backward (how he
hated that word!) and was now a star. Sociometric testing
had its uses! He'd have recognised the writer, even if Anne
hadn't mentioned her name. The phrase '*he never tells
you off for coming to school in the wrong clothes*' was the
main clue. Janet came from a poor family – poor but
spotlessly clean, and their clothes were worn and washed
until they were threadbare.

A Whiter Shade of Pale was at the top of the hit parade and London's Hyde Park was thronged with youngsters demanding that pot be legalized. John Lennon had called it the "dope song" and considered it the only one worth listening to, and said all other pop music at the time was "crap".

Simon Wiseman had wandered along with his biker friend, Malcolm, and they were watching the "posers and pansies making fools of themselves", as Malcolm put it.

"You've never smoked the stuff?" asked Simon.

"You kidding, Si! I like to be in control, mate, not off me bleedin' head. When kids are on that crap you can't believe a word they say or rate a thing they do. Why – have you?"

"No," replied Simon, rather lamely, "but the Beatles do well enough on it. Look at *Sergeant Pepper* ..."

"What about it? Give me rock 'n' roll any day. You won't see me in kaftans and beads. I'm not a poof. What do they think they look like in those poncy clothes? Flowers in yer hair! Do me a favour."

"A joint is supposed to turn you on," responded Simon, with a laugh.

"I don't need it, mate. I've got balls between my legs."

The crowds in the park lurched about, their banners shaking in unsteady hands. Simon noticed how they all looked the same: flower-patterned clothes, kaftans, beads, joss sticks and joints, some with flowers in their hair, some in those long Indian jackets that Ringo Starr wore and all wearing their hair long. All looked happy, but it was difficult to tell the men from the women – or the boys from the girls. Simon wondered how long it would be before the kids at school got hold of the stuff. Some of them – no, all of them – were stupid enough to try it just to look cool. Perhaps the permissive society had gone too far. No, not at all: it hadn't gone far enough. He was sounding just like a schoolteacher or someone from the BBC. They'd just banned Lennon's *A Day in the Life* because it condoned drugs. You didn't need that – not when things had just started to move forward from the 50s.

Harold Wilson was not comfortable with the committee's recommendation that the role of the Lord Chamberlain as censor of theatre drama should be abolished.

"I've received representation from the Palace," he said, "They don't want to ban all plays about live persons but they want to make sure that there's somebody who'd stop the kind of play about Prince Phillip which would be painful to the Queen. Of course, they're not denying that there should be freedom to write satirical plays, take-offs, caricatures: what they want to be able to ban are plays devoted to character assassination ..."

"You can hardly retain censorship of live theatre and leave radio and television free," suggested Dick Crossman."

"That'll all be lined up now," replied Harold, quickly, "because Charlie Hill has already cleaned up ITV and he'll do the same to BBC now I'm appointing him chairman."

Stella Aldridge had done very well in her first year teaching. No one – colleagues or children – had got in the way of what she wanted to achieve. One look from her had been enough to quell any opposition – in the staff or class room. She'd always got her way with a look: it frightened people. Sometimes it frightened them too much.

The weekend had confirmed her worst fears: here was another one who wasn't going to match up to her expectations. They'd driven down to London from Manchester, where her parents lived and where she'd returned to teach, and gone to see Pinter's *The Homecoming*; only they didn't since it had now closed at the Aldwych and opened on Broadway, and so they ended up at The Globe watching *There's a Girl in my Soup*. Watching was all Stella did, since she hadn't spent three years at college studying French and English Literature to spend her time paying attention to rubbish.

The night in the hotel hadn't been too bad although his performance hadn't been a match for Edward French's, who'd dropped her as soon as they left college. There were no wide shoulders, narrow waist, sinewy thighs or muscular buttocks on this one. Rugby player he might be but the beer and the meat pies had produced a lot of spare flesh; he was more eager than challenging.

Stella looked up at him as they drove back along the motorway. She moved slightly, attracting his attention to the cigarette between her fingers. He didn't like her smoking and had said so, much to Stella's annoyance: no one, but no one, told her what to do.

She didn't want a lifetime commitment from any bloke at the moment, but she did want stimulation and inspiration. She'd left college with honours, beating Stephen Last to the Education distinction: that had given her some pleasure. She had wondered whether teaching would give her the intellectual stimulus she needed, and it hadn't; and so she'd found another outlet – theatre. Only it was amateur: and were they amateur! They'd annoyed her and she'd annoyed them. There were so many good plays to perform – Wesker, Pinter, Bolt and Orton for starters – and so what did they choose? Coward! The epitome of waste-of-time theatre except, perhaps, for *The Vortex*, and that was stridently over-written. She'd played Sorel Bliss in *Hay Fever* – God forgive her! –and then quit the company.

She was living at home. Having few friends in Manchester, despite having gone to school in the place, there was no one with whom she wanted to share a flat – or who wanted to share a flat with her. She'd enquired discreetly at school, but no one was interested; they all slid off at 3.30 to their homes, a northern tea and *Coronation Street*. It wasn't easy living at home. Not now – not since college. She'd changed but couldn't help it: her dad knew and her mum disapproved. The quiet reserve hurt Stella because she loved both her parents, and especially her dad who had always been her main source of encouragement.

She wasn't prepared to compromise. She couldn't bear the thought of settling down. She had wondered about going abroad, but was now committed to the school until Christmas at least. It was hard. She'd always been so successful throughout school – and now, what was there to look forward to, to plan for or to arouse excitement? "Get thee on lass!" She laughed at his well-worn phrase. What was it Osborne had said? 'There are no brave causes anymore'? She wasn't going to find her Che Guevara – not in today's world. God, wouldn't that be wonderful – to be the mistress of a man like Che Guevara?

Education wasn't going to bring about change – not of its own accord. It wasn't driven. Change needs to be driven. She couldn't see anyone in education driving anything forward. They were all too … too … wimpy! Where was the light now – the one she'd seen shining in the darkness when she went to college only four years ago? Somewhere there must be … what? Proust on the Left Bank?

"Stop the car," she said.

"What?"

"Stop the car."

"Here – on the motorway?"

"Anywhere. Just stop."

"What – do you need to go that badly?"

"Are you going to stop or do I just open the door and get out?" she replied without looking at him, without giving him the withering look contained in her voice.

He pulled over onto the hard shoulder, looking round to see if there were any police cars about. Stella stepped out of the car and walked away.

"Where are you going? You can't walk off on a motorway. Stella – come back for Christ's sake."

She carried on walking along the hard shoulder and then out onto the carriageway and into the darkness until he could see her no longer. He drove slowly attempting to follow her but she seemed to have disappeared. When he found a place to turn and headed back along the southbound carriageway, the accident had already happened. Cars were cast askew and blue lights were flashing.

CHAPTER 48

Summer of Love

Cynthia Lennon felt an utter fool, standing on the platform, their bags at her feet, watching the train pull away from Euston station. They'd been late, and John had dashed off with the others leaving her to carry the bags. She followed as fast as she could, weighed down by the luggage, but the melee of fans, reporters, police and passengers made it impossible for her to reach the platform on time.

George and Patti, Ringo (whose wife, Maureen, was still in hospital following the birth of their second child), Paul and Jane with Mick Jagger and Marianne Faithful had all made it through to join the Maharishi Mahesh Yogi's party on their way to his conference at a teacher training college in Bangor; but Cynthia with the luggage had been stopped by a policeman.

"Sorry, love," he said, not realising who she was, "You're too late, the train's going."

John had poked his head out of the window and yelled:

"Tell him you're with us! Tell him to let you on!"

Tears streamed down her face as she watched the train pull away. Flashbulbs popped and reporters jostled her as Peter Brown, Brian Epstein's assistant, put his arm round her and said:

"I'll take you to Bangor by car. We'll probably be there before the train."

In the event, Cynthia's car arrived quietly soon after the train, and she was greeted by hugs and kisses from the others and 'admonishments' by John.

"Why are you always last, Cyn? How on earth did you manage to miss that train?"

They stayed in dormitories along with the Maharishi's regular followers: bunk beds, simple chests of drawers. Over two hundred people gathered in the main hall for the introductory seminar. All sat cross-legged on the floor. Cynthia sat next to Marianne who she found to be a gentle person. Cynthia wondered how she would cope in the world of rock and drugs.

The Maharishi explained how, through meditation, anyone could reach a spiritual high 'as powerful as any drugs could induce'. Cosmic enlightenment seemed within John's grasp; the promise of Nirvana was in the air.

"It's fantastic stuff, Cyn," said John, "It's life-changing. The meditation's so simple."

Cynthia wondered whether this time it was a road she, too, could undertake with her husband.

Simon Wiseman smiled when he watched the Beatles press conference that afternoon. There they were – a group of pop stars catching on to yoga, which he'd practised for the last five years. It would change their lives; about that, he had no doubts. Eastern mysticism and transcendental meditation were the way forward – the road ahead that must be followed.

He'd failed his probationary year and, to be honest, he was neither surprised nor disappointed. Teaching wasn't for him. The hypocrisy of that final assembly when they all said they'd be sorry to see him go still stuck in Simon's throat. They'd expected him to make a speech and he'd made one they'd never forget. He'd stood up and told them exactly what he thought of them.

"For the past year," he said, "you've set out to make my life a misery, and you've succeeded. I've had sleepless nights and days fraught with fear and loathing at the thought of facing you lot – especially 2B. If you want teachers to enjoy their work and if you want to learn something – which I doubt – you can start by behaving like decent people, instead of little louts. Your presents mean nothing to me. Your consideration would have meant everything for the past twelve months."

He'd left the stage at that point, and walked from the hall and from the school forever. He wasn't sure what was ahead, except that he was moving up to Staffham to be near Sheila and that a friend had told him the DHSS were always looking for people to dole out the benefits. Sheila's friend – he'd forgotten her name, for the moment – was getting married and they'd been invited to the wedding. He was looking forward to that occasion because Stephen was supposed to be going with Chris Dixon. It should be a gas.

Des had had to face Elizabeth. He knew that and wasn't looking forward to what he feared would be a hurtful confrontation. His intention to go south, "maybe to London", to "save up for their marriage" held no water at all. He was insulting her intelligence and she was holding on to an illusion with her comment that it would "be better having a happy Des every now and then, rather than a miserable one more often".

He made a clean breast of the whole Moira business; telling her straight was the only way he could handle the situation. Elizabeth listened without speaking. Her response had taken his breathe away.

"You should have told me before, Des. You owed me that after what we'd meant to each other. You could have at least been honest with me. I know you feel that you've let me down – and you have because I love you – but we couldn't have gone forward on the basis of a lie. How do you think I'd have felt if we'd got married and then I'd discovered about Moira? I know – you didn't want to hurt me and that Moira is *important to you in quite another way* but we couldn't have built a successful marriage on such an arrangement."

He remembered her only as the girl who'd sat watching him doe-eyed while he played his guitar; but here she was – a woman seeing an impossibly hurtful situation with a degree of honesty he wished he'd possessed. Even her voice was calm despite what he knew must be raging in her heart. She said little more but leaned over, kissed him gently on the cheek and walked from the room.

Her dignity collapsed later in the privacy of her own bedroom, and her mother came and held Elizabeth in her arms.

"It was a boy-girl romance," she said, "we all go through them, Beth."

"I know, mum, but that doesn't make them any less important or the ending any more bearable," and her mother, too, wondered what had become of her child who was now so much more.

Pete Campbell's girl, Glenda, who he'd known since they started training college together in 1962, was over the moon. He was coming back and he was going to take up teaching again; his old school had welcomed his application with open arms. It had been a risk letting him go – not because she didn't trust him but because there were so many ... temptations on the road. Pete would be attractive to any and many women, and women had no scruples when it came to catching a man. Glenda laughed at her own admission, and tripped lightly round the little flat she was getting ready to welcome him.

It wasn't that she was pleased the American trip had been less than successful; it was that, realistically, not many good rock-cum-folk singers (and that was what Pete did best) were going to make it as a living. He'd play on because it was in his blood and he'd become well-known and respected in the area, but it was going to be an unreliable life for a married man with children. Children ... they could get the first one on the road tonight.

Had she tried to stop him, it would have been a mistake – perhaps a fatal one for their relationship. He would always have been hankering after what might have been, but now would know wasn't ever going to come to anything. Now they could create a home and start a family.

Miriam and Patrick stood in the open courtyard of the Karanda Mission Hospital. They had just walked in from the dusty landing strip outside the hospital to which the light aircraft has brought them. There was the huge tree, its leaves and branches shading those who sat in the sun, and across the courtyard walked two nurses in the white and blue uniforms. There were seats all around the courtyard: some with tables, others placed for those who wished to sit alone. Miriam was surprised at the number of people sitting around: all seemed to be waiting for something to happen, all turned to look at the strangers.

"Ever felt you were in a minority group," said Patrick with a laugh.

"Stop it," replied Miriam, "the eyes are all smiling."

The buildings were wooden with corrugated tin roofs, and they were painted yellow or had yellowed in the sun. The tree was covered with purple blossom that fell to cover the earth beneath. Four oxen stood under the tree and had clearly been unharnessed from the two carts that stood beside them. One man lounged in his cart talking to another who was picking his teeth with a piece of straw. Miriam thought they might be local farmers delivering food to the hospital. As Miriam and Patrick waited with their suitcases resting on the sandy ground the men paused in their conversation and smiled.

"Nurse Davison, you are very welcome – you and your husband. You have had a good journey," said the older of the two nurses who approached them.

It wasn't a question; it was a positive statement of belief. Miriam could tell that from the tone. She knew immediately that she was going to feel at home in this place.

Brian Epstein's butler found him dead in his locked bedroom; he had, apparently, died of a sleeping pill overdose. The news arrived in Bangor via one of the reporters who were hanging around the Maharishi's conference waiting for the Beatles to give a press release.

The blood drained from John Lennon's face, and Cynthia knew that life for the four 'boys' would never be the same again. They owed everything to Brian: he had managed their rise to international success, he was an astute businessman, he was their friend and their mentor and he had been kind and thoughtful in remembering their birthdays and anniversaries. They had known him since 1961 when he had begun to orchestrate their lives and careers.

"Christ, Cyn," said John, "what are we going to do?"

He received no answer. Neither Cynthia nor any one of the Fab Four was able to speak; traumatized was the word that occurred to Cynthia as they retreated to the main hall and sat looking at one another.

After some time, they were summoned to the Maharishi's presence. He sat cross-legged in the centre of a room bedecked with flowers, and the Beatles and their followers were asked to sit on the floor and listen. He talked of life's journey and of reincarnation, of this life being a stepping stone to the next. He gave the impression that Brian's spirit was still with them and that they must be joyful to ease their friend's passage beyond this world.

As he listened, the idea began to form in John's mind that grief must be controlled, that the memory must be kept nice, that Brian's spirit was all around them and that a good cry wouldn't get them anywhere. Transcendental meditation was the way forward because it encouraged positive thinking and understanding. India was looming in his thoughts as a place where they could study the Maharishi's way and where they might find peace and love. The Beatles had always been seen as 'leaders of youth' and here was a way to give a lead.

That afternoon they returned to London. In the car, John and Cynthia held hands.

"Oh, Christ, why? Why Brian? I just can't get it into my head," he said.

Cynthia, bereft at the loss herself, could see that John was low, as low as he'd ever been.

Mike Harrison wasn't too keen in being at Woburn Abbey for what had been advertised as 'The Festival of the Flower Children', but the girl, Sue, who he'd seen as a good standby while she finished her final year at Coseley College of Education had been insistent.

"Everyone's going, Mike. It'll be the last chance to let my hair down before I start teaching next term. It'll be like San Francisco, so put some flowers in your hair," she laughed.

"Everyone" wouldn't, he suspected, include his old mate, Paul Crisp, and Amanda, the Lady of the Shackles, who was also completing college that summer. He hadn't seen anything of Paul since they qualified; Amanda's ball and chain was too short.

It had cost him a three quid to get them both in for the three days, and Mike was glad he'd continued to ferry cars backwards and forwards across the country at weekends and in the evenings otherwise he'd never have afforded it – not on a teacher's salary. They'd driven down in a Triumph Herald he was due to deliver after the Bank Holiday, and so they'd arrived in style.

He felt a bit of a prat dressed in psychedelic clothes, and hoped none of the children he taught were there to catch sight of him. He soon found, however, that he merged in well with the crowd. His paisley and beads went well with the surroundings, as did the flowers Sue had painted on his cheeks and one lens of one of his glasses.

"Hey man, you look real," said a youth sitting on the hot ground next to them, "Like not off the rack if you know what I mean. Like you've got it together yourself from the charity shops and your gran's cast-offs and not from Carnaby Street."

"Carnaby Street is a bit out of my scene, man," replied Mike, stifling a snort and getting a nudge from Sue, "Like I don't have the bread ... you know what I mean."

"Cool," said the youth, who must have been all of seventeen, turning his attention to the band.

'Seventeen,' thought Mike, 'He's only a few years younger than me, but I feel so much older.'

The band was called Dantalian's Chariot and the musicians were all dressed in white robes with a white backcloth. This, Sue told him, was one of the great psychedelic bands, and Mike thought that times had moved on since he went to college four years ago; then, it was the uncouth Stones or the polished Beatles. He didn't just feel old, he thought old. Where was the power in a flower? And what was 'happening'? There was a firework happening and a non-stop happening and a flower happening ... even the car park was happening.

Feeling hungry, he looked around for food and saw a group of kids sitting in a circle with carnations in their hair. Those were the ones that had fallen from the hot air balloon – the ones the two lads had fought over. One kid was smoking something. A joint was it? Mike wasn't sure. He told Sue that he was going for food and walked past the group. It had the sweet smell of cannabis. Mike was about to pull it from the boy's mouth when he realized he wasn't at school anymore. It wasn't his responsibility – or was it? Forsaking the urge to do something and feeling older than ever, he made his way to the hot dogs.

"How much?" queried Mike, when the vendor handed him the hot dogs.

"One pound ten, mate."

"Bloody hell, man, it only cost us that to get in for the three days."

"Take it or leave it – and go hungry. We've had to make a special trip to get here and we've had to pay for the pitch."

Mike rummaged in his wallet and pocket, paid up and slouched off. Someone was making a packet out of this little festival. He wondered who it might be, and whether His Grace, The Duke of Bedford was away in Cannes for the Bank Holiday weekend. Thirty shillings for two hot dogs! Still, parking was no problem – there was plenty of room – and they'd be able to find lunch somewhere off site.

"They won't serve you in the village, man," said the youth who'd admired his gear and who'd overheard Mike's comments to Sue, "Not if you're a hippy. They turned us out of the shop.

"It gets better and better," said Mike.

"Don't be so miserable," quipped Sue, nudging him for a second time that day, "We've got the Small Faces to look forward to tonight.

It was relaxing Mike found after he'd forgotten his age and settled into the rhythm of the event. He didn't know how many people were there but there was no pushing or shoving. Everyone just wandered round, looking dazed and chatting, dancing and listening to the groups. The police were relaxed; several officers wore flowers in the helmets.

And many of the girls were beautiful – as advertised – especially with flowers in their hair. He and Sue were sharing a tent, and Mike wondered whether the night might hold any promises for him. She'd indicated several times that they might "settle down". The idea just seemed so ... so final. After all, wasn't 'free love' supposed to be part of the hippie revolution? He might not miss out after all.

It was hot, but as evening settled in the air cooled slightly and Mike and Sue found that many of the 'hippies' were university or college students, much like themselves. The conversations rolled on as the bands played.

"This is a real revolution, man," proclaimed one student from York University, "We're lighting a torch for the future. Politics are dead. Society is dead. Socialism has failed. It's not about delivering food and a place to kip. What we're into is a freeing of the spirit, a raising of human consciousness. We're only at the beginning. We're going to turn the world on its head, get in touch with our real selves, get in touch with other like thinkers ..."

Sue listened politely and Mike thought how attractive she looked with the beads and the flowers and the bandana. Her kaftan was an old shawl of her mother's from back in the days when paisley was previously in fashion. Hunger was going to his head (the youth had been right about the village shop) and the Watney's Red Barrel and the joint at which he'd had a cursory puff.

Strobe lights were flashing from the stage and sparklers were being flung into the crowd who were slinging them back. It was the Small Faces singing *Itchycoo Park*, and Mike thought he recognised the DJ, John Peel, urging the crowd back from the stage as the canopy caught fire.

"... Here is the real revolution – the revolution of the spirit. We're not being dictated to, like we're free," continued the student from York, "We're joining hands round the world ...We're going to replace the old system with something new ..."

Mike took Sue's waist and eased her off through the crowd towards the Londoner who was selling hot dogs at fifteen shillings each. With his stomach fuller – even if his wallet was lighter – Mike made his way towards a group of dancers who'd caught his attention with their incessant drumming. They had a pole – not unlike a maypole but without the ribbons – and appeared to be performing some ritual around it.

One man who was dressed like a Red Indian – with feathers rather than flowers in his hair – began a nervous, twitching kind of movement around the pole. Others joined him in what seemed to be a pre-arranged order. Every now and then the drumming stopped and someone blew a whistle at the sound of which the dancers froze. There were all togged out with beads and belts. Occasionally a dancer would appear to collapse and was then helped from the circle to be offered drink. The dancers were all men, but the women would place flowers and beads about and on the pole whenever the dancers froze. As the dance progressed so the pole disappeared beneath a draping of flowers.

Mike had seen Morris dancing, but nothing like this before. There seemed no end to the dancing, and after about fifteen minutes he nodded to Sue that they might move on, but she seemed transfixed. It was a hot night anyway, despite the cooling since sunset, and the fires didn't help. Soon some of the dancers began to strip as the sweat poured from them. Here was an ancient ritual – not English – about which some of these ... hippies must have heard and were resurrecting. 'But it has no ... roots in our culture,' he thought, and then dismissed the thought, allowing himself to be caught up in the spirit of the night.

When he woke next morning, Mike found that he was in his sleeping bag in their tent and that Sue was snoring softly beside him. He couldn't remember a thing, but the beat of the drums still reverberated in his head.

The little village church in Codsall was filled in the way Kate Walsh had wanted it to be – not only with her relatives but with her friends. She saw them all as they turned to watch her walking down the aisle with her dad: Joan (who'd broken her family holiday at their house in France to come), Sheila, Christine and Heather each with their bloke, or husband and baby in Heather's case. 'To have and to hold ... till death us do part': that was the promise she would make and she knew it to be true. Bill might be a little dull, but he was reliable; he'd be a good provider.

He had also leavened the bread. Her mother had wanted the wedding to take place in a Catholic church; her father had totally opposed the idea. Neither had raised the argument in front of Bill, however, and he had *assumed* the wedding would take place in their parish church. 'Assumed' had taken the day, and they had seen the vicar accordingly. She remembered the occasion well, if only for the amusement afforded by the verger. The lady had come scuttling out of the vestry crying:

"If you're in charge of my immortal soul, God help me."

The vicar had followed and smiled at Kate and Bill, saying:

"Our verger is a little excited today."

He had run them through the rigmarole, knowing full well that neither had ever attended his church, and been ever-helpful in the arrangement of flowers and order of service.

The church did look nice. Chris and Sheila had seen to the flowers the day before, relieving her mother of "yet another worry". They'd even collected the bouquets for her and her bridesmaids – two little cousins who looked "as pretty as a picture" – and the buttonholes for the men, none of whom seemed in the least bothered by the momentousness of the occasion.

She didn't really like one of the hymns, but Bill's mother was in the WI and he was a socialist, and so *Jerusalem* was sung; and at least everyone knew it and their voices rang out, much to the vicar's delight. The other hymn, *Love Divine All Loves Excelling*, had been her choice and she hoped (she knew!) it would be true. The traditional *Wedding March* took them down the aisle and the organist's choice, *The Sound of Music* (a swing into modernity for the church), took them out into the sunshine to face the photographer, their friends and the bombardment of confetti.

The wedding was at 2.00 and the reception (a buffet do that had troubled her mother who thought that everyone should sit down for a meal) was an afternoon one, due to finish at about 5 o'clock, after which everyone would make their own plans for the evening. (Both she and Bill had been bored rigid by receptions that dragged endlessly on into the night.) When the final parting from her friends and family came – as their taxi pulled away from The Bentlands, wrapped in toilet paper and trailing boots and tin cans, on its way to the station, London and, the next day, Jersey – Kate knew that she'd chosen her road and that her life had changed forever.

Wolverhampton and Kingswood, Staffordshire	**1967 – 1969**
Loddon, Norfolk	**2011 – 2012**

Afterword

The destinies of the public figures mentioned in this book are well known and need no follow-on in this novel but those other figures in the story should be mentioned:

Pete Campbell and **Glenda** married in the summer of 1968, after he had completed his second year of full-time teaching and Glenda her third. Pete continued to perform as Glenda had predicted. He also went on to inspire children with the love and joy of music for forty years.

Heather Burton and **Barry Glover** had one more child, a girl, once she had completed her nursing training in the autumn of 1967. Heather went on to join various drama groups, all concerned with social issues, which included the feminist agenda of the 1970s. They divorced in 2000.

Stephen Last and **Christine Dixon** married during the Christmas holiday of 1969. They had four children – three boys and a girl – and Christine left nursing to raise their family, while Stephen continued to teach. He became headteacher of a large primary school at an early age and continued a pragmatic approach to education for forty years. When Christine returned to nursing in 1983, the Salmon Report had done away with the old management structures, and Christine worked her way up to become a Senior Nursing Officer rather than a Matron.

Desmond Smith married Moira in the summer of 1968. They had three children, all girls. He was active in local socialist politics and remained a member of the Labour Party until it moved to the right during the Tony Blair years. He played a leading role in the National Association of Schoolmasters when it united with the Union of Women Teachers.

Simon Wiseman and Sheila Pratt married in the summer of 1968. They had two children, a boy and a girl. They remain friends with Stephen and Christine to this day. Sheila's ambition drove her on to eventually attain the post of Senior Nursing Officer. Simon found as little success in the social services as he had in teaching and left work on the birth of their second child to became one of the first, full-time house-husbands; the arrangement suited them both and gave Simon time to write his book *Kennedy: unravelling the truth*.

Paul Crisp and Amanda Harrelson married in the summer of 1967. Paul taught for forty years and retired – along with many of his college friends – in the summer of 2006. Amanda continued to work after the birth of their two children, relying on her mother to help with the children.

Mike Harrison and Sue married at Easter 1968. They had two children. Mike always found time to deliver cars cross-country – among other part-time work – to supplement his teacher's salary. The divorced, amicably, in 1993, after which Sue remarried happily and Mike recaptured a late bachelor life.

Jenny Pryce married a publican form Coseley.

Susan Paget and **Rodney** had two children, and Susan left teaching to raise her family in 1969. They divorced after eight years of marriage, due to Rodney's serial adultery. Susan remarried in 1992, this time to a solicitor for whom she then worked as a secretary – having left teaching in 1990 following the introduction of the National Curriculum.

Marguerite Bannister married her **Bobby**, and he continues to put his shoes out for cleaning to the present day. Marguerite left teaching on the birth of her first child, never to return.

Elizabeth Sturlson gained a first class honours degree in philosophy and political studies at Leicester University and went on to make her mark, initially, in left-wing politics. She worked as a lecturer at a local polytechnic and wrote for various left-wing journals including the *New Statesman* and *Time Out*. She eventually found work as a researcher for the Labour Party and was involved in the emergence of New Labour as a political force.

Hughie Spragg disappeared somewhere in America.

Kate Walsh and **Bill** had three children, and Kate gave up work to raise her family. When she returned after nine years, nursing had changed completely much to Kate's dismay. She still believes that the matron system, which imbued nurses with high standards of professionalism and an over-riding concern for patient care, has never been equalled as a means of effective management. On her return she attained the rank of Sister and specialised in the care of the elderly.

Miriam Davison and **Patrick** returned to the United Kingdom following the birth of their first child in 1972. Her nursing career spanned many specialisms but she finally settled for paediatrics. She and her husband continue to be devout Christians; they are both involved in evangelism and both teach at their junior church.

Joan Whiting gained a first class honours degree in Law from Oxford in 1970 and went straight on to take her masters. Following her success, and while researching her doctorate, Joan worked for a firm of London solicitors recommended by her father. In 1978 she obtained a post as a legal officer for the National Council for Civil Liberties, which she held for five years. In the 1983 general election, she refused to stand as a Conservative candidate – much to her father's annoyance – and took a post in Brussels working for the European Court of Human Rights. She never married.